Danielle Steel is one of the world's most popular and highly acclaimed authors, with over ninety international bestselling novels in print and more than 600 million copies of her novels sold. She is also the author of *His Bright Light*, the story of her son Nick Traina's life and death; *A Gift of Hope*, a memoir of her work with the homeless; and *Pure Joy*, about the dogs she and her family have loved.

To discover more about Danielle Steel and her books visit her website at www.daniellesteel.com

You can also connect with Danielle on Facebook at www. facebook.com/DanielleSteelOfficial or on Twitter: @daniellesteel

Also by Danielle Steel

Danielle Steel

FAMILY ALBUM

SPHERE

First published in Great Britain in 1985 by Michael Joseph
Paperback published in 1985 by Sphere Books Ltd
This reissue published by Sphere in 2020

1 3 5 7 9 10 8 6 4 2

A CIP catalogue record for this book
is available from the British Library.

ISBN 978-0-7515-7952-9

Typeset in Bembo by Hewer Text UK Ltd, Edinburgh
Printed and bound in Great Britain by Clays Ltd, Elcograf S.p.A

Papers used by Sphere are from well-managed forests and other responsible sources.

MIX
Paper from
responsible sources
FSC® C104740

Sphere
An imprint of
Little, Brown Book Group
Carmelite House
50 Victoria Embankment
London EC4Y 0DZ

An Hachette UK Company
www.hachette.co.uk

www.littlebrown.co.uk

To my family: With all my love
To Beatrix, Trevor, Todd, Nicholas,
Samantha, Victoria, and especially . . .
most especially, with all my heart . . .
to John.
d.s.

'God places the solitary in families,' comforting words from the Bible . . . families, by blood, by obligation, by necessity, by desire . . . and sometimes, if one is very lucky, by love. It is a word that implies solidity, a rock-solid foundation, a place to go home to . . . to grow out of . . . to grow away from, and yet to remember and hang onto . . . the echoes never leaving one's ears or one's heart, the memories carved like painted ivory, from a single tusk, delicately coloured in brilliant hues, and softer ones, faded sometimes, so dim as to be almost forgotten . . . and yet never to be totally forgotten or left behind. The place where one begins, and hopes to end . . . the thing one works hard to build on one's own . . . the pieces like building blocks reaching high into the sky . . . Family . . . what images that conjures . . . what memories . . . what dreams.

Prologue 1983

The sun was so brilliant nearly everyone was squinting, though it was only eleven o'clock in the morning. The tiniest of breezes ruffled the women's hair. The day was so beautiful there was a kind of agony to it, an amazing silence, and all one could hear in the silences were birds, a quiet chirping, a sudden shrieking, and the overwhelming smell of flowers ... lily of the valley, gardenias, freesia, buried in a carpet of moss. But Ward Thayer saw none of it and he seemed to hear nothing at all. His eyes had been closed for several minutes, and when he opened them, he stared for the longest time, almost like a zombie, looking colourless, so unlike the image everyone had of him ... had had for the last forty years. There was nothing dashing or exciting or even handsome about Ward Thayer this morning. He stood immobilised in the brilliant sunlight, watching nothing. His eyes closed again; he pressed his eyelids tightly together, and for a moment he wanted never to open them again, as she had not, as she never would again.

There was a voice, droning softly in the distance, saying something, sounding no different than the hum of insects buzzing near the flowers. And he felt nothing. Nothing. Why? Why did he feel nothing, he asked himself? Had he felt nothing for her? Had it all been a lie? He felt a wave of panic wash over him ... he couldn't remember her face ... the way she wore her hair ... the colour of her eyes ... his eyes flew open brusquely, tearing the lids apart like hands that had been clasped, skin that had once upon a time been grafted. The sun blinded him in an instant, and he saw only a flash of light and smelled the flowers, as a bee hummed lazily past him, and the pastor said her name. Faye Price Thayer. There was a muffled popping sound to his left and the lightning of a camera flash exploded in his eyes, as the woman beside him pressed his arm.

He looked down at her, his eyes adjusting to the light again, and suddenly he remembered. Everything he had forgotten was reflected in his daughter's eyes. The younger woman looked so much like her, yet how different they were. There would never be another woman like Faye Thayer. They all knew that, and he knew it best of all. He looked at the pretty blonde beside him, remembering it all, and longing silently for Faye.

His daughter stood tall and sedate. She was plainer than Faye had been. Her smooth blonde hair was pulled tightly into a knot, and beside her stood a serious looking man, who touched her arm often. They were on their own now, all of them, each one different, separate, yet part of a larger whole, part of Faye . . . and of him as well.

Was she truly gone? It seemed impossible, as tears rolled solemnly down his cheeks and a dozen photographers leapt forward to record his pain, to put on front pages around the world. The grieving widower of Faye Price Thayer. He was hers now, in death, as he had been hers in life. They were all hers. All of them. The daughters, the son, the co-workers, the friends, and they were all there to honour the memory of the woman who would never come again.

The family stood beside him in the front row. His daughter Vanessa, her bespectacled young man, and beside him, Vanessa's twin Valerie, with hair of flame, a golden face, a perfect black silk dress which clung to her breathtakingly, her success stamped on her unmistakably, and beside her an equally dazzling man.

They made such a beautiful pair one had to stare at them, and it pleased Ward to see how much Val looked like Faye. He had never noticed it quite so much before, but he saw it now . . . And Lionel, who looked so like her too, though more quietly. Tall, handsome and blond, sensual, elegant, and delicate, yet at

2

the same time proud. He stood staring into the distance now, remembering the others he had known and loved . . . Gregory and John, lost brother, treasured friend. He thought too of how well Faye had known Lionel, better than anyone perhaps. She had known him better than he knew himself . . . and as well as he himself knew Anne, standing beside him now, prettier than she had been before, so much more confident, and still so young, in sharp contrast to the grey-haired man who held her hand.

They were all there in the end. They had come to pay homage to all that she had been. Actress, director, legend, wife, mother, friend. There were those who had envied her, those she had driven too hard and wanted too much from. Her family knew that best of all. She had expected so much of them, yet given so much in return, driven herself so hard, gone so far. Ward remembered it all as he looked at all of them, all the way back to that first time in Guadalcanal. And now here they were, a lifetime past, and each of them remembering her as she had been, as she once was, as she was to them. It was a sea of faces in the bright Los Angeles sun. All of Hollywood had turned out for her. A last salute, a final smile, a tender tear, as Ward turned to glance at the family he had built with her, all of them so strong and beautiful . . . as she had been. How proud she would have been to see them now, he thought, tears burning his eyes again . . . how proud they were of her . . . finally. It had taken a long time . . . and now she was gone . . . it seemed impossible to believe when only yesterday . . . only yesterday they'd been in Paris . . . the South of France . . . New York . . . Guadalcanal.

GUADALCANAL 1943

Chapter 1

The heat of the jungle was so oppressive that just standing in one place was almost like swimming through thick, dense air. It was a presence you could feel and smell and touch, and yet the men pressed forward wanting to see her . . . to get closer . . . to see more . . . Their shoulders were tightly compressed, as they sat there, side by side, cross-legged on the ground. In the front, way up front, they had folding chairs, but they had run out hours before. The men had been sitting there since sundown, baking, sweating, waiting. It felt like a hundred years that they'd been sitting here in the thick jungles of Guadalcanal and they didn't give a damn. They would have waited half a lifetime for her. She represented everything to them right now . . . mothers . . . sisters . . . women . . . girlfriends they had left behind . . . women . . . Woman. There was an almost audible purr after nightfall, as they sat there, talking, smoking, rivulets of sweat pouring down their necks and backs, their faces glistening, their hair damp, their uniforms sticking to their flesh, and all of them so young, children almost . . . and at the same time children no more. They were men.

By 1943, they had been here for longer than they cared to remember, and everyone wondered when the war would end – and if it ever would. But tonight no one thought about the war, only the men on duty had to worry about that. And most of the men waiting for her now had bought out of being on duty for the night with every kind of currency they could lay their hands on, everything from chocolate bars to cigarettes to cold hard cash . . . anything . . . anything to see her . . . they would do anything to see Faye Price again.

As the band began to play, the air wasn't thick so much as sultry, the heat no longer oppressive but sensual, and they felt their bodies stir in a way they hadn't in a long, long time. It wasn't just hunger they felt for her, it was something deeper and more tender something that would have frightened them if they had felt it too long. They felt the first stirrings of it now as they waited . . . waited . . . every moment seeming an age as a clarinet began to wail. The music wrenched at the gut and was almost painful, and every face, every man, held his breath and was still. The stage was empty in the darkness, and then suddenly, dimly, they saw her, or thought they did . . . it was impossible to be completely certain, a tiny spotlight sought her in the distance. It found her feet and there was a flash of silver, a sparkle in the distance, like falling stars in a summer sky . . . the shimmer of her body as she approached them made their guts ache, and suddenly she stood there before them. Blinding perfection in a silver lamé gown. There was an audible sigh from the men who watched her, a perfect blend of desire and ecstasy and pain. Her skin was like the palest of pink velvet in the dazzling silver gown, the long, blonde hair was almost the colour of ripe peaches and she had worn it down. Her eyes danced, her mouth smiled, she held her hands out towards them as she sang, and her voice was deeper than any woman they remembered. She was more beautiful than any they had known. She moved and the gown revealed endless, exquisite flesh, the pink perfection of her thighs.

'Oh God . . .' one voice murmured in a back row, and around him, half a hundred young men smiled.

They all felt that way about her, had for years. They hadn't believed it when they'd been told she was going to do a show for them. She had been doing shows like this halfway around the world. In the Pacific, in Europe, in the States. A year after Pearl Harbor, the guilt had overwhelmed her, and she'd been touring off and on now for more than a year. Recently, she had stopped to make another film, but she was back on the road now . . . and tonight, she was here . . . with them.

Her voice had grown mournful as she sang to them and, in the front row, the men who watched could see a pulse beating in her neck. She was alive . . . she was human . . . and if they had reached across the makeshift stage, they could have touched her . . . felt her . . . smelled her flesh. It made them almost keen just to watch her, and seeming to look each man in the eye as she sang, Faye Price let no one down.

At twenty-three years of age, Faye Price was already a legend in Hollywood. She had made her first film at nineteen, and from there had rushed headlong into success. She was beautiful, striking, and so damn good at what she did. She had a voice that ranged from molten lava to melted gold, hair that shimmered like a I golden sunset, green eyes like emeralds in an ivory face. But it wasn't the features, or the voice, or the texture of the skin on her long narrow frame that belied the softly rounded hips and full breasts, it was the warmth that lit her from within, the brilliance that exploded in her eyes, the laughter in her voice when she wasn't singing that enthralled the world. She was a woman, in the best and purest meaning of the word. She was someone men wanted to cling to, women wanted to stare at, children loved to look up to. She was the stuff of which dream princesses were made.

From a small town in Pennsylvania, Faye had made her way to New York after graduating from high school, and had become a model. Within six months she was making more than any girl in town. The photographers all loved her, her face was on the cover of every major magazine in the country, but secretly she admitted to her friends that she was bored. There was so little to it, she insisted; all she had to do was stand there. She tried to explain it, and the other girls looked at her as though she were mad. But two men recognised what she was: the man who later became her agent, and Sam Warman, the producer, who knew a gold mine when he saw one. He had seen her pictures on the magazine covers and he thought she was pretty, but it was only when he met her that he realised how fabulous she was. The way she moved, the way she looked into his eyes when she talked to him, her voice, and he knew instantly that this one wasn't looking to get laid. She wasn't looking for a damn thing, not outside herself, Sam instinctively suspected. And everything Abe, her agent, said about her was true. She was fabulous. Unique. A star. What Faye Price wanted, she wanted from within. She wanted a challenge, she wanted to work hard, she wanted to try anything they'd let her . . . and he did. He gave her the chance she wanted. It wasn't difficult for Abe to talk him into that. Sam brought her to Hollywood and gave her a part in a film. It was a small part, and as it was written, it was not an overly demanding role. But somehow she managed to get under the skin of the writer; there were times when he openly admitted she drove him nuts, but she had got what she wanted out of the part, and what she wanted was very, very good; good for the movie, and for her. The part had been small but gutsy, and a light shone through Faye Price's performance that took people's breaths away. There was something magical about her, half girl, half woman, from elf to siren, and back again, drawing on the full range of human emotions, sometimes only using her facial expressions and her incredible deep green eyes. That part had won her two others and her fourth film had won her the Oscar. Four years after her first role, she had done seven films, and in the fifth one, Hollywood had discovered she could sing. And that's what she was doing now, singing her guts out for soldiers halfway around the world. She gave her guts and her heart and her life to these men, just as she did with everything she attempted. Faye Price was no halfway person, and at twenty-three she was no longer a 'girl' in anyone's eyes, she was all woman. The men who watched her on the stage knew that about her. To watch Faye Price move, to hear her sing, to see her before you was to feel what God intended when he created woman. She was the infinite . . . the ultimate . . . and tonight every man who watched her longed to touch her, just for a moment . . . longed to be within the circle of her arms, his lips gently pressed on hers, his hands in the silky blonde hair . . . they wanted to feel her breath on their shoulders . . . hear her moan softly. There was a sudden groan from one of the boys who watched her and his friends laughed at him. He didn't give a damn.

'Holy Moses . . . ain't she fantastic?' The boy's eyes lit up like a child's at Christmas and the men around him smiled. For a long time they had watched her in total silence, but after the first half hour, they could bear it no more. They screamed, they hooted, they keened for her, they howled. And when the last song ended, they screamed so long and hard that she sang five or six more songs for them. Though they couldn't see it, when she left the stage there were tears in Faye Price's eyes. It was so little to do for them, a few songs, a silver dress, a flash of legs, a hint of womanhood shared among a thousand men in a jungle night, five thousand miles from home. And who knew how many of them would live to go home again? The thought of it always tore at her heart. It was why she had come here, why she had to do this for them. And in the months she had done it, she allowed herself to appear more of a siren than she ever did back home. She would have died before wearing a dress slit almost to her crotch in LA, but if that was what they wanted here, and it was clear they did, then that's what she would give them, what harm was there in giving them a little make-believe pleasure from the safety of a stage?

'Miss Price?' She turned quickly as one of the CO's aides spoke to her as she came off the stage. They could still hear the men screaming for her, and she could barely hear the aide's voice even here.

'Yes?' She looked exhilarated and distracted. Her face and chest were wet with perspiration, and he thought her the most beautiful woman he had ever seen. It wasn't just that her features were perfect, it was that you wanted to reach out and touch her . . . hold her . . . she exuded something he had never felt before, at least not at such close range. A kind of magic mixed with glamour, a sensuality that made you want to kiss her, without ever stopping to ask her name. She was about to leave him and go back out to the men begging for her, and instinctively he reached out and touched her arm. He felt everything within him quicken, and then he felt foolish for his reaction. This was ridiculous. What was she after all? Just another film star, dolled up, done up, and if everything about her was so convincing, it was just that she was better than some of the others at the artistry she created. It was all an illusion, wasn't it? . . . But he knew it wasn't as his eyes met hers, and she smiled at him. There was nothing fake about the woman who stood there. She was precisely who she was. 'I've got to go back out there.' She waved towards the din, mouthing her words as she spoke carefully, and he nodded, shouting his.

'The CO would like you to join him for dinner.'

'Thank you.' Her eyes pulled away from his and she left him and went back to give the men another half hour. This time she sang songs that amused them, including two in which they joined her, and at the end a ballad that made them all fight back tears. When she left them, she did it with a look that seemed to envelop each one of them, like a goodnight kiss from their mothers . . . their wives . . . the girls back home . . . 'Goodnight, friends . . . God bless.' Her voice was husky and suddenly the din had turned into silence. Almost no one spoke as they left their places, and quietly went home to bed. Her words rang in their heads for hours. They had screeched and applauded, but they had been ready when she left them, and now they wanted to go back to their bunks and think about her, letting the songs roam in their heads . . . remembering her face . . . her arms . . . her legs . . . the mouth that seemed to kiss them, and then exploded into laughter and then grew serious again. They all remembered the look in her eyes when she had left them. They would remember it for months. Right now it was all they had. And Faye knew that. It was her gift to them.

'She's some woman.' The words were spoken by a thick-necked sergeant, and were unlike him. But no one was surprised.

12

Faye Price brought something special out in each of them. Their guts, their hearts, their hopes.

'Yeah . . .' An echo voiced a thousand times that night by the men who had seen her, and the men who hadn't, who had been forced to be on duty, tried to pretend they didn't feel cheated. And in the end, they didn't have to pretend at all. Her request was unusual, but quickly granted, and the CO was obviously surprised when he heard of it. He had even assigned his aide to take her around. She had requested permission to tour the base, to meet the men on duty that night. By midnight, she had shaken hands with everyone. So that the men who hadn't seen her performance had met her face to face instead, looking into those incredible green eyes, feeling the strong, cool hand she extended, smiling awkwardly at her words. And in the end, each one felt he had special . . . those who had heard her singing, and those whom she had come to see instead. Suddenly, men were sorry they hadn't been on duty, so that she would have come to see them. But all in all, everyone was pleased. And at twelve-thirty she turned to the young man who had taken her around the base, and she saw something warm and friendly in his eyes. He hadn't looked that way at first. But slowly she had won him over, as she had everyone else. He had wanted to say something to her about it all night, but there had never been quite the right moment. He had been so sceptical about her at first, the cool Miss Faye Price from Hollywood . . . who did she think she was, coming to show off to the men on Guadalcanal? They'd been through enough, they'd seen it all. They'd already survived Midway and the Coral Sea, and the hideous naval battles it had taken to win and keep Guadalcanal. What did she know about it? Ward Thayer thought to himself as he first looked at her. But after all these hours at her side, he had begun to see her differently. She cared. She cared a lot. He read it in her eyes. Watching her meet the men's eyes, totally oblivious of her own charms, reaching out only to them with something they had never felt before made you care about her as well. There was a kind of warmth and compassion about her that in turn enhanced her already incredible sexual appeal. There were a thousand things the young lieutenant wanted to say to her as the night wore on, but it was only after she had finished her rounds that she seemed to notice him at all. She turned to him with a tired smile, and for an instant he wanted to reach out and touch her hand, almost to see if she was real. He almost wanted to comfort her. She had had a long, hard night. But then again, they had had a long, hard year . . . two years.

'Do you suppose your CO will ever forgive me for not making it to dinner with him tonight?' She smiled tiredly.

'He may be heartbroken, but he'll live.' In fact, the lieutenant knew that an hour or two before, the CO had been called into a secret meeting with two generals who had arrived by helicopter that night. He would have had to leave Faye anyway. 'I think he'll be very grateful for what you did for the men.'

'It means a lot to me.' She spoke gently as she sat down on a large, white rock in the warm night air and looked up at him. There was something magical in her eyes, and there was a strange tug in his gut as he looked down at her. It almost hurt to look at her, she brought up feelings that he had wanted to leave behind him in the States. There was no room for that here, no time, no one to share the feelings with. Here there was only killing and misery and loss, and anger sometimes, but the gentler emotions were too painful now, and he looked away from her as she stared at the back of his head. He was a tall, handsome, blond man with broad shoulders and deep blue eyes, but all she could see of him now were the powerful shoulders and the wheat-coloured hair. There was something about him that made her want to reach out to him. There was so much pain here, they were all so damn lonely and sad and young . . . and yet with only a little warmth, a touch, a hand on theirs they came alive, and they laughed and they sang . . . that was what she loved about these tours, no matter how tiring they were. It was like bringing new life to all of these men, even this young lieutenant, who was so tall and proud as he turned to face her again, obviously defending himself, or trying to, against all that he felt, and yet not quite able to shut her out after all. 'Do you know, after spending the whole evening with you,' she smiled up at him again, 'I don't know your name.' She knew only his rank, and they had never really been introduced.

'Thayer. Ward Thayer.' The name rang a distant bell, but she didn't know why and didn't really care. He smiled at her, and there was something cynical in his eyes. He had seen too much in the last year and she sensed that easily about him. 'Are you hungry, Miss, Price? You must be starved.' She had performed for hours, and had been touring the base, shaking hands, for three hours since. She nodded now, with a shy smile.

'I am. Do you suppose we should go knock on the CO's door and ask if there's anything left.' They both laughed at the thought.

'I think I can dig something up for you somewhere else.' He glanced at his watch, as she looked at him. What was there about this man? There was something about him that kept making her want to reach out, to ask him who he really was, to find out more. There was something one couldn't know, and yet which one sensed about him. But he smiled up at her now, and he looked young again. 'Would you be terribly offended if we check out the kitchen? I'll bet I can get you a real meal there, if you'd like that.'

She held up a graceful hand. 'A sandwich would be great.'

'Let's see what we can do.' They headed back to his jeep, and drove swiftly to the long quonset hut where the men's meals were prepared and, twenty minutes later, she was seated on a long bench faced with a plate of hot stew. It wasn't what she would have picked for a hot jungle night, but she was so hungry and it had been such a long night that the steaming concoction actually tasted good, and Ward Thayer had a plate of it too. 'Just like "21" eh?' He glanced at her with his cynical grin again and she laughed.

'More or less . . . except it's not hash . . .' she teased and he winced.

'Oh God, don't say that word. If the cook hears you, he'll be only too happy to oblige.' The two of them laughed again, and Faye was suddenly reminded of midnight suppers after school proms back home and suddenly she began to laugh harder as she looked at him, and he cocked an eyebrow over the handsome blue eyes. 'I'm glad you're amused. This place hasn't struck me as funny in well over a year.' But he looked happier now. He was enjoying her company and it showed and, nibbling at the stew, she explained it to him.

'You know . . . just like after the prom . . . when you have breakfast in some diner at five am . . . this is sort of like that, isn't it?' She looked around the harshly lit room and his eyes followed hers and then searched her face again.

'Where'd you grow up?' They were almost friends now. They had been together for hours, and there was something about being together in a war zone. Everything was different here. Faster, more personal, more intense. It was all right to ask questions one would never have asked anywhere else, and to reach out in ways that otherwise one wouldn't have dared.

She answered him thoughtfully. 'Pennsylvania.'

'Did you like it?'

'Not much. We were dirt poor. All I wanted was to get the hell out, which I did, the minute I graduated from high school.'

He smiled. It was difficult to imagine her dirt poor anywhere, and least of all in some hick town.

'What about you? Where are you from, Lieutenant?'

'Ward. Or did you forget my name again?' She blushed as he teased. 'I grew up in LA.' He seemed loath to add more; and she wasn't quite sure why.

'You going back there after . . . afterwards?' She hated the word 'war', and by now so did he. It had already cost him a lot, too much; there were wounds now that would never heal, even

16

if they weren't the kind she could see. But instinctively she knew that they were there.

'Yeah. I guess so.'

'Are your folks there?' She was curious about him, this sad, cynical, handsome young man, with the secrets he didn't want to reveal, as they ate their stew in the ugly, brightly lit mess hall on Guadalcanal. There were stiff blackout covers on all the windows, so the impression was that there were no windows at all. They were both used to that.

'My folks are both dead.' He looked evenly at her, something dead in his own eyes. He had said the word too often by now.

'I'm sorry.'

'We weren't close anyway.' But still . . . her eyes searched his again as he stood up. 'More stew, or something more exotic for dessert? They tell me there's an apple pie hidden somewhere.' his eyes smiled and she laughed.

'No thanks. There's no room in costumes like this for apple pie.' She glanced down at the silver lamé dress, and for the first time in several hours, so did he. He was getting used to her looking like that. It was different from Kathy of course . . . so different in her starched white . . . and eventually, the fatigues she wore . . .

He disappeared for a moment and then returned with a small plate of fruit and a tall glass of iced tea. It was more precious than wine here, ice being almost impossible to make. But he had filled the glass with the precious ice cubes, and she had been on tour often enough to know what a rare gift this was. She savoured each mouthful of the chill drink as a few men came and went, staring openly at her. But she seemed not to mind. She was used to it. She smiled casually at them, always turning her eyes back to Ward, and now she had to stifle a small yawn, as he pretended to look crushed and shook his head, mocking her. He teased a lot, and there was something funny about him. And at the same time something sad.

'Funny, they always do that after talking to me. I put them to sleep every time.' She laughed and took another sip of the iced tea.

'If you'd been up since four o'clock this morning, you'd be yawning too. I suppose you officers hang around in bed until noon around here?' She knew it wasn't true, but she liked teasing him; It quenched some of the sadness in his eyes and she sensed that he needed that. And he looked at her oddly then.

'What makes you do this, Faye?' He suddenly dared to use her first name and he wasn't sure why, but it felt good on his lips, and she didn't seem to mind. She said nothing about it anyway.

'Some kind of a need I guess . . . to repay all the good things that have happened to me. I never really feel I deserve it all. And you have to pay your dues in life.' It was the kind of thing Kathy would have said and tears almost filled his eyes. He had never felt that kind of a need, to pay 'dues', to repay anyone for how fortunate he had been. And now he didn't feel fortunate any more anyway. Not since . . .

'Why do women always feel a need to pay dues?'

'That has nothing to do with it. Some men do too. Don't you, in a way? Don't you want to do something nice for the next guy, if something good happens to you?'

His eyes grew rock hard as he looked at her. 'Nothing good has happened to me in a hell of a long time . . . at least not since I've been here.'

'You're alive, aren't you, Ward?' Her voice was soft beneath the bright lights where they sat, but her eyes bore into him.

'Sometimes that's not enough.'

'Yes, it is. In a place like this, that's a lot to be grateful for. Look around you every day . . . look at the boys wounded and crippled and maimed . . . the ones who're never going home at all . . .' Something about the tone of her voice bore straight to his heart and for the first time in four months, he had to fight back tears.

'I try hard not to think about that.'

'Maybe you should. Maybe it'll make you glad you're alive.' She wanted to reach him, to touch the place that hurt so much. She wondered what it was, as slowly he stood up.

'I don't give a damn any more, Faye. If I live or die, it's all the same to me and everyone else.'

'That's a terrible thing to say.' She looked shocked and almost hurt as she stared up at him. 'What could possibly make you feel like that?'

He looked down at her for an endless moment, silently begging himself not to say anything more, and suddenly wishing she'd go away. But he stared at her; she seemed not to move at all, and suddenly he didn't give a damn who he told. What difference did it make now? 'I got married six months ago, to an army nurse, and two months after that she was killed by a fucking Jap bomb. It's kind of hard to feel good about this place after that. You know what I mean?'

She sat frozen in her seat, and then slowly nodded her head. So that was it. That was the emptiness she saw in his eyes. She wondered if he'd always be like that, or if he'd come alive again. One day. Maybe. 'I'm sorry, Ward.' There wasn't much else one could say. There were other stories much like this, some worse. But that was no consolation to him.

'I'm sorry.' He smiled a quiet smile. There was no point dumping it on her. It wasn't her fault. And she was so different from Kathy. Kathy was quiet and ordinary and he had been so desperately in love with her. And this woman was all beauty and flash, worldly right down to the tip of every brightly polished nail. 'I'm sorry, I didn't mean to tell you something like that. There are thousand stories like that here.' She knew that there were and she had heard most of them before, but that didn't make them any easier to hear. She felt terrible for him, and as she followed him slowly back out to the jeep, she was glad she hadn't had dinner with the CO after all, and she told him so, as he turned to her with that quiet half smile of his that somehow appealed to her, more than any smile she'd seen in Hollywood, at least in the last year or two.

'That's a nice thing to say.'

She wanted to touch his arm, but she didn't dare. She wasn't just Faye Price the actress now, she was herself. 'I mean it, Ward.'

'Why? You don't have to feel sorry for me, Faye. I'm a big boy. I can take care of myself. I have for a long time.' But she saw more than that. She saw what Kathy had, and more. She knew how desperately hurt he was, how lonely, how shocked still by the pretty little nurse's death . . . his wife . . . it had happened two months after they got married, to the day, but he didn't tell Faye that bitter detail as he drove her back to the tent she'd been assigned. 'I still think it's damn nice of you to come out here to see the men.'

'Thanks.'

He stopped the jeep, and they sat looking at each other for along time, each with a lot more to say, but no way to say it here. Where did one start? How did one begin? He had read about her affair with Gable years before, and he wondered if it was over now. She wondered how long he would pine for the army nurse he had loved.

'Thank you for dinner.' She said it with a shy smile and he laughed as he opened the door for her.

'I told you . . . it's just like "21" . . .'

'Next time I'll try the hash.' They were back to joking again, it seemed to be the only route open to them, but as he walked her to the door of her tent, and pulled the flaps back for her, there was something more in his eyes, something quiet and deep and alive in a way he hadn't been a few hours before.

'I'm sorry I told you all that. I didn't mean to lay my troubles in your lap.', He reached out a hand and touched her arm as she looked at him.

'Why not, Ward? What's so wrong with that? Who else do you have to talk to here?'

'We don't talk about things like that.' He shrugged. 'Everyone knew anyway.' And suddenly the tears he had fought back before sprang into his eyes again, and he started to turn away, as she grabbed his arm and pulled him back.

'It's all right, Ward . . . it's all right . . .' And the next thing she knew, she was holding him tight, and they were both crying, he for a dead wife, and she for a girl she had never known, and a thousand men who had died and would continue to die long after she went home. They cried for the agony and the waste and the sorrow that was inescapable here, and then he looked down at her, and gently smoothed a hand over her silky hair. She was the most beautiful woman he had ever seen, and it struck him as odd that he didn't even feel guilty for thinking that. Maybe Kathy would understand . . . maybe it didn't even matter any more . . . she was never coming back to him . . . he would never hold her or touch her again . . . and he would probably never see Faye again after that night. He knew that too, and wished he could go to bed with her. Now. Before he died or she did, or time ended the spark they felt as surely as any bomb.

She sat down slowly on the room's only chair, and looked up at him, as he sat down on her sleeping bag, and they silently held hands, a lifetime of words unspoken but deeply felt, as the jungle roared to life in the distance somewhere.

'I'm never going to forget you, Faye Price. I hope you know that.'

'I'll remember you too. I'll be thinking about you over here . . . I'll be knowing that you're all right every time I think about you.' And he actually believed that she would. She was that kind of girl, despite the fame and the glamour and the silver lamé dress. She had called it a 'costume' and to her that was all it was. That was the beauty of her.

'Maybe I'll surprise you and drop in on you at the studio when I come home.'

'You do that, Ward Thayer.' Her voice was quiet and firm, her eyes still beautiful after the tears.

'Will you have me thrown out?' He seemed amused at the thought and she looked incensed.

'Of course not!'

'I may try it, you know.'

'Good.' She smiled at him again, and he could see how exhausted she was. She had given so much of herself that night.

To the others, to him. And it was after four o'clock. She would have to be up again in less than two hours, in order to move on, to do the next show. She had been working nonstop for months now. Two months on tour, and three months before that, without a day off, on her biggest film so far. And when she went back, there was another film waiting for her. She was a big star, and she had a big career, but none of that seemed to matter here. She was just a pretty girl with a big heart, and given a little time, he could easily have fallen in love with her.

He stood up, almost regretfully, took her fingers in his own, and then lifted them to his lips. 'Thanks, Faye . . . if I never see you again, thank you for tonight . . .'

She left her fingers in his for a long moment, her eyes holding his, 'We'll meet again one day.' He wasn't as sure, but he wanted to believe her words. And then the weight of the moment was too much for him, and he needed to make light of it. 'I'll bet you say that to all the guys.'

She laughed and stood up as he walked slowly to the tent door. 'You're impossible, Ward Thayer.'

He turned and glanced over his shoulder at her. 'You're not bad yourself, Miss Price.' She was just Faye to him now, in his mind, it was difficult to remember who else she was . . . Faye Price . . . the film star . . . actress . . . singer . . . important personality . . . she was just Faye to him, now, for tonight. His face sobered slowly then. 'Will I see you again before you leave?' Suddenly that mattered a lot to him, and to her as well, more than he knew in fact. She wanted to see him again too before she left.

'Maybe we can catch a quick cup of coffee tomorrow morning before things get too crazy.' She knew the crew had probably been up all night, raising hell with the enlisted men, or the nursing staff, or preferably both, singing and playing the band's instruments. It was the same everywhere they went, but they needed to let off steam, and they never seemed to mind staying up all night. The crunch would come the next day when they had to get organised to leave, and then suddenly everything would be totally insane for two hours before they boarded the plane to the next base. She went through it almost every day, and then finally on the plane they would all sleep until the next stop, and then the magic would begin again. She would have a lot to do before they left, to help everybody load up, but maybe, just maybe . . . there would be a spare moment for him . . . 'I'll look for you.'

'I'll be around.'

But when she joined the others at the mess hall the next day at seven o'clock, he was not there. The CO had needed him, and it was almost nine o'clock before Ward found Faye standing with the others while their plane warmed up. There had been a faint look of panic in her eyes which pleased him as he shrieked up in the jeep, and jumped out to speak to her.

'Sorry, Faye . . . the CO . . .' The noise of the propellers drowned him out, and there were frantic orders being given by the stage manager to the rest of the group around her.

'It's all right . . .' She smiled her dazzling smile at him, but he saw that she looked tired today. She couldn't have had more than two hours' sleep, and he had had half of that himself, but he was used to it. She was wearing a bright red jumpsuit today with platform sandals that made him smile. The latest fashions for Guadalcanal . . . and then suddenly Kathy's face flashed into mind and he felt the old familiar pain again. His eyes met Faye's as someone in the distance shouted her name. 'I have to go . . .'

'I know.' They were both shouting above the din.

He grabbed her hand for one moment and squeezed it hard. He wanted to kiss her lips but he didn't dare. 'I'll see you at the studio!'

'What?' She looked distressed; in all her travels among service men, no one had touched her as this man had.

'I said . . . see you at the studio!'

She smiled at him, suddenly wondering if she would ever see him again. 'Take care of yourself!'

'Sure.' There were no guarantees here. For anyone. Even for her. Her plane could have been shot down on its way to their next stop. They all accepted that, realised it, until someone they cared about got hurt . . . a buddy, a roommate, a friend . . . Kathy . . . he shook the image from his mind again. 'You take care too.' What did you say to a woman like her? 'Good luck.' She didn't need much of that, she already had it all. Or did she? He wondered if there was a man in her life, but it was too late to ask now. She had begun to walk away with the others, looking back and waving at him. The CO had suddenly arrived for a last round of thanks, and Ward saw her shaking his hand, as he watched her go, and then she was in the plane, standing in the doorway for a last instant as she waved at him, and then the red jumpsuit disappeared from his life, probably for good, he thought. He hardened himself never to see her again. It was unlikely that he would, he told himself, as Faye told herself the same thing. She found herself looking down at him, wondering why he had hit her so hard. Maybe it was time to go home after all, maybe the men she met on tour were beginning to appeal to her, and that could be dangerous . . . but it wasn't that . . . it was something else about him . . . something she had never felt before. But she couldn't afford those feelings now. He was a stranger to her, she reminded herself, and she had a life to live. A life which didn't include him. He was fighting a war. And she had enough wars of her own . . . on tour . . . in Hollywood . . . Goodbye, Ward Thayer, she whispered to herself . . . good luck . . . and then she sat back and closed her eyes as the plane flew on . . . but his face haunted her for weeks . . . those deep blue eyes . . . it was months before he was completely out of her mind. And then he was. At last.

HOLLYWOOD 1945

Chapter 2

Everyone on the set stood in total silence, and tension was heavy in the air. They had waited for almost four months for this moment, and now that it was here they all wanted to stop it, to keep it from coming, to make it come on another day. It had been one of those magical films where almost everything went smoothly; what seemed like lasting friendships had been made, everyone was crazy about the star, and all of the women were more than half in love with the director. The male lead was Christopher Arnold, and everyone said he was Hollywood's biggest male star. It was easy to see why, the man was a pro. And now they all stood watching him, in his last scene, speaking softly, tears in his eyes. You could have heard a pin drop all the way to Pasadena, and Faye Price walked off the set for the last time, head bowed, real tears streaming down her cheeks. Arnold watched her go, devastated . . . that was it . . . the final scene . . . it was over.

'That's a wrap!' the voice shouted, and there was an endless instant of silence, followed by a shriek, and then suddenly everyone was shouting, laughing, hugging, crying. There was champagne for the entire crew, and it rapidly turned into a raucous party with everyone talking at once, wishing each other well, hating to leave. Christopher Arnold gave Faye a powerful hug, and pulled away a moment later to look deep into her eyes as he held her.

'It's been a joy working with you, Faye.'

'I've enjoyed it too.' They exchanged a long, knowing smile. They had been involved with each other once, almost three

27

years before, and she had been hesitant about doing the film because of that. But it had worked out beautifully. He had been a perfect gentleman from beginning to end, and other than a glimmer of something more than recognition in his eyes on the first day, this was the first sign of their old liaison. It hadn't got in the way of their work at all during the entire three months of making the picture.

He smiled at her warmly as he took his arms from around her. 'I'm going to miss you all over again now. And I thought I was over all that.' They both laughed.

'So will I.' She looked around at the rest of the cast, happily raising hell, and the director, passionately kissing the set designer, who also happened to be his wife. Faye had enjoyed working with them both. Directing had fascinated her ever since she had started acting. 'What are you going to do now, Chris?'

'I'm leaving for New York in a week, and then I'm sailing to France. I want to spend a few days on the Riviera before this summer is entirely over. Everyone tells me it's too soon for France but what have I got to lose? I hear nothing's changed, except for a little rationing.' He looked rakish for a moment as he winked at her. He was twenty years older than she, but on him it looked more like ten. He was probably the best-looking man in town, and he knew it. 'Care to come with me?' As attractive as he was, he no longer appealed to her.

'No thanks.' She gave him an airy smile, and then wagged a finger at him. 'Now don't start that again. You've behaved yourself through this whole picture, Chris.'

'Of course, that was work. This is different.'

'Oh is that it?' She was about to say something to tease him, but suddenly the chaos around them seemed to heighten and a page ran onto the set screeching something Faye couldn't discern. For a moment, panic registered on a number of faces, and then shock, and then there were tears, and Faye still hadn't heard what had happened. She pulled at Chris Arnold's sleeve, her eyes anxious. 'What did he say . . .? What . . .?' Chris was speaking to someone to his right, and Faye was straining to hear above the din.

'My God . . .' He turned to her with a look of amazement. And then without thinking he pressed her to him in a huge hug again, and she could hear his voice tremble when he spoke to her. 'It's all over, Faye . . . the war is over. The Japanese have surrendered.' It had ended in Europe only months before, and now finally it was all over. Tears sprang to her eyes, and she was crying as she hugged him back. Suddenly everyone on the set was crying and laughing, others had joined them, and fresh cases of champagne were opened. Everyone was shouting now. 'It's over! It's over!' No longer the film . . . but the war.

It felt like hours before she left the set to go back to her house in Beverly Hills, and the pain of finishing the film was long since gone. It had been totally eclipsed by her joy that the war was over. It seemed amazing. She had been twenty-one years old when Pearl Harbor was bombed, and now here she was, twenty-five years old, grown up, a woman, at the summit of her career.

This had to be the summit; she told herself that every year. She couldn't imagine anything improving from this point on. How could it? And yet it had. The roles got better and bigger and more important, the praise more lavish, the money more unbelievable each year. The only blemish in it all came when her parents died. It made her sad that her parents were no longer alive to enjoy it with her. They had both died the previous year. Her father of cancer, her mother in a car accident on an icy Pennsylvania road near Youngstown. She had tried to get her mother to come out to live in California, after her father died, but she hadn't wanted to give up her home. So now she had no one. The little house in Grove City, Pennsylvania, had been sold the year before. She had no sisters or brothers. And other than the faithful couple who worked for her in the handsome small house she had bought in Beverly Hills, Faye Price was alone. She seldom felt lonely though; there were too many people around her for that. She enjoyed her work and her friends. And yet, it was odd not having any family now. No one she 'belonged' to. It still surprised her that she had become so successful, and her life had become so lavish, in such a short time. Even at twenty-one, when the war had broken out, her life had been different. But now, ever since her last USO tour two years before, things had settled down. She had bought the house, made six films in two years, and although she had intended to go on tour again she had never had the time. Life seemed to be an endless round of premières and publicity pictures and press parties, and when she wasn't doing that, she was getting up at five o'clock in the morning and going to work on a film. Her next picture was scheduled to start in five weeks, and she was already reading the script for hours every night before she went to sleep, and now that she had finished the film she'd been working on, she could really get down to work. The new one was a sure Oscar for her, her agent had told her. But she always laughed when he said that . . . it was a ridiculous thought . . . except that she had already won one, and been nominated two other times. But Abe insisted this film would be a big one, and Faye believed him. In an odd way, he had become a father figure to her.

She turned her car right on Summit Drive, past Pickfair and the Chaplins, and a moment later reached her own home as Bob, who spent his days in the little gate house, opening the gate for deliveries and friends, or for Miss Price herself, ran out with a smile for her.

'Have a nice day, Miss Price?' He was ancient and white-haired and grateful for the job. He had been working for her now for over a year.

'I sure did, Bob. Did you hear the news?' He looked blank. 'The war is over!' She beamed at him and tears came to his eyes. He had been too old to go to the First World War himself, but he had lost his only son. And now, in this war, it reminded him every day of the grief he and his wife had felt way back then.

'Are you sure, ma'am?'

'Positive. It's all over.' She reached out and shook his hand.

'Thank God.' His voice trembled and he turned his head to wipe his eyes. But he didn't apologise to her when he looked back into the lovely face. 'Thank God.' She wanted to kiss him for all that they both felt, but she smiled, and waited for him to open quietly the large handsome brass gates which he kept shined to perfection at all times.

'Thank you, Bob.'

'Goodnight, Miss Price.' He would come up to the house late for dinner in the kitchen with her butler and maid, but Faye wouldn't see him again until she drove out the next day. And if she chose to stay at home, she wouldn't see him at all. He only worked in the daytime, and at night, her butler, Arthur, drove for her, and would open the gate himself with his key. Most of the time, Faye preferred to drive herself. She had bought a beautiful Lincoln Continental with a convertible top, in a deep shade of blue, and she was perfectly content to drive around Los Angeles herself. Except at night when Arthur drove her out in the Rolls. It had seemed a shocking thing to buy at first, and she had almost been too embarrassed to admit it was hers, but it was such a beautiful machine that she hadn't been able to resist. And there was still a certain excitement as she stepped into it; the rich smell of leather everywhere, the thick grey carpeting beneath her feet. Even the wood in the magnificent car was totally unique, and finally she had decided what the hell. At twenty-five, her success no longer embarrassed her as it once had. She had a right to it, 'more or less', she teased herself, and she wasn't hurting anyone. She had no one else to spend her money on, and she was making so damn much of it. It was hard to know what to do with it all. She had invested some, on her agent's advice, but the rest just sat there and waited to get spent, and she was far less extravagant than most of the stars of her day. Most of them were wearing emeralds and diamonds to the floor, buying tiaras they couldn't afford, sable coats and ermine and chinchillas, to parade around in at openings of other people's films. Faye was far more restrained in what she wore, and what she did, although she did have some beautiful clothes which she enjoyed, and two or three very beautiful fur coats. There was a white fox coat that she adored; she looked like an exquisite blonde eskimo when she buried herself in it on a cold night. She had worn it just the winter before in New York, and she had actually heard people gasp as she walked past them. And then there was a dark chocolate sable she had bought in France, and a sensible mink she kept for 'everyday' . . . 'Just my everyday mink,' she grinned to herself, as she pulled the Lincoln up outside the house. How life had changed since she was a little girl. She had always wanted to have a second pair of shoes, for 'dressing up', but her parents had been too poor back then. The Depression had hit them hard, and both of her parents had been out of work for a long, long time. Her father had wound up doing odd jobs, and hating everything about his life. Her mother had finally found a job as a secretary. But it all seemed so dreary to Faye. That was why the movies had always seemed to magical to her. It was the perfect escape for hours and hours and hours. She would save every penny she could lay her little fingers on, and then off she'd go to sit in the dark, gaping at what she saw. Maybe that was in the back of her head after all when she went to New York to find work as a model . . . and now here she was, walking up the three pink marble steps to her own house in Beverly Hills, as a serious-faced English butler opened the door to her, and in spite of himself smiled into her eyes. He couldn't resist the 'young miss', as he called her in private to his wife. She was the nicest employer they had ever had, they agreed, and certainly the youngest by far. And she had never acquired what they referred to as 'Hollywood ways'. She didn't seem overly impressed with who she was, and she was always pleasant and polite and thoughtful to them. The house was a pleasure to run, and there was very little to do. Faye seldom entertained, and she was working most of the time, so all they had to do was keep things neat and clean, and running smoothly for her, a task Arthur and Elizabeth both enjoyed.

'Good afternoon, Arthur.'

'Miss Price,' he looked extremely prim, 'excellent news, isn't it?' He assumed correctly that she would have heard, and he knew she had when she beamed.

'It certainly is.' She knew that they had no sons to fear for, but they still had relatives in England who had been hit hard by the war, and Arthur had always been deeply concerned for them. He spoke of the RAF as very near to God-like. They had discussed the Pacific theatre as well from time to time, but there would be no war to discuss any more. As she walked into her study, and down at the little English desk to open her mail, she wondered how many of the men she had seen were still alive, how many of the hands she had shaken were no more. It brought tears to her eyes as she thought of it, and she turned to look out into the perfectly tended garden and the pool house beyond. How difficult to imagine the holocaust that had existed over there, the countries that had been destroyed, the people who had died. She wondered, as she often had, if Ward was among them. She had never heard from him, but over the years, he had never quite left her mind. And thinking of him often made her feel guilty that she hadn't gone on tour again; but there had never been time. There never was. Not lately. Not after her parents' death, and the constant demands of her career.

She turned back to her desk now, glancing through a stack of mail from her agent, and assorted bills, trying to force the faces of the past from her mind, but there was so little in her present to occupy her thoughts, other than work. She had had a serious involvement with a director twice her age the year before, and she realised at the end of it that she had been more in love with his work than she was with him. She loved hearing about what he did, but after a while there wasn't much excitement left, and they had finally drifted apart, and there had been no one serious in her life since. She wasn't given to the usual Hollywood affairs, and she had never got involved with anyone unless she

33

truly cared about him. She kept to herself most of the time, and avoided publicity as much as she could. For a major star, she led a remarkably quiet life, but she insisted to her friend and agent, Abe, when he scolded her for 'hiding' too much of the time, that she couldn't work as hard as she did unless she did stay home, to study and prepare for her roles, and that was just exactly what she was planning to do in the next five weeks, no matter how much Abe nagged her to get out, be seen, and have some fun with her colleagues.

Instead, she had promised to go up to San Francisco to visit a friend for a few days, an elderly actress, now retired, whom she had befriended at the beginning of her career. And on the way home she was planning to stop and see friends in Pebble Beach. After that, she had agreed to a weekend with the Hearsts at their vast country estate, complete with wild animals and a zoo, and after that she was coming home to rest and relax and study and read. She liked nothing better than lying around her own pool, soaking in the sun, smelling the flowers, listening to the bees. She closed her eyes now, just thinking of it, and never heard Arthur walk softly into the room. She heard him clear his throat some distance from her and opened her eyes. One never heard Arthur come in. For a man of his size and years, he walked with catlike grace, and now he stood before her, some eight or ten feet beyond her desk, in his tailcoat and striped trousers, wing collar, and carefully starched shirt and tie, holding a silver tray, bearing a single cup of tea. She had bought the china in Limoges herself and was especially fond of it. It was pure white, with a tiny blue flower here and there, as though put there almost as an afterthought, and she saw as Arthur set the cup down on her desk with the white linen napkin she had bought in New York, made in Italy before the war, that Elizabeth had sent in some cookies today as well. Normally, Faye wouldn't have indulged, but she had five weeks before the next picture after all, so why not? She smiled up at Arthur, and he bowed; and silently left the room. She looked around at the things she loved; the shelves lined with books, both old and new, some even very rare, the vases filled with flowers, the sculptures she had begun to buy a few years before, the beautiful Aubusson rug in dusty pinks and pale blues with scattered flowers all over it, the English furniture she had selected so carefully, the silver that Arthur polished till they shone, and beyond her study she could see the lovely French crystal chandelier that hung in the hall, the dining room with its English table and Chippendale chairs and another chandelier beyond. It was a home that gave her pleasure every day, not just because of the beauty of its treasures, but also because of the contrast to the threadbare poverty she had grown up with. It made each object more precious, from every silver candlestick and lace tablecloth to each gleaming antique. Each was a symbol of her accomplishment and its rewards.

There was a handsome living room as well, with a pink marble fireplace, and delicately shaped French chairs. She had blended English with French, a few modern pieces with the old, two lovely Impressionist paintings that had been a gift from a very, very dear friend. And a small but elegant staircase led upstairs. Here, her bedroom was done entirely in mirrors and white silks, like the kind of fantasies she had had as a little girl, enamoured by the cinema. There was a white fox bedspread on her bed, fur pillows on the couch, a white fur thrown on the chaise longue, and a white marble fireplace identical to the one in her mirrored dressing room. Her bathroom was all done in white marble and white tile. And there was another small sitting room, which she often used late at night when she was studying a script, or writing a letter to a friend. And that was all of it. A tiny, perfect gem. Just the right size for her. There were servants' quarters behind the kitchen on the main floor, and a huge garage with a flat over it, where Bob, the gatekeeper, lived. Extensive gardens, a good-sized swimming pool with a small pool house and a bar, and dressing room for her friends. She had everything she wanted here, a world unto itself, she often said. She almost hated to go anywhere any more, and she was almost sorry she had promised to go to San Francisco the following week to visit her old friend.

Once she was there, she had a good time with her. The woman, Harriet Fielding, had been a famous actress on the Broadway stage years before, and Faye had enormous respect for her. Harriet had taught her a great deal, and Faye talked to her about her new role now. There was no doubt it would be challenging. The leading man was said to be difficult, and a prima donna of the worst sort, everyone said. Faye had never worked with him before and wasn't looking forward to it. She hoped she hadn't made a mistake accepting the role, but Harriet insisted that she had not. The part had more meat to it, and required more expertise, than anything Faye had ever done before.

'That's exactly what frightens me!' She laughed with her old friend as they looked out across the Bay. 'What if I fall flat on my face?' It was like having a mother again, being able to talk to her, although Harriet was very different from how her own mother had been. She was more sophisticated, more worldly, more knowledgeable about Faye's work. Margaret Price had really never understood anything about what Faye did or the world she had moved into, but she had certainly been proud of her. She bragged to everyone, and Faye was touched to realise how much her mother cared about it all whenever she went home. But there was no home to go back to now, no one she still cared about in her home town. Instead, there was Harriet, who meant a great deal to her. 'I'm serious, what if I'm terrible?'

'In the first place, you won't be. And in the second, if you do fall on your face, and we all do from time to time then you'll pick yourself up and try again, and do better next time. Probably much better, in fact. What's the matter with you? You've never been cowardly before, Faye Price.' The old woman sounded annoyed, but Faye knew it was all an act. 'Do your homework and you'll be just fine.'

'I hope you're right.' The old woman growled at her in response, and Faye smiled. There was something so comforting about Harriet in many ways. They walked the hills of San Francisco side by side for five days and talked about everything from life to the war, from their careers to men. Harriet was one of the few people Faye really talked to. She was so wise and so bright and so funny. She was a rare, rare, woman and Faye was always grateful to have found her.

When the conversation turned to men, Harriet questioned her, and not for the first time, about why she never seemed to settle down with any one man.

'They're never quite right, I guess.'

'Some of them must be.' Harriet looked searchingly at her young friend. 'Are you afraid?'

'Maybe. But I really don't think any of them have been right. I can have anything I want from them: orchids, gardenias, champagne, exotic evenings, fabulous nights, entrée to some extraordinary parties, and in some cases expensive gifts, but that's never really been what I wanted. None of that seems real to me. It never has.'

'Thank God.' That was one of the reasons why Harriet liked her. 'It isn't real. You've always been smart enough to see that. But there are other men in LA, not just the fakers and the pretenders and the playboys.' Although they both knew that because of Faye's looks, and her star status, she attracted hordes of what Harriet loved to call the 'glitter gluttons'.

'Maybe I just haven't had time to meet the right ones.' And the funny thing was that she could never imagine settling down with any of those men, even Gable. What she wanted was a slightly more sophisticated version of the men she would have met back home, in Grove City, the kind of guy who would shovel snow on a cold winter morning, and cut down a Christmas tree for the kids, and go for long walks with her and sit by a fire, or walk along beside a lake with her in summer . . . someone real . . . someone else she could talk to . . . someone who put her and the children ahead of else, even his job . . . not someone who was looking to hitch wagon to a star and get a great part in someone else's new film. Thinking of that brought her mind back to her new film, and she questioned Harriet again about some of the subtleties of the script and the techniques she wanted to try. She liked being adventurous about her acting – and creative. As long as she wasn't creating a home and a family for someone, the least she could do was put all her creative energies into her career, and thus far she had done that with enormous success, as the whole world knew. But Harriet was still sorry that the right man hadn't come along. She sensed that that would bring out a dimension of Faye that hadn't been touched yet, a dimension which would enhance her both as a woman and an actress.

'Will you come down and watch me on the set?' Faye turned to her with pleading eyes and she looked like a child to the older woman. But Harriet only smiled gently and shook her head.

'You know how I hate that place, Faye.'

'But I need you.' There was something lonely in Faye's eyes; it was the first time Harriet had seen it, and she patted her young friend's arm reassuringly.

'I need you too, as a friend. But you don't need my advice as an actress, Faye Price. You've got more talent than I ever had in my little finger. You're going to be just fine. I know it. And my being on the set would only distract you.' It was the first time in a long time that Faye had felt she needed moral support on the set, and she still felt shaky about it when she left Harriet in San Francisco, later than planned, and began her trip down the coast road to what the Hearsts modestly called their 'Casa'. All the way down, she found herself thinking of Harriet.

For some reason she herself didn't understand, she felt lonelier than she had in years. She found herself missing Harriet, her old home in Pennsylvania, her parents. For the first time in years, she felt as though there were something missing in her life, though she couldn't imagine what. She tried to tell herself that she was just nervous about the new part, but it was more than that. There was no man in her life just then, hadn't been in a long time, and Harriet was right, it was too bad she never did settle down, but with whom? She couldn't imagine a single face that appealed to her at the moment; there was no one she was anxious to see when she got home, and the revels at the Hearsts' estate seemed emptier than ever. There were dozens of guests, and as always, lots of amusing entertainers, but there suddenly seemed to be no substance to the life she led, or the people she knew and met. The only thing that made any sense was her work, and the two people she cared about most, Harriet Fielding, who lived five hundred miles away, and her agent, Abe Abramson.

In the end, after smiling interminably for days on end, it was a relief to head for Los Angeles. When she arrived, she let herself in with her key and walked upstairs into the white splendour of her own bedroom, feeling happier than she had in weeks. It was wonderful to be home. It looked better to her than the Hearsts' grand estate, and she lay across the white fox throw with a happy grin, kicking off her shoes, staring up at the pretty little chandelier, and thinking with excitement of her new role. She felt good again. So what if there was no man in her life? She had her work, and it made her very, very happy.

For the next month, she studied night and day, learning every line in the script, hers and everyone else's as well. She tried out different nuances, spent entire days walking the grounds of her home, talking to herself, trying it out, becoming the woman that she was to play. In the film she would be driven mad by the man she had married. Eventually, he would take their child from her, and she would attempt to kill herself, and then him, and slowly, slowly she would realise what he had done to her. She would prove it in the end, retrieve the child, and finally kill him. But even that final act of violence and vengeance was desperately important to Faye. Would the audience lose sympathy with her then? Would they love her more? Would they care? Would she win their hearts? It meant everything to her.

On the morning that filming was to begin, Faye was at the studio right on time, the script in a red alligator briefcase she always carried with her, her own makeup case made to match, a suitcase filled with a few things she always liked to have on the set, and she moved into her dressing room in a quiet and businesslike way that was a delight to some, and enraged those who could not compete with her. Above all, and beyond anything, Faye Price was a professional, and she was also a perfectionist. But she demanded nothing from anyone that she didn't demand from herself first.

A maid from the studio was assigned to take care of Faye, her clothes, and her dressing room. Some brought their own help, but Faye could never imagine Elizabeth here, and she always left her at home. The women provided by the studio did just as well. This time they assigned a pleasant black woman to her, who had worked with her before. Pearl was extremely capable, and Faye had enjoyed her comments and remarks before. The woman was sharp and had been working around the studio for years, and some of the stories she told made Faye laugh until she cried. So this morning, they were happy to meet again. She hung up all of Faye's own clothes, put her makeup out, did not touch the briefcase because she had made that mistake before and remembered that Faye didn't like anyone else handling her script. She served her coffee with exactly the right dose of milk, and at seven in the morning, when the hairdresser arrived to do Faye's hair, she brought her one soft-boiled egg and a single slice of toast. She was known for working miracles on the set, and taking exquisite care of 'her stars', but Faye never took advantage of it, and Pearl liked that.

'Pearl, you're going to have me spoiled for life.' She looked gratefully at her as the hairdresser went to work on her hair.

'That's the whole idea, Miss Price.' She beamed at Faye. She liked working with this girl. She was one of the best, and she loved talking about her to her friends. Faye had a kind of dignity that was difficult to describe, but she also had warmth and wit and, she grinned to herself, one hell of a pair of legs.

In two hours her hair was done, set exactly the way it was meant to be, and she had put on the dark blue dress that had been assigned to her. Her makeup was done just as the director had specified, and Faye was standing in the wings. The usual excitement had begun. Cameras were being pushed around, script girls were standing by, the director was conferring with light men, and almost all the actors had arrived, except for the other star. Faye heard someone mutter 'as usual', and wondered if this was the way he always worked, and with a quiet sigh, she sat down unobtrusively in a chair. If need be, they'd go on to a scene that didn't call for him, but it didn't bode well for the next few months, if he was late for the first day. She was staring down at the matronly blue shoes she had been assigned by the wardrobe mistress when suddenly she had the odd feeling that someone was watching her, and she looked up into the deeply tanned face of a strikingly handsome man with blond hair and deep blue eyes. She imagined that he was one of the actors in the film, and maybe he wanted to say hello to her before they began. She smiled casually at him, but the young man didn't smile.

'You don't remember me, do you, Faye?' For the flicker of an instant there was that sinking feeling all women get when confronted with a man who gives the impression that he knows one well, although one doesn't remember him at all. Did I really know this man? Did I forget his face? Could it be? . . . but it couldn't have been serious . . . He simply stood and stared, desperately intent, and he almost frightened her. There was a hint of memory somewhere at the very back of her mind, but she couldn't place this man. Had she acted with him before? 'I don't suppose there's any reason why you should.' His voice was quiet and calm, his eyes so serious as he looked at her, as though disappointed that she hadn't recognised him at once, and she was growing increasingly uncomfortable. 'We met in Guadalcanal two years ago. You did a show for us, and I stood in for the CO.'

Oh my God . . . her eyes grew wide . . . and suddenly it came back to her . . . all of it . . . that same handsome face, their long talk, the young nurse he had married, and who had been killed . . . the two of them stared at each other as the memories flooded back. How could she have so nearly forgotten him? His face had haunted her for months. But she had never expected to see him again. As she stood up and held out a hand, he smiled at her. He had wondered for so long if she would remember him.

'Welcome home, Lieutenant.'

He saluted smartly, as he had so long before, and did a little bow, the mischief slowly returning to his eyes. 'Major, now, thank you.'

'I apologise.' She was relieved that he was still alive. 'Are you all right?'

'Of course I am.' He answered her so quickly that she wondered if indeed he was, but he looked well enough; in fact he looked fabulous. She looked up at him, and then she remembered where they were, and the film that was about to begin, if her co-star ever arrived.

'What are you doing here?'

'I live in Los Angeles. Remember? I told you that . . .' He smiled. 'I also told you I'd drop in on you at the studio one day.' She smiled in answer. 'I usually keep my promises, Miss Price.' It was easy to believe that about him. He was better-looking than she remembered, and there was something very dashing about him, and yet restrained. Like a magnificent stallion held in on a tight rein. She knew he must be twenty-eight by now, and he had lost his boyish look. He looked every inch a man. But she had other things on her mind . . . like the star who hadn't yet arrived. It was awkward seeing him here again for the first time.

'How on earth did you get in here, Ward?' She still remembered his name. She smiled gently at him as she asked the question.

Suddenly the mischief in him came back again and he grinned happily. 'I greased a few palms, told them I was an old friend of yours . . . the war . . . Purple Heart . . . medals . . .

Guadalcanal . . . you know, the usual.' She was laughing at him now. He had bribed his way in, but why? 'I told you I'd like to see you again.' But he didn't tell her how often he had thought of her in the past two years. A thousand times he had wanted to write to her, but he hadn't dared. What if they threw her 'fan mail' away, and where would he send the letter to anyway? Faye Price, Hollywood, USA? He had decided to wait until he came home, if he ever did, and there were times when he doubted that. Many, many times. And now here he was. It was like a dream, standing there, looking at her, listening to her talk to him. He had remembered her voice in all his dreams, that deep, sensual voice that had lingered in his head for two years.

'When did you get back?'

He grinned again. He decided to be honest with her. 'Yesterday. I would have come by then, but I had a few things to take care of first.' His lawyers to see, papers to fill out, the house that still seemed too big to him. He was staying in a hotel.

'It's perfectly all right, I understand.' But suddenly she was glad he was here now, glad he had lived, glad he'd come home. He was like the one living example of all the men she had met on tour. He stood before her like someone in a distant dream, someone she had met in a jungle two years ago . . . and now here he was, smiling down at her, out of uniform, just like everyone else, except that there was something special about him, in a way she'd never run into before.

And then suddenly her co-star arrived and everything exploded on the set, and the director began roaring at everyone and she had to do her first scene with her leading man. 'You'd better go, Ward. I've got to go to work.' She felt pulled suddenly, for the first time in her life, between work and a man.

'Can't I watch?' He looked like a disappointed child as she shook her head.

'Not this time. First day is kind of tough for all of us. In a few weeks, when we've all relaxed.' He liked the sound of that. They both did . . . 'in a few weeks' . . . as though they had all the time

43

in the world, and a future to share. Who was this man, she suddenly asked herself as he looked intently at her? He was only a stranger after all.

'Dinner tonight?' He whispered the words on the darkening set and she started to say something to him and shake her head, and then the director roared again and Ward tried to speak to her but she held up her hand. Her eyes met his and she could feel the man's strength. He had fought a war, he had come home, he had lost his first wife, and he had come to see her. Maybe that was all she needed to know about him. For now anyway.

'All right,' she whispered back, and he asked her where she lived. She smiled, and scribbled her address for him, embarrassed that he would see how grandly she lived. It wasn't nearly as lavish as it could have been, but surely by his standards he would be somewhat awed. But there was no time to arrange another meeting place. She just handed the slip of paper to him, and waved him off the set with a grin, and five minutes later, she was getting directions and an introduction to her leading man. He was a powerful, intriguing, and very handsome man. But Faye realised as they worked together for several hours that there was something lacking in him, something. Warmth . . . charm . . . she tried to define it to Pearl in the privacy of her dressing room later on.

'Yeah, I know what you mean, Miz Price. There's two things he ain't got. Heart and brains.' And suddenly, with a burst of laughter, Faye knew she was right. That was what was wrong with him, he wasn't bright. He was also terribly full of himself, which was tiresome after all. There was a fleet of valets, secretaries, and go-fers to attend to his every need on the set, from cigarettes to gin. And when they had finished work for the day, Faye saw him undressing her with his eyes. And then he asked her to dinner that night.

'Sorry, Vance, I've already got a date for tonight.' His eyes lit up like Christmas trees and she could have kicked herself. It wouldn't have mattered if she didn't have a date for the next ten years, she would never have gone out with him.

'Tomorrow night?'

She shook her head, and quietly walked away from him. It wasn't going to be easy working with Vance Saint George, but there were moments when she had thought his performance was actually very good.

And it actually wasn't Vance she was thinking of as she hurried back to her dressing room that night. It was already six o'clock, and she had been on the set for twelve hours, but she was used to that. After she changed her clothes she bid Pearl goodnight, and hurried out to where she had parked her car. She drove towards Beverly Hills as quickly as she could. Bob was still at the gate when she arrived; he let her in and she raced through, leaving the car out front, and not even taking the time to put up the top. She glanced at her watch again. He had whispered eight o'clock, and it was a quarter to seven now.

Arthur opened the door to her, and she raced upstairs. 'A glass of sherry, miss?' he called after her, and she stopped on the stairs for a moment with the smile that always warmed his heart. He was crazy about her, more so than he would ever have admitted to Elizabeth.

'There's someone coming for drinks at eight o'clock.'

'Very well, miss. Shall I send Elizabeth up to run your bath? She could bring a glass of sherry to you now.' He knew how exhausted she got on the set sometimes, but she didn't even look tired tonight.

'No, thank you, I'll be fine.'

'Do you wish your guest to be shown into the living room, miss?' It was a rhetorical question, he knew she would, and was surprised when she shook her head.

'My study, please, Arthur.' She smiled once more at him, and vanished, cursing herself for not arranging to meet Ward somewhere downtown. How ridiculous to play film star with him, poor kid. Well, at least he'd survived the war. That was the important thing, she told herself, as she ran into her dressing room, pulling open all the closet doors, and then dashing into the white marble bathroom to turn on the bath. She pulled out a plain white silk dress that suited her perfectly, and wasn't too showy. It had a grey silk coat that went over it, and she selected a pair of grey pearl earrings from her jewellery box, grey silk pumps, and a grey and white silk bag. All put together, it looked a little dressier than she thought, but she didn't want to insult him either by being too casual. He knew who she was after all. The only problem was that it was she who knew nothing about him. She stopped for a minute, staring into space, remembering him, as she turned off her bath. It was a good question. Who was Ward Thayer after all?

Chapter 3

At exactly five minutes to eight, Faye was downstairs in her study waiting for Ward. She was wearing the white silk dress, and the matching grey coat was tossed over the back of a chair. She paced nervously once or twice, regretting again that she hadn't arranged to meet him elsewhere, but it had been such a shock, his turning up on the set like that, after their brief meeting in Guadalcanal two years before. How strange life was. Here he was again, and she was having dinner with him, her heart was pounding, and she had to admit she was excited about it. He was a very attractive man and there was something a little mysterious about him.

The doorbell broke into her reverie and as Arthur went to answer it, Faye took a deep breath and tried to steady herself, and then suddenly she was looking into the deep sapphire eyes again, and she felt an exhilaration she hadn't felt in years. It was like riding a roller coaster just looking at him. She tried to sound cool as she offered him a drink, and noticed how well he looked in civilian clothes. He wore a simple pinstriped grey suit but it moulded his shoulders to perfection, and he seemed even taller than he had before. She still felt a little strange being here with him, this soldier from a war that was finally over. But it was a nice gesture after all, and if they had nothing in common, she wouldn't have to see him again. She was still impressed with the fact that he had bribed his way into the studio to see her, and there was a definite charm about the man. But she had felt that long before when she had met him in Guadalcanal.

47

'Please sit down.' The silence between them was awkward and she was struggling for something to say to him when she saw him smile. He was looking around with obvious pleasure, and he seemed to notice all the little details of the room: the small sculptures, the Aubusson rug; he even stood up to glance at the collection of rare books she had bought in an auction long since, and she noticed a sparkle in his eye.

'Where did you get these, Faye?'

'At an auction several years ago. That particular set is all first editions and I'm very proud of them.' In fact, she was proud of almost everything she had. It had all been hard earned and meant more to her because of that.

'Mind if I take them down?' He glanced at her over his shoulder and he looked more at ease, as Arthur walked into the room with a silver tray and their drinks. A gin and tonic for Faye and scotch on the rocks for Ward, in her pretty crystal glasses from Tiffany in New York.

'Of course, take a look at them.' Faye watched him from where she sat, as he gingerly removed two books, put one down, and opened the other, examining the fly leaf, and then the back pages of the old leather-bound edition. She saw him smile and then he looked at her with an amused expression.

'That's what I thought. These were my grandfather's. I would have known them anywhere.' He grinned, and handed her one of the books, pointing to an interesting handstamped logo on the back page. 'He put that in all his books. I have a number of them myself.' His words made her curious and reminded her of how little she knew about him, and she attempted to draw him out over drinks as they chatted. But somehow Ward remained vague; he talked about his grandfather's interest in ships, summers spent in Hawaii, and she learned only that his mother had been born there. He didn't say much about his father, and she was unable to learn more. 'And you, you're from the East, aren't you, Faye?' He always seemed to turn the conversation back to her, as though he thought the details of his life were unimportant. He almost seemed determined to remain a mystery to her. Handsome, poised, there was something terribly worldly about him and she was suddenly dying to know more. She would have to draw him out over dinner. He was watching her quietly, with an appreciative look in his eyes.

'I'm from Pennsylvania, but I feel like I've been out here forever.'

He laughed. 'Hollywood does that, I think. It's hard to imagine having another life.' He declined a second drink, glanced at his watch, and stood up, reaching for her coat. 'I think we'd better go. I made reservations at nine.' She was dying to ask him where, but she didn't want to push, and let him help her on with her coat, as they walked slowly into the hall and once again he looked around. 'You have lovely things, Faye.' He seemed to understand the beauty and history of all that he saw and easily recognised a fine English table she had near the door. What he didn't know was the reason why her home meant so much to her: because of the poverty that had come before.

'Thank you, I collected them all myself.'

'That must have been fun.' But it had been more than fun. At the time, it had meant everything to her. Now the objects in her life seemed less important, less real. She was more secure now.

His eyes met hers, and he reached the door and opened it for her before Arthur could help them. He smiled at the English butler and seemed unperturbed by his disapproving stare. Arthur felt it was not proper for the young man to open the door himself, but Ward looked happy and carefree as they stepped outside. The night was warm and balmy, and he ran lightly down the marble steps to the car he'd parked out front. It was a bright red Ford convertible, with more than a few dents, but it had a certain rakish look to it, which amused her. 'What a great car, Ward.'

'Thanks. I borrowed it for tonight.' Which was true, he had. 'Mine is still up on blocks. I just hope I can get it running again.'

She didn't ask him what he had, and slipped into the little Ford as he held the door open for her. The car started easily and rumbled off towards the gate which Arthur had gone ahead to open for them, and Ward sped through with a friendly wave. 'Awfully serious houseman you've got, madam.' He grinned at her and she smiled. Arthur and Elizabeth were so good to her she wouldn't have given them up for anything in the world.

'I'm spoiled, I guess.' She looked faintly embarrassed and he smiled at her.

'There's no harm in that, Faye. You should enjoy it.'

'I do.' She blurted the words out and then blushed as the wind whipped her thick blonde hair into a froth about her shoulders and they both laughed as she attempted to keep it down.

'Do you want me to put the top up?' he asked her as they sped downtown.

'No, no . . . I'm fine . . .' And she was. She enjoyed racing along beside him. There was something wonderfully old-fashioned about what they were doing. Like a Saturday night date back home in Grove City. She didn't feel at all like a film star as she sat beside him. She just felt like a girl, and she liked it, even more than she had expected. The only thing that concerned her was that she had to get up at five the next morning, and she didn't want to stay out too late.

He stopped the car at Ciro's on the strip, and hopped out with ease as the doorman approached him. He was a tall, handsome black man, and his face lit up when he saw Ward. 'Mr Thayer! You're home!'

'I sure am, John, and believe me, it wasn't easy!' They, exchanged a long fervent handshake and a warm smile, and then suddenly the older black man looked with horror at the car.

'Mr Thayer, what happened to your car?'

'Up on blocks for the duration. I'll have it out again next week, I hope.'

'Thank God . . . I thought you sold it for this pile of junk.' Faye was a little surprised at the rude remark about the car, and equally so that they seemed to know him so well at Ciro's, but it was more of the same when they went inside. The headwaiter almost cried as he shook Ward's hand, congratulating him on his return, and it seemed as though every waiter in the place knew him and came over to say hello. They were given the best table in the house, and after ordering drinks, he led her out on the floor to dance.

'You're the prettiest girl here, Faye.' His voice was soft in her ear, and his arms felt powerful around her.

She smiled up at him. 'I don't need to ask you if you used to come here often.'

He laughed at her remark and circled her expertly around the floor. He was the smoothest partner she had known, and she was growing more intrigued by the moment about who he really was. Just a young LA playboy? Someone important? An actor whose name she had never heard before the war? It was obvious that Ward Thayer was 'someone', and she was seriously beginning to wonder who he was. Not because she wanted something from him, but it was strange to be out with someone she barely knew, and had met in such a far-off place, in such an anonymous way.

'Something tells me you're keeping secrets from me, Mr Thayer.'

Her eyes sought his and he laughed and shook his head. 'Not at all.'

'All right, then. Who are you?'

'You know that much already. I told you. Ward Thayer, from LA.' He reeled off his rank and serial number and they laughed again.

'That doesn't tell me a damn thing and you know it. And you know what else?' She pulled away slightly to look up at him again. 'You're enjoying this, aren't you? Making a fool of me, playing mystery man. I suddenly get the feeling that everyone in town knows who you are except for me, Ward Thayer.'

'No, just the waiters . . . that's it . . . I was a waiter . . .' But suddenly, as he said it, there was a flurry in the doorway, and a woman in a skintight black dress walked into the room, her hair an explosion of fiery red. It was Rita Hayworth, and she had come here as she always did, with her handsome husband. She and Orson Welles would dance around the floor so he could show her off and it was easy to see why he was so proud of her. Faye thought instantly that she was the most spectacularly beautiful woman she had ever seen. She had seen her once or twice in the past, though only from a distance, and as she brushed past her now, Faye's breath caught she was so impressed. And then, as though the woman had heard her, she stopped, and quickly turned around. Faye blushed furiously beneath her own mane of peach-coloured hair, and was about to apologise for being rude, when suddenly Rita Hayworth seemed to spring into her arms and the next thing she knew, Ward had been pulled from her, and he and Rita were hugging tightly. Orson was standing a few paces away watching them with interest, and eyeing Faye, and Rita squealed with delight as she pulled away from Ward.

'My God, Ward, you made it! You rotten boy. All these years and not a word if you were alive or dead. Everyone kept asking and I never knew what to tell them . . .' She threw her arms around him again, her eyes closed, her mouth smiling the smile that made grown men cry from desire, as Faye watched in awe. Rita hadn't even seen her she was so happy to see Ward. 'Welcome home, you bad boy, you.' She grinned and glanced at Faye, nodded, recognition dawning in her eyes, and then interest as she glanced back at Ward. 'Aha, I see . . .' she teased him. 'Does anyone know that piece of gossip yet, Mr Thayer?'

'Now come on, Rita, for chrissake . . . I've only been back for two days.'

'Fast work.' She grinned at him, and smiled openly at Faye. 'It's nice to see you again.' Polite empty words. The two women had never been friends. 'Take good care of my friend here.' She patted him on the cheek, and then rejoined Welles, who saluted Ward with a smile from the distance, and as they left for a table at the far side of the room, Faye almost exploded. Ward led her back to their table, and took a sip of his drink, as Faye grabbed his other arm.

'Okay, Major. That does it. The truth.' She was glaring at him in mock fury, and he laughed openly as he set the drink down. 'Before I make a complete ass of myself, I want you to tell me what in hell is going on. Who are you? An actor? A director? A gangster . . . did you used to own this place?' They were both laughing and he was enjoying the game much more than she was.

'How about a gigolo? How's that?'

'That's garbage, that's what that is. Come on, dammit, tell me. First of all, how do you know Rita Hayworth that well?'

'I used to play tennis with her husband. And actually, I met them here.'

'As a waiter, right?' She was amused now. This anonymous soldier she had met in Guadalcanal had a lot of spirit to him. But she was dying to know more. She forced him to look her in the eye and attempted not to laugh. 'Now stop it. Here I am feeling sorry for you taking me out to dinner, embarrassed at having you see my house, and you know lots more important people than I do.'

'That's not what I hear, pretty one.'

'Oh really?' She blushed, and tossed her hair off her shoulders.

'What about Gable?' The blush grew deeper.

'Don't believe everything you read in the papers.'

'Just some things. And that I heard from some of my good friends.'

'I haven't seen him in years.' She attempted to look vague and Ward was too much of a gentleman to press it. And suddenly she looked into his eyes again. 'Now don't try and sidetrack me, dammit. Who are you?'

He leaned towards her and whispered in her ear, 'The Lone Ranger.' She laughed at him and the headwaiter approached their table with a huge bottle of champagne and the menus.

'Welcome home, Mr Thayer. It's good to have you back.'

'Thank you.' He ordered dinner for them both, toasted her with the champagne, and proceeded to tease her for the rest of the evening, until finally they sat in the open Ford outside her front door, and he earnestly took her hand in his own. 'Seriously, Faye, I am an unemployed soldier. I don't have a job, and didn't have one before I left. I don't even have an apartment any more. I gave it up when I was drafted. And they know me at Ciro's because I used to go there a lot before the war. I don't want to pretend I'm anyone important. I'm not. You're the star, and I've been nuts about you since the day I met you, but I'd be lying to you if I pretended to be someone I'm not. I'm just who you think I am, Ward Thayer . . . a man with no home, no job, and a borrowed car.'

She smiled gently at him. If it was true, she didn't give a damn. She hadn't had as nice an evening in years. She enjoyed being with him. He was bright and fun and good-looking. He danced like a dream and there was something warm and virile and exciting about him. He was knowledgeable on subjects she had never dreamt of, and he was different from all the men she'd known over the years. He didn't have that empty Hollywood superficiality about him although everyone certainly seemed to know him. 'I had a wonderful time, whoever you are.' It was almost two o'clock, and she didn't even want to think about how she would feel in the morning. She had to get up in less than three hours.

'Tomorrow night then?' Ward looked hopeful, and suddenly very young as she smiled at him and shook her head.

'I can't, Ward. I'm a working girl. I have to get up at a quarter to five every morning.'

'Until when?'

'Until we finish the picture.'

He looked crestfallen. Maybe she hadn't had a good time after all. And after two years spent dreaming of her, he desperately wanted her to have a good time when she was with him.

He wanted to take her out every night, and wine her and dine her, and sweep her off her feet as never before. He didn't want to wait patiently on the sidelines while she finished her movie.

'Hell, I'm not going to wait that long. How about you get a good night's sleep tomorrow night, and we go out again after that?' He glanced at his watch. 'And I won't keep you out so late next time. I didn't realise how late it had got.' His eyes sought hers and his voice was deep and gentle. 'I had a wonderful time, Faye.' He was head over heels in love with her and he barely knew her. But he had been dreaming of her for the past two years, just like a star-struck kid, and he had promised himself he would look her up when he got home. And now he had, and he wasn't going to let her go until she was just as desperately in love with him. And what Faye didn't know was that what Ward Thayer wanted he got. Almost always.

And now his eyes pleaded with her and she couldn't resist him. 'All right. But you have to have me home by midnight or I turn into a pumpkin. Is that a deal?'

'Cross my heart, Cinderella . . .' He sat staring at her, aching to kiss her, but he didn't dare. It was too soon. He didn't want it to be just like every other date she'd had, with someone pawing her because of who she was. There was so much more to it than that for him. He got out of the car, and came around to open the door, and she stepped out lightly, her hand in his.

'I had such a good time, thank you.' She looked up at him and then he followed her up the pink marble steps. She was half tempted to invite him in for a drink, but then she'd never get any sleep at all, and she needed at least a few hours' sleep before she went back on the set. He stood in the doorway, looking down at her, feeling like the boy next door, and his lips gently brushed the top of her head, as he tilted her chin up with one hand so he could look into the exquisite emerald eyes again.

'I'll miss you in the next few days.'

And then, without even wanting to say the words, she nodded. 'I'll miss you too, Ward . . .' Just as she had missed him in the beginning, after Guadalcanal. He had a way of getting under her skin, after these few meetings, as no man ever had before. It would have frightened her, except that she was having too good a time to be frightened. Especially by Ward Thayer.

Chapter 4

Faye was on the set on time the next morning, and Pearl brought her three cups of stiff black coffee.

'My hair may stand up straight for the rest of the day after this.'

'Yeah, honey, but if you don't drink it all, you may fall asleep in that big dummy's arms during a love scene.'

'That might happen anyway.' The two women laughed. It was no secret between them, even on the second day on the set, that they didn't think much of her co-star. He had arrived late for work again, and had behaved like a complete horse's ass. His dressing room was too hot, and when they set up fans for him, he complained that there was a draught. He didn't like the hair-dresser or the makeup man they had assigned him, and he was still complaining about the lighting and the wardrobe, when in desperation the director told them all to break for lunch. And when she went back to her dressing room, Pearl had the paper open for her. Hedda Hopper's column told her everything she had wanted to know the night before. She read the words carefully and sat staring at them for a moment afterwards, as though to digest them, as Pearl stood watching her, wondering what was in her mind.

'. . . The playboy heir to the Thayer Shipyard millions, Ward Cunningham Thayer IV, is safely home from the war, and back at his old haunts, we're told: Ciro's last night, where he got a warm welcome from Rita Hayworth and her hubbie. And it looks like there's a lovely new lady on his arm. Faye Price, with one Oscar and a lot of handsome beaux to her credit already, one of our favourites (and yours) among them, as we all know. In fact, we've been wondering if the lonely widower would come back for more now, but it looks like Thayer has the inside track. Fast work, Ward. He's only been home for three days! Faye, by the way, is working on a new film with Vance Saint George, and director Louis Bernstein will have his hands full with that combination, no thanks to Faye, we might add . . . and good luck, Ward! In fact, good luck to you both. And will there be wedding bells in their future? Let's wait and see! . . .'

'Boy, they work fast, don't they?' She smiled up at Pearl, half amused, half intrigued . . . 'Playboy heir to the Thayer Shipyard millions' . . . Now she recognised the name of course, though it hadn't rung any bells for her before. Playboy heir . . . she wasn't sure if she liked that. She didn't want him to think she was after his money, nor did she intend to be a notch on the belt of a notorious playboy. Suddenly he seemed a little less appealing than he had the night before, a little less ordinary, less 'real'. He wasn't like the men in Grove City after all. In fact he was extremely different. It bothered her more than she wanted to admit, and after mentioning it only once, Pearl got the hint and didn't mention it again. It was a difficult day anyway. Vance Saint George made a nuisance of himself all day, and when they all left the set at six o'clock, Faye was totally exhausted. She left her makeup on, slipped into a pair of tan trousers and a beige cashmere sweater, the honey-coloured hair flying loose around her face, and she started the Lincoln Continental, just as she heard an insistent horn behind her. She glanced in the windscreen mirror and saw a familiar red car, and sighed to herself. She was not in the mood to talk to anyone, let alone a 'playboy millionaire'. She was a working girl, she'd had two hours' sleep the night before, and she wanted to be left alone, even by Ward Thayer. No matter how attractive he was, she had her own life to lead. And now he was just a 'playboy'.

He hopped out and slammed the door of the little red car and ran over to see her with a smile, his arms filled with white tuberoses and gardenias and a bottle of champagne. She shook her head and grinned at him, almost in despair.

'Don't you have anything else to do with your time, Mr Thayer, except chase poor actresses after they finish a day's work?'

'Listen, Cinderella, don't get excited. I know you must be dead. I just thought these might cheer you up on your way home . . . unless, of course, I could steal you away to the Beverly Hills Hotel for a drink . . . any chance of that?' He looked like a hopeful little boy and she almost groaned.

'Who's your press agent, by the way?' She sounded a little bit annoyed, and his eyes looked worried as he watched her.

'I suppose Rita did that. I'm sorry . . . do you mind very much?' It was no secret that Hedda Hopper disliked Orson, but she had always been fond of Rita. And Ward, but Faye didn't know that.

She smiled. It was impossible to be annoyed with him. He was so ingenuous and generous and obviously happy to see her, and she had to admit that, even knowing he was a playboy, he still had enormous appeal. There was something overwhelmingly attractive about him. There had been, even in Guadalcanal. And now, in his own element, he was even more so. He exuded confidence and sex appeal, and Faye was far from immune to him.

'At least now I know who you are.'

He shrugged with a grin. 'None of that junk means very much, or is very accurate, as you know.' He made no comment about the 'beaux' mentioned in the piece, but he smiled at her in a way that touched her heart. He had a knack for doing that. 'Shall we follow their suggestion, Faye?' There was something funny in his eyes and she didn't know him well enough yet to know if it was serious or playful.

'What was that?' She was so tired she couldn't think and he watched her eyes carefully as he answered

'Remember the bit about wedding bells . . . we could surprise the hell out of them and get married.'

'What a great idea,' she mocked, glancing at her watch and squinting. 'Let's see . . . it's six twenty-five . . . how about at eight o'clock tonight, that way it could make the morning papers.'

'Great idea.' He ran around to the other side of her car, and before she could object, he hopped in beside her. 'Okay, let's get going, kid.' He sat back against the seat matter-of-factly, and grinned at her, and suddenly she was amused at him too. She forgot how tired she was. Actually, she was happy to see him. More so than she meant to be.

'You mean you expect *me* to drive? What kind of marriage is this?'

'You read the papers. It said I was a playboy. Playboys don't drive. They get driven around.'

'That's gigolos. That is *not* the same thing, Ward Thayer.' They were both laughing, and he had moved closer to her on the seat, but she didn't mind it.

'Why can't a playboy be driven too? I'm tired. I had a hard time today. I had lunch with three friends and we drank four bottles of champagne.'

'My heart bleeds for you, you lazy dog. I've been working since six o'clock this morning and you've been drinking champagne all day!' She tried to sound angry but all she could do was laugh as an enormous limousine pulled up for Vance Saint George.

'That's what you need, Faye.' He almost sounded serious and she laughed at him.

'A car like that? Don't be ridiculous. I enjoy driving myself.'

'It's not ladylike.' He assumed a prim expression, and glanced at her. 'Besides, it's not suitable for the victim of a playboy.'

'I'm your victim, am I?'

'Hopefully you will be.' He looked at his watch and then back at her. 'Now what time are we getting married? You said eight o'clock . . . we'd better step on it . . . or would you rather just stop for a drink after all?'

She shook her head, but she was less convincing than she had been before. 'No. I'd rather go home, Mr Thayer. Remember me, I'm the working girl, and I happen to be exhausted.'

'I can't imagine why. You probably went to bed at ten o'clock last night.'

'Nope.' She crossed her arms and grinned at him. 'I had a date with a playboy millionaire.' Now that it was out in the open they were both having a good time with it. It all seemed totally absurd, like a joke on them both, and Faye refused to take it any more seriously than he did.

'No, you didn't!' He attempted to look shocked. 'Who?'

'I can't remember his name.'

'Was he nice?'

'More or less. Terrible liar of course, but they all are.'

'Handsome?'

She looked him square in the eye. 'Very.'

'Now you've picked it up from him, lying again. Come on, I've got some friends you ought to meet.' He put an arm around her and she could smell the spicy fragrance of his aftershave, which was masculine and sexy. 'Let's go have a drink. I promise I'll get you home early tonight.'

'I can't, Ward. I'd fall asleep on the table.'

'Don't worry. I'll pinch you.'

'Were you serious about meeting friends?' That was the last thing she wanted to do tonight. All she wanted to do was go home. She had some new lines to study in the script, and with Saint George performing so poorly she felt an obligation to work even harder to compensate for him. Otherwise, they'd make a botch of the whole movie.

Ward shook his head. 'I was joking about seeing friends. Just the two of us. I'd take you to my place, if you'd come, but I don't have one.' He laughed. 'That makes it a bit difficult.'

'I'll say.'

'I was going to stay at my parents' place, but it's all closed up and it's too damn big. I've got a cottage at the Beverly Hills

Hotel until I find something I like, so I'm afraid all I can offer you is the hotel bar, for the moment.' It would have been highly improper to suggest coming to his cottage for a drink, and he wouldn't have considered suggesting that to her. She wasn't that kind of girl, no matter how big a film star she was, or how many beaux she'd had. There was still more than a hint of the well-brought-up young lady about her, and he liked it that way. The papers weren't far off the mark as to his intentions. 'So what do you say? Half an hour and then I'll take you home. Okay?'

'Okay, okay . . . my God, you drive a hard bargain. I'm glad I don't work for you, Ward Thayer.'

'Ah, my little chickadee,' he pinched her cheek, 'that could be arranged. Now slide over and I'll drive.' He hopped out and got back in behind the wheel.

'Won't you need your car?'

'I'll take a cab and come back for it after I take you home.'

'That's not too much trouble for you, Ward?"

He looked at her, amused. 'Not at all, little one. Why don't you put your head back and rest on the way to the hotel? You look tired.' She liked the tone of his voice, the look in his eyes . . . the feel of his hand as he touched hers . . . she watched him through half-closed eyes as they drove along. 'How's work?'

'Vance Saint George is an awful pain in the neck. I don't know how he's got as far as he has.' Ward knew, but he didn't say anything to her. He had slept with everything that moved, woman or man, and collected favours from everyone in town, but it had to catch up with him someday.

'Is he any good?'

'He would be, if he'd stop worrying about draughts and how much makeup he wears and studied his lines for a change. It's difficult to work with him, he's never prepared, and it delays us for hours.' She sat up and looked out as they neared the hotel.

'I hear you're awfully professional, Miss Price.' He looked admiringly at her.

She smiled. 'Who told you that?'

'I saw Louis B. Mayer at lunch today. He said you're the finest actress in town, and of course I agreed.'

'A lot you know.' She laughed. 'You've been gone for four years. You've missed all my best films.' She sniffed primly and he laughed. He was happy with her. Happier than he'd been in years.

'Yeah, but don't forget, I saw you in Guadalcanal.' He glanced over at her tenderly and touched her hand again. 'How many people can boast of that?' and then suddenly they both laughed, thinking of the thousands of troops she'd entertained. 'All right, never mind . . .' He pulled up in front of the pink hotel, and jumped out, as a doorman rushed to his aid, touching his hat and murmuring Ward's name. And he went to open Faye's door himself, as she stepped out and looked down at her slacks.

'Can I go in like this?'

'Faye Price?' He grinned. 'You could go in wearing a bathing suit and they'd kiss your feet.'

'Would they now?' She smiled at him. 'Or is that just because I'm with Ward Thayer?'

'What a lot of nonsense that is.' But as usual, the headwaiter gave him the best table. This time, three people asked her for her autograph, and when they left the hotel an hour later, much to her dismay someone had called the press, and a flashbulb exploded almost in their faces.

'Damn. I hate that stuff.' She looked annoyed as they took refuge in her car, and the photographer had followed them all the way. 'Why can't they leave us alone? Why do they have to make a thing of it?' She liked her privacy and the same thing had happened to her before. And this time she wasn't even involved with Ward yet. It was only their second date.

'You're big news, kid. It can't be helped.' He wondered then if she objected to being paired off with him; maybe there was someone else. He hadn't thought of that before, but it made perfect sense. And as he drove her home, he brought it up gingerly. 'It won't . . . it won't mess up anything else for you, will it, Faye?' He looked concerned, and she smiled as she saw the worried look in his eyes.

'Not the way you mean. But I don't like to go around advertising how I spend my private hours.' She still looked annoyed and also tired.

'Then we'll have to be discreet about where we go.' She nodded, but they both seemed to forget the vow the following night when he picked her up in his own car, a custom-built Duesenberg he had bought before the war and had left up on blocks in his garage. It was the car the doorman at Ciro's had been referring to, and Faye could see why. It was the most beautiful car she'd ever seen.

He took her to the Mocambo that night, and Charlie Morrison, the grey-haired owner, had run up and almost kissed Ward as he hugged him and pumped his arm. Like everyone else, he was ecstatic over Ward's safe return, and another mammoth bottle of champagne appeared as Faye glanced around the room, wondering who was there. She had been there before of course, and it was the most glamorous place in town, with an entire wall of rare, live birds flying around, while couples danced, and big film stars drifted in and out, just as she did now with Ward.

'I don't suppose our being here will go unnoticed tonight. Charlie may call the papers himself, you know.' Ward looked concerned. 'Do you mind very much, Faye?' He suspected she hadn't been pleased with the photograph that had appeared on page four of the LA *Times* that day, showing them leaving the Beverly Hills Hotel after cocktails the night before and running for the safety of her car.

But she only smiled at him. 'I get the feeling, Ward, that you don't know how to be invisible.' They both knew it was the truth. 'And actually, I'm not really sure I care. Neither of us has anything to hide. It would have been nice to maintain our privacy, but it looks like that isn't in the cards for either of us.'

She had thought about it a lot the night before, and decided what the hell, they had nothing to hide.

'I've never worried about it much before.' He sipped the sparkling wine. He always drank gallons of champagne, it seemed to be almost a trademark with him. 'That's just the way things are' . . . if you're the heir to a shipyard fortune, she thought, and drive a custom-built Duesenberg . . . And suddenly she laughed.

'Little did I know, when I met that nice young lieutenant in Guadalcanal, that he was spoiled rotten to the core, and used to hanging out in a lot of fancy watering holes and drinking rivers of champagne . . .' She teased him and he didn't seem to mind, it was all true, yet there was a great deal more to him. In some ways, he knew that the war had done him good. They were the hardest four years of his life, and he had proved something to himself, that he could survive almost anything: hardship, danger, misery, discomfort. For all four years, he had never once traded on his connections or his name, although of course there were those who knew who he was.

And then there had been the girl he had married. At first, he had thought he would never recover when she'd been killed. It had been a reality he had never faced before, and a grief almost beyond bearing. And now there was Faye with all her magic and her glamour, and underlying it her keen sense of reality, and her enormous talent. He was glad Faye hadn't known who he was at first. She might have felt differently if she had, might have thought he was frivolous. And he was at times, he liked to have fun. But he was capable of seriousness too, as Faye was beginning to discover. There were so many dimensions to the man, as there were to her. And together they were quite a combination. They each liked the other for what they were, not for what they had. They were a good match in a lot of ways, as Hedda Hopper and Louella Parsons both quickly noticed.

'What are your lifetime goals, Miss Price?' Ward teased her over their fourth glass of champagne, although he seemed to be feeling no effect from it, but Faye knew she'd have to slow down or she'd get drunk, and that was something she never did. 'What do you want to be doing ten years from now?' He seemed serious as he asked and she knit her brows and looked at him. It was an interesting question.

'Do you mean it?'

'Of course.'

'I'm not sure. When I think about things like that, I always see two possibilities, like two roads with two very different destinations, and I'm never sure which one I'll take.'

'And where do those two roads go?' He was intrigued by what she said, he was intrigued by everything about her now, even more so than he had been before.

'One road represents all this,' she looked briefly around the room before glancing back at him, 'the same people, places, things . . . my career . . . more films . . . more fame,' she was being very honest with him, 'more of the same, I guess . . .' Her voice trailed off.

'And the other road?' He gently took her hand. 'Where does that one go, Faye?' The room faded around them as he spoke and she looked into his eyes. There was something there she wanted very much, and she wasn't sure yet what it was. 'The other road . . .?'

'It goes to a very different place . . . a husband . . . children . . . a life far, far from all this . . . more like the life I had as a little girl. I can't really imagine it any more, but I know the possibility is there, if I wanted to make that choice. But that's a hard choice to make.' She looked honestly at him.

'You don't think you could have both?'

She shook her head. 'I doubt it very much. The two don't mix. Look at the way I work. I'm up at five, gone by six. I don't come home until seven or eight o'clock at night. What man would put up with that? And I've seen Hollywood marriages come and go for years. We all know what that's like. That's not what I want if I settle down.'

'What do you want, Faye . . . if you settle down, I mean?'

She smiled at him. It was a funny conversation for them to have on their third date. But she was beginning to feel she knew him well. They had seen each other three times in three days, and something strange had happened to them in Guadalcanal so long ago. It was as though a bond had formed and strengthened silently over the years, and it was still between them now, holding them fast, bringing them closer than they might have been had they just met. She thought about his words again.

'I guess I'd want stability, a marriage that would last for years and years, with a man I'd love and respect, and children of course.'

'How many?' He grinned at her and she laughed again.

'Oh, twelve at least.' She was teasing now.

'As many as all that . . . good lord . . . how about five or six?'

'That might do.'

'Sounds like a good life to me.'

'It does to me too, but I still can't imagine it.' She sighed.

'Is your career that important to you?'

'I'm not sure. I've worked awfully hard at it for six years. That might be difficult to give up . . . or maybe not . . .' Suddenly she laughed. 'Enough films like the one I'm working on and maybe I'd give it all up like that.' She snapped her fingers and then he took her hands in his again.

'I'd like to see you give it all up one day.' His face was suddenly so serious that it startled her.

'Why?'

'Because I'm in love with you, and I like that second road you described. That's the fulfilling one. The first road is a road to loneliness. But I think you already know that.' She nodded slowly and stared at him. Was he proposing to her? He couldn't be. She wasn't sure what to say, and slowly she drew her hand away.

'You just got home, Ward. Everything looks different to you right now. You're going to be very emotional for a while . . .' She wanted to discourage him. It was only right. He was moving too quickly . . . for heaven's sake, she barely knew him, and yet it felt like a time which might never come again, and they were both still under the spell of his surviving the war. The magic of wartime was still there for them both, and yet this was very real. And very special.

He retrieved her hand again and kissed her fingertips. 'I'm serious, Faye. I've never felt like this in my life. And I knew it the minute we met in Guadalcanal. I just didn't know what to say to you there. For all I knew I'd be dead the next day. But I'm not, and I'm home, and you're the most incredible woman I've ever known . . .'

'How can you say a thing like that?' She looked upset and he wanted to hold her in his arms, but he didn't dare, not in the middle of the restaurant, with the photographers possibly lurking nearby, and everyone anxious to report what they'd seen. 'You don't even know me, Ward. You saw me perform for two hours in Guadalcanal . . . we talked for half an hour afterwards . . . we've seen each other twice since you got back . . .' She wanted to discourage him now, before it was too late but she wasn't even sure why. It's just that it all seemed to be going so fast, and yet she had this incredible feeling about him, as though she could have walked off into the sunset with him that night, hand in hand, and everything would have been all right for the rest of their lives. But it didn't happen like that. Did it? It couldn't . . . or maybe it did . . . maybe that was 'the real thing' that everyone talks about. 'It's too soon, Ward.'

'Too soon for what?' He looked matter-of-fact. 'Too soon to tell you I'm in love with you? Well, maybe it is. But the fact is, Faye, I am. I've been in love with you for years.'

'Then it's an illusion.'

'No, it's not. You are exactly who I sensed you were. You are smart and realistic and practical. You are modest and warm and funny and beautiful. You don't give a damn who the press agents say you are. As far as you're concerned, you like what you do, you work hard. You are the most decent woman I've ever met, and what's more you're good at what you do, because of all of the above . . . and if I don't drag you out of here and kiss you in the next five minutes, I'm going to go nuts, Faye Price, so just shut up, or I'll kiss you right here!'

Her eyes were worried, but she couldn't help smiling at him. 'What if you figure out that you hate me in six months?'

'Why should I?'

'I probably have habits you'd detest. Ward, I'm telling you, you don't know who I am. And I don't know you.'

'Fine. Then we'll get to know each other.' But he had already tipped his hand to her and he didn't care. 'But I'm going to glue myself to you and drive you nuts till you say yes.' He looked completely satisfied with what he had just said, and drained his glass of champagne with a contented look, and then set it down and looked at her. 'All right with you?'

'Would it make a difference if I said no?'

'Not a bit.' It was the grin she had already come to love, the mischievous spark in the deep blue eyes. He was difficult to resist, and she wasn't even sure she wanted to. She just wanted them both to be sensible. She had had romances with other men before, though admittedly none was quite like him. But she didn't want to be one of those women the press wrote about constantly, in love with this one, engaged to that one, and in the end it all amounted to their being used up, like tired old Hollywood whores. She still cared about things like that, which was another thing he liked about her. In fact, he was convinced that he liked everything, and she suspected the same about him, but she wasn't about to give in, certainly not after three days.

'You're impossible.'

'I know.' He looked pleased with himself, and then suddenly concerned as he leaned toward her. 'Does it bother you that I don't work?' Maybe that was it, the work ethic was bothering her.

'Not if you can afford not to, I suppose. But don't you get bored, Ward?' She was intrigued with what he did with his spare time. She worked so hard, and had for years, it was difficult to imagine just playing tennis and going out to lunch. It sounded deadly to her, but he certainly didn't seem unhappy with it.

'Faye.' He sat back and looked at her. 'I love my life. I've had a good time ever since I was a kid. And when my father died, I told myself that I would never work myself into the ground like he did. He was forty-six when he died, of a heart attack. My mother was forty-three. I think she just worried herself to death about him. They never took a minute to do what they wanted to, to have a good time, hell, they never even spent any time with me. And I swore to myself that when I had kids one day, and even long before that, I wouldn't live like that. There's no reason to. I couldn't spend all that money if I tried, to be vulgar about it,' which he seldom was, as Faye knew, but he was being honest with her and she valued that. It gave her a good insight into him. 'My grandfather did the same damn thing, died at fifty-six of overwork. So what? Who cares how hard you worked when you die. I want to enjoy life while I'm here and I am enjoying it. Let them say what they want to. Let them call me what they want. I'm not going to drop dead from a heart attack at forty-five, or be a stranger to my wife and kids. I'm going to be right there, enjoying life with them, knowing who they are, and letting them know me. I never even knew who my father was, Faye. He was a stranger to me. Like you, I see life divided in two roads. The life they lived that I don't ever want to live, and the one I'm living now, and this one suits me just fine. And I hope to hell it doesn't bother you.' He looked deep into her eyes and took a deep breath. 'Of course, if you want me to, I could always get a job.' She looked at him in shock before she answered. He was serious about all this. But how could he be after just three days? 'You don't have to get a job for me, Ward. What right could I possibly have to ask you to do that?' And if he could afford his lifestyle, why should he do anything differently? He wasn't hurting anyone with the way he lived. She looked at him and spoke softly. 'I can't believe you're serious about all this. Their eyes held for a long time as he nodded, and then silently he led her to the floor and they danced for a long time, without saying a word. And when he led her back to the table, he watched her wondering if he had upset her and praying that he hadn't.

'Are you all right, Faye?' She was suddenly very pensive, and he was concerned that he had frightened her by telling her what was on his mind.

'I don't know.' She looked at him honestly. 'I think you've taken my breath away with all that.'

'Good.' He put an arm around her and squeezed her shoulders, admiring again the navy satin backless dress she wore. She had a flair for dressing with subtle sensuality in a way that pleased him immensely, and he was dying to buy her clothes and jewellery and furs. For the rest of the evening, they kept to lighter subjects, Faye trying to pretend to herself that he hadn't bared his heart already, and he seemed even happier than before to know that she knew what he felt for her. After dinner, he drove her back to her place, and this time she invited him for a glass of cognac, although she was almost afraid to. She knew his thoughts now, and she wondered if it was dangerous to let him inside. And then as she poured his drink, she laughed at herself. Hell, he wasn't going to rape her. She handed him the glass and he wondered at her smile.

'You're so lovely, Faye . . . even more beautiful than I remembered.'

'You need to have your eyes checked.' His praise embarrassed her at times, it was so lavish, and his adoration of her was so clearly written in his eyes. He was a carefree, happy man, with few disappointments and no current worries, and he was clearly very much in love. 'What are you doing tomorrow?' She said it just to have something to say and he laughed.

'I'll tell you one thing I'm not doing. I'm not working.' In some ways, he was shameless about it and it amused her. He had certainly told her all he felt on the subject at dinner, but it was almost as if he were proud of not working. He didn't even mind being called 'the playboy millionaire'. 'I wish you weren't working on a film just now, Faye. We could go out and play.' She could just imagine the trouble they would get into. Lazy afternoons on the beach, days of expensive shopping, maybe a trip or two. She had to admit, the prospect was almost appealing, but she wouldn't even let herself dream about that yet. 'I'd like to take you to the Casino at Avalon Bay one of these nights, but we'd have to spend the night on Catalina Island. I don't suppose you'll have a weekend off, will you?'

Sadly, she shook her head. 'Not till the film is over.' She smiled at him over their cognac, smelling the heady aroma, and thinking of all the fun things they had in store.

'There are a lot of places I'd like to take you . . . Paris . . . Venice . . . Cannes . . . Now that the war is over, we can go anywhere we want.'

She laughed at his words and shook her head as she set down her glass. 'You really are spoiled, my friend, aren't you? One of us has to work at least. I can't just go off halfway around the world.'

'Why not?'

'The studio wouldn't let me. After this film, my agent is going to renew my contract, and I'm sure they'll keep me pretty busy for a long, long time.'

Ward's eyes lit up like Christmas and he stared at Faye. 'You mean after this film, your contract is over?' She nodded her head, amused at his reaction. 'Hallelujah, baby! Why don't you take a year off?'

'Are you crazy? I might as well give it up for good, Ward. I can't just do that.'

'I don't know why not. You're one of the biggest stars they've got, for heaven's sake. You don't think you could take a year off and pick up exactly where you left off?'

'I doubt it.'

'Don't believe that for a second, Faye Price. You could walk out and come back any time you wanted.'

'That's quite a risk, Ward. I wouldn't play games like that with my career.'

He watched her with serious eyes. Things were happening much faster than either of them had expected. 'It's the fork in the road again, isn't it, Faye? . . . Which road do you really want to follow? The old one? Or the other one we talked about . . . marriage and babies . . . stability . . . and a real life . . .' She walked away from him and stared out into her garden, saying nothing, and when she turned around, he saw that there were tears in her eyes. But more than anything she looked angry, and he was startled.

'I want you to stop that, Ward.'

'Stop what?' He hadn't intended to upset her and he was shocked at her reaction.

'Stop torturing me with this nonsense. We hardly know each other. We're strangers. For all I know, by next week, you'll be involved with some little starlet, or Rita Hayworth, or someone else. I've worked like a dog to get where I am, and I'm not ready to give it up yet. Maybe I never will be. But I'm sure not going to do it for some half-crazy ex-GI fresh off the boat from the war, who thinks he's been in love with me for two years because he talked to me for a while when I was on tour. You don't throw your whole life away for that, Ward Thayer. And I don't give a damn how rich you are, or how carefree, or if you've never worked a day in your life. I have. I've worked every day of my life since I turned eighteen, and I don't intend to stop now. I got here, and I'm staying here, until I know it's safe to walk away from it.' He was interested in the work she had chosen . . . 'safe' . . . and she was right. She had worked hard to get where she wanted, and now that she was there she would have been crazy to throw it all away. But in time he would show her that he meant everything he was saying . . . if she would listen. 'I don't want to hear that stuff any more.' The tears were spilling down her cheeks now. 'If you want to see me, fine. Take me to dinner. Dance with me. Make me laugh. But don't ask me to throw away my career for a stranger, however much I might like him, however much I may care . . .' and with that a sob broke from her and she turned her back to him again, her shoulders shaking in the exquisite evening dress by Trigère. He went quickly towards her and put his arms around her, holding her close to him, her back against his chest, his face nestled in her silky hair.

'You'll always be safe with me, babe . . . always . . . I promise. But I understand what you're saying. I didn't mean to scare you. I just got so excited . . . I couldn't help it.' He turned her slowly to face him, and his heart tore when he saw her face wet with tears. 'Oh Faye . . .' He crushed her to him, and then crushed his lips on hers, and instead of pulling back, every inch of her reached towards him. She needed the comfort he had to offer, needed something she saw in him, wanted him more than she had ever wanted any man before.

They kissed for what seemed like hours, his hands caressing her back, his lips seeking her mouth, her face, her eyes, her hands on his neck, and then touching his face as she kissed him, feeling relief from the fear and anger she had felt only moments before. She was crazy about this man, and she was not yet sure why. Except that perhaps she believed what he told her, that she would be safe with him . . . always . . . he offered her a protection she had never had. Not with her parents during the Depression, or on her own, or with the other men she had known. And it wasn't just the money. It was his outlook, his lifestyle, his certainty that he lived in a perfect, carefree world. And it was obvious that he adored her. They had to tear themselves from each other an hour later, in order to avoid something that neither of them wanted yet. He knew that Faye was not yet ready, and would always have regretted succumbing to him so soon. And he had to leave her, for fear that he might lose control. He wanted to take her on the floor of her study, in front of the fire, or upstairs in the silky white bedroom, or in her bathtub . . . or on the stairs . . . anywhere . . . his whole body keened for her, but he knew he couldn't have her so soon. And when they met the next night, the agony was even sweeter, as their lips met instantly, and they spent an hour in his Duesenberg, beyond her gates, kissing like two children, and then laughing as he drove her to the Biltmore Bowl.

There was a big party being held there, and the photographers went wild when they saw him. But this time, Faye didn't seem to resist it. In four brief days, she knew that there was no running away from Ward Thayer. She didn't know where their romance would lead, but she wasn't going to fight it any more. She had worn her floor-length white fox coat to the party, over a black and white satin gown. She looked absolutely exquisite as they walked in, with her hand tucked into Ward's arm. She looked up at him warmly for an instant, and he smiled at her, just as the photographers approached them, and they had a field day with Ward and Faye for the rest of the night. But as promised, he got her home early. The late nights were beginning to wear on her in the morning. But Vance Saint George arrived on the set so late every day that she usually had time to take a nap.

'Did you have fun?' He looked down at her, as she rested her head on his shoulder while they drove home. 'I thought it wasn't a bad party.' It had been to promote a new film, and all the big names had been there.

'I thought it was fun too.' She was beginning to enjoy their nightly outings even more than she had at first. 'If I didn't have this damn film to do, I could really have some fun.'

He laughed at her and tugged at a lock of the golden hair. 'See, that's why I told you not to renew your contract the other night. This is fun, isn't it?'

'It's habit-forming. But I'm a working girl, Ward.' She tried to look at him disapprovingly, but they both laughed.

'That's your choice, but you can choose differently any time you decide to.' He looked meaningfully at her and she didn't answer, and when they reached her house, he kissed her passionately on the lips again, and this time he had to fight himself not to carry her upstairs. 'I'm going.' He said it in a voice of anguished desperation, and she kissed him once more in the doorway. The delicious torture went on for weeks, until finally late one Sunday afternoon in October, a month after their courtship had begun, they were walking in her garden, talking about the war, and other subjects. She had the afternoon off from shooting, and Arthur and Elizabeth were off for the weekend. There was a feeling of peace between them as they wandered. She had begun telling him about her childhood, her parents, her desperation to leave Pennsylvania, the initial excitement of modelling in New York, and then finally the boredom, and then she confessed that at times it was still that way for her now.

'It's as though there's something more I could be doing . . . with my mind . . . not just my face or my lines. I don't want to just memorise other people's lines for the rest of my life.'

It was an interesting confession and it intrigued him. 'What would you rather do, Faye? Write?' As usual, he was aching for her body, but there was nothing he could do about it. At least they were alone for a change. She wasn't rushing to or from work, Arthur wasn't hovering in the doorway with tray in hand, and they weren't going to a party. They were growing hungry for time alone and she had offered to cook him dinner that night. They had spent a lovely afternoon, lazing around the pool, and then walking in the garden. 'Would you like to write a screenplay?' He turned to her and smiled at her expression. She looked frightened at the thought as she shook her head.

'I don't think I could do that.'

'What then?'

'Directing . . . one day . . .' She barely breathed the words. It was quite an ambition for a woman, and he didn't know of any who had directed films before.

'Do you suppose anyone would let you?'

She smiled and shook her head. 'I doubt it. Nobody believes a woman could do that. But I know I could. Sometimes when I watch Saint George on the set these days, I just want to scream,

I know what I want to have him do . . . how I would direct him . . . the instructions I would give him. He's such a simple-minded fool, you have to bring it down to the kind of emotions he can relate to, and believe me,' she looked painfully at Ward and rolled her eyes, 'they're damn few.'

Ward smiled at her and picked a bright red flower to tuck behind her ear. 'Have I told you lately that I think you're amazing?'

'Not for at least an hour.' She smiled appreciatively up at him. 'You spoil me, you know. No one's ever been as good to me as you are.' She looked genuinely happy and he couldn't resist the urge to tease her. They had a comfortable, easy way about them that they both enjoyed. 'Not even Gable?'

'Stop that.' She made a face at him and ran past him, as he chased her, and then suddenly he caught up with her and grabbed her, and they were kissing in an arbour, and suddenly all the breathlessness they both felt overwhelmed them, and Ward felt he couldn't bear to take his hands or lips from her again. It was almost painful when at last he tore himself away.

'It's not easy, you know.' He looked agonised as they walked slowly back to the house and she nodded. It wasn't easy for her either. But she didn't want to make a mistake with Ward. He had made his intentions clear to her right from the beginning, and it was too dangerous to play games with that. He wanted everything from her, her life, her career, her body, her children. He wanted her to give everything up for him . . . and at times it was almost tempting to her. Lately she had even told her agent not to rush into the next contract, although he thought she was crazy. But she said she needed time to think, and it was growing more and more difficult to think when Ward was near her.

'You make me crazy too, you know,' she whispered as they went up the pink marble steps into her study, but it looked so bleak there, so stuffy and much too formal. She went to make them both a cup of tea and then suggested they move to her sitting room upstairs. It was small and warm and cosy, and Ward lit a fire, although they didn't really need it. But it was pretty, and they sat side by side admiring the blaze. 'I've had an offer to do a wonderful film,' she told him, but there was no excitement in her voice as she said it, and she wasn't sure she wanted to do it at all. In fact her agent had been furious at her indecision.

'Who's in it?'

'No one yet, but they have some awfully good possibilities.'

'Do you want to do it?' He didn't sound upset, he was only asking but she took a long time to answer as she stared into the fire.

'I just don't know.' She looked up at him, feeling contented and at peace with life. 'You make me awfully lazy, Ward.'

'What's wrong with that?' He nuzzled his face into her neck, and began to kiss her with one hand lazily sculpting her breast. She gently touched his hand, wanting to push away his fingers, but it felt too good. She had no desire to push him away, hadn't since they'd met, and yet it seemed wiser . . . wiser . . . suddenly all she could feel were those delicious burning fingers, their mouths met, and a passion rose in them both that was difficult to quell. They never seemed to come up for air, as her skirt rose slowly past her knees, and his hand found her thighs. Her whole body trembled as his hand moved up, and then suddenly he moved away. Breathless, anguished, he looked at her, and held her face in both his hands. 'Faye . . . I can't . . . I've got to go . . .' He couldn't stop himself any longer, he wanted her too badly, had for much too long. He looked at her with tears in his eyes, and then he kissed her, just once more, and it was the moment that decided both their futures. The way she kissed him told him that she didn't want him to go, and then silently she stood up and led him across the hall to the spectacular white bedroom, and without waiting a moment longer, he laid her across the white fox-covered bed. He peeled her clothes from her, devouring her flesh, murmuring to her in whispers, as her fingers gently disentangled him from his clothes, and moments later they lay side by side, naked, enveloped in the rich white fur, and then suddenly they were engulfed in each other's bodies, and neither of them thought of resisting or being sensible any more. Faye shouted out for him with a passion that overwhelmed her, and Ward lay within her, his excitement far beyond control. They spent themselves in what would have looked like agony to strangers, and was the purest passion either of them had ever known. And as she lay silent at last, in the circle of his arms, the white fur bedspread soft beneath them, he looked down at her with a love he had never known before.

'Faye, I love you more than life itself.'

'Don't say that . . .' His passion frightened her sometimes. He loved her so much . . . what if one day it stopped? She couldn't have stood it. She knew that now.

'Why not? It's true.'

'I love you too.' She looked up at him with a sated smile, and he bent to kiss her once more, and it amazed him how quickly his body begged for her again, and how hungrily she reached for him, and they made love in her bed for hours, never able to get enough, to make up for the years when they had done without each other. It was as though they had waited for this for much, much too long.

'Now what, my love?' He sat on the edge of her bed at midnight, smiling at her as she rose slowly, stretched, and smiled down on the man she so richly loved.

'How about a bath?' And then suddenly she remembered, and covered her mouth with a look of horror. 'Oh my God, I forgot to give you dinner.'

'No, you didn't.' He pulled her towards him again. 'This suited me just fine.' She blushed faintly and he smoothed the long, blonde hair back from her face, and then followed her to the white marble bath. She filled the tub with warm soapy water, and they slid in together, his feet tickling her in subtle places, as he nibbled on her toes. 'I asked you a question a little while ago.'

She frowned slightly, unable to remember. 'What was it?'

'I asked you, "now what?".'

She smiled at him, mysteriously. 'And I said, "a bath".'

'Cute. But you know what I mean. I don't just want to have an affair with you, Faye.' He looked faintly troubled, and at the same time extremely pleased with the evening they had just spent together in her bed. 'Although, I must admit, it's tempting. But I think you deserve more.' She said nothing. She only watched him, her heart beating faster. 'Will you marry me, Miss Price?'

'No.' She suddenly stood up, and he looked shocked. It was a rapid refusal as she stepped out of the tub.

'Where are you going?'

She turned to look at him, magnificent in her naked beauty in the centre of the white marble bathroom. 'I will not tell my children that their father proposed to me in the bathtub. How can I tell them something like that?' He began laughing as he looked at her in amusement.

'No problem.' He leapt out of the tub, swept her up in his arms, and deposited her soaking wet on the white fox bedspread once more, as he knelt at her feet and looked up at her with blatant adoration. 'Will you please marry me, my love?'

She grinned at him, impish, happy, yet at the same time terrified at what she was doing. But she knew she had no choice now. It was not just because she had slept with him; but it was what she wanted, 'the other road' . . . the good life . . . marriage and babies with him . . . and with him, she was brave enough to do it. For her, it meant giving everything up, but she didn't care. 'Yes.' It was the merest whisper, and he crushed his lips on hers before she could change her mind, and when they came up for air they were both laughing with delight and excitement.

'Do you really mean it, Faye?' He had to be sure . . . had to . . . before he went totally berserk and gave her the world.

'Yes. I do . . . yes . . . yes . . . yes . . .yes!'

'I love you. Oh God, I love you.' He crushed her to him, and she laughed as he held her close to him. She was happier than she had ever been before, and then suddenly he looked at her, grinning, his blond hair tousled, his eyes the purest sapphires as he smiled. 'Tell me something, do you have to tell your children what you were wearing when I proposed? If you do, you're in big trouble, Mrs Thayer.'

'Oh dear . . . I didn't think of that.' She laughed as he held her, and a moment later, he was beside her on the bed again. It was hours before they reached the bathtub again, and they had to fill it with more hot water. By then it was almost four o'clock in the morning and Faye knew she wouldn't sleep before she went to work. Instead, they sat in the bathtub for an hour, talked about their plans, their lives, their secret, when they would make the announcement. They giggled over how shocked everyone would be, not that they were getting married, but that she was giving up her career. And as she said it, she felt a tremor, but it was more excitement than panic. She realised now that secretly, deep within, she had thought about this a great deal. She had always known what Ward wanted from her, and how much he wanted to give her. She regretted nothing now, and suspected that she never would. What was she giving up? A career she had enjoyed, but she had already reached the summit. She had won one Oscar, considerable acclaim, and had made a dozen interesting films. It was time to go now. She had another life to live. A life she wanted more than making films. She lay back in the bathtub, smiling at her future husband, feeling something she had never felt before. A confidence, a peace, a certainty that she had chosen the right road.

'You're sure you won't regret it?' He looked faintly worried, but more happy than anything else. He wanted to start looking for houses with her that afternoon, but she pointed out to him that she had to work, for another month or so at least

'I won't regret it for a minute.' She was absolutely certain.

'When do you think you'll finish this film?'

'I would think by the first of December if Saint George doesn't screw things up too badly before.'

'Then we'll get married on December fifteenth. Where shall we honeymoon? Mexico? Hawaii? Europe? Where do you want to go?' He beamed at her, and her heart swelled with the love she felt for him.

'How did I get lucky enough to find you anyway?' She had never been as happy in her life as she was now. With him.

'I'm the lucky one.'

They kissed and reluctantly left the bath, and a few minutes later, she went downstairs. She made coffee for them both, and brought it up, reminding herself to clear up the bedroom and to leave the empty cups in her sitting room when they left, and he drove her to work in the Duesenberg, as they both almost shouted with delight. The next two months were going to be difficult for them, but they would have a lot to do . . . a lot to look forward to . . . so much to plan for their future.

BEVERLY HILLS

Chapter 5

The wedding took place at the Hollywood Presbyterian Church on North Gower Street, near Hollywood Boulevard, and Faye slowly walked down the aisle in an exquisite ivory satin gown. It was encrusted with the tiniest of pearls in delicate designs and she moved with measured grace, her head held high, her hair piled into an ivory satin crown encrusted with the same miniature pearls, a whisper of a veil floating around her for what seemed like miles. Her hair looked like spun gold as it cascaded over the sides of the pearl-encrusted crown, and around her neck sparkled a diamond choker the height of her swanlike neck. It had been a wedding present from Ward, and a favourite piece of his maternal grandmother's.

Faye had walked down the aisle on the arm of her agent, and Harriet Fielding had come to be matron of honour. Faye had overcome her ferocious protests and her old friend was there, with tears streaming down her face as Abe handed Faye to Ward at the altar. The young couple had beamed at each other, and been more beautiful than any two people in a film. And when they emerged from the church arm in arm, there had been hundreds of well-wishers standing outside to greet them. Fans throwing handfuls of rose petals and rice, young girls screaming for Faye's autograph, women crying, and even men smiling tenderly as they watched them. The couple disappeared into the new Duesenberg Ward had bought several weeks before to celebrate the wedding, as a kind of nuptial gift to himself and his bride, and they drove on to the reception at Biltmore, where they were met by Abe, Harriet, and four hundred friends they

85

had invited. It was the happiest day of Faye's life, and the papers had a field day with the pictures.

But there was even more coverage three weeks later, when they returned from their honeymoon in Acapulco. Faye made the announcement she had decided on two months before, but she had wisely decided to keep the news to herself until then, and even Abe was shocked when she told him. The headlines that night told it all in few words: 'Faye Price Gives Up Career for Millionaire Husband'. It was blunt, and the piece was over-done, but in essence that was her decision, not so much because of Ward's 'millions', although obviously that eliminated any need for her to work, but she felt strongly that she had 'done it', and now she wanted to devote herself entirely to her husband and her future children. And Ward certainly wasn't complaining about her decision. He was thrilled to have her all to himself, to lie in bed with him until noon, make love any time they wanted, eat breakfast on trays in their room, and even lunch if they so desired, dance all night at Ciro's or Mocambo or the homes of their friends. And Ward was having a wonderful time shopping with her, buying her fabulous new clothes to add to her already copi-ous wardrobe. Her three fur coats looked meagre in comparison to the wonders he bought her, two floor-length sable coats in slightly different shades and styles, a fabulous silver fox, a red fox, a silver raccoon; she had every imaginable fur, and more jewel-lery than she thought she could wear in a lifetime. A day hardly went by that he didn't disappear for an hour or two and return with a box from a fur shop or dress store or jeweller. It was like Christmas every day of the year, and Faye was overwhelmed at his generosity and the love he lavished on her constantly.

'You have to stop this, Ward!' She was laughing as she sat naked in the new red fox coat with a string of enormous pearls around her neck and nothing else on the exquisite young body he adored.

'Why?' He sat down to watch her with a happy grin and a glass of champagne. He seemed to drink rivers of it, but he never appeared drunk so Faye didn't really care. And she smiled tenderly at him now.

'You don't have to do all this. I would love you in a grass shack, if we had to wear newspapers to keep warm.'

'What a disgusting thought . . .' He made a grimace and then squinted as he looked at the long, shapely limbs. 'On second thoughts . . . you might look fabulous wearing the sports page, and nothing else.'

'Silly.' She ran over to kiss him again and he pulled her onto his lap and set down his glass. 'Can you really afford all this, Ward? We shouldn't be spending all this money, with neither of us working.' She still felt faintly guilty about no longer going to work, but it was so heavenly spending all her time with Ward that she never really missed her career. As she had told the papers when she retired, she had 'done it'. But she looked at Ward with concerned eyes. He had spent an absolute fortune on her in the three months since they'd been married.

'Darling, we can spend ten times this.' It was a generous thought, though not exactly what he had been hearing from his attorneys. But he knew how conservative they were. They had no flair, no style, no sense of romance. It annoyed him to listen to their petty warnings that he should be more cautious. He knew how large his fortune was, and there was plenty of leeway for a little fun. He could afford what they were spending, for a while at least, and then they'd settle down to a more 'sensible' life, and neither of them would ever have to work. And at twenty-eight, he had no intention of starting. He was having too much fun, he always had had, and now his life with Faye was sheer perfection. 'Where do you want to go tonight for dinner?'

'I don't know . . .' She hated to admit it, but she loved the corny exotic decor of the Coconut Grove with its palm trees and the projections of white ships passing each other in the distance. It always made her feel as though they had sailed away, and the palm trees reminded her faintly of Guadalcanal, where she had first met Ward. 'The Grove again, or are you too tired of it?'

He laughed again, and called the majordomo downstairs to have him make a reservation. They had hired an army of new people to care for their house.

In the end, Ward had decided not to move into his parents' old mansion after all. Instead, he had bought Faye a fabulous new estate that had belonged to a silent movie queen. It had grounds that could almost be called a park, a lake with swans, several lovely fountains, long walks, and a house that looked like a French château. They could easily have the ten children here that he always threatened he wanted. They had filled it with Faye's pretty antiques from her own house, which had sold almost the day she put it up for sale, and they had taken the pieces they liked best from his parents' place, and the rest they had bought together, at auctions and antique stores in Beverly Hills. The new house was already almost fully furnished. And Ward was talking about putting his parents' house on the market. It was too big and dark and old-fashioned for their taste and there was no point in keeping it any longer. His lawyers had always urged him to keep it for a while, lest when he married one day he would want it, and he was sentimental about it anyway, but it was obvious they would never live in it now. And his lawyers were anxious for him to get rid of it. They wanted him to reinvest the money in something that would bring in more income for him and his bride, although Ward wasn't too concerned about that.

He and Faye took a stroll in the gardens that afternoon, and sat by the little lake kissing and talking. They never seemed to tire of each other and these were golden days as they talked about the sale of his parents' house and a dozen other things. Faye looked up with a dreamy smile when Arthur brought them two glasses of champagne on a tray. She was pleased that Ward had let her keep Elizabeth and Arthur and they seemed happy in their new life. Arthur seemed to approve of Ward, most of the time, although at times there was no denying that he behaved like a crazy boy. One day he had even bought her a coach and four white horses to drive around the estate, and there were six shiny new cars in the garage, being constantly polished by one of their two chauffeurs. It was a lifestyle Faye had never seen before, let alone lived, and at times she felt more than a little guilty. But Ward turned everything into such a delight that it didn't seem naughty any more, just fun, and the days flew by faster than she could count them.

'You're not drinking your champagne.' Ward smiled at her. She had never been prettier than she was now, even at the very height of her career. She had put on a few pounds, and there was a glow in her cheeks, and her eyes were the most brilliant green he had ever seen, especially in the sunlight. He loved kissing her in the gardens . . . in the bedroom . . . while going for a drive. He loved kissing her anytime . . . anywhere. He adored his bride and she was crazy about him.

More than anything she was content, and it showed in her face as she looked at him and declined the proffered champagne. 'I think I'd rather have lemonade.'

'Ugh.' He made a terrible face and she laughed, and hand in hand they walked slowly back to the house, to make love lazily before they bathed and dressed for the evening. It was an idyllic life, and in a way Faye knew that these days would never come again. One day they would have children, they would have to grow up themselves, they couldn't spend their life playing forever. But it was fun while they could, and it made their honeymoon days seem to go on forever.

That night at the Grove, Ward gave her a magnificent ring with three huge pear-shaped emeralds in it, and Faye gasped when she saw it. 'Ward! Good heavens . . . but . . .' He always loved her amazement, her delight, at the things he bought her.

'It's for our third anniversary, silly girl.' It had been three months that day, and they were the happiest months of Faye's life, and Ward's. There was not a single cloud on their horizon

89

to worry them. He slipped the ring on her finger, and they danced for hours, but he noticed that tonight she looked a little tired when they went back to their table. They had been up late for several nights, several months in fact, he acknowledged with a small smile, but it was the first time he had noticed it taking a toll on her. 'Do you feel all right, sweetheart?'

'Fine.' She smiled, but she also ate very little, drank not at all, and by eleven o'clock she was yawning, which was usually not her style.

'Well, I guess this is it. The honeymoon's over,' Ward pretended to look crushed, 'I'm beginning to bore you.'

'No . . . how awful . . . I'm sorry, darling . . . I just . . .'

'I know . . . never mind. Don't try to explain.' He teased her mercilessly all the way home, and when he went into the bathroom to undress and brush his teeth, he returned to find her sound asleep, cosy in their big double bed, and appealing in her pink satin nightgown. But he attempted to rouse her to no avail, she was dead to the world, and it was obvious why the next morning. She awoke and was desperately ill immediately after eating breakfast. It was the first time he had seen her sick, and he was frantic and insisted on calling the doctor to the house, despite all her protests.

'For heaven's sake . . . it's just the flu or something. You can't drag the poor man all the way out here. I'm fine.' But she didn't feel it.

'The hell you are. You're absolutely green. Now go to bed and stay there until the doctor comes.' But when he arrived, he saw no reason whatsoever for Mrs Thayer to stay in bed, not unless she intended to stay there for another eight months. According to his calculations, the baby was due in November. 'A baby? A baby! Our baby!' Ward was absolutely beside himself with excitement and relief, and Faye laughed at him as he danced around the room when the doctor left. He was quick to come to her side, begging her to tell him what she wanted, needed, or what he could do to make her feel better. She was delighted at the news and his reaction, and of course as soon as word was out, it made headlines. 'Retired Movie Queen Expecting First Child'. Nothing in their life remained a secret for long, but Ward couldn't have kept it to himself anyway. He told anyone who would listen, and treated Faye like the most delicate piece of glass, and if he had lavished gifts on her before, it was nothing to what he did for her now. She didn't have enough drawers and jewel boxes to keep all the outrageously expensive baubles he bought her.

'Ward, you have to stop! I don't even have room to keep it all any more.'

'Then we'll build a cottage just for your jewels.' He laughed mischievously and all her scolding was for naught. If he wasn't buying jewels for her, he was buying prams and pony carts and mink buntings and teddy bears, and he even had a full-scale carousel built on the estate. He allowed Faye to ride slowly around on it in October when she walked across the grounds to see it for herself.

She had been feeling remarkably well since the first few queasy months, and her only complaint was that she was so large she felt like a balloon about to take off. 'All I need is a basket attached to my heels and they could rent me out for sightseeing trips over LA,' she told a friend one day and Ward was outraged. He thought she looked beautiful, even in her swollen state, and he was so excited, he could barely stand the remaining month to wait. She had reservations in the finest hospital in town, and she was being attended by the fanciest doctor.

'Only the best for my darling and my baby,' he always said as he attempted to ply her with champagne, but she had no taste for it any more, and there were times when she wished he didn't either. It wasn't that he got drunk when he drank, it was just that he drank so much of it when he did, and he seemed to drink it all day long, moving on to scotch when they went out in the evening. But she hated to complain. He was so good to her in so many ways, how could she object to a little thing like that? And she knew he meant well, when he ordered a case of their favourite champagne sent ahead to the hospital, so it would be waiting for them when the big moment arrived. 'I hope they keep it chilled.' He ordered Westcott, the majordomo, to call the hospital and instruct them exactly how to cool it, and Faye laughed.

'I suspect they may have a few other things on their minds, my love.' Although the hospital she would be going to was used to such requests; it was where all the big stars gave birth to their babies.

'I can't imagine what,' he said. 'What's more important than keeping the champagne cooled for my love?'

'Oh, I can think of a few things . . .' Her eyes told him all he wanted to know, and he held her gently in his arms, and they kissed as they always had. He was hungry for her, even now, but the doctor had said that they couldn't make love any more. And Faye could hardly wait until they could again. It seemed an eternity to wait, and his hands roved over her full belly, night after night, loving even that, and wanting her desperately.

'This is almost as bad as before we made love for the first time,' he complained with a wry smile as he climbed out of bed late one night and poured himself a glass of champagne. Her due date was only three days away, but the doctor had warned them that the baby could be several weeks late. First babies often were, so they were prepared for a late arrival, and it was beginning to seem like forever to both of them.

'I'm so sorry, love.' She looked tired now, and for the past few days any kind of movement at all had been exhausting. She hadn't even wanted to walk in the gardens with him that afternoon, and when he told her about the miniature pony he had bought, even that hadn't got her outside. 'I'm just too damn tired to move.' And that night, she insisted that she was too tired even to eat dinner. She had gone straight to bed at four in the afternoon, and now at two in the morning she was still there, looking like a giant pink silk balloon with maribou feathers around her collar.

'Want some champagne, sweetheart? It might help you sleep.'
She shook her head, her back hurt, and she had been feeling queasy for the past several hours. On top of everything she thought she might be coming down with the flu.

'I don't think anything will help me sleep any more.' One thing might have, she suggested lasciviously a moment later, but that was forbidden them.

'You'll probably be pregnant again before you leave the hospital. I don't think I'll be able to keep my hands off you for more than an hour after the baby's born.'

She laughed at the thought. 'At least it's something to look forward to.' She looked doleful for the first time in nine months, and he kissed her gently and went to turn off the lights, but as he did he heard a sharp cry from the bed, and turned in surprise to see her face contorted by pain and then suddenly the pain was gone, and they both looked at each other in amazement.

'What was that?'

'I'm not sure.' She had read a couple of books, but she was still hazy about how to be absolutely certain when labour began. And everyone had warned her that in the last few weeks there could be endless false starts and false alarms, so they both knew that this wasn't likely to be 'it'. But the pain had certainly been sharp, and Ward decided to leave the lights on and see if it happened again. But twenty minutes later, when it hadn't, and he went to turn the lights off again, she gave another sharp cry, and this time she seemed to writhe in their bed and he noticed a film of perspiration on her face when he approached her.

'I'm calling the doctor.' He could feel his heart pound in his chest, and his palms were damp. She looked suddenly very pale and very frightened.

'Don't be silly, darling. I'm fine. We can't call the poor man every night for the next month. It probably won't be for weeks.'

'But you're due in three days.'

'Yes, but even he said it would probably be late. Let's just relax and wait until morning.'

'Shall I leave the lights on?' She shook her head, and he turned them off and slid gingerly into bed beside her, as though he were afraid that by shaking the bed too much he would cause her to explode then and there and have the baby. She giggled at him in the dark, and then suddenly he heard her breath catch, and she reached for his hand and held it tight. She was almost fighting for air when the pain had passed, and she sat up in bed when it was over.

'Ward . . .' He was lying very still, wondering what to do, and the sound of her voice touched him to the core. She sounded so vulnerable and frightened and instinctively he took her in his arms.

'Sweetheart, let's call the doctor.'

'I really feel silly bothering him at this hour.'

'That's his job.' But she insisted that they should wait and see what happened until morning. But by seven o'clock there was no doubt in Ward's mind. This had to be the real thing. And he didn't give a damn what anyone had told her about false alarms, the pains were coming five minutes apart, and she was fighting not to scream as each pain lunged through her. In desperation, he left the room, and called the doctor they had engaged. He seemed satisfied with what he heard, and suggested Ward bring her in at once.

'It'll probably take a while from this point on, Mr Thayer, but it's a good idea to get her into the hospital, and settled in.'

'Can you give her something for the pain?' Ward was desperate after seeing her suffer for the past five hours.

'I'll have a better idea once I see her.' The doctor was noncommittal.

'What the hell does that mean? For chrissake, she can hardly keep control now . . . you've got to give her something . . .' Ward himself was desperate for a drink, something a lot stronger than champagne this time.

'We'll do what we can for her, Mr Thayer. Now just keep calm, and bring her to the hospital as soon as you can.'

'I'll have her there in ten minutes, five if I can.'

The doctor didn't say anything, but he had no intention of getting to the hospital himself in anything less than an hour. He had to shower and shave, he hadn't finished reading the paper, and he knew the ways of obstetrics well enough to know that she wouldn't deliver for hours, maybe even for another day, so there was no point rushing in, no matter how panicked the young father was. He'd say all the right things to him when he arrived, and the nurses could keep him at bay after that. They'd had one man force his way into the delivery room the week before, but the security people had dragged him out and threatened to put him in jail if he didn't behave. But he didn't anticipate any problems with Ward Thayer.

And the doctor was pleased to be delivering her. It was another feather in his cap to be delivering Faye Price Thayer.

But Ward was horrified when he walked back into their room and found her doubled over a pool of water on the white marble bathroom floor, with a look of shock mingled with pain. 'My water just broke.' Her voice was huskier than usual, her eyes wide open and afraid.

'Oh my God, I'll call an ambulance.' But at his words she laughed and sat down on the edge of the tub.

'Don't you dare. I'm fine.' But she didn't look all that fine to him and she looked scared, almost as scared as he was. 'What did the doctor say?'

'To bring you in right away.'

'Well,' she looked into her husband's eyes, 'I'll say one thing. I don't think it's a false alarm.' She looked a little more relaxed then, and he put his arms around her and helped her back to her dressing room. 'What'll I wear?' She stared at the open closets and he groaned.

'Oh for chrissake, Faye . . . anything . . . just make it quick. How about a dressing gown?'

'Don't be ridiculous. What if there are photographers there?' Ward looked at her and smiled.

'Don't worry about it. Come on.' He pulled a dress out of the closet, helped her into it, and gently led her downstairs. He wanted to carry her but she insisted she could walk. A couple of minutes later, she was comfortably tucked into the Duesenberg, the sable lap robe tucked around her legs, as she cautiously sat on a thick pad of towels. The driver pulled up in front of the hospital, and Ward let her out. She was instantly put in a wheelchair and whisked away, and he was left to pace the hall for the next six hours. His demands to see the doctor when he arrived were all in vain, until finally at half past two he saw him striding down the hall, his surgical cap still on, swathed in a blue gown, the mask hanging loosely around his neck, and he met Ward with an outstretched hand.

'Congratulations, you have a fat, handsome son!' The doctor smiled and Ward looked shocked, as though he hadn't quite expected it, even after all these hours of going half mad, pacing the halls. He thought he wouldn't have been able to stand it for another half hour. 'He weighs eight pounds nine ounces, and your wife is doing fine.'

'Can I see her?' Ward could feel his whole body go slack at the news. He was so relieved that it was over, Faye was well, the baby was fine.

'In a few hours. She's sleeping now. It's hard work, you know, pushing these little fellows into the world.' The doctor smiled again. He didn't tell him how hard on Faye it had been, or how close they had come to doing a Caesarean. And he hadn't wanted to give her gas until the head was out. They had waited until the very end and then, put her out, once the baby was born. It made sewing up easier for him, and there was no reason for her to be awake now. Her work was over.

'Thank you, sir.' Ward pumped his hand, and almost ran out of the hospital. He had a present waiting at home for her, a huge diamond brooch with a matching dinner ring and bracelet, all lying in a blue velvet box from Tiffany's. He wanted to get it and bring it back, but more importantly, he needed a drink. Desperately, in fact. He had the chauffeur drive him home as fast as he could, and he almost raced into the house. What an incredible day it had been. With a double scotch straight-up under his belt, he sat down and relaxed, took a deep breath, and realised finally that he had a son. He wanted to shout it from the rooftops he was so pleased, and he couldn't wait to see his wife. He tossed off his drink, and poured a second one, before rushing upstairs to look at the present he had waiting for her. He knew she would be pleased with it, but more than anything he was pleased with her . . . a baby boy! . . . A son! . . . his firstborn. As Ward showered and shaved and dressed to go back and see Faye at the hospital, he thought of all the things he would do with him one day, the trips they'd go on, the mischief they'd get into. His father had never been willing to do anything with him, but everything was going to be different with him and his son. They'd play tennis, polo, go on deep-sea fishing trips in the South Pacific, travel together, have a grand time. He was beaming radiantly when he arrived back at the hospital at five o'clock, and asked the nurse to bring the champagne into Faye's room. But when he tiptoed in, he found her still dozing groggily. She opened her eyes and seemed not to know who he was at first, and then she smiled, the strawberry blonde hair looking like a halo around her pale face. She looked almost ethereal as she stared sleepily at him.

'Hi . . . what did we have?' Her voice drifted off and her eyes closed again, as Ward kissed her cheek and whispered to her.

'You mean they haven't told you yet?' He looked shocked, and the nurse quietly left the room. Faye shook her head. 'A boy! A little boy!' She smiled sleepily at him, and declined the champagne. She didn't seem able to sit up and she still looked kind of green to him, and he was desperately worried about her, even though the nurses insisted everything was fine. He sat for a long time with her hand in his. 'Was it . . . very . . . difficult, sweetheart?' He stumbled on the words and something in her eyes told him that it was terrible but she bravely shook her head. 'Have you seen him yet? Who does he look like?'

'I don't know . . . I haven't seen him . . . I hope he looks like you.' He let her go back to sleep after that. He had showed her the spectacular gift he'd bought for her, and she looked appropriately awed but she was definitely not herself and he suspected she was in a lot of pain but didn't want to admit it to him. He tiptoed down the hall by himself to look at his son. The nurse held him behind the glass window in the nursery, and the baby looked like Faye; he was big and round and beautiful with a fluff of blond hair like hers. And as Ward watched he gave out what looked like a healthy wail, and Ward thought he had never been so proud in his life as he strutted out of the hospital and into the Duesenberg. He went to dinner at Ciro's alone, knowing he would run into all his friends, and he bragged to everyone, handed out cigars, and got extremely drunk on champagne, while in her hospital room, Faye slept, trying to forget how awful it had been.

She left the hospital in less than a week, and by the time she got home, she looked more like herself. She wanted to nurse the baby, but Ward had convinced her that it wasn't practical. She needed her sleep. They had hired a nurse, who took over while Faye regained her strength, but within two weeks, Faye was on her feet again, with the baby in her arms most of the time, and looking more beautiful than she ever had before, Ward said.

They named the baby Lionel, and christened him on Christmas Day at the church where they'd been married.

'He's the perfect Christmas gift.' Ward beamed down at his son as he held him in his arms on the way home, and Faye laughed. Lionel was almost two months old. 'He's beautiful, sweetheart, and he looks so much like you.'

'He's pretty cute, whoever he looks like.' She gazed down at the sleeping infant happily. He had barely cried during the brief ceremony. And once at home, he woke up and didn't seem to object when he was passed from hand to hand. Everyone wanted to have a look at him. All the illustrious and celebrated of Hollywood were there, all the big film stars, producers, directors, from Faye's old life, and Ward's more social friends. It was a dazzling list of names, and the Hollywood people all teased Faye about giving up her career for 'all this' . . . 'Are you just going to go on having babies forever, Faye?' She said she was, and Ward stood at her side and beamed. He was so proud of Faye and Lionel and the champagne flowed like the Seine all day. And that night Ward and Faye went dancing at the Biltmore Bowl. She had made a remarkable recovery. She already had her figure back, and felt well. And Ward thought she had never looked more beautiful. The photographers concurred.

'All set to do it again?' Ward teased. She wasn't quite sure she was. The memory of how painful it had been still lingered with her, but she was crazy about Lionel. It might not be so terrible to do it again, she thought now, though only weeks before she would have shrieked at the idea. 'How about a second honeymoon in Mexico?' he proposed, and she loved the idea. They left shortly after New Year's Day, and had a fabulous time in Acapulco for three weeks. They ran into a number of their friends, but spent most of their time alone, they even rented a yacht and spent two days fishing blissfully. It was the perfect holiday, and would have been even more so if on the last week of their trip, Faye hadn't begun feeling ill. She blamed it on the fish, the heat, the sun, and couldn't imagine anything else. But when she got back, Ward insisted she go to the doctor to check it out, and when she did, she was stunned. She was pregnant again.

Ward was thrilled, and so was she. This was exactly what they had both wanted from the first, and everyone teased them mercilessly this time. 'Can't you leave the poor girl alone, Thayer? What's the matter with you two? Can't you leave her alone long enough to comb her hair?' But they were both happy about it, and this time they made love almost until the end, doctor's advice be damned. Ward said that if she was going to spend nine months out of every ten pregnant, then he wasn't giving her up, and he barely did this time. She went into labour five days late, and it was easier this time. She recognised the symptoms of labour more easily, and it began one hot September afternoon. They barely had time to make it to the hospital, the pains came so hard and fast, and Faye was clenching her teeth with tightened fists when they arrived at the hospital. The boy was born less than two hours after that, and when Ward saw her late that night, he wasn't as upset this time at how sleepy she was. This time he had bought her sapphire earrings with a matching thirty-carat ring. It was another boy, and they named him Gregory, and Faye bounced back just as quickly this time. But this time she vowed to be a little more careful, at least 'for a while'.

When the baby was three months old, she and Ward went to Europe on the *Queen Elizabeth* for a nice long trip. They took the nurse and both boys along, with a separate stateroom for them, and huge suites of rooms in every city where they went. London, Paris, Munich, Rome. They even went to Cannes for a few days in March and the weather was pleasant and warm, and then finally back to Paris and from there home again. It was a wonderful trip for all of them, and Faye was as happy as could be with the husband she adored and her two sons. She was stopped for autographs once or twice, but that happened much less often now. People seldom knew who she was. She was still very beautiful, but she looked different somehow. More matronly perhaps, slightly less glamorous, except when she went out in the evenings with Ward. But she was perfectly content to wear trousers and a sweater and a scarf around her golden hair, and go out with her two little boys. She couldn't imagine a more perfect life, and Ward was so obviously proud of them.

They found all well when they went back, but the gossip in Hollywood was ugly these days. The Hollywood Blacklist had come out months before, and countless actors, directors, writers, and other people they had known could no longer find work. Suddenly the word 'commie' was on everyone's lips, fingers were all too anxious to point in all directions, even towards old friends. It was a sad time for many people, and in a way, Faye was glad she was no longer a part of it. The saddest thing of all was that those who had been blacklisted suddenly found themselves with no friends, as well as no work. People were afraid to be seen with them.

Warner Brothers had put up an enormous billboard outside the studios, 'Combining Good Pictures with Good Citizenship', which told everyone where they stood.

The House Committee to Investigate UnAmerican Activities had been in operation for ten years, but it had never taken itself so seriously, and when in October 1947, the 'Hollywood 10' were given prison sentences for refusing to testify, it was as though the whole town had gone mad, and it made Faye sick to hear the stories that were going around about old friends, people they all knew. By 1948, talented people they had all loved were being forced to leave Hollywood and get jobs as plumbers, carpenters, anything they could. Their Hollywood days were over, and Faye looked pained whenever she spoke to Ward of it.

'I'm glad I'm out of all that. I never thought it would get as ugly as this.'

Ward looked at her carefully. He had to admit, she seemed happy with her present life, but he wondered sometimes if she didn't miss the old days of her film career. 'You sure you don't miss it, babe?'

'Not for a minute, my love.' But he had noticed that she was restless lately, as though she needed something more to do. She had begun doing volunteer work in a local hospital, and she spent a lot of time with the boys. Lionel was almost two years old, and Gregory was ten months old, a precious baby with a happy smile and dancing curls. But Faye was happiest of all when she announced to Ward just days before Greg's first birthday that she was pregnant again.

This time it was more difficult for her. She felt less well than she had, right from the first, and she was much more tired this time. She never seemed to want to go out, and Ward noticed that she was much bigger this time. Although the rest of her looked even thinner than usual, her stomach was enormous almost at once, and by Christmas the doctor suspected why. He examined her carefully, and as she sat up, he smiled at her.

'I think the Easter bunny might have quite a surprise for you this time, Faye, if he waits that long.'

'What's that?' She felt as though she could barely move, and she still had three months to go.

'I have a suspicion, just a faint one, that it might be twins.' She stared at him in astonishment, the possibility had never even crossed her mind. She just thought that she was more tired this time, but now that she thought about it, she was much bigger too.

'Are you sure?'

'No. We can do an X-ray in a while, and we'll certainly know at the delivery.' And that they did. Two beautiful little girls popped out of her, nine minutes apart, and Ward was so beside himself when he saw the two baby girls that he went completely berserk. It was matching ruby and diamond bracelets this time. Two ruby rings. Diamond and ruby earrings, two of everything. And even Greg and Lionel looked surprised when they came home with two babies instead of one.

'One for each of you,' Ward said, lovingly putting one tiny pink bundle into the arms of each little boy. The twins were a big success with everyone. They weren't identical technically, but they might just as well have been they looked so much alike. They called the older one Vanessa, who looked incredibly like Faye: the same green eyes, the same blonde hair, the same tiny perfect features, yet she was the quiet one. It was the younger twin who screamed the loudest whenever she wanted to eat, who smiled first. The same tiny perfect face and huge green eyes, but Valerie had fiery red hair, right from birth, and a personality to match.

'My God, where did she get that?' Ward looked shocked as her red hair began to grow, but as she grew older, her hair, like the rest of her, grew more and more beautiful. She was a startlingly pretty little girl and people often stared at her. At times, Faye worried that Valerie eclipsed her twin. Vanessa was so much quieter, and she seemed to accept living in the shadow of the twin sister she adored. Vanessa was a pretty child too, but quieter, more ethereal; she was happy looking at her picture books, or watching Valerie torment the boys. Lionel was always particularly patient with her, and Greg would grab fistfuls of the bright red hair. It taught Valerie the art of self-defence at an early age, if nothing else. But on the whole, the children had a good time with each other, and people said they were the prettiest lot anyone had ever seen. Two beautiful little girls, toddling around the grounds of the estate, playing with the miniature pony their father had bought several years before, and the two boys cavorting all around, climbing trees, and reducing their beautiful little silk shirts to shreds with glee.

They all enjoyed the carousel now, the pony rides, all the treats their father had bought for them. And he adored playing with them. At thirty-two, he seemed hardly more than a boy himself, and Faye was content with her family. Four children seemed perfect to both of them. She didn't want any more, and Ward was content to stop at four, although he teased her sometimes about still wanting ten. But Faye would roll her eyes at the mention of it. She had her hands full as it was, and she liked spending time with all of them. They went on wonderful holidays; Ward had bought a house in Palm Springs the year before, and they spent part of every winter there. Faye loved going to New York with him to visit friends. They had a good life, in all possible ways, far, far, from the poverty of her early life, and the loneliness of his childhood years.

Eventually, he had confided everything to her. He had led the life of a 'poor little rich boy' as a child. He had had everything materially, but his parents were never around. His father had been working all the time, his mother had been constantly involved with various committees as a volunteer, and in between they had taken extensive trips, but always leaving Ward behind.

As a result he had sworn that he would never do the same thing to his own family. He and Faye took all four children everywhere, on weekends in Palm Springs, on trips, even to Mexico. They enjoyed their company and the children flourished with the attention lavished on them, each in their own way. Lionel had an inclination to be quiet, perceptive, serious, and close to Faye. His seriousness unnerved Ward at times, he was less rough and tumble than Greg, who played football for hours on the lawn with Ward. Greg was more like he himself had been as a child, happy go lucky, athletic, carefree . . . or more as he would have been, had he had the same amount of attention lavished on him. And Valerie only grew more beautiful. She was the most demanding of the four, the most aware of her own charms, and because of that, Vanessa seemed to demand nothing at all. Valerie took her dolls, her toys, her favourite clothes, and Vanessa didn't even seem to notice it. She was happy to give anything up for her twin. She cared about other things, the look in her mother's eyes, a warm word from Ward, a trip to the zoo, holding Lionel's hand, and her own secret life of dreams, as she glanced through a picture book or stared up at the sky as she lay beneath a tree. She was the dreamer of the family. She could lie on the grass for hours, looking up at the sky with her own thoughts, sometimes singing a little song to herself as Faye smiled at her.

'I was like that when I was her age,' Faye said softly to Ward as he glanced at the pretty little blonde girl.

'And what did you used to dream about, my love?' He kissed her neck and took her hand, his eyes as warm as the morning sun. 'Did you dream of being a film star?'

'Sometimes, but I was a lot older than that by then.' Little Vanessa didn't even know what films were.

He smiled happily at his wife. 'And what do you dream of now?' He was so happy with her. She had taken all the loneliness out of his life. And she was fun. That was important to him. His parents had never seemed to have a good time. All his father did was work, as far as Ward could see, and his mother did the same with her endless charities. He had sworn to himself long before that he would never live like that. He wanted to enjoy his life. Both his parents had died young, without ever really enjoying themselves. That was not the case with Ward and Faye. They had a wonderful time. He looked at her again now, so peaceful and beautiful, she almost looked like a painting as she pondered the question he had asked.

'I dream of you, my love . . . and the children. I have everything I want in this world . . . and more.'

'Good. That's the way I always want it to be.' And he meant every word of it, as the children grew up, and time passed by.

Ward still drank too much champagne sometimes but he was harmless and good-humoured, and Faye loved him enormously, even with his occasional boyish flaws, of liking to have too much fun, or drinking a little too much. There was no harm in it.

The lawyers came to see him more than they used to do, about his parents' estate and what was left of it, but she didn't concern herself with it. It was his money after all, and she had enough to do with Lionel, Gregory, Vanessa, and Val. But she noticed around the time that the twins turned two that Ward was drinking more, and it was less champagne and more scotch, which worried her.

'Anything wrong, sweetheart?'

'Of course not.' He smiled, feigning unconcern, but there was something frightened in his eyes these days and she wondered what it was. But he persisted in insisting nothing was wrong, and still the lawyers came, and often called. She wondered what they said to him. And then somehow, it all seemed less important again. The earlier decision was forgotten late one night, and in the throes of passion after going to the Academy Awards with him in April of 1951, they threw caution to the winds, and by late May, Faye was sure.

'Again?' Ward looked surprised, but not displeased, although he was less interested this time. He had too many other things on his mind, although he did not tell Faye that.

'Are you mad at me?' She was concerned, and he pulled her into his arms with a broad grin.

'Only if it isn't mine, you silly girl. Of course I'm not mad. How could I be mad at you?'

'Five children is an awful lot, I suppose . . .' She was faintly ambivalent about it this time too. The family seemed so perfect as it was. 'And if I have twins again . . .'

'Then that'd make six! It sounds fine to me. We might even reach our original goal of ten one of these days.' But as he said it, all four of the children they had ran into the room, shrieking with excitement, falling all over each other, laughing and shouting and pulling hair, and Faye shouted over their heads at him, 'God forbid!' He smiled at her, and all went well and in January, Anne Ward Thayer was born, the smallest child Faye had borne, and she looked so tiny and frail one was almost afraid to hold her. In fact, she was so tiny and delicate that Ward refused to take her in his arms, but he seemed pleased with her. He bought Faye an enormous emerald pendant this time, but somehow he seemed less excited than he had before, and Faye told herself that she could hardly expect him to hire a brass band for their fifth child. But still, she was disappointed that he didn't seem more pleased.

But within days, she knew exactly why. The lawyers didn't even try to talk to Ward this time. They talked to her, feeling it was high time she knew what was going on . . . Seven years after the end of the war, Thayer Shipyard hadn't seen a profit in almost four years. It had been running in the red for years, despite all their pleading with Ward to pay some attention to it, cut down the scale of operations, and face what was happening. They wanted him to go to work in the office at the yard, as his father had. And he had flatly refused. Instead, he had ignored their pleas and not only allowed the shipyard to run itself into the ground, but he had bankrupted the estate as well. He had insisted that he wasn't going to ruin his life by working night and day. He wanted to be with his family. And now there was nothing left, hadn't been in almost two years. And suddenly, as she sat in shocked silence listening to them, Faye looked back remembering when he had begun to seem preoccupied, concerned, drinking more, but he had never admitted anything to her. And for the past two years, without saying a word to her, he had been running on 'empty'. There was no money left at all, there were only monumental debts which he had accumulated with their extravagant lifestyle. Faye Price Thayer sat listening to what they had to say, her face pale, features taut, a frown between her eyes, and she looked as though she were in shock. In a way she was. She almost staggered out of the room when they left her. And when Ward came home later that afternoon, he found her sitting upright in a chair in the library, silently waiting for him.

'Hi, babe. What are you doing downstairs so soon? Shouldn't you be resting?' Resting? *Resting?* How could she be resting when they had no money left, when she should be out looking for a job? All they had left were debts, and as she raised her eyes to his, he knew that something terrible had happened. 'Faye? . . . Darling, what's wrong?' There were tears trembling in her eyes and she didn't even know where to begin. The tears spilled onto her cheeks and she began to sob. How could he have played this game? What was he thinking of? When she thought of all the jewellery he had bought, the cars, furs, the house in Palm Springs, the polo ponies . . . it went on forever . . . and God only knew how bad the debts were. 'Darling, what is it?' He knelt beside her and all she could do was sob, until finally she took a deep breath and gently touched his face with her hand. How could she hate this man? She had never faced it until now, but he was only a child, a boy pretending to be a man. At thirty-five, he was less mature than their six-year-old son. Lionel was already practical and wise . . . but Ward . . . Ward . . . there was the sorrow of an ended life in Faye's eyes as she attempted to calm down and talk to him about what she had heard that afternoon.

'Bill Gentry and Lawson Burford were here this afternoon, Ward.' There was nothing ominous in her voice, only sorrow, for him and for all of them, and Ward looked instantly annoyed. He spun around and walked to the bar, and poured himself a stiff drink. He'd had fun that afternoon, until now. He glanced over his shoulder at his wife, searching her eyes.

'Don't let those two upset you, Faye. They're both a pain in the ass. What did they want?'

'To talk some sense into you, I guess.'

'What's that supposed to mean?' He looked nervously at her as he sat down in a chair. 'What did they say?'

'They told me everything, Ward.' His face went white, as hers had hours before. 'They told me that you don't have a dime left. The shipyards have to be closed down, this house has to be sold to pay our debts . . . everything's going to change, Ward. We're going to have to grow up and stop pretending we live in a fairy land and aren't subject to the same pressures as everyone else in the world.' The only difference between them and everyone else was that he'd never worked a day in his life and they had five children to support. If only she had known. She would never have had this last child. She didn't even feel guilty at the thought, no matter how sweet the new baby was. Their very lives were at stake right now, and she knew in her gut that Ward wasn't going to do a damn thing about it. He wasn't capable of it, but she was. And if he couldn't row the boat to shore, then she would, and that's all there was to it. 'Ward . . . we have to talk about this . . .'

He jumped up and stalked across the room. 'Some other time, Faye. I'm tired.' She leapt to her feet, not caring how weak she still felt. All of that was forgotten now. That was a luxury. Another luxury they could no longer afford.

'Dammit! Listen to me! How long are you going to play games with me? Until they put you in jail for bad debts? Until they throw us out of this house? According to Lawson and Bill, we don't have a dime left, or damn few anyway.' They had been brutally honest with her. They would have to sell everything.

They had just to pay their debts. And then what? That was the question she was asking herself.

Ward stood and faced her then. 'And what do you suggest I do about it, Faye? Start selling my cars? Put the children to work?' He looked horrified; his world was coming down around his ears and he was equipped for no other way of life than this.

'We have to face reality, no matter how frightening it is.' She walked slowly to him then, her eyes alight with green fire, but she wasn't angry at him. She had thought of it all afternoon, and she understood how he was, but she couldn't let him pretend to himself any more, or to her. He had to face the changes that had to be made. 'We have to do something, Ward.'

'Like what?' He slumped slowly into a chair like a deflated balloon. He had thought about it before, and it was beyond his ken. Maybe he had been wrong to keep it from her, but how could he possibly tell her how desperate things were? He never had the heart. So he always bought her a new piece of jewellery instead, and the stupid thing was that he knew she didn't really care about those things. She loved the children and him . . . she did love him, didn't she? That was what always frightened him about telling her. What if she walked out on him? He couldn't bear the thought. And now finally he was looking at her, and he saw hope in her eyes. She wasn't going to desert him after all and suddenly tears filled his eyes and he bent to her and buried his face in her lap, sobbing at what he had done. She stroked his hair and spoke softly to him for what seemed like hours, and when he stopped she was still there. She wasn't going to go away after all, at least not yet, but she also wasn't going to let him run away from it any more.

'Ward, we have to sell the house.'

'But where will we go?' He sounded like a frightened child, and she smiled at him.

'We'll go somewhere else. We'll fire the staff. Sell most of this expensive stuff, the rare books, my furs, my jewellery.' It pained her to think of that, only because he had given her all of it and all of it for important events in their life. She was sentimental about it, but she also knew that the jewellery was worth a great deal and they couldn't hang onto anything now. 'How bad do you suppose the debts are?'

'I don't know.' His face was muffled in her thighs, and she pulled his face up to hers with her hands.

'We have to find out. Together. We're in this together, sweetheart, but now we have to bail out.'

'Do you really think we can?' It was terrifying facing it, even with her.

'I'm sure of it.' At least she told him so, but she was no longer sure of anything.

He felt relief sweep over him at the tone of her voice. Once or twice, between cases of champagne, he had actually contemplated suicide. And he knew exactly how weak he was. He was totally unprepared to face what he had to face now. Without Faye, he couldn't have faced it at all. And with her, it was hardly easier. She forced him to go to the lawyers with her the next day. The doctor had told her not to go out yet, but she totally ignored the rules. After her fifth child, she wasn't as impressed with all that as she might have been after her first, and she wasn't going to let Ward squirm out of it. She stood beside him all the way, but in that sense she was merciless. It had to be faced, by both of them. According to the lawyers, they were three and a half million dollars in debt. She almost fainted when she heard the words, and Ward's face as he listened was a deathly chalk white. The lawyers explained that they would have to sell everything, and if they were lucky they would have a little money left, which they could invest, but they could no longer live on it as they once had. In fact, Bill Gentry looked pointedly at Ward; they would have to go to work, or at least one of them would. They wondered if Faye wanted to go back to her old career, but it had been seven years since she'd done her last film, no one asked for autographs any more, and the papers no longer ran headlines about her as they once had. She was old news. At thirty-two she could certainly make a comeback if she wanted to, but it wouldn't be quite the same thing, and it wasn't what she had in mind anyway. She had another idea, but it was too early to think of that.

'What about the shipyard?' Her questions were intelligent and blunt and Ward was relieved not to have to ask. Somehow it all embarrassed him, and he desperately wanted a drink as Faye pressed on. The lawyers were firm.

'You'll have to declare bankruptcy.'

'And the house? How much do you think we'll get for that?'

'Half a million, if you find someone who falls in love with it. Realistically, probably less.'

'All right, that's a start . . . then we've got the house in Palm Springs . . .' She pulled a list out of her bag. The night before, after Ward had gone to sleep, she had made a list of absolutely everything they owned, right down to the dog. She figured that with a little luck they might collect five million dollars for everything they had. Or at least four.

'And then what?' Ward looked at her bitterly for the first time. 'We dress the children in rags and go begging in the street? We have to live somewhere, Faye. We need servants, clothes, cars.'

She shook her head. 'Car. Not *cars*. And if we can't afford that, we take the bus.' Something in his face suddenly frightened her. She wondered if he could successfully make the change. But he had to, they had no choice, and she was going to help him make it. The only thing she was not willing to give up was him.

At the end of two hours, the lawyers stood up and shook their hands, but Ward's face looked grim. He seemed to have aged ten years in the past two hours, and he hardly spoke a word as they drove home in the Duesenberg. He almost had tears in his eyes realising that it might be the last time they went out in it.

As they walked in the door, the baby nurse was waiting for them. Little Anne had a fever. The nurse was sure that she had caught cold from Val and she was concerned. With a distracted look, Faye went to the phone and called the doctor for her, but she didn't take the baby from the nurse's arms, and when she offered the baby to Faye later on, Faye waved her away with a distracted look and uncharacteristically brusque words. 'I don't have time.' She had other things on her mind. 'Other things' being the demise of their current way of life. The prospect of what she had in store for her was exhausting just to think about. But it had to be done, and she was the one who was going to have to do it all. Ward couldn't cope with it. She would have to do everything, and he was grateful to her when she began tackling it the next day. She called all the estate agents in town and made appointments for them to come to see the house. She called the lawyers again, made appointments with several antique dealers, and began to make lists of what they would keep and what they would sell. Ward watched her stupefied as she sat at her desk at noon the next day, businesslike, matter-of-fact, a frown on her face, and he shook his head, unnerved by it all.

She looked up at him, still wearing a frown, but it wasn't meant for him. 'What are you doing today?'

'Having lunch at the club.' That was another thing that would have to go, all his club memberships, but she didn't say anything to him now. She merely nodded her head, and a moment later he left the room. He didn't come back until six o'clock and when he did he was in a very good mood. He had been playing backgammon all afternoon and had won nine hundred dollars from one of his friends. But what if you'd lost? Faye thought the words silently and said nothing to him, as she went upstairs quietly. She didn't want to see him playing with the twins, knowing he was drunk, knowing all that she knew now. And there was so much to do. Tomorrow she would have to begin firing the help . . . they still had the cars to sell . . . and after everything was done here there would still be the house at Palm Springs . . . tears filled her eyes at the thought of it all, not so much with regret, but more with the sheer weight of it all, and the weight was resting entirely on her. There was no avoiding it. It was like a nightmare, or a very, very strange dream. In a mere twenty-four hours, their entire life had fallen apart; she could barely allow herself to think of it. If she did, she might scream. It was so strange, only days ago, her head had been filled with other things ... the new baby being born ... another spectacular gift from Ward. They were thinking of spending a few weeks in Palm Springs, and now suddenly it was over ... forever ... gone. It was totally incredible. As she walked up the stairs with a heavy heart, wondering what they would do, the nurse waylaid her again, as she had already done several times that day. But Faye had no time for the baby now. There was just too much going on. The woman in white stood at the head of the stairs looking at Faye ominously, a bottle of formula in one hand, as she clutched the newborn babe to her breast, wrapped in an embroidered pink receiving blanket Faye had bought for the twins.

'Would you like to feed the baby now, Mrs Thayer?' The fancy British nanny stared malevolently at her, or at least that was how Faye saw her now, thinking of her salary and also of how she had attempted to make her feel guilty all day.

'I can't, Mrs McQueen. I'm sorry ...' She turned away, feeling the knife of guilt slice at her heart. 'I'm too tired ...' But it wasn't that. She wanted to go through her jewellery before Ward came upstairs. She had made an appointment with Frances Klein the following day, and she had to decide now what she wanted to sell to them. She knew that she would get a fair price from them. And there was no turning back now ... and also no time for little Anne, poor tiny frail child. 'Maybe tomorrow night,' she murmured to the nurse, as she hurried to her room, averting her eyes. It would be easier if she didn't see the child, so recently sprung from her womb. And a week or two before, that was all she had to think about. But not any more ... not now ... With the tears spilling from her eyes, she hurried into her room and closed the door. Mrs McQueen watched her go, shook her head, and headed for the nursery upstairs.

Chapter 6

Christie's picked up the furniture in February. They took all the significant antiques, the six sets of fine antique china Faye and Ward had bought in the last seven years, all the crystal chandeliers, the Persian rugs. They took everything except the bare necessities. And Faye arranged it all so that the children would be in Palm Springs with their nurse, and she urged Ward to go away as well.

'Trying to get rid of me?' He looked at her balefully over the standard glass of champagne he always seemed to hold, except that the glasses were larger nowadays.

'You know better than that.' She sat down next to him with a sigh. She had been labelling furniture all day. Red tags for everything that went, blue for what stayed, and there wasn't much of that. She wanted to sell everything valuable they had. The simpler things they could use when they moved on. It was depressing for everyone, but it had to be faced. They were words Ward had come to hate, but she was merciless. Now that she knew the truth, she wouldn't let him hide from it any more. She was doing everything she could to help, but she wouldn't allow him to lie to himself or to her. It was Faye who dealt directly with the lawyers now, and privately it worried her. She knew that what she was doing was, in some hidden way, emasculating him. But what could she do? Let him go on living the lie? Running up more debts? She shuddered at the thought. To her, it seemed better to face the music now, and then build a new life again. They were still young enough. They had each other, and the kids. Now and then, she was as terrified as Ward. It was like climbing a steep mountainside, but she rarely allowed herself to look down. That was another luxury they could no longer afford. They just had to move on. 'I sold the carousel yesterday.' It was the only subject they talked about any more, what had been sold, what had not. The house still hadn't moved, and it was beginning to worry her. 'I sold it to a hotel, for a decent price.'

'How wonderful.' He got up suddenly and went to fill his glass again. 'I'm sure the children will be thrilled with the news.'

'I can't help that' . . . but you could have, she thought suddenly, and then forced the words out of her mind. It wasn't her fault that they were losing everything. But she wouldn't allow herself to blame Ward either. He had never known any other way of life. No one had taught him to be responsible. And he had always been wonderful to her. In spite of everything, she still loved the man, but sometimes it was difficult not to blame him for what was happening now. It had all been such a sham, for so long . . . if only she had known . . . She found him staring at her, a look of despair in his eyes as he held his glass. For an instant, just an instant, she could glean what he would look like as a very old man. Most of the time, he still looked like a boy, a very handsome, debonair, carefree young man, but now suddenly, in the past two months, he seemed to have taken on the weight of the world and it was ageing him. She had even noticed a few grey hairs mixed in the blond, and there there were new lines around his eyes. 'Ward . . .' She looked across the room at him, wondering what she could say to ease the pain, to make them both better able to live with the truth. And the questions and terror roared through both their minds like trains. Where do we go from here? What do we do now? What happens when the house is sold?

'I wish I'd never dragged you into this.' He sat down, feeling sorry for himself, guilty towards her. 'I had no right to marry you.' But he had wanted and needed her so desperately, especially after the war, after his first bride's death two months after marrying her . . . and Faye had been so remarkable. And she still was. That made it even harder now. He hated what he was doing to her.

She walked slowly to him and sat on the arm of his chair. She was thinner than she had been before Anne, thinner than she had been for years. But she was working hard these days, up at dawn, packing boxes, sorting through mountains of things. She did some of the housework herself, with one of the two remaining maids. The huge staff was reduced to two women who cooked and cleaned for all of them, the nurse who had been with the children for the past six years since Lionel was born, and the baby nurse who had been hired to care for Anne. Eventually, Faye planned to reduce their numbers further to two, but for the moment she still needed these, to help her pack up and close the house eventually. The rest of the staff was long since gone. Arthur and Elizabeth had retired tearfully some six weeks before, leaving Faye after so many years. Both chauffeurs had been fired, the majordomo, and half a dozen maids. Eventually perhaps they wouldn't need anyone at all, if they found a house that was small enough. She hadn't even begun to tackle that yet. She had to sell this one first. And Ward was letting her do it all.

'Wouldn't you rather just have a divorce?' He stared at her, his glass empty in his hand once again. But not for long. Never for long any more.

'No.' She said it loud and clear in the half-empty room. 'I would not. As I recall, the man said "for better or worse", and if things are tough right now, then okay, that's the way it is.'

" 'That's the way it is"? We have the rugs sold out from under our feet, the roof from over our head, our lawyers are lending us money to buy food and pay the maids, and you're just going to shrug it off? And just how do you think we're going to eat after this?' He poured himself another drink, and she had to fight herself not to ask him to stop. She knew he would eventually. Everything would be normal again. One day. Maybe.

'We'll figure something out, Ward. What choice do we have?'

'I don't know. I suppose you think you'll go back to your film career, but you're no spring chicken any more, you know.' She could tell from the way he was beginning to slur his words that he was drunk by now, but she didn't cringe at his words.

'I know that, Ward.' Her voice was painfully calm. She had been thinking about it herself for weeks. 'Something will work out.'

'For who? For me?' He advanced on her menacingly, which was unlike him. But they were both under such strain that anything was possible now. 'Shit, I've never worked in my whole life. What do you think I'm going to do? Get a job at Saks selling shoes to your friends?'

'Ward, please . . .' She turned away so he wouldn't see the tears in her eyes, and he grabbed her arm and pulled her back viciously. 'Come on, tell me your plans, Miss Reality. You're the one who's been so busy making us face up to it all. Hell, if it hadn't been for you, we'd still be living the way we were before.' So that was it, he blamed her and not himself, or maybe he only wished he did. She knew him well, but it didn't stop her from lashing out at him.

'If we were, we'd have five million dollars in debts instead of four.'

'Christ . . . you sound just like those two old maids. Gentry and Burford. They don't know their ass from a hole in the ground. So what if we were in debt?' He shouted the words and walked away from her. 'We had a decent life, didn't we?' He glared at her in fury from across the room, but it was fury at himself, not her, and suddenly she shouted at him.

'It was a lie goddammit! It was only a matter of time before they took the house out from under us and carted the furniture out of here.'

Ward laughed bitterly. 'Oh, I see. And just what do you think is happening now?'

'We're selling it ourselves, Ward. And if we're lucky, we'll have some money left at the end of it. Money we can invest if we're sensible, and maybe live on for a while. And you know what? All that really matters is that we still have each other and the kids.'

But he didn't want to hear what she had to say. He slammed out of the room, and the door shuddered in the frame from the impact as he left. Her hands shook for half an hour after he had left, but she went on packing their things. And three weeks later, they sold the house. It was a sombre day for them, but it was the only way out. They got less than they had hoped for it, but the buyers knew that they were desperate, and it didn't look as good as it once had. The gardeners were all gone and the grounds were already a little run down, the disappearance of the carousel had left some ugly scars. All the really fine furniture was gone, the huge rooms looked barren without the chandeliers or curtains. They got a quarter of a million dollars for the place from a well-known actor and his wife. He wasn't particularly pleasant to Faye, and they never even met Ward. They just strutted around the house, and made comments to their estate agent, as though Faye weren't there. The offer came in the next day, and it took a week of negotiation just to get them up as high as they did. And Burford, Gentry, and Faye all pressed Ward to agree to it. They insisted he had no choice, and finally in desperation, he agreed with them, signed the offer himself, and then locked himself into his study with two bottles of champagne and a fifth of gin. He sat there staring at the photographs of his parents on the wall, and crying silently, thinking of his father's life and the life that now faced him. Faye didn't even see him until late that night when he finally came upstairs. She didn't dare speak to him as he came into the room. She just watched his face, and she wanted to cry just looking at him. It was the end of his whole way of life, and suddenly she was frightened for him, wondering if he could survive the change. She had been poor before, although admittedly not in a very long time, but she still remembered the realities of it. And it wasn't as terrifying to her as it was to Ward. She felt now though as if she had been running for months, and wondered if she was ever going to be able to stop, if they were ever going to be able to find each other again. It was like the worst nightmare of her life, and all their idyllic moments were gone. They were left with the shock of reality, the tragedy of what he'd done, and the dreary ugliness of the rest of their life. But she refused to let it be like that, refused to let him let go and give up, to become a hopeless drunk.

He stood staring at her, as though reading her thoughts, and he looked heartbroken as he walked into the room and sat down. 'I'm sorry I've been such a sonofabitch about all this, Faye.' He sat staring at her and she felt tears in her eyes as she tried to smile at him.

'It's been hard on all of us.'

'But it's all my fault   that's the worst part of it. I'm not sure I could ever have turned the tide, but I could have slowed things down a little bit.'

'You could never have revived a dying industry, Ward, no matter how hard you tried. You can't blame yourself for that.' She shrugged and sat down on the edge of the bed. 'As for the rest . . .' She smiled sadly at him. '. . . it was fun for a while . . .'

'What if we starve?' He looked like a frightened little boy. For a man who had lived on credit for all these years, it was an amazing thing to ask. But he had finally faced those thoughts tonight and the one thing he realised was that no matter how angry he was, he desperately needed her. And she didn't fail him now.

She looked calm when she spoke to him, far calmer than she felt. But she wanted to give him something she knew he didn't have. Faith. Confidence. It was what she could do best for him now. And to her that was what it meant to be his wife. 'We won't starve, Ward. You and I can handle this. I never starved before, even though I came pretty close at times.' She grinned tiredly at him. Her whole body ached from the packing and pushing and moving things around.

'There weren't seven of you then.'

'No.' She looked at him tenderly for the first time in weeks. 'But I'm glad there are now.'

'Are you really, Faye?' His own misery had sobered him hours before. He just couldn't seem to stay drunk tonight, and now he was just as glad. 'Doesn't it frighten you to have all of us pulling on your skirts, and me most of all, I'm more frightened than the kids.' She walked slowly towards him and touched the thick sandy blond hair. It was strange how much he looked like Gregory, and sometimes he seemed even more a little boy than their son.

'It'll be okay, Ward . . . I promise you that.' She spoke in a whisper as she kissed the top of his head, and when he turned his face up to her, there were tears pouring slowly down his cheeks and he had to gulp down a sob.

'I'm going to help you now, babe. I promise . . . I'll do whatever I can . . .' She nodded, and he pulled her face down towards his, and for the first time in what seemed like years, he kissed her lips. Moments later, he followed her to bed, but nothing happened there. It hadn't in a long time. There were too many things on both their minds. But at least the love was still there, battered but not gone. It was all they had left now. Everything else was gone.

Chapter 7

They moved out of the house in May with tears streaming quietly down Faye's and Ward's cheeks. They knew that they were leaving a world and a life that would never come again. Lionel and Gregory were crying too. They were old enough to understand that they were leaving the house for good. It had been their childhood home, and it was beautiful and safe and warm. And there was something frightening about the look in their parents' eyes. Everything was suddenly different somehow, but the children weren't entirely sure how. Only Vanessa and Val seemed less affected by the move. They were only three years old and didn't seem to mind as much, although they felt everyone else's uneasiness too. They thought it was exciting that they were all going to the house in Palm Springs.

Ward drove them all down in the only car they had left. It was an old Chrysler station wagon they had kept for the help, but it served the purpose now. The Duesenbergs were all gone, Faye's Bentley coupé, the Cadillac, and the rest of the fleet of cars they had had.

For Faye and Ward it was like leaving their youth behind them for good. The house in Palm Springs had to be vacated by June. But in the meantime, it gave Faye and Ward a place to leave the children for a few weeks. She had leads to several houses to rent, and the furniture would wait in storage until then. She was going to drive down to Palm Springs with all of them, and then go back to Los Angeles alone to find a house, while Ward oversaw the packing up of the house in Palm Springs. He insisted that it was the least he could do, after all she had tackled things alone in LA. She didn't have to touch a thing this time, she just had to find them a decent place to live. And she knew it wasn't going to be easy to do. With the sale of the shipyard, the house in Beverly Hills, all their furniture, their art, the collection of rare books, the cars, and the house in Palm Springs with most of its contents too, they would have just enough to pay off all of their debts, with about fifty-five thousand to spare, which, carefully invested, would eke out barely enough to support them all. They were going to rent a house, and Faye was hoping she could find something cheap. And as soon as they were all settled in, and the children went back to school in the fall, she was going to see about getting a job. Of course Ward was talking about getting one too. But she had more faith in her own ability to find work, and it would be easier for her. She had worked before, and even if she was thirty-two, she certainly wasn't over the hill yet, not for what she wanted to do. Lionel would be starting first grade, Greg would begin kindergarten, the twins would be in nursery school, so she would have plenty of free time. She was keeping only their nurse to keep an eye on all of them, and the baby as well, and help with the housework and cook. Baby Anne was only four months old and not much trouble yet. It was a perfect time for Faye to leave home. And as she thought of it on the drive to Palm Springs, she suddenly felt guilty about the baby again. The others had all spent so much time with her at the same age, but this time she hadn't had a moment to spare. She had barely seen the baby since she'd been born. But disaster had struck so immediately after her birth, it was impossible even to think of her more than now and then, she had so many other things on her mind. Ward glanced over at her several times as they drove, noticed the frown and patted her hand. He had promised her he would drink less once they got to Palm Springs, and she hoped he would keep his word. The house was smaller there and the children would be much more aware of it if he was drunk all the time. Besides, he had a lot to do, and Faye hoped it would keep him occupied.

*　　*　　*

She went back to Los Angeles two days later, by train, and moved into a small room at the Hollywood Roosevelt Hotel when she arrived. The houses she saw were depressing beyond words. In bad neighbourhoods, with tiny backyards and small ugly rooms. She combed the papers, and called all the agencies, and finally, desperate, by the beginning of the second week, she found a house that was not quite as ugly as the rest, and was large enough for all of them. It had four good-sized bedrooms on one floor. She had already decided to double up the boys, and the twins, and the nurse and Anne could also share a room. The fourth bedroom would be for her and Ward. Downstairs there was a large, somewhat gloomy, cheaply panelled living room, a fireplace that had not worked in years, a dining room that looked out on a bleak little garden, and a big old-fashioned kitchen, big enough to put a big kitchen table in. The children would certainly be closer to her than they ever had before, and she tried to tell herself that it would be good for them, that Ward wouldn't hate it and refuse to live in it, and that the children wouldn't cry when they saw the dreary rooms. The best thing about it was the rent, which was an amount they could afford. And it was in a family neighbourhood in Monterey Park which was a long, long way from their old life in Beverly Hills. There was no kidding anyone about that, and when she returned to Palm Springs, she didn't really try to. She told them all that it would be 'for a while', that it was an adventure they would share, that they would all have chores to do, and they could plant pretty flowers in the garden. And when Ward faced her when they were alone, he stared at her openly and said the words she feared:

'How bad is it really, Faye?'

She took a deep breath. The only thing she could do was tell him the truth. He would find out soon enough for himself. There was no point lying to him. 'Compared to what we had?' He nodded. 'It's grim. But without looking back at that, if we can make the effort not to for a while, it's not so bad. It's freshly painted, it's reasonably clean. The little bit of furniture we have left will fit. And we can make it prettier with curtains and bright flowers. And,' she took another breath, trying not to see the look of devastation on his face, 'at least we have each other. It'll be all right.' She smiled at him but he turned away.

'You keep saying that.' He was angry at her again, as though it were all her fault. And secretly, she was beginning to believe it was. Maybe she shouldn't have forced him to face it all. Maybe she should have let him go on living in debt until they couldn't any more. But it would have all had to be faced sooner or later anyway . . . wouldn't it? She didn't have the answers any more. At least he had kept his word, and packed up the house in Palm Springs, and he hadn't started drinking again until she returned. Then he knew she would take over and he could relax. At least for a while . . . until they moved.

When they closed up the house and drove to Los Angeles all together on a Tuesday afternoon, it felt terribly hot. Faye had already made a little headway in the Monterey Park house before rejoining them in Palm Springs. She had unpacked what she could by herself, hung a few pictures in everyone's rooms, filled vases with flowers, made beds with clean sheets. She had done everything possible to make it look like home, and the children were intrigued when they arrived, like puppies sniffing out their new home, and delighted when they found their rooms and their toys and their own beds. Faye watched them hopefully, but Ward looked as though he were going to faint as he walked into the dark, ugly, wood-panelled living room. He said not a word as Faye watched his face, and fought back tears. He glanced out into the garden with narrowed eyes, glanced around the dining room, noticed a table they had kept from an upstairs den, and instinctively looked up, expecting to see a familiar chandelier that had been sold months before, and then shook his head as he looked at Faye. He had never seen anything like it before. He had actually never been in a home this poor, and instantly it cut him to the quick.

'So much for that. I hope at least it's cheap.' He felt guilt overwhelm him again at what he was doing to her, and all of them.

Her eyes were gentle, as they stood facing each other in their new home. 'It's not forever, Ward.' That was what she had told herself years before, as she longed to escape the poverty of her parents' home. But that had been much worse than this. And this wouldn't be forever either. This time, she was sure of that. Somehow, they would dig their way out.

Ward looked around again sorrowfully. 'I don't think I can take too much more of this.' And at his words she felt anger bubble up inside of her for the first time in months, and when she spoke she roared.

'Ward Thayer, everyone in this family is making the best of this, and you'd damn well better too! I can't turn the clock back for you. I can't pretend this is our old house. But this is our home, *ours*, mine, the children's and yours too.' She was trembling as she stood staring at him and he looked at her eyes. She was determined to make the best of it, and he respected her for that, but he wasn't sure he had the strength to do it too, and when he went to bed that night, he was almost sure he did not. The room smelled of old rot, as though the beams had been damp for years, there was a musty smell about the whole house, and the curtains Faye had hung were from their old servants' quarters and didn't fit. It was like becoming servants in their own home, it was all like an incredible, surrealistic, ugly dream. But it was theirs, and it was real, and she knew they had to make the best of it. He turned to say something to her, to apologise for how badly he was taking it all, but she was already fast asleep, curled into a little ball, huddled onto her own side of the bed, like a frightened child, and he wondered if she was scared too. He was terrified most of the time these days – even the drinking didn't help any more – and he wondered what would happen to the rest of their lives. Was this it for good? They certainly couldn't afford more than this, and he wondered if they ever would again. She said that it was just a stepping stone, an interim place, that one day they would move on, but when and how and to where? In his wildest dreams, as he lay in the ugly, musty bedroom, painted pale green, he couldn't even imagine it.

HOLLYWOOD . . .
AGAIN 1952-1957

Chapter 8

It had been years since he had represented her, and her hand trembled as she dialled. It was entirely possible that he had retired, or perhaps wouldn't have time to speak to her. He had called her when Lionel had been born, and tried to convince her once again to pick up the threads of her career before too much time had passed and it was too late. And it was surely too late now, seven years after she had abandoned her career. She didn't need him to tell her that. But she needed his advice. She had waited until September. The children were all in school, as planned, except, of course, Anne. And Ward was out seeing old friends, trying to get a job, he said, but most of the time he just seemed to be having long lunches at his favourite restaurants and clubs; 'making contacts', he told her when he came home. Maybe he was, but she could see it going on for years and getting them nowhere, not unlike this call . . . if he wouldn't talk to her. She prayed he would, as she gave the secretary her name. There was an interminable pause and she was asked to hold the line, and then suddenly there he was . . . just like the old days, long before this.

'My God . . . a voice from the distant past. Are you still alive?' His voice boomed in her ear as it had years before and she laughed nervously. 'Is it really you, Faye Price?' She was suddenly sorry she hadn't seen more of him over the years, but she'd been so busy with Ward and the kids, and Hollywood was part of another life.

'It's me, the same Faye Price Thayer, with a few grey hairs now.'

'That can be changed, although I don't suppose that's why you called me. To what do I owe the honour of this surprise, and do you have ten children yet?' Abe sounded as warm as he had before, and she was touched that he still had time to talk to her. They had been such good friends once upon a time. Her agent for all the years of her stellar career, he had faded from her life, and now she was knocking on his door again. But she smiled at what he had said.

'Not ten children, Abe, only five. I'm only halfway there.'

'Christ, you crazy kids. I knew from the light in your eye, you meant it way back then, that's when I gave up on you. But you were great while you were up there, Faye. And you could have stayed there for a long, long time.' She wasn't sure she agreed with him, but it was nice to hear. She would probably have started to slip one day. Everyone did eventually, and Ward had spared her that, but now . . . she had to get up the courage to ask what she wanted from him, although he must have suspected the moment he heard her name. He read the papers, just like everyone else, and had heard how much trouble they were in, the house sold, their goods auctioned off, the shipyards closed. It was a quick trip down, just like for some of his stars. But it never changed the way Abe felt about the people he liked. He felt damn sorry for Faye now, with no money, a husband who had never worked a day in his life, and five kids to support.

'Do you ever miss the old days, Faye?'

She had always been honest with him. 'I never have, to tell you the truth.' Not till now anyway, and even then, she had something else in mind.

'I don't suppose you have had time with five kids on your hands.' But she'd have to go out and work again now. He knew that only too well and decided to get to the point, and spare her the embarrassment of crawling to him.

'To what do I owe both the honour and the pleasure of this call, Mrs Thayer?' Though he could guess . . . a part in a play . . .

a small part in a film. He knew her well enough to know she wouldn't ask the moon of him.

'I have a favour to ask, Abe.'

'Shoot.' He had always been direct with her and if he could, he would help her now.

'Could I come and see you sometime?' She sounded like an ingenue again and he smiled.

'Of course, Faye. Name your day.'

'Tomorrow?'

He was startled at how soon she wanted to come in. They really were desperate then. 'Fine. We'll have lunch at the Brown Derby.'

'That would be wonderful.' For just an instant, she thought longingly of the old days. It had been years since she had thought of that. And after she hung up, she walked upstairs with a secret smile. She just prayed he wouldn't tell her she was out of her mind.

When she met him the next day, he didn't say that, but he sat very quietly, thinking of what she had asked. He had been shocked to hear the details of what had happened to their life, and that they were living in Monterey Park. It was so far from where they had begun, light-years away in fact, but she seemed to be holding up. She was one hell of a gutsy girl, always had been, and she was smart enough to do what she had in mind. He just wondered if anyone would give her the chance.

'I read somewhere that Ida Lupino directed a film for Warner Brothers, Abe.'

'I know. But not everyone is going to give you that chance, Faye.' He was honest with her. 'In fact, few will.' And then, 'What does your husband have to say about all this?'

She took a deep breath and looked her old agent in the eye. He hadn't changed much over the years. He was still rotund, grey-haired, sharp, demanding, but kind, and honest to a fault. And best of all, she sensed instantly that he was still her friend. He would help her if he could. 'He doesn't know yet, Abe. I thought I'd talk to you first.'

'Do you think he'll object to your coming back to Hollywood?'

'Not like this. He might if I tried to act again. But the truth is I'm too old now, and I've been gone for too long.'

'At thirty-two, that's a lot of crap. You're not too old, but it would be hard to make a comeback after all these years. People forget. And the young kids have their own stars today. You know,' he sat back and drew pensively on his cigar over dessert. 'I like your idea a lot better. If we can sell it to a studio, it would really be something else.'

'Will you try?'

He pointed the cigar at her. 'Are you asking me to be your agent again, Faye?'

'I am.' She met his eyes and he smiled.

'Then I accept. I'll sniff around and see what I get.' But she knew him better than that. She knew he would turn over every rock and stone until he found something for her, and if he didn't find anything, it would be because there was nothing there. And she was right about him. He didn't call her for six weeks, and when he did, he asked her to come in to see him again. She didn't dare ask him on the phone. She just took the bus from Monterey Park to Hollywood, bumping along nervously, and then running up the steps to his offices. She was breathless when she arrived, but still beautiful he noticed as she sat down. She was wearing a striking red silk dress with a lightweight black wool coat. She had kept some of her clothes from their better days and she looked wonderful. She almost trembled as he watched her face, and he reached across the desk and took her hand. He knew just how anxious she was.

'Well?'

'Relax. It's nothing fabulous, but it's a start. Maybe. If it appeals to you. It's a job as assistant director, at pathetic pay, at MGM. But my friend Dore Schary liked the idea. He wants to see what you can do. And he's well aware of what Lupino is doing at Warner Brothers. He likes the idea of having a woman in his stables too.' Schary had long since had the reputation of being the most forward-thinking of the studio heads, he was also the youngest of all of them.

'Will he be able to tell if I'm any good, if I'm working for someone else?' She was worried about that, but on the other hand, no one would just let her direct by herself for the first time. She knew that too.

Abe nodded his head. 'The director is someone he has under contract, and Dore knows he's no good. If this film turns out halfway decently, it'll be due to you. And the guy is so lazy and drinks so much, he won't even be on the set half the time. You'll have a free hand; what you won't get is much money or much glory out of this. That comes the next time around, if you do a good job this time.'

She nodded. 'Is the picture any good?'

'It could be.' He was honest with her again, outlined the script, told her who the stars would be. 'Faye, it's a chance and that's what you want. If you're serious about this, I think you should give it a try. What have you got to lose?'

'Not much I guess.' She looked at him pensively, thinking over all that he had said, and she liked the sound of it. 'When would I start?' She wanted time to study the script, and she could almost see Abe gulp. He knew how she liked to work, how thorough she was, how studious. He grinned sheepishly.

'Next week.'

Faye rolled her eyes with a groan. 'My God.' It also didn't give her much time to break Ward in to the idea. But this was what she wanted, it was all she knew how to do. She wasn't even sure she knew how to do it, but she desperately wanted to try. She had secretly been thinking about it for months. She looked Abe Abramson in the eye and nodded her head. 'I'll take it.'

'I haven't told you how much.'

'I'll take it anyway.'

He told her the pay, and they both knew it was ridiculous, but the important thing was that she was being given a chance.

'You'll have to be on the set by six o'clock every day, earlier if they want you to. You may work till eight or nine o'clock at night. I don't know how you'll manage with the kids. Maybe Ward can help you out.' Although Abe couldn't imagine that. Ward wasn't that kind of man. He was too used to having an army of help to fulfil his every need. And Abe wondered how much he helped Faye now.

'I still have one woman to help me out.'

'Good.' He stood up. It was just like the old days . . . almost . . . sort of . . . she grinned.

'Thank you, Abe.'

'Never mind that.' His eyes said that he felt sorry for her, but he respected her. She'd bail herself out yet. She was just that kind of girl. 'Come back tomorrow and sign the contract, if you can.' It meant another long bus ride into town, but nothing compared to the ride she would have now every day, getting all the way across town from east to west, to Culver City, and MGM. But she would have walked over ground glass for this job, or for Abe. She knew he would take ten percent from her, and ten percent of what she would be making was hardly worth looking at for him, but he didn't seem to mind. And neither did she. She was thrilled.

She had a job! She wanted to shout as she ran down the stairs. And she smiled to herself all the way home on the bus, and burst into the house the way one of her children would have. She found Ward sitting in the living room, obviously feeling the effects of another champagne lunch with one of his friends, and she dropped onto his lap and threw her arms around his neck.

'Guess what?'

'If you tell me you're pregnant again, I'll kill myself . . . but only after I kill you!' He laughed at her and she shook her head with a smug look he hadn't seen her wear before.

'Nope. Guess again.'

'I give up.' His eyes were red and his words were slurred but she didn't even mind that now.

'I have a job!' He looked shocked and she went on. 'As assistant director on a film that starts next week at MGM.' He stood up so quickly that she had to scramble to her feet so as not to fall on the floor, as he looked down at her.

'Are you out of your mind? What the hell did you do that for? Is that what you've been out doing? Looking for work?' He looked horrified, and she wondered how he thought they were going to support themselves. Fifty-five thousand in bonds was hardly going to do the job for two adults, five children, and a maid. 'Why the hell did you do a thing like that?' He was shouting at her and the children were staring at them from the stairs.

'One of us has to, Ward.'

'I told you, I've been making contacts every day.'

'Great. Then something will turn up for you soon. But in the meantime, I want to do this. It could be a wonderful experience.'

'For what? Is that what you want? Hollywood again?'

'Only like this, not like the old days.' She fought to keep her voice calm, and she wanted to be honest with him. She also wanted the children to go upstairs and stop staring at them, but when she waved them away, they didn't budge, and Ward paid no attention to them at all, these days he rarely did. 'I think we should talk about this when we're alone.'

'To hell with that. We'll talk about it now.' His good looks seemed to vanish as he raged. 'Why didn't you ask me before you did this?'

'It came up suddenly.'

'When?' He was throwing words at her like rocks.

'Today.'

'Fine. Then tell them you changed your mind. You're not interested.'

Suddenly something in her snapped and she could feel fury mounting in her. 'Why should I do a thing like that? Ward, I want this job. I don't give a damn how badly it's paid, or what you think. This is what I want to do. And one day you'll be glad

I did. Somebody has to bail us out of this mess we're in.' Instantly, she regretted the words.

'And you're it. Is that it?'

'Maybe so.' She might as well go on now, the damage was done.

'Great.' His eyes blazed at her as he grabbed his jacket off the back of the chair. 'Then you don't need me around here, do you?'

'Of course, I do . . .' But the words weren't out of her mouth before he had slammed out of the door and Valerie and Vanessa began to cry, as Gregory looked sadly down at her.

'Is he ever coming back?'

'Of course he is.' She walked up to meet them, suddenly feeling tired. Why did he have to make everything so difficult? Why did he have to take it all so personally? Probably because he drank too much, she told herself with a sigh, as she kissed Lionel and Greg's hair, and then reached down to pick up the girls in her arms. She was strong enough to carry both of them. She was strong enough to do a lot of things. Maybe that was the problem with Ward. He didn't like knowing that and it was getting harder and harder to keep that fact from him. She wanted to ask him why he was doing this to her, but she already knew the answer to that. He couldn't cope with what had happened to them, and his choices were to blame her or himself. Either way she paid the price. As she did that night, lying awake until four o'clock, waiting for him to come home, praying that he hadn't smashed up the car and got hurt. He walked in at four-fifteen, reeking of gin and barely able to crawl into bed in the darkened room. There was no point even talking to him now. She would wait until morning and tell him her plan. But when she did, he was not impressed.

'For Heaven's sake, Ward, listen to me.' He was so hung over he could barely see, and she was in a hurry to get to Abe's office in Hollywood, to sign the contract and pick up the script.

'I don't want to listen to that shit. You're as crazy as I used to be. Pipe dreams. That's all they are. You're nuts. You don't know any more about directing than I do, and I don't know a damn thing about any of it.' He looked at her furiously.

'Neither do I. But I'm going to learn. That's the whole point of this job, and maybe the next one after that . . . maybe the next ten films, for all I know. But after that at least I'll know something about it, and what I'm suggesting to you isn't all that insane.'

'Horseshit.'

'Ward, listen to me. Producers are people with a lot of contacts, people who know other people with money. They don't have to have a dime themselves, and they don't even have to like the film, although it helps if they pretend they do. They're go–betweens. They put together the deal. What better job for you? Look at the people you know, the contacts you have. Some of your friends would love to invest in films and get a little bit involved in Hollywood. And one day, if we do this right, we could be a team. You produce, I direct.' He looked at her as though she were out of her mind.

'Why don't you just sign us up for vaudeville? You're goddamn nuts, and you're going to make a fool of yourself.' Finally, she pulled away from him. He didn't want hope yet. He couldn't even begin to see the possibilities, but she could. She could see it all, if he'd only get off his backside and try. She picked up her coat and handbag and looked down at him.

'Laugh at me if you want, Ward Thayer. But one day you'll admit I was right. And if you ever get the guts to be a man again, you might even try my idea. It's not as crazy as you'd like to think. Think about it sometime, if you have time, between drinks.' And with that, she walked out and closed the door.

And for the next two months, she barely saw Ward at all. He was sound asleep when she left the house for the long bus ride she took to get to work every day. She had to leave the house just after four, and the bus took forever to get to MGM. And by the time she got home at night, it was after ten o'clock, the children were sound asleep, and most of the time Ward was out. She never asked him where he went at night. She just fell into bed after a hot bath, a snack, and a glance at the script, and the next day it would begin again. It would have been enough to kill anyone, but she wouldn't give up. The director she was working for hated everything she did, and gave her a hard time whenever she was on the set, but fortunately he was almost never there. And she didn't give a damn what he did; there was pure magic between the actors and herself, and she got something from them that no one else could. It showed in the daily rushes, and more than that it showed in the print they finally showed to Dore Schary. Abe called her at home late in January, a week after they had wrapped up the film and she'd come home to find Ward gone for several days this time. He had told the maid he was going to Mexico 'to see friends', and she hadn't heard a word from him. A small chill ran up her spine as the message was delivered to her, but she forced herself to think that everything was all right and concentrate on the children she'd barely seen since she began working on the film. Abe's call came as she was playing with Anne.

'Faye?' The familiar voice boomed in her ear, and she smiled.

'Yes, Abe.'

'I've got good news.' She held her breath. Please, God, let them like her work. She had been dying over it, waiting to hear. 'Schary says you're fabulous.'

'Oh God . . .' Tears stung her eyes.

'He wants to give you another shot at it.'

'On my own this time?'

'No. As assistant director again, but for more pay. And this time, he wants you to work with someone good. He thinks you'll learn a lot from him.' He mentioned a name that took Faye's breath away. He had directed Faye herself years ago, and she knew what Dore Schary said was true. She would learn a lot from this man. She wanted to direct a film herself, but she knew she had to be patient now. She reminded herself of that as Abe outlined the new deal, and it sounded very good to her. 'What do you think?'

'The answer is yes.' They needed the money anyway, and God only knew where Ward was. This Mexican trip was really the last straw and she intended to tell him that when he came back. That, and a lot of other things too. She wanted to tell him about this new deal. It was wonderful, and there was no one else she could tell. She had been so desperately lonely without him. 'When do I start?'

'Six weeks.'

'Good. That'll give me some more time with the kids.'

He noticed that she didn't mention Ward, and hadn't for quite a while, but he wasn't surprised at that. He wouldn't have given ten cents for the chances that their marriage would survive. Ward was apparently not adjusting to their circumstances, from the little Faye had said, and sooner or later, Faye would dig her way out and leave him behind. It was easy to read the handwriting on the wall, or at least Abe thought so. He had never fully understood how deeply attached to Ward she was. Without family or many close friends, and having given up her old life as a star for him and the kids, she had been totally dependent on him for years and still was. She needed him, just as much as he needed her, or so she thought. It came as an enormous shock when she saw him return from Mexico. He was tanned, healthy, happy, with a long, thin Cuban cigar in his teeth, an alligator suitcase in his hand, and wearing one of his old white linen suits. He gave the impression that the Duesenberg would still have been parked outside if she'd looked. And he only appeared slightly sheepish when he looked at her as he came in. He had expected her to be in bed at that hour. It was well after midnight, but she was studying the new script.

'Have a good trip?' The chill in her voice hid all the loneliness and pain she had felt since he'd left. But she was too proud to let him see that . . . yet.

'Yes . . . sorry I didn't write . . .'

'I imagine you didn't have time.' Something in his face made her feel sudden anger at him. There was sarcasm in her voice, and anger and bitterness. He wasn't sorry he had gone at all. She could see it instantly, and she rapidly sensed the reason why. 'Who were you with?'

'Some old friends.' He set his bags down, and sat across from her on the couch, aware that this was more delicate than he had told himself it would be.

'How interesting. Funny you never mentioned it before you left.'

'It came up pretty suddenly.' Something nasty lit in his eyes. 'And you were busy with your film.' That was what it was really all about. His revenge for her finding a job when he had not, and she knew that too, but it wasn't fair of him.

'I see. Of course then I understand. Next time you leave for three weeks, you might try calling me at work before you go. You may be surprised at how easy I am to reach by phone.'

'I didn't know that.' He was growing pale beneath the tan.

'I guess not.' She looked deep into his eyes and knew the truth. She just didn't know how to confront him with it. But the papers made it easy for her the next day. It was all there. All she had to do was throw it across the bed at him. 'Your press agent's pretty good, and your travel agent must be too. I just don't happen to think much of your taste in girls, or your judgement about who you take along on trips.' There was a gash in her guts that felt as though it would kill her on the spot. But she refused to show him that. She didn't want him to know how much pain he'd caused her with this flagrant affair. And she knew too that it was his way of coping with all that had happened to them, of pretending that he was still part of the world he had just lost. But no matter how hard he pretended all that, it was over for them . . . unless he married that world again.

Ward almost gasped as he read the words. 'Bankrupt million-aire Ward Thayer IV and Maisie Abernathie should be back from Mexico any day. They've been lolling on her yacht outside

San Diego for three weeks, and went down to Mexico to meet friends and play with the fish. They look awfully happy and everyone is wondering what he did with his retired movie queen . . .' Faye stared at him with terror and hatred in her eyes for the first time in her life. 'You can tell them I quit. It won't make headlines any more, but at least it'll clear things up for you and Miss Abernathie, you sonofabitch. Is that how you're going to handle what happened to us? By running around with people like her? You both make me sick.' Maisie Abernathie was a spoiled, self-indulgent heiress who had slept with almost every man they knew . . . 'except me', he used to tease. And now the list included him as well.

Faye walked out of the bedroom and slammed the door, and when he came downstairs, he found that she had left to take the four older children to school. She had been spending most of her time with them for weeks, to make up for the months she'd worked and would work again now. She missed them terribly when she worked, but she wasn't thinking of them as she walked back into the house and found Ward waiting for her, downstairs, in a blue silk dressing gown he'd bought in Paris years before.

'I have to talk to you.' He looked terrified as he stood up, and she brushed past him on her way upstairs. She was going to do her reading at the public library.

'I have nothing to say to you. You're free to go whenever you want. I'll find a lawyer, and he can call Burford.' She was beginning to convince herself that Maisie Abernathie was not only for real, but for good.

'It's that simple, is it?' He grabbed her arm as she swept by, avoiding his eyes. But now she looked him full in the face and it almost frightened him. He had never seen such contempt, let alone felt it, and it almost broke his heart as he realised what he'd done. 'Faye, listen to me . . . it was all a stupid mistake. I just had to get out of here . . . the children screaming all the time . . . you gone . . . this depressing house . . . it was more than I could take.'

'Good. Then you're out of it permanently. You can move back to Beverly Hills with Maisie. I'm sure she'll be happy to take you in.'

'As what?' He looked at his wife bitterly. 'Her chauffeur? For chrissake dammit. I can't even get a job, and you're at work all the time, what the hell do you know about what I feel? I can't stand this life. I wasn't brought up for this . . . I don't know . . .' He let go of Faye's arm and she stared unsympathetically at him. This time he had gone too far. The drinking, the self-pity, the inability to work, the lies as he wasted the last of his money before she found out, she could forgive him all of it, but not this. This was it. But he looked pitifully at her anyway. 'I can't help it. You're stronger than I am. You have something inside you that I don't. I don't know what it is.'

'It's called guts. And you've got them too, if you'd just give yourself a chance, and stay sober long enough to get on your feet.'

'Maybe I can't. Has that occurred to you yet? It has to me. Every day, in fact, until I went away. And maybe that's something I should do for good.'

'What?' She looked blank, but she felt terror crawl up her spine again.

He looked strangely calmer now, as though he knew what he had to do. 'I mean get out of your life, Faye.'

'Now? That's a stinking thing to do.' In spite of what she had said she was horrified, she didn't want to lose this man. She still loved him. He and the children were all that mattered to her. 'How can you do a thing like that to us?' There were tears in her eyes and he forced himself to look away, just as he had forced himself not to think of her in the last few weeks. He couldn't stand the guilt any more. What had happened was all his fault, and there was nothing he could do to help. He had nothing to offer her and she seemed to be doing fine on her own. At least that was what he told himself, and what he was telling himself now, without looking at her. Had he looked, he'd have seen the agony in her eyes as she stared back at him. 'Ward, what's happening to us?' Her voice was husky and hoarse, and he sighed deeply and walked across the room to look out the window at the nonexistent view of their neighbour's unpainted house, and the rubbish in his yard.

'I think it's time for me to get out of here, find a job on my own, and let you forget we ever met.'

'With five kids?' She would have laughed except that she wanted to cry. 'Are you planning to forget them too?' She stared at the back of his head in disbelief. This couldn't be happening to them, except it was. It was like a nightmare or a very bad script.

'I'll send you everything I can.' He turned slowly to face her from across the room.

'Is it Maisie? Are you serious about her?' It was hard to believe, but anything was possible now. Maybe he was that desperate for their old life, and Maisie was certainly part of it. But Ward shook his head.

'It's not that. I think I just need to get out of here for a while.' He looked almost bitter as he said it. 'I feel as though I ought to leave you alone to build a new life for yourself. You could probably wind up married to some successful film star.'

'If I'd wanted that, I could have had it years ago. But I didn't want that. I wanted you.'

'And now?' He felt the first surge of courage he had felt in years. It was all out now. There was no place left to go but up. He had nothing left to lose, if in fact he had lost her.

She stared at him with sad, empty eyes. 'I don't know who you are any more, Ward. I don't understand how you could go to Mexico with her. Maybe you'd better go back to her.' They were words of false bravado, but he snapped at the bait.

'Maybe I will.' He stalked upstairs then in a rage, and a moment later, she could hear him crashing around their bedroom, packing his things. She sat in the kitchen, staring blindly into a coffee cup, thinking of the last seven years and crying bitterly, until it was time to pick the children up at school again.

And when she came home with the kids, he was gone. The children had never realised he was back, so she had nothing to explain to them. She fixed dinner for them that night, lamb chops that were overcooked, baked potatoes that remained like rocks, and spinach that she burned. She wasn't at her best cooking for them, but at least she tried, and all she could think of that night was where he was – with Maisie Abernathie undoubtedly – and had she been wrong to blow up at him? She lay in bed that night, thinking all the way back to Guadalcanal, the good times they had shared . . . the tenderness, the dreams, and she cried long into the night, and finally cried herself to sleep, aching for him.

Chapter 9

The second film Faye worked on was far more difficult than the first; the director was constantly there, making demands on her, giving her orders, criticising what she did. There were times when she would have dearly loved to throttle him, but when all was said and done, he gave her a rare and very special gift. He taught her all the tricks she so desperately needed to know for her new trade; he demanded the utmost from her and got far more than that, and at times he let her take the reins and then corrected her. When they finished the film, she had learned more than she might have otherwise in ten years and she was grateful to him. He paid her an enormous compliment before walking off the set for the last time and there were tears in her eyes as she watched him go.

'What did he say to you?' one of the grips whispered and Faye smiled.

'He said he'd like to work with me again, but he knows he won't. That I'll be directing my own film next time.' She sighed deeply and looked at the actors hugging and kissing and celebrating the end of their hard work. 'I hope he's right.' And he was. Two months later, Abe offered her her first job as director at MGM again, without being assistant to anyone. Dore Schary had given her her big chance, and she had lived up to it.

'Congratulations, Faye.'

'Thanks, Abe.'

'You deserve every bit of it.' The new film would begin in the autumn. It was an enormous challenge and she was pleased. The children would be back in school by then. Lionel was going into second grade, Greg into first, the twins were still in nursery school for this final year, and Anne was not yet two years old, straggling behind the others, anxious to keep up, and somehow always outrun by them. Faye always meant to spend time with her, but somehow she never had enough time. The others clamoured for her; now she would have the script to study and read for several months, eventually the film to do. It was difficult to stop everything and spend time with a baby again. Anne was different from the others; not only younger, but also so much less able to communicate. It was always easier to leave her with the nurse, who loved her so much, and Lionel who had always been especially attached to her.

Faye was excited about the new film, except that day in, day out, she still thought of Ward and wondered where he was. Since the day he'd walked out, they'd never heard from him. She'd read about him in Louella Parsons once, but the piece told her nothing at all. At least it hadn't mentioned Maisie Abernathie.

In light of that, the film gave her something to do. She had been anxious to keep her mind occupied since finishing the other film. She had asked Abe for a lawyer's name several months before, but somehow she had never got around to calling him, although she promised herself that she would. Something always came up, and the memories would flood her again.

Then suddenly, one day in July, Ward appeared at her front door. The children were playing in the back, in the yard they had all so carefully planted with flowers. The nurse had built a swing for them, proud of their accomplishment and ingenuity. Suddenly, there he was, in a white linen suit and a blue shirt, looking more handsome than he ever had before. For an instant, she felt the old familiar pull towards him, but she reminded herself that he had walked out on her, and Lord only knew who he was involved with now. She felt shy as she looked at him, and lowered her eyes before glancing up at him again.

'Yes?'

'May I come in?'

'Why?' She stared at him nervously and he looked uncomfortable, but it was obvious he wouldn't go away until she let him in to talk to her. 'It'll upset the children if they see you here.' They had only recently stopped asking for him and she assumed that Ward was planning to disappear again.

'I haven't seen my children in almost four months. Can't I at least say hello to them?' As she hesitated, she noticed that he was thinner than he had been before. It made him look younger than he had in years. She hated to admit to herself how handsome he was. There was no point falling in love with him all over again. 'Well?' He wasn't backing off and finally she stepped back and held the screen door open for him. The house looked even uglier to her than it usually did, seeing it again through his eyes, as he stepped inside and looked around. 'Well, nothing's changed here.' It was a simple statement of fact and it riled her immediately.

'I suppose you're living in Beverly Hills again?' There was a sharp edge to her voice that cut through him like a knife, just as she had intended it to. He had hurt her terribly when he left, and he was probably just coming back to torment her again. She instantly assumed the worst.

He turned to her quietly. 'I'm not living in Beverly Hills, Faye. Do you really think I would leave all of you in a place like this and go back to Beverly Hills myself?' He looked horrified and Faye just stared at him. Somehow that was exactly what she had assumed.

'I don't know what you'd do, Ward.' She certainly hadn't noticed the cheques rolling in from him, but they had been managing on the income from their small fund and her salary. Actually, she wondered what he'd been living on for the past few months, but she had no desire to ask.

And at that point, the children came running in. Lionel stopped in the garden doorway, shocked to see him there, and then advanced slowly towards him with wide eyes. But when Greg saw his father, he thundered past Lionel and hurled himself into his arms. The twins followed suit. Anne simply stood staring at him, with no idea who he was. She didn't remember him and she looked up at Faye and held her hands out to be picked up. Her mother obliged, watching the other four climb all over Ward, laughing and screeching now as he tickled them. Only Lionel seemed more cautious than the other three, and he looked towards Faye again and again, as though needing to know what she thought of it. 'It's all right, Lionel.' She said it gently. 'You can play with your dad.' But he remained on the fringe, watching them. And at last, Ward talked them all into getting cleaned up, with the promise of taking them out to lunch for a hamburger and an ice-cream cone.

'Do you mind?' he asked her after the children had gone upstairs.

'No,' she looked at him cautiously. 'I don't.' She looked nervous as she faced him now, but he seemed equally so. Four months was a hell of a long time. They were almost strangers again.

'I have a job, Faye.' He said it as though he expected trumpets to play and she resisted the urge to smile.

'Oh?'

'In a bank . . . it's not a very important job. I got it from one of my father's friends. I just sit at a desk all day and collect a cheque at the end of the week.' He looked surprised, as though he had expected it to be more painful than that, like surgery.

'Oh?'

'Well, aren't you going to say anything, dammit?' He was angry at her again. Suddenly, she was so damned hard to please, and she had never been like that. Maybe going back to work had taken its toll on her. He knew she didn't just sit at a desk all day waiting for her cheque on Friday afternoons. He took a deep breath and tried again. 'Are you working these days?' He knew she couldn't be, or she wouldn't have been at home playing with the kids, at least it hadn't been that way when he was around.

'No, not for another month. I'll be doing my own picture this time.' She was instantly annoyed at herself for saying too much. It was none of his business any more what she did, but it felt good telling him anyway. It had always felt good telling him everything.

'That's great.' He seemed to hop from one foot to the other, watching her, not sure what to say to her. 'Any big stars in it?'

'A few.'

He lit a cigarette. He had never smoked before. 'We haven't heard from your lawyer yet.'

'I haven't had time to take care of it.' But that wasn't entirely true. She had been free for several months, not that he could know that. 'You will.'

'Oh.'

And then the children came thundering down. He took all four of the older ones to lunch, offering to drive them in his new car. A 1949 Ford. It still looked practically new and Ward glanced apologetically at her. 'A Duesenberg it's not, but it gets me back and forth to work.' She resisted the urge to tell him she still took the bus. The station wagon had finally died the month before, leaving them with no transportation at all. 'Would you like to come to lunch with us, Faye?'

She started to say no, but the children begged her so loudly that it was easier just to give in and go, and part of her was curious about him; where he had been, what he had done, where he was living now. She wondered if he was still involved with Maisie Abernathie, but she told herself she didn't care any more, and almost convinced herself until she saw the way the waitress looked at him and then she felt herself flush. He was still a very handsome young man, and women certainly seemed to notice him, more than men ever noticed her. But then, she still wore her wedding band, and everywhere she went, she dragged five children along.

'They're wonderful.' He praised her on the way home, as the four children pushed and shoved each other on the back seat of the dark blue Ford. 'You've done a good job with them.'

'It isn't as if you've been gone for ten years, for heaven's sake, Ward.'

'It feels like it sometimes.' He was silent for a little while and then glanced at her when they paused at a red light. 'I sure miss all of you.'

She wanted to blurt out, 'We miss you too,' but she forced herself to say nothing at all, and was surprised when she felt his hand on hers. 'I've never stopped regretting what I did, if that counts at all.' His voice was so low the children couldn't hear, and they were making such a ruckus they wouldn't have heard anyway. 'And I've never done it again. I haven't gone out with another woman since I walked out of our house.' 'Our house', strange words from him, referring to that awful place, and what he said touched her heart as her eyes filled with tears, and she turned to look at him. 'I love you, Faye.' They were the words she had longed to hear for four months and instinctively she reached out her arms to him. They were at the house by then and the children tumbled out of the car. Ward told them to go inside, and he would be there in a moment. 'Babe . . . I love you more than you'll ever know.'

'I love you too.' Suddenly she began to sob, and pulled away to look at him with ravaged eyes. 'It's been so awful without you, Ward . . .'

'It was just as terrible for me. I thought I'd die without you and the kids. Suddenly, I realised all we had, even without our old life and a big house . . .'

'We don't need all that.' She sniffed and smiled. 'But we do need you.'

'Not as much as I need you, Faye Thayer.' He looked at her hesitantly. 'Or is it Faye Price again?'

She laughed through her tears. 'Not a chance!' And at the same time noticed that he was still wearing his wedding band too. At that exact moment, Greg was calling to him from the house.

'I'm coming, son! Just a minute.' He shouted back. There was so much left to say, but Faye slid slowly out of the car.

'Go ahead. They've missed you too.'

'Not half as much as I've missed them,' and then, with a look of desperation in his eyes, as he reached out and grabbed her arm, 'Faye, please . . . can we try again? I'll do anything you want. I stopped drinking as soon as I left. I realised what a complete jerk I had been. I've got a lousy job, but at least it's something . . . Faye . . .' Tears filled his eyes and suddenly he couldn't contain his feelings for her any more. He bowed his head and began to cry. After a moment he looked at her honestly. 'I didn't know what to do with myself when you went to work. I felt as though I wasn't a man any more . . . as though I never had been . . . but, oh God, I don't want to lose you, Faye . . . please . . . oh babe, please . . .' He pulled her into his arms, and Faye felt as though her heart had found its home again. She had never really given up on him. She wasn't even sure she ever could. She put her head on his shoulder and the tears began to flow again.

'I hated you so much for a while . . . or at least I wanted to . . .'

'I wanted to hate you too, but I knew I was the one who was wrong.'

'Maybe I was too. Maybe going back to work wasn't the right thing, but I didn't know what else to do.'

He shook his head. 'You were right,' and then he smiled at her through his own tears, 'you and your crazy ideas about making me a producer one day . . .' He smiled tenderly at her. What a good woman she was, how lucky he was to have her back in his arms, even for an hour or two.

She was shaking her head at him. 'That wasn't a crazy idea. It's possible, Ward. I could teach you everything you need to know. You could hang around the set on this next film.' She looked hopeful but this time he shook his head.

'Can't. I'm a working man now. Nine to five and all that.'

She laughed. 'All right, but you could still be a producer one day, if that's what you want.'

He sighed and put an arm around his wife. 'Sounds like pipe dreams to me, my friend.'

'Maybe not.' She looked up at him, wondering what life would bring. At least it had brought him home to her again.

He stood in the doorway to the ugly house in Monterey Park, looking at her. 'Do we give it another try? . . . No . . . more correctly, will you give me another chance, Faye?'

She looked at him long and hard, and slowly a small smile dawned in her eyes. It was a smile born of wisdom and disappointment and pain. She was no longer a young girl. Life was no longer the same as it had been a few years before. Her whole world had turned upside down, and she had survived. Now this man was asking her to walk along beside him again. He had hurt her, deserted her, cheated on her, betrayed her. And yet, deep inside, she still knew that he was her friend, that he loved her, and she him, and that she always would. He didn't have the same instincts that she had, and was not nearly as well equipped to survive. But perhaps, side by side, hand in hand . . . maybe . . . just maybe . . . in fact, she was sure of it. More important, she was sure of him again.

'I love you, Ward.' She smiled up at him, feeling suddenly young again. It had been an endless few months without him. She never wanted to live through that again. She could survive anything but that, even poverty.

He stood kissing her then, as the children looked on, and suddenly they all began to laugh. Greg pointed at them, laughing the hardest of all, as Ward and Faye began laughing too. Life was sweet again, as it had been long before, only better now. They had both been through hell and back, not unlike Guadalcanal in some ways. But they had won the war. Finally. And now life could begin again. For all of them.

Chapter 10

Ward gave up his furnished room in West Hollywood, without ever staying there again, and he moved back into the ugly house he had hated so much in Monterey Park, without ever noticing this time how dreary it was. It looked wonderful to him as he carried his bags up the stairs to their room.

They had three idyllic weeks before the children went back to school, and Faye began her new film. And when she did, he insisted that she take the car, while he took the bus to work, which saved her hours on the bus at 4 and 5 am, and she was grateful to him. He was nicer to her than he had ever been before. And if it was no longer emerald pendants and ruby pins, it was dinners he had prepared for her with his own hands, and then kept warm until she came home, little presents he bought when he got paid, like a book, or a radio, or a warm sweater for her to wear on the set. It was messages he left for her when she was so tired she wanted to cry, and the hot baths he ran with bath oil he had bought. He was so good to her, at times it almost made her cry. Month after month he proved to her how much he loved her, and she proved the same to him, and from the ashes of their old life emerged a stronger relationship than they had ever had before and memories of the ugly months began to fade. Still they rarely allowed themselves to reminisce about the old days. It was too painful for both of them.

In many ways Faye enjoyed her new life. Her first job as director went very well, and she was given three pictures to do in 1934, all with major stars. Each of them was a major box-office hit. She had begun to make a name for herself in

Hollywood again, not as a pretty face or a big star, but as a director with a fine mind, a great gift, and amazing power with her stars. She could get a heartrending performance out of a rock, Abe Abramson said, and Dore Schary didn't disagree with him. They were both proud of her, and when the first offer of 1955 came in, Faye demanded what she had wanted from them for years. She had been grooming him ever since he came back, and she knew he was ready now. Her agent almost fell off his seat when she explained her conditions to him.

'And you want me to tell Dore that?' He looked shocked. The guy didn't know a damn thing about pictures and Faye was out of her goddamn mind as far as Abe was concerned. He had thought she was crazy when she took him back. It was the first time he had ever disagreed with her, but he never told her what he thought. Not then. But he did now. 'You're nuts! They'll never buy a package like that. He has no background at all. The guy is thirty-eight years old, Faye, and he has no more idea how to be a producer than my dog.'

'That's a disgusting thing to say, and I don't give a damn what you think. He's learned something about finance in the last two years; he has a sharp mind, and he has some influential friends.' But more importantly than that, Ward had finally grown up, and Faye was enormously proud of him.

'Faye, I just can't sell a package like that.' Abe was sure of it.

'Then you can't sell me, Abe. Those are my terms.' She was as hard as rock, and Abe wanted to reach across his desk and strangle her.

'You're making a big mistake. You're going to blow everything. If you screw this up, no one will ever touch you again. You know damn well how hard it was to sell a woman director at first. And everyone is just waiting for you to fall on your face. No one else will give you the chance Dore gave you, not again . . .' He was running out of arguments, and she held up a hand, bare of rings except for her simple gold wedding band which she hadn't taken off since her wedding day. All the other jewellery Ward had given her had been sold long ago. She didn't even miss it any more – it was part of another life, another time.

'I know all of that, Abe. And you know what I want.' She stood up and looked down at him. 'You can do it if you try. It's up to you. But those are my terms.' He wanted to throw something at the door after she left.

But he was even more stunned when MGM accepted her terms.

'They're even crazier than you are, Faye.'

'They said yes?' She was in shock as she clutched the phone.

'You two start next month. At least he does. He starts first and then you come into it once the film gets under way. Producer, director, with your own offices at MGM.' He still couldn't get over it, and he sat at his desk shaking his head. 'Good luck . . . and listen, you'd both better get your asses in here and sign the contracts right away before they come to their senses and change their minds.'

'We'll come in this afternoon.'

'Damn right,' he growled. And when they did go in Faye was proud of Ward again.

It was a terrible thing to say, but the hard times had been good for him. There was an air of quiet maturity about him now, and intelligence. Abe began to think he might just pull it off after all, and he knew she'd do everything to help. He wound up shaking hands with both of them and kissing Faye's cheek, wishing them luck, and shaking his head once they had left. You never knew . . . it was possible . . . just possible . . .

The film was a huge box-office hit, and their career took off after that, producing and directing two to three films a year. In 1956 they were finally able to leave the house Ward had hated so much, although now neither of them had time to notice it. They rented another house for two years. And in 1957, five years after they had left, they were in Beverly Hills again. Not in the grandiose splendour they once had known, but in a pretty, well-kept house with a garden front and back, and five bedrooms, which gave them an office at home, and a modest swimming pool. The children were enchanted with it, and Abe Abramson was happy for them. But not as happy as Ward and Faye Thayer were. They had made it back. It was like returning from the war all over again, and they clung to their careers for dear life, appreciating every moment of it.

BEVERLY HILLS . . .
AGAIN 1964–1983

Chapter 11

His office at MGM looked out at nothing in particular, and he glanced out without much interest, while giving dictation. When Faye walked in, she looked across the room at her husband's profile, and smiled to herself. At forty-seven years of age, he was as handsome as he had been twenty years before. More so perhaps – his hair had turned white and his eyes were the same wonderful deep blue. His face was lined, but his body was still long and lean and sinewy, and he was holding a pencil as he measured his words. It was about their next film, slated to go into production in three weeks, and almost on schedule this time. He was fearsome about that. Ward Thayer Productions went out on time, and were expected to come in on time too. And God help those who didn't cooperate with him. They never worked for him again. He had learned a lot in the last ten years. Faye had been right. He was a genius at producing films, more so than anyone had suspected at first. He learned to budget everything well in advance, and came in with investment money from sources that boggled everyone. He tapped the resources of his friends at first, but after that he became ingenious at going out to corporations for funds, conglomerates looking to diversify. As Abe Abramson had said about Ward, 'He could charm the birds off trees,' and he had again and again. He and Faye had worked long into the night for months, figuring it all out together for the first few years. But after the first half-dozen films, Ward was really on his own. She stuck to her directing. He put the packages together long before she got involved in the directing and together they produced hit after hit. They were often called Hollywood's Golden Team. And although they had their flops, most of the time they could do no wrong.

Faye was so damn proud of Ward. She had been for a long time. The drinking had stopped, there had been no other women in his life since that distant interlude when they had been separated in 1953. He had worked hard, done well, and she was happy with him. Happier even than they had been in those early fairy-tale years. Those years no longer seemed real to her, and Ward seldom mentioned them any more. She knew he still missed that life, the easy life, the trips, the estate, dozens of servants . . . the Duesenbergs . . . but they had a good life now. Who could complain? They enjoyed their work, and the kids were almost grown up.

She smiled quietly at Ward now, and glanced at her watch. She would have to interrupt him soon. And as though he had sensed her in the room, he turned and smiled at her, their eyes met and held, in the way that people still envied them after all these years. There was something very special about Ward and Faye Thayer, a love which still burned brightly and was the envy of all their friends. Their life hadn't been without pain. But there had been rich rewards too.

'Thanks, Angela, we can finish the rest this afternoon.' He stood up and came around the desk to kiss his wife. 'Time to go?' He pecked Faye on the cheek and she smiled up at him. He still wore the same after-shave after all these years, and it was always like an announcement that Ward had been in the room. If she closed her eyes, it still conjured up the same romantic images of long before, but there was no time for that today. Lionel was graduating from Beverly Hills High. They had to be there in half an hour, and the other children were waiting to be picked up at home.

Faye glanced at the handsome sapphire and gold Piaget watch he had given her the year before. 'I think we should go, sweetheart. The troops are probably hysterical by now.'

'No,' he grinned at her, as he grabbed his jacket and followed her out, 'only Valerie.' They both laughed. They knew the children well, or thought they did. Valerie was by far the most high-strung, ebullient, excitable, with the worst temper coupled with the most strident demands. She lived up to her red hair, most of the time, in sharp contrast to her more subdued twin. And Greg had lots of energy too, but he used it differently; all he thought about were sports, and lately girls. And then there was Anne, their 'invisible child', as Faye referred to her some-times. She spent most of her time in her room, reading, or writing poetry. She always seemed separate from the rest. She always had. And it was only when she was with Lionel that a different side of her came out, that she laughed and joked and teased, but if the others pushed her too hard, she would retreat again. It seemed to Faye that she was always saying to the others 'Where's Anne?' and sometimes they even forgot to ask. It was difficult to know the child, and she was never quite sure she did, which seemed an odd thing to say about one's own child, but it truly seemed to apply to Anne.

Ward and Faye waited for the elevator at MGM. They had their own complex of offices now, handsomely decorated all in white and bright blue and chrome. Faye had redone it all herself two years before, when Thayer Productions Inc. officially estab-lished permanent offices at MGM. In the early days they had had temporary offices there, and then they had set up shop half-way across town, and as a result, spent half their lives in cars driving to meetings with the MGM staff. But now they were both independent and at the same time part of MGM, subcon-tracting to them for two years at a time, working on their own projects as well as those they undertook for MGM. It was an ideal position to be in, and Ward was satisfied with the way things had worked out, although he privately thought it was all because of Faye. He told himself that, and once confessed it to her, although she disagreed violently with him, insisting that he didn't appreciate his own worth. And he didn't of course. She had always been so much more the star, so much more in control of everything. She had known everyone in the industry for years and they respected her. But they respected him too now, whether he admitted it to himself or not, and Faye wished he would. It was difficult to convince him of how important he was. Somehow he was never quite sure. But in another way, that was part of his charm, the boyish ingenuousness that had followed him into middle age, and still gave him the appearance and the sweetness of youth.

Their car was parked in the car park, a black convertible Cadillac they'd had for two years. They kept a huge station wagon at home for when they went out with the kids, and Faye had a small bottle-green Jaguar she loved to drive. But somehow, even at that, they never seemed to have enough cars. Now that both Lionel and Greg could drive, they were always fighting over the station wagon, a situation which was about to end, unknown to Lionel, that afternoon. As a combination graduation and birthday gift, they were giving him one of the new little Mustangs that had just come out. It was bright red, convertible, with white sidewalls and red upholstery. Faye had been even more excited than Ward when they picked it up the night before, and they had sneaked it into their neighbours' garage. They could hardly wait to give it to the boy that afternoon. They were all going to lunch at the Polo Lounge to celebrate, and there was to be a party for him at the house that night.

'It seems incredible, doesn't it?' Faye looked over at Ward as they drove home, and she smiled nostalgically. 'He's going to be eighteen . . . and graduating from high school . . . it seems like yesterday doesn't it, when he was just a little thing learning to walk?' Her words conjured up images of the old days, and Ward was thoughtful as they drove along. All of that had changed forever twelve years before, and it still saddened him sometimes when he thought of it. That had been such a good life, but so was this, and that didn't even seem real any more. It was a lost world, and he glanced at Faye now.

'You haven't changed a bit since then, you know.' He smiled appreciatively at her. She was still beautiful, her hair was still almost the same peachy blonde, and she coloured the grey so it didn't show. At forty-four, her figure was still good, her skin clear and smooth, and the green eyes still danced with emerald fire. He looked older than she did now, by quite a bit, but it was because of his white hair. His blond hair had turned early, but it suited him. It was in sharp contrast to the youthful face, and she often thought that she liked him better like this. He looked more mature. She leaned over to kiss his neck as he drove.

'You lie beautifully, my love. I look older every year, but you're still pretty dashing, you know.'

He chuckled with a look of embarrassment and pulled her closer to him. 'You're going to be cute thirty years from now, you know that? Necking with me as we drive along . . . pulled over maybe . . . catching a quickie in the back seat . . .' She laughed at the thought, and he noticed the long, graceful neck he had always loved, amazingly still free of lines. He often thought that she should have stayed in films herself. She would still have been beautiful, and she knew so much about the art. He was reminded of it every time he saw her direct, but she was so damn good at that too. There was very little Faye Thayer couldn't do. The realisation of that used to bother him, but he was proud of her now. She was just one of those people who could do many things well. But the odd thing was that he was too, although he didn't recognize it, and would have argued, and often did, when Faye told him that. He didn't have the self-confidence she had, even now, or the drive, or the assurance that let her cast herself at anything, sure that she could accomplish it.

She glanced at the Piaget watch again now. 'Are we late?' Ward frowned as he looked at her. He didn't want to let Lionel down. He wasn't as close to him as he was to Greg, but Li was his oldest son after all, and this was his big day, and when he saw the car . . . Ward smiled again.

'We're not late yet. What are you smiling at?' Faye looked at him curiously.

'I was just thinking of Li's face when he sees the car.'

'God, he's going to die!' She giggled to herself again, and Ward smiled. She was so crazy about that boy, always had been, almost too much so, he thought sometimes, and too protective of him. She was never willing to let him take the physical risks Greg took, or be exposed to as many things. He didn't have Greg's physical strength, she always said, or his ability to take hard knocks, emotionally or otherwise, but Ward was never as sure. Maybe he would have been tougher, if Faye had given him a chance. In other ways he was so much like her, he was as quietly stubborn as Faye herself had always been, as determined about what he wanted to do, at all costs, as certain. He even looked like her; if you squinted they could almost have been twins, and spiritually, they were, to the exclusion of everyone else sometimes. If Ward had been honest about it, he would have been jealous of the boy sometimes. She was so close to him as he grew up, they confided in each other so much, that it left everyone else out, especially Ward, who resented it. Lionel was always polite to him, pleasant, but he never went out of his way to seek him out, to go anywhere with him . . . not like Greg, who bounded up to Ward the moment he came home, every night for the last sixteen and a half years, or ever since he could walk anyway. Sometimes Ward even found him asleep on his side of the big double bed when he got home at night. Greg would have some urgent adventure to relate to him and wanted to be sure he woke up when they got home. The sun rose and set on his dad, and Ward had to admit that that kind of passionate approval was hard to beat, and it made Lionel's shy aloofness seem even more difficult to penetrate. Why even try when you had a child like Gregory panting at your feet? But he knew he owed something to his oldest son. He had just never been quite sure what.

Even the car had been Faye's idea. It would make his commute to UCLA in the autumn so much easier, and his summer job too. He was working at Van Cleef & Arpels, the jewellers, on Rodeo Drive, doing errands and odd jobs, and he was thrilled. It wasn't the kind of job Ward would have wanted for him, and Greg would have hated doing something like that, but Lionel had got the job for himself; he had gone in for the interview with his hair freshly cut, dressed in his best suit, and he had obviously impressed them despite his age, or maybe they had known who his parents were. But whatever it was, he had got the job, and when he announced it to the family that night, it was one of those rare times when he had seemed almost childlike in his excitement, instead of more composed and mature. Greg had looked nonplussed, and the twins had been none too excited at the news. But Faye had been especially pleased for him; she knew how badly he had wanted the job, and he had got it all on his own. She had urged Ward to congratulate him too, and he had, but he had to admit he hadn't been all that pleased.

'You sure you wouldn't rather go to Montana in August with Greg?' He was going to work on a ranch for six weeks, and before that he was going camping in Yellowstone Park with a group of boys and teachers from school, but that was exactly the kind of thing the elder boy hated most.

'I'd be a lot happier here, Dad. Honest . . .' His eyes were wide and green as Faye's, suddenly terrified they wouldn't let him take the job, and he had tried so hard . . . but his father had backed down rapidly at the look on his face.

'I just thought I'd ask.'

'Thanks, Dad.' Lionel had disappeared into the solitude of his room. Ward had built on to the house several years before; they had no guest room any more, and the maid slept in a tiny apartment built over the garage, but now each of the children had their own room in the main house, even the twins, who had been relieved finally to sleep apart, although they didn't admit it at first.

Ward and Faye drove into the driveway on Roxbury Drive, and the twins were already waiting on the front lawn. Vanessa was in a white linen dress with a blue ribbon on her long, blonde hair. She was wearing new sandals, and carrying a white straw bag, and both parents thought instantly how pretty she looked, as did Val, but in a far more striking way. She was wearing a bright green dress that was so short it was closer to her crotch than her knees. It was low-cut in the back, and defined her lush figure perfectly, and unlike her twin, she did not look anywhere near fifteen. She was already using makeup most of the time, her nails were freshly done, and she was wearing cute little green French heels, but Faye sighed and glanced at Ward as he stopped the car.

'Here we go again . . . our resident siren on the march . . .'

Ward smiled benevolently and patted his wife's hand. 'Let it go, babe. Don't get into an argument with her today.'

Ward squinted at her appraisingly, still from the safety of the car and then laughed. 'Just tell people she's your niece.' He looked gently at his wife then. 'She's going to be a beauty one day.'

'I'll be too old and senile by then to appreciate it.'

'Just let her be.' He always said that. It was his answer to everything, except Lionel of course. In Lionel's case, he always had to be told, reprimanded, made to conform. Ward expected everything from him. Always too much according to Faye. Ward had never been able to understand how different the boy was, how creative he was, how sensitive, how totally unique were his needs. But Val . . . she was something else . . . headstrong, demanding, belligerent. She was surely their most difficult child . . . or was it Anne, so constantly withdrawn? . . . sometimes Faye couldn't decide which was worse. But as she stepped out of the car, Vanessa came bounding towards her with that clear easy smile, and she decided to be grateful for the easy one today. It was simpler that way. She told her how pretty she looked, put an arm around her and kissed her cheek.

'Your brother's going to be so proud of you.'

'You mean Alice in Wonderland here?' Val sauntered up, seething inwardly as she noticed her mother's arm around her twin; she had been watching intently when she kissed Vanessa's cheek. 'Don't you think she's a little old for that look?' Valerie was everything mod, and in contrast, Vanessa looked like innocence itself. And now that she had come nearer, Faye could see a thick black line on Val's upper eyelid that made her physically cringe.

'Sweetheart, why don't you take some of that makeup off before we go? It's a little early in the day for all that, isn't it?' It was easier to blame it on the hour, rather than her age. Fifteen seemed than a little young for Cleopatra eyes to Faye, and this sort of thing had never been her style anyway. But Valerie had adopted absolutely none of her mother's ways, or Ward's. She seemed to have her own ideas about everything, and God only knew where they came from; surely not from any of them, she told herself. She was straight out of a teenage film about Hollywood, with some of its worst features exaggerated until her mother wanted to scream. But Faye attempted to remain calm now, as Val stood in front of her and visibly dug in her little green heels.

'It took a lot of time to put this on, Mother. And I'm not taking it off now.' 'Make me' were the only words she forgot to add, and Faye wasn't sure she could have anyway.

'Be reasonable, sweetheart. It looks a little overdone.'

'Who says?'

'Come on, squirt, go take that shit off.' Greg had bounded out, wearing khaki slacks and a blue oxford shirt, a tie that was more than slightly askew and looked as though it might have spent the night under the bed for several years. His loafers were all banged up, and his hair wasn't quite lying down the way he wanted it to. But despite his obvious contrast to his father's far more debonair style, he was clearly a carbon copy of him, and Faye smiled as he glanced at Val with a shrug. 'It really looks dumb.' But his words only enraged Val more.

'Mind your own business . . . you're nothing but a dumb jock anyway.'

'Well, I can tell you one thing. I wouldn't go out with a girl with all that goop on her face.' He looked her over and it was obvious that he didn't approve. 'And your dress is too tight. It makes your boobs stick out.' She blushed faintly but was instantly furious with him. She had wanted them to, but she didn't want her hateful brother to point it out. 'Makes you look like a tart.' He said it matter-of-factly but her eyes flew open wide and she took a swing at him, just as Ward came out of the house again and shouted at them both.

'Hey, you two! Behave! This is your brother's graduation day.'

'He called me a tart!' Valerie was furious with him, and Vanessa looked bored. They went through it all the time, and she secretly thought he was right – not that that would influence Valerie anyway. She was so headstrong and determined, she'd do exactly what she wanted anyway, or make their lives miserable for the rest of the day. They'd all been through it before, at least ten thousand times, with her.

'She looks like one, doesn't she, Dad?' Greg was defending himself against her ferocious swing, and standing nearby, Faye heard the wrinkled blue oxford shirt rip.

'Stop it!' It was useless, but they exhausted her when they behaved like this. They usually did it when she was bone-tired, after a bad day on the set. Gone were the days of quietly reading them stories at night by the fire, but she hadn't been home for most of that anyway. The baby-sitters and the maids had taken her place over the years, and sometimes she wondered if this was the price she had paid for it. There were times when they were completely out of control, like now. But Ward stepped in and grabbed Val's arm, speaking to her firmly in a voice that quieted her down.

'Valerie, go and wash your face.' There was no ambiguity to what he said, no space for argument, and she hesitated for a moment, as he looked at his watch. 'We leave in five minutes, with you, or without, but I think you should be there.' And with that, he turned his back on her and looked at Faye. 'Where's Anne? I couldn't find her upstairs.' She didn't know any more than he did; she had come home from the office with him.

'She was here when I called. Van? Do you know where she went?'

Vanessa shrugged. It was impossible to keep tabs on that kid, she came, she went, she didn't talk to anyone, most of the time she was reading in her room. 'I think she was upstairs.'

Greg gave it a moment's thought. 'I thought I saw her go across the street.'

'To where?' Ward was beginning to get impatient with them all. It was begining to remind him of those unbearable family holidays they used to take, to places like Yosemite, until they could finally afford to send them all to camp and have a little peace. It wasn't that he didn't enjoy his family, he did, but there were times when they all drove him nuts, and this was one of them. 'Did you see where she went?' He noticed silently that Val had disappeared into the house, hopefully to take some of the makeup off, or maybe even the dress, although that seemed too much to hope, and it was. She emerged while they were still hunting for Anne, the thick black line on her eyelids had diminished by slightly less than half. The dress was just as tight and green. 'Valerie, do you know where Anne went?' He looked at her exasperatedly, ready to kill them all.

'Yeah. She went to the Clarks'.' Simple. Finally. That child was always getting lost. He remembered the time he had spent three frantic hours hunting for her in Macy's in New York, only to find her outside, sound asleep in the back seat of their rented limousine.

'Would you mind running over to get her please?' He could see that the mod beauty queen was about to object, but after one look at her father's face, she didn't dare. She nodded, and ran across the street, the tiny miniskirt clutching her shapely rear. He glanced at Faye with a groan. 'She could be arrested in an outfit like that.'

Faye smiled at him. 'I'll go and start the car.' And out of the corner of her eye, she saw Valerie escorting their youngest child back across the street. She was dressed more appropriately than the rest in a pretty pink shirtwaist dress, perfectly pressed, the right length. Her hair was shining clean, her eyes bright, her red shoes were freshly shined. She was a pleasure to look at, in sharp contrast to her far more flamboyant older sister. She piled into the station wagon into the farthest row of seats, not because she was angry at anyone, but because it was where she liked to sit.

'What were you doing over there?' Greg asked as he got in, in front of her with one of the twins on either side. Anne was sitting alone, although usually Lionel or Vanessa sat next to her. It was no secret that she didn't get along with Val, and she didn't have much in common with Greg. It was Lionel whom she adored, and Vanessa who took care of her when no one else was around. Those were always Faye's orders to them. 'Vanessa, see to Anne.'

'I wanted to see something.' She said nothing more, but she had seen it . . . the graduation gift . . . the beautiful little red Mustang . . . and she was so happy for him. She didn't say anything to anyone all the way to the school. She wanted it to be a surprise, and when they got out, Faye wondered if she knew. But she said nothing at all, just followed the others into the auditorium, and sat down at the end of the row. It was one of the happiest days of her life, and one of the saddest too. She was happy for him, but she was sad for herself. She knew that in the autumn, Lionel would be moving to an apartment he would share with friends on the campus of UCLA. Mum had thought he was too young, but Dad had said it might do him good. She knew why he had said that, because he was jealous that Li was so close to Mum. But now he would be gone. She couldn't imagine not living with him any more. He was the only person she could talk to. He always had been. It was always Li who took care of her, even made her lunch for school, and made it with things she liked to eat, not dried-up old bologna, or rotten leftover cheese. That's what Vanessa or Valerie would have done. But Lionel made her things like egg-salad sandwich, or roast beef, or chicken or turkey. He brought her books she loved to read. He talked to her late at night, explained how to do her maths. He was her best friend. He always had been . . . and he tucked her in at night when Mum and Dad were at work. He had been more like a mother and father to her than they had ever been. And suddenly as she saw him on the stage, in his white mortar board and white robe she felt tears in her eyes. It was like watching him get married . . . almost . . . just as bad in some some ways. He was marrying a new life. And one day soon, he would be leaving her.

Greg watched him with envy, wishing he were the one graduating this year, if he ever did. His grades hadn't been good all junior year, but he had promised Dad he would pull them up next year lucky creep . . . going to college . . . although Greg didn't think much of his choice. He thought UCLA was a dumb school. He wanted to go to some place like Georgia Tech where he could be a big football star, even though Dad was talking about somewhere like Yale, if he could get in, of course he could play football there . . . he almost drooled at the thought . . . and the girls . . .!

Valerie was watching a boy in the third row. Lionel had brought him home a few weeks before and he was the best-looking guy she had ever seen. With smooth jet-black hair, dark eyes, he was tall, had clear skin, and he danced like a dream. He was also going steady with some stupid senior girl. But Val knew she was a lot better-looking than his steady girl, if she could just talk to him a couple of times . . . but of course Li wouldn't cooperate. He never fixed her up with anyone. And then there was John Wells, Greg's best friend. He was cute, but he was so shy. He blushed every time she talked to him. And he was going to UCLA eventually too. That would really be a coup to land a college boy, but for the moment her only success had been with three boys in her own sophomore class and they were all drips, and all they wanted was to feel up her boobs. She was saving the rest for a college man! Like the guy in the third row . . .

Vanessa was watching her twin, almost reading her mind. She knew her too well. She even knew which boys she would like. It was really a pain how boy crazy she was, and she had been like that since seventh grade. Vanessa liked boys too, but it wasn't an obsession with her; she was more interested in writing poetry and reading books. Boys were okay, but there had been no one special yet. And she was beginning to wonder if Val had already gone all the way. She hoped not. It would ruin her life if she did. Of course there was the pill . . . but you couldn't get it unless you were over eighteen, or something, or engaged. She knew that one of the girls in the junior class had got it by pretending she was twenty-one, but she couldn't imagine doing that, or wanting to.

Faye would have been relieved if she could have read her thoughts. She worried about those things too. But her mind wasn't on Greg, or Anne, or the twins, it was entirely concentrated on her older son, standing so beautiful and innocent and tall, singing the school song, his diploma in his hand, as the sunlight streamed into the room. She looked at him, knowing that this moment would never come again, he would never be this young, or this pure. Life was just beginning for him and she wished so many things for him as the tears poured down her cheeks and Ward silently handed her his handkerchief. She turned and looked at him with a bittersweet smile. How far they had come, and how dear they all were to her . . . especially Ward . . . and this boy . . . she wanted so badly to protect him from all the pain in life . . . all the disappointments, the sorrows, and instinctively, Ward put an arm around her shoulders and pulled her closer to him. He was proud of the boy but he wanted very different things for him.

'He looks so sweet,' she whispered to Ward. In her eyes, he was still a little boy.

Ward whispered back, 'He looks like a man.' Or at least he hoped that one day he would. For the moment, he still had the slightly effeminate look of youth, and sometimes Ward wondered if he always would. He looked so much like her . . . and just as he thought that, he saw Lionel look out and into the crowd until he found Faye's eyes, and the two of them stared at each other lovingly, to the exclusion of all else. It made Ward want to pull her back, for her own sake as much as the boy's, but the two of them were beyond anyone's reach. They had always shared something that no one else could touch.

'He's such a wonderful boy.'

It made Ward doubly glad that Li would be moving out in the fall. He needed to get away from her. And he was even more sure of it when Lionel raced to hug Faye tight after the ceremony. The other boys were all standing around, holding hands with awkward-looking girls.

'I'm free, Mum! I'm not a high school kid any more!' He had eyes only for her, and she was so excited for him.

'Congratulations, sweetheart.' She kissed him on the cheek and Ward shook his hand.

'Congratulations, son.'

They all hung around for a while, and then went to lunch at the Polo Lounge at the Beverly Hills Hotel. And just as Anne knew he would, he sat with her in the very last seat on the way there. No one thought it strange. He had sat next to her back there for years, just as Faye and Ward had sat in front, and then Greg and the twins in between.

The crowd at the Polo Lounge was the same as it always was at lunch, showy, dressed in silks and gold chains and miniskirts, directors and writers and film stars, people asking for autographs and phones being rushed from one table to the next, as people pretended to get important calls. Faye went outside at one point and called Lionel to congratulate him, and everyone laughed, except Ward. They acted like lovers sometimes, and it always bothered him. But the boisterous group had a good time anyway. And after lunch, they all went home and swam in their pool. Some of the kids' friends dropped by, so no one noticed when

Ward and Faye sneaked away stealthily and went next door to the Clarks'. Ward drove the car almost up to the pool, honking frantically as Faye laughed, sitting on a towel in the front seat, in her wet bathing suit, as the kids stared, not understanding any of it at first, except that obviously their parents had gone berserk. And then Ward hopped out, walked over to his son, and handed him the as tears filled the boy's eyes, and he threw his arms around his father's neck, crying and laughing all at once.

'You mean it's mine?'

'Happy graduation, son.' There were tears in Ward's eyes too. He was touched by the boy's delight, it was a special moment that would never come again. With a shriek, Lionel hugged him again, while from the sidelines Anne watched him and beamed.

He invited everyone to pile into it, and Ward and Faye stood back as the children did, sitting on each other, on the seats, on the back of the car with the top down. 'Take it easy, Li,' Faye admonished him, and Ward took her hand, and led her a few steps back.

And for an instant, just an instant, before he started the car and drove away, he paused, and met his father's eyes, perhaps in just that way for the first time, and the two men exchanged a smile. There was no need for any more thanks than that. And as they drove away, Ward felt as though he had just made contact with his son for the first time, finally.

Chapter 12

That night there were a hundred people, most of them kids, invited to celebrate Lionel's graduation with a barbecue. And Ward and Faye had arranged for a rock band to play under a tent in the backyard. It was the biggest party they'd given in years, and the whole family was excited about it. Greg was wearing a wrinkled striped T-shirt and jeans. His blond hair looked uncombed, and his feet were bare. Faye was about to send him back upstairs but he escaped, and when she said something to Ward, he said what he always did, 'Let him be, babe, he's all right.'

His wife looked at him disapprovingly. 'For a man who used to spend his time changing shirts three times a day and wearing white linen suits, you certainly don't seem to expect much of your son.'

'Maybe that's why. That was twenty years ago and it was outdated then. People don't live like that any more, Faye. We were practically dinosaurs, albeit lucky ones. Greg has more important things on his mind.'

'Like what? Football? Girls? The beach?' She expected more of Greg, like the kind of things Lionel did. But Ward seemed happier with their jock than with their more intellectual child. It didn't make sense to her, and it always seemed unfair that he expected so much less of Greg, and never appreciated Lionel's outstanding accomplishments, but the matter couldn't be resolved in one night. It was a difference they had always had, sometimes more vociferously, but this was a special day and she didn't want to fight with him. It was funny, they actually fought very seldom, but occasionally about the children they disagreed violently and exchanged harsh words . . . particularly about Lionel . . . but not tonight . . . please not tonight she thought to herself, and decided to give in about Greg.

'All right . . . never mind . . .'

'Let him have a good time tonight. It doesn't matter what he wears.'

'I hope you feel the same way about Val.' But it was a real challenge to both of them not to say anything to her. She was wearing a skintight white leather minidress with a fringed skirt with matching boots that she had apparently borrowed from a friend.

Ward leaned over and whispered to Faye as he poured her a drink at the bar, 'What street corner does her friend work on? Did she say?' Faye laughed and shook her head. It seemed to her that she had had teenagers for so long that almost nothing surprised her any more. It prepared her well to deal with the actors at MGM. None of them could be more impossible, more difficult, more unpredictable, more argumentative than any teenage kid, although many of them tried.

'I think poor Vanessa tries to counteract Val's effect,' Ward said to Faye. She had worn a pink and white party dress that looked more suitable for a ten-year-old, and pink ballet shoes, with her hair done Alice in Wonderland style again. The two couldn't have been more opposite and Faye suspected it was no mistake. And looking around at all of them, Lionel in a light tan summer suit, looking handsome and dignified with a pale blue striped shirt and one of his father's ties, working at looking extremely grown up, the new car prominently parked on the front lawn, Greg in his wrinkled clothes . . . Valerie in the white leather dress . . . Vanessa in her childish garb . . . all of them individuals certainly, it reminded Faye of something again, and she looked at Ward over the drink he had handed her. 'Have you seen Anne?'

'She was around the pool with some friends a while ago. She's all right. Lionel will keep an eye on her.' He always did, but tonight was a big night for him, and Ward had even looked the other way when he saw him pouring himself a glass of white wine. He had to allow the boy let off some steam for a change, and if he got roaring drunk on graduation night, what harm could it do? It might dent his impeccable image for a change and that might do him good too. He just had to keep Faye busy enough not to keep an eye on him, and eventually he invited her to dance. Valerie watched them, horrified, Vanessa was amused, and eventually Lionel cut in and danced with Faye himself, and Ward went around to chat with friends, and make sure that none of the kids were getting too desperately out of line. A few of them were pretty drunk, but they were all Lionel's age, and this was their graduation night too. Ward felt that they had a right to get a little crazed, as long as none of them drove home, and he had given stern instructions to the parking valets. No one got the keys to his car if he appeared inebriated, and that applied to adult as well as child.

He spotted Anne sitting by the pool talking to John Wells, Greg's best friend. He was a sweet boy who worshipped the ground Greg walked on, and Ward suspected that Anne had a crush on John, but he wasn't likely to return her sentiments, considering that she was only twelve. She had some growing up to do, although Lionel treated her as though she already was. It was amazing how mature she could be sometimes. Far more than the twins, or even Greg at times. He wondered what she was saying to John, but she was so skittish and shy that he didn't dare approach them now, for fear that he would scare her off. She seemed to be having a good time, and a little while later, Lionel joined them, and Ward saw John look up with a smile, his admiration for Li matching Anne's . . . the wonder of kids . . . Ward smiled to himself, and went to retrieve Faye from a group of neighbours and friends. He wanted to dance with her again. He still thought she was prettier than any girl there, and it showed in his eyes as he slipped an arm around her waist.

'Care to dance?' He tapped her on the shoulder and she laughed when she saw who it was.

'I certainly would.'

The band was good. The kids were all having a good time. And Anne was enjoying herself with Lionel and John. They both treated her like an adult, which was more than most of the other kids did. She was tall for her age, and she had the same ripe peach-coloured hair that Faye had had in her youth. One day she would be a beautiful girl, but she never quite felt like one. She thought she wasn't as pretty as Faye, or as spectacular as Val, and she thought Vanessa had quietly distinguished good looks. But Lionel always told her that she was the best-looking of them all and she told him he was nuts. She pointed out her knobbly knees, what she described as 'wimpy, weird hair', because it framed her face in a soft fluff. She was just starting to develop breasts and she felt awkward about that too. She felt awkward about everything, except when she was with Lionel. He made her feel wonderful about everything.

'How do you like your new car?' John was smiling at the older brother of his friend, secretly admiring how neatly he tied his tie. He loved the way he dressed, but he would never have dared say that to him.

'Are you kidding?' Lionel grinned boyishly. 'I'm crazy about it. I can't wait to get it out tomorrow and really go for a spin.' He smiled at Greg's friend. John had been hanging around their house for years, and he had always liked him. He was more interesting than most of Greg's jock friends, although he had discovered that by accident one day when he'd talked to John when Greg was out. Most of the time, John pretended to be like the rest of them, but Lionel correctly guessed that it was camouflage he wore, and there was a lot more to him than just football and bikes, and the rest of it, which had never interested Lionel very much. 'I start work next week, and it's going to be great having my own car.'

'Where are you going to work?' John sounded interested, and Anne watched the exchange, saying nothing, as usual. But she was listening to her brother, and watching John's face. She had always thought he had beautiful eyes.

'Van Cleef & Arpels. It's a jeweller in Beverly Hills.' He felt a need to explain it to him. None of Greg's friends would have had any idea what that was.

But John laughed and, watching him, Anne smiled. 'I know that. My mother goes there all the time. They have pretty stuff.' Lionel looked both surprised and pleased. John hadn't gagged at the thought of Lionel working there. 'Sounds like a nice job.'

'It is. I'm looking forward to it.' He beamed, glancing in the direction of the car again. 'Especially now.'

'And UCLA in the fall. You're lucky, Li. I'm sick to death of high school.'

'It won't be long now. You've only got a year to go.'

'It feels like an eternity.' John groaned and Lionel smiled.

'And then what?'

'I don't know yet.' That wasn't unusual. Most of his friends hadn't figured that out.

'I'm doing cinematography.'

'That sounds wonderful.'

Lionel shrugged modestly. He had won photography awards ever since he was fourteen, and he had started getting into films two years before. He was ready for everything UCLA could offer him, and excited about going there, in spite of what his father said. His father had wanted him to go to a gung-ho school in the East. And he had the grades, but it had absolutely no appeal for him. He could sell that line to Greg.

He looked at John with a friendly smile. 'Come and see me at school sometime. You can have a look around while you're making your mind up about schools.'

'I'd like that a lot.' John looked at him intently, and for a moment the boys' eyes met and held, and then quickly John turned away, and a moment later he spotted Greg. He seemed anxious to leave them then, and Lionel invited Anne to dance.

179

She blushed furiously at the thought and refused to dance with him, but after he had insisted for a while, she relented and followed him onto the floor.

'What's that?' The boy who had wandered into the house with Val had followed her into the den, and he was determined to get a hand up her skirt, which didn't look too hard. But a coveted object pushed onto a shelf in the bar had caught his eye. 'Is that what I think it is?' He was impressed. This was the first house he'd been in that actually had one of those, even though you sure heard about them a lot in LA.

'Yeah. So what? Big deal.'

'It sure is.' He stared at it in awe, and then reached a hand out to touch it so he could tell his dad when he picked him up. 'Whose is it? Your mum's or your dad's?'

It seemed to cost her something to admit it to him. 'My mum's. You want a beer, Joey?' And then he almost fainted. There was another one. They had two!

'My God! She's got two of them. What for?'

'Oh for chrissake. I don't remember. Now do you want a beer or not?'

'Yeah. Yeah. Okay.' But he was much more interested in hearing what her mother had won the Oscars for. His dad would ask him later, and so would his mum, but Val didn't seem to want to talk about them. 'She used to be an actress, didn't she?' He knew she was a director now. Everyone knew that. And her dad was a big producer at MGM. But Valerie sure didn't talk about it much. She was more interested in booze and boys. At least that was the reputation she had, and he could almost see up her white leather skirt when she sat down. But actually all he glimpsed was a long expanse of inner thigh.

'Did you ever smoke dope?' He hadn't but he didn't want to admit it to her. He was fifteen and a half years old, and he had met her in school that year, but he'd never taken her out. He hadn't had the guts. She was beautiful, and terrifyingly mature.

'Yeah. Once.' And then he couldn't help himself. He had to ask again. 'Let's talk about your mum.'

That was it. She jumped to her feet, her eyes blazing with rage. 'No, let's not!'

'Don't be so uptight for chrissake. I'm just curious, that's all.'

Val looked at him with contempt as she strode to the doorway and looked back. 'Then ask her, you creep!' And with a flash of her red mane, she was gone, and he stared at the empty doorway in despair and whispered to himself:

'Shit.'

'Oh?' Greg stuck his head in to see who was there, and the boy blushed and jumped to his feet.

'Sorry . . . I was just relaxing in here . . . I'll go back outside.'

'That's okay. I do that here all the time. No sweat.' He grinned and disappeared, in hot pursuit of some dark-haired girl, and Joey went back outside. And eventually they all wound up in the pool late that night, in clothes, in bathing suits, in suits, in dresses, in sneakers and bare feet and shoes. They had a wonderful time and it was 3 am before the last guest went home, and when they were all gone, Lionel walked upstairs with Ward and Faye, and all three of them yawned sleepily as Faye laughed.

'We're a lively bunch . . . good party though, wasn't it?'

'The best.' Lionel smiled, and kissed his mother goodnight, and when he sat down on his bed in the terry robe he had put on to cover his bathing suit, he sat and stared at the wall for a minute, thinking of the day . . . the diploma . . . the white gown . . . the car . . . the friends . . . and the music . . . and funnily enough, he found himself thinking of John, and what a nice kid he was. He liked him better than even some of his own friends.

Chapter 13

The day after the graduation party dawned like any other working day for Faye and Ward. The kids could sleep it off until
noon, but they had to be at the studio by nine. Their next film
would be starting soon and the two of them had mountains of
work on their desks. It always seemed to require so much disci-
pline to go on, to work, no matter how tired they were, especially when Faye was actually directing the film. Then she was
always at the studio before six o'clock, often before the actors
were there. But she had to be there, to breathe the air, to get the
feel of it. In fact, while they were shooting, it was always difficult to force herself to go home, and sometimes she did not.
Sometimes she slept in a dressing room, eating, sleeping, and
thinking the script, making it become almost a part of her, until
she knew every character as though she had been born in their
skin in another life. It was what made her so demanding of the
actors who worked for her, but she taught them a kind of disci-
pline they never forgot, and most of the actors in Hollywood
talked of Faye Thayer with awe. Her kind of talent was a gift,
and she was so much happier than when she had been acting
herself. This was the fulfilment she had been looking for, and
Ward loved seeing that light in her eye, the light that came only
when she was thinking of her work. It made him a little jealous
sometimes because he liked what he did, but not with the same
determination, the same fire, as she seemed to feel. She breathed
her very soul into her work. And he was thinking of that now.
In a few weeks he was going to lose her to their new film, but
they both thought it was the best one they had ever done. They

were both extremely excited about it, and more than once Faye had said how sorry she was that Abe Abramson was no longer alive. He would have loved this film. But he had died some years before. He had lived long enough to see their success, to see her win the second Oscar of her life, this one for directing, but he had died after that, and she still missed him sometimes, as she did now. She lay back against the seat, looking at Ward and thinking of the night before.

'I'm glad the kids had a good time.'

'So did I.' He smiled at her, but he was painfully hung over, and these days that was rare. He often wondered how he used to drink as much as he did. He couldn't take it any more, without paying a tremendous price for it. Youth ... he smiled to himself ... a lot of things changed when you added a few years and a few grey hairs ... and other things did not. In spite of the hangover, he and Faye had made love that morning after he got out of the shower. That always got his day off to a good start, and he gently put a hand on her thigh now. 'You still drive me wild, you know ...'

She blushed faintly and looked pleased. She was still in love with him. Had been for nineteen years, longer if you counted the time they had met in Guadalcanal in '43 ... that would make it twenty-one ... 'It's mutual, you know.'

'That's good.' He looked pensive as he pulled into the MGM car park. The guard at the gate had smiled as he waved them in. You could set your clocks by those two, he thought to himself ... nice people ... with nice kids ... and they worked hard. You had to hand it to them. 'Maybe we should put a communicating door between our offices, and a lock on my door,' Ward suggested.

'Sounds good to me,' she whispered in his ear, and then playfully nipped his neck before sliding out. 'What have you got going today, love?'

'Not a hell of a lot. I think almost everything is squared away. What about you?'

'I'm meeting three of the stars.' She told him who. 'I feel like I need to do a lot of talking to all of them before we start, so that everyone's prepared. So that they all know where we're going with this thing.' It was the most challenging film she'd done. It was about four soldiers during the second world war, and it wasn't a pretty film in that sense. It was brutal and painful and tore your guts out, and most studio heads would have assigned a male director to it, but Dore Schary still trusted her, and she wasn't going to let him down. Or Ward. It hadn't been easy for Ward to raise the money for this film, in spite of their names. But people were afraid that no one would want to see a depressing film. After the assassination of John Kennedy the year before, everybody wanted comic relief, not serious film, but both Ward and Faye had agreed from the start, when they read the script, that this was it. It was a brilliant film, the screenplay was magnificent, as the original book had been, and Faye was determined to do right by it. Ward knew she would, but he also knew how nervous she was.

'It's going to be okay, you know.' He smiled at her just outside her office door. They both knew it would be, but he also knew that she needed reassurance from him, and he knew that even more certainly as she answered him.

'I'm scared to death.'

'I know you are. Just relax and enjoy yourself.' But she didn't do that until they started the film, and then she plunged into it even more fully than she usually did. She never got home before midnight or one, was gone again by five am, and often didn't come home at all. Ward knew it would go on for months that way, and he had promised her he would keep an eye on the children for her, and he tried. She had always worked that way. When she was directing a film she was totally involved, and when she was finished she spent her life folding shirts, doing laundry, driving car pools. She took special pride in it, but right now, even the children were far, far from her mind.

★　　★　　★

Ward came back to the studio to pick her up late one night; he didn't trust her to drive when she was that tired, or that wrapped up in her work. He was afraid she'd wind up in a tree off the motorway somewhere, so he came to pick her up, and she collapsed on the front seat of his car like a little rag doll. He leaned over and kissed her cheek. She opened one eye sleepily and smiled at him. 'I may not survive this one . . .' Her voice was deep and hoarse. She had drunk gallons of coffee all day long, and talked endlessly, urging them on, begging for more from them, and her actors hadn't disappointed her. She looked at Ward and he smiled.

'It's going to be great, babe. I've been watching the dailies all week.'

'What do you think?' She had seen them herself, and she kept seeing what was wrong and never what was right, but in the last two days she had seen a ray of hope. The actors were really working hard, as hard as she was, to give it their all. 'Think it'll fly?' She looked terrified as she asked. His judgement was better than anyone else's she knew and she trusted him implicitly, but he was smiling at her.

'It'll fly right over the moon, love. And that Oscar is going to fly into your hands again.'

'Never mind that. I just want it to be good. I want us to be proud of it.'

'We will.' He was sure of that, and he was always proud of her, just as she was of him. He had come so far, for a man who had never worked a day in his life until he turned thirty-five. It was miraculous what he had done with himself, and she never lost sight of that. She was always proud of him, more so than he knew. Much, much more.

She laid her head back on the seat again. 'How are the kids?'

'They're okay.' She didn't need the petty aggravations now. The cleaning woman was threatening to quit, Anne and Val had had a major fight, and Greg had put a dent in the car, but they were all minor problems he could handle himself. Still, he was always grateful when she finished work and went back to running the house. He often wondered how she stood the daily irritation of it all. It always drove him nuts, though he didn't tell her that. 'They're all busy. The twins have been baby-sitting every day, Greg leaves for the ranch next week.' He didn't add aloud, Thank God. At least it would be quieter without the phone ringing, and doors slamming, and half a dozen of Greg's friends playing catch with a favourite vase. 'We hardly see Lionel now that he has a job.'

'Does he like it?' She opened her eyes. She would have asked him herself but she hadn't seen him in weeks.

'I think so. He hasn't complained anyway.'

'That doesn't mean much. Li never complains.' And then she thought of something else. 'I should have lined something up for Anne. I just didn't think we'd get going so soon.' But the money had come in, the set had been free. Everything had fallen into place, and instead of late September, they had started in June. That was unusual, and Faye didn't want to make trouble by saying that she wasn't free to start, but it meant deserting her kids for the summer, which was complicated, and Anne had steadfastly refused to go to camp. 'What's she doing all day?'

'She's all right. Mrs Johnson is there till I come home. She has friends over and they hang around the pool. I told them I'd take them to Disneyland next week.'

'You're a saint.' She yawned and smiled at him at the same time, and she leaned heavily on him as they walked into the house. The girls were still awake. Val's hair was set in giant curlers, and she was wearing a bikini that would have made Faye gasp if she had the strength. She made a mental note to say something to her the next day, if she had time, and saw the child. They listening to music in the den, and Vanessa was in a nightgown and talking to a friend on the phone, oblivious to the noise that Valerie was making.

'Where's Anne?' Faye asked Val and she shrugged, mouting the words to the song. She had to ask again before Valerie answered her.

'Upstairs I guess.'

'Is she asleep?'

'Probably.' But Vanessa shook her head. She had the uncanny knack of listening to several conversations at once and often did. Faye went upstairs to kiss her youngest child goodnight. She already knew that Greg was out with friends, and a note in the kitchen had said Lionel was having dinner with some people from work, which accounted for everyone. She liked knowing where all her children were, and she often worried about that on the set. Ward was more relaxed than she was about letting them do what they wanted, and she wanted him to keep a tight rein on them, but he never did. He would have gone mad if he had, that and run the house.

She gently opened the door, and as she came up the stairs, she could have sworn she saw a light, but the room was dark now. Anne was curled up in her bed, her back to the door, and Faye stood there for a long moment, and then walked to her, and gently touched the soft halo of hair. 'Good night, little one,' she whispered and then bent to kiss her cheek. She closed the door again and walked on to her own room with Ward, telling him about the film again and sinking into a hot bath before going to bed. A few minutes later she heard the girls come upstairs; they pounded on her door and yelled goodnight, and she didn't see Vanessa go to her younger sister's room. The light was on again, and Anne was reading *Gone With the Wind*.

'Did you see Mum?' Vanessa searched her face and saw something strange in her eyes, something hidden and distant that was almost always there, except with Li. Anne shook her head. 'How come?' She didn't want to admit that she had turned off the light and pretended to be asleep, but Vanessa guessed. 'You played possum, didn't you?' There was a long hesitation again and the girl shrugged. 'Why?'

'I was tired.'

'That's bullshit.' It made her angry. It was infuriating and so typical of her. 'And it's not nice. She asked for you the minute she came in.' Anne's face didn't give an inch, and her eyes said nothing at all. 'I think that was crummy of you.' She turned and started to leave the room, and Anne's voice reached her as she got to the door.

'I don't have anything to say to her.' Vanessa looked at her and walked out, never understanding the truth that Lionel understood so well. Anne was afraid that her mother had nothing to say to her. She never had. She had never been around when she was a little girl. It was always nurses or baby-sitters or maids, or one of the other children baby-sitting for her, while her mother worked, or went out or did something else. She was always 'tired' or 'had something on her mind', or 'had to read this script' or had to 'talk to Dad'. So what was there left to say now? Who are you? Who am I? It was easier to talk to Lionel and avoid her . . . just as she had avoided Anne for so long. Now she had to pay the price for it.

Chapter 14

Faye was still deep into the film when Lionel moved into an apartment with four friends, and began classes at UCLA. He stopped in to see her the following week on the set just to catch up. He stood by waiting patiently for a break. He always enjoyed watching her work, and finally, after an hour of three retakes on a very gruelling scene, she dismissed them all for lunch, and glanced up to see her son. She had been so intent before that she hadn't even noticed him arrive. Pleasure instantly warmed her face and she hurried over to give him a kiss.

'How's everything, sweetheart? How's the apartment, and school?' She felt as though she hadn't seen him in years, and she was suddenly lonely for all of them, especially him. She hadn't felt the full blow of his absence yet. She was so used to having him around, to having those wonderful chats with him and now he was gone. But she had been so busy at work that she hadn't had time to notice it yet. 'Do you like your place?'

His eyes lit up enthusiastically. 'It's pretty nice, and the other guys are fairly neat. Thank God there's no one like Greg.' He grinned, and she laughed, thinking of the familiar chaos of Greg's room. Nothing had changed.

'Have you been home at all since you moved out?'

'Just once or twice to pick some stuff up. I saw Dad, and he said you were okay.'

'I am.'

'It looks great.' He nodded toward the stage she had just left, and she was pleased. Like his father, he had a good eye for successful films. She got too caught up in details to see the whole, and they were better at that. They could stand back and see it differently. 'That was some scene.'

She smiled. 'We've been working on it for a week.' And as she spoke, their big star, Paul Steele, whose scene it was, wandered over towards them, casting a glance at Lionel, and looking more seriously at Faye. He was as much a perfectionist as she, and she loved working with him. This was the second picture they'd done and she was very pleased with him. He was one of the up and coming stars of Hollywood. Paul sat down next to Faye.

'What did you think?'

'I think we got it the last time.'

'So do I.' He was glad that she had felt it too. 'I was getting worried by yesterday. I didn't think I'd ever get this scene right. I stayed up all last night working on it.' She was, as always, impressed with him.

'It showed. Thanks, Paul. That kind of dedication is what makes it work.' But damn few actors were willing to work like that. He was. And he stood now, and looked at Lionel with a smile.

'You must be Faye's son.' People always noticed and both Faye and Lionel laughed.

'How'd you guess?'

Steele squinted with a grin. 'Oh, let's see . . . the hair . . . the nose . . . the eyes . . . Listen, kid, all you need is the same hairdo and a dress and you could be twins.'

'I'm not sure I'd approve of that,' Faye laughed. 'In fact, I can tell you right now, I wouldn't.'

'So much for that.' Paul laughed.

'I was very impressed by your last scene, Mr Steele.' Lionel was deeply respectful of him, and Steele was touched.

'Thank you.' Faye introduced them formally, and Paul shook his hand. 'Your mother is the toughest director in town, but she's so good it's worth all the blood, sweat, and tears.'

'My my, such compliments.' All three of them laughed and Faye glanced at her watch. 'We have about an hour, gentlemen. Can I invite you both to lunch in the commissary?'

190

Paul made a grisly face. 'Christ, torture yet. Can we do better than that? My treat. My car is right outside the studio.' But they all knew there wasn't much outside the studio, and they didn't have much time. 'All right, all right. I give in. Indigestion, here we come.'

'It's not that bad.' Faye tried to defend it to no avail. Paul and Lionel both disagreed with her vociferously and the three-some walked to the commissary. Paul inquired if Lionel was in school, and he explained that he had just started at UCLA, majoring cinematography.

'That's where I went. Have you had time to figure out if you like it yet?'

'It seems great.' Lionel grinned happily, and Paul was amused. He was so young, but as they talked over lunch, it was obvious that he was a bright kid. He was intelligent and sensitive, knew a great deal about his chosen field, and talked intensely with Paul until Faye said they had to get back. And once they did, Lionel seemed to linger, wanting to absorb the atmosphere. Paul invited him into his dressing room, while he put his makeup on again and the studio hairdresser did something different to his hair. He was a prisoner of war in the next scene, and Lionel was dying to stick around but he had to get back to school. He had three more classes that afternoon.

'That's too bad. I've enjoyed talking to you.' Paul looked at him with a genuine smile. He was sorry to see him go. He liked the boy . . . too much perhaps . . . but he wasn't going to let it show, out of respect for Faye, and this very young boy. He wasn't in the habit of corrupting anyone, and virgins weren't quite his thing. But Lionel seemed anxious to see him again, much to Paul's surprise.

'I'd like to come back and watch some more. I have a free afternoon at the end of the week.' He looked at Paul Steele hopefully, like a child waiting for Santa Claus, and Paul wasn't quite sure if it was the film he was excited about, or something else, so he proceeded carefully. 'Maybe I could come back then?'

Lionel's eyes searched his, and Paul was no longer sure what he saw, boy or man.

'That's up to your Mum. She runs this show. She's my boss too.'

They both laughed and Lionel agreed. 'I'll ask her what she thinks.' Paul worried for a moment that she would think he had put him up to it; he made no secret of his preferences. 'See you Friday, I hope . . .' Lionel looked at him hopefully, and Paul turned away. He didn't want to start anything . . . he did . . . but it wasn't right . . . and he was Faye Thayer's son . . . Christ, life was complicated sometimes. He lit a joint after the boy left, hoping to calm down again but it only made him long for him more.

When he went back to the set there was a hunger and loneliness in him that was almost an ache, and it came across in the film. They got the scene on the first take this time, an almost unheard of victory, and Faye congratulated him. But he was cool to her, and she wondered why. She thought nothing of his being pleasant to Lionel. She knew Paul well enough to know that she had nothing to fear from him. He was a decent man, and whatever he did with his spare time, he wouldn't take advantage of her son. She felt sure of that, and she wasn't upset when she saw Lionel on the set again on Friday afternoon. When he was younger, he had often dropped in to watch her work. Lately, he hadn't had as much time, but it was no secret that he loved the making of films. And now he would be making a career of it. She was actually pleased to see him there, and although he didn't show it at first, so was Paul Steele.

'Hello, Paul.' Lionel said the words hesitantly, and the moment they were out, he wondered if he should have called him Mr Steele. Paul was only twenty-eight years old, but he commanded great respect in the industry and Lionel was eighteen, and felt like a kid around him.

'Hi.' Paul looked casual as he walked past, on his way to someone's dressing room, praying that their paths wouldn't cross again. But late that afternoon, Faye offered him a glass of wine when they took a break. Lionel was standing there, obviously in awe, and Paul couldn't resist the urge to smile at him.

'It's nice to see you again, Lionel. How's school?' Maybe if he pretended to himself the boy was just a child, it would be easier. But nothing was easy when he looked into those eyes. They were impossible to resist. They were so much like hers, but deeper, more compelling, sadder and wiser in some ways, as though he were keeping some terrible secret inside him. And instinctively, Paul knew what the secret was. At his age, he had had the same secret himself. It was a lonely place to be until someone held out a hand to you. Until then you were a freak living in a lonely hell, frightened of your own thoughts and what other people would think if they knew. 'What did you think of today's take?' There was no point treating him like a child. He was a man. They both knew that. And Paul looked him in the eye.

'I thought it was very, very good.'

'Would you like to see the dailies with me?' Paul liked to see them whenever he could, so that he could correct his mistakes. They were important to his work, and Lionel was flattered beyond words that Paul should invite him into such a special world. His eyes were huge with awe, and Faye and Paul laughed. 'Now, listen, if you look like that, I won't let you watch. You've got to realise most of what you'll see is crap. Embarrassing crap, but that's how we learn.'

'I'd love to see the dailies with you.'

They watched them at around six o'clock, and as they took their seats and the lights went off, Paul felt Lionel's leg inadvertently touch his knee. He felt a thrill rush through him that was almost painful to refuse. But he carefully moved his leg away and forced himself to concentrate on what was on the screen, and afterwards when the lights came up, Lionel discussed what he'd seen with him, and amazingly they felt the same way about the same scenes. The boy was brilliant about film; intelligent, intuitive, and he had an instinct for style and technique. It was hardly surprising, he had grown up with it. But Paul was still impressed. He was dying to talk about it with him some more as Faye got ready to leave the set. She had to leave early tonight. For her seven-thirty was midafternoon and she glanced at them both, amused, as they rattled on.

'Have you got your car with you, love?' Faye asked him. She looked tired tonight and was longing to go home and unwind; it had been a gruelling week, and they were doing a scene at dawn the next day. She had to be up before three.

'Yes, Mum. I drove here.'

'Good. Then I'll let you boys talk yourselves out. This old lady's going home. Before I fall on my face from sheer exhaustion. Goodnight, gentlemen.' She kissed Lionel's cheek, waved goodbye to Paul, and hurried outside to her own car. Ward had gone home ahead of her to have dinner with the kids. Paul was stunned when he looked at his watch after that. It was almost nine o'clock, and they were the last ones on the set. He hadn't had anything to eat since lunch, and from something he had said he knew Lionel hadn't either. What harm could there be in having a bite to eat?

'Do you want to go out for a hamburger, Lionel? You must be starving.' It seemed harmless enough to ask, and Faye's son looked pleased.

'I'd like that, if you don't have anything else to do.' He was so young and humble it was embarrassing, and Paul smiled and put an arm around his shoulder as they walked to their cars. There was no one else around, so it couldn't be misconstrued.

'Believe me, talking to you is the most fun I've had in weeks, maybe even months . . .'

'That's a nice thing to say.' He smiled at Paul as they reached his car. Paul was driving a silver Porsche, and Lionel had the red Mustang he was so proud of.

'What a great car!'

'I got it for graduation in June.'

'That's some gift!' Paul looked impressed. At his age, he had bought a clunker for seventy-five dollars, but his parents weren't Ward and Faye Thayer, and he didn't live in Beverly Hills. He had come to California from Buffalo when he was twenty-two, and life had been beautiful ever since, especially in the past three years. His career had taken off meteorically, at first thanks to one fortuitous romance with a major producer in Hollywood. But after that, the breaks he got were thanks to his own strengths and abilities. There was no denying it, and few did. No matter what you thought of Paul Steele, he was damn good. Most of the people who had worked with him didn't have ugly things to say about him. He was a decent man, fair to work with, he kept to himself most of the time, and if you got to know him well, he could be fun. Between films, he was a wild man sometimes, smoking a lot of dope, snorting a little cocaine, he was into poppers, and there were rumours about orgies at his place, and kinky sex, but he took advantage of no one; no one got hurt, and working as hard as he did, he had to do something to let off steam, and he was still young after all.

He took Lionel to Hamburger Hamlet on Sunset, and had him follow him there in his car, driving carefully. For some reason, he found himself anxious about the kid. He didn't want him to get hurt, physically or in any other way. He liked him, more than he'd liked anyone in a while. It was just a damn shame that he was only eighteen. That was rotten luck. He was so damn beautiful and so fucking young. He couldn't take his eyes off him as they ate, and afterwards they stood outside, Lionel not even sure how to thank him for the honour and the rare treat, Paul dying to invite him up to his place, but afraid of how it would sound so they stood there, awkwardly, as Paul looked at him. He wished he knew what Lionel knew of himself, but he still wasn't sure of that. If the boy knew, maybe it would be different, but if he didn't suspect as yet . . . just looking at him, Paul was already sure, but was Lionel? And then suddenly, as they stood there in the car park, Paul knew he had to take the bull by the horns, so to speak. Maybe he'd even ask him eventually. Maybe he was wrong. Maybe they could be friends. But he couldn't let him go . . . not yet . . . not now . . . not quite so soon.

'I know this sounds dumb, but would you like to come to my place for a drink?' He was almost embarrassed to say the words, but Lionel's eyes grew wide with delight.

'I'd love it.' Maybe he did know . . . Paul was going crazy trying to figure it out, and there was no way to guess.

'I live in Malibu. You want to follow me again, or leave your car here? I could drive you back afterwards.'

'Wouldn't that be a lot of trouble?' Malibu was an hour from there.

'No, not at all. I never go to bed very early. And I may not go to bed tonight at all. We shoot at four am tomorrow, and I work better on calls like that without going to bed.'

'Will my car be safe?' They looked around, and decided that it would. The hamburger place was open all night, so people would come and go, and no one would dare break into it with people around. That decided, Lionel slid into the passenger seat of Paul's Porsche and instantly felt that he had died and gone to heaven. It was like being lifted into another world. Sitting on the smooth black leather seats, the dashboard looked like the panel of a plane and with a shift of gears they took off. Paul turned the stereo on as the music of Roger Miller singing 'King of the Road' filled their cars. It was almost a sensual experience getting to Malibu. Paul was dying for a joint, but he didn't want to smoke dope in front of the boy, and he was a little bit afraid of what he might do if he did, so he refrained, and they talked from time to time on the brief drive, listened to the music as they flew along, and by the time they reached the house on the beach, Lionel was totally relaxed with his new friend.

Paul put his key in the lock, and let them in, and the house just continued the same mood. There was a full ocean view with soft lights, a sunken living room filled with couches and soft cushions, huge plants and recessed lights that highlighted a few pieces of art Paul loved. There was a handsome bar, a wall of books, and a stereo that seemed to fill the whole world with soft music as Lionel sat down and looked around. Paul threw his leather jacket on the couch, poured them each a glass of white wine, and came to sit down with him.

'Well,' he smiled, 'you like?' He had to admit, he was proud of it. For a poor boy from Buffalo, he had come a long, long way, and he was happy here.

'My God . . . it's so beautiful . . .'

'It is, isn't it?' He didn't disagree. They could look out at the beach, the sea. The whole world seemed to lie at their feet, and when they finished their wine, Paul suggested a walk. He loved to walk on the beach late at night, and it was only eleven o'clock. He kicked off his shoes, and Lionel did the same. They walked out onto the smooth white sand, and Lionel thought he had never been as happy as this. He felt something he had never felt before, and he felt it each time he looked at this man. And it was confusing to him. He fell silent after a while, and on their way back, Paul stopped and sat down on the sand. He looked out at the ocean, and then at Lionel and suddenly the words just came. 'You're confused, aren't you, Li?' He had heard his mother call him that and wondered if he'd mind the familiarity, but Lionel didn't seem to object, and he nodded his head, almost relieved to admit what he felt to this man who was becoming his friend.

'Yes . . .' He wanted to be honest with him, maybe then he'd understand what he felt himself. He felt both very old and very young. 'I am.'

'I used to feel like that too. Before I came out here from Buffalo.' He sighed in the night air. 'I used to hate it there.'

Lionel smiled. 'It must be very different from this.' They both laughed, and as the laughter subsided, Paul looked at him.

'I want to be honest with you. I'm gay.' Suddenly he was terrified. What if Lionel hated him for that? . . . What if he jumped up and ran away? . . . It was the first time he had been afraid of that kind of rejection in years and that frightened him. It was like taking a giant step back . . . back to Buffalo . . . to being in love with Mr Hoolihan at baseball practice in the spring and not being able to say anything . . . just watch him in the shower and want so desperately to touch his face . . . his arm . . . his leg . . . to touch him anywhere . . . to touch him there . . . he turned to Lionel with frightened eyes. 'Do you know what that means?'

'Yes, of course.'

'I don't mean just that I'm a homosexual. I assume you'd understand that. I mean do you know the special kind of loneliness that can mean to a man?' Paul emptied his soul into his eyes and Lionel nodded, never taking his eyes from him. 'I think you do know, Lionel . . . I think you've felt the same things I have. Haven't you?'

Tears slowly ran down Lionel's cheeks as he nodded his head, and suddenly he couldn't bear looking into those eyes any more; he dropped his face into his hands and began to cry, and a thousand years of loneliness welled up in him. Paul took him in his arms and held him there until he stopped, and then he lifted his chin until he looked into his eyes again.

'I'm falling in love with you. And I don't know what to do about it.' He had never felt as free as he did just then. It felt wonderful to admit it to him, and Lionel felt his whole body turn to fire. Suddenly he understood things he had never understood before about himself . . . things he had never wanted to know . . . or was afraid to think about . . . he knew them all as he looked into this man's eyes. 'You're a virgin aren't you?'

Lionel nodded and his voice was hoarse. 'Yes, I am.' He was falling in love with him too, but he didn't know how to say it yet. He prayed that in time he would, that Paul wouldn't send him away . . . that he would always, always let him be with him . . .

'Have you ever slept with a girl?' He shook his head silently. That was how he had known. He had never wanted to. Ever. It just wasn't there. 'Neither had I.' He sighed and lay back on the sand with a sigh, gently taking Lionel's hand and kissing the palm over and over again. 'Maybe it's easier like this. The choice was made for us a long time ago. I've always believed that about people like us. I know we have nothing to do with the choice, and it's there even when you're a very little boy. I think I knew it way back then, but I was afraid to know.'

Lionel felt braver now. 'So was I . . . I was afraid somebody would find out . . . would know . . . would see my thoughts . . . my brother is this all-out jock, and my father wanted me to be like that. And I just couldn't be . . . I couldn't . . .' Tears filled his eyes again, and Paul held his hand tight in his own.

'Does anyone in your family suspect?'

Lionel quickly shook his head. 'I never really even admitted it to myself until tonight.' But now he knew. He knew for sure. He wanted it to be like this. With Paul. And no one else. He had waited for him all his life and wasn't going to lose him now.

But Paul was watching him carefully. 'Are you sure you're ready to admit it now? You can never go back again. You can't really change your mind . . . some do, I guess, but I always wonder how convinced they are . . . I don't know . . .' He looked up at Lionel as they lay on the the sand side by side. He was propped up on one elbow and looking down at him, and there was no one around for miles. The houses were lit up behind them like jewels, a thousand engagement rings he was offering him . . . a crown . . . 'I don't want to do anything you're not ready for.'

'I am . . . I know I am, Paul . . . it's been so lonely until now . . . don't leave me out there again . . .' Paul took him in his arms and held him tight, and he couldn't bear it any more. He had done what was right. He had offered him a choice. He had never taken advantage of anyone and he didn't intend to start now with this boy.

'Come on, let's go home.' He stood up gracefully on the sand, and held out a hand to Lionel, who sprang up beside him easily. With a carefree smile, Lionel followed him home, hand in hand, as they talked, suddenly more animatedly. Suddenly he felt as though a thousand-pound weight had been lifted from him. He knew who and what he was, and where he was going now, and suddenly it was all right. It wasn't as frightening any more. They reached the house a few minutes later, and walked back inside, feeling invigorated by the night air. Paul poured them each another glass of wine, took a sip of his, and lit the fire, and then he disappeared into another room, and left Lionel with his own thoughts and his wine, and when he returned, the lights were dim, the room was dark, the fire was lit, and he stood naked in the centre of the room, beckoning to him. He said nothing, and Lionel didn't hesitate. He stood up and followed him.

Chapter 15

Paul drove Lionel back to his car at the hamburger place at four in the morning, and they stood in the car park, looking at each other. It seemed odd to be back here. So much had happened since they had eaten here. It was remarkable. Lionel felt as though he had wings. It had been the most beautiful night of his life, and he felt a relief he had never experienced before. He finally knew what he was, and Paul had made it seem all right . . . more than that he had made it beautiful. And Lionel didn't know how to begin to thank him now.

'I don't know what to say . . . how to thank you . . .' he said, shifting from one foot to the other, smiling shyly at his friend.

'Don't worry about it. Do you want to see me tonight?'

Lionel could hardly breathe, and he felt excitement stir in him again. He hadn't known how incredible it would be, but with Paul it was. 'I'd like that a lot.'

Paul narrowed his eyes, thinking of where they could meet. 'How about meeting me back here again at eight? Just wait in your car, and then you can follow me out to the house. If I'm not too wiped out, we can make something to eat, or stop on the way. Sound okay?' It wasn't the way he usually liked to woo his men, but he was working long hours just then on the film.

'Sounds great.' Lionel beamed and then yawned sleepily as Paul laughed and tousled his hair.

'Go home and get some sleep . . . lucky boy. I'm going to be working my ass off all day.'

Lionel looked at him sympathetically. 'Say hi to my Mum.' And then suddenly he looked shocked at what he had said.

Paul laughed. 'I don't think I'd better do that just yet.' If ever. He wasn't at all sure how Faye would react to knowing that her older son was gay. 'If she asks, I'll just tell her we had a hamburger and you went home. Okay?'

Lionel nodded. What if he slipped? What if he himself said something to someone one of these days? It was a frightening thought, or was it? . . . Eventually people would have to know. He didn't want to live in hiding for the rest of his life. But on the other hand, he didn't want to tell anyone just yet . . . not yet . . . he wanted it to be his secret with Paul. 'Have a nice day . . .' He wanted to reach out and kiss him right here in the car park, but he didn't dare, and Paul gently touched his cheek with warmth in his eyes.

'Take care of yourself today . . . get some rest, love.'

Lionel felt the power of his loving in his words, and his heart tugged as he watched him go. He waved as the silver Porsche drove away, and slipped into his own car, with his own thoughts. He could hardly wait until that night came, and when it did, he was waiting in his car, in a clean shirt and sweater, impeccable suede slacks, his hair neatly combed and a new brand of after-shave he had bought just that afternoon. Paul recognised all the preparations as he stepped out of the car, and he was touched. He hadn't even had time to shower before leaving the set, but he didn't want to be late. He put an arm around Lionel and they hugged, and it was obvious that the boy was happy to see him again. Li was thrilled.

'How was your day, Paul?'

'Great. Thanks to you.' He smiled generously and the boy beamed. 'I remembered all my lines, sailed right through every-thing, but we worked our asses off this afternoon.' He looked down at himself. He was still wearing fatigues from the set, but no one had said anything when he left. 'Let's go home, so I can clean up and change.' He would have liked to take him to a gay bar afterwards for dinner, or at least a drink, but he wasn't ready to introduce him to the gay world yet. Instinctively, he sensed that Lionel wasn't ready. He wanted this to be special, something that existed only between them, and Paul was willing to play the game for a while, staying away from his usual friends to be alone with him. Lionel decided to ride in the car with him again, and they stopped at a market on the way to Malibu. They bought a six-pack of beer, some wine, the makings of a salad, a bag of fresh fruit, and two steaks. It was a wholesome dinner for two, and Lionel said he knew how to cook.

As it turned out, he was as good as his word, and when Paul stepped out of the shower with a towel wrapped around his waist, Lionel handed him a glass of wine with a smile. 'Dinner will be ready in five minutes.'

'Great. I'm starving.' But then, Paul set the wineglass down, and reached over to give Lionel a kiss. As they parted, their eyes held, and Lionel's heart soared. 'I missed you today.'

'So did I.'

The towel slipped slowly from around Paul's waist, and he whispered at the boy as he fumbled hungrily with his belt. 'Will the steaks burn if they wait?' Not that he really cared . . . he didn't care about anything just now except this young flesh . . . Lionel was one of the most exciting lovers he had had in a long time. He was so enthusiastic and new, every inch of him smelled sweet and good, his body was so young and firm. He tore the suede trousers down until he found what he sought, and Lionel groaned as Paul's mouth found him there. A moment later, they were tangled on the wet floor, dinner forgotten, their bodies locked in passion.

Chapter 16

The affair went on through the fall, and Lionel had never been happier in his life. He was doing well in school, and Paul was still working on the Thayers' film. Once in a great while, Lionel dropped by the set, but it was too hard to pretend with Paul right there. He had to fight to keep his eyes away, and he was afraid that his mother would see.

'She doesn't know everything, you know,' Paul teased him once. 'Even if she is your Mum. And I think she could take it if she knew.'

Lionel sighed. 'I think so too . . .' But when he thought of Ward '. . . My Dad couldn't though. He'd never understand.'

Paul nodded, agreeing with him. 'I think you're right there. I think it's hard for fathers to accept their sons.'

'Did your parents know about you?'

Paul shook his head. 'They still don't. And I'm still young enough that they can understand why I stay single out here. But ten years from now, they'll really be on my back.'

'Maybe you'll be married and have five kids by then.' They both laughed at the absurd possibility. It appealed to Paul not at all. He had no bisexual leanings whatsoever. Women had never turned him on. But Lionel did. They spent most of their nights making love in his huge bed, or on the couch in front of the fire . . . or the floor . . . or the beach. It was an entirely sensual, erotic relationship, and everything about each of them turned the other on. Lionel had the key to the Malibu house now, and sometimes he went there straight from school, or else he'd go back to his own place and meet Paul in Malibu when he finished working later on. But he hadn't spent a night in his own apartment in months, and his roommates teased him every chance they got.

'Okay, Thayer . . . who is this broad? What's her name? When are we going to lay eyes on her, or is she one of these easy dames you hide from your friends and just screw all the time . . .?'

'Very funny.' He tried to fob them off, he put up with their jokes, their admiration, their jealousy, wondering what they would say if they knew the truth. But he knew the answer to that. They would call him a fucking filthy little faggot and probably throw him out.

'Have you told any of your friends?' Paul asked him one night, as they lay naked in front of the fire, having just made love.

Lionel shook his head. 'No.' All he could think of were the boys he shared the apartment with. Typical freshmen jocks, or young intellectuals, all dying to get laid and working hard at it all the time. Their sex lives were far less active than Lionel's, but in a totally different vein. They would have been horrified if they could see him now. Yet he was so happy like this. He looked tenderly at Paul, who was watching him carefully, as though trying to read his mind.

'You going to hide all your life, Li? It's the shits. I did myself for a long time.'

'I'm not ready to come out yet.' They both knew that.

'I know.' And Paul hadn't pushed. He didn't take him anywhere, although the boy was absolutely beautiful and his friends would have all drooled enviously, but he didn't want word to get out. It was only a matter of time, once he did go out with him, before people found out who he was. Faye Thayer's son . . . and then the shit would hit the fan. Paul wanted to spare them both that, and that seemed wise for both of them. Particularly for Paul, whose career could have been jeopardised if Faye or Ward went berserk when they heard, and they might well. The boy was only eighteen after all, and Paul had just turned twenty-nine. It could make a real stink, and it wouldn't do Paul any good. His PR agent still linked his name with actresses whenever possible. People cared about that stuff. No one wanted to hear that their idol was gay.

At Thanksgiving, Lionel spent the day with his family, feeling separate and grown up and strange and different from them now. He didn't have anything to say, he discovered, listening to them. Greg was so childish, and the girls seemed as though they came from another world. He couldn't talk to his parents now, and only Anne was bearable as he waited for the day to tick by. He was relieved when, after dinner, he could finally leave and go back to Paul. He had told his parents that he was going up to Lake Tahoe with friends, though of course he was spending the weekend quietly with Paul. Paul only had another few weeks of shooting left, and they were both relaxed.

It seemed only moments later when Christmas had arrived. Lionel did all his Christmas shopping as soon as he got out of school for the holidays and he dropped in on the set one afternoon, while Paul was in his dressing room.

He didn't see his parents anywhere, so Lionel just drifted into the little room he knew well by now and flopped down in a chair. Paul was smoking a joint, and he offered it to Li, but he had never enjoyed it as much as Paul said he did. He took a quick hit, and gave it back, and the two men sat back and smiled at each other. Paul touched Lionel's thigh. 'If we weren't here, I'd have a great idea.' The two men laughed. They were so easy with each other sometimes they forgot there was something to hide. Paul leaned forward and they kissed.

Neither of them heard the door or the single step, but Lionel was sure he heard a sharp gasp and he pulled away to see Faye standing there, her face frozen with shock and tears in her eyes. Lionel jumped to his feet instantly, and slowly Paul stood up, as the three of them stared at each other.

'Mum, please . . .' Lionel held out a hand to her, tears also in his eyes. He felt as though he had just put a knife to her heart, but he didn't move and neither did she. She just looked at them both, and then she sank slowly into a chair. She didn't feel as though her legs could hold her any more.

'I don't know what to say. How long as this been going on?' She looked from Lionel to Paul.

Paul didn't want to make things worse for either of them. And it was Lionel who spoke up, as he dropped his hands to his side with a defeated look. 'A couple of months . . . I'm sorry, Mum . . .' He began to cry, and Paul's heart went out to him. He stood up and went to his side, looking down at Faye. He owed it to him to stand by the boy now, but he knew how great the cost might be. She could destroy his career if she chose . . . it had been an insane thing to get involved with her son. He regretted it now, but it was much, much too late. The damage was already done.

'Faye. No one's been hurt. And no one knows. We haven't gone anywhere.' He knew she would be relieved to know that and she lifted her eyes to him now.

'Was this your idea, Paul?' She wanted to kill him, but part of her told her that she was wrong, that it wasn't entirely his fault. She looked sorrowfully up at her son's tear-stained face.

'Lionel . . . is this . . . has this happened before?' She wasn't even sure what questions to ask, or if she had a right to know after all. He was a man, and if Paul had been a girl, would she have asked for the details? But the facts of this affair actually frightened her. She knew very little about homosexuality, and she wanted to know even less. There were plenty of gay men in Hollywood, but she had never made it her business to research exactly who did what to whom, and now suddenly it was her son standing there . . . her son had just been kissing a man . . . she wiped the tears from her cheeks, and looked at them both again, as Lionel sighed and sank into the chair across from her.

'Mum, this was the first time . . . I mean with Paul. And it isn't his fault. I've always been like this. I think in my heart I've known it for years, I just didn't know what to do, and he . . .' He faltered, glancing up at Paul almost gratefully, and Faye thought she felt sick. '. . . he introduced me so gently to all this . . . I can't help it. This is what I am. Maybe it's not what you want, and you'll never be able,' he gulped down a sob, 'to love me again . . . but I hope you will . . .' He went to her and put his arms around her, burying his face in her dress, and there were tears in Paul's eyes too as he turned away. He had never been involved in anything like this, even with his own family. Lionel looked up at Faye again then. 'I love you, Mum . . . I always have . . . I always will . . . but I love Paul too . . .' It was the most grown-up moment of his entire life, and perhaps he would never have to be this grown up again. But right now he had to stand up for who and what he was no matter how much pain it caused her. She put her arms around her son and held him close kissing his hair, and at last she took his face in her hands and looked hard at him. He was the same little boy he had been for the past eighteen years, to her, and she loved him just as much.

'I love you just as you are, Lionel Thayer. And I always will. You remember that.' She looked deep into his eyes. 'No matter what happens to you, or what you do, I'm behind you all the way.' She glanced at Paul, as Lionel smiled through his tears. 'I just want you to be happy, that's all. And if this is what your life is, then I accept it. But I want you to be careful and wise about what you do, who you see, how you handle yourself. You've chosen a difficult life. Don't fool yourself about that.' He already suspected it, but it was less difficult with Paul, and less difficult than hiding from himself all these years. She stood up again then and stood looking at Paul, her eyes bright with tears.

'I only want one thing from you. Don't tell anyone about this. Don't ruin his life. He may change his mind one day, give him that chance.' Paul nodded silently, and she looked back at her son. 'And don't say anything to your father about this. He won't understand.'

Lionel visibly gulped. 'I know he won't . . . I . . . I can't believe how great you've been, Mum . . .' He wiped the tears off his face again and she smiled through her own.

'I happen to love you a lot. And your father does too.' She sighed sadly, looking at the two men. It was difficult for anyone to understand. They were both so handsome, so virile, so young. It was a terrible waste, no matter what anyone said, and she had never thought it a happy life. Certainly not for her son. 'Your father will never understand, no matter how much he loves you.' She hit the hardest blow then. 'It'll break his heart.'

Lionel choked again. 'I know.'

Chapter 17

They finished the film five days after New Year's Eve, and the wrap party was the best Paul had ever seen. It was a major event that went on almost all night, with everyone leaving at last with the usual kisses and hugs and tears. For himself, he was relieved. No matter how understanding she had been, it had been difficult working with Faye for the last few weeks, and he knew the strain had shown in the quality of his work, although most of the important scenes had been in the can long since.

He suspected that she had felt the tension too, and he wondered nervously, as he had several times recently, if she would give him a part again. He loved working for her, but he felt as though he had betrayed her this time. And maybe he had. Maybe he should have walked away from the kid, but he had been so damn beautiful, so fresh, so young, and he had convinced himself that he was falling in love with him. He knew differently now. He was a sweet boy, but he was just too damn young for him. Unsophisticated, naïve, he would be fabulous in ten years, but just then there was't enough substance for a man of Paul's age. He felt like his father most of the time, and he was missing his old friends, the gay scene, the parties and orgies he went to, to let off steam, from time to time. It was an awfully sedate little life staying home night after night, staring into the fire. The sex was good, particularly lately with the help of a little amyl nitrate, but he knew that it wouldn't last long. It never did with him. And then he'd have to live with the guilt of that. Life was just too damn complicated sometimes, he thought to himself as he drove home. But when he found Lionel, looking like a sleeping god, curled up in his bed, he had second thoughts about it ending for a long, long time. He quietly peeled off his own clothes, and sat down at the edge of the bed, running a finger down the endless length of Lionel's leg as he slept, and then stirred, and finally opened one eye.

'You look like a sleeping prince . . .' It was a whisper in the darkened room, lit only by the moonlight from the beach, and Lionel smiled and held out his arms to him sleepily. It was more than any man could want, Paul thought to himself as he abandoned himself to the pleasures of the flesh. They slept late the next day and went for a long walk on the beach. Afterwards, they talked about life. But it was in those moments he realised again how young Lionel was. He smiled at him in a certain way he had, and Lionel looked annoyed.

'You think I'm just a baby, don't you?'

'No, I don't.' But he was lying to him. He did.

'Well, I'm not, and I've seen a lot.'

Paul laughed and it enraged Lionel more, and eventually it led to one of their rare fights, and that night Lionel went back to his own place. As he slid into his own bed for the first time in weeks, he wondered if things were going to be different now, with Paul out of work. He would be free all the time, and Lionel had to go to school. He was diligent about that, despite his affair with Paul.

Within weeks, it became obvious that it did complicate things somewhat. Paul was restless much of the time; he was reading scripts, trying to decide what he wanted to do next; he was still nervous about Faye, and by spring he was tired of his schoolboy love. It just didn't give him enough. It had lasted six months, which was a long time for him. Lionel sensed it before Paul said anything. It was painful for both of them when it ended, but Lionel finally confronted Paul with it. He couldn't stand the strained silences between them any more, and suddenly the house in Malibu seemed oppressive to both of them.

'It's over, isn't it, Paul?' He didn't look quite so young any more, but he was, Paul reminded himself. He wasn't even nineteen. Christ. They were eleven years apart. Eleven years. And he had just met a forty-two-year-old man who had turned his legs to mush. He had never had an older lover before, and he was anxious to spend some time with him. But he couldn't with Lionel hanging around his neck. He looked at the boy now, and he had no regrets for what they'd done. He wondered if Lionel did, but he had never seemed to in all these months. He seemed to have found his niche in life. He was happy, his grades had soared. He seemed to have found himself. Maybe it was worth it after all. Paul smiled sadly at him. It was time to be honest and call it a day.

'I think it might be, my friend. Life is like that sometimes. And we've had a good run, wouldn't you say?'

Lionel nodded, looking sad. He didn't want to let go. But it hadn't been good for a while, except in bed. It was always good there, but they were both healthy and young, there was no reason for it not to be. And now he wanted to know the truth. 'Is there someone else?'

Paul was honest with him. 'Not yet.'

'But soon?'

'I don't know. And that's not the point.' Paul got up and walked around the room. 'I just know I need to be free for a while.' He turned back to look at Lionel. 'It's not like the other world, Li. People don't fall in love and get married and live happily ever after with thirteen kids. It's a lot harder for our kind. It's pretty rare for people to stay together for a long time. It happens, sure, but most of the time it's a one-night stand, or a couple of days, or even a week, or if you're lucky six months like us . . . and then, there's nowhere to go, and that's it.'

'That's not good enough.' Lionel looked upset. 'I want more than that.'

Paul smiled. He was wise to his way of life. 'Good luck. You may find it, but most of the time you won't.'

'Why not?'

Paul shrugged. 'Not our style maybe. We're all too interested in good looks, beautiful bodies, a tight little ass, a body as young as yours . . . and all of us know we won't be young any more one day.' He was already starting to feel like that. He was envious of Lionel sometimes, which made him bitchy with him. But this older man made him feel beautiful and young, as Lionel was to him.

'What do you want to do now?'

'I don't know. Travel for a while maybe.'

Lionel nodded. 'Can I still see you sometimes?'

'Of course . . .' And then he looked up at the boy. 'It's been wonderful for me, Lionel . . . I hope you know that . . .'

But Lionel looked far more intensely at him. 'I'll never forget you, Paul . . . never . . . for the rest of my life . . .' He went to him, and they kissed. Lionel stayed there that night. But the next day Paul drove him home, and without being told, Lionel knew that he wouldn't be seeing him again. Not for a long, long time anyway.

Chapter 18

In June 1965, the entire Thayer family found itself sitting in the same row of the auditorium of Beverly Hills High as it had the year before. But it was Greg graduating this time, and it characteristically lacked the solemnity of Lionel's graduation the year before. Faye didn't cry this time, although both she and Ward looked deeply moved, and Lionel was there looking very grown up in another new suit. He was going into his sophomore year at UCLA and loving it. The twins looked far more grown up than they had at fifteen, too. Vanessa had given up looking like Little Bo Peep. She was wearing a red miniskirt and Louis heels with a red and white blouse Faye had bought for her in New York, and had a little red patent-leather shoulder bag. She looked young and fresh, with her hair hanging down her back in a sheet of gold. Only Valerie had made a negative comment on what she wore, but she always did, grumbling that she looked great, if you didn't mind looking like a peppermint stick. She had chosen to look more subdued, she felt, and was also wearing a miniskirt, but hers was black, and her sweater was too tight once again this year. There remained about her a look of startling maturity. The lush figure, the makeup more subtly done now, the red hair in a breathtaking mane that eclipsed all else but her dress. She actually looked very pretty, or would have for cocktails in Beverly Hills. She was just somewhat overdressed for a high school auditorium at 9am, but they were all used to that by now. Faye was just grateful she hadn't chosen to wear something with a plunging décolletage, and the miniskirt was, remarkably, one of her most modest ones. 'Thank God for small favours,' she had whispered to Ward as they got in the car, and he had grinned. They were quite a bunch, and they were all growing up. Even Anne had matured. She had grown breasts and softly rounded hips, was thirteen now, and mercifully hadn't got lost this year before they had to leave for the ceremony. Greg's graduation gift had been no surprise. He had badgered them so badly for it, that Ward had given in and presented it with a flourish the week before. It was a yellow Corvette Stingray convertible, and he was even more excited than Lionel had been about his, if that was possible. It was actually a fancier car than Lionel's little red Mustang but that had been Ward's idea. And Greg roared up and down their street, and then vanished to pick up all his friends for a ride. Ward had been certain that he would either crash or be arrested within the hour, but somehow they had all survived, and nine of his closest friends had arrived whooping and screeching as they careered down the street, burning rubber as they turned into the drive, and then all of them had leapt out of the car outside the house and headed for the pool. Ward wondered if he'd made a terrible mistake. Greg certainly didn't have Lionel's calm ways, and Ward just prayed that he would drive sensibly when he got to the University of Alabama. He had won a football scholarship, and he could hardly wait to leave. He was going back to the ranch in Montana to work for a month again. But then he was going to the university on August 1st to begin football practice with the team and their famous coach 'Bear'. Ward could hardly wait to fly down and see him in his first game. Faye knew she was going to be doing a lot of that this year, but she didn't mind. She had promised to go whenever she could, although they'd be winding up a film in the autumn, and starting another after the first of the year, but she'd do what she could.

They watched Greg receive his diploma, as Lionel had last year, but Greg merely grinned sheepishly – unlike his more poised brother. He waved to his family and friends, and then took his seat again, his broad shoulders almost knocking his friends off their seats. He was the big hero in school for getting a football scholarship, and Ward was so proud he could hardly see. He had told everyone he knew, and he had looked at Lionel almost reproachfully when he heard the news. Lionel was currently doing an experimental film on ballet and the dance, and there were times when Ward wondered what went through the boy's mind. He was certainly different from their younger son, but at least he was doing well in school. And Faye seemed to see a lot of him at lunch. He hadn't had much time himself. He'd been putting together the package for another big film deal, and he had a lot on his mind. But the boy looked all right. At least none of their brood had gone haywire with this flower child nonsense, and none of them were into drugs, although he frequently warned Faye to keep an eye on Val. That child was too damn seductive by far, and she seemed to have a knack for hanging out with older boys. She had turned up with some character in May who admitted to being twenty-four, and he had squashed that romance fast enough. But there was denying she was hard to control. There was one in every brood, he'd been told, and Val was theirs. But so far, despite the wild garb, the makeup, and the older boys, she seemed to have stayed within the bounds of some kind of propriety.

The party they gave Greg that night differed radically from Lionel's the year before. By midnight everyone was not only drunk on beer, but most of them were naked in the pool. Faye wanted to have them all thrown out, but Ward prevailed and told her to let them have their fun. He wanted to send Anne and the twins to bed, and Faye said that was impossible. You either had to close the whole show down or let them be, but the police made the decision for them shortly after two o'clock. They told them to turn the music off and tone it down. Every neighbour on their street had complained, especially the couple next door, when a chorus line of twelve hefty young men had appeared on the front lawn, and mooned them before leaping into their pool. Ward had thought the whole thing in good fun, but he was amused by almost everything Greg did. Faye was slightly less amused. There had been no complaints at all over Lionel's party the previous year. By the time the police came, Greg was sprawled out on a chaise longue, a towel wrapped around his naked waist, and an arm draped across his date, both of them drunk on beer and sound asleep. Neither of them woke up when the rest of the guests left, talking about what a great party it had been. Faye was just grateful that none of them had come into the house. Only one couple had wandered in and had been necking heavily in Greg's room, but Faye had seen them tiptoeing in and had asked them to go outside immediately. Sheepishly they had, and they had left early with a few others, who wanted to do some serious groping before going home. But for the most part they were more interested in pushing each other into the pool and consuming as much beer as they could before they had to leave.

And when the last guest left, Lionel and John Wells were still sitting a little distance from the pool, in a comfortable old double swing, under a tree. They were talking about UCLA, and Lionel was telling him which classes he liked best, and about his projects in film. John had got his dream fulfilled, and he had been accepted there too.

The swing moved slowly back and forth as they watched the revellers beyond. Lionel had escaped quite a while before, and John had found him sitting in the swing: 'I've been thinking about fine arts a lot,' John said. He was still Greg's best friend, officially, but in the last year they seemed to spend less and less time together. John was still on the football team too, but he didn't care about it as much as Greg did, and he was relieved to be free of it now. He never wanted to play football again, no matter how well suited to it he was. Greg had told him he was nuts. He had been offered a football scholarship at Georgia Tech, and had actually turned it down. Oddly enough, the friendship hadn't been as close after that. Greg just couldn't understand his giving up an opportunity like that. He had stared at his childhood friend in disgust and disbelief, and every time they met now, John felt as though he had to explain it again, as though he had committed an unpardonable sin. And in Greg's eyes he had. But Lionel didn't seem to care. And he had always been fond of John.

'They have a good fine arts department. And a great drama department of course.' Lionel knew he hadn't chosen his major yet.

'I don't think that's my style.' John smiled shyly at the older boy. He had always admired him.

'Are you living on campus next year?'

John looked hesitant. 'I'm not sure. My mother thinks I should live in the dorm, which doesn't appeal to me much. I think I'd rather live at home.'

Lionel looked pensive for a time as they moved gently on the swing. 'I think one of my roommates is moving out.' He looked thoughtfully at John, wondering how he would fit in. He was still very young, but he was a decent kid. He didn't smoke, didn't drink, didn't seem to raise too much hell, certainly nothing like Greg. He was a lot like Li's roommates, most of whom Lionel liked. Occasionally, they got rowdy on Saturday nights, but they weren't completely wild, and unlike a lot of other freshmen and sophomores, they didn't choose to live like pigs. They kept the apartment fairly clean, two of them had girlfriends who slept there a lot, but they didn't bother anyone, and Lionel came and went as he pleased. No one asked him a lot of questions any more. Sometimes he wondered if they knew, but no one said anything, and no one asked. It was a good group, and John Wells might just make a good fifth. 'Would you be interested, John? The rent is pretty cheap.' He looked at him. 'How would your parents feel about your living off campus first year? Actually, it's just across the street, but it's not the dorms.' He grinned, and looked just like Faye as he did. He had grown from boyhood into manhood that year, and he was a beautiful young man. People often stared at him in the street with his graceful build, long limbs, big green eyes, and golden hair. And he wore quiet clothes that set off his good looks in a casual way. He could have been in films if he'd wanted to, but that end of the camera had never appealed to him. He looked at John now, and the younger boy felt something stir in him. 'What do you think?'

His eyes lit up with quiet excitement as he glanced up at Lionel. 'Boy, I'd love to find a place like that. I'll ask them tomorrow, first thing.'

Lionel smiled. 'No rush. I'll just tell the others I know someone who's interested. I don't think anyone is worried about it yet.'

'How much is it? My dad'll want to know.' John's parents were de comfortable, but careful. He was the oldest child of four, and they were going to have four in college in the next four years, not unlike the Thayers, although Lionel's dad worried less than John's. But Ward had two or three successful films under his belt every year, and John's did not. He was a plastic surgeon in Beverly Hills, and his mother did a little decorating for her friends when she had time. She looked great though. She had had her eyes done the year before, her nose bobbed several years before that, and that summer she was going to have implants done in her breasts. Besides, she looked great in a bathing suit. His sisters were pretty nice-looking too, he always thought. Greg had gone out with two of them, and one of them had had an eye on Lionel for years. But he had never seemed interested, and John had never wondered why.

'Divided by five, the rent only comes to sixty-six dollars a month, John. It's a five-bedroom house in Westwood, and the landlady is pretty good about staying off our backs. There's no pool, and there's only room for two cars in the garage. You'd have a good-sized bedroom, looking out on the front, and you share a bath with two other guys. The room comes with a bed and a desk. You'd have to supply the rest yourself, unless Thompson wants to sell his junk. He's going East to Yale for the next two years.'

'Wow!' John's eyes were all alight with excitement. 'Wait till I tell my dad!'

Lionel smiled. 'Want to come by tomorrow and have a look at it? There are only going to be two of us there this summer, which will make the rent pretty steep. But it's too much trouble to move back in here,' he shrugged and looked vague, 'and I don't know . . . it's easier. Once you move out, I think it would be hard to come home again.' Especially in his case; there would be so many questions asked that he didn't have to contend with now. And he liked the freedom he had. With only one other boy that summer, it would almost be like his own place. He was looking forward to it.

'Yeah, I know . . . can I come and see it tomorrow?' It was Saturday and Lionel didn't have any plans. All he was going to do was sleep late and do some laundry. He had been invited to a party that night, but he was free all day.

'Sure.'

'Nine o'clock?'

John looked like a five-year-old kid waiting for Santa Claus to come, and Lionel laughed. 'How about noon?'

'Great.' They abandoned the swing then, and Lionel gave John a ride home. After he dropped him off at the miniature French mansion where he lived in Bel Air, with the regulation Cadillac and Mercedes parked outside in plain view, he drove slowly home, thinking about John. He felt something he couldn't deny, but he didn't know if it was appropriate in this case. He suspected not, and he had no intention of taking advantage of him. The offer of the room in his house was sincere. He wasn't setting John up, but he had to admit, having him so close could be difficult, or . . . and as his thoughts whirled around while he pulled up in front of the house he shared with the four other boys, he suddenly wondered if Paul had felt that way about him. There was an odd kind of responsibility to reaching out to someone like John . . . especially if it was the first time . . . and Lionel suspected it would be . . . He almost shook himself then.

What was he thinking of? What if John didn't feel that way at all? He'd be crazy to make a pass at him. He reminded himself of that several times as he brushed his teeth and went to bed. He was crazy to even consider it, he told himself as he lay in the dark, trying not to think of him again. But John's innocent young face kept coming to mind again and again . . . the powerful legs . . . broad shoulders . . . narrow hips . . . he could feel himself becoming aroused, just thinking of him . . . 'No!' He said it aloud in the dark, and turned over, instinctively stroking himself, as he tried to force John out of his mind. But it was impossible, and his whole body shuddered with desire, as he thought of John diving into the pool earlier that night . . . and all that night, as he slept, Lionel dreamt of him . . . running on a beach . . . swimming in a deep tropical sea . . . kissing him . . . lying at his side . . . He awoke with a dull ache that refused to go away, and he took his bike out and went for a long ride before anyone else got up, anxiously waiting for noon, and promising himself that he was going to tell John the room had been rented to someone else. That was the only way out. He could have called, but he didn't want to. He would tell him when he came to the house at noon . . . he would . . . that was the best way . . . tell him to his face . . . that was the only way.

Chapter 19

When Greg woke up the morning after his graduation bash, he had the worst hangover of his life, and he had already had quite a few. His head throbbed, his stomach was upset. He had woken up twice during the night and thrown up, once on his bathroom floor, and he thought he would die when he tried to stand up at eleven o'clock the next day. But his father saw him staggering downstairs, and handed him a cup of black coffee, a piece of toast, and a glass of tomato juice with a raw egg in it. Just looking at it made him feel sick again, but his father insisted that he force it down.

'Make an effort, son. It'll do you good.' He seemed to speak from experience, and Greg trusted him, so he did his best, and was amazed when he felt a little better afterwards. Ward handed him two aspirins for his head and he gulped them down, and he felt almost human by noon, as he stretched out in the sun at the pool. He glanced over at Val, her lush figure poured into a bikini Faye didn't like her to wear when there was anyone else around, but with family it was all right. It was barely more than a piece of string, but Greg had to admit, it looked great on her.

'Great party, wasn't it, Sis?'

'Yeah.' She opened an eye and looked at him. 'You sure got drunk enough.'

He looked unconcerned. 'Were Mum and Dad mad?'

'I think Mum would have been, but Dad kept telling her it was your graduation night.' She grinned. She had had quite a few beers too, and the music had been good. They had all danced a lot before passing out.

'Just wait till it's your turn. You'll probably go nuts.'

'It's my turn next.' Except that she would have to share it with Van. That was the one thing she hated about being twins; you always had to share everything with someone else. And Faye had never understood that she wanted to be separate, to do things by herself, to have her own friends. She always treated them as though they were one, and Valerie had spent her whole life fighting that, making a point of how different they were, at all costs. And still nobody understood. It ruined everything. But not for much longer.

Only two more years at home, and then she was moving out. Vanessa said she was going to college in the East, but she knew exactly what she was going to do. She was going to take classes at acting school. Not UCLA drama school – the real thing, the kind working actors went to between jobs, and she was going to start looking for work. She'd get her own apartment. She wasn't going to waste her time going to college. Who needed that? She was going to be an actress, and a bigger one than her mother had ever been. She had set that goal for herself years before, and she had never swerved from that desire.

'What are you looking so uptight about?' Greg had been watching her, and she was wearing an ominous frown. She usually looked like that when she was plotting against some poor slob she had the hots for. But she only shook the long red hair back now, and shrugged. She hadn't told anyone what she was going to do. They would just give her a hard time. Greg would try and talk her into being a physical therapist, or an acrobat, or getting a dumb athletic scholarship somewhere, Vanessa would try and talk her into going to school in the East with her, Lionel would have some other dumb idea, like going to UCLA because he did. Mum would make speeches about education, Dad would tell her how bad makeup was for her skin, and Anne would look at her as though she were a freak. She knew all of them too well after sixteen years of living with them.

'I was just thinking about last night,' she lied and he lay back in the hot sun again.

'Yeah . . . it was the best.' It occurred to him then to ask what had happened to his date. 'Dad took her home. She almost threw up in his car.' Val grinned and he laughed.

'Christ, he didn't say a word.'

'Lucky it wasn't one of us, he'd have had a fit.' They both laughed and Anne wandered by on her way to the swing with a book.

'Where are you going, squirt?' Greg squinted at her in the sun, noticing what a trim figure she was getting in a bathing suit. Her waist seemed to be shrinking by the hour and he could have got both hands around it, and her breasts were almost as big as Val's. Their little sister was getting all grown up, but she wasn't the kind of kid you could say something about it to. She was the most restrained of all of them, and she never gave him the impression that she liked any of them much, except Lionel of course. It seemed to Greg that they had barely heard her speak since their older brother moved out. 'Where are you going, kid?' He repeated the question as she walked past them expressionlessly. She never had anything much to say to Greg. She had never liked sports and she always thought his girlfriends were dumb. And she had her worst fights with Val, who glared at her ominously now. She thought Anne's bathing suit looked suspiciously like one of her own, but she wasn't quite sure, and Anne could feel her eyes examining her.

'Nowhere.' She walked past them without saying another word, holding tight to her book. Greg whispered to Val once she was past:

'She's a weird kid, isn't she, Val?'

'Yeah, I guess.' Val wasn't interested. She had just figured out that the bathing suit wasn't hers. Hers didn't have a yellow stripe down the sides.

'Growing up a lot though. Did you see those tits?' He laughed. 'They're almost as big as yours.'

'Yeah? So what?' Val sucked in her already flat stomach as she stood up and pushed out her breasts. 'She's got short legs anyway.' She didn't look like any of them. Her looks had never been as striking as the other four. Val looked at her own legs now, trying to decide if she had taken enough sun for one day. If she took too much, she'd burn, although she had more tolerance than most redheads. She noticed that Greg was already starting to fry. 'You better watch out. You're turning red.'

'I'll go inside in a little while. John said he'd come by, and I want to go downtown to get extra floor mats for my car.'

'What about Joan?' She was the little blonde her father had had to escort home the night before. She had the biggest boobs Val thought she'd ever seen. They were almost gross, and everyone in school said she was an easy lay. And that seemed to suit Greg perfectly.

'I'm seeing her tonight.' He had been sleeping with her for the last two months, ever since they'd heard about his football scholarship to the University of Alabama.

'Are you doubling with John?' She knew he had no special girlfriend and she was always hoping to be asked to be his date, but Greg had never suggested it, and neither had John.

'No. He said he had other plans.' He glanced at Val. 'Why? You got the hots for him, little Sis?' He was the worst tease of all, and in years past they had had some almost lethal fights. He loved to bait her, and she always went for it, as she was about to now.

'Hell, no. I just wondered. I've got a date,' she lied again.

'With who?' He knew her better than that.

'None of your business.'

'That's what I thought.' He lay back with a grin and she wanted to strangle him. Anne watched them silently from her distant hiding place in the old swing. 'You don't have a date with anyone, smartass.'

'The hell I don't. I have a date with Jack Barnes.'

'Bullshit. He's going steady with Linda Hall.'

'Well.' Her face was bright red and not from the sun. From the distance, Anne could tell she had just told a lie . . . she knew them all so well, better than they knew her. 'Maybe he's cheating on her.'

Greg sat up and stared at his sister carefully. 'Not unless you're putting out the way she is, Sis. Which brings up a question I've been meaning to ask . . . are you?'

Val's face looked like it was on fire. 'Screw you.' She wheeled on her heel and flounced into the house, and he laughed again as he lay down in the sun. She was a hot number, his little Sis, he had heard it from a couple of his friends whose younger brothers had gone out with her. But supposedly she would do anything except the real thing. He knew she was still a virgin, at least he thought she was, and he also knew she had lied about Jack Barnes. He suspected too that she had always had the hots for John Wells, but John had never seemed interested in her, and he was just as glad. That was a little close to home for his taste, and she wasn't John's type. He went for quieter, less showy girls. He was still pretty shy, and Greg was almost sure he hadn't done it yet either. Poor kid. He'd better hurry up. He was probably the last guy in their class who hadn't got into someone's pants yet, at least that was what they said. And it was getting embarrassing for Greg to have a friend like that. Hell, people would start to think John was queer, and worse yet, if they hung out together, they would say it about him. But he smiled to himself then. With what he'd been up to with Joan, there was no chance of that.

'Boy, this is a nice place.' John was looking around the house in Westwood rapturously, as though it were Versailles, or a Hollywood set, instead of a shabby student house across from UCLA. My dad thought the rent was cheap. Mum was a little nervous about my not living in the dorm, but Dad said that as long as you were here, you could keep an eye on me.' He blushed, feeling stupid for what he had just said. 'I mean . . .'

'That's okay.' Lionel was fighting to repress his dreams of the night before, and he had the oddest feeling of reliving a film he had seen once before, only this time he was cast as Paul. It was like a variation of *déjà vu*, and he couldn't seem to escape his thoughts as he showed John around. Lionel's own room would be across the hall from John's, but he was sure that if he was willing to give up the only room in the house with its own shower, he could have the room adjoining John's. The other guys would have killed to have his room, and he would have been willing to give it up if . . . he pushed the thought out of his head, and forced himself to concentrate on John, and the tour of the house he was giving him. 'There's a washing machine in the garage. No one uses it for weeks, and then everyone wants to use it all in one night.' Lionel smiled.

'My mum said I could bring my laundry home.' Lionel couldn't help thinking how unlike Greg he was, it was most odd that they were friends, except that they had gone to school together for thirteen years, and he suspected that it was habit more than anything else. Had he thought about it, John would have admitted he was right. He and Greg hadn't had much in common for the last couple of years, and especially in the last few months. They seemed to disagree about everything, from the football scholarship to the class whore Greg was sleeping with. John couldn't stand being around her, and as a result he had been seeing less and less of Greg. He had been spending more time alone, and it was almost a relief to be talking to Lionel, someone sensible, who even went to the same school he'd be going to. 'I really love this place, Li. It's great.' It could have been a barn and he would have fallen in love with it. It was all so grown up, so collegiate, and so cool, and it comforting knowing Lionel would be there. He felt shy about starting out in a new school, and he had hated the idea of the dorm, after living at home with four sisters for eighteen years. It was going to be so foreign to him, but not now, not with Lionel, here.

'Would you want to stay here this summer, John? Or move in in the autumn before school starts?' Lionel could feel his heart pound and he hated himself. What difference did it make when the kid moved in? Leave him alone, he wanted to shriek, and he was suddenly sorry he had suggested it at all. It was just going to make things difficult for him. It had been a stupid idea, but he couldn't back out now, and he had told two of the boys that morning before John arrived. They were pleased he had found someone. It saved them the trouble of placing an ad, or calling friends.

'Could I move in next week?'

Lionel was momentarily shocked. 'So soon?'

'Oh no . . .' John blushed nervously '. . . not if that's inconvenient for you. I just thought that since Tuesday is the first, it would be easier from the standpoint of the rent . . . and I have a summer job at Robinson's. I could live here while I work.' It was a department store, and Lionel was faintly reminded of his job the year before at Van Cleef & Arpels. He had enjoyed that and was as sorry he couldn't do it again, but he wanted to work in film this year. It made more sense for him, and if he was lucky he would get credit from UCLA for the work, if the project turned out well.

No, no . . . you're right, John. I hadn't thought of that. And the room is free. I just thought you'd want to think about it for a while . . .' It was too late, he had offered the room to John and now he wanted it. He would have to live with what he'd done, no matter what the cost to himself.

'I don't need to think about it, Li. I think the room is great.' Shit. Lionel stared at the tall dark-haired boy, with the exquisite body that had tormented him the night before, and there nothing left to say.

'Fine. I'll tell the other guys. They'll be thrilled. It saves them a lot of headaches.' And then, in an attempt to make the best of it, 'Do you want help moving in?'

'I don't want to bother you . . . I thought I'd borrow Dad's car and move some stuff in tomorrow.'

'I'll come pick you up.' John's face lit up like a child again.

'I really appreciate it, Li. You're sure it's not too much trouble?'

'Not at all.'

'Mum said she had a bedspread and some lamps and some other stuff.'

'Great.' Lionel could feel his heart sink, as he wondered what he had got himself into. John looked up admiringly at him.

'Can I take you to dinner tonight, Li, to thank you for all this?' Suddenly Lionel was embarrassed by the boy's sincerity, and he was touched. 'That's all right, John. You don't have to do anything like that. I'm glad it worked out.' But he wasn't. He was scared. What if he lost control? If he did something dumb? If John found out he was gay? But suddenly he felt John's hand on his arm and a chill ran down his spine. He wanted to tell John not to touch him again, but he'd think he was nuts.

'I can't thank you enough, Li. It's like a whole new life.' He was so relieved to get away from the kids at Beverly Hills High. He just didn't feel like them any more. He hadn't in years, and he had hidden it for so long. Now he could start a new life somewhere else. He wouldn't have to try as hard, or listen to the jocks, or run away from the girls, or pretend to get drunk on Saturday nights . . . even the locker room had become a nightmare for him . . . all those boys . . . all those jocks . . . even Greg . . . especially him . . . and he knew he was different from them. And yet with Lionel he didn't feel as though there were something wrong with him. He was so quiet and understanding, and he felt so comfortable with him. Even if he didn't see him much at the new house, it was nice to know that he'd be there once in a while, that their paths would cross, that he could talk to him sometimes. He looked into his eyes now and he wanted to cry with relief. 'I've hated school so much, Li. I can't wait to get out.'

Lionel was surprised. 'I thought you liked it, John. You're a big football star.' They wandered into the kitchen, and Lionel handed him a Coke, which he took gratefully. He was even more grateful it wasn't a beer. It would have been if it had been Greg.

'I've hated that for the last year. I'm just sick of all that shit.' He took a sip of the Coke, and sighed with relief. It really was a whole new life. 'I hated every moment I spent on that damn football team.'

Lionel was stunned. 'Why?'

'I don't know. I just never gave a damn about it. I was good at it, I guess, but I didn't really care. You know they actually used to cry in the locker room when they lost a game. Sometimes the coach cried too. As though it really mattered that much. All it is is a bunch of big guys beating each other up on a field. It just never turned me on.'

'Then why did you play?'

'It meant a lot to my dad. He played in college before he went to med school. And he always used to kid me that if they smashed up my face, he'd fix it for me, for free.' John looked disgusted at the thought. 'That didn't increase the appeal much.' He smiled slowly at Lionel. 'Being here is going to be like a dream.'

Lionel smiled at him. 'I'm glad you like the room. It'll be nice having you around, although I'm not here much. But if there's anything I can do . . .'

'You've done enough, Li.'

True to his word, Lionel went to pick him up the next day, put the top down on the little red Mustang, and made three trips to help him move in his stuff. He seemed to have mountains of it, but he performed miracles and Lionel hardly recognised the room by Sunday night. He stopped in the doorway and stared.

'My God, what did you do?' He had stapled fabric to one wall, hung plants, put up simple curtains and a handsome painting over the bed. Two lamps provided warm light, there were posters on the other wall. It looked like an apartment in a magazine, and there was a small white flokati rug on the floor. 'Did your mum do this for you?' Lionel knew she was a decorator and he couldn't imagine John doing all that in a matter of hours. There were even orange crates with the same fabric stapled on them, with magazines in baskets, and cushions giving the impression of a window seat. It was a small haven, and Lionel was impressed beyond words and it showed.

'I did it myself.' He looked pleased at the effect on Lionel. Everyone said he had a talent for interior design, he had always been able to take a room and change it in a matter of hours, using whatever materials were at hand. Even his mother said he should do something with his innate ability – he was better than she was, she claimed. It took her months to achieve the effects she struggled for. 'I love doing stuff like that.'

'Maybe one of these days, you can wave a magic wand over my room. It still looks like a jail cell, and I've lived here for a year.'

John laughed. 'Anytime.' He glanced around. 'Actually, I had two extra plants, and I was going to ask you if you wanted them.'

Lionel smiled at him. 'Sure. But they'll probably die the first time I walk into the room. I don't exactly have a knack with anything green.'

'I'll take care of them for you. I'll water them when I do mine.' The two young men exchanged a smile and Lionel looked at his watch. It was seven o'clock.

'Want to go out for a hamburger?' The very words had a ring of *déjà vu* again, and he was reminded of Paul. It was even more eerie when John agreed and suggested they go to the very place he had gone with Paul the first time. It made Lionel silent and moody for the first part of the meal. He was thinking of that first night when he had gone to Malibu with Paul. He hadn't heard from him in months, but had seen him drive past once, on Rodeo Drive, in the passenger seat of a beige and brown Rolls with a handsome, older man at the wheel. They had been talking animatedly as Lionel watched, they were smiling at each other, and Paul had laughed at something the other man said.

And now here he was again, with John . . . his younger brother's best friend. It felt odd. Even more so when they went back to the house they now shared. The other two living there just then were both staying at their girlfriends' that night, and the others had already moved out at the end of the school year.

'Thanks for dinner.' John smiled at him as they sprawled comfortably in the living room and Lionel put a record on. Two of the bulbs were burned out in the room's main lamp, and the light was unintentionally dim. John lit a candle on the coffee table and glanced around. 'This room could use a little help too.'

Lionel laughed. 'You're going to have this place in shape in no time, but I think the other guys will discourage you a little bit. When they're here, this place always looks like someone just threw a bomb into the room.'

John laughed too. 'My sisters keep their rooms like that.' His face grew more serious. 'I've never lived with men before, except my dad of course. I'm so used to having girls around all the time, this is going to be weird at first.' And then he smiled. 'That must sound crazy to you.'

'No, it doesn't. I've got three sisters too.'

'But you've had Greg around too. I've always been so close to my mum and the girls. I'll bet I miss them for a while.'

'It's good training for when you get married, to have that many women around.' Lionel smiled again and wondered to himself if he was testing him. He told himself that wasn't fair. John was just a kid . . . but he was the same age he had been when he met Paul . . . but Paul was so much more experienced . . . and he was the experienced one now. Not as much as Paul had been, but more so than this boy. But where did you start? How did you ask someone something like that? He tried to remember what Paul had said to him, but the words escaped him now . . . he remembered that they had gone for a long walk on the beach . . . and Paul had asked him something about being confused. But there was no beach here, and John didn't look confused to him. He was a trifle shy, and he was far less rowdy than Greg, but he was a happy, pleasant, young . . . yet Lionel could never remember seeing him seriously involved with a girl.

They chatted on for a while, and finally Lionel got up and said he was going to take a shower. John said he'd do the same. It was ten minutes later, when John knocked on the bathroom door and pologised, shouting into the shower where Lionel stood, not to think of him, as rivulets of hot water purified his mind and his flesh.

'I'm sorry, Li . . . do you have any shampoo? I forgot mine.'

'What?' Lionel pulled aside the curtain so he could hear and saw John standing there, naked save for a towel wrapped around his waist. He felt his body stir, and pulled the shower curtain closed again so John couldn't see.

'I said, do you have any shampoo?'

'Sure.' He had already used it and his hair was wet and clean. 'Here.' He handed it to John, who disappeared with a thanks and a smile, and he returned with it in a little while, wearing his towel again, his hair wet and dark, his body rippling with the muscles football had built for him, and Lionel was wandering naked around his room, putting things away and humming to himself. He had the radio on, and Lennon and McCartney were singing 'Yesterday', as John handed the shampoo back to him.

'Thanks.' He seemed to linger in the door, and Lionel turned away, wishing he would go. He didn't want to start anything, and he didn't want anyone to get hurt. His way of life was his own and he wasn't looking to drag anyone else into it, when suddenly he felt John's hand on his back, and it was as though his whole body was electrified. It was going to be agonizing having the boy around and hiding his secret from him. Without turning, he grabbed a white terry-cloth robe from a nail on the wall, struggled into it, and turned around, but he had never seen a more beautiful face than John's, there was sorrow and pain and honesty there. And their faces were only inches apart, as John looked at him. 'I have to tell you something, Li. I should have told you before.' There was anguish in the boy's eyes, and Lionel ached for him, wondering what it was.

'Something wrong?'

The younger boy nodded and sank down slowly on the edge of the bed, looking sadly up at him. 'I know I should have told you before I moved in, but I was scared you wouldn't . . . you'd be pissed.' He looked up at him, frightened, but honest. He came right to the point. 'I think you should know I'm gay.' He looked as though he had just admitted he had just killed his best friend, and Lionel's jaw almost dropped he looked so stunned. How simple it all was. How brave he was to speak up, not knowing what Lionel would do or say. His heart went out to the boy and he sat down on the bed next to him and started to laugh. He laughed until tears came to his eyes, and John looked at him nervously. Maybe he was hysterical, or maybe he just thought it was so disgusting it was ridiculous. It was a relief when he finally stopped laughing long enough to speak, and he was stunned when Lionel put his hands on his shoulders as he did.

'If only you knew the things I've been telling myself since you moved in . . . I've been torturing myself . . .' It was clear that John didn't understand. 'Baby, so am I.'

'You're gay?' John looked appalled and Lionel started laughing again. 'You *are?* But I never thought . . .' And yet that wasn't true, there had been a faint, hesitant current between them for the last year and yet neither could accept the possibility that the other understood. They talked about it for the next two hours, lying on Lionel's bed, friends at last. Lionel told him about Paul. And John confessed to two brief, terrible affairs. There had been no love in either of them for him, just terrible, anguished, tortured, guilt-ridden sexual release, one with a teacher from his school, who had threatened to kill him if he talked, the other with a stranger, an older man, who had picked him up on the street. And the only purpose the two affairs had served was to show him what he was. He had suspected it for a long time, but he had always thought it was the worst thing that could ever happen to him. People like Greg Thayer would never have talked to him again. But Lionel was so different, he understood it all, and he looked at the younger man sympathetically now, from his vantage point of nineteen. And John was curious about one thing.

'Does Greg know?'

Lionel was quick to shake his head. 'Only my mum. She found out last year.' He told John how. It still hurt thinking of how shocked she had been, but she had been wonderful to him since then, understanding, compassionate, she accepted him as he was. 'Everyone should be lucky enough to have a mother like her.' She had far exceeded his hopes and dreams.

'I don't think my mum could accept it . . . and my dad . . .' He almost cringed at the thought. 'He always wanted me to be sue a jock. I played football for him, and I kept thinking, I'm going to get my teeth kicked out doing this, and I hate it, I hate it.' His eyes filled with tears as he looked at Li. 'I did it for him.'

'I wasn't as good as you were. But my dad had Greg to pin his hopes on. I always let him carry the ball, so to speak.' He smiled gently at the new friend he had known for years. 'It took the heat off me in some ways, but I paid the price I guess. My father has never approved of me. And if he knew . . . he'd die.' They had so much guilt for so many years, for what they were not, for what they could never be, and in the past year, for what they had done. It was almost too much to bear at times. Lionel thought of it now as he looked into John's eyes. 'Did you know about me?'

John shook his head. 'I don't think I did. I wished a lot though sometimes.' He smiled honestly up at Li and they both grinned, as Lionel tousled the damp black hair that framed his face.

'You little shit. Why didn't you say something?'

'And have you knock my teeth down my throat, or call the cops, or worse yet . . . tell Greg?' He shuddered at the thought, and the thought of something else. 'Are all the guys in this house gay?'

Lionel was quick to shake his head. 'None of them, and I'm pretty sure of that. You get a feel for that when you live with people. And they all have girls stay here pretty regularly.'

'Do they know about you?'

Lionel looked at him pointedly. 'I'm damn careful that they don't suspect, and you'd better be the same, or they'll throw us both out.'

'I'll be careful. I swear.'

Lionel found himself thinking again of changing rooms to the one that shared the bathroom with John, but he forgot the room and looked up at John instead, lying across his bed, and suddenly he felt relief and desire wash over him, as he remembered his dreams of the night before. He reached out to touch John, lying back on the bed, waiting for Li's lips and his hands and his touch, his youthful flesh rippling with excitement and begging for him. Lionel found him with his mouth, and his tongue danced hot fire up John's thighs, as he groaned, and discovered something at Lionel's hands that he had never had before. This time there was nothing clandestine, nothing frightening, nothing embarrassing about the love that Lionel lavished on him for the next couple of hours, until, satisfied and peaceful, they lay in each other's arms and slept. They had each found something that they had been looking for, for a long time, without ever knowing it.

Chapter 20

School began in the autumn without event. Lionel and John had never been happier, and no one at the house knew. Lionel had changed rooms before the others came back from their summer plans, and the arrangement worked out perfectly. John and Lionel both locked their doors at night, and no one had any idea who spent the night in whose bed, as they tiptoed back and forth stealthily, whispering late at night, and keeping their moans of ecstasy dimmed. It was only on the rare nights when no one was there at all, sleeping at girls' houses, or going skiing over a long weekend, that they allowed themselves a little more liberty. But they were cautious that no one should know, and for once Lionel didn't even say anything to Faye. He just said that school was going well. He didn't offer any romantic news, and she didn't to pry, although she suspected there was someone in his life from the happy look in his eyes. She just hoped it was someone decent who wouldn't make him unhappy eventually. From what she knew of the homosexual world, there seemed to be so much unhappiness, promiscuity and infidelity, it wasn't a life she wanted her eldest child condemned to. But she knew that there was no alternative for him, and she accepted that.

In November, whe invited Lionel to the Première of their latest film. He accepted with delight, and she wasn't surprised to see John Wells with him. She knew that John was renting a room in the same house as Lionel, and going to UCLA as well, but at the end of the evening when they went to Chasen's for supper and champagne with the twins and a number of business associates and friends, she suddenly wondered if she didn't see something special pass between their eyes. She wasn't quite sure of it, but she sensed something, and she thought John looked much more mature than he had in June, as though he had grown up a lot in the last few months. She suspected something, but she said nothing to anyone, of course. She was startled when Ward questioned her as they got undressed that night. She was talking to him animatedly about the film, the audience response, the favourable reviews they hoped to get, and she was stunned when he interrupted her with a worried frown, standing in his trousers with a bare chest.

'Do you think John Wells is queer?'

'John?' She looked amazed, but in her heart she knew she was stalling for time. 'My God, Ward, what a thing to say . . . of course not, why?'

'I don't know. He looks different to me suddenly. Didn't you notice something about him tonight?'

'No,' she lied.

'I don't know . . .' He walked slowly to his closet and hung up his jacket, still wearing the same frown. 'I just get a funny feeling about him.' Faye felt her whole body grow cold. She wondered if he had the same suspicions about their son. And like Lionel, she wasn't at all sure he could survive knowing the truth, although maybe he would have to one day. In the meantime, she was dedicated to keeping the truth from him. 'Maybe I should say something to Lionel. Warn him . . . he may think I'm nuts, but if I'm right, he may thank me some day. Greg thought there was something wrong with him when he turned down that scholarship at Georgia Tech. Maybe he was right.'

Faye looked suddenly annoyed. 'Just because he doesn't want to play football doesn't mean he's gay for chrissake. Maybe he's interested in other things.'

'You never see him with girls.' They didn't see Lionel with girls either, but Faye didn't point that out to him. And she knew Ward just assumed that Lionel kept his love life to himself. He did not assume he was carrying on with men, just because he didn't see the girls. But she didn't point that out to him either.

'I think you're being unfair. It's like a witch hunt, for God's sake.'

'I just don't want Lionel living with some damn queer, and not realising it.'

'I'm sure he's old enough to figure it out for himself. If that's the case.'

'Maybe not. He's so wrapped up in those crazy films of his. Sometimes I think he's completely lost in his own world.' Well, he had noticed that much about his eldest son at least, she told herself.

'He's a remarkably creative boy.' She was anxious to get Ward off the subject of John. And she had to admit, there had been something different about him tonight. But instinctively, she felt a need to protect him. She suspected that he was involved with Lionel. Lionel still didn't look gay, and John was only just beginning to, and he had talked a lot about decorating and interior design. Maybe it was time she said something to Lionel about him. 'Have you seen Li's last film, sweetheart? It's beautiful.'

Ward sighed and sat down on their bed in his shorts. He was still a beautiful man, and at forty-eight he was as well built as his sons. 'Just between us, Faye, I have to tell you it's not my cup of tea.'

'It's a whole new wave, sweetheart.'

'It still isn't something I understand.'

She smiled at him. He was so good at what he did, but he was rarely open to new ideas. He put packages together for her films, but he was interested in none of the new and more exotic trends in films. He had hated the Cannes film festival that year. But he loved the Academy Awards and had been disappointed when she hadn't won another one. He had bought her a beautiful emerald ring to make up for it, and it reminded her of the old days before 1952 when everything changed for them. 'You ought to give Li's films a chance, love. One of these days he's going to surprise the hell out of you and win an award for one of those odd little films.' She was convinced of it but Ward didn't look impressed.

'Good for him. Did you hear from Greg today? He said he'd call about the weekend he wants us to come down.'

'No, he didn't call and I'm not sure I can. I've got meetings with the new script writer every day for the next three weeks.'

'Are you sure?'

'More or less. Why don't you ask Lionel to go with you?'

Ward didn't look sure, but in the end he did, and it gave him the perfect opening to ask him about John when he extended the invitation to him.

'You don't think he's a fag, do you, Li?'

Lionel forced himself to keep a blank look in his eyes. He hated that word and it took every ounce of restraint not to lash out in defence of his friend. 'For heaven's sake, what makes you say a thing like that?'

Ward smiled. 'You look just like your mother when you say that.' But then his face sobered rapidly. 'I don't know. He looks different to me suddenly and he talks about decorating all the time.'

'That's ridiculous. That doesn't make him gay.'

'No, but chasing men would. Watch out he doesn't go after you. And if you sense anything weird about him, throw him out of that house. You don't owe him a thing.' For the first time in his life, Lionel had to fight the urge to punch his father out, but he managed to appear calm until he left his parents' house. He drove all the way back at eighty miles an hour, wanting to kill somebody, mainly his dad. When he reached the house, he slammed the front door, and a moment later, slammed the door to his room and locked it. It was one of the few times his room-mates had ever seen him out of control, and everyone looked shocked. A while later, John wandered into his own room and locked his door as well. He walked quickly through the bathroom that now joined their two rooms.

'What's wrong, love?' Lionel looked up at John with fire in his eyes, and he had to admit to himself that John *was* beginning to look gay. In spite of the well-muscled physique, there was something smooth and pure about his face, he was wearing his hair differently, and his clothes were almost too perfect, too stylish, too neat, but he loved the boy, loved his talent, his warm heart, his giving ways, his body, his soul, he loved everything about him, and if he were a girl, they would already have been engaged and no one would have been surprised. But he was not, so everyone called him queer. 'What's wrong?' He sat down in a chair and waited for Lionel to unload.

'Nothing. I don't want to talk about it.'

John looked at the ceiling quietly and then back at his friend. 'That's a dumb way to handle it. Why not get it off your chest?' And then, suddenly he suspected it had to do with him. 'Did I do something to upset you, Li?' He looked so worried and hurt, that Lionel walked over to him and gently touched his cheek. 'No . . . it has nothing to do with you . . .' But it did, and he didn't know how to explain to him. 'It's nothing. My father just pissed me off.'

'Did he say something about us?' He had correctly sensed that Ward had been staring at him the other night. 'Does he suspect?'

Lionel wanted to be vague, but John was too sharp. 'He might. I think he's just feeling around.'

'What did you say?' John looked concerned. What if he said something to the Wells? They had so much to hide. What if they had him arrested or sent away, or . . . it was terrifying thinking of it all, but Lionel kissed his neck and spoke to him soothingly. He knew how worried he got.

'Relax. He's just talking off the top of his head. He doesn't know anything.'

John had tears in his eyes. 'Do you want me to move out?'

'No!' Lionel almost shouted the word. 'Not unless I go too. But we don't have to do that.'

'Do you think he'll say something to my dad?'

'Stop being so paranoid. He just made some cracks and he pissed me off, that's all. It's not the end of the world.' But to pacify Ward, Lionel went to Alabama with him, to watch Greg play ball, and it was the most boring weekend he had ever spent in his life. He hated football almost as much as John, and he had nothing to say to Greg. Worse yet, there were endless painful silences with his dad, who went berserk when one of their star players suffered an injury and the coach put Greg in his place, just in time for Greg to score a touchdown in the last two and a half seconds of the game and win for his team. Lionel tried to feign the same excitement as Ward felt but it just wasn't there, and he was desperately relieved on the flight home, as he talked about films to him, and tried to explain what he was working on. But as he had felt that he might as well have been on the moon as he watched Greg play, so his father looked at him as he described his latest avant-garde film.

'Do you really think you can make money with something like that one day?' Lionel looked at him, stupefied; it was a goal that had never entered his mind. They were trying out new techniques, stretching the language of film to its utmost. Who gave a damn about making money on it? This was much more important than that, and the two men stared at each other in confused disbelief, each convinced that the other was a fool, yet feeling the burden of pretending that they respected the other's views. It was a terrible strain for both of them, and they both looked relieved to see Faye waiting for them at the gate. Ward talked endlessly about Greg's extraordinary touchdown, crushed that she hadn't watched it on TV, and Lionel looked at her as though he couldn't have stood a moment more. She laughed to herself, knowing them both so well and how different they were, yet she loved them both, just as she loved her other son, and the girls. They were just all very different people, who needed different things from her.

She dropped Ward off at home first, and then said that she would run Lionel home, and come back in time for a drink with Ward. It gave her a few minutes to talk to her eldest son, and commiserate over the boring weekend he had had.

'Was it terrible, love?' She smiled at the look on his face, and he groaned as he leaned his head back against the seat after they dropped his father off at home. He had never felt so exhausted in his entire life.

'Worse. It was like going to another planet and trying to talk their language all weekend long.' She wondered if it was just the boredom of the sport, or the strain of pretending to be straight, but she didn't ask.

'Poor thing. How was Greg?'

'The same.' He didn't need to say more to her. She knew how little they had in common. Sometimes it was hard to believe that they were both her sons. And then she asked him what she had worried-about all weekend long.

'Did your father ask about John?'

Lionel's face went tense and he sat up again. 'No. Why? Has he said anything else to you?' He sought her eyes, he still hadn't admitted anything to her, but he knew that she knew without being told, and he wasn't sure what she thought. He had a feeling that she thought it was too close to home, and in some ways she was right.

'I think you ought to be careful, Li.'

'I am, Mum.' He sounded very young and her heart went out to him.

'Are you in love with him?' It was the first time she had asked, and he nodded with serious eyes.

'Yes.'

'Then be careful, for both your sakes. Do the Wells know about John?'

Lionel shook his head, and Faye felt a ripple of fear course up her spine as she drove home alone again. One day it would all come out, and someone would get hurt . . . maybe a lot of people would . . . John, Lionel . . . the Wells . . . Ward . . . she didn't care so much about John and his family, although she was fond of them . . . but she was terrified about what it would do to Ward . . . and Lionel . . . She thought that Lionel could probably weather the storm. He was growing up, unconsciously preparing himself to face that one day, not just from his father, but from everyone. Lionel wasn't the kind of man to hide for the rest of his life. But Faye wasn't sure if Ward would survive the shock. It would destroy a part of him, she knew that, and it terrified her. But there was nothing she could do. Lionel had promised her to be discreet. At that moment, he had just locked his bedroom door, and was quietly kissing John and then sighed as he told him how lonely the weekend had been.

Chapter 21

On Christmas Day, Lionel joined his family for their traditional Christmas dinner. Greg was home for a few days, although he had to go back early to play another game, and Ward was going with him. After that, they were flying to the Super Bowl. Ward wanted Lionel to come too, but he insisted that he had other plans. Ward looked annoyed, but Faye distracted them all with an enormous turkey, and champagne for all. Valerie drank a little too much, and everyone teased Van. She looked absolutely beautiful in a new hairdo and a new dress. She was in love for the first time, with a boy she had met at a school dance several weeks before, and she suddenly looked grown up. Even Anne had changed remarkably this year. In the past few months, she had sprouted up, and she was as tall as the twins, though she hadn't come into her own yet, but she was getting there. Lionel reminded them all as he toasted her, and she blushed, that she would be fourteen in a few weeks. After dinner, Lionel and Anne sat by the fire and talked. He saw her less than he would have liked to these days, not so much because he was living out of the house, but because of his work on the film, but it was clear that he still adored her, and it was mutual. And then she surprised him by asking about John, and there was an odd look in her eyes when she did, as though she had a crush on him, and he was surprised that he hadn't realised it before. But everything about her was so hidden and so clandestine, it wasn't surprising that he hadn't noticed it.

'He's fine. I guess he's doing all right in school. I don't see him very much.'

'He's still living at your house though, isn't he? I saw Sally Wells the other day, and she said he loved it there.' Sally Wells was Anne's age, but she was far more mature, and he prayed that Sally hadn't figured things out and told Anne, but it didn't look as though she had. Anne still had that light of innocence and hope in her eyes.

'Yes, he's still there.'

'I haven't seen him in a long time.' She looked at Lionel wistfully and he wanted to laugh she looked so sweet, but he didn't say anything.

'I'll tell him you said hello.' She nodded and the others came in. Ward lit a fire, and they were all pleased with their gifts, and Ward and Faye looked over each other's heads and smiled. It had been a good year all around.

Lionel was the first to leave, as was John at the Wells' home. The other boys were all gone for the holidays. They had the whole house to themselves, so they didn't have to hide and lock their bedroom doors. It was wonderful being able to relax and be themselves. It was a strain being careful all the time, especially for John, who seemed to be growing more obviously effeminate day by day. Now he could fill the house with flowers, and spend long hours in bed every afternoon with Lionel, who was taking a break from his film over the holidays. The two boys took long walks, and talked a lot, and came home to cook and drink hot toddies or white wine by the fire.

It was almost like being grown up, John teased, so much so that they didn't even bother to lock the front door, and never heard Lionel's father walk in the day after Christmas Day. He had stopped in to see if he could talk Lionel into flying South with him after all, and watching Greg play, before all three of them went to the Super Bowl. But the thought went right out of his head, as he walked quietly in after no one had answered his knock. He found the two boys lying near the fire, fully dressed, but with John's head nestled in Lionel's lap, Li's head bent low, saying something endearing to him. Ward stopped and uttered an almost groan, as the two boys jumped and looked up. Lionel's face went white. They both scrambled to their feet, and without thinking, Ward advanced toward John angrily, and took a vicious swing at him, making his nose bleed at once, and then he swung at Lionel, but Li grabbed his arm and stopped the blow before it reached his face. There were tears in his eyes, and his father was crying with rage, screaming obscenities at both of them.

'You little sonofabitch . . . you whore . . .!' The words were meant for John, but he was shouting them at his son, too, his eyes blinded by fury and tears. He couldn't believe what he had just seen. He wanted them to take it back, to tell him it wasn't true, but it was, and there was no hiding from it now. Lionel felt physically sick as he held his father away from him, and John had begun to cry. It was a nightmarish scene and Lionel was attempting to keep calm. He felt as if his whole life was in question now, and he had to explain it to him. Maybe he would understand . . . he had to try desperately to explain how different he had always been from Greg . . . from all of them . . . how he had felt... he didn't even feel the tears pouring down his cheeks, or the blow when his father finally freed his hands and slapped his face.

'Dad, please . . . I want to talk to you . . . I . . .'

'I don't want to hear any of it!' He was trembling from head to foot and Lionel was suddenly terrified he would have a heart attack. 'I never want to see you again! You two fag bitches!' He looked at them both. 'You scum!' And then at Lionel. 'You're not my son any more, you little queen. I never want to see you in my house again. I won't pay another dime for your support. You are out of my life from now on, is that clear? And stay away from my family!' He was sobbing and shouting and he advanced menacingly on John again. All his dreams had been shattered at once. His elder son was queer. It was more than he could bear, more than losing his fortune years before or the threat of his losing his wife shortly after that . . . in his eyes, this was even worse than a death. It was a loss he would never understand, and in some ways a loss he was inflicting on himself, but he didn't realise that. 'You're through! Is that clear?' Lionel nodded his head numbly and, staggering towards the door he had come in only moments before, Ward almost fell blindly down the stairs as he left. The shock was too much for him. He went straight to the nearest bar, had four scotches straight up. At eight o'clock Faye called Lionel with a worried voice. She hated to bother him, but it didn't make sense. They had been expecting guests at six o'clock and Ward hadn't come home. They said he had left the studio early that afternoon, and she couldn't imagine where he'd gone.

'Darling, did your father call you today?' Lionel was still numb. John had been sobbing on the couch for hours, aghast at what had been said, the end result, and the fear that Ward would tell his parents too. Lionel had tried to calm him and had forced him to put an ice pack on his swollen cheek and nose, and he felt an anguish in his own heart that no one could soothe now. His voice was still trembling when he answered the phone, and he couldn't answer at first. And then suddenly, with an icy chill, she realised something was wrong. 'Li . . . sweetheart, are you all right?'

'I . . . yuh . . . I . . .' The words were unintelligible, and suddenly he began to sob too. John sat up and stared at him. He had been so calm, so strong, and suddenly he was falling apart. 'Mum . . . I . . . can't . . .'

'Oh my God . . .' Something terrible had happened to him . . . maybe Ward had got hurt and they had called Lionel. She felt panic rise in her throat. 'Calm down. Now come on . . . tell me what happened . . .'

'Dad came . . . by . . .' There were great terrible gulping sobs locked in his chest and they were begging to come out. 'He . . . I . . .' And then suddenly she knew.

'Did he find you and John?' She imagined the worst, that he had found them in bed and she felt faint at the thought. She herself wouldn't have enjoyed that scene no matter how tolerant she was of her son. And Lionel was beyond being able to reassure her as to what his father had seen.

He could only force out a single word before collapsing totally on the phone. 'Yes . . .' It was moments before he could speak again. 'He said he never wanted to see me again . . . that I wasn't his son . . .'

'Oh my God . . . darling, calm down. You know none of that is true, and he'll come to his senses eventually.' She talked to him for over an hour, their guests having gone home after several cocktails some time before. She offered to go over and talk to them, but he wanted to be alone with John, and she was just as glad. She wanted to be home when Ward returned.

When he did, she was horrified by the condition he was in. He had stopped at several bars after the first one, and he was drunk and staggering, but he still remembered having seen Lionel and John and what he now knew of them. He looked at Faye with hatred and despair. He had turned on her too.

'You knew, didn't you?'

She didn't want to lie to him, but she didn't want him to feel there had been a conspiracy to keep it from him for years. 'I suspected about John.'

'Fuck that little sonofabitch . . .' He reeled toward her and she saw that there was blood on his shirt. He had fallen and cut his hand on the way out of the last bar, but he wouldn't let her come to him. 'I mean you knew about our son . . . or should I call him our daughter now?' He reeked of booze and she fell back as he approached and grabbed her arm. 'That's what he is, did you know that? Did you know?'

'Ward, he's still our child, no matter what he does. He's a decent human being and a good boy . . . it's not his fault if that's the way he is.'

'Whose fault is it then? Mine?' That's what he was really worried about. Why had Lionel turned out that way? He had tortured himself over it from one bar to the next, and he didn't like any of the answers that came to mind . . . he had let Faye have too much of a hand with him . . . he hadn't spent enough time with him himself . . . he had frightened him . . . he hadn't loved him enough I . . . he had always favoured Greg . . . the reproaches were legion, but they all amounted to the same thing. His son was queer. Where had he learned? How had it happened? How could it happen to him? It was a personal affront to his own manhood . . . his son was a fag . . . the words burned through him like fire, and he looked into Faye's eyes with tears in his own eyes again.

'Stop blaming yourself, Ward.' She slipped her arms around him and led him to their bed, where they sat side by side, as he leaned heavily against her.

'It's not my fault.' It was the whine of a frightened child, and she felt sorry for him. She had asked herself the same questions too the year before, but maybe it was harder for him. She had always known it would be. He wasn't as strong as she was, as sure of herself, or what she had given their kids.

'It's not anyone's fault, not yours, not mine, or his, or even John's. It's just the way he is. We owe it to him to accept that.' But as she said it, he pushed her away from him and stood up unsteadily, grabbing her arm until she winced.

'I will never accept it. *Never!* Do you understand? That's what I told him. He's not my son any more.'

'Oh yes, he is!' Now she was furious too and she wrenched her arm away from him. 'He is *our* son, whether he is crippled or maimed or impaired, or deaf or dumb, or mentally ill, or a murderer, or whatever he is . . . and thank God, all he is is a homosexual for chrissake. He is my son until my dying day or his, and he is your son until then too, whether you like it or not, or whether you approve of him or not.' She was crying now too, and Ward was shocked at her words and the vehemence with which she spoke to him. 'You can't banish him from your life or mine. He is not going anywhere. He is our son, and you'd damn well better accept him as he is, or you can go to hell, Ward Thayer. I'm going to let you put that boy through any more misery than he's already been through. It's hard enough on him as it is.'

Ward's eyes blazed into hers. 'That's why he's the way he is. Because you've protected him all his life. You make excuses for him, you let him hide in your skirts.' He sat down in a chair and began to cry again, as he looked up at her. 'And now wearing your skirts, damn you. We're lucky he isn't walking around in a dress for chrissakes.' The way he spoke of their son tore at her heart so terribly that she reached out and slapped him hard across the face, and he didn't move from where he sat. He just looked at her with eyes so cold and hard that they frightened he. 'I never want to see him in this house again. And if he comes here, I will throw him out myself. I told him, and I'm telling you, and I will tell everyone else, and if any of you disagree, you're welcome to leave too. Lionel Thayer no longer exists. Is that clear!' She was speechless with rage, and she would have liked to kill him with her bare hands. For the first time in her life, even with all that had happened to them before now, for the first time she was sorry that she had married him and told him so, before slamming out of the room.

She slept in Lionel's room that night, and the next morning at breakfast Ward broke her heart again. He looked as though he had aged ten years overnight, and she remembered now what she had said to Lionel before. She had been afraid then that the truth would kill Ward, and it looked now as though it might, but by the time she was finished, she wished it would. He drank a cup of coffee in silence, stared at the paper without picking it up, and then spoke up in a numbed, flat voice to all of them. Oddly enough, it was one of the few times that they had all had breakfast together in months. But Greg home for another day before going back for his big game, the twins were both up, which was miraculous, and Anne had come downstairs only moments after them. They all sat there now staring at Ward, as he told them that, in his eyes, Lionel would no longer exist from that day forth, that he was a homosexual and having an affair with John Wells. The girls sat and stared at him in open horror and Vanessa began to cry, but Greg looked as though he might throw up. He jumped to his feet, shouting at his dad as Faye gripped her chair.

'That's a lie!' He said it more in defence of his old friend than his brother, who was, in some ways, a stranger to him. 'That's not true.' His father looked as though he might hit him and pointed at his chair.

'Sit down and shut up. It is true. I walked in on them yesterday.' Anne's face turned to ash, and Faye felt as though her entire family, her whole life, were being destroyed. She hated Ward for it, for what he was doing to all of them, and most of all their firstborn. 'Lionel is no longer welcome in this house. As far as I'm concerned, he doesn't exist. Is that clear? You are all forbidden to see him again and if I find out you have, you're welcome to leave too. I will not support him, or see him, or speak to him ever again. Does everyone understand?' They all nodded woodenly, and all eyes were damp, and a moment later he was gone. He got in his car, and drove to Bob and Mary Wells, as Faye sat at the breakfast table staring at them all, and they stared back at her. Greg was fighting back tears, and he kept thinking of what his friends would say when they found out. It was the worst thing he could think of, and he wanted to die. Most of all he wanted to kill John Wells, the phony little shit . . . he should have known when he wouldn't take the scholarship to Georgia Tech . . . fucking fruit . . . he clenched his fists and looked at them all helplessly as Vanessa searched Faye's eyes.

'Is that how you feel, Mum?' Vanessa asked. There was no point asking if it was true, no matter how unbelievable it was. Their father had said he had walked in on them, and none of them could imagine anything worse. It sounded mysterious and frightening and terrible, and they all imagined obscene acts going on before his eyes, instead of two boys in front of a fire, with one's head in the other's lap. But it had all been very clear, and there was no argument now.

Faye looked at them all and then at Vanessa again. She spoke in a measured, quiet voice, and she thought she had never known such pain. He had destroyed everything she had built for almost twenty years. What would happen to these children now? What would they think of Lionel? Themselves? Their father for banishing their eldest brother from their lives, their mother for letting him do it? . . . She had to speak up. To hell with Ward. 'No. That is not how I feel. I love Lionel, just as I always have, and if that is how he feels, and what he is, and he is a decent upstanding man, no matter what his sexual preferences are,' it was time to be honest with them, 'I will always stand by him. And I want you all to know that right now. Whatever you do, wherever you go, whatever mistakes you make, and whatever you become, whether it be good or bad, or something I approve of or not, I will always be your mother and your friend. You can always come to me. I will always have a place in my heart and my life and my home for you.' She went then and kissed each of them as they cried, all four of them, for the brother they had just lost at their father's hands, for the disappointment they felt, the shock of the secret revealed. It was all a little beyond their ken, but their mother's message was clear.

'Do you think Daddy will change his mind?' Val's voice was subdued, and no one had noticed Anne slip away a moment before.

'I don't know. I'll talk to him. And I suppose in time, he'll come to his senses, but he just can't understand it right now.'

'Well, neither can I.' Greg slammed a fist into the table and stood up. 'I think it's the most disgusting thing I ever heard.'

'How you feel about it, Greg, is up to you. I don't give a damn what they did. As long as they don't hurt anyone, as long as that's the way they are, I accept them as they are.' She looked her son in the eye and saw the distance between them now. He was too much like Ward. His mind was closed, and now so was his heart. He ran upstairs and slammed the door, and once he had left, Faye noticed that Anne was gone. She knew what a blow it would be to her, and she resolved to go upstairs and talk to her, but when she did, the child's door was locked and she wouldn't answer her. The twins went to their rooms too, and the entire family acted as though someone had died. Faye called Lionel a little while later, and he and John knew by then that Ward had gone to the Wells.

They were all hysterical and Bob and Mary Wells had called. There had been rivers of tears, and after the phone call, John had gone to the bathroom and thrown up. But for all the shouting and screaming and reproaches they directed at both boys, they wanted John to know that he was still their son, that they did not share Ward Thayer's view, that they still loved him, and they accepted Lionel as well. It brought tears to Faye's eyes when she heard, and she was secretly pleased when Lionel told her that Bob Wells had thrown Ward out of their house.

Faye went to see both boys that afternoon. She wanted Lionel to know again how strongly she supported him, and mother and son stood holding each other for a long time, and then she turned and hugged John. It wasn't easy to accept, and it wouldn't have been her choice for her son, but it was what he was. And she also wanted him to know that he would always be welcome in their home, that he was still part of the family no matter what his father said, and that from now on, she would be supporting both his school career and his living expenses. If his father wanted to cut him off, that was up to him, but Faye would always be there for him. She would take the responsibility on now, and Lionel cried as she told him, and promised to get a job to help support himself. And John did too. His parents had already told him earlier that they would continue to support him as long as he was in school, that nothing was going to change for him.

But Ward stuck to the same party line, when he returned that night. He had disappeared all day, and Faye could tell from the way he looked when he got home that he had been drinking all day. He reminded everyone at dinner that night that Lionel was

254

no longer welcome in his house, that he was dead as far as he was concerned, and as he said the words, Anne rose and stared at him with hatred in her eyes.

'Sit down!' It was the first time he had ever spoken harshly to her, and she stood up to him, much to everyone's surprise. It was a time in their family that no one would forget soon.

'I won't. You make me sick.'

He walked around the table and grabbed her arm, forcing her into her seat, but she wouldn't touch her food, and then with measured tones she stood up at the end of the meal and glared at him.

'He's better than you are.'

'Then get out of my house.'

'I will!' She threw her napkin onto her plate, which was still full, and disappeared into her room. They heard Greg's car roar away moments after that. He was having trouble coping with it all. Vanessa and Valerie looked at each other with concern. They were both frightened for Anne and what this could do to her.

That night she slipped out of the house, and hitched a ride to Lionel's house. She rang the bell, and knocked on the door. She could see lights upstairs, but they wouldn't answer her and when she went to the corner and called on the pay phone there, no one answered the phone. They had heard it ring, and they were sitting quietly in the living room. But it had been such a nightmarish twenty-four hours for them that they couldn't take any more. John thought that maybe they should answer the door. But Lionel disagreed.

'If it's one of the guys coming home early, they've all got the key. It's probably my father drunk again.' They'd been through enough. They both agreed about that. They didn't even look out the window to see who it was. And downstairs Anne fished a pencil out of her coat pocket, and tore a piece of newspaper off the garbage can, scribbling a note to Lionel. 'I love you, Li. I always will, A.' Tears filled her eyes. She had wanted to see him again before she left, but maybe it didn't matter now . . . she slipped the piece of paper into the mailbox. That was all he needed to know. She didn't want him to think she had turned on him too. He had to know she never would. But she couldn't stand it any more. It had been unbearable ever since he moved out, and now it would be worse. She would never see him. She had only one choice, and she was surprised at how relieved she felt.

That night as they all slept, she quietly packed a small duffle bag, and slipped out of her bedroom window, as she had done when she had gone to see Li. There were easy footholds all the way down the side of the house. She had used them before, plenty of times. And she slipped quietly down now, wearing sneakers and jeans, her hair in a long blonde braid, a warm parka on. She knew it would be cold up there. She had everything she cared about in the one small bag. She didn't even look back as she left the house. She didn't give a damn about any of them, any more than they did about her. She stealthily crept down the road, and walked all the way into LA, and there she hitched a ride on the motorway heading north. She was surprised at how easy it was. She told the first driver that she went to Berkeley and had to get back after the Christmas holiday. He didn't ask her anything else, and drove her all the way to Bakersfield before dropping her off.

And by then, Faye had found her note. She had left the door unlocked, and the note on her bed.

'That makes two of us you're rid of now, Dad. Goodbye, Anne.' No word to anyone else. Nothing to Faye. Her heart almost stopped when she found the piece of paper left on Anne's bed, and they called the police immediately. She called Lionel too, and he had found the scrap of newspaper by then. It was the worst time in her life Faye could ever recall, and she wondered if she'd live through it, as she waited for the police to arrive. Ward was sitting, stunned, in a chair in the den, the note still in his hand.

'She couldn't have gone very far. She's probably at a friend's.'

But Valerie took care of that hope. 'She doesn't have any friends.' It was a sad statement about Anne, but they all knew it was true. Her only friend had been Lionel, and her father had banished him. Faye sat watching him with unspoken rage, as the bell rang. The police had come. She just prayed they would find Anne before something happened to her. There was no telling where she had gone, and she had already been gone for hours.

Chapter 22

After the first driver who picked her up left her in Bakersfield, it took Anne several hours to catch another ride, but this one took her straight up to Fremont, and she caught another ride easily from there. It took her a total of nineteen hours to get to San Francisco, but on the whole she was surprised at how easy it was, and all of them had been nice to her. They thought she was just another college kid, 'a flower child' two of them had teased. None of them would have guessed that she was a few weeks shy of being fourteen years old. And when she reached San Francisco, she walked down Haight Street, feeling as though the streets were paved with gold. There were young people everywhere, in bright, homemade clothes. There were Hare Krishnas in soft orange robes with shaved heads, boys with hair to their waists in jeans, girls with flowers braided into their hair. Everyone looked happy and pleased with life. There were people sharing food on the streets, and someone offered her an acid tab for free, but she smiled shyly and refused.

'What's your name?' someone asked, and she whispered softly, 'Anne'. This was the place she had longed to be for years, free of the strangers she had been related to and hated for so long. She was glad, in a way, that it had come to this. Lionel had John now, and maybe soon she would have someone too. Lionel would know that she loved him no matter what, and as for the others . . . she didn't care. She hoped she'd never see them again. On the way north, she had thought seriously about changing her name, but once on the streets of the Haight-Ashbury, she realised that no one would care. There were others who looked even younger than she, and no one would suspect she'd come here. She had said nothing to anyone. And a girl named Anne was as anonymous as anyone could be. Her looks were plain, her hair an ordinary blonde, unlike Vanessa's pale golden hair, or Val's which looked like flame. The twins couldn't have got away with this, even if they wanted to. But she knew she could. She could fade into any crowd. She had been doing it at home for years. No one knew when she was there, when she was not, when she arrived, or when she disappeared, and she was so used to everyone asking 'Where's Anne?' that she knew that she could easily do the same thing here.

'Hungry, Sister?' She looked up to see a girl in what looked like a white bedsheet wrapped around her spare frame, with a tattered purple parka over it. The girl was smiling at her and held out a piece of carrot cake. Anne suspected it might be laced with acid or some other drug, and the girl in the parka saw her hesitate. 'It's clean. You just look like you're new here.'

'I am.'

The girl with the carrot cake was sixteen and she'd been here for seven months, having come from Philadelphia in late May. Her parents hadn't found her yet, although she'd seen their ads in the 'Personals', but she had no inclination to respond. There was a priest who roamed the streets, offering advice, and to make contact with their parents, if they wished. But not too many did, and Daphne wasn't one of them. 'My name is Daff. Do you have a place to stay tonight?'

Hesitantly, Anne shook her head. 'Not yet.'

'There's a place on Waller. You can stay for as long as you like. All you have to do is help keep it clean, and help cook the food on the days they assign.' They had also had two outbreaks of hepatitis recently, but Daphne didn't tell her that. Outwardly everything was beautiful and loving here. The rats, the lice, the kids who died from overdose were not something one discussed with a neophyte. And no matter, those things happened everywhere, didn't they? This was a special time in history. A time of peace and love and joy. A wave of love to counteract the useless deaths in Vietnam. Time had stopped for all of them and all that mattered was the here and now, and love and peace, and friends like this. Daphne gently kissed her cheeks and took her hand, leading her to the house on Waller Street.

There were roughly thirty or forty people living there, mostly in Indian garb of rainbow hues, although there were some in patched jeans too, and outfits with feathers and sequins sewn on. Anne felt like a plain little bird in her jeans and an old brown turtleneck she'd worn on the trip, but a girl who met her at the door offered to lend her a dress, and she found herself suddenly wearing a costume in faded pink silk. It had come from a thrift shop on Divisadero Street, and she slipped her feet into rubber thongs, unbraided her hair, and wove two flowers into it. By that afternoon she felt and looked like one of them. They ate an Indian dish, and someone had baked bread, she took a few hits on someone's joint, and she lay back on a sleeping bag feeling full and warm and content, looking around at her new friends, feeling a warmth and acceptance she had never felt before. She knew she would be happy here. It was a lifetime away from the house in Beverly Hills, her father's angry edicts about Lionel . . . the perfidies of the people she knew . . . the stupidity of Gregory . . . the selfishness of the twins . . . the woman who called herself her mother that she had never understood . . . this was where she belonged now. Here on Waller Street, with her new friends.

When they initiated her three days after she arrived, it seemed suitable and right and loving. It was a supreme act of love in a room filled with incense, as a fire blazed warmly in the hearth, and the hallucination carried her from heaven to hell and back again. She knew she would be a different person when she woke up again. They told her that before she ate the mushrooms, followed by the tiny tab of LSD absorbed into a sugar cube. It took a little while for it to take hold on her mind, but when it did, there were friendly spirits there, and a room full of people she knew. Later, there were spiders and bats and terrifying things, but they held her hands while she howled and screamed, and when she felt her body racked with pain, they sang her songs, and cradled her as her mother never had . . . even Lionel had done nothing like this for her . . . she crossed a desert on her hands and knees, and then at last she came to an enchanted forest, filled with elves, and she felt their hands on her, and felt the spirits singing to her again. And now the faces that had hovered over her all night, and waited for her to be free of the evil of her past life, came forward towards her.

Already, she felt purified, and knew that she was one of them. The evil spirits had been killed, they had left her, and now she was pure . . . now they could complete the ritual with her. Gently, they peeled away her clothes, and washed her with oils, each one gently massaging her tender flesh . . . she had come far that night, and parts of her were sore, but the women gently massaged her, getting her ready now, reaching slowly into her, and stretching her as she screamed. She fought them at first, but they whispered so gently to her, and she could hear the music now. They had her drink something warm, and poured more oil on her, as her two guardians tenderly massaged her most secret place and she writhed beneath their hands, howling with agony and joy, and then her new brothers came, the spirits who would belong to her now, to replace the others she had left behind, and each of them knelt beside her as the sisters crooned, and one by one the brothers entered her, as the music grew louder, and birds flew high overhead . . . there were sharp arrows of pain at times, and waves of ecstasy, and again and again they came into her, and held her there, and left again, until the sisters returned, kissing her now and reaching far far into her until she could feel no more, and heard no sound. The music had stopped. The room was dark. Her past life was gone. She stirred, wondering if it had all been a dream but when she sat up and looked around, she saw them there, waiting for her. She had been gone for a long, long time, and she was so surprised at how many there were. But she recognised each one of them, and crying, she held out her arms and they came to her, embracing her. Her woman-hood was complete, her sisterhood was sure. They gave her another acid tab as a reward, and this time she soared with them as one of the flock, dressed in a gown of white, and when the brothers and sisters came to her again, she was one of them this time, kissing them too . . . touching the sisters as they had touched her. This was her privilege now, they explained, and this was an expression of her love for them and theirs for her. She was to participate often in the ritual in the next few weeks, and when a new face arrived in the house on Waller Street, it was Sunflower who greeted them, with her blonde hair woven with flowers and her gentle smile . . . Sunflower who had once been Anne . . . she lived mostly on LSD, and she had never been as happy in her life.

'I'hree months after she had come to them, one of the broth-ers took her as his own. His name was Moon, and he was tall and thin and beautiful, with silver hair and gentle eyes. He took her to bed with him every night, and cradled her, and in some ways he reminded her of Lionel. She went everywhere with him, and often he would turn to her with his mystic smile.

'Sunflower . . . come to me . . .' She knew the magic of what pleased him now, knew best how to warm the herb potions he drank, when to bring him drugs, when to touch his flesh. And now, when a newcomer arrived, and they performed the ritual, it was Sunflower who went to the sisters first, gently pouring the warm oil over them, welcoming them to their tribe, and letting her swift fingers prepare them for the rest of the tribe. Moon was always very proud of her, and gave her extra acid tabs because of it. It was strange how different life was now from what it had once been. It was filled with bright colours and people that she loved, people who loved her too. There was nothing left of the lonely ugliness of her life. She had forgotten all of them. And when, in the spring, Moon felt her belly and told her she was with child, and could no longer participate in the ritual, she cried.

'Don't cry, little love . . . you must prepare for a much greater ritual than that. We will all be there with you when this tiny moonbeam pierces the skies and comes to you, but until then . . .' He cut down on her acid tabs, although he let her smoke as much marijuana as she wished. And he laughed at her when it increased her appetite.

The baby was just beginning to show when she walked down Haight Street one day, and saw a face she knew she recognised from the past, but she wasn't quite sure who it was. She returned to Moon in the house on Waller Street with a pensive air.

'I've seen someone I know.'

It didn't particularly worry him. They all saw people they knew at times, in their minds and hearts, and occasionally in more concrete ways. His wife and child had died in a boating accident just before he had walked out of his house in Boston one day and come here. He saw them in his mind's eye, much of the time, especially during the ritual. For Sunflower to see someone she knew now surprised him not at all. It was a sign of her rising to a higher state, and that pleased him. This child, who was part his, would bring her even higher before it came. 'Who was it, child?'

'I'm not sure. I can't remember his name.' He had let her have one of the rare acid tabs he allowed her the night before, and the name Jesus kept coming to her mind, but she was sure it wasn't him.

Moon smiled at her. Later, she would have more mushrooms and acid again, but she had to remain pure for the coming child, she could have only just enough to keep her in an enlightened state. But she could not soar too high now, or it would frighten the child. And this baby belonged to all of them after all. They had all shared in it, the brothers and the sisters. Moon felt certain that it had been conceived during her first night, when she was the centre of the ritual. The child would be specially blessed and as he reminded her of that the name John came into her mind, clearly, and then suddenly she remembered him.

Chapter 23

'Are you sure?' Lionel stared at him disbelievingly. John had done this to him twice before. They had both dropped out of school three months before, much to everyone's despair, and they had come to San Francisco to search for Anne. Ward had refused to hear about it from Faye, and Bob Wells was afraid they were using it as an excuse to drop out of school, go to San Francisco, and join the gays living freely there.

But Lionel insisted that Anne would go there. It was a haven for runaway kids, and though he didn't tell his parents, he felt certain that the runaways could live there for years without being recognised or turned in. There were thousands of them, crushed into tiny apartments, living like ants in the houses of the Haight-Ashbury, the houses painted a riot of colours, with flowers and rugs and incense and drugs and sleeping bags everywhere. It was a place and a time that would never come again, and Lionel instinctively felt that Anne was part of it. He had felt it from the first moment he'd arrived. It was just a question of finding her, if they could. He and John had combed the streets for months without success, and there wasn't much time left for them. They had promised to return to school by June for the summer session to make up for the time they'd lost.

'If you don't find her in three months,' Bob Wells had said, 'then you have to give up. You can only search for so long. She could be in New York, or Hawaii, or Canada.' But Lionel knew he was wrong. She would come here to search for the love she felt she'd never had from them. John agreed with him, and now he was certain that he'd seen her walking in a daze near Ashbury, wrapped in a purple bed sheet, with a crown of flowers on her hair, her eyes so glazed he almost wondered if she had seen him at all. But for an instant, just an instant, he had been certain that she had known who he was, and then she had drifted off again. He had followed her to an old broken-down house that seemed to be housing an entire colony of obvious druggies and runaways. The smell of incense wafted right out into the street, and there must have been twenty of them on the steps, singing an Indian chant, and holding hands, crooning and laughing softly and waving at friends. And as she came to the stairs, they parted like the Red Sea for her, helping her up the stairs through their midst, as a grey-haired man waited for her in the doorway, and then carried her inside as John watched. It was the strangest sight he had ever seen and he tried to explain it to Lionel, describing her again.

'I have to admit, it sounds like her.' But the others John had found had too. Every day they split up and wandered through the Haight-Ashbury looking for her. If she was there, it was amazing they hadn't found her yet. And at night, they went back to the hotel room they had rented with the money Lionel had borrowed from Faye. They usually ate a hamburger quietly somewhere; they never went to a single gay bar. They kept to themselves.

In the mornings, they started all over again. It was a labour of love, the like of which Faye had never seen. She had flown up several times to join them in their search, but as Lionel finally explained, she only hampered them. She stood out in the crowd of flower children; her shirts were starched, and even with her jewellery reduced to a minimum it was still too much – her jeans were too clean. She looked exactly what she was, the mother of a runaway from Beverly Hills, looking for her child, and they ran from her like rats. Finally, Lionel had told her straight out. 'Go home, Mum, we'll call you if we see anything. I promise.' She had gone back then to work on a film. She had urged Ward to take a co-producer on this one, because he was drinking so heavily, and things had gone from bad to worse with them. He still refused even to speak to Lionel. And when Lionel called her to report on what he had seen in the Haight-Ashbury, the moment Ward heard his voice, he hung up on him. It made communication with Faye extremely difficult for Lionel and Faye was furious. Eventually, she put in a separate phone for Lionel to call her on. But she noticed that the children avoided their brother as well; they were afraid of what their father would do if they talked to him. The twins never answered the phone Lionel called her on, as if Ward would know if they had talked to him. They had taken him at his word, and Lionel was abandoned by all save Faye, who loved him more than ever before, out of compassion, her own loneliness, and for what he was doing to find Anne. She spoke to Mary Wells as often as she could and expressed her gratitude for John's help. They seemed to have accepted the situation gracefully. They loved their son, and they accepted hers as well. It was far more than she could say for Ward, who had never spoken to the Wells since the morning Bob had thrown him out, the day he'd broken the news to them.

Things were no longer the same between Ward and Faye either. He had actually gone to the Super Bowl with Greg despite Anne's running away. He had insisted that the police would find her eventually, and when they did he would punish her, and put her on restriction for the next ten years if that was what it took to put some sense into her. But it was as though he couldn't cope with anything more, and he left with Greg, and had a great time at the Super Bowl. He seemed surprised to learn that the police had not located Anne when he came back, and in the ensuing weeks, he began pace the floor at night, pouncing on the phone the moment it rang. He finally understood that it was serious, and the police had told them bluntly that it was possible that their daughter was dead, or that she was alive and they would never find her again. It was like losing two children at once, and Faye already knew that they would never recover from it. She had buried herself in her work to ease the pain, to no avail, spending whatever time she could with the twins when they were free. But they felt it too. Vanessa was quieter than she had ever been before, her big romance died shortly after it began, and even Valerie was more subdued. She hardly seemed to wear makeup any more or go out. Her miniskirts were less intentionally shocking and her wardrobe hadn't grown. It was as though they all waited to hear something that they might never hear again, and as each day passed Faye grew more fearful that her youngest child was dead.

She began going to church, which she hadn't done in years, and she said nothing at all to Ward when he didn't come home at night. At first, he came home at one or two o'clock, when the bars closed, and it was easy to see where he'd been, but eventually he began not to come home at all. The first time it happened, Faye felt sure he had been killed. But when he walked in at six o'clock the next morning, tiptoeing in with the newspaper under his arm, there was a look on his face which frightened her. He wasn't drunk, he was not hung over, he offered her no explanation at all, and suddenly she remembered a name she hadn't thought of in years . . . Maisie Abernathie . . . she remembered when Ward had gone to Mexico with her for five days fourteen years before, and Faye knew that although it obviously wasn't the same girl, it was the same look on his face . . . the same way of avoiding her eyes, and suddenly she completely withdrew from him. He came home less and less, but she was so numbed by pain and tragedy that she felt nothing any more. She was barely hanging on to her own sanity. Her days were filled with work, her nights were filled with guilt, and in between she did whatever she could for the twins – but their entire family had fallen apart in a few brief moments.

Eventually she heard the rumours at MGM. He was involved with the star of an important daytime TV show, and according to rumour, the affair was serious. She just prayed that it wouldn't turn up in the columns so she wouldn't have to explain it to the girls. She had enough on her hands just then, and just when she thought she couldn't stand any more Lionel called her. He had gone out with John that afternoon and followed the girl John had been so sure was Anne, and he was sure of it now too. She looked drugged and completely dazed, and she was heavier than she had been before, and wrapped up in what looked like a purple sari, but they were both sure it was Anne.

Tears rolled down Faye's cheeks as she listened. 'Are you sure?'

Lionel said that they almost were, as sure as they could be. She was so dazed-looking and so wrapped up in her strange garb, surrounded by the members of her odd little sect, it was difficult to get close enough to her to find out if it was Anne. It wasn't as if one could yell 'Anne' and have her wave back. Lionel hated to raise his mother's hopes and then disappoint her. 'No, we're not sure, Mum. And we wanted to know what you want us to do now.'

'The police told us to call them.'

'What if it's the wrong girl?'

'Apparently, it happens all the time. She'll probably turn out to be another runaway they're looking for. They said not to hesitate to call if we think we know where she is, and there's a Father Paul Brown up there who knows every kid there. He helps them out all the time.' The boys knew who he was, and agreed to contact him as well as the police. 'Do you think I should fly up tonight?' She had nothing else to do at night now once she left work. She never saw Ward. He made almost no pretence about coming home at night, and he seemed to be waiting for her to confront him about it, but she didn't have the strength. She wondered if the rumours were true, that it was serious. It seemed incredible after all these years to get divorced, except that that looked extremely likely now . . . if they could just find Anne . . . and get Lionel back in school first . . . then she could deal with Ward's affair . . . and a divorce . . . Her private line for Lionel rang at midnight that night, and she knew it could only be he. Ward never called any more when he wasn't coming home and he would call her on their usual line.

She picked the phone up and held her breath. 'Li?'

'The police think it's her too. We pointed her out to them today. They have half a dozen undercover cops working narcotics details out there, and looking for runaways. And they have been to talk to Father Brown. Apparently her name is Sunflower. He knows who she is. But he doesn't think she's as young as Anne.' Anne would be fourteen and a half by now, but she had always looked older than her years, as they all knew, especially recently. He also didn't tell Faye the rest of what Father Brown had said, that she was living in a sect that indulged in strange sexual and erotic practices that involved group sex. They had all been busted several times, but it seemed impossible to prove either what went on, or that any of them were in fact minors. Everyone claimed to be over eighteen, and it was impossible to prove differently. He had also told them that LSD was involved heavily in what they did, and 'magic mushrooms', as peyote was called. The worst of it was that this girl they were following was with child. But he didn't dare tell Faye that yet. If it was the wrong girl, there was no point worrying her about that. 'Mum, do you want her arrested, or just questioned?' They had never come this close before, and Faye felt her heart sag as she thought of her child. It had been five months since she had seen Anne, and God only knew what had happened to her in that time. She didn't dare think of it, and forced herself to concentrate on what Lionel had asked.

'Can't they just take her away, and have you have a good look at her?'

Lionel sighed. He'd been over that all day with them. 'They can, if it turns out to be Anne. But if not, and if the girl isn't a runaway, and is of age, she can sue them for false arrest. Most of those hippies won't, but they're pretty cautious about that. I guess they've been burned a couple of times.' He sounded so tired, her heart went out to him, and Faye sighed. She wanted Anne back, at all costs.

'Tell them to do whatever they have to, sweetheart. We've got to know if it's her.'

He nodded at his end. 'I'm meeting the undercover guys at ten o'clock tomorrow morning. They're going to stake out the house, and follow her again. If we can just talk to her, we will. If not, they'll bust her for being under the influence, or something like that.'

Faye sounded shocked. 'Is she on drugs?'

Lionel hesitated as he looked at John. They were both sick to death of the Haight-Ashbury, the filth, the drugs, the scum, the scams, the kids. They were almost ready to give up, but now . . . if it could be her . . . 'Yeah, Mum. It looks like she is. If that's Anne. She doesn't look too great.'

'Is she hurt?' There was such anguish in Faye's voice that it tore at his heart.

'No. Just spaced out. And she's living in a pretty strange place. It's some kind of Eastern sect.'

'Oh Christ . . .' Maybe she had shaved her head. Faye couldn't imagine it. The whole place had been beyond her when she had gone up to meet Lionel and John to look for her before. She had actually been relieved when they had sent her away. But now she wanted to go back. She suddenly sensed that it could be Anne this time, and she wanted to be there too. She could still envisage her as she had been the day she was born. It was hard to believe it was so long ago.

'We'll call you tomorrow, Mum. As soon as we know something.'

'I'll be in the office all day.' And then, 'Should I make a reservation on an afternoon flight, just in case?'

He smiled into the phone. 'Just hang on. I'll call you either way, whether it's Anne or not.'

'Thank you, sweetheart.' He was the dearest son a woman could want, and so what if he was gay. He was a better son to her than Greg had ever been, although she loved them both, but Greg lacked his sensitivity. He would never have dropped out of school for three months to look for Anne. In fact, when he had come home at Easter, he had said that he thought

Lionel was nuts. Ward had glared at him instantly for speaking the forbidden name, and she had to control herself not to lash out at him in front of Greg. She had had all she could take, and maybe it would be a relief to get a divorce from him. But she couldn't think of that now. All she could think about was Anne.

She lay awake long after speaking to Lionel, thinking of Anne when she had been a little girl, the things she had done, the funny things she'd said, the way she'd hidden so much of the time, the way she'd clung to Lionel. The timing of her birth had been unfortunate, Faye realised now, but that was no one's fault. Disaster had struck only weeks after she'd been born, and Faye had had her hands full selling the house, their antiques, her jewellery, moving them all into the hideous little house in Monterey Park, and then Ward leaving them, and her trying to support them all herself. Anne had more or less got lost in the shuffle of it all. The others had been just old enough not to need her quite as much, and she had given all her time to them before that. But not to Anne . . . never to Anne . . . she had worked ever since then, and Anne had got tossed in with the pack. Faye could remember moments now when the nurse had come to her, months after Anne had been born, asking if she wanted to hold the child, or give her her next bottle, and Faye had told her, 'Not now . . . I don't have time.' She had brushed her off again and again, and Anne had paid the price for it. How could you tell a child like that that you *did* care, that you always had, but that you just hadn't had the time . . . what right did one have to the child if one had no time for it? And yet, when she had been conceived, their life had been so easy, and she had had all the time in the world. Bad timing, bad luck . . . bad mother, she told herself again and again as she lay in the big empty bed, thinking about Anne, and wondering if it was too late, if Anne would hate her for the rest of her life. It was possible, she recognised that now. Some things could never be mended again, like her relationship with Ward . . . and with this child . . . and his

271

with Lionel . . . the fabric of their family seemed to have been irreparably rent in the past few months, and it weighed on her like a rock.

She got up at six o'clock, having slept not a wink all night. But she couldn't sleep now, wondering if the girl Lionel had seen was Anne. She showered, and dressed, waited for the twins to leave for school, and then went to her office at MGM. It amazed her that Ward was making no pretence at all. He didn't even call her, or try to explain where he had spent the night. Once in a while he came home, and she asked no questions of him. And now, when he did show up, he slept in Greg's room, and they spoke not at all.

She caught a glimpse of him as she walked down the hall later that morning, but she said nothing to him. She didn't want to say anything about Anne yet. There was no point until she was sure she had been found, and it wasn't sure at all. Not until she got the call just after noon and her heart almost stopped. Her secretary told her Lionel was on the line, and she hit the button hurriedly on her phone.

'Li?'

'It's okay, Mum, relax.' He was shaking from head to foot, but he didn't want her to know that. It had been hairy getting her out of them, but the police had handled everything, and no one was hurt, not even Anne. She was a little dazed. But she didn't even seem upset to have been removed, although the old guy had been. He had waved a staff at them and said the gods would punish them for stealing his child. But she had just let them carry her away, and she had smiled at Lionel, and now she seemed to know who he was. But she was also very high on dope, and it was possible that when she came down, she would be mad as hell. They were prepared for that. The cops were used to it and there was a doctor standing by.

Faye held her breath, and then her words exploded on the phone. 'Is it Anne?' She closed her eyes.

'Yes, Mum, it is. And she's all right. More or less . . .' They had found her at last.

He looked at John again. The last months had formed a bond between them that they both knew would last for the rest of their lives. It was as though they were married to each other by now. But Lionel forced his mind back to his mother at the other end of the line. 'She's fine, Mum. We're at Bryant Street, with the police, and they'll remand her into my custody, if you want. I'll bring her home in a day or two when she's had a chance to adjust.'

'Adjust to what?' He had a lot to tell her, which he couldn't tell her yet. Not over the phone at least. She was going to have to get prepared.

'She's been away from us for a long time, Mum. It takes a little adjustment to get used to the real world again. She's led a very different life for the last few months.' He was looking for a tactful way to say it to her, but he hoped she never heard the tales the police had told him. They knew the sect well, and their rituals. She would have died if she knew what Anne had been through, although Anne looked none the worse for wear. In fact, Lionel thought she looked happier than she had in years, except that most of that was probably the drugs, and she was probably not going to be nearly as happy when she came down from them. The police had discussed the possibility of bringing charges for being under the influence, but since she was fourteen years old, and had probably been coerced, they had decided not to press any charges at all. They wanted to know if the Thayers wanted to press any charges against the members of the sect for abducting or seducing her, and Lionel knew his parents would have to decide that. Faye was still trying to decipher what Lionel was telling her.

'Is she on drugs?'

He hesitated, but the truth had to be told. 'I'd say so, yes.'

'Hard drugs? Like heroin . . .' Faye's face went pale at her end. Her life would be over if that was the case, people never got off heroin, but Lionel was quick to put her mind at rest.

'No, no, more like marijuana, and probably some LSD and other hallucinogens.' He was becoming very expert about all that, and Faye sighed.

'Are the police holding her?'

'No. I thought I'd take her back to our hotel, let her take a bath and unwind . . .' (ie, come down . . .)

'I'll catch the next plane up.'

Lionel gritted his teeth, He wanted desperately to clean her up before Faye arrived, and the 'next plane' didn't give him much time, also there was something else that Faye would have to know, and it was easy to see now. 'Mum, there's something you ought to know . . .' She had known instinctively that there was something he wasn't telling her. Anne had been hurt . . . something . . . 'Mum?'

'What is it, Li?'

'She's pregnant, Mum.'

'Oh my God.' At that, Faye burst into tears. 'She's fourteen years old.'

'I know that. I'm sorry, Mum . . .'

'Do they have the boy?'

He didn't have the heart to tell her that the child had probably been fathered, not by a 'boy', but by the thirty or so male members of the sect. Instead, he was vague and said they'd have to leave that to Anne. It was difficult for Faye to regain her composure after that, and she made a hasty note on her office pad, 'Call Dr Smythe'. He would arrange an abortion for her. He had taken care of the star of one of her films the year before, and if he wouldn't do a child of Anne's age, she'd take her to London or Tokyo. She didn't have to go through with this. She'd probably been raped. Somehow, the. idea that Anne was pregnant was more horrible than the rest of this whole grim affair and she had to remind herself to be grateful that the girl had been found at all. She was still crying when she hung up the phone, and buried her face in her hands for a moment before taking a deep breath, blowing her nose, and straightening her shoulders to go down the hall to see Ward. He had to be told. Anne was his child too, however little he and she had in common now. She wondered how they would handle the division of their business life. So far they had gone on as before, but that couldn't go on forever either. And now that Anne had been found, Lionel would be coming home. And she had no excuses left not to confront Ward. She stopped outside his office, and his secretary jumped nervously.

'Is Mr Thayer in?' But she knew he was. She had seen him only moments before.

The secretary looked at her anxiously, dropped a pencil on the floor, and then tried to avoid Faye's face. 'No . . . he's not . . .'

'That's a lie.' Faye wasn't in the mood to listen to garbage from anyone. 'I happen to know he's in.' It was a guess, but it worked.

'He's not . . . well, he is . . . but he asked not to be disturbed.'

'Fucking on his office couch again?' Faye's eyes blazed. She knew exactly what was going on, and in their offices. He had one hell of a nerve. 'I didn't know we used the casting couch here quite so much.' She advanced towards his office door and the secretary gasped as Faye turned towards her. 'Don't worry. I'll tell him I overpowered you.' And with that, she opened the door and stepped in. And the scene which met her eyes was reasonably sedate. He and Carol Robbins, the star of 'Follow my World', the daytime soap, were both fully dressed and talking across the desk, but he was holding her hand, and everything about them suggested that they were deeply involved. She was a pretty blonde with long legs and enormous tits. She played a nurse on the show, and the men loved to watch her buttons strain. Faye looked directly at Ward as he let go of the girl's hand, and looked at his wife nervously. She never acknowledged the presence of the girl, and kept her eyes directly on his.

'They found Anne. I thought you'd want to know.'

His eyes grew wide, and it was obvious that he cared a great deal. For a moment, he completely forgot the girl in the room, and looked only at his wife. 'Is she all right?'

'Yes.' She didn't tell him about the drugs or the pregnancy. She didn't want the girl to know. It would have been all over Hollywood by dinnertime. 'She's fine.'

'Who found her? The police?'

Faye shook her head. 'Lionel.' There was a look of victory in her eyes as she watched his face go taut. 'I'm going up there in two hours. If I can, I'll bring her home tonight. You can stop by and see her tomorrow when she's had some sleep.'

He looked surprised at what she said. 'Is there any reason why I can't come home tonight?'

Faye smiled a small bitter smile at that, and finally allowed her gaze to drift to the full-breasted girl sitting across from him.

'That's up to you. Tomorrow seems plenty of time to me.' She looked back at him then and he blushed beneath his white mane and as she looked at him, she saw how much he had aged in the past six months. He was going to be fifty years old soon, but he looked older than that. He had been carousing with this girl, and drinking heavily for the last five months, and before that he had had two severe shocks. It had all taken a toll, but she didn't feel sorry for him. She had aged too, and he had done nothing for her. He had deserted her, and sought solace with this girl. She was almost sorry she hadn't done something like it herself, but she had been too worried about Lionel and Anne. She would have enjoyed an affair just then. But she'd have plenty of time for one now, and at forty-six she wasn't completely over the hill. She looked at him now with utter contempt. 'I'll have Anne call you when we get back, if she wants to talk to you.' He looked horrified at the tone of her voice, the look in her eyes, and he glanced nervously at the buxom blonde, as Faye walked out of his office and closed the door. Outside, his secretary was shredding a Kleenex waiting for him to come out and murder her, but Faye looked perfectly calm as she walked out and nodded to her and hurried down the hall. She had to be at the airport in an hour, and she was just throwing a toothbrush she kept in her desk into her handbag when Ward stormed in.

'Just what do you mean by all that shit?' His face was red, and she couldn't know that he had just told Carol to go home. She had left in tears, accusing him of dumping her, which he was considering seriously. He was still married to Faye, as far as he was concerned, although she seemed to have forgotten it. And the affair had been begun for 'fun' supposedly and had got out of hand in the last few weeks.

Faye looked up at him uninterestedly. Part of it was an act, although part of it was for real. 'I don't have time to talk to you. My flight is at three o'clock.'

'Fine. Then we can talk on the plane. I'll come up with you.'

'I don't need your help.' Her eyes were cold and his were sad.

'You never did. But she's my child too.' Faye was momentarily silenced by that.

She looked up at him finally, unable to resist the urge to hurt him again, he had already hurt her so much recently. 'Are you bringing your friend?'

He looked down at his wife. 'We have to talk about that one of these days.' She knew it too, and she nodded at him, but they didn't mean it quite the same way.

'I wanted to get things settled with Anne and Lionel, before I tackled you on that. But I guess in a few weeks, everything will be relatively normal again, as much as it ever will be. I'll have time to talk to a lawyer then.'

'Have you already made up your mind?' He looked depressed, but he wasn't surprised. He hadn't done anything to prevent her from deciding that, and it was probably too late now. He felt defeated by life. His marriage was over, his son was a queer, his daughter had run away from them, and God only knew what had happened to her since she had. It was devastating to contemplate it all, but Faye seemed unswayed by all of it. She was remarkable. She never drowned. She just kept swimming until she reached the shore again, and she looked as though she just had. He was happy for her. 'I'm sorry it's come to this.'

She spoke quietly as she stood up. She was ready to leave. 'So am I. And I would assume that you're the one who's made up his mind. You don't even call to make excuses any more. You just don't come home at all. I'm surprised you haven't just moved your clothes out yet. I keep coming home at night, expecting to find your things gone.'

'Nothing has reached that point, Faye.'

'I don't see how you can say that. You've walked out, you just haven't bothered to explain it yet.' It seemed wrong to be fighting when Anne had just been found. They should have been shouting with relief, except that there was so much bitterness between them now. And they had avoided each other for so long.

'I haven't known what to say to you, Faye.'

'Apparently. You just walked right out of our lives.'

He knew it was true, and it was the second time in their life he had done that, but he didn't have the strength she had. Carol had come along, and it had made him feel like a man again. It softened the blow of his son turning out to be gay . . . it was no longer a reflection on him . . . he was okay . . . but in the process he had walked right over Faye. He saw that now. But how could he explain it to her? There was no way that he could. She walked past him to the office door.

'I'll call you as soon as we're back.'

Ward looked at her sheepishly. 'I made a reservation on the three o'clock flight too. I figured that was the one you'd be on.'

'There's no point in both of us going up.' She really didn't want him along. She had enough on her mind, especially with Lionel saying Anne might be on drugs, and the pregnancy they'd have to get rid of as soon as possible. All she needed was Ward making excuses for what a sonofabitch he'd been. She didn't want to hear it now. It just wasn't the time. She looked at him in exasperation and he begged with his eyes.

'I haven't seen her in five months, Faye.'

'Couldn't you wait another day?' He didn't move from where he stood, and she looked at him and sighed. He was just making this more difficult. She looked suddenly resigned. 'Fine. I have a studio car downstairs.' She turned and walked out the door, and he followed her. He said not a word to her on the way to the airport; it was clear that she had no desire to talk to him. Their seat assignments were not together on the flight, and when the man at the desk attempted to do them a favour and shift some other people around, she discouraged him. There was no doubt in Ward's mind as they boarded the plane separately, that his marriage to Faye was over. And the bitch of it was that the other girl didn't mean a damn to him. She had just been a way of confirming his own masculinity to him and soothing the pain, but it was too late to try and explain that to Faye. She agreed to share a cab to Lionel's hotel with him, although she looked him straight in the eye and laid down the law to him.

'I just want to make things clear to you, Ward. Those two boys have just devoted five months of their lives to finding her. They gave up a term in school, and they've gone looking for her every day. If it were up to the police, we still wouldn't know where she was. So if you say one ugly word to either of them, I am never ever going to see you again, and I will sue you for every dime you've got, just to get even with you. If you want a friendly divorce, my friend, be decent to your son and John Wells. Is that clear?' Her eyes were rock hard, and his wore the same look of sorrow she had seen in them all day. He looked like a beaten man these days, but it was his own damn fault as far as she was concerned.

'And if I don't want a friendly divorce?'

'Then don't even try and ride into the city with me, Ward.' She raised an arm to hail a cab for herself and he pulled it down harder than he had meant to, but he was desperate now.

'That isn't what I meant. Why are you so sure I want a divorce? I haven't agreed to that. I haven't said anything at all about that.'

She laughed bitterly at him outside the airlines terminal. 'Don't be ridiculous. I've hardly seen you for the last four months, you never even come home at night, and you expect me to stay married to you? You must take me for an even bigger fool than I am.' Besides which he had caused damage which she suspected could never be repaired.

'You're not the fool, Faye, I am.'

'I completely agree with you. But this is neither the time nor the place to discuss it.' She looked at him with immeasurable irritation. 'I really don't know why in hell you came along.'

'To see Anne . . . and talk to you . . . it's been so long, Faye . . .'

'That's not my fault.'

'I know that. It's mine.' He seemed perfectly willing to take the blame. As though he had come to his senses at last. But it was too late. For both of them.

She looked at him sceptically now. 'What happened, did your little soap-opera nurse call it quits this morning when I walked in on you in your office?'

'No. As a matter of fact, I called it quits with her.' More or less. She had left in a rage because he said he was going to San Francisco with Faye, and he had told her he'd talk to her about it when he got back. But he had every intention of telling her it was over between them, whether Faye wanted to stay married to him or not. She was twenty-two years old, and he was beginning to feel ridiculous with her. It was all over. It had been foolish and insane, but it was what he had needed at the time. What he needed now was Faye. He knew now that he always had, yet she had been so locked in her own pain that he couldn't reach her any more. They had had nothing to give each other for a short time, yet all he wanted now was another chance – if she'd listen to him, but she was showing no sign of it now. She had hailed a cab, yanked open the door, and was staring at him.

'Are you coming, Ward?'

'Did you hear what I said? I told you, it's over with that girl.'

'I don't give a damn.'

'Fine. Just so you know where we stand.'

'And just so you know where we stand, Ward; we stand finished. Over. Finito. Through. Is that completely clear?' She gave the driver the address and sat back against the seat.

'I don't happen to agree with you.'

She was so furious she wanted to punch him, but she had to restrain herself. She attempted to lower her voice so the driver wouldn't hear, and went on arguing with him. 'You've got one hell of a fucking nerve. For half a year, you abandon us, shit all over me, and make a fool of yourself with a girl almost thirty years younger than you are, and now magnanimously you decide to come back. Well, go fuck yourself, Ward Thayer. I want a divorce.' She saw the driver glance in the windscreen mirror, but Ward took no notice of him.

'I want to be married to you.'

'You're a sonofabitch.'

'I know I am. But we've been married for twenty-one years and I don't want to quit now.'

'Why not? You had no trouble quitting five months ago.' But they both knew why. The shock of Lionel had been too great for him. She had always known it would be, and she felt a stirring of compassion for him now.

'You know what that was all about.'

'That's no excuse for walking out on me.'

'I had no other way to prove my masculinity again.'

'That's a miserable excuse.'

'But it happens to be true.' He stared out the window and then back at her again. 'You'll never know what that did to me.'

'And now? Are you going to punish him again?'

'I'm grateful that he found Anne.' But his voice told its own tale.

'But you'll never forgive him, will you?'

'I can never forget what he is.'

'He's your son, Ward. And mine.'

'It's different for you.'

'Maybe. But I love him anyway. He's an extraordinary young man.'

Ward sighed. 'I know that . . . I don't know what I feel any more. I've been hurting and confused for so long, it's not easy to sort out now . . . and there's Anne . . .' Faye frowned, thinking of what Lionel had said. She wondered if she should warn Ward, if that would be too much of a shock for him too.

Her voice was gentle for the first time in months when she spoke to him again. 'Lionel thinks she's on drugs.' He immediately looked up at her with a worried frown.

'What kind?'

'He's not sure yet. Marijuana, LSD . . .'

'It could be worse, I guess.'

'It is.' Faye went on. 'She's pregnant too.' Ward closed his eyes and then opened them again and looked at her.

'What's happened to us all in the last six months? Our whole damn life has fallen apart.'

She smiled gently at him. What he said was true. But in time, they would put it together again, they'd crawl out of it. They had before. He looked at her, and took her hand.

'We've both been through hell.' She didn't disagree with him, and she didn't pull her hand away. They needed each other now, if only for the next few hours, and she was suddenly glad he had come along. Even if they never saw each other again after this.

The cab hurtled into town, as they both sat, lost in their own thoughts, thinking of their little girl.

Chapter 24

They arrived at the San Marco Hotel shortly after five o'clock. It was a small unassuming hotel off Divisadero Street, and had been John and Lionel's home for more than four months. Faye looked up at it for an instant before hurrying inside with Ward on her heels. She knew that their room was on the third floor, from her last trip up, and she headed quickly up the stairs before the desk clerk could say anything to her. She didn't want to talk to anyone now. She just wanted to see Anne. She even forgot that Ward was with her, as she rapped softly on the door. A moment later Lionel appeared. He looked at her through the narrow opening, seemed to hesitate, and slowly opened the door. And from where she stood, Faye could see the still form lying there, her back to her. She was wearing Lionel's bathrobe, her hair had grown long and her feet were bare, and for an instant Faye thought she was asleep. Then she turned slowly to see who it was, her face tear-stained, her eyes dark-rimmed and huge in the suddenly narrow face. Faye was instantly taken aback, but she didn't want to let on. Anne had completely changed in the five months she'd been gone. She was thinner, looked more grown-up, and there was something so different about her face that Faye wasn't even sure she would have recognised her. She was almost sure she would not have from a photograph and was grateful that John had.

'Hello, sweetheart.' Faye advanced slowly towards the bed, almost afraid she'd frighten her away, like a wounded bird. Anne gave a soft moan and huddled further into a ball as she turned away again. She was coming down from the hallucinogens she

283

had taken on and off for so long, and Lionel and John had been feeding her orange juice and candy bars to keep up her strength. And a while before they had forced her to eat a hamburger they had brought in. She had thrown up after eating it, but she looked better now; at least to John and Li. They had seen what she looked like when the police first picked her up several hours before, and Lionel had cringed at the thought of his mother seeing her then. He looked from her to his parents now, and he was stricken by the look in his mother's eyes. He didn't dare look directly at Ward. It was the first time he had seen him since that terrible day when he had walked in on him with John. But at least he had come, if not for them, then for Anne.

'She's not feeling too hot, Mum.' He spoke to her in a soft voice and Anne didn't turn around as John handed her another candy bar which she took in a trembling hand. She felt hungry and sick all at once, and she didn't want to be here. She wanted to go back to them . . . to the Haight . . . to Moon . . . to the ritual . . . she belonged with them . . . Tears choked her throat as she tried to swallow a bite of the candy bar, and she lay back and closed her eyes.

'Is she sick?' They spoke of her as though she weren't there, and Lionel hated to explain it all to them.

'She's just coming down from some of the stuff she's been on. She'll be all right in a few days.'

'Can we take her home tonight?' Faye was anxious to get her home, to have her seen by the doctor who had taken care of her for years, and to get her to Dr Smythe before it was too late for him to take care of the other problem. She hadn't seen Anne from the front yet and didn't know how far along she was, but she assumed that it wasn't too late. There was no reason to think it was. But Lionel was shaking his head in answer to what she had said, and Faye frowned.

'I don't think she's up to travelling yet, Mum. Give her a day or two to adjust.'

'To what?' Faye looked shocked. 'To us?'

Ward stepped forward for the first time, and avoided his son's eyes while speaking to him. 'Has she seen a doctor yet?' Lionel shook his head. 'I think she should.' He walked slowly around the bed, and looked down at his youngest child. She was still filthy, caked with dirt, her face stained with tears, and the eyes were huge in her face. He gently sat down and stroked her hair, feeling tears sting his own eyes. What had brought this child to that? How could she have run away from them? 'It's so good to see you again, Anne.' She didn't shrink from his hand, but she watched him like a frightened animal. He let his eyes rove slowly down her limbs, and they stopped midway and moved on. He tried not to register the shock he felt. It was much too late to do something about the pregnancy. He turned towards Faye with a look of despair and then stood up, and glanced at Lionel again. 'Do you know a doctor in town?'

'The police gave us a name. He thought they should examine her anyway. And they want to talk to you and Mum.' Ward nodded; at least he was able to speak to the boy, but he couldn't bring himself to look at John. The room's only bed, a double that looked barely that wide, on which Anne lay now, spoke for itself and he tried not to think of it. One drama was enough, and he wanted to speak to the police now. He took out his pen and jotted the names down of the men who had cooperated in finding her, and particularly the two who had brought her in. Lionel said they would have all the details, and Ward shuddered at the prospect of hearing them. But he knew they would have to know eventually.

Faye went over and sat on the bed next to Anne, as Ward had, but this time the girl flinched. It was like having a desperately sick child and visiting her in the hospital. Faye's eyes were riveted to her face and Anne started to cry.

'Go away . . . I don't want to be here . . .'

'I know, sweetheart . . . but we'll all be going home soon . . . to your own house . . . and your own bed . . .'

'I want to go back to Moon and my friends.' She sobbed. She was a fourteen-year-old girl and she sounded like she was five. Faye didn't ask who Moon was. She assumed that he was the father of the child. As the thought came to mind, she glanced down at Anne's belly, assuming it would still be flat, and she gasped in shock as she saw it sticking out. Faye knew from experience she was at least four or five months gone. She decided to ask right away, much to Ward's chagrin. He didn't want to push her yet. Lionel was right. She needed time to adjust to all of them again. She had gone far, far away, and she had been away from them for a long time.

'How pregnant are you, Anne?' She wanted her voice to sound gentle when she asked, but she instantly knew it did not. It sounded nervous and harsh and sharp and Lionel looked at them in despair.

'I don't know how pregnant I am,' Anne answered her with closed eyes. She refused to look at her any more. She hated her. She always had. And she hated her even more now. It was her fault that they had taken her away, her fault they wouldn't let her go back. She had always ruined everything for all of them, pushing them all around, doing everything her way. But she wouldn't this time. They could take her anywhere, and she would escape again. She knew how easy it was now.

'Haven't you seen a doctor yet?' Faye sounded shocked. Anne shook her head again, her eyes closed. And then slowly she opened them.

'My friends took care of me.'

'How long has it been since you had a period?' It was just like talking to the police, only worse, Anne thought. At least they didn't ask her questions like that. She knew she didn't have to answer her. But she always did. Faye just had that kind of way about her. As though she expected everyone to do what she said, and Anne did now.

'Not since I left home,' Faye knew only too well that was five months before, and she cringed at the thought. It must have happened almost as soon as she left.

'Do you know who the father is?' It was an outrageous thing to ask so soon, and Lionel glanced at Ward, wishing he would stop Mum from asking her those things. Anne wasn't ready to be pushed, and he was afraid she would run away again before they got her home. And maybe this time they wouldn't find her. Lionel was afraid of that, but Anne only smiled at the memories.

'Yes.'

'Is it Moon?'

Anne shrugged. But Faye was in no way prepared for what came next.

'Yes. It's all of them.'

Faye's breath caught. That couldn't be right. There had to be some mistake. 'All of them?' She stared uncomprehendingly at the child who was a child no more. She was a woman now, a twisted broken one, but nonetheless she was no longer a little girl, and she was expecting a baby of her own. Suddenly Faye understood and a look of horror came into her eyes.

'Do you mean to tell me that the entire commune fathered this child?'

'Yes.' Anne looked sweetly at her, and sat up for the first time. As she did the room reeled, and she looked to Lionel for help. He came to her and supported her as John handed her a glass of orange juice. They had both suspected something like that from what the police had told them about the sect, but Faye and Ward were not prepared, and now that Anne was sitting up, she looked even more pregnant than she had lying down.

Ward took over now, thinking of what had happened to his innocent child. He looked firmly at Lionel, ignoring Anne. 'I'm going to call those inspectors now.' He had every intention of seeing all those sonsofbitches in jail, and Faye was crying softly as they left the room. She clung to Ward when they got downstairs, and she didn't care who was looking at them now.

'My God, Ward, she'll never be the same again.' He was as afraid as she, but he refused to admit that to her. He was going to help her now, just as Faye had helped him so long ago, given him a career he could never have found himself, taught him everything he knew until he could fly on his own. He would do everything he could, and if she still wanted a divorce afterwards, he would accept it gracefully. She had a right to that after what he'd done. He still felt shaky now, looking at Lionel and John, but he couldn't allow himself to think of that now. They both had to stop blaming themselves, he for Lionel's homosexuality, and Faye for what had happened to Anne. He knew that they were both consumed with guilt, but to what end? It did neither child any good. 'She'll be all right, Faye.' He wished he believed his own words, but above all, he wanted to convince her.

'She's got to get rid of that child, and with the drugs she's been on, God only knows what it will be. It'll be a vegetable.'

'Probably. Do you think it's too late for an abortion?' He looked at his wife hopefully and she laughed bitterly through her tears.

'Did you see her, Ward? She's five months pregnant, at least.' It suddenly dawned on her that she might have even been pregnant when she left home. She didn't think she was, although who knew any more with Anne.

They went to the police station at Bryant Street immediately, and then went upstairs to speak to the juvenile authorities. There were apparently hundreds of cases like this one now. Children were migrating from all over the States, coming to the Haight-Ashbury. Some of them did a lot worse than losing their virginity – some of them lost their lives. There were stories of eleven-year-olds overdosing on heroin or jumping out of windows on LSD. There were illegitimate children being born to thirteen- and fourteen- and fifteen-year-olds, delivered in hallways as their friends sang. One girl had bled to death only six weeks before, and an ambulance had never been called. As they listened, Faye was deeply grateful they had found her at all. She steeled herself to hear the tale they told about the sect Anne had been living with. She wanted to kill them all when she'd heard all of it, and Ward was insistent that he wanted the entire sect put in jail, but the police were discouraging. It would be difficult to bring charges against all of them, and it was impossible to accuse an entire tribe of statutory rape on one girl. Above all, was this what they wanted for Anne? Wasn't it just easier to take her home, get her good psychiatric help, and let her forget the whole thing, instead of subjecting her to a lengthy trial, which wouldn't even come up for a year or two, if not longer than that, and which they probably wouldn't win? The kids would have disappeared by then, their own families, many of them moneyed and influential, would bail their children out. It just didn't make sense. In a year or two, it would all seem like a distant dream, the police said. A nightmare she would soon forget.

'What about her pregnancy? What about this Moon?' Faye wanted to know. And they told her that nothing concrete could be proved against him. He held none of them against their will, and none of the members of the sect would ever testify against him. They doubted that Anne ever would herself, and later they discovered the police were right. She had an unreasoning love for the man, and she refused to talk about him to anyone, even Lionel. It was hopeless, Faye and Ward finally agreed. And as wrong as it seemed, the police were right perhaps. It was best to take her home, get help for her, deliver her safely of the monstrous child, and let her forget it all, if only she'd be willing to. Lionel thought she would, in time, and John said nothing at all. He was still terrified of Mr Thayer, and frightened he would lose control and hit him again, although Lionel swore he wouldn't let that happen again. Ward showed no sign of losing control, except when he spoke of Moon or one of them. His rage was directed at them now, much to John's relief.

They took turns staying with Anne that night, and the next morning the three Thayers discussed the trip home, while John sat with her. Faye was anxious to get her back, and maybe even check her into a hospital, though Lionel thought they should wait a few days. She was fairly clear now, but she was extremely paranoid. He thought she should have a few more days to come down. Ward agreed with Faye, but he couldn't imagine getting her on a commercial airline in the dishevelled, disorientated condition she was in. Eventually, a compromise was reached. Ward called MGM and chartered the studio plane for all of them. It was to pick them up in San Francisco at six o'clock that night and fly them back to Los Angeles. He wanted to see the police once more, and after that he talked to his lawyer, who basically agreed with them. No charges were brought, and at four-thirty that afternoon, they bundled Anne up in a bathrobe Faye had bought for her on Union Street, and they took a cab out to the airport. She sobbed all the way. The four of them felt like kidnappers as the young cab driver stared at them all angrily. Hardly a word was said, and she didn't have the strength to walk, so Ward carried her onto the plane. For the first time in two days, he had a stiff drink once they boarded the plane, and the two boys and Faye all had a glass of wine. It was a difficult trip for everyone and Lionel and John were feeling the strain of being with Ward. He never really spoke to them. Whenever possible he addressed Faye and let her pass the message on, as though he was afraid to contaminate himself by speaking directly to either of them. When the MGM limo dropped the boys off at their place on the way to the Thayer house, John heaved an enormous sigh of relief.

'I just don't know what to say to him.' He took a big gulp of air and looked apologetically at Lionel, who understood perfectly.

'Don't feel badly. Neither do I. But he's just as uncomfortable with us.' It had been an uneasy truce, and Lionel felt sure that he hadn't changed his mind, and wouldn't rescind the family ban on them. Lionel felt no more welcome in the family home than he would have three or four months before, and he was right.

'He acts like being gay is a contagious disease and he's afraid to catch it from us.'

Lionel grinned. It was good to be home, or so he thought. Faye had continued paying for their rooms at the house at UCLA for all these months, and they hadn't seen their roommates since they had dropped out in January. But they couldn't go to Lionel's parents' house or the Wells'. They would have been upset by the tales about Anne. So they walked up the steps now, home for the first time in months, anxious to unpack and settle in.

They were talking about starting the summer sessions in a few weeks. They could both go back to real life now, whatever that was, but they had forgotten what it was like to pretend and hide, and suddenly as they walked into a room full of sophomore and junior boys, drinking beer, they both remembered the agony they had forgotten, after five months of living in the hotel while they looked for Anne. They had to go back into hiding now, and it depressed them both as they put their things away. Lionel wandered into John's room, and they exchanged a look. Suddenly, they wondered if everyone knew about them. They felt as though it could be clearly seen, and Lionel wasn't even sure he cared any more. Yes, he was gay. Yes, he was in love with John. He adopted an almost belligerent air as he went to the kitchen and helped himself to a beer, but no one said anything. Those who knew were glad he had found Anne. One of the others had a runaway sister too, a twelve-year-old, and they hadn't found her yet. Her parents were afraid she was dead, and her brother was convinced she was in San Francisco too. They talked about it for a little while, and Lionel thought there was a funny look in the boy's eyes, as though he wanted to ask him something but didn't dare.

At the Thayer house, everyone was subdued. The twins had been shocked when they had seen Ward carry Anne in. They didn't realise she would look that sick, and when she stood up on shaky legs and they saw her belly sticking out, Vanessa had actually gasped, and Valerie couldn't believe her eyes.

'What's she going to do?' they questioned Faye later that night, who thought she had never felt so tired in her life. She didn't have the answer to that herself.

They took her to the doctor the next day, and were relieved to hear that he could find no evidence of abuse on her.

Whatever she had done, she had done willingly, and there were no marks, no scars. He estimated that the baby was due on October 12, suggested that she recuperate for six weeks after that, assuming the baby came on time, and could comfortably be back in school after the Christmas holiday. She would have lost exactly one year from the time she left, and she could finish eighth grade after the baby came, and go on to high school the following year. They made it sound so easy as Anne stared at them and, with the doctor standing by, Faye brought up what she had discussed with him. It was too late for an abortion of course, which would have been the easiest solution for her, assuming she would have agreed, though Faye would have seen to that. And it was impossible to tell just how many drugs she had taken since she'd conceived, or what effect they'd had. But even if the baby had minor disabilities as a result, there were plenty of childless couples who would be happy to adopt, even with some small defect. The Haight-Ashbury culture had been a real boon for them. There were dozens of babies being put up for adoption now, babies born of girls who would never have got pregnant a few years before. These were mostly girls from middle-class homes, sleeping with boys of the same ilk, in communes that had sprung up. And once the babies came, they weren't interested in them. Some were, of course, but most were not. They wanted to be free, to enjoy their days of sunshine and peace and love, without the burden of responsibility. The doctor would be happy to help, he explained. Why, just in Los Angeles, he knew four couples anxious for such a child. All of them would give the baby a good home, and it would be a blessing for Anne. She would go back to the life of a fourteen-year-old girl, and forget it ever happened. Faye and the doctor smiled and Anne looked at them, horrified, struggling not to scream.

'You want to give my baby away?' She started to cry, and Faye tried to put an arm around her, but she fought her off. 'I'll never do that! Never! Do you hear me!'

But there was no doubt in Faye's mind. They would force her to give the child up. She didn't need to drag some little mongoloid around for the rest of her life, to remind her of a nightmare they all wanted to forget. No, absolutely not. She and the doctor exchanged a speaking look. They had four and a half months to convince her of what was best for her.

'You'll feel differently about it later on, Anne. You'll be happy you gave it up. And it may not be normal anyway.' Faye tried to keep her voice matter-of-fact, but she was panicking inside. What if she ran away again? If she insisted on keeping the child? The nightmare refused to end, and all the way home, Anne huddled on the far side of the car, looking out the window with tears running down her cheeks. When Faye stopped the car at home she tried to reach for her hand, but Anne pulled it away and refused to look at her. 'Sweetheart, you can't keep that child. It would ruin your life.' Faye was sure of it, and Ward agreed with her she knew.

'Yours or Dad's?' She glared at her mother now. 'You're just embarrassed I got knocked up, that's all. And you want to destroy the evidence. Well, what are you going to do with me for the next four months? Hide me in the garage? You can do anything you want, but you can't take my baby from me.' She ran out of the car and Faye lost control, screaming at her as she went. The last few days had been too much for her. The last few months in fact.

'Yes we can. We can do anything we want! You're not even fifteen years old!' She hated herself for saying the words, and by that afternoon, Anne was gone again. But she only went to Lionel's this time, and sat sobbing out her tale to him and John.

'I won't let them take it away from me . . . I won't . . . I won't!' She looked like such a baby herself, it was hard to imagine her with a child. And even though she had grown up in the Haight, she was still so young. Lionel didn't know how to tell her, but he agreed with their mother. As did John. They had talked about it the night before, as they lay in bed, whispering so the other boys wouldn't hear. It had been so much better in the hotel, but now they had to face real life too, not unlike Anne.

'Baby,' Lionel looked at her compassionately, and gently took her hand in his. He looked just like their mother when he did, but Anne never wanted to see the resemblance between the two of them. If she had, she might have loved him less than she did. The fact that he did look so much like Faye was the one thing that brought him a little closer to Ward, though not much any more. 'Maybe they're right. It would be a terrible responsibility, you know, and it's not really fair to impose that on Mum and Dad.'

She hadn't even thought of that. 'Then I'll get a job and take care of it myself.'

'And who'll take care of it while you work? See what I mean? Baby, you're not even fifteen years old . . .'

She started to cry. 'You sound just like one of them . . .' And he never had before. She couldn't stand it from him too. She looked up at him with heartbroken eyes. 'Li, it's my baby . . . I can't give it up.'

'You'll have others one day.'

'So what?' She looked appalled. 'What if they'd given you away because one day they'd have me?'

He had to laugh at the example, and he looked at her so tenderly. 'I think you ought to give it some thought. You don't have to make your mind up right now.'

She agreed to that at least, but when she got home, she got into a huge fight with Val, who demanded that she stay inside the house whenever her friends came around.

'I'll be the laughing stock of school if everyone knows you're knocked up. And you'll be going there in a year yourself, you don't want everyone knowing that.'

Faye admonished her that night for being unnecessarily cruel, but it was already too late. Anne had gone to her room after dinner and packed her bags, and at ten o'clock she was standing in Lionel's living room again.

'I can't live with them.' She told him why, and he sighed. He knew how difficult it was for her, but there wasn't much he could do for her. He gave her his bed that night, and told her they'd figure it out the next day. He called Faye to tell her where she was. She had already called Ward, and Lionel got the impression that he was going to spend the night at home, but he didn't ask. He told his roommates that he was going to sleep on the floor, but of course he slept with John, and reminded Anne to be careful of what she said, because his roommates didn't know that they were gay. The next day, when the three of them went out for a walk, he was embarrassed at the questions she asked, but he tried to be honest with her. 'Do you and John really sleep together every night?'

He started to say something and then changed his mind. 'Yes. We do.'

'Like husband and wife?'

Lionel saw John blush out of the corner of his eye. 'Sort of.'

'That's weird.' She didn't say it meanly and Lionel laughed.

'I guess it is. But that's the way things are.'

'I don't know why people get so upset about that, I mean like Dad. If you love each other, what difference does it make what you are, I mean a man and a woman, or two girls or two men?' He wondered just exactly what she had seen in the commune, and remembered what the police had said. She had probably had numerous homosexual experiences now too, but he didn't ask her that, and hers would have been drug-induced, and as part of a large group probably, given the sect's practices. Lionel didn't want to ask anyway. She might not even have remembered what she'd done. It was very different from what he and John shared, which was a genuine love affair. But he looked at her now. It was odd how she floated between being a woman and a child.

'Not everyone sees it that way, Anne. It's frightening to some people.'

'Why?'

'Because it's different from the norm.'

She sighed. 'Like me being pregnant at fourteen.'

'Maybe.' That was a tough one. And it brought to mind what they were going to do about her. He and John had talked about it for half the night, and they had an idea. Lionel had talked to Faye about it. In some ways it would be easier for Faye and Ward too.

Lionel had been right of course. He had always been an intuitive child, and he wasn't wrong this time. Ward had spent the night. His father answered Faye's phone, but he said not a word to Lionel, and they were back on their old terms of his no longer existing in the Thayers' life. Now that he had found Anne, they could dispense with him again, or at least Ward could. He handed the phone to Faye, and she proposed the idea to Ward when she hung up.

'Lionel wants to know what we think of their taking an apartment near school, and letting Anne stay with them until the baby comes. And after that, she can move out, come back here, and they'll find a roommate to rent her room. What do you think?' She looked at him carefully over coffee. It was nice to have him back in a way, even if it was for one night, or two. He gave her some support in these difficult times. He frowned now, thinking of Lionel's idea.

'Can you imagine what she'd be exposed to with those two?' The thought made him sick and Faye bridled instantly.

'Can you imagine what she did herself in that disgusting commune, Ward? Let's be honest about this.'

'All right, all right. We don't have to go into that.' He didn't want to think about things like that with his little girl. Nor did he want her with John and Lionel, in a fag nest somewhere. But it was obvious that she was not going to come home to them, and it might take some of the strain off him and Faye for a while. The only ones home now were the twins, and they were never there. They were always out with their friends, especially Val. He looked at Faye. 'Let me think about it.'

He still wasn't sure he liked the idea, but the more he thought it over, the more he had to admit that it wasn't such a bad idea. The boys were relieved when Faye told them that. They had come to realise how impossible it was living with the other boys in their old house, and neither of them wanted to pretend any more. At twenty, Lionel was ready to admit he was gay, and John was too.

Faye helped them find a small but attractive apartment in Westwood, not far from where they'd been living with the rest of their friends, and offered to decorate it for them, but John worked his magic in a matter of days, with whatever he had at hand, and Faye couldn't believe how pretty it was. He had bought yards of pale grey flannel and pink silk, and transformed the place, putting fabric on the walls, upholstering two couches they bought for fifty dollars at a garage sale, finding prints in back streets, reviving plants that had looked beyond hope. It looked like a sophisticated apartment done by a professional decorator, and John was thrilled with her praise. His mother was even more proud of him, and bought them a beautiful mirror for over the fireplace. She felt sorry for poor little Anne, and was grateful it wasn't one of her girls.

Anne had never been happier in her life than she was with them. She kept the apartment clean for them. It was even better than the commune she said one night, as John taught her to make roast duck. He was a fabulous cook, and made dinner for them every night. Lionel had gone back to school, for the summer session in cinematography, to make up for the time he had missed, and he'd be caught up by autumn. But John had taken a big step. He knew he didn't want to go to UCLA. He dropped out permanently and got a job with a well-known decorator in Beverly Hills. The guy had the hots for him and it was a pain in the neck rebuffing his advances every day, but the decorating experience he got was fabulous. He got none of the credit and did all the work, but he loved the homes he got to work on, and he told them both about his job every night. He had had it since July, and by late August the guy had finally got the message and was leaving him alone. He had told him about Lionel and that it was serious, and the older man had laughed, knowing it was only a matter of time. 'Kids,' he had laughed. But he was pleased with John's work, so he let him be.

Faye dropped in on them from time to time. Ward had moved back in with her, and they were trying to put the pieces together again. She spoke to Lionel about it when they were alone, but not in front of Anne, and she inquired if he had made any progress about getting her to promise to give up the baby when it came. It was less than two months away now, and the poor thing looked huge. She was uncomfortable in the heat, and the apartment wasn't air conditioned, though John had bought them all fans. He was insisting on paying for half of the apartment now, since he had a job and Lionel was in school, and Faye was touched by how hard he worked and what good care he took of all of them. She looked at her son tenderly one day.

'You're happy, aren't you, Li?' It was important to her to know that. He meant so much to her. And she was fond of John; she always had been, but she was more so now, after him helping to find Anne.

'Yes, I am, Mum.' He had grown up beautifully, even if he wasn't what she and Ward had expected him to be. Maybe that didn't really matter after all. She asked herself a lot of questions about that at times, but it was still impossible to discuss it with Ward.

'I'm glad. Now what about Anne? Will she give the baby up?' The doctor had a couple who were definitely interested. She was thirty-six and he was forty-two; they were both sterile, and the agencies said they were too old to adopt. She was Jewish and he was Catholic, and with all of that there was absolutely no hope, except this way. They didn't even mind the risk of the baby's possible defects from drugs. They were desperate and insisted they would love him or her anyway. And in September, Faye insisted that Anne at least meet them, to give them a chance. They were very nervous and very sweet, and they almost begged the child to give her baby to them. They promised her that she could come to visit him sometimes, although the doctor and their lawyer discouraged that. It had led to some terrible incidents once or twice, and a kidnapping once, after the papers had been signed. It was better to make a clean break, they said, but they would have agreed to anything. The woman had shining black hair, and beautiful brown eyes, a good figure, a bright mind. She was a lawyer, originally from New York, and her husband was an ophthalmologist with features similar to Anne's. The baby could even have looked like them, if it looked like Anne at all, and not the rest of the commune, Faye thought to herself. They were lovely people and Anne felt sorry for them.

'How come they can't have kids?' Anne asked as they drove away and her mother took her back to Lionel's.

'I didn't ask. I just know they can't.' Faye was praying she would be reasonable. She wanted Ward to talk to her too, but he was away. He had begged Faye to come with him, he thought they needed a 'honeymoon' as he put it, now that they were back together again. She had been touched, but she just didn't feel comfortable leaving Anne until after the baby was born. If something happened to her, if she delivered early, which the doctors said teenagers sometimes did . . . and he had warned her that girls in their teens had the hardest time, even harder than women her age, which surprised her. She was forty-six years old now, and babies were the farthest thing from her mind. But she was frightened that Anne would have a hard time, and she refused to go away with Ward. They had some time between films, but she was trying to spend as much of it as she could with Anne. Instead, Ward went to Europe with Greg. Faye thought it would do them both good to get away.

Anne hadn't agreed to anything by the time the baby was due. She was so enormous she looked as though she was having twins, and Lionel felt desperately sorry for her. She seemed to be having pains all the time, and he suspected that she was scared.

He didn't blame her at all; he would have been terrified. He just hoped he was home from school when the baby started to come. If not, John had promised to take a cab home from work and get her to the hospital. It was a lot easier to reach him than Lionel. She had had some crazy idea about having it at home, like they did at the commune, but they had squashed that, and Faye had made them swear that they would call her right away. Lionel had promised, but Anne had begged him not to.

'She'll steal my baby, Li.' The big blue eyes pleaded with him and his heart went out to her. She was frightened all the time now, of everything.

'She won't do anything of the sort. She just wants to be there with you. And no one is going to steal the baby. You have to make up your own mind.' But he was still trying to influence her. He thought his mother was right. At fourteen and a half, she didn't need the burden of a child. She was still a baby herself. And he was even more sure of it the night she began to have labour pains. She panicked and locked herself in her room, sobbing hysterically, and he and John had alternately threatened to break down the door. Eventually, while he talked cajolingly to her, John went out on the roof, slipped in through the window, unlocked the door, and let her brother in. She was sobbing hysterically on the bed, convulsed with pain, and there was water all over the floor. Her waters had broken an hour before, and the pains had grown severe. She threw her arms around Lionel's neck and sobbed, clutching him with each pain.

'Oh Li, I'm so scared . . . I'm so scared . . .' No one had told her it would hurt this much. On the way to the hospital in the cab, she moaned and dug her nails into his hand, and refused to go away with the nurse. She hung on to him and begged him to stay with her, but when the doctor came, he told her to be a good girl, and two nurses wheeled her away while she screamed.

Lionel was visibly shaken and John was pale as they spoke to the quiet older man. 'Can't you give her a sedative?'

'I'm afraid not. It may slow her labour down. She's young, she'll forget it all afterwards.' That seemed difficult to believe and he smiled sympathetically at them. 'It's hard on girls her age, they're not really prepared to go through childbirth, physically or mentally. But we'll get her through and she'll be just fine.' Lionel wasn't as sure. He could still hear her screaming from down the hall, and he wondered if he should be with her. 'Have you called your mother yet?' Li shook his head nervously. It was eleven o'clock at night, and he wasn't sure if they'd be asleep. But he knew she'd be furious if they didn't call, so he dialled his old home number with trembling hands. Ward answered and Lionel spoke at once.

'I'm at the hospital with Anne.'

Ward didn't waste time handing the phone to Faye. For once, he spoke to Lionel himself. 'We'll be right there.' And he was as good as his word. In ten minutes, they were at UCLA Medical Center, looking slightly rumpled, but wide awake. The doctor made an exception, and let Faye stay with Anne, at least as long as she was in the labour room. None of them were prepared for how long it would take. Even the doctor didn't know, although he was usually good at predicting that, but again with teenagers, nothing was sure; she could race through it or it could take three days. She was dilating well, but she would stop at each stage for long hours, begging for release, for drugs, for anything, clutching at her mother's hand, trying to sit up to leave and then collapsing with the pain, clawing at the walls, and begging the nurses to let her go. It was the worst thing Faye had ever seen, and she had never felt so helpless in her life. There was nothing she could do to help the child, and she only left her once to go outside and say something to Ward. She wanted him to call the lawyer first thing the next morning, in case Anne agreed to give the baby up after it was born. They would have her sign the papers immediately. They had to review them again in six months, to make them permanent, but by then the baby would be gone, and hopefully she'd have started a normal life again. Ward agreed to call him the next morning, and she suggested he go home since it could take hours. The three men agreed. Ward dropped Lionel and John off, without saying much to them, and the two boys went upstairs. They were surprised to realise that it was already 4 am and Lionel never got to sleep that night. He crept stealthily out of bed and called the hospital several times, but there was no news of Anne. She was still in the labour room, and the baby had not been born. And she was still there the following afternoon when John came home from work, and found Lionel still sitting by the phone. It was six o'clock and he was amazed.

'My God, hasn't she had the baby yet?' He couldn't imagine it taking so long. She had gone into labour around eight o'clock the night before, and had already been in terrible pain when they got her to the hospital. 'Is she all right?'

Lionel looked pale. He had called the hospital what seemed like a thousand times, had even gone there for a few hours, but his mother didn't even want to come out to talk to him. She didn't want to leave Anne. He noticed a couple waiting nervously in the waiting room with the Thayers' lawyer, and he correctly guessed who they were. They were even more anxious for the baby to come than the Thayers were. And the doctor was guessing only a few more hours now. They had seen the head all afternoon, and she was ready to push, but it was going to be a while. And if there was no progress by eight or nine o'clock that night, he was going to do a Caesarean.

'Thank God,' John said, and both of them found they couldn't eat. They were too worried about her. At seven, Lionel called a cab. He was going back to the hospital.

'I want to be there.'

John nodded. 'I'll come too.' They had spent five months looking for her, another five living with her now. John felt as though she were his little sister too, and the house didn't seem the same without her clothes and her books and her records spread around. He had threatened to put her on restriction once, if she didn't pick up her clothes, and she had laughed and teased him and said she'd tell the whole neighbourhood he was queer. He was desperately sorry for her now. It sounded like a grisly ordeal and when he saw Faye Thayer's face shortly after nine o'clock, he could only begin to imagine what the child was going through.

'They just can't get it out,' Faye reported to Ward, who was back at the hospital too. 'And he doesn't want to do a Caesarean on a child her age, unless he absolutely has to.' What Anne was going through was worse than anything Faye had ever seen. She was shrieking and begging, half delirious with the pain. There was absolutely nothing they could do for her, and the nightmare went on for another two hours, while Anne begged them to kill her . . . the baby . . . anything . . . and then finally, the little head emerged, and as the rest of him came, slowly, tearing his mother wickedly and causing her as much grief as possible right till the end, they all understood why it had been such agony for Anne. The child was huge, just over ten pounds, and Faye couldn't think of worse punishment for her narrow frame. It was as though each man who had entered her had contributed to this child, and he had emerged full grown, a composite of all of them. Faye stood watching him, with tears in her eyes, tears for the pain he had caused Anne, and for the life which would never touch theirs again.

Hours before, Anne had agreed to give him up. She would have agreed to anything then. And the doctor slipped a gas mask on her face now. She never saw the child, never knew how big he was, never felt them sewing her up, and Faye silently left the delivery room, feeling sorry for her own child, for the pain she had borne, for the experience she would probably never forget, the child she would never know, unlike her own, who had caused her joy and pain over the years, but none of whom she regretted having. And now her first grandchild was to be given away, and she would never see him again. He was put in a polyethylene basket and rolled away to the nursery, to be cleaned up, and given to someone else.

Half an hour later, as she and Ward left the hospital, she saw the woman with the dark hair holding him, with tears streaming down her face and a look of love in her eyes. They had waited fourteen years for him, and they accepted him as he was, not knowing who his father was, or what damage the drugs had done. They accepted him with unconditional love, and Faye held tightly to Ward's hand as they left, and took a deep gulp of the night air. The doctor had said that Anne would sleep for several hours. She would be heavily sedated now, thank God, and that night, as she lay in her bed, Faye cried in Ward's arms.

'It was so horrible . . . she screamed so terribly . . .' She sobbed uncontrollably now. It had been almost unbearable watching her, but it was all over now. For all of them. Except the couple with Anne's child. For them it had just begun.

Chapter 25

They kept Anne in the hospital for a week, in an attempt to let the wounds heal, both physically and mentally. The doctor told Faye that they would heal with time. They kept her on Valium, and Demerol for the pain. She had been torn badly by the baby's heed because he was so large. But more than that, they all recognised that she would have emotional scars from this. A psychiatrist came to talk to her every day, but she would say nothing at all to him, she just lay in bed and stared at the ceiling or the wall, and every day after an hour he went away. She said nothing to Faye, or Ward, or the twins, or even Lionel when he and John came, carefully, at a different time from Faye and Ward. Lionel brought her an enormous stuffed bear, and he hoped it didn't remind her of the lost child. The baby had left the hospital three days after it was born. His new parents took him away in an elaborate blue and white outfit by Dior, and two blankets his new grandmother had made. They had sent an enormous arrangement of flowers to Anne, but she had them given to someone else. She wanted no reminder of them. She hated herself for what she had done, but in those first few hours after she woke, she felt so terrible that she never wanted to see him again. It was only now that he was gone that she wished she could have seen his face, just once . . . so she would remember him . . . her eyes filled with tears at the thought. Everyone said she had done the right thing, but she hated them all, and herself most of all. She told Lionel that now, as John fought back tears. If it had been his sister, he would have died for her, and he tried to cheer Anne up now. Even if the jokes were in bad taste, they were heartfelt. He felt terrible for her.

'We could always redo your room in black. I have some great black corduroy at the shop . . . we could drape black tulle over the windows, a few little black spiders here and there.' He squinted artistically, and for the first time in a week she laughed. But when it was time to go home, it was Ward and Faye who came for her. They had talked to Lionel earlier that day, or at least Faye had, and explained that they were taking Anne home now. He and John were free to rent her room to a friend, or do whatever they liked with it. The purpose had been served, and now Anne had come home to resume her life with them.

Anne was even more depressed when she found that out, but she didn't have the strength to argue with her parents now. She sat in her room for the next few weeks, refusing to eat most of the time, telling the twins to get the hell out when they stopped in to say hello to her, which admittedly they seldom did, although Vanessa really did try more than once. She wanted to reach out to Anne, with records, and books, and a bunch of flowers once or twice. But Anne steadfastly refused to be wooed by the gifts. She kept her heart closed to all of them. And it was Thanksgiving before she joined them for dinner again. Lionel was conspicuously not there, nor was Greg, who was playing a big game at school, and Anne returned to her room as soon as possible. She had nothing to say to any of them, even Vanessa, who tried so hard, and Faye, whose grief still showed in her eyes. Anne hated them all. All she could think of was the baby she had given up. He was exactly five weeks old now. She wondered if for the rest of her life she would remember exactly how old he was all the time. She could almost sit down now, which was at least something, Lionel reminded her when he stopped by, when he knew for sure their father was out. Ward knew he was coming to see Anne, and he didn't say anything, just so he didn't have to see him himself, or John. He hadn't changed his mind about any of that, and at Christmas, Faye begged him to let her invite Lionel to share Christmas dinner with them, but Ward refused to bend.

'I've taken a position, and I intend to stick by it. I disapprove of his way of life, and I want the rest of the family to know that, Faye.' He was totally intractable, but she argued with him day and night about it. He hadn't always been a saint. He had betrayed her more than once. But Ward was outraged that she would dare to compare his heterosexual indiscretions with Lionel's homosexuality.

'I'm just trying to point out that you're human too.'

'He's queer, dammit!' He still wanted to cry when he thought of it.

'He's gay.'

'He's sick and I don't want him in my house. Is that clear once and for all?'

It was pointless. She couldn't budge him an inch. And sometimes, she was almost sorry he had come back. Their marriage was definitely not what it had once been, and the issue of Lionel didn't help anything. It was a constant source of friction and despair between them. Mercifully, they had started another film, and she was out most of the time. And she was grateful for Lionel stopping by. Someone had to talk to Anne. She had been through such an ordeal, and Lionel had always been able to talk to her. It seemed so wrong to her to close the door on him and she hated Ward for it. She looked at him angrily now. And yet, always beneath the anger, was the love she had always felt for him. Ward Thayer had been her world and her life for so long that, sinner or saint, she could never imagine a life without him.

On Christmas Day, Lionel was not there, and as soon as the family left the table, Anne left and went to their house. The Wells had made an excuse for not inviting Lionel although they would have welcomed their son, but somehow inviting his lover made too much of a reality of it, even for them. So John and Lionel had chosen to celebrate Christmas alone. They were joined after dinner not only by Anne, but also a few of John's friends from work and a gay friend of Li's from school.

Anne found herself surrounded by a dozen gay young men, and she didn't feel the least bit uncomfortable. She was far more comfortable with them than the rest of her family. She was looking more herself again now. She had lost all the weight she had gained, and her eyes were a little brighter. She looked older than her years, and far more mature. She would turn fifteen in a few weeks, and go back to her old school to finish eighth grade. She was dreading it. She was going to be a year and a half older than everyone, but Lionel said she just had to grit her teeth and go, and in a way she was doing it for him.

They let her have half a glass of champagne, and she stayed with them until after nine o'clock. She had saved up and bought Li a cashmere scarf, and a beautiful silver pen from Tiffany's for John. They were the best friends she had, and the only family she cared about. John drove her home that night in his secondhand VW bug, while Lionel stayed with their friends. She knew the party would go on for several hours, but Lionel had wanted her to go home. He didn't think she belonged at evenings like that. Sometimes they talked pretty openly, and some of their friends weren't as discreet as John and Li were. She had hugged her brother when she left, and she kissed John's cheek before she got out of the car.

'Merry Christmas, love.' He smiled at her.

'Same to you.' She gave him a quick hug and hopped out, and ran upstairs to her room to try on their gifts to her. They had given her a beautiful soft pink angora sweater with a matching scarf from Li, and little pearl earrings from John. She could hardly wait to put them on and when she did, she preened in front of the mirror with a happy smile. She was so happy with the gifts that she hadn't even heard her sister come in. It was Val, watching her admire herself. She was annoyed and in a rotten mood. Greg had promised to take her out with his friends, and at the last minute, he had backed out. Vanessa had a date with a serious beau she had, and Val was left at home to cool her heels. Even Ward and Faye had gone to friends' for a drink and Valerie and Anne were left alone. Val stared at her.

'Where'd you get the sweater and scarf?' She would have liked to try them on, but she knew Anne would never offer them.

Valerie helped herself to most of Vanessa's clothes, but Anne kept her door locked most of the time, and never offered them anything, nor did she ask anything of them. She kept to herself, as she always had, even more so than before.

'Li gave them to me.'

'Playing favourites, as usual.'

Anne was hurt by the remark, but it didn't show. It never did. She was a genius at hiding what she felt. She always had been. 'It's not as though you and he have ever been close.' It was a grown-up remark and the honesty of it took Valerie by surprise.

'What does that have to do with anything? He's my brother, isn't he?'

'Then do something for him some time.'

'He's not interested in me. He's all wrapped up in his fags.'

'Get out of my room!' Anne advanced on her menacingly, and she took a step back. There were times when the intensity in Anne's eyes frightened her.

'Okay, okay, don't get all worked up.'

'Get out of my room, you whore!' But she had said the wrong thing. Val froze in her tracks and looked viciously at Anne.

'If I were you, I'd watch that. I'm not the one who got knocked up and had to sell my kid.'

It was more than Anne could bear. She swung at Val and missed, and Valerie grabbed her arm and slammed it into the door. There was a sharp crack, and both girls looked shocked, as Anne freed her arm, and swung at her again. This time she didn't miss. She punched Val squarely in the face and stared at her, holding her arm. 'The next time you talk to me, I'm going to kill you, you bitch, is that clear?' She had hit a nerve so painful and raw that she might almost have lived up to her words, but just then Faye and Ward walked in. They saw Val's face, saw Anne clutching her arm, and they easily guessed that the two had exchanged words. They reproached them both, and Ward made ice packs for both girls, but Faye insisted on driving Anne to the hospital for an X ray. As it turned out the arm was badly strained but not cracked after all, and they bandaged it for her. By midnight, they were home again, and they had hardly come in the door when the phone rang. It was Mary Wells and she was hysterical. At first, Faye couldn't understand what she was saying . . . something about a fire . . . and the Christmas tree . . . and then a chill ran down her spine . . . had it been at their home or John's? She began to shout into the phone, trying to find out what had happened to her, but eventually Bob came on the line. He was crying openly, as Ward picked the extension up, and they heard the words at the same time.

'The boys' Christmas tree caught fire. They left it on when they went to bed. John is . . .' He could barely go on, and they could hear his wife sobbing in the background, and somewhere far, far in the distance, there were Christmas carols. They had had friends over when the news came, and no one had thought to turn the music off. 'John is dead.'

'Oh my God . . . no . . . and Li?' Faye whispered the words into the phone as Ward closed his eyes.

'He's badly burned, but alive. We thought you should know . . . They just called us . . . the police said . . .' Faye couldn't follow the rest of it, she sank into a chair as Anne watched her with terrified eyes. They had forgotten all about her as she stared at her mother now.

'What happened?'

'There's been an accident. Li's been burned.' She could hardly absorb it all and her breath was coming short and fast. That had never happened to her before, but for a moment, she had thought they were going to tell her Li was dead . . . but it was John . . . John . . . poor child . . .

'What *happened*?' Anne was crying now, and the twins had come to the top of the stairs. Faye looked up at them in disbelief. It wasn't possible. She had talked to him only hours before.

'I don't know . . . Li and John's Christmas tree burned . . . John was killed . . . Lionel was taken to the hospital . . .' She leapt to her feet as the girls began to cry, Vanessa instinctively

310

taking Anne in her arms, and the younger girl letting her. Faye turned to see Ward crying softly as he grabbed his car keys again. They left a moment later, as Anne lay on the couch and sobbed, and Vanessa stroked her hair with one hand, while holding Val's hand with the other.

In the hospital, Faye and Ward found Lionel being treated for severe burns on his arms and legs. He sobbed uncontrollably as he tried to explain it to Faye.

'I tried . . . Mum, I tried . . . Oh God, Mum . . . but the smoke was so thick . . . I couldn't breathe . . .' As they both sobbed, he told her of the fumes, of how he had tried to give John mouth-to-mouth after dragging him outside, but it was too late and he could barely breathe himself. The fire department had arrived as he collapsed. He had woken up in the hospital, where a nurse inadvertently told him that John was dead of toxic fumes. 'I'll never forgive myself, Mum . . . it's my fault . . . I forgot to turn the lights off on the tree . . .' The enormity of the loss engulfed him again, as Faye sat and cried with him, reassuring him, holding him as best she could with his bandages and salves, but he seemed to hear none of it. He was so hysterical about John that he didn't even feel the pain from his burns. Ward stood by helplessly, watching them as Faye and the boy cried, and for the first time in months, he felt something for his son. He looked down at him gently and suddenly he remembered him as he had been so long ago . . . running on the lawn . . . playing with the pony cart at their old house, before everything had changed . . . it was the same boy he was looking at now, except that he had become a man, and they didn't understand each other any more. But it was hard to remember that as he lay in his bed and cried, thrashing the bandaged arms, and at last Ward took him in his arms and held him close, the tears running down his cheeks, as Faye watched them both, heartbroken at what had happened to John . . . and feeling guilty at how grateful she was that it had not been her son.

Chapter 26

The funeral was devastating. It was the most painful thing Faye had ever seen. Mary Wells was hysterical, and Bob cried even harder than she did. John's four sisters looked as though they were in shock, and as they rolled the casket away, Mary tried to throw herself on it and had to be restrained. Lionel stood so tall and thin and pale in a dark suit Faye didn't know he owned that she thought he would faint where he stood, and on his one unbandaged hand, she noticed for the first time with a shocked glance that he wore a narrow gold wedding band. She didn't know if Ward had ever noticed it, but she knew what it meant. As she stared at it, she knew what John had meant to her son, and she looked at his face. It was the greatest loss of his life so far, and possibly one of the worst he would ever endure.

Anne stood as close to him as she could, crying softly into a handkerchief, looking up at him to make sure he was all right. There was no question about what would happen afterwards. Ward and Faye had discussed it the night before. Lionel was coming home to stay with them for a while. After the funeral he and Ward took a walk. Greg had escaped almost the moment they got back to the house. John had been his friend for most of his life, but he didn't seem to feel the pain so much.

'What can I say?' He shrugged to Val after the funeral. 'The guy was a fucking fag.' But he had also been his friend, and Valerie remembered the crush she had had on him, to no avail. They all knew why now.

Faye kept a discreet eye on Anne, she had been through a great deal in the past few months, but she seemed to be all right now . . . unlike Lionel, who walked along woodenly at his father's side unable to think of anything but his fight through the flames and his inability to get to John. He had thought of it again and again and again in the past three days. He would never allow himself to forget . . . never . . . it was all his fault . . . he had forgotten to turn the Christmas-tree lights off when they went to bed . . . they had drunk too much wine . . . and those damn little fucking blinking lights . . . why hadn't he remembered them . . . it was all his fault . . . he might as well have killed him with his bare hands.

He said as much to his father now. He had nothing in common with Ward any more, but he had to talk to someone. He wondered if John's parents blamed him.

'They should, you know.' He looked at his father with broken eyes and Ward felt his heart melt towards the boy he had tried so hard to hate for the past year. Now one of them was dead, and it had to end. Faye was right. They were lucky it hadn't been Li. These moments with him now were like a gift.

'We blamed you both for a lot of things in the past year. And we were wrong.' Ward sighed and looked out at the trees as they walked along. It was easier than looking his son in the eye, something he hadn't done in almost exactly a year, even after Li and John had rescued Anne. 'I didn't understand what made you the way you are. I thought it was my fault, so I took it out on you . . . and I was wrong . . .' He looked at Lionel, and saw tears coursing slowly down his cheeks, tears mirrored by his own. 'I was wrong to blame myself. Just as you're wrong to blame yourself now. You couldn't have done anything, Li . . .' They stopped walking and he took the boy's hands in his own. 'I know how hard you must have tried,' his voice broke, 'I know how much you loved John.' He didn't want to know but he did. And now he pulled Lionel close to him, their cheeks touching, their hearts beating against each other's chests, their tears falling on each other's shoulders as they cried and Lionel looked at him, seeming like a little boy again.

'I tried, Daddy . . . I did . . . and I couldn't get him out fast enough . . .' Great sobs broke from him, and Ward held him tight, as though to keep him safe from harm.

'I know you did, son . . . I know . . .' There was no telling him it was all right For John, it would never be all right again. And Lionel felt he would never recover from it. It was a loss that none of them would ever forget, a lesson dearly learned.

When they went back to the house, the others were waiting for them. It was a quiet dinner that night, and afterwards they all went to their own rooms. Almost everything Lionel owned had been destroyed in the fire, except a few things he had forgotten which were still at his parents' house; some jewellery that had been darkened by the smoke, but not lost, and his car, which was parked outside now. He was sleeping in his old room. Quietly Faye went about shopping for him in the next few days, and bought a few things she knew he'd need, and he was touched. Ward lent him some things, and the two men spent more time together than they had in a long time.

Greg went back to school, and the day of her birthday, Anne went back to school too, for the first time in a year. It was painful and difficult but it was what she had to do. Anyway, it distracted her. A few weeks later, the bandages came off Lionel's arms. The scars were there, scars they could all see, unlike those he wore deep inside. And no one had mentioned the fact that he had not gone back to school. He wasn't ready yet.

He took them all by surprise when he asked Ward to lunch one day. He looked across the table from him at the Polo Lounge, and he looked far older than his years, Ward thought as he watched him quietly. He didn't understand his way of life any better than he had before and he was sorry that that was what he preferred, but he respected him now. He liked his values and his views and his reasoning and it disappointed him all the more when Lionel told him he wouldn't be going back to school.

'I've thought about it a hell of a lot, Dad. And I wanted you to be the first to know.'

'But why? You only have a year and a half left. That's not so bad. You're just upset right now.' At least he hoped it was that. But Lionel shook his head.

'I can't go back, Dad. I don't belong there any more. I've had an offer to work on a film, and I want to get out there and do that now.'

'And then what? In three months you're through with that and you're out of work again.' It was a business he knew well.

'Just like you, huh, Dad?' he teased. Ward smiled, but he still wasn't pleased with the news, although he respected him for telling him man to man. 'I've just had it with school. I've got to try my wings.'

'You're only twenty years old. What's your rush?' But they both knew he had lived a lot for his age, in part because of John. He had suffered, and lost someone he dearly loved. He couldn't go back to being a child again, no matter how much Ward wanted him to, and although he resisted admitting it, Ward knew it too. John's death had changed all of them, it had allowed him to form a bond with his son again. But Lionel would never be as young, or as carefree, as he had been before. Maybe he was right to give up school, but Ward was sorry anyway. 'I'm sorry to see you do it, son.'

'I knew you would be, Dad.'

'Who's offering you the job?'

Lionel grinned. 'Fox.' The competition of course. And Ward laughed and put a hand to his heart as though he had been shot.

'What a blow. I wish you'd stay out of this damn business.' He meant what he said but Lionel shrugged.

'You and Mum seem to like it a lot.'

'And sometimes we get good and tired of it.' He had been feeling that way for a while, and he wanted to talk Faye into taking a trip with him. She had finished a film and would be free for a while, and she had no excuses now. Then as he looked at Lionel, he had an idea. 'You're not moving out right away, are you?'

'I thought I'd start getting organised one of these days and look for a place to stay. I don't want to get in your way.'

'Not at all.' Ward smiled apologetically at him, remembering how harsh he had been. 'Would you be willing to stay for another month and keep an eye on the girls?'

'Sure.' Lionel looked surprised. 'How come?'

'I want to take your mother away. She needs a break, and so do I.' They hadn't had five minutes alone since he had ended his affair and moved back into the house nine months before, and it was high time they went on a trip together. Lionel smiled at the thought.

'I'd be happy to do that, Dad. It would do you both good.'

Ward smiled at him as they left the restaurant. They were friends again. Friends as they had never been. Man to man . . . no matter how odd that seemed. And that night Ward told Faye about his plans. 'And I don't want to hear any arguments. No excuses. Nothing about work or the kids, or the actors you have to talk to about the script. We're leaving two weeks from tonight.' He had ordered the tickets that afternoon. They were leaving for Paris, Rome, and Switzerland, and instead of arguing, her eyes lit up.

'Are you serious?' She looked at him, amused, and put her arms around him.

'I am. And if you don't come willingly, I'll kidnap you. We're going to stay away for three weeks, and maybe four.' He had checked her production schedule secretly that afternoon and knew she could stay away for that long.

She followed him upstairs that night with a lighter step, and pirouetted in her nightgown as he teased her about Paris and Rome.

'It's been too long since we did something like that, Faye.'

'I know.' She sat down quietly on the bed and looked at him. They had almost lost each other twice; they had almost lost two children . . . a daughter . . . and a son . . . they had given up a grandchild and their son's lover had died. It hadn't been an easy time for any of them. And if anyone had asked her a year before if her marriage could have been saved, she would have told them no. But now, as she looked at him, she knew she still loved the man, with all his faults, with his affair, with the times he had failed her, even with the anguish he had inflicted on their son. She loved Ward Thayer. She had for years, and probably always would. She had few illusions about him after twenty-two years, but she loved the man he was. And that night, when they went to bed, they made love as they had done years and years before.

Chapter 27

Paris was exquisite that spring. They wandered along the Seine, went to Les Halles for onion soup, strolled down the Champs Élysées, went to Dior, and then lunch at Fouquet's and dinner at Maxim's and the Brasserie Lipp. They had drinks at the Café Flore and the Deux Magots and they laughed and cuddled and hugged and kissed over cheese and wine. It was exactly what Ward had wanted it to be – a second honeymoon, a place to forget all the sorrows of the past year or two, the children, the films, the responsibilities. When they reached Lausanne, Faye sat looking out at Lac Léman and smiled at him.

'You know, I'm glad I married you.' She said it matter-of-factly as she sipped her coffee and ate a croissant, and he laughed at her.

'I'm awfully glad to hear that. What made you decide?'

'Well,' she mused, staring out at the lake, 'you're a nice man. You make a mess of things sometimes, but you're smart enough and decent enought to go back and straighten things out.' She was thinking of Lionel, and she was relieved that he and the boy were friends again. And she was thinking of his affair too.

'I try hard. I'm not as smart as you are sometimes, Faye.'

'Bullshit.'

'You sound like Val.' He looked disapprovingly at her and she laughed.

'Well, I'm no smarter than you are. Just more stubborn sometimes.'

'I don't always have the guts to hang on the way you do. Sometimes I want to run away.' He had done it twice so far, but she had taken him back both times and he was grateful for that. But he was surprised at what she said next.

'Sometimes I want to run away too, you know. But then I worry about what would happen if I did . . . who would keep an eye on Val . . . make sure Anne was all right . . . Vanessa . . . Greg . . . Li . . .' She smiled at him. 'You. Somehow, I'm so damn egocentric that I figure none of it would run right if I disappeared, which isn't true, but it keeps me hanging in.'

'I'm glad.' He smiled at her and took her hand. They still had romance between them after all these years. 'Because you're right. None of it would run right if you disappeared, and I'm glad you never have.'

'Maybe one day I will. I'll run off and have some wild affair with a grip on the set.' She laughed at the thought, but Ward did not look amused.

'I've worried about that a few times. There are some actors I'm not crazy about you working with.' It was the first time he had admitted that to her and she was touched.

'I always behave myself.'

'I know. That's why I keep such a good eye on you.'

'Oh it is, is it?' She tweaked his ear, and he kissed her, and a little while later they went inside, forgetting Lac Leman and the Alps, and their children and careers. They only thought of each other for their remaining days abroad, and they were both sorry when they boarded the plane to go home. 'It was a beautiful holiday, wasn't it, love?'

'It was.' He smiled at her, and she slipped a hand into his arm, and leaned her head on him.

'I'd like to spend a lifetime doing that one day.'

'No, you wouldn't,' he laughed, 'you'd go stark staring mad. By next week, you'll be knee deep in your new picture, and telling me how impossible everyone is, that none of the costumes fit, the scenery stinks, the locations are no good, no one knows their lines. You'll be tearing your beautiful blonde hair out by the roots. Without that, you'd be so bored you couldn't stand it . . . could you?' She laughed at his accurate description of her business life.

'Well, maybe I'm not quite ready to retire yet, but one of these days . . .'

'Just let me know when.'

'I will.' And she looked as though she might.

But he was right. Two weeks later, life was just as he had described; she was going totally nuts, her biggest star was giving her a rough time, two others were on drugs, another drank on the set and showed up drunk every day after lunch, an entire set had burned to the ground, the unions were threatening to walk out. Life was back to normal again, but all the same they were both revived after their trip. Lionel had the girls well in hand when they got back. Anne seemed to have settled back into school; the twins were behaving, more or less; the news from Greg was good; and a month later, Lionel moved out again. He had found a place on his own, and although Faye knew he would be lonely without John, she thought it might do him good. He was doing the film for Fox, and it was going well, he said, whenever he called. The only problem they had was with Anne, who had wanted to move in with him. Lionel had discouraged her. He told her that she didn't belong with him now. That he had to live his own life, and so did she, that it had been right for a time, but no more. Now she had to make a life for herself in school again, make new friends, revive old friendships if she wished. She belonged with Ward and Faye, he told her.

Anne watched him in tears as he moved out one Saturday afternoon and she spent the rest of the day in her room. But the next day, she went to the cinema with one of her friends, and Faye decided there was hope for her. She hadn't mentioned the pregnancy in a long time, and she never mentioned the baby she had given up. Faye prayed that she would forget it all if that was possible.

And Faye tried to forget it herself as she dived into her film, stopping only for the Academy Awards, which were at the Santa

Monica Civic Auditorium that year. She persuaded Lionel and the twins to come. She thought that Anne was too young, so she stayed home in lonely isolation, as usual, refusing to even watch the awards on TV.

Faye didn't think she'd win, and she kept telling Ward all that night as she got dressed that it was ridiculous to get worked up about it, they didn't mean anything any more . . . not like when she was young . . . when she was acting . . . when it was the first time. 'And after all,' she looked at him, as she fastened pearls around her neck, 'I've already won two.'

'Show-off.' He teased her and she blushed.

'That's not what I meant,' she replied. She looked ravishing in a black velvet dress that showed off the still firm perfectly rounded breasts and he slipped a hand inside her dress now until she shooed him away. She wanted to look perfect tonight. Everyone would be so beautiful and young, and she was forty seven now . . . forty-seven . . . how did it all happen so fast? It seemed like only last year when she was twenty-two . . . and twenty-five . . . and she was madly in love with Ward Thayer . . . and they were dancing at Mocambo's every night. She looked dreamily at Ward, remembering the distant past, and he kissed her gently on the neck.

'You look beautiful tonight, my love. And I think you're going to win.'

'Don't say that!' She didn't even want to think of it. Things had been wonderful between them ever since they got back from their trip. There was an aura of romance which shut out everyone else sometimes, but she didn't mind. She loved being alone with him, in spite of the children they loved so much. They needed just each other at times. As they left the house that night with the twins, all dressed up in long gowns and the strings of pearls Faye had lent each of them, Faye saw Anne standing in her room and stopped in to kiss her goodnight. She looked like a lonely lost child and Faye was sorry they hadn't invited her too, but she was so young, just fifteen . . . and it was a Monday night after all, she had told

Ward. Anne had school the next day. Yet, she reproached herself for not taking her. 'Goodnight, sweetheart.' She kissed Anne's cheek nervously, and her youngest looked up at her, still with that puzzled air that always seemed to be asking her who she was. She had hoped that after she had sat through childbirth with her, they would be friends, but it hadn't worked out that way. Secretly, Anne blamed her for causing her to give up the child, and as soon as she had come home from the hospital, the doors had closed again. There was no getting close to her. Except for Lionel, of course. He was both mother and father to her.

'Good luck, Mum.' She called it out carelessly as they left, and then helped herself to something to eat.

They picked up Lionel at his place on the way. He looked very handsome in an old tuxedo of Ward's, and he jabbered with the twins in the back seat of Faye's Jaguar. Ward complained all the way that it wasn't driving well again; he didn't understand what she did to it. It was one of those nervous nights, when you pretend you're not thinking what you really are.

Everyone was there, Richard Burton and Liz, both of them nominees for *Who's Afraid of Virginia Woolf?*, and she was wearing a diamond the size of a fist. The Redgrave sisters were there, both of them nominated as well . . . Audrey Hepburn, Caron, Mel Ferrer. Faye was up against Antoine Lebouch, Nichols, and more for best director. Anouk Aimée, Ida Kaminska, the Redgraves, and Liz Taylor were vying for best actress. Scofield, Arkin, Burton, Caine, and McQueen for best actor. Bob Hope kept everyone amused as emcee, and then suddenly it seemed they were calling Faye's name . . . she had won the best director award again. She flew towards the stage with tears in her eyes, still feeling Ward's kiss on her lips, and suddenly there she was, looking at all of them, the golden statue clutched in her hands, just as she had held it so long ago when she had won the best actress award for the first time in 1942 . . . a hundred years ago, it seemed and only last night . . . twenty-five years . . . The thrill was still there for her.

'Thank you . . . all of you . . . my husband, my family, my co-workers, my friends . . . thank you.' She beamed and left the stage, and she could hardly remember what happened for the rest of the night.

They came home finally at 2 am, and though she knew it was too late for the twins to be out, it was a special night. They had called Anne from the Moulin Rouge but she hadn't answered the phone. Val had suggested that she was probably asleep, but Lionel knew better than that. It was her way of shutting them out, of getting back at them for not including her. And, like his mother, he knew they had made a mistake by not bringing her.

Long afterwards, they dropped Lionel off on the way home, and he kissed his mother's cheek again. The twins were strangely silent for the rest of the drive home. Vanessa was half asleep, and Val hadn't said anything to Faye all night. She was seething with anger over her mother's award. Lionel and Vanessa were well aware of it, but Faye seemed not to realise how jealous Val was of her.

'Did you have a good time, girls?' Faye turned to look at them in the car, thinking of the Oscar she had won. They had taken it away to be engraved, but she felt its presence as though she still held it in her hands. It was impossible to believe it had happened to her again. Now she had three. She beamed at Val, and was startled to see something chilly in her eyes, something she had never recognised quite that clearly before. It wasn't just anger this time, it was jealousy.

'It was all right. You must be pretty pleased with yourself.' They were unkind words, and no one else seemed to hear them quite the way Faye did, but they were aimed straight at her heart, and Val had hit her mark.

'It's very exciting. It always is, I guess.'

Val shrugged as she looked at her. 'I hear they give them out of sympathy sometimes.' The comment was so outrageous that Faye laughed.

'I don't think I'm quite over the hill yet, although you never know.' And of course it was true, sometimes they passed one up and then made it up the next year, although they denied that it worked that way, but everyone felt that it did. 'Is that what you think this was, Val?' Her mother searched her eyes. 'Sympathy?'

'Who knows?' She shrugged indifferently and looked out of the window again as they drove up to the house. It irked her that Faye had won and she made no secret of it. She was the first to leave the car, to reach her room, to close the door, and she never mentioned the Oscar again, not even to Anne the next day. Or when her friends mentioned it in school, and congratulated her. That seemed strange, she had nothing to do with it after all and what did she care anyway? So she just shrugged and said, 'Yeah, so what? Big deal.' And changed the subject to something that interested her like the Supremes. She was sick of hearing about Faye Thayer. She wasn't so hot. And one day, she would show all of them, she would be an actress who would make Faye Price Thayer look pale by comparison. She only had a few months left before she could get out there and show them her stuff, and she could hardly wait. She'd show them all. To hell with her mother . . . three Oscars? Bullshit. So what anyway?

Chapter 28

The twins graduated from high school two months after Faye won the Academy Award, and Greg came home for the summer just in time to attend the graduation ceremony at his old school.

This year their eyes were dry. Ward leaned over to Faye halfway through the ceremony to say 'I feel as though they should be giving *us* a diploma by now.' Faye giggled softly and rolled her eyes. He was right, and they would be back again four years from now, for Anne. It seemed to go on forever. In two years, Greg would be graduating from the. University of Alabama. They seemed to be spending half their life watching young people line up in gowns and mortarboards. But it was touching when the twins got theirs, in spite of how many times they'd seen it before. They wore simple white dresses beneath their gowns, Vanessa's totally plain with a high neck and embroidered hem, Val's a slightly too dressy organdie with a pair of very sexy high heels that showed off her legs. But the shoes weren't Faye's biggest disagreement with her. Valerie had staunchly refused to apply to any college, East or West. She was going to model, act, and in her spare time go to acting school, and not the drama department at UCLA, but the kind where 'real actors' went between jobs, to perfect their skills. She was sure she would find herself in classes with Dustin Hoffman and Robert Redford and she was equally sure that she was going to set the world on fire, despite everything Ward and Faye said to her.

It had been a heated argument for the past several months, and she was more stubborn than either of them. In desperation, Ward had told her he wouldn't support her if she didn't go to school, and that seemed to suit her fine. Someone had told her about a coven of young actresses in West Hollywood; for only a hundred and eighteen dollars a month, she could have a bed and share a room. Two of the actresses had jobs on soaps, one of them did porno films (though Val didn't tell her parents that), one was a big star in a horror film the year before, and there were four others who modelled regularly. It sounded like a whorehouse to Faye, and she told Val so, but the twins were nearly eighteen now, and Valerie reminded her of it constantly. It was an argument which they couldn't win. A week later, they knew that she would be moving out. Vanessa had done exactly as she planned. She had applied to a handful of schools in the East, been accepted by all of them, and was going to Columbia in the fall. She was staying at home until the end of June, and then she was going to New York to work for two months before starting school. She had got a job as a receptionist in a publishing house and she was very excited about it. Meanwhile Greg was going to Europe with friends. Only Anne was staying home this year. They had tried to talk her into going to camp, but she insisted that she was too old. She wanted to go camping with Lionel for a week or two, but he was working on a new film for Fox and didn't have time. Ward and Faye were starting a biggie too. Ever since the Academy Award, the offers had been rolling in with even greater regularity than before. Faye had three projects lined up back to back for the next year, and no spare time at all. Ward reminded her that it was a good thing they'd made the trip to Europe when they had, and she agreed.

The twins' graduation party was the rowdiest of all, and Faye looked at Ward in exhaustion as the last guest left at 4 am. 'Maybe we're getting too old for this.'

'Speak for yourself. Personally, I think seventeen-year-old girls are a lot more attractive than they used to be.'

'Watch out for that.' She wagged a finger at him, and lay down on their bed, before leaving for work at five. There was a big scene she wanted to set up, and Ward was going to spend the day with Lionel and Anne. Val had a hot date, Vanessa had her own plans. God only knew where Greg was, or with whom, but undoubtedly it involved sports, beer, or girls, and he seemed relatively well able to take care of himself, so Faye went to work happily just as Ward fell asleep.

The summer seemed to whiz by. Valerie moved into the apartment she loved so much. There were actually nine girls living there when she moved in. It was a huge house, and half the beds had no sheets on them at all. In the kitchen there were six bottles of vodka, two lemons, three bottles of soda, and no food at all in the fridge, and she hardly ever saw any of the other girls. They had their own lives, boyfriends, some of them had their own phones. Val had never been happier in her life, she told Vanessa just before she left.

'This is just what I've always wanted to do.'

'How's acting school?' Vanessa asked, wondering how they could have shared the same womb, same life, same house. Two people couldn't have been more different than they.

Val shrugged. 'I haven't had time to enrol yet. I've been busy going to go sees.' But in August she struck oil. Vanessa was already long gone, staying at the Barbizon in New York, and looking at apartments with a friend from work. The job at Parker Publishing was actually pretty dull as all she did was answer phones, but she was looking forward to Columbia. Valerie called her late one night to tell her that she had a walk-on in a horror film. 'Isn't that great?'

It was three o'clock in the morning and Vanessa yawned, but she didn't want to take the wind out of Val's sails. She was pleased she'd called. 'What do you get to do?'

'I walk across the set, oozing blood from my eyes and nose and ears.'

Vanessa repressed a groan. 'That's wonderful. When do you start?'

'Next week.'

'That's great. Have you told Mum?'

'I haven't had time. I'll call her this week sometime,' but they both suspected Faye wouldn't be quite so thrilled, although they didn't voice it. She never seemed to understand anything Val did, or so Val felt, and she was never pleased for her, and probably wouldn't be about this. But *she* had started small too. Hell, she had done soap ads in New York for a year before they discovered her. And this was straight into film, as she said to Van, who didn't remind her that their mother had never had to walk across a set bleeding from the nose and eyes and ears. 'How's your job, Van?' She was feeling magnanimous, usually she didn't really care about anyone but herself, as Vanessa knew only too well.

'It's okay.' Vanessa yawned again. 'Actually, it's pretty dull. But I met a nice girl from Connecticut. We thought we'd try and find a place together near Columbia. She's going there too.'

'Oh.' Val already sounded bored, and decided to hang up. 'I'll let you know how things go.'

'Thanks. Take care.' They were oddly close, and yet not; linked to each other somehow, but with nothing in common at all. It was a bond Vanessa had always felt and never quite understood. She envied other sisters who seemed so close. She was close to neither of hers, and had always longed for a sister she could talk to and confide in, which was what was so nice about the girl from Connecticut.

In California Anne was discovering that too. She had discovered a girl walking down Rodeo Drive one day eating an ice-cream cone, and swinging a bright pink purse from her arm. She looked like an ad in a magazine, and she had smiled at Anne. Anne thought she was beautiful, and had noticed her an hour later, eating lunch at the Daisy, sitting by herself, as Anne stopped there for a hamburger. Her mother had given her money for two new pairs of shoes, and she had been wandering along Rodeo Drive, watching the people stroll in the bright sun. It was a hot day, but there was a nice breeze, and she found herself sitting at the next table from the girl with the pink purse. They smiled at each other again, and she spoke up easily. She had soft brown hair, which fell almost to her waist, and big brown eyes, and she looked about eighteen Anne thought; but she was surprised to learn they were the same age, almost to the day.

'Hi, I'm Gail.'

'I'm Anne.' The conversation would have ended there, left up to her, but Gail seemed to have lots to say. She told her that she had seen this neat skirt at Giorgio's, it was white leather, and real soft, and they had great boots too. Anne was impressed at the places where she shopped and told her about the shoes she'd seen further up the street. They discussed the Beatles, Elvis, jazz, and eventually got around to schools.

'I'm going to Westlake next year.' She looked unimpressed and Anne's eyes grew wide.

'You are? So am I!' It was another happy coincidence, in addition to their age. She told Anne honestly that she had had glandular fever, and then a bout of mononrvoin, and all in all she'd missed a year of school. She was fifteen now, and she was a year behind, she shrugged. Anne felt as though good fortune had just walked into her life for the first time.

She was honest with her too, to a point; there were some things she intended never to tell anyone, like about the baby she'd given up, but there were other things she could say. 'I dropped out for a year, and I'm a year behind too.'

'That's fabulous.' Gail looked thrilled and Anne grinned. No one had ever reacted that way before, and she knew instantly she liked this girl. She was ready for a friend. And she was bored around the Thayers' pool alone every day. Maybe Gail would like to come by some time. 'What did you do when you dropped out?' She looked fascinated by her adventurous new friend, and Anne tried to look blasé.

'I went up to the Haight-Ashbury for a while.'

Gail's eyes grew huge. 'You did? Wow! Did you take any drugs?'

Anne hesitated for a fraction of an instant and shook her head. 'That stuff's not so hot.' She knew differently, but she also had experience of the price you paid, and she realised that this girl knew nothing of that life. She looked clean and neat and pretty and well dressed and a little spoiled. She was what some people described as a Jewish American princess, and Anne was intrigued by her. All the girls at her old school were so dull, and practically no one had even talked to her when she came back from the Haight, but this girl was nothing like them. She had style and looks and obviously a great personality, and they were attracted to each other instantly. By the end of lunch, they were giggling and having a great time, and the maître d' was giving them angry looks for tying up two tables outside, until, finally, Gail suggested they take a walk back up Rodeo Drive.

'I'll show you the boots at Giorgio's if you want.' Anne was even more impressed when she discovered that Gail had a charge account there, and everyone seemed anxious to help her buy something. Usually, when kids went into places like that, the salespeople were anxious to get rid of them, but not Gail. Everyone called her by name, they even offered Anne a Coke from the bar. They had a great time even though Gail had decided she didn't like the boots that much after all and they were giggling again when they left.

'I'll show you the shoes at the place I went.' It was the most fun she'd had in years, ever probably. The two had hit it off, and they were having a wonderful afternoon, with nothing else to do. 'Your mum must buy a lot of stuff at Giorgio's for them to be so nice.'

Gail was quiet for a minute, staring into space, and then she looked at Anne. 'My mother died of cancer two years ago. She was thirty-eight years old.' They were such shocking words that Anne just stared at her. It was the worst thing she had ever heard, much worse than anythng that had happened to her in some ways. Even though she and Faye weren't close and there were times when she hated her, still to have her die that way would be terrible, and she could still see the pain in Gail's eyes now.

'Do you have sisters and brothers?'

'No. Just my dad.' She looked at Anne honestly as they walked along. 'That's why he kind of spoils me, I guess. It's like I'm all he has left. I try not to take advantage of that, but it's hard sometimes.' She smiled and Anne noticed that there were freckles dusted across her face. 'I like getting my way, and he gets so upset when I cry.'

Anne laughed. 'Poor man.'

'What are your parents like?'

Anne hated to even talk about them, but after Gail's confidence it seemed unfair not to share something with her. 'They're all right.'

'Do you get along with them?'

Anne shrugged. The truth was that she did not, and never had. 'Sometimes. They weren't too crazy about it when I took off.'

'Do they trust you now?'

'I think so.'

'Would you do it again?' Gail was curious about her new friend.

But Anne shook her head. 'No, I wouldn't.'

'Do you have sisters and brothers?' They had reached the shoe shop and were wandering inside, as Anne nodded her head. 'Two of each.'

'Wow!' Gail smiled the dazzling smile which showed how she could have been a child actress if she'd wanted to. 'Lucky you!'

'That's what you think!' Anne knew better and rolled her eyes.

'What're they like?'

'My older brother, Lionel, is neat. He's going to be twenty-one.' She didn't tell Gail he was gay. 'He dropped out of school too, and he's making films for Fox.' She said it like a pro and Gail impressed again. 'My other brother is a jock and goes to University of Alabama on a football scholarship. He'll be a junior this year. And my sisters are twins. One of them just went East to go to Columbia, and the other one is trying to be an actress here.'

'Wow! That's neat!'

'Lionel is . . . we've always been close . . . the others are . . . well,' she shrugged again, dismissing them at one blow, 'a little strange at times.' It was what they said about her too, but she didn't care what they said now. She had a friend of her own now.

Gail bought two pairs of the same shoes in different colours. A few minutes later, she looked at her watch.

'My dad's picking me up at four, in front of the Beverly Wilshire. Do you want a ride somewhere?'

Anne hesitated. She had taken a cab from home, but it would be fun to ride with Gail. 'You don't think he'd mind?'

'Not at all. He loves doing stuff like that.' Giving strangers rides? Anne laughed. Gail was naive in some ways but she liked that about her. They crossed Wilshire Boulevard, and stood in front of the sumptuous hotel, waiting for the car to arrive. Anne was impressed when she saw his car. He was driving a two-toned grey Rolls, and Gail waved frantically until he stopped. Anne thought she was kidding at first, because of the fancy car, but a stocky, thick-shouldered man, with features much like hers, leaned over and opened the door. Gail hopped in and beckoned to Anne, explaining her instantly to the man at the wheel of the Rolls. 'Hi, Daddy, I made a new friend. She's going to the same school as me next year.' He didn't look upset that she was hitching a ride, and warmly shook her hand. He wasn't a handsome man, but he had a kindly face, Anne decided. His name was Bill Stein, and Anne gathered that he was a lawyer in the entertainment world. She was sure he would know who her parents were, but she didn't offer their names. She was just Anne.

He took them to Will Wright's on Sunset Boulevard for ice cream. And he had a surprise for Gail that night, he said. They were going to dinner at Trader Vic's and then to a film with some friends. The funniest thing of all was that the film was one of Ward and Faye's, but Anne only said that she had seen it and liked it a lot, and then they talked of other things. All the time, she felt his eyes on her, as though he were trying to figure out who she was, but more as though he were trying to draw her out. The odd thing was that she felt safe with him, and comfortable in a way that she rarely did with anyone. When they dropped her off, she hated to see them go, and she watched the grey Rolls disappear, anxious to see Gail again. She had given her her phone number on the drive home, and Gail had promised to call the next day and come over to swim in the pool. Anne could hardly wait. She wondered if Mr Stein would drop her off. She was surprised to see her own father at home when she walked in, until she glanced at the clock and saw that it was almost six o'clock.

'Hi, sweetheart.' He looked up at her from the glass of wine he was pouring himself. Faye wasn't home yet, and dinner wouldn't be for a couple of hours. He wanted to relax and watch the news, maybe take a swim, and enjoy his glass of wine. He didn't drink much any more, only wine. He was surprised to see Anne looking so pleased with herself, he couldn't imagine over what. Most of the time, she still hid in her room. 'What did you do today?'

She looked at him for a long moment and then shrugged. 'Nothing much.' And then she disappeared upstairs, as usual, and closed her bedroom door, with a smile this time, thinking of her new friends.

Chapter 29

The Barbizon for Women had provided a pleasant home for Vanessa since she had arrived in New York. There were only women living there, it was a nice neighbourhood at Sixty-third and Lexington, there was a swimming pool, and a coffee shop downstairs. It met all her needs, and she was hardly there anyway. Louise Matthison lived there too. They went to Long Island at weekends, to people Louise knew, and eventually they found an apartment to share. It was on 115 Street on the West Side, and she knew her parents would have died if they'd seen the neighbourhood. But it was close to Columbia, and all the kids lived up there. She didn't like it as much as the Barbizon, but there was more freedom there. They moved in a month before school began, and took turns buying groceries and doing household chores.

It was Vanessa's turn to do the shopping, and she struggled up the stairs one day with a bag in each arm. There was an ancient elevator which never worked, and she was afraid she'd get stuck in it anyway. It was easier just to stagger up the stairs to the third floor, but as she did so on a hot August afternoon, after work, she found someone staring down at her. He was tall and he had auburn hair, a pleasant face, and he was wearing a T-shirt and shorts, and carrying a stack of papers in one hand.

'Do you need help?' She looked up at him and was about to decline, but she liked the look of him. There was something matter-of-fact and intelligent about the man that appealed to her instantly. He was the kind of man she had hoped to meet at Parker when she took the job. But she never seemed to meet

334

anyone there who excited her, and this young man had something that appealed to her now. She wasn't sure what it was, maybe it was just the stack of papers he held. It looked like a manuscript to her, and she wasn't far wrong. That was exactly what it was, he explained, as he set her bags of groceries down outside her door. 'Just moved in?' He had never seen her before, and he'd been living there for years. He had moved in when he'd gone to graduate school, which he'd finished the year before. But he'd been too lazy to move out; he had too many papers lying around. He was doing research for a thesis on philosophy, and he was thinking about writing a play, but he forgot about it all now, as he looked at the slim girl with the long, blonde hair. She nodded in answer to his question, and dug her key out of her bag.

'I moved in with a friend two weeks ago.'

'Starting graduate school next month?' He knew the type. He'd been dating them for years. He'd been at Columbia since 1962, and five years, almost six in fact, was a long time. But she was smiling at him, amused. Lately, people had begun to think she was older than she was. It was a refreshing change after years of people thinking her less sophisticated and much younger than her twin.

'No. Undergraduate, but thanks for the compliment.'

He smiled ingenuously. He had nice teeth, and an attractive smile. 'Not at all. Well, see you sometime.'

'Thanks again for the hand.' He clattered down the stairs with his manuscript in hand, and Vanessa heard a door slam on the second floor. She mentioned him to Louise that night, who grinned as she set her hair in rollers for work the next day.

'He sounds cute. How old do you think he is?'

'I don't know. Old, I guess. He said he was working on his thesis, and he was carrying a manuscript.'

'Maybe he was just putting you on.'

'I don't think so. He had to be pretty close to twenty-five.' Louise immediately lost interest in him; she had just turned

335

eighteen, and she thought nineteen was old enough. Twenty-five wasn't even fun. They just wanted to climb into bed the first time around, and Louise wasn't ready for that.

As it turned out, Vanessa was right, or pretty close. He was twenty-four, and they met each other again one Sunday night as the girls came home from a weekend in Quogue. They were juggling suitcases and tennis rackets, Louise's oversized hat, and Van's camera, and they were climbing out of the cab that had just brought them from Penn Station all the way uptown. He had parked his battered MG across the street and was watching them He thought Vanessa had great legs in the shorts and sandals she wore. She looked a lot like Yvette Mimieux, right down to the turned-up nose, and she had fabulous green eyes, he had noticed that the day they had met on the stairs. He sauntered across the street, wearing shorts and a T-shirt again, and loafers without socks.

'Hi, there.' They hadn't introduced themselves and he didn't know her name, but he volunteered to help with the bags. He was juggling both tennis rackets, a suitcase in each hand, and his own briefcase, which was no small feat, and Vanessa was awkwardly attempting to help and thanking him, as everything fell in a heap in front of their door and he looked at her. 'You guys sure drag a lot of stuff around.' And then in a soft voice, as Louise stepped inside, 'Want to come down for a glass of wine?' Vanessa was tempted to, but she had the feeling he was putting a fast move on her. She didn't go to men's apartments, and she didn't really know who he was. He could have been the Boston Strangler for all she knew, but he seemed to read her mind. 'You won't get raped, I swear. Not unless you agree.' He looked her over appraisingly and she blushed, as he wondered exactly how old she was. She looked about twenty-one but she had said she was an undergraduate. Maybe twenty, or even nineteen. She had a calm, tranquil air, and a healthy blonde beauty which appealed to him. He was dying to spend some time with her.

Instead of going downstairs with him, she invited him in to join her roommate and herself for a beer. It wasn't what he would have preferred, but since he seemed to have no choice, he accepted gracefully, put the rest of their stuff inside the hall, closed the door, and looked around at what they'd done to the place. It had all been painted pale yellow and there were plants and magazines, and a lot of rattan, and some Indian prints, and there was a photograph of a large family on the wall. A massive group standing next to a swimming pool. It looked very Californian to him, and he inquired who they were, and then suddenly recognised Van, standing next to Valerie, with Lionel next to her.

'Those are my folks.' She said it simply and he didn't question her about who they were, and then suddenly Louise laughed as she strolled by with a beer can in her hand.

'Aren't you going to ask her who her mum is?'

Vanessa blushed to the roots of her hair and she could have killed her friend. She hated talking about that, but Louise had been impressed ever since she had discovered that her mother was Faye Thayer. She had seen all her films, including the ones she had acted in years before.

'Okay.' The tall young man with auburn hair looked at her with an obliging smile. 'Who's your mum?'

'Dracula, who's yours?'

'Cute.'

'Want another beer?'

'Sure.' He liked the way her eyes danced when she smiled, and he was curious now, as he glanced at the photograph again. There was something familiar about all of them, but nothing specific came to mind as he looked at Vanessa again. 'Are you going to tell me, or do I have to guess?'

'Okay, big deal. My mum is Faye Thayer.' It was easier to get it over with than to play coy. It wasn't all that important to her, and she hadn't bragged about it since third grade. In fact, she had learned to keep her mouth shut most of the time. It wasn't easy being the child of a celebrity, let alone one who had won three Academy Awards. Somehow, it made people expect more of you, or else they were quick to criticise. And Vanessa liked getting by quietly in life. The boy was looking at her now, with narrowed eyes, as he nodded his head.

'That is very interesting. I like her films. Some of them.'

'So do I.' She smiled. At least he hadn't fallen over himself the way some people did. 'What did you say your name was again!' He had never really said. It had all been pretty casual as he carried their bags upstairs.

'Jason Stuart.' He smiled at her. She certainly didn't seem stuck up about who she was. Her friend was a lot more impressed. He glanced at the picture again. 'Who are all the other kids?'

'My brothers and sisters.'

'That's quite a mob.' He was impressed. He was an only child, and large families had never appealed to him much. He liked his life the way it was. His parents were older and had retired to New Hampshire, and everything would come to him one day, not that there was much. His father was a lawyer, with a small country practice now, though he wasn't really interested in pursuing it any more, and he did as little as he could. Jason had thought he might like to go into law too, but when he thought of it seriously, writing had a lot more appeal to him. He was going to write a play, after his thesis, he told Vanessa over their third beer. It wasn't so much that he liked to drink, but the heat was killing them. The whole building seemed to be baking after a day of it, and after Louise went to bed, they went outside to get some air. They walked along Riverside Drive for a while, he telling her about New England, and she talking about Beverly Hills.

'I'd say they're worlds apart, wouldn't you?' He smiled down at her again. She seemed mature for her age, and quiet, and unassuming. She laughed a little later on and told him about her twin.

'We're worlds apart, too. All she wants to do is be a big star. She just got a part in a horror movie with blood streaming out of her ears.' He made a face and they both laughed. 'I'd like to write a screenplay one day, but you couldn't pay me to act.' And then, for no reason in particular, she thought of Lionel, and she had a feeling he would like this man, and that Jason would like him. Both of them were honest, unpretentious, and bright. 'My brother's making films too.'

'You people must be quite a group.' Overwhelming at best.

'I suppose we are. I'm used to us. And everyone's going their own way now. There's only one left at home.' Poor little Anne with her runaway days in the Haight, and the baby she'd had to give away. Vanessa felt sorry for her sometimes, although she didn't understand her now any better than she ever had. They all seemed so far away now, as though they were part of another world. She wondered when they would all be together again, or if. It seemed unlikely now, although she had promised them she would try to come home for Christmas this year. But who knew what would happen between now and then, or where Lionel or Val or Greg would be.

'Do you like your family?'

'Some of them.' For no reason in particular, she was honest with him, though she had no reason not to be, as long as she didn't tell him too much, about Lionel or Anne, but she had no intention of doing that. 'I'm closer to some than others. My older brother is really neat.' She had come to respect him more and more for standing up for what he was. She knew how difficult it had all been for him.

'How old is he?'

'Twenty-one, his name is Lionel, and my other brother Greg is twenty, then there's Val, my twin, she's eighteen too, obviously, and Anne is fifteen.'

'Your folks sure didn't lose any time.' He smiled and Vanessa smiled back, and they walked slowly home, as the river drifted nearby. And he walked her to her door. 'Want to have lunch tomorrow?'

'I can't. I have to work.'

'I could come downtown.' The idea didn't really appeal to him much. He wanted to stay uptown and write, but she appealed to him a lot.

'Wouldn't that be too much trouble for you?'

'Yes.' He looked at her honestly. 'But I like you. I can spare an hour or two.'

'Thanks.' She left him then.

He picked her up at the reception desk at Parker's the next day, and they went for a long walk, and wound up eating avocado sandwiches in a health-food restaurant he knew. He was interesting to talk to, he took himself seriously in some ways, and he thought Vanessa should too. He thought writing screenplays was junk, and he suggested she think about writing a serious play.

'Why? Because that's what you want to do? Films don't have to be junk, you know.' He liked the way she stood up to him, and he invited her to dinner that night too, though she turned him down. 'I promised I'd meet Louise with some friends.' He was dying to come along, but he didn't let on. He wondered if there was another man involved, which there was. But the boy was Louise's date. Vanessa just didn't want to look too anxious to him. But she liked him just as much as he liked her. She thought of him all that night, as they ate spaghetti and clams on Houston Street, and it seemed hours before they came back uptown. When they did, she noticed that his light was still on. She wondered if he was writing or just hanging out, and she made as much noise as possible clattering up the stairs and slamming their door, hoping he'd call. He didn't call for two days. He had decided to play it cool, and when he did, she was gone for the weekend. They didn't meet again until the middle of the following week, when he saw her coming home from work one night, looking hot and tired, after an endless ride on the bus uptown.

'How've you been?' He smiled and she looked pleased. She thought that he had forgotten her.

'Pretty good. How's your play?'

'I haven't done a thing. I've been working on that damn thesis all week.' He told her that he was going to do substitute teaching at a boys' school that autumn, to make ends meet. He wasn't too excited about it, but it would leave him plenty of time to write, and that was what mattered to him most. Vanessa was impressed by how serious he was. But he was serious about a lot of things, and he was developing a serious interest in her.

This time when he asked her out, she was free. They went to a little Italian restaurant uptown, and they drank a lot of red wine, and talked until almost one o'clock, and then took a leisurely walk home, with Vanessa glancing over her shoulder now and then, hoping they wouldn't be mugged. She wasn't used to New York yet, and it was hardly a lovely neighbourhood. But Jason put a powerful arm around her, sensing her fears, and she felt safe with him. He walked her slowly upstairs, and seemed to hesitate on the second floor, but she began the next flight up, and he gently touched her arm. 'Want to come in for a drink?' She had drunk enough, and she suspected what he had in mind. It was almost 2 am, and she was asking for it if she went to his place. She wasn't ready to make that kind of commitment yet, to anyone, not even to him, and she liked him a lot.

'Not tonight, Jason, but thanks.' He looked disappointed, as he walked her to her door, and she felt just as disappointed when she went inside. For the first time in her life, she really wanted a man. She had always had fun playing with boys before, but she wasn't like Val. She didn't need conquests, or ache with desire for anyone. There were boys that she liked, but never that much. Until now. Suddenly, she knew from the unfamiliar stirrings she felt that she wanted to sleep with him.

She tried to distract herself for the next few days. She went out with Louise and her friends. She even had lunch with her boss at Parker, and she could see that he had the hots for her but she couldn't even stand his touch on her arm. As she went home at night all she could think of was the tall boy with auburn hair on the second floor, and it was almost a relief when she ran

straight into him that weekend. She was going to the laundro-
mat with her things. Louise had gone to Quogue again, and she
was alone for a change. But she didn't tell Jason that. She didn't
want to encourage him.

'How've you been, kid?' He tried to make her feel very
young, and ashamed for not going to bed with him. And she
did. But she didn't let on.

'Fine. How's the play?'

'Okay. It's been kind of hot to work.' She could see that he
had a tan, and had probably been spending time on the roof. His
parents had wanted him to come to New Hampshire for a few
days, but he liked it better in New York. It was so damn dull up
there, and there was an additional lure to town now. He could
almost feel a throbbing pulse being in the same building with
her. No one had turned him on that much in a long time, and
he almost resented it. It made him curt with her now. 'See you,
kid.' It was obvious where she was going, and he could calculate
how long she'd be gone, and when he heard a step on the stairs
an hour later, he swiftly opened his door. And he had guessed
right. She was carrying a bag of clean laundry upstairs and she
turned to look at him as she heard his door open. 'Hi. Want
some lunch?'

She felt her heart pound as she met his eyes, wondering if that
was all he meant, or if he meant more. 'I . . . okay . . . sure . . .' She
was afraid to turn him down again, for fear he wouldn't ask her
again. It wasn't easy being young and in New York for the first
time, even worse if you were a virgin and he was an older man of
twenty-four. She followed him into his apartment, and dropped
her bag of laundry near the door, glad that she had put her personal
things near the bottom where they wouldn't fall out.

He made tuna sandwiches for them both, and cold lemonade,
which she liked. She was surprised at how relaxed she was, as
they sat and talked and munched potato chips from the bag.

'Do you like New York?' She could feel his eyes bore into her
and she had to concentrate on his words. There was something

intense happening between them, but oddly enough it didn't frighten her. She felt as though she were almost floating on a wave of his thoughts, and the air beneath them was soft, warm, and sensual. The air around them was deathly still, and it felt as if there was a thunderstorm brewing that afternoon, but the only world that seemed to exist was in that room between them.

'I like New York a lot.'

'Why?' His eyes dug deep into her soul, as though he were looking for someone, for something that she had brought with her, and she met his eyes now.

'I don't know yet. I'm just glad I'm here.'

'So am I.' His voice was soft and sensual, and she felt herself physically pulled towards him, unaware of his hands pulling her close, his hands reaching for her thighs, touching them, caressing her, kneading her flesh, and then suddenly she felt his lips on hers and his hands on her breasts, and desire exploding from beneath her legs as his fingers moved deftly there, and she was breathless as they lay back on his couch, and then suddenly she was begging him to stop. He seemed surprised, and sat up, looking down at her where she lay.

'Don't, please . . .' He had never raped anyone before, and he had no intention of starting now. He looked almost hurt, and didn't understand what was happening, as tears sprang to her eyes. 'I don't . . . I've never . . .' And yet she wanted him, and suddenly he understood and he held her close to him, and she could feel his warmth and smell the sweetness of his flesh, it had the smell of lemon spice and she wasn't sure if it was soap or eau de cologne, but she liked the smell, and she knew she liked him, and he was looking down at her gently now, having understood everything, but it only made him want her more.

'I didn't realise . . .' He leaned away from her and gave her room to breathe and think. He didn't want to overpower her. Not now, not the first time. 'Would you rather wait?' She was embarrassed for her honesty but slowly she shook her head. She didn't want to wait at all, and a moment later, he was carrying her to his bed, as though she were a little rag doll, and he laid her gently down, and peeled away the few clothes she wore, her shorts, the sleeveless shirt, the underpants, the bra. She felt like a little girl beneath his hands, and he slid into bed next to her, turning away after he shed his clothes, so he wouldn't frighten her. He thought of everything, and he touched her everywhere, and she lay in bed with him in ecstasy as the thunder and lightning came. She was never quite sure if the storm were real or part of what he made her feel. But when they were spent, he lay next to her and the rain beat on the windowpane, and she smiled at him. There was blood on his sheets but he didn't seem to care, he said her name again and again, and touched her face with his hands; and her body with his lips and then he parted her legs again and let his tongue play with her until she screamed. Then he entered her again, and this time the storm was not in the sky, but only in her head as she shouted his name in ecstasy, and she felt herself drift away in his powerful arms.

Chapter 30

'Action!' The director screamed for the eleventh time, and Valerie had to dash across the set again with red paint streaming from her ears and down her cheeks, and from her nose. And each time she had to wash it off, in order to start again. It was the most tedious thing she had ever done, except that after this she would be a big star . . . she just knew it . . . someone would discover her . . . and she would end up playing a role with Richard Burton, or Gregory Peck, or Robert Redford . . . even Dustin Hoffman wouldn't be bad . . . The director shouted 'Action' for the nineteenth time and she did it again. The paint kept running into her hair and he was yelling at the makeup man that it was the wrong consistency. And when he yelled 'Cut' again, Faye tiptoed off the set. Valerie had never known she was there, and Faye was embarrassed for her. It was a pathetic little role, as she told Ward that afternoon. In fact, it was worse than that, it was embarrassing.

'I wish she'd do something decent with herself like go to school.'

'Maybe she'll make something of herself, Faye. You did.'

'That was almost thirty years ago for God's sake. Times have changed. She can't even act.'

'How can you tell in a role like that?' He was trying to be fair, and he thought Faye was being unduly harsh.

'Let's put it this way, she doesn't even walk across a stage well.'

'Would you, with paint pellets shoved up your nose, and into your ears? Personally, I think she's a hell of a good sport.'

'I think she's a damn fool.'

345

But she got another role like the first, as soon as she completed that, and she was thrilled although Faye was worried about it. Faye tried to ask her tactfully if she was happy doing films like that, but Valerie took it as a slur and there had been pure hatred in Val's eyes when she had answered her.

'You started with soap flakes and cereal, I'm starting with blood, but basically it's the same. And one day, if I want to, I can be right where you are.' It was an ambitious goal, and as he watched the two women spar, Ward was sorry for Val. She so desperately wanted to compete with Faye that she forgot to be herself sometimes. Unlike Anne, who seemed to have come into her own finally, in the last few months. She seemed quieter, more mature, and she seemed to love her new school. She had a new friend, whom she spent time with constantly, a child whose mother had died a few years before apparently. The two girls went everywhere as a team. The father doted on his child, and seemed willing to chauffeur them everywhere, take them to every possible kind of show and game, drop them off, pick them up. It was a blessing for Ward and Faye. Since the last Academy Award, they had had no free time at all. They were grateful to Bill Stein for taking such good care of Anne. Ward knew vaguely who he was, their paths had crossed once or twice, but in a strictly friendly way. He seemed like a nice man, and if he spoiled his child, it was understandable, she was the only one he had, and he had no wife. He had no one else to spoil, except now Anne, and of course Gail.

He was always giving Anne nice things, a sweater when he bought one for Gail, a little red Gucci bag, a yellow umbrella from Giorgio's on a day when it was pouring with rain, and he wanted nothing in return from her. He just had a sense of how lonely she was, and how little time Faye and Ward spent with her. It made him happy to do little things for her, just as he did for Gail.

'You're always so nice to me, Bill.' He let her call him that, in fact he wanted her to, he had said so several times, and she finally did, still feeling a little shy with him.

'Why shouldn't I be? You're a nice person, Anne. We enjoy your company.'

'I love you both too.' The words had poured out of her starved little soul, and his heart went out to her at times. He suspected that there was a sorrow there that no one knew, and he didn't know what it was, but it never left her eyes, no matter how much love you lavished on her. He knew she had run away to the Haight almost two years before, and he wondered if it was something that had happened there. He asked Gail about it once, but she didn't seem to know.

'She never talks about it, Dad. I don't know . . . I don't think her parents are very nice to her.'

'I suspected that too.' He had always been honest with Gail.

'It's not that they're mean to her or anything. They're just never there. No one is. Her brothers and sisters are all grown up and gone, and she's always alone there with the maid.' Most nights she even ate dinner alone, but she was used to it by now.

'Well, she doesn't have to be any more.' The Steins took her under their wing, and Anne basked in the warmth of the love they gave. She was like a little flower in full bloom, and Bill loved to watch her play with Gail. They did homework together sometimes, or just sat and talked, and sometimes they dived into the pool, or giggled for hours at some private joke. He loved to buy them both pretty things, and make them smile. Life was short, he had learned that when his wife died. He was thinking of her one day, as he sat by the pool with Anne. It was a warm autumn day, and Gail had just gone inside to get them something to eat.

'You look so serious sometimes, Anne.' She was comfortable with him now, and she didn't look frightened at what he said, although she had sometimes at first. She was afraid he would ask her something she didn't want to tell anyone. 'What do you think about then?'

'Different things . . .' My brother's friend who died . . . the baby I gave up . . . already at fifteen, there were ghosts that haunted her, but she didn't tell him any of that.

347

'Your days in the Haight?' He had wondered about that and she didn't run away from him. Her eyes met his, and he saw something there that broke his heart. There was a pain in her which no one could reach. He hoped he would one day. She was like another daughter to him, and he was surprised at how much she had come to mean to them in a few months. They were deeply attached to her, and she to them. Other than Lionel and John, they were the first people who had ever taken care of her, or given a damn, or so she thought.

'Sort of . . .' And then she surprised herself by opening up more than she'd planned to him. 'I gave up something once that I cared about very much . . . sometimes I think of it, even though it doesn't change anything.' There were tears in her eyes and he reached out and touched her hand, with tears in his own.

'I didn't give up something, but I lost someone I loved very much. Maybe that's a little bit the same thing. A kind of loss. Maybe it's even worse if you give it up willingly.' He thought she was referring to someone she had loved, and wondered how someone so young could have cared so much. It never crossed his mind that she had given up a child. She and Gail still seemed so innocent to him, and he cherished that. But her eyes reached out to him now with wisdom far beyond her years.

'It must have been terrible for you when she died.'

'It was.' It surprised him that he could say the words so easily to her. But she seemed so understanding as they sat holding hands by the pool, like old friends. 'It was the worst thing that ever happened to me.'

'That's like what happened to me.' She had a sudden urge to tell him about the baby she'd given up, but she was afraid he would never let Gail near her again. There were things better left unsaid, and she stopped herself now.

'Was it terrible, sweetheart?'

'Worse than that.' Every day she wondered where he was, whether she had done the right thing. Maybe he was sick, or he had died, or the drugs she had taken had affected him after all,

348

although there was no sign of it at the birth, they said . . . Her eyes met Bill's now, and he looked so sadly at her.

'I'm so sorry, Anne.' He held her hand tight, and she felt warm and safe. In a little while Gail came out with lunch for all three of them. She thought Anne slightly subdued, but she got that way sometimes. It was just the way she was. She didn't see anything different in her father's eyes that day, though he seemed to watch Anne a lot after that. Anne noticed it sometimes, as he sat looking at her, and one day when they were alone, waiting for Gail to come back from a friend's, she got a chance to talk to him again. She had arrived a little bit before the time she had arranged with Gail, and Bill had just come out of the shower and was wearing a robe. He told her to make herself at home, and she stretched out in the den with a magazine, but then she saw him watching her. She put the magazine down and felt everything she had held built for so long. Without saying a word, she stood up and walked to him. He took her in his arms, and kissed her hard, and then he forced himself to pull away from her. 'Oh, God, Anne, I'm so sorry . . . I don't know what . . .' But she silenced him as she kissed him again, and he was stunned. He knew instinctively that she was no novice at this, and as her hands sought him beneath the robe, he knew that there were secrets about Anne that no one knew. He gently took her hands away and kissed her fingertips. His body was straining for her, and she had stroked him so enticingly, he felt half mad, but not so crazed that he would let her get hurt or do something insane. She was just a child, in his eyes. And he knew this was wrong. She was a fifteen-year-old girl, almost sixteen, but still . . . 'We have to talk about this.' He sat down on the couch next to her, turned towards her, pulling the robe tight, and looked into her eyes. 'I don't know what happened to me.'

'I do.' She spoke the words so gently that he thought he had dreamed what she said. 'I'm in love with you, Bill.' It was the truth, she was, and he was in love with her. It was madness for them. He was forty-nine years old and she was fifteen. It was wrong . . . wasn't it? He had to remind himself of that as he looked at her, and he couldn't help himself. He kissed her again. He felt tortured by the waves of passion that he felt and he took her hand in his.

'I love you too, but I won't let this happen to us.' He sounded anguished as he spoke. There were tears in Anne's eyes. She was terrified he would send her away. Maybe even for good. And she couldn't have lived through that.

'Why not? What's wrong with it? It happens to other people too.'

'But not at your age and mine.' They were thirty-three years apart, and she wasn't even of age. Maybe if she had been twenty-two and he fifty-five and not the father of her best friend. Anne was shaking her head frantically. She wouldn't lose him now. She refused. She had already lost too much in her short life, and she wouldn't lose him too, no matter what he said.

'That's not true. It happens to other people just like us.'

He smiled at her. She was so earnest and so sweet, and he loved her so much. He realised that now. 'I wouldn't care if you were a hundred years old. I love you. That's all. I won't give you up.' The melodrama of it made him smile again, and he kissed her lips to silence her. They were so sweet, and her skin in his hands was like velvet to the touch. But this was wrong. Technically, it was statutory rape, even with her consent. He knew that, and he looked at her now.

'Have you ever done this before, Anne? Honestly. I won't be angry at you.' He had a gentle way of bringing out the truth, and it was always easy for her to be honest with him.

She knew what he meant, more or less. And they were both grateful Gail was late. 'Not like this. When I was . . . in the Haight . . .' It would be so difficult to explain to him, but she wanted to now. 'I . . .' She sighed horribly and he was sorry he had asked.

'You don't have to tell me anything you don't want to, Anne.'

'I want you to know.' She tried to make it brief and clinical, but it still sounded terrible to her. 'I lived in a commune, and I took LSD. I took other things too, but mostly that, some peyote . . . a lot of dope, but mostly acid. And the group I lived with had strange practices . . .'

He looked horrified. 'You were raped?'

Slowly, she shook her head, her eyes never leaving his, she had to be honest with him at all costs. 'I did it because I wanted to . . . and I did it with all of them, I think. I don't remember much any more. It was like being in a trance and I don't know what's memory and what's dream . . . but I was five months pregnant when my parents brought me back. I had a baby thirteen months ago.' She knew now that she would remember the date for the rest of her life. She could have told Bill how many days past thirteen months. Five to be exact. 'And my parents made me give him up. It was a boy, but I never saw him. It was the worst thing I ever went through.' There was no way to describe to him what she had been through. 'And giving him up was the worst mistake I ever made in my life. I'll never forgive myself. Every day, I ask myself where he is, if he's all right.'

'It would have ruined your life, sweetheart.' Gently, with one hand he stroked her face, so desperately sorry for her and the pain she had been through. She was so different from Gail. She had seen so much of life. Too much, at her age.

'That's what my parents said,' she sighed. 'I don't think they were right.'

'What would you do with a baby now?'

'Take care of him . . . just like his other mother does . . .' Her eyes filled with tears and he held her close. 'I should never have given him up.' He wanted to tell her he'd give her another baby one day, but it seemed an outrageous thing to say, and then they heard Gail's key in the lock. Bill moved quietly away from her, with a last look, a last touch, an ache of desire, as he pulled his robe close, and they both smiled for Gail.

351

For the next two months, Anne met him whenever she could, just to talk to him, to go for walks, to share her thoughts with him. Gail knew nothing of it, and Anne hoped she never would. It was forbidden fruit for both of them, and yet they couldn't stop. They needed each other too much now. He confided in her too. The relationship was chaste, but they couldn't hold out for much longer, and when Gail's grandmother invited her for the Christmas holidays, they made a plan. Anne would tell her parents that she was going to stay with them. And from Christmas Day until Gail returned, Anne would stay with him. It was thought out ahead of time and planned. Almost like a honeymoon.

Chapter 31

Louise had long since figured out what was going on between her roommate and the man on the second floor. She didn't disapprove, although she thought he was too old for Van. Twenty-four was already a man. And she was sorry she didn't see more of Vanessa now, but she had her own friends too, and Columbia kept them more than busy enough with assignments and projects and homework and exams. The months flew by and it was hard to believe that the Christmas holidays had already rolled around. The weather was cold and crisp, and just after Thanksgiving, they had had their first snow.

Vanessa was enchanted with it and she and Jason had thrown snowballs at each other in Riverside Park. There was always so much for them to do, the Cloisters, the Metropolitan, the Guggenheim, the Museum of Modern Art, the opera, the ballet, concerts at Carnegie Hall, and always the lure of Off Broadway for him. Jason led a full cultural life, and now he always took Vanessa along. She hadn't seen a film with him since she'd arrived, except some old ones at a festival at the Museum of Modern Art. He continued to disapprove of all that, and he worked on his thesis while she studied for exams. Somehow she loved his seriousness, and his purism about his philosophies. To her, it made him not rigid, but more lovable.

'I'm going to miss you a lot over the holidays.' She was lying on his couch with a book on her lap. As she looked at him, he appeared terribly serious with his glasses on. He peered over them with a smile.

'It'll probably be a relief to get back to Plastic Land,' which was what he called LA, 'you can go to the cinema with your friends every day, and eat tacos and french fries,' he had a horror of those things too, 'before you have to come back here again.' She laughed at his visions of Los Angeles. According to him, people were running everywhere with hamburgers and tacos and pizzas in their hands, wearing curlers in their hair, dancing to rock, and going to trashy films. It made her laugh even more to think of what he would have thought of Val. She was making another horror film, and in this one she was covered in green slime, hardly his idea of what fine cinema should be. But it would be fun to see them all again too. Sometimes she thought Jason took himself too seriously, but she was enjoying their affair, and she had told the truth. She would miss him over the holidays.

'What are you going to do?' He still hadn't decided the last time they'd talked about it. She thought he should go home, but didn't seem keen on the idea. She noticed that his parents never called, and that he rarely mentioned them. She didn't call home that often either, but she still considered herself close to all of them. As Vanessa looked up, she saw Jason smiling at her. There was a tender side of him that she really loved and she could see it now. She reached out a hand to where he sat at his desk, and he kissed it and smiled.

'I'm going to miss you too, you know. And it'll probably take me weeks to straighten you out again.'

'One of these days, you'll have to come to California with me.' But neither of them was ready for that. Her family sounded terrifying to him, and the prospect of bringing him home frightened her too. That would mean that it was serious, or so her parents would think, and it was not. It was just a lovely first affair. She expected nothing more of it than that or so she told herself. 'I'll call you, Jase.'

She repeated exactly the same words to him as they stood at the airport on December 23. He had decided not to go home,

354

but to work on his thesis instead, which sounded like a lonely way to spend the holidays to her. But he said he'd be fine, and she promised to call every day. He kissed her long and hard before she boarded the plane, and then she was gone in the huge silver bird in the air, and he dug his hands into his pockets, and wrapped his scarf around his neck, and went back out into the cold air. It was snowing again. It frightened him to realise how much he had fallen in love with her. He had wanted it to be a casual affair, even the convenience of living in the same building appealed to him. That had nothing to do with it now. He liked everything about her; she was serious, intelligent, beautiful, kind, and wonderful in bed, and his apartment seemed like a tomb as he unlocked the door, and sat down at his desk and stared. Maybe he should have gone home after all. But it was so depressing for him. Life in their small town was so limited, and his parents always smothered him, he couldn't stand it any more. As much as he loved them, he wanted to be free. His father drank too much. His mother had become so old, he knew it would depress the hell out of him, and he was happier in New York alone. It had been almost impossible to explain to Vanessa before she left, her family was so different from his. She had actually been happy to go back. And he could hear it in her voice when she called him that night. She called almost as soon as she got off the plane.

'Well, how's Plastic Land?' He tried to sound less glum than he was and she laughed.

'Still the same. Except you're not here, and that's what's wrong with it.' She loved LA, but now she had come to love New York too. Because of him. 'Next time you have to come out.' He almost shuddered at the thought. He couldn't face a family like that, high-powered, shiny, totally involved in the film world. He could imagine Faye cooking breakfast in gold lamé high heels, and the image of it made him laugh as he talked to Van.

'How's your twin?'

'I haven't seen her yet. I thought I'd drop by tonight. It's only eight o'clock here.'

'That's because they don't know how to tell the time,' he teased, and his face looked youthful and sad as he did. He missed her so much. The next two weeks were going to be unbearable. 'Give her my best.' They had talked to each other on the phone several times, and she sounded like fun, although totally different from Van.

'I will.'

'Let me know if she's turned green.' He had teased her mercilessly about the green slime film, telling her that that was typical Hollywood and probably the best they could do. Except Vanessa had taken umbrage at that. Her mother had made beautiful films in her life, and one day they'd probably be in the archives of the Museum of Modern Art too. She was still eighteen, and they were her family. He went easy on it after that. But he would have been horrified, Vanessa thought, if he could have seen the place where Val lived.

She borrowed her father's car and drove to the place Val shared with at least a dozen other girls. Vanessa thought she'd never seen such chaos and filth in her entire life. There was stale food left on plates in the living room from God knew when, and unmade beds in every room, some even without sheets; an empty tequila bottle lay on the floor; there were stockings hung in the bathroom in all shapes and hues, and everywhere hung the rancid smell of too many perfumes. In the midst of it all sat Val, happily doing her nails and telling Vanessa about her part in the film.

'And then I come out of this swamp . . . I hold out my arms like this,' she did so, almost knocking over a lamp, 'and I scream . . .' She demonstrated that too, and Vanessa covered her ears. It seemed to go on for hours, and she was actually impressed. She grinned at her twin. It was good to see her again, even here.

'You've developed quite a range with that in the last few months.'

Val laughed. 'I get plenty of practice every day.'

Vanessa looked around again. 'How do you stand this place?' Between the smell, the filth, the disorder, and the girls, Vanessa knew she would have gone mad in two days, but Valerie seemed oblivious to it all. In fact she seemed happy there, happier than she had been at home by far, and she said as much to her twin.

'I can do whatever I want here.'

'And what does that include?' Vanessa was curious about what she'd been up to the last three months. Val knew about Jason, although Vanessa hadn't gone into details about her affair, and she didn't intend to now. 'Any big new heart throbs since I left?'

Valerie shrugged. There were a number of men in her life, one she cared about, and three she was sleeping with, but she knew her sister would be shocked so she didn't say anything. It didn't mean that much to her. A little dope, a little booze, a terrific piece of ass in some boy's apartment or rented room. There was so much going on in Hollywood that it didn't seem so terrible to be a part of it, and all of them in her apartment passed the pill around like after dinner mints. There was always an open box somewhere in the house. Someone had told her not to mix brands, but they seemed to work anyway. And if there was a slip, she could always get rid of it. She wasn't as dumb as her little sister, Anne. 'What about you?' Valerie turned the tables on her, as she started on the nails on the other hand. 'What's that guy like you're with all the time?'

'Jason?' Vanessa feigned innocence and Val laughed.

'No. King Kong. Is he cute?'

'By my standards yes, but probably not by yours.'

'That means he has a harelip and a club foot, but he's cute and you think he's serious.'

'More or less. He's working on his PhD.' Vanessa sounded proud of him and Valerie stared at her. He sounded horrible to her. She hated intellectuals, she liked all the Hollywood types, especially long hair, open shirts, the California beach-boy look.

She looked at Vanessa suspiciously. 'How old is this guy?'

'Twenty-four.'

'You think he wants to marry you?' That horrified her, but Vanessa was quick to shake her head.

'He's not that type and neither am I. I want to finish school, and come back here to write screenplays.' She and Jason argued about that all the time. He thought she had too much talent to write 'junk', but she insisted that some films were very good. 'It's just nice for now.'

'Well, watch out you don't get knocked up. Do you take the pill?' Vanessa was embarrassed by the directness of her twin, and shook her head. She hadn't even admitted that she was sleeping with him, but Val knew her better than anyone. "You're not?" Valerie was appalled at her naïveté.

'Jason takes care of it.' She blushed beet red and Valerie laughed as a girl in a red satin G-string walked through the room. And with that she glanced at Val again. 'Has Mum seen this place?' She couldn't imagine that she had, or she would have had Valerie out of it in two hours, or possibly less.

'Just once. And we cleaned it up pretty good before she came. No one was here that day.'

'Thank God. She'd have your head for this, my friend.' But that would have applied to just about anything Val was doing these days, from the little snorts of cocaine, to the pipes filled with hashish, to the men she was experimenting with, to the roles she played in horror films. As she said to Van bitterly, 'She never wants me to have any fun.' Someone had just offered her her first porno role but she had turned it down. She had been terrified her mother would hear of it. But as Vanessa drove back to the house, she had the feeling that Valerie was going bad. She was way out of control, and she was just eighteen. But she knew her well enough to know that there was no stopping her. She was rolling wildly down a hill, and it would all end somewhere. Vanessa just hoped she didn't get hurt on the way.

'How was Val?' Her father glanced at her as she came in, and read something in her eyes that she wouldn't have said to him.

'Okay.'

And then, 'Just how bad is that place?' They couldn't have known how bad it really was. But she wondered. If they knew other things. Hollywood was a small town, and if she was sleeping around, they were liable to hear of it.

'It's not that bad. Just a lot of girls running around making a mess, and leaving dirty dishes on the floor.' That was the least of it, but it was all she felt safe telling them. She tried to make it sound better than it was, for Valerie's sake. 'Just a magnified version of our rooms.'

'As bad as that?' He laughed, and reported that Greg was coming home the next day. And a little while later, Anne came in with a glow in her eyes that Vanessa had never seen before.

'Hi, kiddo.' She stood up and kissed her cheek, and she could have sworn that she smelled a man's after-shave in her hair, though she wasn't sure. Little Anne was growing up. She was about to turn sixteen after the holidays, and Vanessa noticed that she was becoming beautiful. Her dress was short, her legs were long and slim, and she was wearing beautiful little red shoes and a ribbon in her hair. Vanessa smiled at the image that had developed in three short months. She looked as old as Vanessa herself. 'When did you get so grown-up?' Ward glanced at her admiringly too. She had settled down beautifully in the last few months, and she had made new friends in her new school. Especially Gail Stein, who seemed like an awfully nice girl, even if she was a little spoiled. So what if she wore Vuitton bags and Jourdan shoes, she was a nice, decent, wholesome girl, and her father took good care of her. It was a pleasant change from the agony of what had happened in the Haight, and he and Faye were both grateful for that.

Anne didn't waste much time with them and disappeared quickly into her room. She did the same thing on Christmas Day, after they ate, but they were all used to it. Anne had been hiding in her room for years, but tonight she was packing a bag. The next day she was moving in with Bill for the holidays

Chapter 32

Anne had explained to her mother weeks before that Gail had invited her to spend ten days with them until they went back to school. At first Faye had balked, but Anne had preyed cunningly on her maternal sympathies, reminding her that Gail was an only child, without even a mother to keep her company. Since her mother's death, the holidays were hard for her. That had done the trick with Faye, eventually.

'She only lives a few miles from here, Anne. Why can't you both stay here! Why do you have to sleep over at her house?'

'It's too confusing here. And you and Dad are out all the time anyway. What difference does it make?' There had been panic in her eyes and Ward saw it too. He didn't want her going wild on them again. They'd all been through enough two years before. Maybe it was better to give in to her on small things like this.

'Let her go, babe. There's no harm in it. Gail's father seems to sit on her like an egg about to hatch. They'll be fine. And she can always come home, if you want.'

'Will anyone else be there?' Faye never trusted anyone, not where her children were involved, and this time she was right.

'Just the cleaning lady and the cook.' He also had a gardener but that didn't count, she knew. And in fact, none of them did. Both women were leaving for the holidays as soon as he put Gail on a plane to her grandmother's in New York. But Faye had no way of knowing that. When Anne left the house with her small valise, it was filled with her prettiest clothes, and her frilliest nightgowns, including two new ones she had bought just for this. She called a cab after everyone left the house, and left a

360

note, 'See you on the 3rd. I'll be at Gail's.' The cab pulled up on Charing Cross Road in Bel Air ten minutes later, and Anne felt her heart pound. He was waiting for her in the living room. Gail had left only hours before, and the maids were gone. They were finally alone. They had planned it for months, and now suddenly they were both terrified. All morning, he had asked himself if he was insane. He was practically raping a fifteen-year-old girl, and he had long since resolved to take her home as soon as she arrived.

He tried to explain it as they sat in his cosy den. There was a tiger skin on the floor, and photographs he had taken of Gail over the years hung on the walls, Gail in first grade . . . Gail in a funny hat . . . Gail eating an ice-cream cone when she was four . . . but his eyes were riveted to Anne's now, and they saw nothing in the room. She only saw him, this man she so deeply loved, who wanted to send her away now.

'Why do I have to go? . . . Why? We planned it for weeks.'

'But it's wrong, Anne. I'm an old man. You're a fifteen-year-old girl.' He had thought about it all night as he tossed and turned, and he had finally come to his senses. He wasn't going to let her change his mind now.

'I'm almost sixteen.' There were tears in her eyes, and he smiled as he smoothed her hair back from her face. But just that small touch electrified him again. This was forbidden fruit of the sweetest kind, and he mustn't let her stay even an hour, or he couldn't be responsible for what he would do. He knew himself too well. He had never felt this way for anyone – it was just one of life's cruel jokes that she was a fifteen-year-old girl. 'I'm not even a virgin, Bill.' She said it sadly with heartbroken eyes. She loved him so much; he was all she wanted in life. He was the reward for all the loneliness and pain she had had.

'That's beside the point, sweetheart. Your other experiences don't count. They were drug-induced, hallucinating dreams. You don't even have to think about them any more. That's all behind you now. It's not like making a decision to become involved with a man. This is something neither of us could handle for very long. And then what do we do? Someone would get hurt, and I don't want it to be you.' He didn't tell her that it could also be him, that he could wind up in jail for sleeping with her, if her parents found out. And they might, no matter how carefully they had planned. She had told Gail not to call her at home, that she couldn't talk anyway, with all the brothers and sisters around for the holidays. And she was going to call Gail herself every day, so that she wouldn't have a reason to call. They had thought of everything. He was breaking her heart now: she didn't care if she got hurt, she didn't care if she died, as long as she could be with him.

She looked at him with deep, sad eyes. 'If you make me go, I'll run away again. You're all I have to live for, Bill.'

It was a terrible thing to say and it tore at his heart. She had been through so much and she was so young, and in some ways she was right, she was far more mature than most girls her age, certainly more than Gail; but she had also been exposed to more. The Haight-Ashbury, the commune, the baby she had given birth to, her difficulties with her parents. It seemed unfair to hurt her again, but this was for her own good, he told himself as he stood up, her hand gently held in his. He was going to drive her home himself – but she wouldn't move. She just sat looking at him, with that broken look, those heartrending eyes. 'Baby, please . . . you can't stay . . .'

'Why not?'

He sank down on the couch next to her. He could only fight her for so long, and if she didn't go soon . . . it wasn't fair to him . . . he was only a man after all. 'Because I love you too much.' He took her gently in his arms, and kissed her, with every intention of taking her home after that. But his iron resolve began to melt as he felt the hot molten lava of her tongue reaching into his mouth, and instinctively his hand went between her legs. They had been getting bolder and bolder for weeks now, each time they were alone. 'I want you so much, little one . . .' he whispered hoarsely into her neck, '. . . but we can't . . . please . . .'

'Yes, we can,' she whispered back. She was melting into the couch, pulling him down with her, and all his arguments began to drift away . . . maybe just this once . . . just once . . . they would never do it again . . . and then suddenly he came to his senses, and pulled away from her. His legs were shaking when he did, but he shook his head and stopped.

'No, I won't do this to you, Anne.'

'I love you with all my heart.' She looked like a stricken child.

'And so do I. I'll wait for the next two years for you, if that's what we have to do. And then I'll marry you. But I will not ruin your life.'

Suddenly she laughed, and it was the laugh of a very young girl as she kissed his cheek. 'I love you so much. Do you mean you'd really marry me?' She was stunned and delighted and pleased and happier than she'd been in a long time.

'I would.' He smiled gently at her. It had been a difficult hour for him, for both of them, but more so for him, and he hadn't slept all night. But he meant what he said to her now. He had thought of it before. He even thought that Gail might approve of it one day. Other men had married girls less than half their age. It wasn't the worst thing he could do. 'If you were crazy enough to marry me, that is. In two years, you'll be eighteen and I'll be fifty-one.'

'Sounds great to me,' she grinned.

'How about when you're thirty and I'm sixty-three?' He was testing her now and watching her eyes. He was serious about proposing to her. He could think of nothing else in life he wanted more, but there was no reason why they couldn't have both, his happiness and hers. He wanted to take care of her, to keep her from sorrow for the rest of her life. He sensed that her parents had done precious little for her since the day she was born, certainly less than he did for Gail. But Gail was an only child, and Anne was the last of five, and from what he had heard, she had been born into their lives at a difficult time. Still that was no excuse. He would spend the rest of his life making it up to her. Everything. Even the baby she had given up.

'That sounds fine to me.' She was responding to his second question about the difference in their ages, and she looked genuinely unimpressed. 'I can count too, you know. And when I'm sixty, you'll be ninety-three. How does that sound to *you*? You sure you won't want someone younger by then?' She was teasing him now and they both laughed as he began to relax. It had been a nightmarish morning, filled with terror and guilt, but this was more like the easy moments he had known with her before, although he had never proposed to her.

'Shall we call it definite then? We're engaged?' He smiled at her and she smiled back at him, and then leaned forward to kiss him again.

'We're engaged, and I love you with all my heart.' He kissed her so tenderly in answer to what she said that their bodies seemed to become almost one, and he had to remind himself to pull away again, though he didn't really want to any more . . . and if he was going to marry her one day . . . wouldn't it be all right now . . . just this once? . . . to seal their vow, as it were. He sat back, looking into her eyes, knowing he couldn't think straight any more.

'You make me crazy, you know.'

'I'm glad.' She looked like a woman as she said the words, and her eyes bored deep into his. 'Can I stay for a while?'

There was no harm in that. They had done that before, when Gail had other plans and the maids were off weekends. The only difference was that then they knew everyone was eventually coming back, and now they were totally alone. He offered to heat the pool so they could swim, and she thought it a fine idea. She didn't bother with a bathing suit, and dived neatly in from the diving board. He watched the smooth velvet of her flesh stretched over her long, graceful limbs. She was a beautiful girl, although no one in her family seemed to have noticed it yet. She was just 'little Anne', the quiet one who hid in her room. But she wasn't hiding now. He shed his clothes and dived in after her, and they swam like porpoises beneath the surface of the pool, and then leapt high, catching each other by the waist, and slowly he brought her to him. He couldn't stand it any more. He wanted her too much. Their bodies met and held as he caressed her back and neck and kissed her tenderly. He led her from the pool, wrapped her in a towel, and then carried her inside the house. There was nothing left to say. He couldn't fight it any more, she looked like a delicate princess as he laid her on his bed, and smiled down at her, his own body still firm, his muscles hard, his legs strong. They would have beautiful children together one day, he thought to himself, though he wasn't thinking of babies now. He was thinking only of her, as he touched every inch of her, caressing and kissing and letting his tongue dance over her, and from some distant part of her, she remembered a kind of loving she had never really known before, and she gently caressed him until he could bear it no more and their bodies joined as one. Her whole body arched with pleasure at his touch, and they seemed to dance there together for hours, sailing high into the sky, until at last they exploded like the sun.

Chapter 33

Their days together were the most idyllic either had ever known. There were no drugs this time, no hallucinogens, no rituals, no make-believe, only Bill and the tenderness and beauty he brought to her life, and the joy she brought to his. For ten days they allowed themselves to forget how difficult it would be for the next two years. They stayed within the confines of the house and grounds, but they ran and they played, they listened to music, and he gave her a glass of champagne, only one, on what he called their wedding night. They took long baths in his tub, and he read to her, and at night in front of the fire he combed her hair, and he loved her in ways she had never been loved before. It was the kind of fatherly love he had always had for Gail, enhanced now by the love he had once had for his wife and yet had no one to share with for several years. He poured his soul out to Anne, and she gave hers to him. She was happier than she had ever been in her life. She cried on their last night. She had dutifully called Gail every day, who reported that she was having fun in New York. But she had never bothered to call home. They knew she was all right, and they knew where she was. They had no idea what she was up to, but that was her secret now, and they would have to live with it for the next two years.

'What if Gail ever found out?' she asked as they lay in bed. She had hardly worn clothes for the past ten days, they made love all the time, and he seemed unable to get enough of her. He had made love more in ten days than he had in the past ten years. He sighed now, thinking of what she had asked.

'I don't know. At first, I think she'd be shocked, but I think she'll accept it in time. I think the best thing is if she doesn't find out for a year of so, she'll be older then and more mature, and better able to accept what we feel.' Anne nodded, agreeing with him. She agreed with him about almost everything. 'I think the most important thing is that she know eventually that our love can be shared with her too, that it won't shut her out. I love her just as I once did. But I also love you now. I have a right to get married again one day, after all . . . it just may surprise her a little when it's one of her friends.' Anne suddenly envisaged herself in a white veil with Gail as the maid of honour, and she smiled to herself. It was a lovely dream, but it was still a long, long way off. A lot could happen in two years.

She knew that better than anyone. She had told him about Lionel and John, about their being gay, and taking her in until the baby was born, and how nice they had been . . . and John dying in the fire, and how heartbroken Li still was. It had been a year and he still wasn't the same. He lived alone, and except for work, he never went out. He took her to lunch now and then, but he was so quiet it frightened her. Bill understood what she described. He had felt that way when his wife died, but he had had Gail of course to cheer him up. He began to feel he knew everything about Anne now, all her secrets, her fears, the way she felt about Faye; she was convinced that her parents had never loved her at all, and it saddened him for her. 'We're going to have to be very careful, little one. Not just with Gail. But with everyone.'

'I know that. I've kept secrets before.' She looked mysterious and he laughed and kissed the tip of her breast, which hardened instantly.

'Not like this, I hope.'

'No,' she smiled, and a few minutes later, they made love again. He didn't even feel guilty about it any more. This was what was, and it was his, and he wouldn't lose it now. He would never give her up. He would stand by her for the rest of their life together and he promised that as he took her home the following afternoon. They both looked tired, they had stayed up all night to make love and talk, and he had to pick Gail up at the airport in two hours, and that night, the maids would be back. The fairy-tale honeymoon was over now; now they had to walk carefully, hand in hand, and into what their life would be like for the next two years. But there would be moments like this again. Holidays they could go on, stolen weekends, a night here and there. He had promised her that, and her eyes were still alight with his love as she walked in her front door, carrying her suitcase in one hand. She stopped, listening, as she heard the Rolls Royce purr as it drove off.

'You sure look tired.' Her mother glanced at her as she came in. They hadn't filmed that day. It was a Sunday afternoon and she looked at Anne's eyes. She looked happy enough though. 'Have a good time, sweetheart?'

'Mm hmm . . .'

'It was probably one long pyjama party for ten days.' Ward smiled. 'I don't know what it is about girls your age, they never want to get dressed.' She smiled and disappeared into her room without saying anything, but as Vanessa glanced at her she saw something more than her parents did, though she wasn't sure what it was. It made her uneasy about the girl, and she wanted to talk to her before she left. But there was never time. Anne went back school the next day. There were some friends Vanessa still wanted to see, and the next night she had to pack, and then she was gone, without ever finding out what had lit Anne's eyes up like that.

Chapter 34

Everyone went back to their own lives, Val to her life with her horror films, a smattering of drugs, a new man in her bed whenever possible, and Vanessa back at school in New York. Greg was having trouble with his grades, but promising to pick up, and Anne didn't seem to give anyone any trouble. She spent most of her time at her friend's, but everyone was used to it by now. They never saw her any more. She had turned sixteen, and barely had a night to spare for her family to celebrate it. Gail and her father had taken her to the Bistro for a celebration with them the next day, but Faye didn't see anything wrong with it. They were awfully nice to her, and she reminded Anne to buy a gift for Gail now and then, just to show that she appreciated it.

In Febuary, Lionel called Faye at the studio and asked if he could have lunch with her and Ward. It was unusual for him to do something like that, and she hoped it meant good news in his life, like an exciting film or even a job change, or an announcement that he was going back to school. But neither of them were prepared for what he announced to them instead.

He seemed to hesitate, as though afraid to cause them pain, and Ward suddenly felt sick. Maybe he was going to tell them that he was in love with another man, and he didn't want to hear about it. But Lionel dived in quickly, there was no way to ease the words. 'I've been drafted.' They both stared. Vietnam was in full swing and it was on everyone's minds. Ward looked horrified. As much as he loved his country, he didn't want to sacrifice either of his sons for a war which stank, in a place he didn't give a damn about, and Faye's jaw almost dropped at the first thing Ward said.

'Tell them you're gay.' It was the first time he had used the word and Lionel smiled and shook his head.

'Dad, I can't.'

'Don't be shy, for chrissake. It may save your life.' This was exactly why he had told Greg to pull up his grades. All he needed was to get kicked out of school and sent to Vietnam. But Lionel had the perfect excuse. He hadn't really worried about him. 'Be sensible, boy. Either that or go to Canada.'

'I don't want to run away, Dad. It just wouldn't be right.'

'Why not, for chrissake?' He pounded the table in the commissary but no one looked. There was so much action and noise that no one noticed anyone, no matter what they wore or did or said. You could have walked in naked, screaming at the top of your lungs, and everyone would have figured you were practising for a part. But Ward was serious with him now. 'You have to get out of it, Li. I don't want you to go.'

There were tears in her eyes, as Faye listened to the two men. 'Neither do I, sweetheart.'

'I know, Mum.' He gently touched her hand. 'I'm not happy about it either, but I don't feel like I have a choice. I talked to them yesterday, and I think they know what I am, they also know my film background, and they'd want me to do something with film.' Ward and Faye both looked relieved.

'Do you know where?'

He took a breath. 'Probably in Vietnam for a year, and maybe in Europe for a year after that.'

'Oh my God.' Ward's face went white and Faye started to cry, and it was a dismal two weeks while Lionel wrapped up the details of his life, gave up the small apartment he had, left his job, and moved in with Faye and Ward for a few days before he left for boot camp. They were grateful to have the time with him and they both left work early every day. But the last night was rough. Everyone cried as they toasted him. They all stood in the doorway and waved the next day at 6 am as the cab drove away, and Faye collapsed Ward's arms and sobbed. She was afraid she would never see him again, and as he held her, Ward cried just as hard. It was a heartbreaking time for all of them. Anne and Bill went for a long, long walk, and Anne voiced to him what her parents were afraid to say; that he had never recovered from John's death and maybe he had gone to Vietnam to let himself be killed. It was a sobering thought.

'I'm sure that's not true, sweetheart. He's just doing what he thinks he has to do. I went to war once too, you know. Not everyone gets killed. And if he's working in film, I'm sure he'll be pretty safe.' It wasn't entirely true. He knew that those boys often got hit, riding low in helicopters to get the best shots. He just prayed that her brother would be sensible, and that her assessment of his psychological state was wrong. But Ward and Faye were secretly afraid of it too.

Only Val seemed certain that he'd be fine. She was so involved in her own life, it was difficult for her to think of much else. She had just landed a part in a monster film being made outside Rome. It was an international cast and the whole thing was being dubbed, but she had no lines in it anyway. There were a number of old stars in it, all of them failing badly and long since out of work.

'Isn't that great?' She had called Vanessa to tell her she'd be coming through New York. Only for one night, but it would be fun anyway. Vanessa had invited her to stay to meet her 'friend'.

Valerie hurtled off the plane wearing a red leather skirt and purple tights, a purple fur, and suede boots that looked like neon signs. The sweater she had on was cut almost to her waist, and her hair was still the same wild mane. Suddenly as Vanessa glanced up at Jason in his subdued forest greens and charcoal grays, she coughed and wondered what she had done.

'My God, is she for real?' he whispered to Van, but her beauty was undeniable, no matter how ridiculous her clothes were, and Vanessa grinned.

'Plastic Land at its best.'

She threw herself into Vanessa's arms, kissed Jason a little too lovingly for a first time. Her perfume was too heavy and as they kissed, Vanessa could smell marijuana in her hair. They went to Greenwich Village that night, to listen to some jazz, and then came back and talked in Jason's apartment until four o'clock. He poured tequila until they ran out, and Valerie pulled out a box of joints.

'Help yourselves.' She lit one expertly as Jason watched, and he followed suit, but Vanessa hesitated. She had only tried it once before and she didn't think much of it. 'Come on, Sis, don't be a square.' Vanessa did it to be a good sport, and insisted it had had no effect, except that they all found themselves combing the yellow pages for an all-night pizza joint, and settled for emptying Louise and Van's refrigerator instead, laughing and giggling as Jason stared at Val. He couldn't get over how different she was from Van, and he was still staring at her the next day as she got back on the plane, this time in a lime-green leather suit her parents had never seen. She had borrowed a lot of her wardrobe for the trip from the girls she roomed with and no one seemed to care. No one knew what belonged to whom any more, and she was only going to be gone a few weeks, unless she got more work, once she was over there.

'Ta ta, guys. Take care of yourselves.' And then she winked at Van. 'He's okay.'

'Thanks.' The two young women kissed, and Jason waved as she boarded the plane. It was like having been hit by a cyclone for two days.

'How on earth did she wind up like that, with you the way you are?' He couldn't figure it out and Van laughed at him. He looked as though he were in shock.

'I don't know. We're all different I guess, even if we are one family.'

'Apparently.'

'Want to trade me in for Val?' She was always afraid of that. Valerie was so much more spectacular, and outrageous, with her

372

box of joints, her loose morals, her wild red hair. She got the feeling that she would have gladly slept with Jason, if Vanessa would only have disappeared, but she knew her sister too well, and was careful of that. She had lost too many boyfriends to her over the years to ever trust her again with a man, though she didn't hold a grudge for it. It was just the way Val was, and it didn't mean anything to her.

'Not yet.' Jason looked enormously relieved to have found the quieter twin.

But he did not look relieved when Vanessa made a suggestion several months after that. Their affair had been continuing comfortably. In fact, she had moved in with him downstairs, and Louise had found another roommate in no time at all. The deal they made was that if her parents called, they would cover for her, tell them to hold on, and come downstairs and bang on the door so she could run up and talk to them. But they seldom called. And if they had come to town, Vanessa would have moved back in for a few days, but so far they hadn't come. They were too busy with their latest film. Lionel was still in Vietnam, but miraculously thus far all had gone well, and Valerie still hadn't returned from Rome. She had got another bit part once there, this time in a cowboy film, which was new for her, and she had modelled a few times in Milan, she'd said on the phone. What she didn't tell Faye was that it was without clothes.

But whatever the case, they were spread all over the world now, and the only one left in LA was Anne. Ward wanted to rent a house in Lake Tahoe for two weeks, and he wanted to know if Van could be there. Lionel would be on leave, Greg would be through with his summer job, Val said she'd be home from Rome by then, and Anne said she'd go if she could bring Gail. What he wanted was a commitment from Vanessa, who wanted to bring Jason along. Jason looked horrified at the thought.

'To Plastic Land? For two weeks?'

373

'Come on, you'll be finished with your thesis by then, and Lake Tahoe's for real. Besides, I want you to meet my family.' That was precisely what he feared. He imagined that they all looked like Val and he would be devoured by the enemy. He was a small-town boy and he had no defences against them. 'You already know Val, so they won't all be strangers to you.'

'Oh God.' He did everything to talk her out of it in the next few weeks, but she absolutely refused. She had taken a summer job in a bookstore downtown, and she bugged him about it when she came home every day. 'Isn't there something else we can talk about? Robert Kennedy's been killed, the politics in this country stink, your brother is in Vietnam. Do we have to talk about holidays now?'

'Yes.' She knew he was scared but she couldn't imagine of what. They were a harmless bunch, at least in her eyes. 'We are going to talk about it, until you agree to come.'

'Shit!' He had shouted at her because he really loved her a great deal. 'All right! I'll come!'

'Christ, was that a big deal!' It had only taken two months. When she called her parents, they were stunned. Other than Anne's little friend Gail, Vanessa was the first one to ask to bring 'someone' along.

'Who is he, sweetheart?' Faye tried to sound casual as she frowned at her desk at MGM. She was suddenly frightened that he wasn't good enough, or didn't have Vanessa's best interests at heart. How could she know if the guy was decent or not? Vanessa was still so naïve about everything. She had run into Valerie the week before with some character who looked like a hairdresser and he had been so stoned Val was practically holding him up. She was going to have to spend some time with that girl. Ever since she'd been in Rome she had gone totally wild, and rumours were beginning to reach Faye that she didn't like at all, mostly about the people she ran around with. But she knew herself that it was almost impossible to control Val. Now she turned her mind to Vanessa again, and this mysterious friend she wanted to bring out, knowing that Vanessa's taste in men was far more sedate than Val's. She didn't even know what Ward would say, although the place he had rented was certainly big enough. There were a dozen bedrooms, and it was right on the lake. Actually, it sounded like a nice idea to her too, and it would be wonderful to have them all around again. 'Who is this boy again? Is he at Columbia with you?' She didn't want to nag, but she knew it probably sounded like it to her child.

'Not any more. He's just finishing up his Ph.D.'

'How old is this boy?' Now Faye was really upset.

'Sixty-five.' She couldn't resist teasing her mother but Faye was not laughing with her. 'Come on, Mum. Relax. He's only twenty-six. Why?'

'Isn't that a little too old for you?' She was fighting to keep her voice relaxed, but without much success.

'Not that I've noticed. He still walks pretty well. He can dance . . . ride a bike . . .'

'Stop being cute. Is it serious? Why do you want to bring him home with you? How involved are you with this man?' The questions came faster than Vanessa could answer them, and she was glad she had called when Jason was out.

'No, it's not serious. He's just a good friend' . . . I live with him, Mum . . . She would really have been thrilled at that. 'Why don't you ask Val questions like that and get off my back?' Why did she always have to take the brunt of it? They had always done that to her. They let the boys do what they wanted, they couldn't control Val, and Anne wouldn't talk to them, although she suspected that all of them had deeper secrets than hers. Greg had been banging everything in skirts for the past three years; God only knew what Val was into now; and Anne had had that secret look . . . but the heat wasn't on them, it was on her, because she was decent to them. It wasn't fair. But the gentleness of her mother's voice touched her heart, with the next question.

'Are you in love with him, sweetheart?'

Vanessa hesitated. 'I don't know. I just like him very much, and I thought he'd get along with everyone.'

'Is he your steady beau?'

Vanessa smiled at the term and they were friends again. 'More or less, I guess.'

'Well, I'll speak to your father about it, and see what he says.' But after asking fewer questions than Faye, of course, he said yes, and told Faye to relax, which was easy for him to say. She had five children to think about, and to her that's what they still were.

Chapter 35

They arrived at Lake Tahoe separately. Ward wanted a few days alone with Faye, and he was pleased that the house they had rented was even better than they'd hoped. There was a small tower at each end, a huge living room downstairs, a dining table that seated eighteen in a panelled room with an enormous fireplace. Upstairs there were twelve bedrooms, which was more than enough for all of them. The decor was rustic and cosy, with quilts and antlers and pewter plates everywhere. There were Indian baskets and bearskins on the floor, and it was exactly what Ward had had in mind, he noted, as he arrived with Faye. They took over what was obviously the master suite, with a huge old-fashioned bathroom and a dressing room. They sat looking out over the lake the next day, holding hands and remembering their holiday a year before Switzerland.

Faye looked wistful thinking of it, and turned to him. 'I'd like to retire to a place like this one day.'

'My God, you?' He smiled. He couldn't imagine anything more incongruous than his beautiful, worldly, elegant wife, winner of three Academy Awards, most important female director in the world, and trend-setter of sorts, giving it all up to sit staring at a lake for the next forty years. She was only forty-eight years old after all and he just couldn't imagine it. 'You'd go stark staring mad in three days, if not two.'

'That's not true, sweetheart. One of these days I'm going to surprise you and give it all up.' There was so little left that she hadn't done, that she still wanted to do. More and more often now she thought that she might like to give it all up. She had been directing films for more than fifteen years and that was almost long enough. He was surprised at how serious she looked.

'You're too young to retire, babe. What would you do?'

She smiled at him and nuzzled his neck. 'Stay in bed with you all day.'

'Sounds good to me. Maybe you *should* retire if that's what you have in mind.' He smiled, thinking of the next two weeks they had ahead of them. 'Think you can survive two weeks with our brood?' He was looking forward to it, especially to spending some time with Lionel and Greg. It had been years since he'd been outdoors with his sons, and he was relieved to know that Lionel was surviving Vietnam. There were tears in his eyes, as Li hopped out of his rented car two days after that. He was the first to arrive, and Ward embraced him with both arms. 'My God, you look tall and tanned, boy.' He looked wonderful to him. And he seemed to have grown up overnight. At almost twenty-two he looked five or six years older than that, and Ward couldn't help noticing that he didn't look gay at all. He wondered if maybe he had changed his mind, but that was too much to ask and when he hinted around at it later that night, Lionel laughed at him. It was the first time they had talked as friends in years. But Ward respected the films he was making in Vietnam, and the constant danger he was in.

'No, Dad.' He said it very gently, with kind eyes. 'I haven't "changed my mind".' Ward looked embarrassed and Lionel smiled. 'It doesn't work that way. But there hasn't been anyone since John if that's what you mean.' His face sobered thinking of his lost love. It had been a year and a half, and he still missed him terribly. In some ways, it was easier being in Vietnam. He didn't have to see the places where they had once been. It was a whole new life. And Ward could see how painful it still was for him.

They had a pleasant day and a half before the others began to arrive. First, Jason and Vanessa from New York. They flew to Reno and rented a car, reaching the house in the late afternoon. Vanessa got out and stretched, and Jason looked around, surprised at how beautiful it was. As Lionel came across the lawn to them, Jason was surprised. He spotted instantly what Van's brother was, and he wondered why she hadn't told him he was gay.

'Hello.' He had warm eyes, and he looked a little bit like Van. 'I'm Lionel Thayer.'

'Jason Stuart.' The two men shook hands, commenting on how pretty the place was. There was a spectacular view of the lake, and a moment later, Faye and Ward came up from the beach in bathing suits. He with a fishing pole but no visible results and Faye teasing him all the way, in a black maillot that set off her still-beautiful shape. Now he could see where the real resemblance was. Lionel looked exactly like Faye. And although Jason wouldn't have admitted it to Van, it was impressive meeting her. She was beautiful and intelligent, and her eyes danced with a million ideas. She made everyone laugh, and she had a deep sexy voice. He thought she was one of the most interesting women he'd ever met, as they sat deep in conversation that night. She was quizzing him about his thesis, his plans, his ideas, and he suddenly realised how difficult it must have been to have grown up with her. She was so damn beautiful, and so bright, it would have been impossible to compete with her. It explained to him now why Vanessa was so quiet and subdued and her twin sister so wild. Van had obviously chosen not to compete at all, but to lead her own quiet life, and Val was still fighting every inch of the way, but in a way that ensured she would never win. She was trying to be more spectacular, more beautiful; she was trying to beat her at her own game, and she could only lose at that. Lionel had gone into film, but in a totally different vein, and he was curious to meet the other two now. Greg arrived next, talking constantly of playing ball, drinking beer, chasing girls. It was almost exhausting to be in the same room with him, but whenever Jason watched Ward talk to him, he saw his eyes light up. This was his adored son, his hero, his jock. And he could only begin to imagine the pain it must have caused Lionel for most of his life. He attempted to talk to Greg once or twice,

379

the day he arrived, but he had nothing much to say, and he always seemed to have something else on his mind.

And then finally Val arrived with Anne. She had stayed in town as long as she could, and agreed to drive her sister up, although she wasn't in the mood to leave town just then. There was a new horror film being cast, and she didn't want to get passed up. But she couldn't do everything, and she knew there would be another one being cast in two weeks. They were practically a speciality with her now, and she didn't care how much her friends made fun of her. She was working almost all the time, and she was making regular money.

'Come on,' everyone teased once they'd all arrived. Lionel turned off the lights in the living room, 'Let's hear it, Val, the famous Valerie Thayer scream.' She had done dozens of them now, and everyone begged as she laughed, and then finally, standing up in the dark, near the fire, she began to clutch her throat, made a hideous face, and let out a long piercing scream. It was so convincing that they all watched her, horrified, thinking she was choking at first, and then realising what she had done. She was doing it for them, and she seemed to go on for hours and then suddenly, collapsed in a heap. The audience was thrilled and they clapped and cheered, Jason loudest of all. He and Van had gone canoeing with her that afternoon, and she'd been funny as hell. He was rapidly becoming one of her most ardent fans. And to prove that it was mutual, she had calmly handed him a frog on the way back to the house. He had jumped, Van had screamed, and Val had accused them both of being ridiculous.

'Hell, I worked with two hundred of them at once on the film I did in Rome.' Then suddenly all three of them started to laugh, and they raced each other back to the house. It was like being kids again. Lionel, Ward, and Greg had gone off fishing somewhere that day, and returned with several which they tried to convince Faye to cook, but she told them it was their treat instead. Lionel thought that Greg was a little quiet, and he wondered if there was anything on his mind. But all in all, everyone was having fun. Faye had spent a quiet afternoon, lying on the beach with Anne. Anne hadn't wanted to go canoeing with Jason and the twins, or fishing with the boys, and Faye wasn't even sure she wanted to lie on the beach with her. But she had nothing else to do, so she stuck around, and read a book. In the end, her friend Gail had decided not to come along. She didn't want to intrude on their family reunion, and had gone to San Francisco with her father instead, which left Anne felling lonely again. She wrote a letter, and went quietly into the house at one point, and Faye had glimpsed her on the phone. Faye suspected that she was just at the age when she didn't want to leave her friends, and she wasn't thrilled about the trip, but it was doing them all good. By the second week, they were all relaxed and brown. Ward and Jason were great friends, the twins hadn't enjoyed each other as much in years, and Greg seemed to have relaxed finally. Even Anne was having fun, and she went on a long walk with Vanessa one day, when Jason had driven Faye into town. Vanessa glanced at her, thinking again how grown up she looked now. She was sixteen and a half, but her experiences seemed to have matured her far more than her years.

'I like your friend.' She said it quietly, and Van was reminded of how withdrawn she had always been.

'Jason? So do I. He's a nice guy.'

'I think he likes you a lot too.' They both nodded. It was obvious that he did, and that he even enjoyed her family now. He had been so frightened of what they would all do to him. He had finally confessed that he thought it would be like being in a line-up, or being interrogated by each of them, and instead they all had foibles and weird traits of their own. He liked them all, even shy little Anne, who was looking at her big sister curiously now. 'Think you'll marry him?' Vanessa knew that everyone was wondering that, but she was only nineteen and she didn't want to think about that now. Not for several years.

'We never talk about it.'

'Why not?' Anne looked surprised.

'I still have a lot to do. I want to finish school . . . do my own thing . . . try to write . . .'

'That could all take years.'

'I'm not in a rush.'

'I'll bet he is though. He's a lot older than you. Does that bother you, Van?' She wondered what her sister would think of the thirty-years between her and Bill. Their difference was nothing compared to that.

'Sometimes. Why?'

'Just curious.' They had sat down on a rock, and were dangling their feet in a stream. Anne was staring into the water, dreamy-eyed, and Vanessa saw something in her eyes that made her wonder what went on the younger girl's head. They were only three years apart, but sometimes it felt more like ten, and it felt as though Anne were the older of the two, almost as if she had lived too much and felt too much pain. She turned to Vanessa then as though reading her thoughts. 'I'd marry him if I were you, Van.' She looked old and wise and Vanessa smiled.

'Why?'

'Because you may not find one as nice as him again. A good man is worth anything.'

'Is that what you think?' Vanessa looked at her, seeing something unreadable in her eyes again, and she suddenly sensed that there was a man in her life, possibly an important one. It was hard to tell with Anne. She gave so little away, but there was something there that was more than any young girl knew, and she turned her face away, as though to keep Vanessa from seeing what was there. 'What about you? Anyone special in your life?' She tried to keep her voice light and sound casual, but Anne instantly shrugged, almost too fast.

'No, nothing much.'

'No one at all?'

'Nope.'

Van knew she lied but there was nothing she could say, and eventually they put their sneakers back on and walked back. That night she said something to Li; he knew her so well.

'I think Anne is involved with someone.'

'What makes you say that?' He wasn't in touch with her doings any more. He had been in Vietnam for six months by then, and she didn't confide in him now.

'Just a feeling . . . I can't tell you why . . . but she looks different . . .' She couldn't put her finger on it and her brother laughed, and looked into her eyes instead.

'What about you, Sis? How serious is your attachment to this guy?' She wondered if they would all ask her before they left, and she grinned.

'Relax. Anne asked me the same thing today. I told her it's just for now.' She was being mostly honest with him. How could she know now what the future would bring?

'Too bad. I think he's nice.'

She looked at him and grinned, teasing him for the first time in years. 'You can't have him, he's mine.'

He snapped his fingers and grinned. 'Aw shit.'

Greg came up behind them just then, and looked from Lionel to Van. 'What's this all about?' But Vanessa didn't explain it to him. She just said something nonchalant, and went off to find her much-talked-about, apparently popular friend. She found him with Val, who was teasing him mercilessly about how straight he was. Ward and Faye were sitting on the porch drinking wine, and Anne was probably somewhere, inside, on the phone, calling a friend again.

'Probably Gail.' Her mother smiled at Ward, and he shrugged. All was well. There was no need to pry. They were seeing plenty of all of them, and he was happy to say he liked them all. Not all of them were turning out the way he'd planned. He'd had other hopes for Lionel, of course, and he would have liked to see Val going to school instead of learning how to scream, but Anne was back on the right track, Vanessa was certainly doing well, and Greg was their star of course. Although less than Ward thought, as he was admitting to Lionel at that particular point, down near the beach, as they sat on a log, watching the sun go down. Lionel had finally discovered what Greg had been worrying about ever since they'd arrived. It had spilled out like a hundred dollars' worth of groceries from a torn paper bag.

'I just don't know what to tell Dad, Li . . . if I get kicked off the team . . .' He closed his eyes, unable to finish the thought, but Lionel's face looked grim. It would be a terrible disappointment to Ward, but there was more to it than that, as he knew only too well. He saw boys like Greg every day, lying dead on the ground, their guts spilling through bullet wounds as his camera whirred.

'What the hell did you do a dumb thing like that for?' They had caught him smoking dope in the spring, and benched him, un-beknownst to Ward, who thought he'd hurt his foot. But his grades were so bad that there was a possibility they might not even let him back on the team.

'Christ, they could even throw me out of school if they wanted to.' There were tears in his eyes, but it felt good to talk about it at last. It had been killing him for weeks.

Without thinking, Lionel grabbed his arm and looked intensely in his eyes. 'You can't let that happen. You've got to go back and work your ass off to get those grades up. Hire a tutor if you have to, do anything . . .' He knew what he spoke of, though Greg had no idea of what was out there. But he was scared anyway.

Greg looked at him in utter despair. 'I may have to cheat.'

Lionel groaned and shook his head. 'No, you dumb ass.' It was like being kids again, and at least the confidence felt good now. They had never really been friends, not in years, not since they had begun to grow up and Lionel had sensed the difference in himself. And certainly not since Greg had known the truth about him. But funnily enough, Lionel had been the one he had come to know. He had wanted to talk to him for days. He didn't know Jason well enough, and he couldn't tell his dad, but he had to tell someone what was happening to him. Lionel was glaring at him furiously now. 'If you cheat, you asshole, they'll throw you out for sure. You have to do everything by the books. Because if you don't, and they throw you out, they're going to grab you up so fast for Vietnam that your head will spin. You're exactly what they want. Young, healthy, strong, and dumb.'

'Thanks.'

'I mean that. And when I say dumb, I mean a lot of things. I mean you're not old enough to be out there in the jungle worrying about your wife and kids. You'll just watch your buddies die and want to go out there and kill Charlie Cong. And you're healthy and young . . .' Lionel's eyes filled with tears. 'I watch kids like you die out there every day.' He hated to go back, but in a few weeks he would have to, and Greg looked at him now with new respect. He was surviving it somehow and he had become a man, if you could call it that. He was still confused about why Lionel was the way he was, but he listened to him now. He knew he was right, and he was scared to death.

'I've got to get back on that team.'

'Just keep your grades up so they don't throw you out of school.'

'I'll try, Li. I swear.'

'Good.' He ruffled his hair as he had when they were kids, and the two brothers smiled as the sun went down. Greg put an arm around Lionel's shoulders, and it reminded them of their days at camp.

'I hated you then,' Greg said and they both laughed at the memories. 'And I really hated Val and Van.' He started to laugh then. 'I guess I hated everyone. I was jealous of all of you. I wanted to be an only child.'

'You were in some ways. You were always the closest to Dad.' Greg nodded, not denying it. 'But I didn't realise it then.' It impressed Greg that Lionel was so philosophical about that. In recent years, that closeness to Ward sometimes embarrassed him, and he quickly changed the subject now. 'At least I never hated Anne.'

Lionel smiled. 'None of us did. She was too little to hate.' But she wasn't little now. She was all grown up, or almost.

Anne had just hung up the phone from talking to Bill again. It was agony being without him, and she called him collect three or four times a day. Everyone had noticed it, but they all thought she was calling Gail. Only Vanessa continued to think Anne was involved with a man, but there was no way to find out, she wasn't telling anyone.

On the whole, they had all had a wonderful time, and on the last night, Valerie sat on the floor next to her door, lying in wait for Jason and Van. Every night, she had heard Vanessa scurrying down the hall to him, and tonight when she heard the patter of feet scampering past, she waited two minutes and then ran and knocked on Jason's door. She could hear a giggle, then a gasp, and then Jason's baritone said, 'Come in.' She stepped inside, and advanced on him with an amorous air, and as he stared at her in surprise, she pounced on the bed, almost killing her twin, who screamed. And then suddenly, they knew she was teasing them, and everyone laughed, and they talked long into the night. Eventually, they went to find Lionel and Greg and everyone went downstairs to raid the ice box and drink beer. It was the perfect end to a perfect holiday and as they all went their separate ways the next day, they took with them the memory of what fun it had been.

Chapter 36

Much to her amazement, Vanessa was able to convince Jason to spend a few days in LA. Having met her family already, and come to know them fairly well, he had nothing to fear from them, and he was curious to see the place he had maligned for so long. He only agreed to stay for two days, and Valerie saw to it that he had a wonderful time. She took them everywhere, to every studio, every party, every 'in' restaurant, every set. Vanessa had never seen as much of Hollywood in her life as she did in those two days.

Faye and Ward were already back at work on the packaging of a new film, and Anne disappeared into her own life. Lionel flew back to Vietnam, via Hawaii and Guam. After two days, Jason and Vanessa flew back to New York, and everyone picked up the threads of their real lives again.

Vanessa went back to Columbia for her sophomore year, and Greg to Alabama for what should have been his senior year. But it didn't last long. As soon as he returned he knew he was off the team, and after staying drunk for a week to recover from the blow, he missed two important make-up exams he had left over from the previous term. By October 15, he'd been called in to see the dean. He was being 'invited to leave'. They were sorry to see it happen to such a fine boy. They suggested he go home and think about it for the rest of the school year, and if he was ready to settle down after that, they would be happy to see him come back. But six weeks after that, coming home with his tail between his legs, and seeing heartbreak in Ward's eyes, he found the army had a different invitation for him. He was being drafted.

He sat home, all one afternoon, stupefied, and was still sitting there when Anne arrived. She came home later and later now, always going after school with Gail to do homework at her house, and then Bill would drive her home when he got in from work. It gave them a few minutes alone, and was a routine she counted on. Generally, when she came back to the Thayer house at night, there was no one there except the maid anyway. But since Greg had come home, things had changed a bit.

She let herself in with her key, and saw him sitting there looking as though someone had died. She stopped and stared at him. She was tall and beautiful and grown up now, but he didn't notice that. He simply looked at her unseeingly.

'What happened to you?' She had never been close to him, but she was sorry he'd been kicked out of school. She knew how much the football team meant to him, and he'd been depressed ever since he got back, but he looked worse today, and something major had to be wrong.

He raised frightened eyes to her. 'I got my draft notice today.

'Oh no . . .' She sat down across from him, realising instantly what it meant. It was bad enough having Li there. They were still sitting there talking about it, when Ward and Faye walked in. It was early for them and they were in a good mood. Things were going well and the cast was taking shape beautifully. Ward stopped and looked at them as soon as he walked in the door. He could see instantly on Greg's face that something was wrong and he was afraid that it was Lionel.

'Bad news?' He said the words as fast as he could, so they could answer him just as fast.

Greg nodded his head. 'Yeah.' He handed the notice to him wordlessly, and reading it, Ward sank into a chair. A moment later he handed it to Faye. All they wanted was for Lionel to end his tour there, but now they would have Greg to worry about too. It didn't seem fair to have both of them there.

Faye looked at Ward. 'Isn't there some kind of law against that?' Ward shook his head and looked back at Greg. It said he had to report in three days. They certainly weren't wasting any time, and it was already December 1. He thought of Canada again. But it seemed wrong with Lionel there. As though Vietnam were good enough for him to risk his life, but not for Greg. It was clear that he had to go.

He reported to Fort Ord just as the paper said, on December 4, and was sent to Fort Benning, Georgia, for basic training for six weeks. They didn't even let him come home for Christmas Eve, and it was a bleak holiday this year. Val had gone to Mexico with a group of friends; Vanessa had gone to New Hampshire with Jason finally; Greg was in basic training; Lionel in Vietnam; and Anne straining to run out of the door. She had made the same arrangement with Bill this year, and in a few weeks she would turn seventeen with only one more year to go, they told each other constantly.

Greg was shipped out on January 28, and sent straight to Saigon, and from there he went to Bien Hoa Air Base north of Saigon. He didn't even have a chance to touch base with Lionel, who had only three more weeks to serve there. He was being sent to Germany after that, and he could hardly wait. He'd had enough of that stinking war to last a lifetime – if he survived. Too damn many men he knew were killed the day before they went home. He was holding his breath until the plane touched down in Los Angeles and not before. But he also knew that Greg was in Vietnam, and he tried several times to contact him, to no avail. His CO had lost no time at all, sending all the fresh recruits to combat areas the day they arrived at Bien Hoa. It was a hell of a welcome to Vietnam.

And he stayed there for exactly two weeks. On February 13 the Army I Corps staged several actions and rocket attacks against the Viet Cong, destroying two villages, and taking prisoners for several nights. Greg had his first taste of blood and death and victory. The best friend he'd made in basic was shot in the gut, but the doctors said he'd be all right. The only good thing about it was that he'd be going home. Dozens of other boys died, seven disappeared, which frightened everyone, and Greg himself had the opportunity to shoot two old women and a dog, which he found both frightening and exhilarating, like running across the goal line with the ball in your arms. And then at 5 am, with the jungle rustling to life, and birds hooting and cackling all around, Greg was sent ahead with a party of other men, and he stepped on a mine. There wasn't even a body to reclaim after that. He disappeared in a cloud of blood as his buddies watched and most of them were wearing him as they headed back to camp. They staggered in, two of them badly maimed, all of them in shock. The news reached Lionel later that day. He sat staring blankly at the words on the paper someone had handed him. Regret. Gregory Ward Thayer was killed by a mine today. Killed in action. And then only the name of the CO. A ripple went down his spine, as it had as he looked down at John's face outside their charred apartment when the fire engines had arrived. He had never loved Greg as he'd loved John. He would never love anyone like that again. But he and Greg were brothers, and now suddenly he was gone. He thought of his father's pain too when he would hear the news, and suddenly a shaft of agony pierced through him.

'Sonofabitch.' He screamed the words outside his hotel, and then he leaned against the wall and cried, until someone came and peeled him away. He was a good guy, even though people knew what he was. But he didn't bother anyone. They felt sorry for him now. They all knew that his brother had been killed that day. Someone had seen the telegram from the front lines, and news travelled fast in Saigon. Everyone knew everything that was happening. Two boys sat up all night with Lionel, watching him drink and cry. And the next morning, they put him on the plane. He had survived a year in Vietnam, made more than four hundred short films to show in the States, many of them on the news all over the world. And his brother had only lived nineteen days. It wasn't fair – but nothing about the place was, not the rats or the disease or the wounded children screaming everywhere.

Lionel stepped off the plane in LA looking shell-shocked. He would never see his brother again. He had a three-week leave before going to Germany. Someone drove him home, he remembered later on. He felt the way he had when John had died, and that was only two years before . . . twenty-six months in fact . . . he had the same terrible numb feeling now.

He rang the doorbell because he no longer had a key, and his father stood there staring at him. They had got the news the night before. Everyone was there, except Vanessa, who was flying home that afternoon.

There would be no burial, because they weren't sending him home. There was nothing to send, except their fucking telegrams. And Lionel stood staring at Ward, as the older man let out a groan of agony. The two men fell into each other's arms, partly out of relief that Lionel was still alive, and the grief that Greg was gone. Eventually, Ward led him inside, and together they cried for a long time. Lionel held him in his arms like a little child, as Ward keened for the boy he'd loved so much, the boy he'd pinned all his hopes on, their football star. Now he was gone and there was nothing to send home. Nothing at all. They had only their memories.

They moved like wooden people for the next few days. Lionel was vaguely aware that Van was there and Val was staying with them, Anne . . . but no Greg . . . there would never be a Greg again. There were only four of them now.

They had a memorial service for him, at First Presbyterian Church of Hollywood. All his high school teachers came. Ward sat thinking bitterly that if those bastards in Alabama had let him stay on the team, or at least kept him in school, he would still be alive. But hating them didn't help anything. It was Greg's own fault for flunking out. But whose fault was it that he'd been killed? It had to be someone's fault, didn't it? The minister's voice droned on, saying his name, and none of it seemed real. Afterwards, they all stood outside, shaking people's hands. It was hard to believe that Greg was gone, that they would never see him again. Ward glanced at Lionel a thousand times, as though to be sure he was still there. And the girls were there too. But it would never be the same again. One of them was gone. For eternity.

Chapter 37

A few days after the memorial service, Vanessa went back to New York, and Val moved back to her own place again. Lionel spent most of his time alone in the house. His parents and Anne were never there. They were at work, she was in school, and he felt a hideous magnetic attraction for Greg's room. He remembered the days when he and John had been friends, and now they were both gone . . . together again somewhere. It all seemed so unfair, and he wanted to scream all the time.

A couple of times he went out for a drive, just to get some air. His old Mustang was still at the house. He had left it there when he went to Vietnam. Greg's car was there too, but he didn't want to drive it now. It was sacred, and just looking at it hurt his soul.

He took the red Mustang out one afternoon, a week before he was due to leave for Germany, and he decided to stop for a hamburger before he went home. It seemed like the first time he'd been hungry in weeks, and as he parked the car and walked inside, he noticed a two-tone grey Rolls Royce and thought that he had already seen it somewhere, but he wasn't sure where, and he wasn't really interested. He sat down at the counter and ordered a hamburger and a Coke, then glanced in the mirror ahead of him, and as he did he sat up straight. Behind him, reflected in the mirror that he faced, was his youngest sister with a much older man. They were holding hands and they had just kissed. She was drinking a milkshake, and he looked as though he were teasing her. They were laughing and then he saw them kiss again. He was horrified, the man looked as old as Ward. He wanted a better look, but he was afraid to turn around. Then suddenly he remembered who he was. It was the father of her friend . . . what was her name? . . . Sally? . . . Jane? . . . Gail! That was it!

As the couple left, the older man had an arm around the girl and they kissed once more, outside, without ever noticing him. The couple sat in the car for a long time, and Lionel could see their lips meet again, and finally they drove off. He stared, his hamburger forgotten, his appetite gone. He left his money on the counter, and drove home rapidly. When he got there, she was upstairs, the door to her room closed, and Faye and Ward had just got home. Lionel looked as though he had just seen a ghost, but none of them looked very well these days; they were all still mourning Greg. Ward looked and felt like an old man suddenly. At fifty-two, one of his brightest hopes was gone, and Faye looked tired and pale. But Lionel looked worse than either of them. Faye noticed it as he entered. He was fighting with himself about whether to tell them or not. They had enough on their minds, but he didn't want her getting into trouble again. They had all been through that once before, especially Anne, and she didn't need that again.

'Is something wrong, sweetheart?' Faye asked him gently as he sat down in the den. But everything was these days. Ward glanced at him despairingly, and Lionel decided it was unfair to say anything. He would talk to her himself first . . . but what if she ran away again? This time he couldn't stay to help them out. He couldn't spend five months looking for her with John. There was no time to waste. He sighed deeply and sat back in the chair, looking at them both, and then got up and closed the door. When he turned around and faced them again, they could both see that something was wrong. 'What is it, Li?' Faye looked at him with frightened eyes. Had one of them got hurt? Vanessa in New York? . . . Val on a set? . . . Anne? . . .

He decided to come right to the point. 'It's Anne. I saw her this afternoon . . . with a friend of hers . . .' His heart turned over as he thought of it. He was older than Ward. And he could just imagine what he'd been doing to her.

'Gail?' Faye looked even more nervous now. They hadn't monitored the friendship much. She seemed all right, and her father seemed very nice too, and the girls went to the same school. But Lionel totally stunned her with his next words.

'Not Gail, her father, Mum. They were at a hamburger joint where I went, kissing and holding hands.' Ward looked as though he'd been punched. He couldn't take much more now. And Faye stared at him in disbelief.

'But that can't be. Are you sure it was Anne?' He nodded slowly. There had been no question of it. 'But how is that possible?'

'Maybe you should ask her that.'

Faye's heart almost stopped, thinking of all the times she had stayed there, and they had never questioned it. What if Gail hadn't even been there? Or worse yet, if she had . . . if the man was really I sick . . . Faye began to cry. They couldn't go through any more, and most particularly not with her. God only knew what her involvement was with this man. Faye jumped instantly to her feet. 'I'm going to get her down here right now.' But Ward reached out and touched her arm.

'Maybe we should all calm down first. It could all be a big mistake. Maybe Lionel misinterpreted what he saw.' He looked apologetically at his son, but he didn't want it to be true. He couldn't handle another tragedy, and God only knew what the child was into now. She was seventeen now. It would be harder to control her than it was at fourteen, and that had been hard enough.

Faye turned to her husband with a determined look. 'I think we should talk to her.'

'Fine. Then talk to her, but don't accuse.' Faye had the best possible intentions when she knocked on Anne's door, but the moment Anne saw her face, she knew that disaster had struck, and when she followed her mother downstairs to the den, she was stunned when she saw her brother there.

'Hello, Li.' But there was nothing friendly about them, or even about him. He nodded at her, and Ward was quick to take the floor.

'Anne, we'll get right to the point. No one's accusing you, but we want to know what's going on. For your own sake of course.' A premonition of disaster gnawed at her, but she held firm, and her eyes gave nothing away. She just searched their faces. She couldn't believe that even if Lionel had seen anything, he would actually betray her, but she was wrong. To her mind, he had. She would never forgive him, she told herself afterwards. 'Your brother thinks he may have seen you somewhere today. You may not even have been there, sweetheart,' and in his heart of hearts, he was begging her not to have been. He didn't want to have to deal with it, to face some man his own age, and accuse him of rape, which was what it was with a seventeen-year-old girl. 'It was a hamburger place.' He turned to Lionel. 'Where was it, son?' Lionel filled in the address and Anne felt her heart stop. 'But the important thing is that he thought he saw you with a man.'

'So? Gail's father took me for a milk shake on the way home.' She turned on Lionel angrily, and she looked beautiful when she did. This was no child any more. She was a woman now. Lionel was singularly aware of it that afternoon. It explained everything for the past year, why she had adjusted so well to her new school, why she was never at home. 'You have a filthy mind.' She spat the words at him.

'You were kissing him.'

She stared furiously at the boy who had once saved her life. 'Then at least I'm not gay.' It was a vicious thing to say, but he didn't give a damn. Without saying a word, he reached out and grabbed her arm, as her parents watched horrified.

'He's thirty years older than you, Anne.'

'Thirty-three to be exact.' Her eyes blazed. To hell with all of them. They couldn't do anything to her now. It was too late. She belonged to Bill. She always would. And she turned on all of them now. 'And I don't give a damn what any of you think. Not one of you has been decent to me over the years,' she hesitated for only an instant, glancing at Li, 'except you, but that was a long time ago. But you,' she glared at her parents hatefully, 'you've never been here for me. He's been there for me more in the last two years than you ever were, with your films, and your business deals, and your romance with each other and your friends. You never even knew who I was . . . and neither did I. Well, I do now, and I have since I met Bill and Gail.'

'Is it a *ménage à trois?*' Lionel was prepared to be just as vicious with her, as their parents looked on.

'No, it's not, as a matter of fact. Gail doesn't even know.'

'Thank God for that. You're a fool, Anne. You're an old man's tart. It's no different from what you did in the Haight, except for the hallucinogens. You're an old man's whore.' There had been an older man there too, Moon. She remembered him still. But this was nothing like that. She struck out at her brother, freed her arm and swung at him, but he stopped it before it reached his face. Suddenly Ward and Faye were on their feet as one, and Faye was shouting at them.

'Stop! This is disgusting. For chrissake, stop it, both of you!'

'What are you going to do about her, Mum?' Lionel was furious. She had fucked up her life again. Why did she keep doing that? But she was adamant.

'You can all go screw yourselves. I'll be eighteen years old in ten months, and there isn't a damn thing you can do to me then. You can torture me all you want now, you can even keep me from seeing him. But in ten months, mark my words, I'll be married to him.'

'You're out of your mind if you think he'll marry you. All you are is a piece of ass to him.' The funny thing was that it felt good to shout at her, as though he could shout at the fates that had killed Greg and John. At least he could let some of the feelings out now, and besides, he was furious with her.

'You don't know Bill Stein.' Anne said the words in a calm measured way, as Faye watched her face, and suddenly she was afraid. She was serious about this man, and Faye couldn't help asking her.

'You're not pregnant again, are you?'

She looked at her with hatred. 'No, I'm not. I learned that lesson once. The hard way.' No one disagreed with her. And now Ward came forward with a set face and a frown.

'I just want you to know that in ten months or ten years, you are not marrying this man. I am calling my lawyer, and the police tonight, and I'm bringing charges against him.'

'For what? Loving me?' She looked at her father derisively. She had no respect for either of them. They had done nothing for her, and she knew she meant nothing to them. Maybe they were just angry that someone did love her, she told herself. But her father went on to explain his plans.

'It is statutory rape to have sexual intercourse with a girl your age, Anne.' Her father's voice was cold. 'He can go to prison for that.'

'I'll testify against all of you.' She looked panicked now.

'It won't change anything.'

She was suddenly frightened for him. What if he was right? Why had Bill never said that to her? She had to protect him now. She looked at her father desperately. 'Do anything you want to me, but don't hurt him.' The words struck Faye like a blow, she cared enough about this man to sacrifice herself. It was frightening that she loved him so much, and what if they were wrong? But they couldn't be. He had obviously taken gross advantage of her. But Faye looked at Ward.

'Why don't we talk to him first, and see what he says. If he promises never to see her again, maybe it would be simpler not take any legal action against him.' Ward was difficult to convince, but eventually Faye got through to him. They forced Anne to call, and demand that he come over immediately. She had to tell him why, and he could hear her crying on the phone.

He entered the Thayer house, to find a kangaroo court waiting for him. Ward let him in and he had to control himself not to attack him then and there. Lionel was standing by. Bill recognised all the players in the piece, especially Faye. He had come alone, and he faced Anne sobbing hysterically across the room. Instantly, he went to her, smoothed her hair, dried her cheeks, and then realised that they were all staring at him.

He had no excuses to make. He admitted it all. He sympathised totally with Ward, and told him he had a daughter the same age, but he also tried to tell them some things about Anne, about how lonely she had been, how marked by giving up her child, how guilty over what had happened in the Haight-Ashbury. He explained how her earliest memories of their seeming indifference went back to when she was a tiny child, and she had felt rejected by all of them all her life. He made no excuses for himself, but he explained to them who Anne Thayer was, and her parents sat there, realising what a stranger she had been to them. This unknown child, who had come to reject them eventually too, had found Bill Stein, and sought everything from him, and in his own loneliness he had nurtured her. Perhaps it was wrong, he admitted with damp eyes, but it was sincere. He echoed exactly what Anne had said to them, though in a kindlier tone. In less than a year, he planned to marry her, with or without their consent, or even Gail's, once she found out. He would have preferred everyone to wish them well, but this had gone on long enough, and if he could have married her sooner, he would. She could continue school, she could do anything she wanted to, but when her eighteenth birthday came, he would be waiting for her, whether they would continue to let him see her now or not.

As he quietly said the words, she sat there and beamed at him. He hadn't let her down, and he was willing to risk anything for her. He was exactly what she had always believed him to be, and the three other Thayers were shocked, most of all Ward, who stared at this unexciting-looking man and couldn't understand what his daughter saw in him. He wasn't beautiful or young, handsome or debonair. He was actually rather banal, and his looks were very plain. But he had offered something to their child that they had never been able to give her. Whether they wanted to see it or not, she was happy with him. She sat there now, blooming quietly in the sunlight of his love. They really didn't care what was done to them in the next year. Both were willing to wait, and after that it was clear what their plans were. Suddenly both Ward and Faye believed they would. One couldn't fight them at all, no matter how wrong it might be, or how great the age difference, or how big a fool they thought Anne was.

After he left, and they had lectured Anne, Ward and Faye talked quietly in their room. They didn't know what to make of him, and they had told her they didn't know if there would be charges or not. Bill had gone home to make a clean breast of it with Gail, and would be happy to speak to them at any time. He wasn't really apologetic with them. After two years of loving her, he felt he had relatively little to apologise for. He hadn't hurt her or abandoned her, used her, or done anything terribly wrong. By now she was almost eighteen, and it didn't seem shocking to be lovers any more. He suspected Gail would be stunned at first, but she would get over it too. And they had their lives to lead, Anne and Bill. Both had made that perfectly clear to everyone.

'What do you think?' Faye sat in a chair and looked at Ward. He still couldn't see what she saw in the man, and she was only seventeen years old. It was mind boggling.

'I think she's a damn fool.'

Faye sighed. This was worse than some of the films she'd done. 'So do I, but that's our opinion, not hers.'

'Apparently.' He sat down across from his wife, and took her hand. 'How do they get themselves into these things? Lionel with his damn inclinations to something I don't understand, Val with her crazy career, Vanessa living with that boy in New York, and thinking we don't know about it.' Faye smiled, they had talked about it before. She thought she was so exotic and unusual, and it was so transparent, they all knew what was going on, but they didn't really mind. She was twenty-years old and he was a nice boy. 'And now Anne with this man . . . Good God,

Faye, he's thirty-three years older than she is.' It still wouldn't sink in.

'I know. And he isn't even beautiful.' Faye smiled. 'If it was someone who looked like you, I'd understand at least.' At fifty-two he was still as handsome as he had been twenty years before, though in a different way. He was still long and lean and elegant, as was she. This man had none of that. It was difficult to see his appeal, except that he had kind eyes, and he seemed to care a great deal for her. She looked up at her husband then. 'Do we have to agree to this, Ward?' She didn't mean legally, she meant practically for the next ten months.

'I don't see why we should.'

'Maybe we'd be smarter if we did. You can't fight City Hall.' They had learned that again and again, with Lionel, with Val . . . Vanessa . . . now Anne. They did what they wanted to . . . except poor Greg. And Ward looked at her now.

'You mean agree to her having an affair with him openly?' He looked shocked. 'She's only seventeen years old.' But they both knew that she was far older than that, in her soul, she had been through a lot, and it had weathered her.

'She's been doing it for the last year or so anyway.'

Ward narrowed his eyes at his wife. 'What makes you so liberal suddenly?'

She smiled tiredly at Ward. 'Maybe I'm just getting old.'

'And wise.' He kissed her again. 'I love you babe.'

'I love you too, sweetheart.' They agreed to think about it for a few days, and that night they had dinner with Lionel. Anne stayed in her room and no one urged her to come down.

There was enough strain on them as it was, and in the end, they decided to give in. They urged her to be discreet, not to become the talk of the town. Bill Stein was moderately well known in the entertainment industry. He was a respected lawyer and had several well-known clients, and they were sure he wasn't anxious for the publicity either. The whole idea was to keep it as quiet as possible, and then marry, as they planned to, after the first of the year. He gave her an enormous engagement ring, which she only wore when she went out with him. A pear-shaped solitaire that she called her Easter Egg. It was ten and a half carats, and she had been embarrassed when she showed it to Gail. Gail had been very decent to them. It had been a shock to her too at first, but she loved them both a great deal. She wished them well, and they both decided to go to summer school, so that they could graduate before the Christmas holidays. That way Anne wouldn't have to go to school, once she married Bill. And then Gail thought she should leave them alone, at least for a while. Besides, it would be embarrassing to live with them at first. And she wanted to go to the Parsons School of Design in New York.

Lionel was still angry with Anne when he left for Germany. He didn't approve of the man, no matter what anyone said.

'You got off easy, if you ask me,' he told her the day he left, and she'd looked coldly at him. She would never forgive him for turning her in, she said.

'You're a fine one to be making judgements about someone else.'

'Being gay doesn't impair my mind, Anne.'

'No. But maybe your heart.'

He almost wondered if she was right, as he left. He didn't feel the same way about anything any more, ever since Vietnam. He had seen too many people die, lost too many people he cared about . . . and two he deeply loved . . . John and Greg. It was difficult to imagine loving anyone again. He had no desire to in fact, and wondered secretly if that was why he was so angry with her. He couldn't understand her happiness, because his was long gone, with John, and could never come again, and her life stretched ahead of her, with promise and excitement and as much sparkle as her enormous engagement ring.

Chapter 38

On January 18, 1970, Anne Thayer and Bill Stein stood at Temple Israel on Hollywood Boulevard, with their families and a handful of friends watching them. Anne hadn't even wanted to go that far, but Bill had urged her to anyway.

'It'll be easier for your parents, sweetheart, if you let them plan a little something.' But Anne had no interest in it. For almost two years she had felt like his wife, and she needed no fanfare now. Gail thought it was silly of her. She was so unlike girls her age. She wanted no wedding dress, no veil.

It looks so barren, Faye thought to herself, remembering the magnificence of her own wedding day. Anne wore a simple white wool dress with a high neck and long sleeves, simple pumps, her blonde hair in a single braid with baby's breath in it, and she carried no bouquet. She came to him simple and stark, wearing no jewellery save the large diamond he had given her. The wedding ring was a wide band of diamonds too. She looked so innocent and young that it looked almost incongruous on her hand. But she noticed none of that. She saw only Bill. It was all she had wanted since the day they met, and she came quietly to him now, on her father's arm, and then Ward stepped back, feeling again how little any of them had known her in the last eighteen years. It was as though she had slipped through their lives too quickly, too silently, living behind a locked door, always disappearing. Suddenly, it seemed as though his entire memory of her childhood was saying, 'Where's Anne?'

They had a small luncheon at the house, which was all Anne would allow them to do. There were flowers everywhere, and the champagne was very fine. Faye looked quiet and restrained in a green silk suit that set off her eyes. But somehow she didn't feel like the mother of the bride. It all felt like a charade, as though they were playing games, and eventually Gail would go home with her dad. But when they left in the grey Rolls that night, Anne went with them, and she turned to kiss Faye and Ward goodbye. Faye had an overwhelming urge to ask her if she was sure, and yet when she saw her daughter's eyes, there was no question there. She had given herself to the man she loved, and she was a woman now.

Gail was more subdued than usual, but she was happy for Bill and Anne. She and Anne had both graduated a few weeks before, and the couple would fly to New York with her now. She was going to Parsons School of Design, and would live at the Barbizon as Vanessa once had. After they dropped her off, Bill and Anne were flying on to San Juan, and then to St Thomas and St Martin's from there, ending up in St Croix. They would be gone for several weeks, and were in no hurry to come back. Bill wanted to take her shopping in New York too. There were several jewellers whose wares he wanted her to see: Harry Winston, David Webb, a few others he liked, and then there was other shopping too. 'Bergdorf's, Bendels, Bloomingdale's,' the two girls shouted in unison that night.

'You spoil me too much!' She smiled and kissed his neck, she wanted nothing more from him than his love. He wanted to buy a few pretty things for Gail too.

'Well, Mrs Stein, how does it feel?' He smiled at her that night as they lay on his big bed, legally this time, for the first time in two years.

'It feels wonderful.' She grinned like a little girl, still wearing her braid, and now a lacy nightgown that had been a wedding gift from Val, although it was clear she didn't approve of them. None of them did, but more than that they didn't understand. They never had . . . except Li . . . once upon a time. He hadn't been at the wedding though. He was still in Germany, waiting to be released in a few weeks. Van had been back in New York, deep in her junior year. It didn't really matter to Anne, the only one she had wanted there was Bill, and she looked happily at him now, pondering the past. It was as though none of it had ever been real, only this. 'I feel as though I've been married to you all my life.' And the funny thing was he felt that way too.

'So do I.' His friends had all made comments of course. But eventually they pretended to understand. There were lots of hits on the shoulder, slaps on the backs, surreptitious winks. 'Cradle robbing, eh, old man?' They all envied him; some of them said unkind things behind his back, but he didn't give a damn. He was going to take care of his little gem for the rest of his life, and as she looked up at him with trusting eyes, she knew he would.

They slept locked in each other's arms that night, grateful again that they could do anything they wanted now. They had a lazy breakfast with Gail, and that afternoon they all packed, and flew to New York, as planned, that night. Anne thought briefly of calling Ward and Faye to say goodbye and then somehow she never got around to it. She had nothing to say to them anyway, she told Bill, as the plane took off.

'You're awfully hard on them, love. They did their best. They just never understood very well.' In her eyes, that was the under-statement of the year. They had robbed her of her child, threatened to bring charges against Bill, they had passed her over, passed her by, they would have totally destroyed her life, if it hadn't been for him. She looked gratefully up at him again, as they sat in first-class, he with 'his two girls' as he called them. Anne sat in the middle, and while Bill napped on the flight, she chatted with Gail. They were looking forward to the two days they would share in New York, before Gail moved into the Barbizon, and she and Bill flew on to their honeymoon. Meanwhile, they would share a suite at the Pierre.

For the next two days, they did nothing but shop. Anne had never seen so many beautiful things in her life, except in her mother's films. He bought Gail a beautiful little mink coat, in a sporty cut, with a matching hat. He told her she'd need it to keep warm, and a mountain of ski clothes, a new pair of skis, half a dozen dresses from Bendel's, six pairs of Gucci shoes, and a gold bracelet she'd been crazy about at Cartier's, with a little screwdriver to put it on, which the girls loved. Anne loved it so much, he surprised her with one too. But there were even more goodies for his young bride: a full-length mink coat for evening wear, a short one for day, dresses and suits and blouses and skirts, boxes and boxes of beautiful shoes, Italian boots, an emerald ring, a beautiful diamond pin, huge pearl earrings from Van Cleef that she loved, and two more gold bracelets she had admired, and on the last day of the trip, he gave her a splendid piece from David Webb. It was a lion embracing a lamb, all in a single massive hunk of gold, and it was so beautiful that one could only stare at it as it dangled from her arm.

'What am I going to do with all this?' She pranced around their hotel room in her underwear, waving at the beautiful furs and clothes hanging everywhere, the shoe boxes, the handbags, the fur hats, and in her suitcase were half a dozen jewellery boxes. It was almost embarrassing, except that he enjoyed it all so much too. He bought a few things for himself too, like a fur-lined raincoat, and a new gold watch, but he was far more interested in shopping for her. Even Gail thought it was fun. She had so many pretty things he'd given her over the years that she begrudged Anne nothing now. They were almost sisters anyway, and her father would still have bought her anything she desired, perhaps even more so now. He was far too generous, both girls told him on their last night, but they enjoyed every minute of it, and Vanessa's eyes almost fell out of her head when she and Jason met them in the Oak Room for drinks. Anne glided gracefully across the room in beautifully cut red slacks and a creamy silk shirt, a red alligator Hermès handbag to match, and a mink coat that people stopped and stared at, even in New York. As she approached, the diamonds sparkled on her hands; you could see the Webb bracelet in all its glory on her arm, and two small rubies in her ears. She looked so lovely and so poised that Vanessa barely recognised her as the same girl.

'Anne?' Her jaw almost dropped as she stared at her. She was wearing her hair in a simple braid again, with soft wisps of blonde fluff framing her face, her makeup was simple and in good taste, but everything she wore, from her jewellery to her boots looked like something out of *Vogue*. Vanessa hadn't imagined her that way, as she laughed and sat down. Vanessa could see that Jason was impressed too.

'We've been shopping an awful lot.' Anne's voice was as soft as it had always been, and she looked at Bill quickly with a shy glance, as he laughed. 'He's been spoiling me too much.'

'I can see that.'

She ordered a Dubonnet, which was the only drink she liked. Vanessa and Jason had already ordered scotch. Bill had a martini on the rocks, and Gail had white wine. They all chatted amiably about nothing much. The young people reminisced about Lake Tahoe almost two years before, and Anne asked Jason about his job. He had timed it all perfectly. He received his Ph.D. weeks after he turned twenty-six. He had successfully evaded the draft for more than eight years, and now he had a job teaching literature at NYU. It didn't excite him very much, and he'd been doing it for the past year. He was still working on his play, but he was getting nowhere with it.

'I keep trying to get Vanessa to collaborate on it with me, and she won't.'

'I can hardly keep up with school,' she explained to Bill, whom she thought pleasant and fatherly. She still had another year to go at Columbia. It was all she could think of now. She wanted to finish and get a job herself. She seemed inclined to stay in New York, but Anne suspected it was because of Jason. They had been together for two and a half years, and she wondered if she'd ever marry him. Gail asked the same thing after dinner that night and Anne shrugged pensively. She didn't quite understand the relationship they had, she had the feeling they were just moving along parallel tracks, pursuing their own lives. They had no desire for a permanent bond; more important than that, no need. And neither of them mentioned having kids. All they talked about was their work, their jobs, their writing, his play.

'Sounds pretty boring to me,' Gail suggested, 'though at least he's cute.' He was that, but not in a way that appealed to Anne. She thought Bill the most handsome man in the world. As they went home in a cab that night, Vanessa talked to Jason about it.

'I don't understand that kid at all. She's practically a child, and there she is married to that old man, running around in diamonds and mink coat.'

'Maybe those things are important to her.' Jason couldn't understand it either but he had always thought she was a nice girl. Not as intelligent or interesting as Van, but maybe that was hard to say. She was so young and so withdrawn it was hard to know what she was.

But Vanessa was shaking her head. 'I don't think they are important to her. I don't think she gives a damn about any of that stuff. He just wants to give her all that, and she probably wears it to please him.' She was right on that score, she knew her sister that well, the only one in the family who would have loved the glitter and the furs was Val. Eventually Greg would have liked the good life, if he'd lived. The others had simpler tastes, and their parents did now too, contrary to their early life. But it had no importance for them any more, hadn't for years, Van knew. 'I just don't see what she sees in a man his age.'

'He's awfully good to her, Van, and not just materially. He can't do enough for her. If she's thirsty, she has a glass of water in her hand before she can speak up; if she's tired he takes her home; if she's bored, he takes her out to dance, to Europe, to see friends . . . you can't beat that.' He smiled at the girl he loved, suddenly wishing he did more for her. 'A guy his age thinks of all that stuff, he's got nothing else to do,' he teased, and she laughed.

'That's no excuse. You mean I don't get a diamond ring the size of an egg?'

He looked at her soberly as they walked into the house. 'Is that what you want someday, Van?'

'Nope.' She sounded sure of it and she was. She wanted other things in her life. Like him. Maybe a couple of kids one day, eight or ten years down the road. Stuff like that.

'What do you want?'

She shrugged pensively as she threw her coat on a chair. 'Maybe to publish a book one day . . . good reviews . . .' She couldn't think of anything else, and she didn't want to tell him that she might want him and a baby or two. It was too soon to think of that, let alone talk about it.

'That's all?' He looked disappointed.

She smiled at him, softening, 'Maybe you too.'

'You've got that now.'

She sat down on the couch and he lit a fire. They were comfortable here, with their books and papers all around, the Sunday *Times* still spread out on the floor tangled with his sneakers, and her shoes, his glasses on the desk. 'I really think this is all I want, Jase.'

He looked pleased. 'You have mighty simple tastes, my friend.' He held her close, and then, 'Are you serious about the book?'

'I hope so. After I finish school and get a job.'

He sighed. 'It's so damn hard to write them.' He knew that only too well. 'I still think we should collaborate on a play.' He looked at her hopefully and she smiled. He had always felt that their styles would mesh well.

'Maybe one day.' They kissed and he laid her back on the couch and slipped a hand into her blouse. It was a far cry from the scene between Bill and Anne at the Pierre. She was lying on the satin bedspread wearing a marabou-trimmed peignoir and his tongue ran lazily up her thigh. The diamonds on her hand sparkled in the dim light. He touched her where she liked it most, and she arched her back with a moan, as he pulled the peignoir from her. It drifted slowly to the floor. The feelings were the same as Jason and Vanessa. The love, the desire, the commitment to each other through thick or thin. It was all the same, in sneakers, or marabou.

Chapter 39

In May, Bill and Anne went back to New York for a few days. Anne wanted to see Gail, and he had business there. They stayed at the Pierre again, and he took her to the jewellers he liked best, and insisted on buying her some new things. The weather was beautiful, and she had just bought a beautiful white dress and coat at Bendel's which she wore to lunch with him at Côte Basque. He was very proud of her as she walked into the room. She was still totally unaware of herself, and she moved like a doe as she approached him across the room, seeing no one stare at her, seeing only his eyes smiling at her. But he saw something else; that same empty, nervous look that had been there for months. He hoped it happened soon, and he knew why it was so important to her. He wanted a baby too, but not as desperately as she did.

'How was Bendel's today?'

'Pretty good.' She still talked like a child sometimes, but she didn't look like one any more. She was wearing her hair down, and he had had a woman he knew in LA teach her how to put makeup on. Suddenly she looked more like twenty-five than eighteen. Gail had noticed it too, and had obviously approved. She had a new boyfriend now, and was loving New York. Bill insisted that she stay at the Barbizon, but she was threatening to move out by the autumn and get her own place, and Anne had been assigned to work on him. 'I just bought this today.' She waved at the dress and coat with a perfectly manicured hand, and he noticed that she was wearing the new pearls he had just bought her in Hong Kong. They were huge and almost didn't look real. 'You like?'

'I love.' He kissed her gently on the lips, and the waiter took their order for drinks. He had wine, she had Perrier, and they both ate a light lunch. She loved the quenelles at the Côte Basque, and he had a spinach salad and a steak. They weren't really doing justice to the exquisite cuisine, but he had another meeting to attend, and she was off to Bloomingdale's, and then she was going to meet Gail at school.

Bill wondered sometimes if she should be going to school too; she needed something more to do than get her nails done and shop and wait for him to come home at night. She needed something more than keeping her temperature chart every day. She had to think of something else, but he was afraid to tell her that. He just kept reassuring her it would happen soon. They had both had one child, so they knew they were each capable of it, it was just a matter of time, the doctor had told her that too. 'Have you called your sister yet, sweetheart?' She shook her head vaguely, playing with the cookie she had taken from the tray. 'Why not?' She still avoided most of the Thayers, even Lionel, whom he knew she had once loved so much. It was as though she wanted to shut them all out of her life now. She had him, and she wanted nothing else, but he didn't think it was right. It would have broken his heart if Gail had done that to him, although he knew that the Thayers had never been as close to her as he was to Gail.

Anne shrugged. 'Mum said she had exams when I talked to her last week.' It was obvious she had no interest in calling Van. And she never called Valerie in LA, she hadn't talked to her in months.

'You can still give her a call. She might have time for a quick drink.'

'I'll call her tonight.' But he already knew she would not. She would lie around, thinking, counting forward and back . . . fourteen days from . . . and the next morning she would wake up at the crack of dawn and take her temperature again. He wanted her to stop and just relax about it all. She was getting so uptight about it she was losing weight. He was thinking of taking her to Europe in July to take her mind off things, and he wanted Gail to come too, but she had a summer job with Pauline Trigère, and she refused to go anywhere.

'What do you think, sweetheart?' They were strolling up Madison Avenue towards his meeting place, and he was trying to interest her in the European trip. He had to interest her in something. What if a baby never came, or it took years? She couldn't spend her whole life waiting for that, and it was beginning to dim the pleasure they had shared. It was all she could think about, all she could talk about sometimes, as though she could replace the baby she'd given up. He didn't dare tell her that she never would, no more than he could replace his wife. He loved Anne just as much, but it was all different now, and once in a great while, there was still that empty ache of missing her, just as he knew that Anne would always regret that child. There would always remain a lonely void for her, a void which no one could fill, no husband, no child. He looked at her tenderly. 'St Tropez would be fun. We could rent a boat.' She smiled at him then, he did so much for her, and she was always aware of it.

'I'd love that. And I'm sorry I've been such a drip. I guess we both know why.'

'Yes, we do.' He stopped right on Madison Avenue and took her in his arms. 'But you have to let Mother Nature take her own sweet time, and besides, it's fun trying, isn't it?'

'Yes.' She smiled at him. But he still remembered how she had cried when she got her last period, and the angry scene they'd had when she told him it was all Faye's fault. That if it hadn't been for her she would have had a three-and-a-half-year-old son now, and Bill had looked so hurt . . . 'Is that what you want?' he had asked, and she had screamed, 'Yes, it is.' He felt so sorry for her, he had even suggested they adopt a three-year-old boy, but she wanted their own. She wanted to have 'her own baby' again. It was pointless to try and tell her she could never replace the one she'd given up. She was determined to have a baby by Bill, immediately, if possible. Her mother suspected that when they had lunch one day, and the veiled look in her eyes accused Faye just as they had for years. She had never forgiven her, and possibly never would.

Now, on Madison Avenue, she looked sadly at Bill. 'Do you think it'll ever happen?' She had asked him that a million times since January, and it had only been four months since their wedding day. They had used precautions until then, no thanks to her, he reminded her several times. But he knew why she wanted to be careless. It was the same thing again. That desperation to have a child, to fill the void, to relive the past differently this time. She had never forgiven herself for giving that child up, or Faye for making her . . .

'Yes, I think it will happen, little love. Six months from now you'll be wallowing around like a whale, telling me how miserable and uncomfortable you are, and hating me for it.' They both laughed and he kissed her again and left for his meeting, as she headed for Bloomingdale's, and it tore at her heart when she passed the racks of baby clothes. She stopped for just a moment and fingered them wistfully, wanting to buy something just for good luck, and then afraid it would jinx her instead. She remembered when she had bought little pink shoes when she'd been pregnant before. She had been so convinced it would be a girl, Lionel and John had teased her about it.

The memory was still painful now, as she walked away, and it hurt to think of John. She wondered how Lionel was. They seldom spoke any more. Things had never been the same since he had told her parents about Bill, and she seemed to have nothing to say to him now. The last she'd heard, he was still looking for a job at one of the studios, anxious to get back into film. She sighed, and took the escalator downstairs. There was a riot of colour everywhere, silk flowers, patent-leather bags, bright suede belts in rainbow hues. She couldn't resist, and came home with bags of it, most of which she knew she'd never wear, unlike the diamond bracelet Bill gave her that night to ease the pain. He knew how unhappy she was about not getting pregnant yet. But he was sure she would. She was healthy and young and just trying too hard, and the doctor had told her as much. He told her so again the week before they went to St Tropez. 'Just relax and don't think of it,' he said, which was easy for him to say. He was fifty-eight years old, and had learned to be more philosophical about life.

Deep down she was still upset but for the three weeks that they played on the beach at St Tropez, Anne had never looked happier in her life. She wore blue jeans and espadrilles, bikinis and bright cotton shirts, and she let her hair go wild, in a haze of blonde bleached even paler by the sun. She was a beautiful girl, and growing prettier by the day. He was pleased to see she had even gained a little weight, and when they went to Cannes to shop, she didn't fit into her usual size, she had to move up one. He teased her when she had trouble zipping up her jeans again. He told her she was getting fat, but a question dawned which he didn't even dare voice to her. In Paris he was sure of it when she was too tired to walk along the Seine, fell asleep on the way to Coq Hardi for lunch, and turned green when he suggested a Dubonnet. He didn't say a word to her, but protected her like a mother hen with a chick, and when they got back to LA, he reminded her that she hadn't had a period since they left a month before. For the first time in six months, she hadn't even thought of it, and suddenly her jaw dropped as she made rapid calculations in her head, and then grinned nervously at him.

'Do you think . . .?' She didn't even dare say the words and he smiled gently at her. It hadn't taken so long after all. Six months wasn't long at all, except it had been to her, so anxious to conceive.

'Yes, I do, little one. I've thought it for the last few weeks but I didn't want to get your hopes up, so I didn't say anything.' She squealed and threw her arms around his neck, and he tried to

413

calm her down. 'Let's wait till we're sure, and then we'll celebrate.'

She went for the test the next day, and when she called them breathlessly that afternoon for the results, they were positive. She was so stunned, she just sat there and stared at the phone. When Bill came home she still looked dazed, and he whooped with delight. He noticed, as she wandered around in her bathing suit, that she had already subtly changed shape. She wasn't as angular as usual, everything seemed softer and more round.

'I am . . . I am . . . I am . . .' She was so excited she danced with glee, and he took her out to celebrate at the Beverly Hills Hotel, but she fell instantly to sleep, as he found himself dreaming of the baby they would have. He was caught up in it too, and he was thinking of transforming the guest room into a nursery. They could put another maid's room over the garage, and put one of the maids there . . . then put the nurse in what was now the maid's room . . . his mind whirled around all night as she slept, and the next day he came home for lunch to see how she was and celebrate again. It seemed to make no dent at all in their sex life, and she had never looked happier than she did then. She constantly spoke of their 'little boy', as though it had to be a boy, to replace the one that was gone . . . he would have been almost four years old by then, Bill knew . . .

They spent Labor Day weekend quietly with friends. People were getting used to her now, and although they envied Bill, they didn't make as many cracks as they once did. She looked more grown up than she had nine months before. Especially now – the pregnancy had given her a certain maturity.

They were planning to go to New York in the next few weeks, to see Gail, and the doctor said it was all right for Anne to go, but the day before they left, she began spotting lightly, and he put her to bed to rest. She was terrified of what it meant, but the doctor insisted that it happened all the time. Most women had some spotting in the first few months, it meant nothing at all, he said, except that after three days it hadn't stopped, and Bill was growing anxious now. He called another doctor he knew, who said the same thing. But Anne was strangely pale under her tan, mostly from fright. She barely moved from her bed all day long, except to go to the bathroom, and Bill came home for lunch every day to see how she was, and he left the office earlier than usual. They would just have to wait and see, both doctors said, but neither of them was concerned, until after a week of consistent bleeding, late one night she began to have terrible cramps. She woke with a start, and grabbed Bill's arm. She was barely able to speak she was in such pain, and she felt as though a hot poker were forcing its way through her, pushing everything down between her legs and on her lower back. Bill called the doctor, frantically wrapped her in a blanket, and took her to the hospital. Her eyes were wide with fear, and she held his hand tightly, as she lay in the emergency room. She begged him not to leave her, and the doctor let him stay, but it wasn't a pretty sight. She was in terrible pain and bleeding copiously, and within two hours, she lost the baby she had wanted so desperately. She sobbed in Bill's arms.

They put her out and wheeled her away to do a quick D and C and when Anne woke up in the recovery room, Bill was there again, with grief-stricken eyes filled with concern as he held her hand. The doctor had said there was no explanation for it, some foetuses were just wrong and the body eliminated them. It was best that way he said. But Anne was inconsolable as she lay in bed at home for weeks. They told her she could get up, but she had no desire to at all. She lost fifteen pounds, looked like hell, and refused to talk to anyone or go anywhere. Eventually, Faye got word of it in a roundabout way. Lionel called Anne to say hello, and Bill told him. He called Faye, who in turn called Anne to see how she was, but she wouldn't speak to anyone, Bill said in despair. And she flatly refused to see Faye. She got hysterical when Bill even mentioned it, screaming again that it was all her fault, that if she hadn't made her give the other baby away, she would have him now. She hated everyone, even Bill at times, and it was November before he could get her to travel with him again, or go anywhere, Gail was upset at how drawn she looked when she finally came to New York with Bill.

'She looks terrible.'

'I know.' He worried about her all the time, but there was nothing he could do except get her pregnant again, and that could take time. 'She took it very hard.' It had already been two months and she never talked about it, but it was easy to see how the miscarriage had ravaged her, and even the jewellery he bought didn't excite her very much. Nothing did. Not even the trip to St Moritz at Christmastime.

Finally, in January, she began to revive. It had been a terrible time for her, and the six weeks' depression the doctor had predicted for her had turned into three months. At least now she was over it, for the most part. She was back to her old life, of shopping and seeing a few friends. She called Gail in New York more often again, and she had set up her temperature charts again. This time it paid off in two short months. She found out she was pregnant on Valentine's Day.

The baby only lasted six weeks – she lost it on the first of March, two weeks after she found out. Bill braced himself for what she would go through again, but she was quieter about it this time. Silent, withdrawn, she rarely mentioned it, even to him, and in some ways that worried him more. He would rather have seen her cry all the time, at least she would have got it out of her system. Instead, there was something closed and dead in her eyes. She put the temperature charts away for good, threw the basal thermometer away, and talked about redoing the guest room in green or blue. It tore at his heart even more than the time before, but there was nothing he could do for her. Late one night, she confessed to him in the dark that she thought it might be because of all the drugs she took several years before. But that was five years ago, he reminded her, and he was convinced it had nothing to do with it. But she clung to her guilts and her regrets, and the memory of the relinquished child. It was obvious she believed she would never have one now, and he didn't even dare argue with her. It put a terrible silent pressure on him now whenever they made love, but at least she wasn't still taking her temperature. That was a relief of sorts.

She continued to avoid her parents like the plague, particularly Faye, and Bill brought her news of them from time to time. He had heard they were putting together an enormous package, and looking for a star.

'Maybe they'll give Val the part,' he said to distract her one day as they ate lunch by the pool. Even if he hadn't given her a child, she reminded herself constantly, he had given her a beautiful life, and happiness. She was cared for as never before. And it was she who had failed him, she felt, not being able to give him a child. But it didn't seem to matter as much to him as it did to her, and she laughed now at his suggesting Val for her parents' film.

'Only if they're doing a horror picture and need a star with a fantastic scream.' She described Val's famous scream to him, and he laughed as he listened to her. She was coming out of it more quickly this time and he was relieved.

But the suggestion he had just made to his wife was not as outlandish as it seemed. In their offices, Faye and Ward had a hundred résumés spread around, and there was another fat stack of rejects on the floor. They had thought of everyone and no one was right for the part. They wanted someone new and fresh, and beautiful. Someone who seemed real. And Ward looked at Faye with the same idea Bill had had, only he was serious.

'Val?' Faye sighed deeply and looked intensely at Ward. 'I don't think that's a good idea.' She had never put her own children into any of her films. For two decades she had kept her two worlds separate and now they were threatening to collide. Besides which, Val wasn't easy, and she and Faye seldom got along. Also, she had no experience with quality films. Yet, what a great gift to give her. 'I don't know, Ward . . .'

'Well, we've thought of everyone else in this town. And unless you want to start looking in Europe or New York, we're going to have to start looking under flat rocks. Why don't you give it a try?'

'What if it doesn't work?'

'Then you fire her.'

'My own child?' She looked shocked.

'I don't think you'll have to.' Ward wouldn't let go of his idea. 'This could change her whole life, Faye. It could be the chance she needs. The fact is that she's got the ability, she just hasn't had the vehicle.'

Faye smiled at him ruefully. 'You sound like her agent. Baby, don't do this to me, Ward. She's not right for the part.' It wasn't true, but it would have been easier if it were.

'What makes you say that?' He took a framed photograph off his desk and handed it to Faye. 'She has exactly the look you want, doesn't she?'

Faye smiled at her husband. 'All right. I give up.' But she looked happier than she had in a very long time. Ward smiled in answer. He was proud of her, and they both knew it wasn't going to be easy. He was convinced that this was right, and he would do everything possible to help them.

And the truth was that he was right. Val did have exactly the look she wanted for the star, but what a challenge it would be to work with her own daughter. On the other hand, it could be the chance of a lifetime. For Val anyway.

Faye stood up with a smile, and Ward walked towards her.

'You're terrific, do you know that?' He said it with a smile and Faye looked at him ruefully.

'Just be sure you tell that to your daughter.'

Chapter 40

'You want me to do *what*?' Val shrieked at her agent through the phone. She'd been sitting at home doing her nails, wondering whether to go out to eat that night or not. There was nothing in the refrigerator as usual, but three of the girls had been talking about stopping at Chicken Delight on the way home, and Val didn't feel like going out. She was sick of the men she'd been seeing lately. All they wanted was to get laid. And after a while it was all the same. She had given up her virginity six years before, and she couldn't even remember all the men she'd slept with any more.

'I want you to read for Faye Thayer,' her agent repeated again.

She started to laugh. 'Do you realise who you called?' He had made a mistake obviously. 'This is *Val* Thayer.' She wanted to add 'you jerk', but she restrained herself. She was going to read for another part later that week, in a film about drugs. It wasn't much of a part, but it would pay the rent and it was something to do with herself. She wasn't ready to admit defeat yet. She had been acting for four years, and she knew she'd get a big break one of these days, though not reading for her mum. That was the funniest thing she'd heard in months.

'I'm serious, Val. Your mother's office just called.'

'You're out of your mind.' She put the bottle of nail polish down. 'This is a joke. Right? Okay, so ha ha. Now why did you call?'

'I'm telling you why I called.' He was beginning to sound desperate. Faye Thayer's office didn't call him every day, and it made him nervous too. He was a small agent on Sunset Strip, and he supplied actors and actresses and models for B films and horrors, soft porn, and live topless shows. Faye had been furious when Val said she had signed up with him. 'She's serious, Val. They want you there tomorrow at nine o'clock.'

'What for?' She could feel sweat break out under her arms. Why would they call her agent and not her?

'They want you to read cold.' He had offered to pick up the script so Val could study it that night but they had refused, at least the secretary had. And she said that Mrs Thayer wasn't available. Val was to report at 9 am the next day, that was it. Were they interested or not? He had pounced on it of course, but now he had to convince Val.

'What am I supposed to read?'

'All I know is it's a part in her new film.' It was the strangest thing she'd ever heard, and she finally agreed to show up there the next day, but she couldn't resist calling home that night. Her parents were out, as it turned out, and the maid must have off, because no one was there. It made her sad to call the house, there used to be so many people there, and now they were all gone. It was the same way Faye felt when they came home late at night. But all Val could think of tonight was the mysterious part she was supposed to read for the next day. She hardly slept all night, and she was up at six o'clock the next day, washing and drying her hair, doing her face, checking her nails again. She decided to wear a plain black dress, just in case they were serious. It was a little dressy for nine o'clock and it was very low-cut, but her breasts were creamy and full, and her legs were long. It was the kind of outfit she would have worn to read for anyone else, so she decided not to do anything different for Faye Thayer. She tried to tell herself that this was no different from reading for anyone else, as she drove to the studio. Her hands were shaking as she pushed open the door, and she had taken so long to touch up her makeup and do her hair once more that she was half an hour late when she arrived. The secretary looked at her disapprovingly, and she saw Faye check her watch as she walked in, and then glance at the low décolletage, but she looked at her daughter with a smile, and she seemed as nervous as Val was. Ward and two other men were sitting in another part of the room, conferring quietly, with tables spread all around, and photographs of other actresses that they were checking out. They glanced up once and she saw her father wink at her. But it was her mother she had to concentrate on now. Her mother, the woman she had always resented, who was finally giving her her big chance now.

'Hello, Valerie.' Her voice was gentle, and her manner more professional than Valerie was used to. It was as though she were trying to tell Val something without saying the words, and giving her all the encouragement she could. As she watched her, Valerie began to feel calm. She forced herself not to think of the three goddamn Academy Awards and only the script at hand. Suddenly it meant everything to her. She hadn't had a big break yet, but she knew she could act, and if this killed her, she was going to do it. Faye Thayer watched her face, and examined every inch of her, wishing her well, almost praying for her. 'We'd like you to read for a part today, Val.' As she said it, she handed the script to her.

'That's what my agent said. What kind of part is it?'

'It's a young woman who . . .' She went on to describe the part, and Val wondered again why she had called her. She wanted to ask her why she had called, but she decided not to say anything.

'Can I have a few minutes to study it?' Her eyes were intense. She had always been so jealous of Faye, of her looks, of her past, her success, the acting career she had walked away from as a young girl. And now here she was, reading for her. It was the strangest development of her entire career. Her mother nodded now. Val saw that she was getting old. She was only fifty-one, but the last few years had taken their toll.

Suddenly she wanted the part, wanted it more than anything in the world. She wanted to show this woman she could act. She knew Faye didn't think she could, and she wondered whose idea it had been to give her a chance. Probably her dad's.

'Take ten minutes in the other room and then come back in.' The voice was warm, the eyes worried. What if she couldn't do it? Val read her mother's fears clearly. This was a side of her that her children never saw, the consummate professional, the director who demanded guts and heart and flesh, the woman who had given her whole life to her work. And suddenly Val saw it all, who she was, what she did, how demanding she could be. But it didn't frighten her. She was sure she was equal to the task. She almost went into a trance as she studied the lines, feeling the role, making it part of her. And when she walked back into the room, she looked like a different girl. Ward and the other men glanced up at her, and watched her act. She didn't read. She raged and she stormed, and she spoke, and she never glanced at the paper once. Ward's heart went out to her. He knew how hard she had worked, and how badly she must want this now. There were tears of joy and pride streaming down Faye's cheeks when Val finished. The two women exchanged a long glance, and suddenly Val began to cry too, and the two women hugged and laughed and cried, as Ward watched them. And then finally, laughing through her tears, Val looked at them both. 'Well? Do I get it?'

'Hell, yes!' Faye was quick to answer and was stunned when Val gave her now famous scream.

'Hallelujah!'

Chapter 41

Val started work on the film in May, and she had never worked so hard in her life. Her mother worked herself and everyone else to the bone, demanding the utmost from them, working for long, gruelling hours, demanding everything Val had in her guts. But it was no more than she asked of herself, or the other actors who worked for her. That was how she worked, and why her work was so good, it was why she had won the Awards Val had sneered at for so many years. She wasn't sneering now. She was loving it. She could barely crawl home every night, and she ended most of her days on the set in tears. At twenty-two years of age, she had never worked so hard in her life, and wasn't sure she ever would again. And if she did, it would be because she wanted to. No one would ever demand so much from her . . . or teach her so much . . . she knew that too. And she was happy and proud and grateful.

She had been working for three weeks when her co-star, George Waterston, offered her a ride home. She had seen him around Hollywood before, and she knew he hadn't been pleased when he'd heard who would be playing opposite him. He had wanted a big star, and Faye had to work hard to convince him to give her a try. The deal had been that if she was no good, she'd be canned. Val knew all of that, from the scuttlebutt on the set, and she knew it now, as she saw Waterston looking into her eyes. She wondered if he was her enemy or her friend, and she found she didn't really care. She was too tired to give a damn, and she really needed a lift. Her car had been in the shop for weeks, and she had taken a cab to work. So she looked up at him gratefully.

'Sure . . . thanks . . .' She didn't even have the energy to talk on the way home, after she gave him the address, and she was horrified when she fell asleep and he woke her up outside her house. She gave a sudden start as he touched her arm and stared at him, mortified. 'Did I fall asleep?'

'Guess I'm not as interesting as I used to be.' He had brown hair and blue eyes, a strong, somewhat weathered face. He was thirty-five years old, and Val had admired him for years. It was all part of the dream that her life had become, starring in a film with this man. People were already saying that she had got the part because of who her mother was. But she didn't give a damn. She was going to prove them all wrong. She was going to knock them dead as Jane Dare, the woman she played, and she looked apologetically at her co-star now.

'I'm so sorry . . . I've been so tired . . .'

'My first film for Faye, I was like that too. I even fell asleep behind the wheel of my car once, and woke up just before I hit a tree. By the end of it, I was even afraid to drive. But she gets something out of you that no one else does, a piece of your soul... or your heart . . . by the time it's all over, she doesn't even have to pull it out of you any more. You want to give it to her.' It was exactly what Val was already beginning to feel, along with a whole rainbow of new feelings of love and respect for her mother.

'I know . . . I still can't believe she gave me the part.' She looked up at him honestly. 'She's never liked anything I've done before, and I haven't done much. I mean, I've had a lot of roles in films, but nothing as big as this.' He already knew that, and for the first time in weeks, he felt sorry for her. He hadn't liked her at all at first. She looked like a little tart, and he figured Faye was playing favourites with her, but he soon saw that he was wrong, and now he saw that the poor kid was so scared. It must have been hell for her working for Faye, and with him as a co-star. She was in a world of pros, and she was still a kid, he realised now, feeling something entirely new for her.

'She used to scare me to death.' He laughed, relaxing with Val. She didn't look as cheap as she had at first. She hardly wore any makeup any more, and she wore sweatshirts and jeans. There was no point wearing anything low-cut or dressed-up, she just took it off the moment she arrived, and she was beginning to live the role of Jane Dare, who was very different from Val. 'Your mother is something else, Val.' It was the first time he had called her by name, and she smiled at him.

'You know, I forget she's my mother when I'm on the set. She's just this woman screaming at me, making me so mad I want to kill her sometimes.'

'That's good.' He approved. He knew Faye well, and how she made him feel too. 'That's what she wants you to feel.'

Val sighed, comfortable in the big roomy car. It was a white Cadillac convertible with a red interior, and she hardly had the strength to open the door to go home. Then, feeling nervous, she turned to him. 'Do you want to come in for a drink or something? I don't know what there is to eat, maybe nothing at all. But we can call out for a pizza if you want.'

'How about going for a pizza somewhere?' He looked at the Rolex watch on his arm and then glanced back at her. 'I could have you back in an hour. I want to study tomorrow's scene again tonight.' And then he had an idea. 'You want to work on it together?'

She smiled at him disbelievingly. It couldn't be true. She studying lines with George Waterston for a film they were in? It had to be a dream. She decided to answer him quickly, before the dream disappeared. 'I'd love that, George. If I don't fall asleep again.' He laughed at her and he was as good as his word. They had a quick pizza on the way, went to his house in Beverly Hills, and read their parts together for two hours, trying different intonations, different moods, until they reached one they liked. It had the same feeling as the drama classes she had loved so much except that this was for real. And at exactly ten o'clock, he drove her home. They both needed their sleep for the next day. He waved casually at her as she let herself into her house, floating on a cloud. It was a pleasure not to be mauled by some kid, or some guy who looked like a pimp. She wondered why she had never met anyone like George before. And then she laughed at herself. Half the women in the world wanted to meet a man like him, and she was working with him every day.

The picture was going well, and Val had worked at his place several times. She would have had him to hers, but there was too much chaos there. He told her he thought she should move out and get a decent place. He was becoming almost a big brother to her, introducing her to his friends, and teaching her the ways of the upper echelon in Hollywood. 'It looks like hell to live in a place like that, Val.' He could say anything to her now. They worked together twelve hours a day, and studied for two or three hours every night. 'Guys will think you're cheap.' It was exactly what had been happening to her for years, until this reprieve.

'I could never afford anything better than that.' She was telling him the truth and he looked surprised. The Thayers were certainly among the more important people in Hollywood, and it seemed strange that they wouldn't subsidise her. He said as much and she shook her head. That wasn't her style. 'I haven't taken anything from them in years. Not since I moved out.'

'Stubborn little thing, aren't you?' he said, smiling at her. Lately she had noticed a warmer bond between them. She was coming to rely on him. Almost too much, she warned herself. The film they were working on was an unreal world, and sooner or later it would end. But he was so easy to be with, so friendly, so warm, and he knew so much. He even had a fourteen-year-old son whom she liked. He had married at eighteen, divorced at twenty-one, and his ex-wife was married to Tom Grieves, the big baseball star. He saw his son on weekends and occasional Wednesday nights, and he had asked Val to join them a couple of times. She got on well with the boy, whose name was Dan. George told her he had wanted to have lots of kids, but he had never remarried, although she knew from the gossip around

426

town that he had lived with several big stars. It was in early June that they wound up in the papers together for the first time.

Faye saw it too, and showed it to Ward before they left for work. 'I hope she's not getting involved with him.'

'Why not?' Ward suspected they were; he had always liked George. He thought he was one of the more decent people around town.

But Faye was looking at it from a different view. She had a single-minded goal in her mind when she was working on a film. 'It will distract her from her work.'

'Maybe not. He might teach her something.' Faye grunted something unintelligible, and they left for work. As usual, she was worried about Val. Ward had been right of course, she was fabulous in the part, though she didn't want to say too much to Val yet, it might throw her off. She was almost sorry they were all going to Vanessa's graduation in a few weeks. She didn't like socialising with her stars during a film, but it couldn't be helped in this case. She would keep as far away from her as she could, and hoped she'd understand. She was coming to love the child more and more, but right now she was also her director. And that mattered more. Right now.

When George heard Val was going to New York, he wanted to come too. 'I haven't been there since last year. And hell, I could bring Dan.' It was the strangest relationship. They went everywhere together now, and he had never laid a hand on her. She was sorry about it too. Yet they were becoming friends and she didn't want to spoil what they had. 'I could bring Danny too. I usually stayed at the Carlyle.'

'I think my mother's staying at the Pierre with my brother and sister and brother-in-law.' Bill had suggested it to them, and Faye had let him reserve the room. They were slowly becoming friends, and Ward had played tennis a few times with him.

But now George had an idea. 'What about staying uptown at the Carlyle with us? Faye won't want to hang around you too much anyway.'

Val knew that, and her father had explained it, so George's suggestion was perfect.

'She never talks to her stars. She says it confuses her. She can only deal with one identity at once. And right now, in her head you're Jane Dare, she doesn't even want to see Valerie Thayer or George Waterston.' The character he played was a man named Sam, and Val nodded now, understanding better. And she liked the idea of staying at the Carlyle with them.

'You're sure Danny won't mind having me around?'

'Hell, no. He's crazy about you.' And he certainly seemed to be as the three of them flew to New York, first-class. George signed several autographs as Val and Danny watched, and eventually they started teasing him, begging him for one too. She played cards with Dan while George slept, and they all watched the film, elbowing each other ferociously. It was one of George's recent films.

There was a limo waiting for them at the airport in New York, and it drove them straight to the Carlyle, where George had reserved a three-bedroom suite. There was a kitchenette, and a piano, and an airy living room with a view of the park. It was on the thirty-fourth floor, and Danny looked thrilled with it all. They ordered room service instantly, and went to dinner at '21' that night.

'Well, kid.' He spoke softly to her later that night in the bar after Danny had gone upstairs. 'It's going to be all over the world that you're having an affair with me. Think you can take the heat?' She laughed and said yes, and the crazy thing was that they were just friends. A little while later, they sat and listened to Bobby Short make magic on the piano at the Carlyle, and then they went upstairs to their rooms. She knew the rest of her family was in New York by then too, and the next morning Vanessa called, wanting to have lunch with her. She was excited about Val's film and wanted to hear all about it. They had had dinner with Ward and Faye the night before and she wouldn't say a thing.

'So you have to tell all.'

'Okay. Can I bring George to lunch?' She didn't feel right abandoning him and the boy, but Vanessa didn't understand.

'George who?'

'George Waterston.' She said it so casually that Vanessa almost fell off her seat at the other end.

'Are you kidding? Is he here with you?'

'Yup. We flew in together, with his son. He thought it would be fun to be here for a few days while I watch you graduate. Speaking of which, congratulations! At least one of us is educated now!' Vanessa had no interest whatsoever in her education now.

'George *Waterston*! Val, I can't believe you!' She covered the phone with her hand and told Jason the news, whispering loudly to Val after that. 'Are you involved with him?'

'No. We're just friends.' But Vanessa didn't believe a word of it as she told Jason when she hung up. If he had come all the way to New York with her, they had to be more than just friends.

'You never know. You guys out in Plastic Land are weird. I've always said that.' He smiled at her then. They were moving the following week. They had found a loft in Soho, and they could hardly wait to move there. They had promised to show Ward and Faye, and there was no longer any pretence about where Van lived. She lived with him, and intended to continue doing so. Faye had questioned her about it the night before, hoping to hear that they were planning to get married one of these days, but they seemed to have no intention of it. Jason accused Van of torturing her after they went back to the Pierre and he and Vanessa were alone again. 'Poor woman, she's so anxious for you to be respectable. We could at least get engaged, you know.'

'That would spoil everything.'

'You're nuts.'

'No, I'm not. I don't need a piece of paper with you. There's a lot of stuff we both want to do first,' she reminded him, his play, her book, she had to look for a job now. But he was finished with school now and thinking of settling down. Vanessa was in no rush. She was still young enough to feel as though she had forever. Although she was in an enormous rush to meet Valerie's friend.

They made a date for lunch at PJ Clark's and promptly at one o'clock, Valerie and George Waterston, and his son Dan walked in. George was wearing jeans, a T-shirt and Gucci shoes with no socks, and Danny looked like any kid anywhere, in a blue shirt and khaki slacks. He was dressing up a lot these days, ever since he had developed an interest in girls. He had a huge crush on Val, who was wearing a red leather gypsy dress. But Vanessa had eyes only for George and she practically drooled. Valerie teased her about it halfway through lunch. Jason and George were getting on like a house on fire, and Jason had talked endlessly to Dan about sports, and promised to take him to a Yankee game before he left for the Coast again. It was an entirely congenial group, and Vanessa couldn't help but notice the change in her twin. She was calmer, more confident, more subdued, not so loud. She looked peaceful and happy and fulfilled, and it was difficult to believe she wasn't in love with this man. He certainly looked as though he were in love with her, and they talked about the film a little bit. Valerie still couldn't believe she'd got the part, as she told Van about the horrifying interview with her mother and how terrified she had been.

'That woman has always scared me to death.' It was the first time in her whole life she had admitted it, and Vanessa looked at her, surprised. She really had changed. It was almost as if she had finally grown up and become herself, and Van found herself liking her better than she had for years.

'I always thought you were jealous of her, not scared.'

'Both, I guess.' Valerie sighed, with a smile at George. 'She still scares the shit out of me at work, but I don't resent her as much. I see how hard she works. I guess she's deserved every-thing she's got. I could never admit that to myself before.'

'I'm impressed.' Vanessa spoke softly to her, and the two men exchanged a glance. It was extraordinary to think that these two young women were twins. Vanessa was so quiet, so intellectual, so hell bent on success in a totally different field. She didn't even want to go back to Los Angeles any more. Her life was in New York, with Jason and her friends, the publishing world she wanted to break into. She wasn't even talking about writing a film any more, just her book. And Valerie, with her flaming red hair and brilliant good looks was so much a part of the film milieu, but the best part of Hollywood now, not the rubbish. Without realising it, her whole outlook had changed in the past two months. The days of screams and green slime were gone for good. And one could already sense about her the aura of a big star. Faye saw it too. It was the same aura she had once had herself. Or very close to it.

At the graduation the next day, she looked at all of them, quietly. Anne, so impeccably dressed in her expensive clothes, with little diamonds sparkling at her ears, her arm tucked in Bill's; Vanessa so pretty and serious in her cap and gown; Valerie so incredibly beautiful it was startling except that she seemed unaware of it, which was wonderful; and Lionel, who looked happier than he had in two years. Faye wondered if there was a new man in his life, but she never wanted to ask, and of course neither did Ward. What he did was his own business now, he was twenty-five years old after all, and they had accepted him, as they had all of them, though some of that acceptance was still unilateral, Faye knew. She knew that Anne was still angry at her for the child she had given up ... Val still jealous of her success ... Vanessa had grown away from her now ... and Lionel had his own life ... poor Greg was gone. She missed him now, as she so often did, that shock of red hair, the passion for sports, the girls he loved to chase. He had been closer to Ward than to her, but he was her son too, and she tightened her hand on Ward's arm, knowing that he would be thinking of him too, and it was painful for both of them.

But it was all laughter and smiles that afternoon when they went to the Plaza to celebrate. Faye had arranged for a table covered with white flowers in the Edwardian Room, and Vanessa was stunned beyond words when Ward handed their graduation gift to her. They had debated about it long and hard, and they finally decided to include Jason too. It was a way of giving their approval to her way of life. They had given her two tickets to Europe, with a fat cheque to cover all their fun, and reservations at some of the finest hotels. It was going to be a fabulous trip for both of them, and Faye was relieved to hear that Jason could get away too, as soon as they moved to Soho the following week. He had quit his job to work full time on his play.

'Well, you two, that ought to keep you out of trouble for a while.' Ward smiled at them. He still wished they would get married, but it didn't seem to be on the cards. At least not yet. And he was also wondering about George Waterston and Val. George had gone off with his son for the afternoon, but Ward was aware that Valerie was staying with them, and he was curious about how far the involvement went, and he hadn't said a word about it all day. Then of course there were Bill and Anne. And Bill seemed to get on very well with the rest of the mob. Vanessa had invited Gail, and she sat chatting with Lionel. She was crazy about her studies in design, her summer job with Bill Blass this year. Lionel was talking animatedly about the film he was working on. Everyone was happy and young. It warmed one's heart to look at them as he said to Faye, as they strolled slowly back to the Pierre. He tucked her arm in his, and pulled her to one side, spoke to a man standing next to a hansom cab, and the next thing she knew, she was driving around Central Park, with Ward holding her hand. He kissed her gently once or twice and she smiled. She was still crazy about him after a lifetime. 'I must say, that's quite a group we've got.' His mind ran over them again as they clomped along through the park, and Faye didn't disagree with him. She hadn't said much to Val, and she hoped that George would explain it to her. He knew her methods of working well. 'You're better-looking than all of them though, babe.'

'Oh my love.' She kissed him and smiled. 'Now I know you're as crazy as I always thought.'

'Just crazy about you.' He kissed her again then, and they held hands together for a long time, happy with each other and their lives. They had come a long, long way side by side.

Chapter 42

'Do you want to go to dinner tonight, sweetheart?' Anne shook her head as she lay on the bed at the Pierre. It had gone well after all, even though she really hadn't wanted to come, but Bill thought they should, and it was a good excuse to see Gail. Seeing Gail had been what finally convinced her. He even offered her a trip to Europe, with New York as a stop on the way, but she wasn't in the mood, and she was very tired again. She had been for months, ever since the first miscarriage. She never really seemed to have bounced back, and Bill worried about her.

'Why don't we order room service and eat here?' She knew that Gail was going somewhere with Lionel. She enjoyed his company and she had a lot of gay friends, but Anne hadn't wanted to go along. She thought that Bill would be bored, and she knew she would too. Jason and Vanessa were going to celebrate, Val had her film star, and she had no desire to see her parents. Once in a day was more than enough for her. But Bill thought it a shame to waste a night in New York.

'Are you sure?'

'I really don't feel up to going out.'

'Do you feel sick?' It was beginning to remind him of when Gail's mother had first been sick, and he wanted her to go back to the doctor.

But when they got back the next week, she resisted him. 'I don't need to see the doctor. I feel fine.' She looked at him stubbornly and he wouldn't give in to her this time. Some things were just too important to him, and she was the most important of all. He never wanted to lose her. Ever.

434

'You don't feel fine. You feel like hell. You wouldn't even go out with me in New York.' She had ordered room service and gone right to sleep, and she was doing almost the same thing every night. He had the feeling she was sleeping all day too. 'If you don't make an appointment yourself, I'll do it for you, Anne.' And in the end, that was exactly what he did. He made the appointment, pretended to pick her up for lunch, and took her to his doctor in Beverly Hills. She was furious.

'You lied to me!' It was one of the few times she had screamed at him, but he led her inside like a little girl, and she glowered at them both. The doctor found nothing wrong with her. Her glands seemed fine, her chest was clear, her blood count was all right, and then without saying anything to them, he had an idea. He did the test with the blood he had taken from her arm, and he called Bill with the results that night, and he was stunned when he heard. Stunned and thrilled and afraid. She was pregnant again. This time he hadn't even thought of it. And he was afraid to put her through another disaster again.

'Just have her do what she's doing now. Her body knows what she needs. She needs lots of rest, good food, as little stress as possible. All she has to do is lie low for a couple of months and she'll be fine.' Bill nodded, and went into the other room to talk to her. She was watching TV, and she was thinking of calling Gail, and he encouraged her to now, with a quiet smile.

'I think you should, sweetheart.'

'How come?'

'To tell her the news.'

'What news?' Anne looked blank.

He leaned over and kissed her tenderly on the lips, 'The news that you're pregnant again.'

Her eyes grew wide. 'I am? Who told you that?'

'The doctor just now. He just called. He didn't even tell us he was running the test, but you are.'

'I am?' She looked stunned and then suddenly she threw her arms around his neck, fighting back tears. 'Oh Bill . . .' She didn't even dare say the words this time. She didn't even tell Gail. She didn't tell anyone, until the ominous three-month period had passed, and this time all went well. By September, the doctor was no longer concerned, and the baby was due in February, possibly on Valentine's Day. Her other child would have been five and a half years old by then, though neither of them mentioned that. They just talked about this child, and Bill knew how badly she wanted it. He treated her as though she were walking on eggs. They took no trips, barely went out, Anne rested constantly, and Bill spoiled her even more than he had before.

Faye called her several times, and said she hoped it was all going well, but Anne's voice was cold on the phone. She and her mother had been through this before, and she remembered the pressure she had put on her then. She hated talking to her now, because it reminded her of it. She even hated talking to Lionel, because it reminded her of living with him and John, waiting for her first baby to be born.

Gail called them as often as she could from New York, and asked how big she was. Anne laughed and claimed she was huge, and when Val saw her one day on Rodeo Drive, she laughingly agreed. It was November by then, and they had finished the film a month before. It was being edited day and night, because Faye wanted it released over the Christmas holidays. Everyone was working on golden time by then, but they wanted it eligible for the next Academy Awards so it just had to be out by year's end. And when Anne ran into Val, she noticed that George Waterston was parked in his Cadillac at the kerb, waiting for her. She couldn't help wondering if they were still 'just friends', as Val claimed. But one thing was sure, Val looked even more beautiful than before, and she was picking up a dress at Giorgio's for a party that night. Anne had just been in to pick up a few things to wear over the holidays. Bill wanted her to get out a little bit and she had outgrown everything she owned, even her maternity clothes.

'How do you feel?' Val asked, seeming genuinely concerned. All of them knew how much the baby meant to her, and why. Anne laughed. She was enjoying her pregnancy, in spite of the discomforts of it.

'I feel fat.'

'You look great.'

'Thank you. How's everything with you?' They rarely called each other any more. It was difficult to believe they had grown up in the same house once. But they hadn't really. Val had grown up only recently, and Anne had grown up at Bill's.

'I just got an offer for another role.'

'Not with Mum again, is it?'

Val was quick to shake her head. Working with her mother had been an experience she would never forget, and she would always be grateful for it, but she wasn't anxious to do it again soon. Most of the actors who worked for her said that, even George. 'Once in three years is about it with her,' he had said, and Val figured it was true. 'No, with someone else.' She named the director and the stars and Anne was impressed. 'I haven't decided yet. There are a couple of others I might do.' Her career had finally taken off 'overnight', after five years of screams. Anne was pleased for her. That night she told Bill.

'She's going to be the hottest thing in Hollywood one day. Just like your mum was once.' It was easy to believe now; she was talented and beautiful and she had that smell of success about her. You could just see she was someone when she jumped out of a car, not like the old days in a tight black dress and sequined high heels. She had come a hell of a long way, and Anne thought George was responsible for the happiness she saw in Val's eyes.

'I think they're more than just friends, don't you?' She was trying to get comfortable in a chair but it was impossible until he put some pillows behind her. She thanked him with a kiss.

'I think so too. But I think they're smart to keep it quiet. He's a big star, and they don't need the headache of all that publicity.'

437

In fact, they had kept it from everyone, even Dan, for as long as they could. But eventually, they had had to tell him, and now Val was quietly living with them in the Hollywood Hills, in a beautiful house that was entirely walled in, surrounded by thick trees. Even the *papparazzi* hadn't caught onto them yet, and it had been going on for three months. Val had never been so happy in her life. When they'd come back from New York and gone back to work on the film, something different seemed to have happened between them. They were so close they understood every breath, every pause – it was like magic on the set every day, and Faye felt it too and was thrilled by it.

She didn't interfere with them, she just let it roll, and by August, when Dan went away with his mum, Val quietly moved in with George. They explained it to Danny when he came back, and George was even talking about getting married, although neither of them was in any rush. They wanted time to be sure. Val was sure it was going to come out one of these days, but they were ready now. In fact, they were waiting for it.

'Do you think you could stand living here forever, with an old man, and a young boy?' He was kissing her neck the afternoon she had run into Anne, and told him how huge she was.

'It sounds like the good life to me . . . of course,' she put on a wistful face that convinced even him, 'it's not as nice as where I used to live before I moved here.'

George gave a roar and tousled the wild red hair. 'You mean that whorehouse full of old hens? It's a wonder you didn't get arrested just living there!'

'George, what a thing to say!'

'It's true!' She had finally even told her parents she was living with him, and she was relieved that they were pleased. She was all grown up now, but somehow it still mattered to her, especially now, after working with Faye. She had new respect for her after what she had seen, and for the first time in her life she felt as though her mother respected her. Faye had even helped her

438

find a new agent, and they had had a long talk one day after the film was wrapped up.

'Val, you are very, very good. You know, your father thought that all along. He told me so. I have to admit, I had my doubts, but you're one of the best and you're going to go a long, long way.' Those words meant everything to her, and she couldn't believe she was hearing them from Faye Thayer.

'I used to hate you, you know.' It was a terrible thing to say and there were tears in her eyes as she did. 'I was so jealous of you and those damn Oscars in the den.'

'They don't mean anything, Val.' Faye's voice was soft, but Valerie shook her head. 'You five wonderful people are my Oscars.'

'I used to say they didn't matter, but they do. They mean how hard you've worked, how good you are. And you're wonderful, Mum . . . you really are the best.' The women had both cried then, holding each other close, and Val was still warmed by the memory. She had finally made peace with her. It had taken a long time, but she had. And she hoped that Anne would one day too. The ghosts would never leave her eyes until she did, and she said that to George too. She told him everything. He had become more than just her lover, he was her very best friend.

'You know, I kind of envy your brother-in-law.' He said it as they were stretched out in front of the fire that night, and Val looked at him, surprised.

'Bill? Why? You have everything he has and more. Besides,' she grinned, 'you have me, what more could you want?'

'Of course.' He smiled back at her, but there was a longing in his eyes she hadn't seen before. He was a quiet man, with values she liked, ideals that were easy to respect, and a stable way of life, all of which was very unusual for a Hollywood idol, which he was. 'I envy him that kid.'

'The baby?' She was startled by his words, children were something that she rarely thought of. She thought of having them one day, but not for a long, long time. Her career was important to her, she had worked hard for it, and she was just beginning the exciting climb to the top. She was nowhere near ready to step down yet, unlike Faye at almost her age. Faye had been twenty-five when she retired, Val was almost twenty-three. 'Would you really want a baby now, George?' He was at the height of his career too. It would have been difficult for both of them, although the idea appealed to her for a later date.

'Maybe not now, but someday soon.'

'How soon?' She rolled over on her stomach, propped her face on her hands, and looked worriedly at him.

'How about next week?' He was teasing her and he laughed at the worried look in her eyes. 'I don't know, a year or two. But it's something I'd like to do again one day.' Dan was a nice boy, and Val was fond of him too.

'I wouldn't mind that.'

'Good.' He looked pleased, and a little while later, in front of the fire, he peeled her clothes slowly from her, and said something about practising, as he made love to her.

Chapter 43

'How do you feel, sweetheart?' Bill looked at her solicitously, and she laughed.

'How would you feel, if you looked like this? Like shit. I can't move, I can't breathe. If I lie down the kid strangles me, if I sit up, I get cramps.' It was already February 9, and she was five days from her due date, but despite the complaints, she seemed to be enjoying it. She wanted the baby so much that she didn't seem to really care how big she got, or how uncomfortable she was. She just wanted to hold him in her arms and finally see his little face. She still thought it was going to be a boy, but Bill was secretly hoping for a girl. He claimed he was more used to them.

'Do you want to go out for something to eat?' She laughed and shook her head. Nothing fitted, not even her shoes, and she only had three ugly dresses she could wear. She had stopped going to Giorgio's to buy dresses to go out, because she never wanted to go out, and she didn't now. She was too uncomfortable to go anywhere. She just wanted to wander around the house barefoot and in the loosest things she owned, preferably a nightgown. And that night, after they ate some soup and a small soufflé, which was all she had room for now, they went for a walk near the house, but even that was too much for her. She huffed and she puffed and she had to sit down on a huge rock outside someone's house. He almost wondered if he'd have to go and get the car for her, but she insisted that she could get home again. She looked so vulnerable and so huge that he felt desperately sorry for her, but she seemed to accept it as the way things were, and the next day she even got up and made him breakfast before he left for work. She seemed to be brimming with energy and she said something about cleaning the baby's room again, which he thought unnecessary, but she seemed hell-bent on it when he tried to discourage her, and as he left, she was dragging the vacuum across the floor. He was worried about her, so much so that he decided to drop by again before lunch, and when he did, he found her quietly lying on the bed with his stopwatch in her hand, timing contractions as she did the Lamaze breathing she had learned this time. She looked at him with a distracted look and he hurried to her side.

'Is this it?'

She smiled peacefully at him. 'I wanted to be sure before I dragged you home from work, or lunch at the Polo lounge.'

He looked suddenly nervous as he took the stopwatch from her hand. 'You shouldn't have vacuumed the baby's room.'

But she only laughed. 'I have to have this kid sometime, you know.' Her due date was only four days away now. He cancelled his lunch and called the doctor for her, and then told his secretary that he wouldn't be in for the rest of the day. But try as he would, he couldn't make her go to the hospital yet. Even the doctor said she could wait a while, but Bill was afraid they'd wait too long at home.

She remembered her last experience only too well, when it had taken days for the baby to be born. There was no reason to rush now, and the breathing was helping her control the pain. Bill made her a little cup of soup, and sat quietly in the bedroom with her, and now and then she got up and walked around. Then at four o'clock, she looked at him with a distracted frown. She couldn't stand up any more, or talk through the pains. She knew it was time to go, and he hurried to her dressing room to get her bag, and then rushed back again. As she changed her clothes her water broke all over the white marble bathroom floor, and then suddenly the pains were coming hard and fast and the breathing hardly helped. Bill looked as though he were going to panic and she was trying to reassure him while he helped her get dressed at the same time. But the pains were coming too hard and fast now.

'I told you we shouldn't have waited this long.' He was terrified. What if she had it there? What if the baby died . . .

'It's all right.' She tried to smile at him, and he kissed her hair, and finally they got her dress on and he swept her off her feet, and carried her barefoot to the car. 'I need shoes.' She almost laughed, but the pains were too sharp. She clutched at him instead, and he ran back for the sandals she wore all the time now, and drove to Cedars Sinai Hospital with his foot solidly on the gas, barely stopping for lights. The Rolls had never been used as an ambulance before, but he was desperate now. She was giving little sharp screams with each pain, and she said she could feel the head. He left the car doors open as he rushed her inside, and the nurse went out to lock his car up for him, as Anne panted and tried to breathe, and he tried to help. They called for her doctor to come downstairs. There was no time to get her to maternity, and Anne was half crying now as she lay on the gurney in the emergency room.

'I can feel the head . . . oh God . . . Bill . . .' The pressure was unbearable, and it felt as though a bowling ball was tearing her apart as she looked desperately at him. He winced every time another contraction came. He had never seen his first child born; it wasn't done in those days, and he wasn't sure he was ready to see it now. He hated seeing Anne in such agony but the nurse said it was too late to give her anything. She had told him how awful it had been for her last time, and he didn't want it to be that way again, but she was half sitting up, and the nurse told him to hold her shoulders as she groaned horribly.

'You can push now, Anne,' the nurse said as though they had been friends for years. 'Go on . . . as hard as you can.' Anne's face grew red and he felt her strain with every ounce of strength she had and she was crying when she stopped.

'It hurts too much . . . I can't . . . I can't . . . oh God . . . Bill. The pains . . .!' And then suddenly, she was pushing again, and the doctor was there, in cap and gloves and gown. He swiftly took an instrument, and helped Anne make room for the head that emerged triumphantly on the next push. The baby was born in the emergency room, with his parents looking on. He wore a startled look and Bill thought he looked blue at first, but within seconds, he was bright and pink and wailing angrily as Anne cried and laughed all at once and Bill kissed her face and her hands, and told her how wonderful she was. 'He's so beautiful . . .! He's so beautiful . . .!' It was all she could say again and again as she looked from the baby to Bill, and a moment later, wrapped in an emergency-room blanket that was much too big for him, she was holding him in her arms. She hadn't seen the first child she had borne, and she couldn't see enough of this one. She insisted he looked just like Bill, and a little while later, with Bill walking proudly at her side, they rolled her upstairs to a private room in maternity.

'And next time, I'll thank you to come in right away, so I don't have to deliver you at the front door.' The doctor pretended to look stern and they all laughed. Bill was immensely relieved. It had looked so terribly painful and he had been so frightened for her. And now there she was laughing and smiling, with her baby in her arms. She didn't even want to give him up to send him to the nursery for a bath, but the nurse talked her into it, and a little while later they cleaned her up too. Then she and Bill called Gail and she cried when she heard the news. Anne wanted her to be godmother, just to confuse things a little more. And after that he wanted her to sleep a little bit, but she was too high on the news. The baby she had wanted so much had finally been born, and she felt a warmth in her heart she had longed for, for years. She could barely wait for them to bring him back from the nursery, and she rang for the nurse, who brought him back with a smile, looking very pink and clean, and she put him at Anne's breast, showing her what to do, as Bill watched with tears in his eyes. He had never seen anything so beautiful and knew he would remember it for the rest of his life.

444

Anne called Valerie that night, and Jason and Van, and Lionel, and finally her parents, although she had hesitated about that, and everyone was excited for her. They were naming him Maximilian, and would call him Max Stein, and Faye was just so happy for Anne. She had known only too well how desperately she wanted this child. When she came to see her the next day, she came hesitantly, with a huge teddy bear for Max, and a bed jacket for Anne. It looked like one she had worn in the hospital herself when Lionel was born.

'You look beautiful, sweetheart.'

'Thank you, Mum.' But there was always a gulf between them which nothing could bridge, it was an irremediable gap, and Bill felt it too when he came back from the house, where he had made sure everything was the way Anne wanted it. She was going home the next day.

Max was brought in, and they all oohed and ahhed, and Faye agreed that he looked like Bill. Val and George dropped by, and the nurses wanted George's autograph, and Val's too. The film was a huge hit, and posters of Val were plastered all over town. Everyone knew her now. Faye smiled as she sat back in the hospital room, and watched the two girls chat. Val was laughing about something Anne had said, and she was telling her what having the baby was like, as Bill and George stared wondrously at little Max.

Bill drove them proudly home the next day, and they settled Max in his nursery. He seemed happy and content, and he nursed a lot. Bill took a few days off just to be with them. 'You know,' she looked at Bill happily a few days after they got home, 'I'd do it again.' He stared at her and groaned. He wasn't sure he would. He was still impressed by the hideous pain she'd been in, even for such a brief time. It hadn't seemed all that brief to him, and it wasn't something he'd want to put her through again.

'Are you serious?' He looked shocked.

'I am.' She looked down at the baby, cosily tucked in at her breast, and she smiled up at Bill. 'I would, you know.' He realised it was the price of having a twenty-year-old wife, and he leaned over and kissed first Anne, and then Max.

'You're the boss.'

She laughed and her eyes looked different now. It wasn't what she had thought. The pain of the past was not completely gone, and she knew now that it never would be. But there was someone else now, someone else she could love. She would never know where that other baby was, what he was like, who he would be when he grew up, unless he sought her out. He was gone forever from her life, irretrievably lost, but she could move on now. The pain was finally dim, and no longer acute. She had Max now . . . and Bill . . . and even if they never had another child, she thought to herself, she was glad to have them. They were enough.

Chapter 44

The night of the Academy Awards, Anne turned to Bill with a worried look, asking him if she looked fat. She was wearing a pale blue and gold dress, with sapphires and diamonds on her hands and ears and throat, and he thought she had never looked more beautiful. She didn't look quite as gaunt as she once had, and she had lost that beaten look. She looked peaceful and content, and everything about her glowed.

'You look better than any film star.' He helped her on with a white mink wrap, and they hurried out to the car. They didn't want to be late. They had promised to meet Faye and Ward at their place and give them a ride. Valerie was going separately, with George, and Lionel had said he would meet them there. And once united at the Music Center, where the awards were held, they were definitely a striking group, the men in black tie, the women in jewel-coloured gowns, all of them looking faintly alike, not in their dress, but their allure. Valerie was wearing a dazzling emerald-green dress, her hair done high on her head, and emeralds she had borrowed from Anne sparkling in her ears. Faye looked resplendent in a shimmering grey gown from Norrell. They were quite a group. And in New York, Vanessa was curled up in jeans, watching it on television with Jason, wishing she was there.

'You just can't imagine how exciting it is, Jase.' Her eyes lit up as she saw people she knew, and again and again as the camera swept Val's face. And this year he felt it too. He had never really cared about the Academy Awards before, and before Vanessa came into his life, he had never even bothered to watch. But now, they were prepared to sit there all night. They sat through the boring ones, the special effects, the humanitarian awards, the sound effects, the screenplays, the songs.

Clint Eastwood was host for that portion, Charlton Heston having been delayed by a flat tyre. The award to the best director went to a friend of Faye's this year, and although George was nominated, he didn't win, and neither did their film. But then Faye was introduced to give the next award. 'The Best Actress', she said, qualifying it, reeling off the names of those who had been nominated by the Academy. And as Van and Jason watched they saw each tense face, and then finally a composite on the screen of each of them, Val sitting stone still, clutching George's hand, as they both seemed to hold their breath, and Faye looked out at her.

'The winner is . . . Valerie Thayer for *Miracle*.' The screams in the Soho loft could have been heard all the way to LA as Vanessa danced around, overwhelmed by the news. She screamed and cried, and Jason pounded the bed, tossing all the popcorn in the bowl onto the floor, and in Hollywood, Valerie was shrieking too. She ran headlong towards the stage with a last look over her shoulder at George, and a thousand cameras took her photograph as she looked at him, blew a kiss, and then joined her mother on stage. The Oscar was handed to her, and tears streamed unabashedly down Faye's face. She approached the microphone for an instant and said, 'You'll never know how much this girl deserves this award. She had the meanest director in town,' and then, as everyone laughed, she stood back, and hugged Val, and Valerie cried copiously, and thanked everyone for all they had done for her, and then crying harder still, she attempted to thank Faye.

'A long time ago, she gave me life, and now she has given me even . . .' she could barely go on '. . . more than that. She's taught me how to work hard . . . to do my best . . . she gave me the biggest chance of my life. Thank you, Mum.' The entire audience smiled through their tears as she held the coveted Oscar aloft. '. , , and Daddy, for believing in me . . . and Lionel and Vanessa and Anne for putting up with me for all these years . . .' She choked hard, but forced herself to go on, '. . . and Greg . . . we love you too . . .' And then, triumphantly, she left the stage, and flew into George's arms. It was the last award and they all went out to celebrate after that. She called Vanessa and Jason, the first chance she got, and everyone talked to them, although no one made much sense. Everyone was hugging her and shouting, kissing George, squeezing Val, hugging Ward and Faye. Even Anne was beside herself with glee and at Chasen's afterwards, Lionel had his new friend join them. He was someone George had acted with once a few years before, and had liked, and he fitted into the group easily. He was about George's own age, and he and Lionel appeared to know each other well. Faye realised then that this was the man responsible for the look in Lionel's eyes these days. It was the first time she had seen that look since John and she was glad for him. She was glad for all of them , , Val, of course . . . Anne with her baby . . Li . . . Van . . . they were just fine. And that night she stunned Ward by suggesting something he hadn't heard from her in a few years.

'What do you say we retire one of these days, kid?'

'That again?' He laughed. 'I think I've figured it out. Every time you don't get an Academy Award, you want to retire. Is that it, my love?' She laughed at the thought and shook her head. She was so happy for Val, she didn't begrudge her anything. She had earned every bit of it.

'I wish it were as simple as that.' She sat down on the bed and unclasped her pearls. They were the first gift Ward had ever given her, and the only pearls she hadn't sold when they lost their fortune years before, and they were very dear to her, as he was, as their life together had been. But she was ready for a change now. She had known it for a long time. 'I just think I've done everything I want to do, love. Professionally anyway.'

'That's terrible.' He looked upset. 'How can you say something like that at your age?'

She laughed, and she was still so damn beautiful it amazed him sometimes. 'I happen to be fifty-two years old, I've made fifty-six films, had five children, one grandchild,' she refused to count the other one, he was gone to them all and had been for more than five years, 'have a husband I adore, have made lots of friends. In brief, that's it, folks. I think I want to go and play now. All our kids are all right, they seem happy, we've done our best. This is when they write, "The End" across the screen, dear.' She smiled at him and for the first time in their life together he thought she was serious about it.

'What would you do if you retired?'

'I don't know . . . spend a year in the South of France maybe. Go play somewhere. We don't have anything in the works.' She hadn't liked anything she'd seen lately, and maybe this was what she had been waiting for, Val's Academy Award so she could leave. There was something sweet about ending with that film, the film that had begun Val's career in a big way, like a legacy she could leave her child, a special gift.

'You could write my memoirs,' Ward teased

'You do that. I don't even want to write my own.'

'You should.' They had certainly had a full life. He looked at her quietly. It had been a long, exciting night, and she might not mean what she said, although he suspected that she did. 'Why don't we think about this for a while, and see if you still feel that way in a month or two. I'll do anything you want.' He was almost fifty-six years old and he wouldn't have minded playing in the South of France. In fact, it sounded pretty good to him, like the old days almost, and they could afford it again now, although they no longer spent money as they once had. No one did any more. 'Let's think about this.'

When they discussed it again, they decided to leave in June. They agreed to make it a year off at first, to see how it felt. They rented a house in the South of France for four months, and after that they rented an apartment in Paris for six. Faye made a point of seeing each of their children before they left. Her suspicions about Lionel had been correct, this new man in his life was one he cared about a great deal. It seemed to be a good match for him, and they were living quietly together in Beverly Hills. It was the man Faye had met the night of the Academy Awards, and Faye liked him very much.

Valerie was deeply engrossed in preparing for a new role, and she and George were talking about getting married sometime that year, after George finished his new film too. Faye made her promise to come to France for their honeymoon. Val insisted they wouldn't make a fuss and would just sneak away to tie the knot, but they'd come to France for their honeymoon afterwards, and probably bring Danny too. The visit with Anne was more difficult, Faye always found it so hard to talk to her, but she went to see her one afternoon, and found her happily taking care of little Max. Faye thought she didn't look terribly well, and wondered why until Anne confessed that she was pregnant again, which startled Faye.

'Isn't that awfully soon?'

Anne smiled at her. How soon they forgot. 'Li and Greg were a year apart.' And then suddenly Faye smiled. It was true. You wanted them to be different, to be happier, better, safer, and always wise, and instead they did half the things you did yourself and had forgotten about . . . Val's acting . . . Anne's passion for a big family . . . the others had struck out on different paths, but they took parts of their parents with them too. Greg would have been just like Ward as a young man, had he lived . . . and now here was Anne, repeating history too.

'You're right.' The two women's eyes met, in a different way from how they had in a long, long time. It was as though Anne were facing her now, as though it had to be done, before Faye left. Perhaps they would never have quite this chance again. One could never be sure. 'Anne . . . I . . .' She didn't know where to begin. There were twenty years to unfold . . . or maybe five . . . a lifetime of never quite reaching a child that she loved, and she didn't want to miss her now. 'I made a lot of mistakes with you. I don't suppose that's a secret to either of us, is it?'

Anne looked at her honestly, with her child in her arms, and there was no anger in her eyes now. 'I don't think I ever made it easy for you . . . I never understood what you were all about.'

'Nor I you. My biggest mistake was that I never had time. If you had only been born a year or two before you were . . .' But who could have changed all that? It was history now. Along with everything else that had happened to her . . . the Haight . . . the pregnancy . . . the child she had given away. Their eyes met again, and Faye decided to say what was on her mind. She reached a hand out to Anne, and took the hand that wasn't holding Max in her own. 'I'm sorry about the other baby, Anne . . . I was wrong . . . at the time, I really thought we were doing the right thing . . .' Both women's eyes filled with tears, as Max lay in Anne's arms. 'I was wrong.'

Anne shook her head, the tears spilling onto her cheeks. 'I don't think you were . . . I don't think I really had a choice then. I was fourteen years old . . .'

'But you never got over it.' Faye knew that now.

'I've accepted it. It was right at the time. Sometimes that's the best you can do.' And with that, she took her mother in her arms, and held her there with Max. It was like saying 'I forgive you for what you did', but more importantly, she had forgiven herself. And now she could go on. As she walked her to her car later on, she held her hand again. 'I'm going to miss you, Mum.'

'I'm going to miss you too.' She was going to miss all of them, but she was hoping they would all come to France at one point. Once, after all, none of them had been a part of her life. And she had to let them go now. They had accepted her, in the end, and she had accepted them. All of them.

On the way to France, she and Ward stopped in New York and saw Jason and Van, happy in their loft, he writing his play, she working at a publisher's and writing her book at night. There was no talk of marriage there, but no hint of either of them going anywhere. And as Ward and Faye flew to France, she smiled over at him. 'They're all quite something, aren't they?'

'So are you.' As always he looked proud of her. He had been for thirty years . . . since the day they'd met on Guadalcanal... if only he'd known then what he knew now . . . what a full life he had lived with her. He said as much as she reminded him that it wasn't over yet, and he kissed her over the champagne the stewardess had just handed them, as a woman stared at her and whispered to the man she was with . . . *she looks just like a big film star I used to love thirty years ago* . . . the man smiled at her. Everyone looked like someone to her. And Ward and Faye went on chatting quietly, planning their year in France. Eventually they spent ten years there.

They never quite understood how the time went so fast. The children came and went. Valerie married George, and they finally had a child, a little girl they named Faye, after her. Anne had four more, and everyone teased her that she should have been as lazy as their mother and had twins. Vanessa published three books, and Jason was still working on his plays; he had moved to Off Broadway now, from Off Off Broadway, and Faye was impressed at how good his productions were when they saw one once in New York. Valerie had won the Academy Award again, and finally so had George. Everyone was doing well, and after eleven years abroad, at the age of sixty-four, Faye quietly died in her sleep one night. They were in Cap Ferrat for the autumn, in a beautiful villa they had bought there, which they wanted to leave to their children one day. It would make a perfect place for them to come, all of them.

And now she came home to them, with Ward looking stunned. He was sixty-seven, and she had been his whole life from the age of twenty-five years . . . forty-two years . . . He brought her home to Hollywood, the place she had loved, which she had conquered so many times, as an actress, a director, a woman . . . as his wife . . . He remembered those desperate years when he had lost everything, when she had pulled them all together so valiantly, and started a new career, with all of them in tow, when she had helped him get back on his feet . . . and he remembered the years before . . . and the years long afterwards, as they made film after film for MGM . . . and the big break she had given Val . . . what he could not remember any more were the years without her. That wasn't possible. It couldn't be true . . . it hadn't been true . . . and yet it was true now. He was alone, she was gone. Anne and Bill met him at the plane, and mercifully, they had left the children at home. They watched the casket being lowered from the belly of the plane, as the wind whipped Anne's hair, and in the twilight she looked so much like Faye. She was thirty-one years old, and her mother was gone . . . Her eyes rose towards Ward's, and she quietly took his hand. She and Bill had talked about it the night before, and they could at least offer him that. They had built a guesthouse behind their house in Beverly Hills, and it would be nice if he came to live there. Ward and Faye had long since sold their old house in Beverly Hils. They hadn't lived there in years. And Anne looked up at him now, as Bill watched.

'Come on, Daddy, let's go home.'

For the first time, he suddenly looked old. He couldn't believe she was gone. Anne wanted him to rest. There was a lot they had to do, and the funeral would be in two days' at the church where they'd been married, and then Forest Lawn. And everyone would be there of course . . . everyone who had ever been anyone . . . everyone except Faye Thayer . . . but her family would be there. All of them. And Ward . . . it was difficult to imagine a world without her. He couldn't imagine it at all, as tears slid quietly down his cheeks, as they drove into the night, with Faye in the hearse behind . . . he could imagine her everywhere, if he just closed his eyes . . . she was still there with him, as she would be with all of them . . . always, for the rest of time. Her films would live on . . . the memories . . . the love and above all the family, each one of them, touched by her, a part of her, just as she had been a part of them.

STARTING FROM THE CHILD

THIRD EDITION

11·2010

STARTING FROM THE CHILD

Teaching and learning in the Foundation Stage

THIRD EDITION

JULIE FISHER

 Open University Press

Open University Press
McGraw-Hill Education
McGraw-Hill House
Shoppenhangers Road
Maidenhead, Berkshire
England SL6 2QL

email: enquiries@openup.co.uk
world wide web: www.openup.co.uk

and Two Penn Plaza, New York, NY 10122289, USA

A catalogue record of this book is available from the British Library

ISBN (pb) ISBN 10-0335223842
         (pb) ISBN 13-9780335223848

Library of Congress Cataloging-in-Publication Data
CIP data has been applied for

Typeset by BookEns Ltd, Royston, Herts.
Printed and bound in the UK by Ashford Colour Press Ltd, Gosport, Hants.

The *McGraw·Hill* Companies

to my friends and colleagues in Oxfordshire

CONTENTS

LIST OF BOXES AND FIGURES

PREFACE TO THE THIRD EDITION

Writing this third edition of *Starting from the Child* has caused me to reflect on the period of unprecedented change that has faced those of us working in early education over the past 10 years. For much of that time we have been in the government's headlights. On occasions this has been cause for celebration, as policies and strategies have acknowledged the critical role of early education in laying the foundations for future learning and living. On other occasions this has brought about immense frustration, as successive initiatives have rained down upon the sector, frequently before previous initiatives have bedded down and frequently before previous initiatives have been adequately or rigorously evaluated. Nevertheless, it is this ever-changing context in which children are learning and in which practitioners are teaching that this new edition of *Starting from the Child* seeks to address.

These changes in context have led me to make a couple of decisions about the scope of this edition. Firstly, because I know this book will now be read by an increasing number of practitioners in the private and voluntary sectors, I have used more inclusive terminology so that the word 'teacher' has been replaced, where appropriate, by the words practitioner, adult or educator. Secondly, while I have referred on many occasions to the Early Years Foundation Stage, I decided early on to keep the focus of this book on the 3–5 age range. This should not in any way suggest that I do not appreciate the critical nature of the first three years or their impact on the years from 3–5 and beyond. But I felt that to address the full 0–5 age range in a book such as this would dilute the detailed way in which I have been able to talk about the learning environment, the role of the adult and the experiences of children in foundation stage education.

Those of you who have read previous editions will see some significant rewrites which, I hope, capture key elements of current research and policy. In particular I have completely restructured Chapters 7, 9 and 10 to respond to feedback from readers about what they would find particularly valuable. Those who are familiar with the book may also notice a change in Chapter 4 and the 'Triangle' of classroom experiences. The 'Triangle' has perhaps been the most influential outcome of this book and many practitioners now use it as an effective way of planning for learning in their foundation stage settings. Following the extensive amount of in-service work I have done around the 'Triangle', I have amended the use of the term 'adult-intensive' learning to 'adult-focused'. This is mainly because adult-intensive and adult-initiated sound too similar and, when abbreviated, have the same initials! So, more recently, I have been using adult-focused (a–f) instead of adult-intensive (a–i).

This book remains a tribute to the early years educators with whom I work day in and day out. Those who inspire me and challenge my thinking and extend my understanding. I am so grateful to all those who have shared their thoughts and ideas and allowed me to use their material in this book. Many of those practitioners work in Oxfordshire, and it is in recognition of their vision, their expertise, their energy and their enthusiasm and with grateful thanks for all that I learnt in my 11 years there as early years adviser that I dedicate this new edition to them.

The first edition of *Starting from the Child?* had a question mark after the title that I removed when writing the second edition. Now, as I finish this third edition, my belief is stronger than ever that a child-centred pedagogy is the only effective way to capture and harness the incredible powers of young children as thinkers and learners. There is every evidence that the best practitioners continue to challenge all those external agendas that threaten to inhibit the exceptional capabilities of young children. They place the child at the heart of every learning experience and defend every child's right to an educational experience that is liberating and enriching. There is not one expert practitioner that I have met who, in their thinking, planning and evaluation, does not start from the child.

ACKNOWLEDGEMENTS

So much of this book has been influenced by the principles and practice of colleagues with whom I have had the privilege to work. I still want to record my thanks to those whose support and encouragement first enabled me to write. To Paula, without whose inspirational practice this book would never have been written. To Janet Moyles, who not only encouraged me to write but opened the doors for me to do so. To Keith Postlethwaite, at the University of Reading, who read my early work, took it seriously and gave me the confidence to continue. To both Angela Redfern and Carol Boulter who accepted the time-consuming role of 'critical friend' and helped so much to challenge and refine my early thinking and writing. To Tina Bruce for her thought-provoking and supportive comments. To my colleagues in the Early Years Curriculum Group who have continued to be a source of inspiration and professional friendship, ideas and critical evaluation over many years. More recently, I have been privileged to be part of the Oxfordshire Early Years Team and I am so grateful to all my colleagues – not just in the team, but across the county in their different roles – for the generous way in which they have shared their experiences, their ideas and their enthusiasms. Finally, my loving thanks go once again to David, who continues to understand why I need to write and speak and lecture and lobby, and who supports me as I do so, and to Sophie, for giving me new perspectives on everything I do.

COMPETENT YOUNG LEARNERS

What children know and can do

Introduction

Before starting statutory schooling at the age of 5, young children have developed a range of skills, knowledge and understanding at a speed that will never again be repeated in their lives. The years from 0 to 7 are a period in human development when the capacity to learn is, in John Brierley's words (1994), 'at flood-readiness'. All the evidence shows that, in their early years, young children demonstrate a variety of characteristics that make them natural and successful learners. However, when those same children begin their more formal education it can be a different story. Children who have been motivated and determined become disillusioned and disaffected (Barrett 1989; Smith 1995); children who made sense of things and had begun to form their own personal construct of the world become confused and disorientated (Donaldson 1978; 1992); children who posed a thousand and one questions become quiet and uncommunicative (Tizard and Hughes 1984; Cousins 1999). It seems that education can inhibit some of the most prominent characteristics of competent young learners.

So how can there be such a gap between some children's learning before they begin at school or their early years setting and the learning that follows? Is it simply a question of ratios – too many children and not enough adults? Are those adults not sufficiently knowledgeable about how young children learn and how to support that learning? Is there too much pressure from external agendas to follow children's interests and preoccupations? It would seem that at the root of the dichotomy between learning and educating lies a failure on the part of many educators to learn from those who have been most successful in the teaching and learning process in the child's pre-school years at home. If more time were spent observing the strategies of children as

learners, prior to the constraints of the educational setting, and more
notice taken of the strategies of the significant adults with whom
children learn in their homes and communities, then there might be
more chance of schools and other early years settings mirroring the
successes of children's earliest learning environments.

The influence of experience on heredity

All early childhood educators need to study the learning of children
from birth. The development of every child is the result of a unique
interaction of experience with heredity. While genetic programming
determines many of the characteristics displayed by any human being,
a variety of environmental influences combine to affect the development of the brain and consequently the individual (Shaffer 1993). The
balance between these two key factors varies within each child, but the
impact of 'nurture' on 'nature' will determine the characteristics which
differentiate one child from another and make their development
unique. Hereditary influence means that given the same set of
experiences, one child's abilities will differ from another's, irrespective
of the experiences they have. Equally, a child raised in a particular set
of environmental circumstances can have their genetic programming
nullified and their hereditary advantages erased (Meadows 1993).

Until fairly recently, the emphasis in education has been to make up
for the deficits of a poor set of hereditary circumstances (Anning 1991).
In the 1960s and 1970s there was 'a naive belief that compensatory
education would serve to combat the known effects of social disadvan-
tage on children's educational achievements' (Anning 1991: 5). While
many research studies have now discredited such assumptions, there is
other evidence that highlights the negative effects on development of a
poor set of environmental factors (e.g. Smith 1995). Mia Kellmer Pringle,
the first director of the National Children's Bureau, identified four
human basic needs that have to be met from 'the very beginning of life
and continue to require fulfilment – to a greater or lesser extent –
throughout adulthood' (1992: 34). In Chapter 2 she identifies:

- the need for love and security;
- the need for new experiences;
- the need for praise and recognition;
- the need for responsibility.

Jennie Lindon in her book on child development (1993: 11–12) also
identifies some basic needs of young children:

- the need to be cared for physically;
- the need to be kept safe;

- the need for emotional well-being.

All these needs have to be met by the caring adult if children are to thrive and make the most of their developmental opportunities. Research cited by the Carnegie Corporation of New York (1994) provides substantial evidence that *lack* of certain experiences, and inappropriate or impoverished environments in the early stages of learning, may have long-lasting detrimental effects on the development of children. The report, drawing on research that illuminates the workings of the nervous system, highlights the critical importance of the first three years of life. The results of the research led to five key findings that are of profound significance to all those who are concerned with the development and education of young children:

- brain development that takes place before age 1 is more rapid and extensive than previously realized;
- brain development is much more vulnerable to environmental influence than was ever suspected;
- the influence of early environment on brain development is long lasting;
- the environment affects not only the number of brain cells and number of connections among them, but also the way these connections are 'wired';
- there is new scientific evidence for the negative impact of early stress on brain function.

(Carnegie Corporation 1994: 7–9)

These findings give a clear rationale for creating learning environments that offer experiences sensitive to the needs of young children and appropriate to their development, because the results of these experiences – good or bad – stay with children forever. The fact that the effects of early experiences appear to be cumulative only adds to the need to safeguard the environmental influences determining the development of all young children:

> an adverse environment can compromise a young child's brain function and overall development, placing him or her at greater risk of developing a variety of cognitive, behavioral, and physical difficulties. In some cases these effects may be irreversible.

(Carnegie Corporation 1994: xiii)

New understandings about brain development

More has been learnt about the brain during the 1990s than in all previous scientific history (Greenfield 1997; Pinker 1997; Rose and

Nicholl 1997; Jenson 1998; Wolfe and Brandt 1998). By nine months' gestation, human beings have most of the neurons (nerve endings) in their brains that they are ever likely to have (Greenfield 1997). At birth, a child's brain contains around 100 billion neurons, each with the capacity to contribute to that individual's knowledge and understanding of skills and concepts that will determine their unique growth and development (Pinker 1977; Bruer 1999). Of particular importance to those in early education is the evidence that it is not the *number* of brain cells that is important, but how they become connected to each other that makes them effective (Greenfield 1997; Diamond and Hopson 1998). It is the use to which the neurons are put that determines the growth of a brain's functions (Calvin 1996). Growing neurons can adapt sensitively to changing circumstances in order to make the best of a situation (Greenfield 1997) but the key to growth is whether the neurons are sufficiently stimulated to make contact with other neurons and make a firm connection (Cohen 1997; Diamond and Hopson 1998). Brain activity and growth go hand in hand. It is not only a question of 'use it or lose it' says Susan Greenfield (1997: 115), but 'use it as much as you can'.

In the first three years of life, the neural connections are established at a phenomenal rate. By the age of 5 or so, they begin to tail off and are virtually complete by age 10 (Gammage 1999). However, this does not mean that after age 3 no worthwhile learning can take place, or that if connections are not made by age 3 then an individual has lost the opportunity for development and growth. Some writers, in their eagerness to exhort the benefits of early learning, have suggested that if a child has not been fully stimulated by age 3 then their opportunities for learning and development become closed off. Mercifully for most of us, this is not the case! The brain may not 'grow' more neurons, but it does go on making connections and these can be stimulated at any age (Bruer 1999). However, it does seem that there are critical periods in development where experience has significant effects on brain functioning. In other words, the best time to master a skill associated with a system is when a new system is coming on line in the brain (Sylwester 1995; Pinker 1997; Bruer 1999). Language is a good example. It is easy for a 2- or 3-year-old to learn any language, but if that person waits until age 18 or 50, learning a new language will be more difficult because the systems governing this process may have been used for something else. However, not all critical periods happen in the first three years, nor do all cognitive systems show such effects (Bruer 1999). As educators, it is important that we do not make claims for early learning that are overly expansive. Nonetheless, a realization of the critical importance of brain connections to human growth and development should challenge educators to ensure that the learning environments that are created, and the support that adults give to young children as they learn, maximize their drive to make as many connections as they can with what they already know and understand.

Brain development in children under two

In their influential text *How Babies Think* (1999) Gopnik *et al.*, suggest that studying babies makes us think about the brain in a new way. They explain that such studies show how flexible, sensitive and plastic the brain is and how deeply influenced it can be by the outside world. New technology has given researchers the opportunity to reveal that even newborn babies have a pre-programmed repertoire of skills and competences to ensure communication with and inclusion into the community into which they are born. They can mimic their mothers by pulling faces and poking out their tongues, they can discriminate human faces and voices from other sights and sounds and they can discriminate the sounds not only of their own language but of every language, including languages they have never heard. Within the first nine months, before those babies can walk or talk or even crawl, they can tell the difference between expressions of happiness, sadness and anger. This acute sensitivity, documented by a growing number of researchers (notably Trevarthan 1971 onwards), enables us to understand why the experiences of babies in their earliest days and months impact so profoundly on their sense of well-being, self-confidence and resilience as they develop.

Two other recent books have also alerted us to the importance of the very first year of life in laying down the foundations of children's emotional and social well-being and, in particular, the vital contribution of the interactions that take place between babies and the adults who care for them. In *From Birth to One* (2003), Maria Robinson demonstrates how important it is for an adult to understand the influence of their interactions, reactions and behaviour towards their child and, in turn, to understand the child's impact on themselves as an adult. All children, she says, need to feel secure, and that emotional security is learnt from the ongoing relationship with their adult carer(s), based on the patterns of behaviour in the first year. Babies make secure attachments to their primary carer when they have their basic needs, such as being wet or feeling hungry, responded to promptly and appropriately (Bowlby 1971, 1975, 1981). Where a normal attachment develops, the emotions that babies show at times of stress or distress are soothed and managed by the caregiver and, over time, babies are helped to regulate their own reactions through the meaning given to their behaviour and the response of that caregiver. Where this cycle of attunement is disturbed, through separation from the primary caregiver or through neglect, then babies end up with overwhelming feelings of frustration, loneliness and panic.

In her book *Why Love Matters* (2004) Sue Gerhardt explains that these earliest emotions, in turn, shape the baby's nervous system and that the neural pathways formed by these early experiences can affect the way we respond to stress and how we cope with relationships throughout our lives. Gerhard, too, stresses the crucial impact of early interactions between babies and their primary attachment figure, emphasizing that emotions become organized through engagement with others and not in isolation. She provides evidence to suggest that 'expectations of other people and how they will behave are inscribed in the brain outside conscious awareness, in the period of infancy, and that they underpin our behaviour in relationships through life' (p. 24). It is clearly imperative that practitioners who have responsibility for the care of children under the age of two are aware of the immense responsibility that they hold for providing the constant, reliable, loving care that all babies demand and the consequences for babies if they do not. There needs to be greater understanding that this care is not just about responding to a baby's physical needs – their wet nappy or hungry tummy – but about an openness to intimacy on the part of the carer, and a willingness to form emotional loving relationships with a child and their family if that child is to thrive and develop without emotional deprivation or undue stress.

What do young children learn?

Given an appropriate environment in which they thrive, what is it that young children are learning? Shaffer claims that 'we change in response to the environments in which we live' (1993: 5). The educators in Reggio Emilia, a town in northern Italy renowned for the quality of its pre-school provision, see the environment as a 'third teacher', creating enriching situations and 'helping the children to be the direct agents and constructors of their own learning processes' (Spaggiari 1997). But change and development lies particularly in our response to the actions and reactions of the people around us. We behave in new ways because of our observations of and interactions with important people in our lives and are affected by the events we experience together. Young children come to make sense of their world by observing, imitating, investigating and exploring. They learn attitudes, skills, strategies and concepts that enable them to understand and be understood.

Positive *attitudes* to learning arise from children's motivation to learn, to succeed in the face of many odds, and to master the exciting and intriguing world around them. The posing of personal problems teaches children the value of concentration and perseverance in the successful acquisition and honing of skills and understandings. Success fuels their motivation and determination to succeed and enhances their confidence and self-esteem as learners. The infinite range of new and exciting things to discover and explore stimulates young children's curiosity and engages their eagerness to be both successful and competent.

Important *skills* are learnt as a result of establishing patterns of behaviour that ultimately become automatic. Young children repeat movements or actions time after time in order to become expert and succeed at the goals that they have set themselves. Skills usually develop in the course of activities that the child sees as being worth while and which give them the motivation to continue, sometimes through failure after failure, to succeed. Children are motivated by the response of others, particularly their parent or carer, and this response sustains them through the frustrations of learning to stand unaided, throw a ball towards someone else or make their desire for food clearly understood.

In the course of learning skills, children develop their own peculiar set of *strategies* for trying out, rehearsing or repeating what they have done. Some children prefer to look and think before they act. Some try and try again until something comes right. Some prefer to imitate, some to instigate. Some ask questions and others wait for answers. Whatever strategies are developed, they are tailor-made by each child. They are chosen because they serve the child's individual purpose and because they work. These strategies become part of the characteristics of the child as a learner and are the basis of all strategies that will be adopted if the child is left to learn alone.

The understandings or *concepts* that children learn are generally arrived at through a process of abstraction of the principles that underpin a number of different experiences. Children come to understand about size, colour, the past or the seasons through a variety of first-hand experiences, leading them to see and understand the conceptual links between one experience and another. In this way children become able to generalize abstract principles from concrete experiences. It is almost impossible to rush this transition from concrete to abstract because if children are forced to establish connections then it is likely that they will make inappropriate ones (Brierley 1994; Robinson and Beck 2000).

We know that children *do* make the wrong 'connections' and that, once made, these misunderstandings – or alternative understandings –

can take a great deal of unlearning. The work of Wynne Harlen, Roger Osborne and others reveals that children have views about a variety of topics and that they are very often different from the views of 'experts'. However, to children they remain 'sensible, useful views' (Harlen 1985: 76) and can remain uninfluenced or be influenced in unanticipated ways by teaching. The views that children hold are a result of their personal endeavours to construct their own meaning for, and understanding of, the experiences that they have had (Postlethwaite 1993). They work for the child who has constructed them and since they serve the child's purpose reasonably well, they may not readily be displaced by the explanation of someone else especially, as Postlethwaite says, as these explanations are often more complex than their own.

Readiness for learning

Inherent in beliefs about the competences of young children is an attitude towards the concept of 'readiness' for learning. If children are viewed as competent young learners, then it follows that they have predispositions to learn from their earliest days and, as such, are ready for learning from birth (and, many would say, before). The consequence of this view is that children are never *not* ready to learn and the notion of children 'emerging' into literacy (Hall 1987), numeracy (Hughes 1986) and so on, assumes engagement in concepts that at one time would have been deemed inappropriate for young minds. The work of Donaldson (1978), Bruner (1986), Hughes (1986) and others, however, has encouraged the view that children are ready for learning if learning is adapted to the intellectual proclivities of children (Watson 1998).

Once again we are drawn to the behaviours of parents and carers who appear to make these adaptations instinctively. Parents, it seems, adapt naturally to their child's intellectual tendencies, attributing consciousness and intentionality to their child's actions from the very beginning of their lives (Trevarthen 1980, 1992; Stern 1985). When parents talk to their child they do so as if expecting a response, often long before the child seems capable of giving one. In this way, suggests Watson, children's early learning is aided in spontaneous and incidental ways by older and more experienced members of their community, who give structure to the child's earliest, hesitant inclinations to explore the world (1998).

A child is ready to learn when their cognitive disposition and what is to be taught are matched. Parents may make this match instinctively knowing, as they do, so much about the body of beliefs, expectations and assumptions that their child brings to a learning situation. Early childhood educators do not have the benefit of sharing each child's complete learning history and one of the most complex challenges of teaching is to become as knowledgeable as possible about the cognitive dispositions of a large number of children in any one group.

Much of the influence of Jean Piaget stemmed from his view that children progress through various stages of development that determine their current level of skills and competence. Readiness for learning, he believed, depended on the child's developmental stage, and progress from one stage to the next could not be rushed. This view of development influenced many teachers to adopt a relatively passive role in children's progress (Darling 1994). Activities were planned that reflected the notion of readiness with titles such as 'pre-reading', 'pre-number' and so on. The role of the educator was to bring children to a state of readiness to engage fully in significant skills or concepts and children were taken through a whole range of early stages of learning in preparation for their arrival at the next stage of development. Piaget's notion of readiness was ultimately challenged by a number of researchers, notably Margaret Donaldson (1978), who believed that children should be actively encouraged to move towards the 'disembedded' thinking that characterizes learning in primary schools. The work of Lev Vygotsky (1978) has also been highly influential in this debate about readiness. Vygotsky believed that instead of matching teaching to existing development, teaching had to proceed in advance of development in order to challenge and extend children's maturing functions. He believed that learning comes in advance of development when progress is stimulated and guided by the expertise of others. This notion of readiness places the emphasis not so much on *when* to teach, but rather *how* and *what* to teach.

The characteristics of successful early learning

Young children may be inexperienced learners, but their competence should no longer be underestimated. Loris Malaguzzi, who inspired the development of the pre-schools in Reggio Emilia, said 'our image of the child is rich in potential, strong, powerful, competent and most of all, connected to adults and to other children' (1993). Modern technology has made it possible to investigate the very beginnings of human thinking, and researchers have documented critical development in the pre- and postnatal months of life. From the beginning, humans demonstrate intention-directed behaviour (Trevarthean 1992). They are both intellectually and interpersonally engaged, or predisposed to be so, much earlier than previous theories allowed (Watson 1998). The young child is clearly emerging cognitively, linguistically, physically, socially and emotionally and – most significantly – this critical development usually occurs when the child is receiving no formal education. Children have the capacity to draw conclusions about the world when the knowledge that they need has not been formally taught to them.

Given an environment in which they are cared for and in which they can thrive, young children display a range of competences that make their early learning dramatically successful.

- Young children display positive *attitudes* and *dispositions* to learn. The determination for mastery over their environment drives them to persist and persevere – often in the face of difficulty and initial failure – to succeed in their objectives.
- Young children develop personal *skills* and *strategies* that work for them in their quest to understand the world. These strategies are chosen instinctively and fulfil children's purposes for the particular task in hand.
- Young children have developed *understandings* and sometimes *misunderstandings*. Each piece of knowledge acquired, each small piece of sense that is made, fits into each child's personal cognitive jigsaw.

The construction of this personal cognitive jigsaw has many parallels with the construction of the traditional wooden puzzle. At first, the pieces of cognitive jigsaw are picked seemingly at random. Sometimes the piece fits straight away, sometimes it is turned round and round – with astonishing patience – before the fit is finally made. Sometimes the piece is turned round and round and a fit is made and only subsequent pieces show that piece to be in the wrong place. Sometimes the piece is turned round and round, does not quite fit but is jammed in anyway because it is more satisfying to have reached a solution than to have to start again.

It is the skill of the educator to be aware of the pieces of the jigsaw that the child already has in place and whether or not they have been fitted together correctly. If they have not, then supporting the child to review the construction of their cognitive jigsaw is as delicate and difficult an operation as persuading the child to select an alternative piece of wooden puzzle. The 'teacher' – whether an adult or another child – needs to be informative without being imposing. Imposition simply leads to the learner becoming confused and disaffected. Confusion arises because the links between the pieces have been made by the teacher and not by the learner. Disaffection occurs because the initiative has been taken away from the learner and the construction no longer makes personal sense.

The expertise of the child's first educators

We have seen that young children's early learning is not only the result of their own predispositions to learning, but also the result of interactions with significant others in their family and their community at large. It is important to appreciate the strategies that parents use which make them such successful educators, very often without realizing it.

- Crucially, of course, most parents *love* and *care* about their children and have a genuine interest in their actions, ideas and development. Parents may be very busy, be feeling under the weather, be preoccupied with other things – but the bond between them and their children surfaces under all manner of stresses and strains to reassure the child of the strength of the relationship between them (Sylva and Lunt 1982).
- Parents *operate in the real world*. They talk to their children in kitchens and bathrooms, they take them to shops and playgrounds and cinemas, they eat with them in front of the television or in McDonald's. Parents and their children are surrounded by a cacophony of visual, aural and tactile stimuli – sights and sounds that constantly fascinate children and cause them to ask what, how and why?
- Usually, parents give children *time* to learn; time to pose meaningful questions and to come up with their own theories and hypotheses; time to try things out, to make mistakes and to try again; time to leave things be, to return to them at will and to revisit things when the time is right; time to be distracted and to take a detour from their original path or goal and to learn by accident rather than design.
- Very often, parents are in a *one-to-one situation* – or at least one and a very small group situation – when these questions are asked. Although every parent knows that feeling of being asked one question too many, research into the interactions between children and their parents and children and their teachers (Tizard and Hughes 1984; Wells 1986) reveals that however brief, not to say curt, parental responses might be, parents still interact far more frequently with their children than the early childhood educator with their 10, 20 or 30 children. In the home, children are able to talk about a range of topics, to initiate and sustain conversations and to ask questions endlessly, and all of these factors make the home 'a powerful learning environment' (Tizard and Hughes 1984).
- In these situations, parents usually *respond to*, rather than *initiate* learning. The child wants to know, wants to know what to do, wants to know what to do next – and the parent is there to supply the

appropriate piece of the jigsaw, there to support and to facilitate the developing learner.

Studying children and their parents can offer those of us in educational settings many lessons about effective early learning. It is so important that practitioners draw on the expertise of parents and enable them to inform and to go on informing the school or setting about their child. It can be too easy to pay lip service to the notion of a partnership with parents, but early childhood educators should not forget that it is *they* who join the already established learning partnership that exists between the parent and their child.

How do young children learn?

While it is possible to identify the learning characteristics of young children, it is altogether more difficult to try and understand exactly how they learn. There is no conclusive evidence on this subject, although there have been a number of influential theories over the course of the last two centuries. The theories have grown and developed one from the other and many have, at some point or another, had an impact on the way in which children have been educated (see Entwhistle 1987; Wood 1988; Anning 1991).

Young children learn by being active

Any personal study of young children reveals almost non-stop activity in the quest for skills, strategies and understandings. The work of Jean Piaget and other contemporary theorists of child development emphasize that 'being active' does not necessarily mean 'moving around', however. Being active means that the young child *engages* with experiences, actively (as opposed to passively) bringing their existing knowledge and understanding to bear on what is currently under investigation. Being active is what causes children both physically and cognitively to construct their own view of the world, to personalize the experience and to apply it in ways that make sense to them as individuals (Piaget 1929; Bruce 2004).

Young children learn by organizing their own learning experiences

The work of Chris Athey at the Froebel Institute has provided a new framework for studying the patterns of children's behaviour as they learn. These early patterns of behaviour (or schemas, as they are defined) are seen in babies, and become more complex and more numerous as the child develops. By becoming familiar with these behaviours, the observer realizes that actions are not performed in isolation but are one of a set of experiences coordinated by the child (Nutbrown 2006). Athey, in her book *Extending Thought in Young Children* (2007), illustrates how such patterns can be represented in children's play, their thinking and their language. Once in tune with these categories of behaviour, adults have a valuable framework for observing children's actions. Schemas are a way of understanding the learning behaviours of children and, as such, give adults and educators an appreciation of what is currently interesting and absorbing the child. 'It is through schemas, and the fitting of content to different schematic threads, that children's own construction of reality and subsequent continuity can be identified' (Nutbrown 2006).

Young children learn by using language

The language development of young children is a staggering phenomenon. The increase in young children's vocabulary and their growing capacity to use language for a range of purposes is powerful evidence of an innate drive to make meaning and to communicate. The research of Gordon Wells and his team on the Bristol Language Study concluded that in the early stages children's linguistic systems are more or less in place and a basic vocabulary of several thousand words is acquired. From that point on, however, what is learnt and the order in which it is learnt becomes 'progressively more dependent on experience – on having opportunities to hear the relevant functions, meanings, and structure used appropriately and to use them oneself' (Wells 1986: 32).

Wells sees language as a code to be cracked, but that before the child attempts this, he or she has already become familiar with the code in use. Language development relies on children hearing and using language in meaningful interactions. In order to work out for themselves how language is organized, children need the collaborative help of 'conversational partners' who 'provide clear and relevant feedback', enabling children to evaluate the appropriateness of their current hypotheses. This does not mean that it is necessarily best for adults to overtly teach children the use of language. As in other areas of their development, children construct their own internal models of language and rather than adults teaching children, says Wells (1986: 48), 'it is children who teach adults how to talk in such a way as to make it easy for them to learn'.

Language provides not only a means of acting on the world, but also for reflecting on that action in an attempt to understand it (Harlen 1985). Piaget argued that language is a *medium*, a method of representation within which thought takes place. Vygotsky, on the other hand, believed that speech transforms the way in which children learn, think and understand and is, therefore, a *tool* of thought (Wood 1998). The theories of Jerome Bruner draw and build on the work of both Piaget and Vygotsky. His assertion is that the internalization of language is an instrument of thought and that the very young child uses language 'almost as an extension of pointing'. All of these theories depend on the understanding that thought, action and language are inextricably bound together in children's development. The successful development of all three is dependent on experiences being embedded in what is meaningful for the child.

Young children learn by interacting with others

Children may well be active learners in a highly individualistic sense, but they construct their personal meanings within the framework of a social and cultural context (Vygotsky 1978; Wood 1998). The young child is a social being, playing, talking and living alongside others, watching what they do and imitating them, questioning what is seen and responding to questioning, drawing on the knowledge and expertise of others to interpret and make meaning of experiences (Richards and Light 1986; Wells 1986; Dunn 1988). Everything that young children learn is influenced by the culture in which they grow up and the community in which they live. The writing of Vygotsky emphasized the significance of social contexts for learning, whereby adults – or other more expert members of the community – help children to acquire skills and understandings that they might not accomplish, or accomplish less speedily, alone. Vygotsky refers to the gap between what children are able to do alone and what they can achieve with help, as the 'zone of proximal development'; in other words:

> the distance between the actual developmental level as determined by independent problem solving and the level of potential development as determined through problem solving under adult guidance or in collaboration with more capable peers.
>
> (Vygotsky 1978: 86)

The work of Jerome Bruner (1968, 1985, 1990) and Wood *et al.* (1976) extends this notion, adopting the metaphor 'scaffolding' to describe the guidance and interactional support given by the adult or expert until the child is able to take over tasks for themselves. In this model of learning, children are not passively absorbing the strategies of the adult, but take an active, inventive role (Smith 1993), reconstructing the tasks through their own understanding while the adult or educator provides what Bruner (1985) describes as a 'vicarious form of consciousness'.

Implications for classroom practice

What then are the implications for educational practice of the issues that this chapter has raised? What strategies do early childhood educators need to consider if they are to build on what is known about how young children learn?

Young children learn by being active

If young children learn naturally by being active and engaging in a range of exploratory experiences then the primary responsibility of the school or early years setting is to plan opportunities that facilitate and support these instinctive strategies. Children need opportunities to engage with a range of materials and stimuli. They need time and space to explore, investigate and question. They need a range of play experiences and appropriate resources of good quality. They need, in other words, a learning environment that offers concrete experiences that are relevant, meaningful and worthy of active involvement. If children are to continue their struggle to make sense of the world, then the world must be worth the struggle. Clearly, before children start school or playgroup or nursery or children's centre, the incentive and motivation to learn have been sufficient. It is up to practitioners to make children's new learning environments equally worth while.

Young children learn by organizing their own learning experiences

Athey (1990) reminds us that in order to tap into the personal constructs of the child, early childhood educators need to focus on the underlying processes of their thinking and cognition. When practitioners are concerned with the sense that children are making of their own learning then this provides a rich source for planning and development. Observation and appreciation of children's schemas can offer practitioners a starting point for planning experiences that capture children's current interests and preoccupations. If a child is focusing on a trajectory schema – a fascination with things moving or flying through the air (see Bartholomew and Bruce 1993 for further definitions of schema) – then 'he or she needs to be provided with a range of interesting and stimulating experiences which extend thinking along that particular path' (Nutbrown 2006). When children are absorbed by something in this way, it is far more productive for practitioners to go with and plan for that interest. Starting from the child becomes increasingly difficult when there is an external curriculum to be taught (Chapter 3 addresses this issue in depth); however, early childhood educators who believe in working with rather than against the interests of children will make time to observe and record the ways in which they organize their own learning experiences. Nutbrown says that those who become interested in children's schema development come to know that children will pursue their schemas, whether adults like it or not!

Young children learn by using language

The work of Margaret Donaldson demonstrates the importance of young children's experiences being embedded in contexts that are meaningful to them (1978). Her work, and that of researchers studying the relationship between language development in the home and at school, emphasizes the importance of the contexts in which the adult and the child have shared experiences in common from which to draw shared meanings (Anning 1991). Edwards and Mercer (1987) claim that the establishment of mutual understanding and shared meanings is something with which educators also must be concerned. They suggest that of the points at which education commonly fails is when 'incorrect assumptions are made about shared knowledge, meaning and interpretations' (1987: 60). Practitioners and children need to share a 'common knowledge' about the discourse that forms the basis for communication in the setting in order for the learning that comes from interaction to be most effective.

Children use language to learn and therefore learning environments must give them opportunities to use language in a variety of ways. It is language that affords young children the means of making sense of their experiences and of internalizing their actions. In order to capitalize on the power of language to influence both thought and action, experiences must encourage talk as a key process through which young children learn. It is heartening to see in recent government documentation, fresh affirmation of the critical nature of speaking and listening as precursors for competence in reading and writing as well as for understanding across all curriculum areas and the development of good social relationships (DfES 2005). Talking something through, either alone or with others, is an important way of grasping new ideas, understanding concepts or clarifying feelings and perceptions. Young children need opportunities for discussion, for explanation, for description, for narration and for speculation. In learning environments where talk is recognized as a powerful and natural medium for learning, young children are able to make meaning of what is new in terms of what is familiar. Through their talk, they create a context that is personal to them and one that relates to their own experiences.

Young children learn by interacting with others

If learning is socially constructed then early childhood educators clearly have a critical role, a role at one time devalued by misunderstandings about the nature of 'child-centredness' and 'discovery learning' (Blenkin and Kelly 1987). It is the skilled intervention of the practitioner that will move children from their present to their future potential. Interactions with children must facilitate this progress through Vygotsky's 'zone of proximal development' and practitioners must arrange things, says Athey (1990), so that knowledge is actively constructed and not simply copied. Early childhood educators need to have regular conversations with children. These conversations need to be designed to find out what children already know and understand (see Chapter 2) or to support, through questioning or answering questions, the child's current thinking. Such interactions in Reggio Emilia are described as 'a ball which is passed along. At times the children throw it, at times we (the adults) do' (Malaguzzi 1992). It is so important that children and adults alike see themselves as co-constructors of knowledge where both parties contribute to an exchange of ideas and views and questions in order to come to new insights and fresh understandings.

Recent material from the Coram Family Research Unit on 'Listening to Children' (Lancaster 2003) promotes adult–child relationships that uphold children's rights to be listened to as competent individuals who should have their views, concerns and aspirations taken into account and who should participate in decisions that are important to them. This influential work promotes the view that young children are competent to express their views and supports adults to increase their skills of listening so that children's voices are heard.

Other children are also part of this social construct, and practitioners have to look at 'the context in which learning takes place in schools (sic) as well as at the nature of specific learning tasks' (Pollard and Tann 1993). The topic of children working together and learning together is discussed fully in Chapter 6, but there is growing evidence of the importance of peer tutoring in classroom contexts – whether it is planned or not (e.g. Forman and Cazden 1985; Galton & Williamson 1992; Rogoff & Toma 1997; Rogoff *et al.* 2003). Effective teaching acknowledges the role of *all* those who have knowledge and understandings to contribute to the development of individual learners. Descriptions of learning in the pre-schools in Reggio Emilia constantly emphasize the significance of groups of children learning together, sometimes including adults in those groups and sometimes not. In *Making Learning Visible* (2001), there are powerful examples of how 'learning groups' create a dynamic synergy that 'extends beyond the learning of individuals to create a collective body of knowledge' (p. 286).

Conclusion

When children start attending an educational setting they are already competent learners. Competence has evolved from the fusion of the child's natural predisposition to learn and the support he or she has received while learning from birth. This chapter suggests that those responsible for the more formal stages of children's education need to look to the characteristics of children's successful early learning environments in order to develop models of teaching that will lead to the continuation of effective learning throughout the child's educational journey. In the following chapter we examine how early childhood educators establish the range of competences that children bring from home and the wider world and how those educators come to find out what children already know about and can do.

CONVERSATIONS AND OBSERVATIONS

Learning about individual children

Introduction

If we acknowledge that children bring to their school or setting a wealth of skills, knowledge and understandings, then a key task of the early childhood educator is to identify precisely what it is that children already know and can do in order to build on their existing competences. This immediately defines the experiences of both adults and children. If children already know and can do a range of things, then it puts the educator in the role of learner alongside their children. The adult must find out the extent of children's competences to ensure that the planned curriculum is appropriate to these particular children. This leads to planning that is tailor-made for each child because the foundations of learning are unique (Fisher 2000). Each child has their own personal history of experiences, which will determine not only what they need to learn next, but how they will do so most effectively.

Establishing the starting points for children's educational experiences is not a task that takes place only when a child begins in their new school or setting. Practitioners need to establish the starting points for children's learning throughout their education as part of the ongoing cycle of teaching and learning. All too often in schools, in particular, the planned curriculum establishes its starting points from the learning objectives on written documentation, and considers 'previous experience' to be what has been 'covered' in previous teaching time. However, children continue to learn in and from a range of contexts that are nothing to do with educational settings, and it is always necessary to discover what knowledge and understanding children bring with them from their previous life experiences in order to plan a curriculum that matches their current learning needs.

The 'teacher' as learner

Placing themselves in the role of learner, effective early childhood educators make assessments of children's knowledge, skills and understandings before finalizing the planning of an appropriate curriculum. Often, assessment is seen as the end of the teaching process, undertaken to discover whether children have learnt what was planned and taught. However, the more crucial place for assessment is at the start of the cycle of teaching and learning, when practitioners find out what children already know and can do so that the next experiences planned are relevant and meaningful. This process should happen not just when children start at their new school or setting but at the beginning of each fresh learning cycle. Assessment is a tool that comes before and after learning. Before it establishes what is currently known and after, it establishes what has been learnt that is new. This chapter is concerned with the two key ways in which practitioners establish, at the beginning of the teaching and learning cycle, what children already know and can do, as part of a continuous process of reviewing and refining children's learning opportunities. The first strategy is to have *conversations* with those who know about the child as a learner. The second strategy is to make *observations* of the child in action as a learner.

Having conversations

Early childhood practitioners need to have informative conversations with a range of people who have knowledge of the child as a learner. These conversations need to inform the practitioner about:

- what interests the child;
- what motivates the child to learn;
- how the child perceives him or herself as a learner;
- what the child already knows about and can do;
- what the child would like to know about or do.

Having a range of conversations gives practitioners a range of perspectives on each child and these perspectives help to form a rounded and balanced picture. Each perspective is valid and needs to be valued, and each contributes something fresh to the practitioner's understanding of the child and their needs. Putting together this profile is rather like undertaking a detective investigation as the practitioner gathers together the pieces of the evidence that they need in order to make hypotheses and judgements upon which to proceed in their work.

Conversations with children

Successful conversations with children are based on relationships where adults listen respectfully to what children have to say (Cousins 1999; Chilvers 2006). Conversations with children – where children do most of the talking – provide early childhood educators with evidence of children's responses to learning and to experiences. They offer the children's version of what they have just experienced – not the *intended* learning outcomes, but the *actual* learning outcomes. They reveal how children have approached an activity or experience, what they found interesting, what strategies they used for making sense of the world and where any misunderstandings might be. Such conversations give practitioners hard evidence of children's development. When children have to put into words what they have experienced and learnt, then their thoughts and language give clear evidence on which to build the next stages of learning. At this age, oral evidence provides more detailed and reliable information than recorded evidence. The capacity of young children to think and understand far outstrips their capacity to represent that knowledge and understanding in recorded form and written evidence can present a very impoverished version of their expertise. Young children can be limited by their capacity to record, to write or draw what they have done or understood. They can be limited by their understanding of the task or the worksheet. They can be limited by the page or sheet that simply requires that boxes are filled in and leaves no space for their original thoughts or interpretations. Since the Foundation Stage in schools and settings has been subjected to inspection by the Office for Standards in Education (Ofsted), there has been great concern among early years practitioners that evidence of children's achievements must be in written form. It is often believed that a child's picture, model or talk does not carry the same weight as a piece of writing, and worksheets are increasingly in evidence. This is very misguided. A child is far more complex a learner than can ever be evidenced by a worksheet. If practitioners want to have evidence of what a child knows and understands then they must collect the richest and most powerful evidence available – the child's own actions and the child's own words. The very act of articulating ideas and understandings reveals a wealth of information about the child's learning: what they have understood, what they have misunderstood, what skills they have used and what they have enjoyed. Conversations with children offer the practitioner a marvellous assessment opportunity as they reveal needs *and* interests, and can be a critical moment in the cycle of teaching and learning.

It is crucial, however, that conversations are meaningful to the child and that the practitioner genuinely wants to find out about what he or she is asking about. Questions should demand answers that the practitioner does not already know, otherwise the questioning technique is simply being used as a checking device, to discover whether children are paying attention or not. Young children are all too aware of whether adults' questions are genuine. This is scathingly exemplified by 5-year-old Sonnyboy who responded to his teacher's meaningless questioning with a question of his own: 'Why do you keep asking the kids questions when you knows all the answers? Like ... like ... what colour is it then? You can see for yourself it's red ... so why do you keep asking them?' (Cousins 1990: 30).

Skilful, open-ended questioning leads children to share their own thoughts, ideas and perceptions with the practitioner and teaches the adult something more about the child. Effective questioning is not about checking that a child has absorbed the adult's teaching points but should show that the practitioner is joining in the child's own quest for knowledge and understanding. Such questions:

- stimulate children's curiosity and thinking;
- challenge children to modify their ideas;
- generate a fresh point of view;
- take children's learning forward;
- ask: What do you think? What might happen if? What do you imagine will happen?
- ensure the process is given more emphasis than the outcomes.

The following questions show how the practitioner can close down or open up children's thinking and reasoning.

CLOSED	OPEN
What colour are the bricks in your tower?	Why did you choose red bricks for your tower?
Can you make the boat move?	How can you make the boat move without touching it?
Can you stick these two pieces together?	How can you join these two pieces together?
Did the fox catch Rosie in the story?	I wonder why the fox didn't catch Rosie in the story?
Is this big enough to fit in here?	How can you find out if things are big enough to fit in here?
Are you writing orders for the shop?	How can Ellie help you to write orders for the shop?
Do the wheels on you model go round?	How did you make the wheels on your model go round?
Have you changed your idea?	Why did you decide to do it differently?
What do tadpoles turn into?	What do you think will happen to the tadpoles?
Do you need a nail for those two bits of wood?	How did you get the two bits of wood to stay together?
Have you made a rocket?	Where is your rocket going to?

Does your house need a door?	Can you find a way to put a doorway into your house?
Do you want a funnel?	What might happen if you used the funnel on the end of the pipe?
Can you make a bag for those letters? (mail)	How could you carry all those letters (mail) around without dropping them?
What do plants need to grow?	Why do you think this plant is drooping so much?
Shall we make an appointments book?	How can you remember what time all your customers are coming to have their hair done?
Do birds like to eat berries?	I wonder why so many birds come and sit on that bush?
Shall we put the bonfire out?	What is a good way to put the bonfire out?
What are all the little lights called that are in the sky at night?	I wonder how the stars stay up in the sky?
What do fish like to eat?	I wonder how long it will take before the fish come up to eat their food?
Which bear is the tallest?	How can we find out which bear needs the longest bed?

Conversation with parents

Conversations with parents and with carers add to the developing picture of the child as a learner. Parents bring their knowledge of the child in a variety of contexts that the early childhood educator may never be privileged to see. A good case for home visiting is made when practitioners recount what they have learnt from seeing the child in the surroundings of their own home, and how relationships change when parents meet teachers on their own territory (see Edwards and Redfern 1988 for a very practical account of the development of partnerships with parents and Liz Brooker 2002, who traces the learning experiences of Bangladeshi families in the Midlands through the eyes of the children and families as well as the school).

Conversations with parents should take place well before the child starts at their new school or setting, when the child starts and after the child has started. The conversations need to acknowledge the expertise that parents have about their own children and the understanding that parents have about their children's current needs and interests. They should be respectful of the parents' own perspectives and not seek to mould the parents' views to coincide with those of the setting. If early years practitioners want to know about children in order to build on the children's existing abilities, then a significant part of that knowledge comes from the home, and practitioners need to acknowledge this by providing a range of opportunities to listen to and record parental knowledge, attitudes and ideas. Parents have a fresh, different and crucial perspective on their child's development, their attitudes to learning and their growing skills and competences. We all know that children can behave as two different beings – both in attitude and approach – at home and in the setting, and it is an impoverished profile of the child as a learner that only takes account of the child in the context of the school, pre-school or nursery.

> It would not make sense to try to educate a child without taking account of the most significant people in his/her environment, and trying to work with them. It is through the home context that school becomes meaningful, or not, to a family.
>
> (Bruce 1991: 15)

Before children start school/setting

From the time a family first makes contact with a school or setting, or that school or setting first makes contact with a family, there are opportunities for a dynamic partnership to be established. To enable this to develop, Foundation Stage settings could offer some of the following:

- an invitation to use resources, a toy library and/or to borrow books;
- invitations to special events such as performances or fêtes;
- invitations to share amenities such as a hall or family room.

These informal contacts are invaluable for building confidence between parents, children and staff. From such beginnings a more formal induction process can evolve naturally.

Parental entitlement

Each setting needs to think carefully about how they help *all* parents and children to feel valued and welcomed at the beginning of their school life. Practitioners may want to consider the extent to which, in their setting, parents have an entitlement to:

- share their greater knowledge of their child, prior to entry, and throughout their time in the setting;
- enter a partnership with the setting that takes account of differences in culture, language and style;
- sufficient time and opportunity for regular formal and informal communication with staff;
- dialogue with practitioners where parents' opinions and ideas are listened to, valued and have influence;
- communicate their aspirations for their children;
- comment on and contribute to the records of their child's achievements in all areas of development.

Parental partnership

In order to facilitate a partnership with parents, Foundation Stage settings may need to initiate many or all of the following strategies:

- visit families at home (remembering that some parents may prefer to meet in the school or setting);
- design an entry profile for completion by parents and children;
- use photographs and/or a video camera to record everyday and special events;
- communicate aims and routines using visual material;
- share activities taking place in the setting by making a range of small books;
- use home/setting diaries, either audiotaped or written and using community languages where desirable;
- organize a range of times during the day and evening for meetings and appointments;
- organize a crèche for younger children;
- arrange for someone at meetings who can speak the community languages;
- enable an outreach worker/key worker/friend to attend with a family if support is required;
- adopt a flexible and imaginative response to the needs of families and the community;
- respect the variety and depth of information that parents convey about their children;
- recognize the diversity of values within the wider community;
- give parents opportunities to express their own expectations of the setting;
- give parents opportunities to express their hopes for their children both inside and apart from the setting;
- give parents opportunities to express their own fears and misgivings;
- ask parents to describe:
  - their child's interests,
  - what their child can do,
  - their child's health,
  - what is special to the child,
  - what the child hopes to do at the setting,
  - their child's likes and dislikes,
  - the history of their child's experiences,
  - their child's friends,
  - people who are important to the child,
  - what the child fears about the setting;
- share the strengths and achievements of the child in the setting;

- discuss ways in which parents and the setting can work together to support the child's learning.

Conversations with parents can benefit all parties concerned. It benefits early childhood practitioners because of their increased knowledge of the child, it benefits parents by making them genuine partners in their child's learning and it benefits children, who see home and their setting as mutually interested in their education.

Conversations with other adults

The third group of people with whom early years educators need to have conversations are those adults who have experience of the child as a learner before or beyond their current setting. Providing continuity for children's learning requires an appreciation of what has taken place before and what will take place after the child moves into or away from their current learning environment. When the Foundation Stage was introduced in England in 2000, one of its prime objectives was to make children's experiences across different providers and between different sectors as smooth and seamless as possible. This meant that new partnerships needed to be forged between those working in Foundation Stage classes and those working in playgroups, between those in private nurseries and those in nursery schools. In other words, between all settings that would share a child during their Foundation Stage experience. For the child, this phase of their educational journey from age 3 to the end of their reception year (when they would be 5) was to be given common goals and common guidance to enable practitioners, wherever they were working, to know about the principles that underpin early childhood education and how those principles looked in practice (for a very accessible exploration of early years principles into practice see May *et al.* 2006). Many local authorities have worked to produce assessment and planning guidance that enables those working in different sectors to develop processes and practices that are similar, so that the child's experiences are more constant no matter how many transitions they experience.

The issue of transitions in the early years remains an undesirable feature of early education in this country. At a time in their lives when children most need stability and continuity, they are faced with discontinuity and disruption. If anyone was to suggest that a child in Year 6 or Year 10 should start their day with one provider and move to another at lunchtime and then possibly on to a third at the end of the day, each with their own expectations and demands, then there would be a public outcry. Yet, in England, this situation has simply been accepted for a Foundation Stage child. However, a growing awareness of the importance of young children's attachments to their primary caregivers (Howe *et al.* 1999; Cairns 2002), as well as a marked increase in the number of children coming into the care of professionals, rather than families, for many hours a day at a very young age, has prompted concerns for this state of affairs (Biddulph 2005; Belsky *et al.* 2007). Early childhood educators as well as parents and other professionals are beginning to voice these concerns in growing numbers (see Selleck 2006).

The problem with different settings in different sectors is not just whether or not they deliver the same curriculum. Different settings very often have different adult to child ratios; they have different accommodation and resources; they may have different aims and values and they can often have different expectations of behaviour. Indeed, one of the hardest aspects of transition for children (especially where these are happening in one day) is where expectations of them and their behaviour are different. Where in one setting, for example, children have to ask to go to the toilet and in another they do not. Where in one setting children are expected to find and replace their own resources and in another they are found and replaced by the adults. Where in one setting guns and sword play are permitted and in another they are banned.

None of these differences are desirable for the child trying to make sense of the world and coming to their own understanding of rules and constraints. However, while such a situation exists, then the only way for different settings to improve the situation for children is for staff to talk together, to get to know the way each other works and to try and come to some agreement about common ways of planning for children's learning, observing and assessing their learning and sharing information that impacts on their leaning.

For those teaching children in their final year of the Foundation Stage, another crucial transition will be into Key Stage 1. The outcomes of the national Foundation Stage Profile have shown that the aim that 'most children will achieve and some, where appropriate, will go beyond the Early Learning Goals by the end of the foundation stage' (DfEE/QCA 2000) has been far too ambitious. What we now know from the national data is that the vast majority of children enter Year 1 without achieving all the Early Learning Goals. This has profound implications for Year 1 teachers and their curriculum planning (Fisher 2006). Many good schools now realize that the task of the Year 1 teacher is to continue and complete children's Foundation Stage experience before moving on to the Key Stage 1 programmes of study. Many innovative projects have begun in local authorities (e.g. OCC 2006) to support Year 1 teachers to move from the didactic teaching styles of recent years, brought about mainly by the constraints of the literacy hour, and the new more responsive and child-centred methodology required of Foundation Stage practice. Conversations between Foundation Stage and Key Stage 1 colleagues are crucial here if children are to have a seamless transition from one key stage to the next (for further support on this process see National Assessment Agency 2005).

Finally, into this melting pot of 'other adults', come all those who have professional knowledge of the child but are not necessarily their educators. Speech therapists, psychiatrists, pre-school teacher counsellors and so on all have a view of the child that gives their educator greater understanding of how that child learns and how they can best support and extend their learning. Conversations with other adults must permeate the practice of every early childhood educator if they are to truly see themselves as one contributor among many to the child's successful learning journey.

Making observations

The other key mechanism for finding out what children already know and can do is through observations of them while they are in action as learners. Children are naturally active learners (Bruce 1987; EYCG 1992), so it is imperative that to learn about them early childhood educators should watch them in action. If our objective is to find out the full range of what children know and understand, then this cannot be achieved by limiting the observations that are made. Children should be observed while they are engaged in a range of activities, both adult-initiated and child-initiated, which should occur:

- in familiar learning contexts;
- in an environment that encourages confidence and builds self-esteem;
- alongside a range of peers;
- when a child is working with an adult;
- when the child is working independently;
- at different times of the day and week.

Adult-initiated and child-initiated activity

Observations of children need to encompass activities that have been self-initiated and those that have been initiated by the adult. Self-initiated activity gives children opportunities to make choices and decisions of their own. It enables children to demonstrate their independence as well as their social skills in choosing to work with others. Self-initiated activity gives children control over situations, and sometimes their peers, and puts children in rare positions of learning power (Warham 1993; Claxton 2002). Appropriately resourced and supported, child-initiated activity can bring about some of the most creative and innovative learning in the classroom (Whitehead 1993).

Adult-initiated activity also has value of course. A key purpose of education is to broaden the range of children's knowledge and experience and this is appropriately planned for by the specialist practitioner. In adult-initiated activities there are opportunities for children to work with a variety of adults and peers for a range of purposes. Children engage in ideas and actions that are new to them and which they may not have discovered for themselves.

Both kinds of experience – adult-initiated and child-initiated – are important and one without the other will not give children sufficiently broad and balanced opportunities for learning. Equally, one without the other will not give the early childhood educator a sufficiently rounded picture of the child as a learner. Box 2.1 illustrates the importance of knowing as much about the young learner as possible.

Box 2.1   Example 1: Building a balanced profile

A student on teaching practice was building a very thorough profile of a 6-year-old boy in her class and was using it to try and establish why his behaviour was antagonistic and why she had such difficulty in engaging and sustaining his interest. When we looked at the profile together it became clear that she had made observations of the child when engaged in activities which *she* had initiated. Although she was aware that he 'liked making things', she had no observations of his involvement in self-selected tasks from which she might make judgements about future, more appropriate, planning. For the next few days she observed the child engaged in self-initiated activities and soon found that he did indeed enjoy making things, particularly with construction kits, and was very skilful at it. Talking with him about his models, she found that he was very knowledgeable about aeroplanes and regularly visited air shows with his father. When working on his self-selected tasks, she was amazed to see that he was cooperative and supportive to other children who worked alongside him. The student learnt that there was another side to this child. She saw a side of him that, observing him in directed situations, she might never have seen. By combining her knowledge of the child in both situations, she was able to plan teacher-initiated tasks that incorporated the positive aspects she had learnt about the child through her observations of his self-selected activity.

Familiar learning contexts

If educators are to observe children and to have conversations with them in contexts in which they will be at their best, then it is necessary for the environment in which these activities take place to be familiar and comfortable. None of us perform well – or at least naturally – if we feel insecure in new surroundings and with new people. Children need to feel at ease in their environment and to feel confident in the people around them to show what they know and like and can do. This is important to remember when children have just made a transition from one setting to another. Even if it is from the pre-school across the playground or the class down the corridor, there will be so many strange and unfamiliar things to which children will be giving their attention, that they may not have the concentration to show off their learning powers! It is easy to forget just what preoccupies children when they are uncertain. In Oxfordshire we asked our 4-year-olds what they felt about starting school (OCC 2005) and then every reception year child completed a questionnaire about what they felt about moving into Year 1 (OCC 2006). The responses reminded us so powerfully that far from being concerned with the curriculum or planning and assessment procedures, the children were preoccupied with toilets, spiders (mainly in the same context), where to put their coats and lunch boxes, being knocked over in the playground, their new teacher and being with their friends. Young children need to be helped to be secure by adults who listen to their concerns, their aspirations and their views and who understand that these must be attended to before any effective learning can take place. It is also a strong reminder that planning for transitions must take account of the voices of children and their parents and carers, every bit as much as of the practitioners involved (Fisher 2006).

There are some children for whom the new and unfamiliar poses a particular challenge. These are the children made vulnerable or traumatized by their life experiences and situation. For such children, transitions can dredge up old fears and current uncertainties. They have a low threshold of resilience to change and may not have developed the protective factors that enable them to adapt easily to what is new (Pugh 2002). As we saw in Chapter 1 there are children in almost every classroom and early years setting who may find change difficult because they did not have secure attachments to caring adults in the first two years of their lives (Robinson 2003; Gerhardt 2004). Children whose parents were too ill, too busy, too neglectful to respond to their children in ways that made their babies secure and soothed. There are children who cannot cope with transitions in school or pre-school because change is a painful and constant factor of their home lives. Children who are taken into care and then returned to birth families; children fleeing to a refuge, and then returning home; children being sent out of the blue to family members because a parent falls ill, and then being returned without warning when that parent comes home. Not knowing where you live, to whom you belong, who will be there for you at the end of a day, requires constant readjustment and increasing resilience. This resilience can be a thin veil between coping and collapsing, or an impenetrable wall to guard against future hurt. These multiple transitions in children's home lives can damage the capacity to attach to new people and manage new situations and will make the task of facing a transition in school or in their early years setting all the harder to deal with.

Then there are also those children who are normally settled and secure and for whom a tragic experience can be suddenly undermining, leaving them vulnerable and open to uncertainty. Loss, separation or bereavement in its many forms can cause even the strongest child to find yet another transition one thing too many to bear. For vulnerable children the need to have learning environments that are secure, engaging and playful is crucial. Adults need to be reliable and expectations adaptable. Adults must be sensitive to what may be innocuous to a secure child but cause deep trauma to another. Everyday early childhood experiences such as bringing in photos of you when you were a baby if you are adopted; being asked to bring in your most treasured possession when, as a refugee, you had to leave everything behind when your family fled; being asked to compare the colour of your hair for a mathematical graph when yours is covered by a hijab can all set back the learning of a vulnerable child and cause them unnecessary hurt and upset.

An environment that encourages confidence and builds self-esteem

Confidence and self-esteem are built in a myriad of ways and many of these have already been mentioned in this chapter. Children's self-image is enhanced when their culture and traditions are respected and acknowledged by the early childhood practitioner and used in the planning of an appropriate curriculum. Young children's feelings and attitudes are crucial to their achievements in all aspects of life and this has been recognized and celebrated in both *Birth to Three Matters* (DfES 2003a)and the *Curriculum Guidance for the Foundation Stage* (QCA/DfEE 2000) and now in the new *The Early Years Foundation Stage* (DfES 2007). It is important that those of us working in the field of early childhood education fight to preserve the affective elements of the curriculum and to sustain the social and emotional aspects of children's development. Rosemary Roberts (1995a) has examined how children's feelings affect their attitudes to school and shows how self-esteem can be the key to effective teaching and learning. As early childhood educators we can help to build self-esteem through the response that we give to children and to their attitudes, ideas and efforts. This does not mean heaping them with empty praise but supporting them in the self-assessment of their achievements and encouraging them in the development of their abilities (see Box 2.2).

Box 2.2   Example 2: Responding to children's work

A teacher of a vertically grouped class of Year 1 and Year 2 children wanted to develop the children's ability to evaluate their own work. She wanted them to move away from relying on her for decisions about whether what they had done was 'enough' or 'good enough'. She suspected that this reliance stemmed from the fact that, as she had set the tasks, the children believed that only she could judge the quality of the results. So she decided to change the entire way in which she introduced activities to the class. After the initial discussion and the introduction of the activity, she would ask the children what they thought was important in completing the task. She supported the children in thinking through the processes, the skills, the knowledge and the understandings they might need to demonstrate in the course of the activity and what the outcomes might be. They then decided which of these were the most important and these were recorded on a large sheet of paper and left pinned to the wall. At the end of the session the children would gather with their work and then review their own efforts against the criteria, which the class had collectively compiled. In this way the children were developing their personal responses to their own work and in the process were being challenged to use their initiative and to take responsibility for their learning and its outcomes. The teacher reported growing confidence and self-esteem as the children became involved in setting their own criteria for achievement in this way.

To have positive self-esteem children need self-confidence and this can be powerfully developed when children are encouraged to use their initiative, to make decisions and to be responsible for sharing in the planning and the evaluation of their own work. If we want children to develop positive self-esteem, then we have to show them that they are capable, however young they are, of decisions that have an impact on their own experiences and their own lives. The United Nations Convention on the Rights of the Child (Office of the High Commissioner for Human Rights 1990) recognizes all children's need for special protection because of their age and vulnerability. However, it also recognizes their competences and their right to have their views listened to and respected (Articles 12 and 13). Children whose voices are heard grow in confidence and self-esteem (Lancaster 2003). Sometimes practitioners must listen more carefully to those whose voices are uncertain. Liz Brooker's research for 'Starting school – young children learning cultures' (2002) demonstrates how disempowering it can be for children when there is a clash of culture between home and school. She writes of the experiences of Bangladeshi children making the transition from their home culture to school and how parenting practices, perspectives on childhood and beliefs about work and play all make a difference to how the children adapt to their new learning environment. As educators we must be aware of our children's histories, their cultures and their life experiences. Children who are proud of their cultural heritage, their gender, their family and themselves have been profoundly affected by the attitudes of those around them and the early years practitioner is a critical part of that network of influence (Siraj-Blatchford 1994). If we are to make observations of children that reflect the best that they can do, and in which they have the confidence to share with us what they know, then we must give them an environment that encourages their confidence and builds their self-esteem.

A range of peers

As early years practitioners, we are rightly concerned with the social development of children. As with all other aspects of their development, the social experiences of children before they start at school or their early years setting will vary enormously. Some may have come from large, extended family groups, including brothers, sisters, uncles, aunts and grandparents. Some may have had significant periods of time with childminders or at a day nursery and have become used to playing and being alongside their peers. For some children, however, their new school or nursery or children's centre will be their first introduction to the competition, collaboration and cooperation that is required when you are one among a number of others, all vying for space, resources and attention. Like all skills, being sociable is something you get better at with practice. The more people you meet, the more you learn to adjust and adapt to differences in attitudes and behaviour. Some people are better at this than others; some children are better at this than others. Home circumstances, life experiences and general dispositions will mean that certain children are ready to manage a range of social situations while others need support to increase their social skills. The more opportunities children have to learn alongside the full range of children in their group or class, the more opportunities they will have to learn those social skills that will make life in the setting, and life in general, a more positive and pleasurable experience. Children should be supported to communicate and cooperate with a range of others irrespective of their gender, race, physical attributes or ability. A profile of the social development of the child is best founded on observations of children alongside a range of peers, demonstrating a whole range of characteristics, attitudes and behaviours.

Children working with an adult

There will be many opportunities for early childhood educators to observe children while they are working alongside them. By supporting a child, or facilitating their activity, the adult is able to observe and, if appropriate, to record what the child says and what the child does as evidence of their growing conceptual awareness or skill development. They can also observe *how* the child approaches tasks, what strategies they use for solving problems, their persistence and motivation and their attitudes in general. What has to be remembered is that the presence of the adult will, to a lesser or greater degree, alter the behaviour of the child; to what extent depends on the task and also on the sensitivity of the adult. If a child is engaged in an adult-initiated activity and that adult is close by, then the child may frequently look to the adult for affirmation that they are doing the task 'right'. Some research in a reception class (Fisher 1996) illustrated the impact of the task on children's reliance on the teacher (see Box 2.3).

Box 2.3   Example 3: Building independence

As a researcher, I spent one day a week for two years in the same reception class, observing the interactions throughout the day between the teacher and members of her class. There was very clear evidence that the more directed the task, the more frequently the child went to the teacher for help and, particularly, affirmation. As the teacher's aim was to make the children more independent and to give herself more time to focus on her planned activities, this observation presented her with an instant strategy for achieving both aims at once. If she wanted to be less interrupted, and have time to work with particular children or do an observation, then the rest of the class had to be engaged in tasks that were less prescriptive and over which they had more control. The teacher changed the balance in the activities she planned. The activities where there was an adult present were more directed and the activities where children were working independently were more open-ended. Once this new way of planning was established, the teacher reported far fewer interruptions by children engaged in independent activities.

When an early years practitioner gives a child a task and then sits with them while they tackle it, then the child's approach and the amount of support they look for will have a significant impact on the process and probably the outcome of the task. This is not to say that a practitioner should not work alongside a child – far from it. The practitioner's role in supporting, challenging, guiding and extending children's learning is critical (see Chapters 1 and 4), but it is important to be sensitive to the impact the presence of an adult can have on the process and outcome of any activity.

Children working independently

When children play or work independently, they display different behaviours and often different strategies and skills than when they work under the direction of an adult. Dependent on how much independence they are used to, an observation of children working alone usually reveals fresh insights into the children as learners. Children's responses will be affected by whether the task is self-chosen or initiated by the practitioner, whether they have been told to collaborate or whether they have chosen to do so, and whether or not there is a required outcome. Whatever the task, the conversations of children working independently usually reveal far more about children as learners than is revealed when they work on tasks where adults are present.

Different times of the day

Children are no different from adults; some are 'larks' – those who wake up bright and perky and irritatingly cheerful straight away, and some are 'owls' – those who begin sluggishly, but improve as the day goes on. Observation of children at different times in the day shows us that some children take a long time to settle in the morning, while others can concentrate almost immediately. There are some children who are adversely affected by breaks in the learning day – assembly, television and so on – whereas others seem to take these in their stride. Many children are affected by playtimes and lunchtimes and take a long time to settle afterwards. My reception class research showed that it can be the period from break to lunchtime that is the most disrupted. After lunchtime, children were tired but usually more able to settle to their various tasks than after break when they were still wound up from rushing around, and needed more intervention from adults to engage in their activities (Fisher 1996). The great advantage of the planned provision in the best quality early years settings is that there are long periods of time for sustained experience and activity, uninterrupted by such things as playtime and hall time. Young children need time to develop their thinking and to explore what is intriguing and preoccupying them at that moment. Practitioners know well that if a child's attention has been taken by an unexpected incident or discovery, then the child will not focus on any intended activity until their curiosity and interest in the unexpected has dwindled. Likewise, being removed from a learning experience just when it becomes intriguing and just when the child has become deeply engaged is both frustrating and counter-productive. Young children often take longer to become engrossed in something because they can take a while to make sense of new resources, experiences and situations. When much of the world is still new and maybe confusing, then finding the right pieces of cognitive jigsaw can take time. The wise adult gives a child sufficient time to enquire, investigate, explore and play so that the child reaches their own satisfactory conclusions without being disrupted just at the most important moment of personal discovery.

As we have just seen, young children will be at their best at different times in the day as well as in different learning situations, and so it is important that when we observe them we take this into account. The introduction of the literacy and numeracy strategies in England (DfES http://www.standards.dfes.gov.uk/primary/) brought about an unwelcome return, in many schools, to a timetable based on similarly ill-conceived notions about when children are 'at their best'. These schools have adopted a timetable where literacy takes place across all classes until break-time followed by numeracy from break-time to lunch (or the other way round). All other aspects of the curriculum are subsequently squashed into afternoon sessions and all reports on current curriculum provision show that the teaching of art and design, physical education, science, information and communication technology (ICT) and the humanities are being squeezed into smaller and smaller amounts of time. For the youngest children, some of whom attend only part time, this diet has not been adequately modified. Consequently, these Foundation Stage children are receiving only literacy and numeracy education, frequently in a form that is inappropriate for their age and stage of development. Not only that, but these literacy and numeracy experiences are disembedded from those meaningful experiences found in more integrated learning environments. The impact of creative and physical skills and experience on children's capacity to develop number concepts and literacy are well documented (e.g. Edwards and Knight 1994; EYCG 1998) and it is an impoverished curriculum that offers these two crucial aspects of education in such an isolated way. The principles of the new Early Years Foundation Stage (DfES 2007) should ensure that children, up to and including Year 1 it is hoped, have a more broadly based and rounded curriculum experience. But there needs to be greater understanding on the part of many managers and governors that young children's experiences often need to be different and distinct from those that are appropriate for children who are older. It may look neat and tidy if all curriculum planning, records of assessment and timetables are uniform from reception to Year 6, but this will *not* necessarily meet the learning needs of children.

The purpose of observations and conversations

Early childhood educators who want to find out about children choose strategies that tell them the most. Unless those strategies leave room for the practitioner to learn from the process, then the strategies will not be informative but merely affirmative. Practitioners come to know what they already know and teaching remains rooted in *assumptions* about what children need to know next.

Having made an observation or recorded important elements of a conversation, the practitioner needs to translate these records into appropriate action. The professional skill of the early childhood educator is in knowing what it is that they have seen or heard in relation to each child's development. They have to make decisions about whether what they have seen or heard means that something particular needs to be planned and whether the individual has needs that have not previously been identified. Much of what has already been planned will remain relevant, but ongoing assessments of children inform the fine-tuning of short-term plans (see Chapter 3) and enable practitioners to ensure that time is spent on a curriculum that starts from the needs and interests of the child.

Conclusion

Having conversations with children and observing them in action acknowledges the competences with which children come to their new school or setting, not only at the beginning but throughout their educational careers. Observations and conversations are tools for assessment that recognize children's individual competences as the baseline against which their future learning needs should be identified. Such assessment practices define the role of the early childhood educator as being that of a learner, alongside their children, finding out about and then building on what children already know and can do. The assessment practices described in this chapter are the starting point for planning rather than the finishing point. The next chapter explores how practitioners use the information gained through initial assessments of children to plan an appropriate curriculum for the needs of each child.

3

PLANNING FOR LEARNING

Decisions about appropriate experiences to support and extend learning

Introduction

Acknowledging the child as a competent learner should ensure that the starting point for planning an appropriate curriculum is the child's developing skills and understandings. These competences are established through the initial assessments of children described in the previous chapter. What children already know and can do should determine the experiences that are planned for their development (Bruce 1987; DES 1990; EYCG 1992; Ball 1994; Fisher 2002). However, in England, the imposition of an externally imposed National Curriculum and the introduction of first the Desirable Learning Outcomes (DfEE/QCA 1998) and then the Early Learning Goals (QCA/DfEE 2000) challenged the plausibility of such a notion. Many practitioners have felt torn between their early years principles, rooted in the ideals of child-centredness, and their statutory obligations to meet an agenda purporting to meet the needs of all children rather than those of the individual learner. The recent introduction of the Early Years Foundation Stage (DfES 2007) has done little to assuage such concerns. While its principles indeed exhort practitioners to 'deliver personalized learning, development and care to help children to get the best possible start in life' (DfES 2007a: para 1.7), there are concerns that its structure could lead inexperienced or poorly trained practitioners to rely on predetermined 'development matters' (DfES 2007b, p. 22 onwards) to plan for children's experiences rather than from evidence gleaned from 'Listen, look and note' (DfES 2007: para 2.6). The insistence on the use of six areas of learning as the framework for observing, planning for and assessing children's 'progress' from birth promotes a view of learning that is too formal, too compartmentalized and too rigid for the breadth and richness of experience that babies and toddlers need (see Abbott and Moylett 1997; Lindon 2000; Manning-Morton and Thorp 2001) and the nurturing and care that they must have to flourish as the 'strong child' of *Birth to Three Matters* (DfES 2003a). While there is much that is informative and appropriate in the Practice Guidance for the new statutory framework, the fact remains that it is underpinned by a pervading emphasis on goals, outcomes and targets – particularly over the teaching and assessment of phonics (for an informed and balanced overview of the current phonics debate see Wyles and Styles in press; Torgerson *et al.* 2006)

So, there remains a perceptible tension between the interests of young children as learners and the interests of their educators, brought about by successive and excessive government initiatives. Early years educators, like all of the teaching profession, have goals to reach, targets to meet and standards to raise. These are the outcomes by which they are inspected and against which they will be judged. But this external agenda inevitably puts pressure on practitioners to cover the curriculum rather than allow children, in Lilian Katz's words, to *uncover* it (Katz 1998). There is a pervading concern among some practitioners that to detour from the planned path, to encourage children to divert or digress, will mean that outcomes will not be achieved and that somehow this equates to failure. It is a real dilemma that the standards agenda, so beloved of recent UK governments, has attainment in a narrow range of subjects, as a marker of effectiveness. High attainment has always been easy if you narrow the range of things that are to be attained. Look how many children in the 1960s and 1970s got to the 'top' of their reading scheme – but could not transfer any universal reading skills to other texts. Likewise, working constantly to arrive at goals and targets can mean rushing through the vital processes of learning and not having time to revisit experiences and opportunities over again – a necessary and crucial aspect of children's developmental needs (Bruner 1960). However, the Foundation Stage and, now, the Early Years Foundation Stage, are aptly named. Foundations have to go broad and deep before a building of quality can emerge. Foundations must be firm but flexible, skillfully connected to what already exists and strengthened when construction is on poor ground. If the foundations of learning are to be adequate, then it may be some time before any measurable outcomes emerge. However, once constructed, the structure should reach higher and be more adaptable than anything constructed with narrower, more hurried, less secure foundations (Fisher 2002b).

The notion of child-centredness

Early childhood education is rooted in a belief that children should receive an education designed to meet their own individual needs. Child-centred thinking has its roots in the work of philosophers such as Rousseau and Dewey and stemmed, as described by John Darling (1994) in his review of child-centred education, 'from radical dissatisfaction with traditional practice'. This practice was characterized by an emphasis on content over process and on the memorizing of facts rather than an understanding of concepts. Classes were taught as a single entity, with little or no account taken of individual differences in previous experiences, current understandings or rates of progress. The time-honoured metaphor that children were 'empty vessels to be filled' made the classroom roles of children and teachers very explicit. It was the duty of teachers to fill the vessels with knowledge and the duty of children to learn what was being taught, and if they did not, then the onus of blame was well and truly on *their* shoulders.

Yet long before such practice was established, there was a commitment to the notion of children as individual learners. As early as 1762, Jean-Jaques Rousseau declared in *Emile* that 'Nature provides for the child's growth in her own fashion, and this should never be thwarted' (Rousseau [1762] 1976). His approach to thinking about children and their development was taken forward by such writers as Pestalozzi, Froebel and Dewey, each developing and revising the work of the others until a powerful philosophy for the education of young children was formed. However, it was not until the 1960s that this philosophy really began to have any impact on practice in Britain. The main reason for the change in pedagogy was the public endorsement of a more child-friendly approach by official reports, most notably *Children and their Primary Schools* (CACE 1967). The Plowden Report promoted a more liberal view of education, encapsulated in the celebrated quotation:

> at the heart of the education process lies the child. No advances in policy, no acquisitions of new equipment have their desired effect unless they are in harmony with the nature of the child, unless they are fundamentally acceptable to him [*sic*].
>
> (CACE 1967: para 9)

Child-centred education is concerned with the *development* of children. It is seen as a natural progression that is best aided by adults who, in Darling's words, 'have an appreciation of and respect for the ways of children' (1994: 3). This is an important element. Part of the criticism of child-centred practices was that the child was able to choose and control their own actions and that the role of the educator became diminished for fear of being accused of 'interfering' with this natural development (see Blenkin and Kelly 1987; Darling 1994).

Interestingly, it was the work of Jean Piaget (1896–1980) that did much to fuel this misconception. Piaget believed that children pass through certain stages of development and could not operate at the later stages before passing, in their own good time, through the earlier ones. This theory supposed that children passed through these stages irrespective of adult support and that the best an adult could do was interfere! The obvious assumption was that if children passed naturally through these stages of development, then the most dangerous thing one could do was to rush them through the process.

This theory led to the notion of 'readiness' (see Chapter 1), with educators believing that they had to *wait* until a child was ready to learn something rather than being in a position to move them on or extend them beyond the stage where they were. Such a notion rendered the teacher somewhat impotent. Knowing the next stage of development and perceiving the learning needs of the child are of restricted use if you believe that it is damaging to use such knowledge. The other facet of Piaget's work that apparently diminished the role of the educator was his emphasis on the child as an individual explorer of the world, discovering and making sense of new situations through action and self-directed problem-solving (Bruner and Haste 1987). Piaget's influence on thinking and practice in the 1960s and 1970s caused many practitioners, as well as critics, to believe that the role of the adult had been sidelined and that children were to be encouraged to do as they please. The power of these assumptions can be seen all too clearly in the series of Black Papers written between 1969 and 1977 (see Cox and Dyson 1969a, 1969b, 1970; Cox and Boyson 1975, 1977) and the impact of the resultant conservative backlash is, I would suggest, still being felt today.

Much of Piaget's work became challenged even by those who acknowledged his tremendous contribution to the development of our thinking about children and their learning. One of the most influential challenges came from his colleague Margaret Donaldson. In her book *Children's Minds* (1978) she argued for a fresh interpretation of Piaget's views based on her own research in which she replicated some of Piaget's tests but using significantly different methodology. She and her colleagues found that by setting Piaget's tasks in contexts that were familiar to the children and using language that was clear and relevant to the tasks, a significantly greater number of children were able to complete the tasks than had succeeded in Piaget's original tests (Piaget and Inhelder 1956). Donaldson's work adds powerful weight to the notion of the young child as a competent learner and the critical role of the adult in extending those competences:

the normal child comes to school with well-established skills as a thinker. But his [sic] thinking is directed outwards on to the real, meaningful, shifting, distracting world. What is going to be required for success in our educational system is that he should learn to turn language and thought in upon themselves. He must be able to direct his own thought processes in a thoughtful manner. He must become able not just to talk but to choose what he will say, not just to interpret but to weigh interpretations. His conceptual system must expand in the direction of increasing ability to represent itself. He must become capable of manipulating symbols.

(Donaldson 1978: 88–9)

It was the work of Lev Vygotsky (1986–1934) that firmly reinstated the role of the educator to a central place in the developmental journeys of children. Vygotsky saw children's cognitive development operating at two levels; the present level and the potential level. He believed that the role of more knowledgeable others is to move the child from the actual to the potential next level of understanding. The task of the adult is to encourage children to do *without* help what they can do only at present *with* help (Anning 1991). In other words, children's learning can be extended by the right intervention at the right time.

Teachers have a highly interactive role in a Vygotskian framework. Children's development is static unless they are able to work in their zone of proximal development. Teaching does not wait upon development but propels it.

(Smith 1993: 56)

This support for children's learning is what Wood *et al.* (1976) have called 'scaffolding', and this offers an appropriate metaphor for the notion of child-centredness in its aim to offer experiences, resources and interactions that match the level of competence and maturity of the child. The work of Jerome Bruner (1915–) is of particular relevance to early years practitioners here, because he works from an analysis of children's learning, to a model of classroom pedagogy and then to a curriculum framework. It is the very fact that the National Curriculum attainment targets and the Early Learning Goals work in precisely the opposite way that seems to set them at odds with the notion of child-centredness.

Comparisons between the pioneers and modern theorists

The child-centred notions of Rousseau, Dewey, Pestalozzi and others can be seen clearly in the principles and practice of the early childhood educators such as Froebel, Montessori and Steiner. Tina Bruce's book *Early Childhood Education* (1987) takes the threads of influence even further by comparing the principles of those early pioneers with the work of more modern theorists such as Piaget, Vygotsky, Bruner and Mia Kelmer Pringle, founding director of the UK National Children's Bureau. The '10 common principles of the pioneers' (Bruce 1987) is a valuable framework for the development of good early years practice in current settings. These principles have been adopted and developed in many subsequent documents (e.g. EYCG 1992; Roberts 1995b). The Oxfordshire Early Years Team (1996) adapted them to reflect their work with children from birth–8 years, and the adaptation in Box 3.1 offers indicators of those early years principles in practice.

Box 3.1   Principles of early childhood education

 1 *Childhood is seen as valid in itself. It is a stage of life and not simply a preparation for the future.*
 • experiences and environment should be appropriate to the age and developmental stage of the child;
 • experiences should be relevant to the child's *current* needs;
 • each child should be valued for themselves, what they are, what they know and what they can do;
 • learning at this stage may improve later performance but, first and foremost, learning enables children to achieve their present potential and enriches and fulfils their present life (Moss and Penn 1996).

 2 *The whole child is considered to be important; social, physical, intellectual, moral and spiritual aspects of development are related.*
 • all aspects of the child should be considered in planning resources and experiences;
 • the balance between these areas needs to be sustained once children begin statutory schooling;
 • *all* areas of development should be observed and assessed in order to inform future planning.

 3 *There is potential in all children that will emerge powerfully under favourable conditions. Each child is unique and special, with individual ways of learning.*
 • every child should be known well by at least one adult;
 • children should be valued with full regard to their gender, race and ability;

- the environment should be sufficiently flexible and responsive to meet the range of children's learning styles and strategies;
- children need time and space to produce work of quality and depth (EYCG 1992).

4 *Parents are the first and continuing educators of their children. Schools should value and build on parental expertise.*
- schools and settings need to establish systems where parents can tell staff about their child;
- schools and settings should develop a partnership with parents and carers based on mutual respect and a shared interest in the child;
- parents should be involved in the process of assessment and contribute to decisions about future plans for their child.

5 *Learning is holistic and interconnected. The young child does not separate experiences into different compartments.*
- short-term planning should be sufficiently flexible to make space/allow time for the children's spontaneous interests;
- planning should identify the understanding, skills and attitudes that are important for developing learners; activities and themes should support rather than determine these objectives;
- broadly based and integrated experiences are appropriate when working within the National Curriculum.

6 *Young children learn through exploration, play and talk.*
- young children learn most effectively by doing rather than being told (EYCG 1992);
- play should occur throughout the day, alongside adult-directed activity;
- play is given status when it is valued, assessed and used to extend learning;
- children should be encouraged to initiate conversations and pose questions.

7 *Our starting points for supporting learning are what children can do and what they can nearly do.*
- children should be helped to identify their own targets and achievements;
- observation-based assessment should be the basis for planning;
- adults should sensitively support and extend children's learning to the edges of their potential.

8 *Intrinsic motivation is recognized and valued as a powerful force for learning.*
- autonomy (physical, social and intellectual) and self-discipline are emphasized;
- children should have substantial periods of uninterrupted time for sustained self-initiated activity;
- children should have a range of opportunities to make choices and decisions.

9 *The relationships that children establish with adults and other children are of central importance in their development.*
- the education of young children should be the responsibility of appropriately trained and experienced educators with a knowledge of child development;
- children need planned experiences that encourage the interpersonal and cognitive skills necessary for collaboration and cooperation;
- educators should be aware of themselves as models.

10 *Children's education is seen as the total experience of, and interaction with, their environment.*
- children's educational experiences should draw on their personal context of family, culture and community;
- there should be provision and planning for an indoor and outdoor environment of equal quality;
- the way in which we talk and respond to children throughout their time in school should create a climate that nurtures self-esteem.

The translation of early years principles into practice has been particularly influenced by the writing of Geva Blenkin, who espouses a commitment to a developmental view of education and argues cogently for a concept of education:

> not as a device for the transmission of certain bodies of agreed knowledge and values or as a process of moulding people into some predetermined shape, it is of the enhancement of capacities, the widening of every person's horizons of appreciation and understanding, the maximization of everyone's potential, the development of everyone's powers of self-direction, autonomy, understanding and critical awareness.
>
> (Blenkin and Kelly 1987: 11)

In Chapter 2 of *The National Curriculum and Early Learning*, Blenkin, in Blenkin and Kelly (1994: 29), draws together four broad themes of early childhood education which, based on the principles of a developmental curriculum, are peculiar to this stage of education:

1   The young child is dependent on adults and is new to institutional life. The process of learning to be a pupil is thus of great importance.
2   Rates of development and learning are at their most rapid during this stage of education, and they are highly susceptible to environmental constraints and advantages. The young child, therefore, needs to be stimulated by a wide range of experiences rather than confined to a narrow and restrictive programme.
3   Although social interaction is important at every stage of learning, it is of particular importance at this early stage, since young learners are not able to make sense of experiences that are represented in a more formal or abstract way.
4   Early education must not only provide a rich array of practical experiences but it must also nurture the playfulness of children. For secure mastery of skills or knowledge depends on play, because it is through play that the child is able to test out, informally and personally, what is newly learnt.

As early years practitioners, we are challenged to plan a curriculum that:

* focuses on process rather than content or outcomes (or targets or goals);
* offers a wide range of experiences rather than a restrictive one (or imposed one);
* emphasizes first hand, real experiences that contextualize learning (rather than a diet of workbooks or worksheets);
* emphasizes active learning and play (rather than passive learning and pencil and paper activities).

It would seem that the fundamental tenants of good early years practice fly in the face of the National Curriculum, national literacy and numeracy strategies and Foundation Stage goals, which often fail to recognize 'what a complex and subtle matter is the learning of pupils in their early, formative years' (Blenkin and Kelly 1994: 197).

Current documentation supporting early years practice

The new *Early Years Foundation Stage (EYFS)* 'sets the Standards for Learning, Development and Care for children from birth to five' (DfES 2007). In drawing together the principles and pedagogy of the *Curriculum Guidance for the Foundation Stage, Birth to Three Matters* and the *National Standards for Under 8s Daycare and Childminding,* the EYFS is a central part of the UK government's 10-year strategy for improving outcomes for children, young people and families and reducing inequalities (DfES 2004).The principles of previous documentation have been brought together in fours 'themes' – A Unique Child; Positive Relationships; Enabling Environments and Learning and Development, which are broken down into 'commitments' describing how the principles can be put into practice. There are many messages that support the view that children are competent learners from birth who can be 'resilient, capable, confident and self-assured' (DfES 2007a: para 1.11). Much is made of ensuring positive attitudes to diversity and difference and the subsequent need to focus on each child's individual learning, development and care needs (e.g. 2007a: para 1.14). There are strong messages about promoting partnership with parents and other educators engaged in the care and education of the children from birth to age 5 (e.g. 2007a: para 1.16) and of the need to improve the continuity of children's experiences from one Foundation Stage setting to the next (2007a: para 1.16; 2007b: para 1.13).

Having promoted the EYFS by celebrating that the different documents named above would be brought together in order to establish one cohesive phase of education from birth to age 5, it is a puzzlement that in the final materials there are separate documents for those aspects of the framework that are statutory and those that are guidance. Inevitably this suggests that some aspects are more important than others and, when one sees that the section on Play, for example, sits in the Practice Guidance (2007b: paras 1.16–1.20) and not as a statutory requirement, then the principles about child-focused planning sound somewhat hollow.

The EYFS was a golden opportunity to learn from previous undesirable elements within existing early years documentation and frameworks. While there is much to commend in the EYFS, it has done little to resolve the tensions between meeting the needs of individual children and meeting the wider political agenda. Its 'principled approach' pays lip-service to starting from the child, for it then delivers a structure for observation, planning and assessment that promotes reliance on a sequential and compartmentalized formula that in no way reflects the idiosyncratic and meandering learning pathways of individual children. My major concerns about the EYFS are these:

- Observation and analysis of the *needs of babies and toddlers* are not easily categorized into areas of learning suitable for children when they begin statutory schooling. The Areas of Learning and Development (DfES, 2007: p. 22 onwards).
- There is now irrefutable evidence of the importance of *high-quality outdoor environments* in promoting development and learning in the

early years. However, the EYFS has not established even an aspirational target that all settings in the EYFS should have access to a safe and secure outdoor area for learning. The inadequate guidance is that children should have 'access' to an outdoor play area that might be in an 'appropriate nearby location'. To my mind there should be a requirement not only that every funded setting should have access to its own outdoor area, but also statutory requirements as to its size.

- Despite declaring one of its chief purposes to be the improvement of quality and consistency through a set of universal standards (2007a: para 1.2), the statutory requirements of the EYFS have not established *ratios* that are consistent across the different sectors. Although the Practice Guidance reports that 'many schools consider it good practice to employ a full-time level 3 practitioner in order to meet the needs of this particular group', reception classes (for children age 4–5 years in school) can still legally operate with one teacher for 30 children. This is discriminatory practice. There is a suggestion here that somehow the higher the qualification of the adult, the higher the ratios can be. But as we have seen in Chapter 2, the role of the adult is to observe and listen to children in order to support their learning and development. However well qualified the practitioner is, he or she only has one pair of eyes and one pair of ears. When reception class teachers do not have the full-time support of a specially qualified and experienced classroom assistant – all day, every day, then both the teacher and the children are disadvantaged.

- Finally, despite all the evidence and lobbying to the contrary, there has been no alteration of the *Early Learning Goals*. Four years of evidence from the Foundation Stage Profile (the statutory assessment of all children in England at the end of their Foundation Stage experience) has shown that there are certain Early Learning Goals that were set developmentally too high. Those for Calculating, Writing, and Linking Sounds and Letters have consistently been attained by less than 30 per cent of the nation's children. This is not because the teaching of these aspects of the curriculum is poor, but because the Goals are set at a developmental stage which is beyond that which most children are ready to reach. Not only does the EYFS not acknowledge this, but the only change made to the Early Learning Goals is in response to the Rose *Independent Review of the Teaching of Early Reading* (2006), when the Early Learning Goal for Linking Sounds and Letters, attained by just 29 per cent of children in 2006, has been made harder.

Similarities and differences between young learners

When considering similarities and differences, I believe that it is helpful to reflect on the need for different approaches between teaching and assessment. When making assessments, children *must* be seen as individuals. The educator is looking for what the individual knows, understands and can do. Having made these assessments that are concerned with the individual, however, it will then be seen that certain children have similar needs as well as having those that are different. The learning environment and teaching opportunities can thus be planned to meet either the similarities or the differences. On some occasions, a group of children can be taught something in the same way at the same time, because the practitioner has identified that they are all at a similar stage of developmental understanding. This similar need can be addressed at either group time or as an *adult-focused* activity. At other times there will be a group of children who can be encouraged to work together on an *adult-initiated* activity that is set up to achieve the same potential learning but, during which, an individual or the whole group might decide to take that learning elsewhere. In this way, the planning is intended to meet similar needs but the outcome might reveal differences. For much of the time, Foundation Stage children need to be engaged in *child-initiated* learning, responding to the experiences and opportunities offered by the learning environment in their own differentiated and personalized way.

While I do believe that there are tensions between the National Curriculum and a developmentally appropriate early years curriculum (see Blenkin and Kelly 1987) and between the Early Learning Goals and notions of learner-centred education and between the Early Years Foundation Stage and personalized learning, I also believe that there are ways of looking at the apparent dichotomies that may make the application of one not wholly incompatible with the constraints of the other (e.g. EYCG 1998). Some of the answers to easing the tension lie within a better definition of the major stages of curriculum planning. Staff in schools and settings have been increasingly required to plan in depth at each stage – long, medium and short term. Definitions of these stages have been prolific and sometimes conflicting. While not wishing to add to the plethora of definitions, I would suggest that the answer to this fundamental early years dilemma of planning for different needs is to see long- and medium-term planning as meeting one set of needs and short-term planning as meeting a different set. Long- and medium-term planning are about the *curriculum* and about subjects and areas of learning. Short-term planning is about the *child*. If we can make and sustain this differential, then it may be possible to maintain a developmental position while meeting the requirements of the external agenda.

Stages of planning

Long-term planning is concerned with children's entitlement to a *broad and balanced* curriculum and is achieved through the appropriate allocation of time to the Areas of Learning and Development in the Early Years Foundation Stage, the National Curriculum (where appropriate), religious education and other curriculum aspects required, particularly, in the reception year.

Medium-term planning addresses *continuity and progression* from one stage in each area of learning/subject to the next, and from one setting or class to the next. It draws on schemes of work and the long-term plan and identifies the concepts, skills, knowledge and attitudes to which children will be introduced over a specified time. It is at this stage that the curriculum may be most effectively organized by linking together different areas of learning/subjects through themes or topics. Medium-term planning should also record the ongoing learning that will take place alongside any planned topic work, and which simply does not fit in with a current theme such as 'Ourselves' or 'Journeys', for example, elements of mathematical development or personal and social education.

Short-term planning is concerned with *differentiation* and planning for the needs of specific groups and individual children. It provides the detail of activities, experiences, resources, groupings, adult support and teaching strategies that are identified through ongoing observation and assessment of children in action.

Long-term planning

Long-term planning usually takes place well before the start of the new academic year. In many schools and settings this stage of planning is formalized in planning cycles that identify the elements of the areas of learning or subjects to be addressed by topics in different terms and over different years. Many schools and settings I know use a planning sheet that has on it the 'Development Matters' aspects of the EYFS, which might be appropriate for the age and stage of the children for whom they are responsible, and highlight in different colour pens those that will be the focus for each term. Long-term planning should show that the statutory requirements of the curriculum are being addressed over the course of the children's time in the setting. This stage of planning is about children's entitlement to the curriculum and practitioners need to demonstrate that what is being planned covers the breadth of the curriculum and that there is an appropriate balance between the different areas of learning.

Now while it may attribute to overall 'effectiveness' (Ofsted 1994a), long-term planning cannot purport to be concerned with the developmental needs of individual children because practitioners have frequently not yet met the children to whom the planning relates! Even if the children are known, their needs will have changed in many ways between the time when the planning is undertaken and the experiences take place. So the long-term plan cannot have activities or experiences earmarked but should be seen as a framework for ensuring curriculum coverage.

Medium-term planning

It is at the medium-term planning stage that I feel most difficulties lie. Medium-term plans are usually written at the start of a new term or half-term, or at the beginning of a theme or topic for younger children. Although the children may now be known to their practitioners, their developmental needs may not be. Children's needs change rapidly at this stage in their development – too rapidly to be predicted, with accuracy, even several weeks in advance. So it is important that medium-term planning also addresses subjects and areas of learning rather than children. The most important feature of medium-term planning is that it should identify the concepts, skills, knowledge and attitudes that constituted the planned learning for that period of time, and it should show how the children's learning will build on and progress from that which has gone before. It may also show how the teaching of potential skills or knowledge, for example, will be integrated and linked together into themes or topics. However, all too often, on carefully produced planning sheets, there is a column for the activity or task that will be the vehicle for the intended learning outcomes. If a decision is made that this activity or that task will be appropriate for a child before their actual needs are known, then the decision may be the wrong one. There is a lot of sense in pencilling in possible activities and accumulating a bank of ideas from which to draw, but activities are only the vehicles for learning and planning must be sufficiently flexible to change activities and to accommodate the needs and interests of individual children, once they are known.

Topic work

Topic work acknowledges the fact that children do not naturally compartmentalize their learning into subject areas or areas of learning.

It seeks to capitalize on the notion of cross-curricular learning, with its intention of mirroring the real-life learning of children in a range of contexts. However, cross-curricular learning and topic work are not necessarily the same thing and the one may not be a useful vehicle for delivering the other. Cross-curricular learning emphasizes the opportunities for children to cross the boundaries between traditional subjects and see the application of skills and the consolidation of concepts in experiences and activities that enable such cross-fertilization to occur. In an effective early learning environment most activities and experiences offer learning potential across most areas of the curriculum all at the same time and it is only in adult-focused learning that the outcomes are limited to one particular curriculum element. Topic work, however, while rooted in this notion, has been hijacked by the agenda of teachers and other early years practitioners. Increasingly, as topics become planned by whole staff teams together, the links that are made between areas of learning are not seen by the child but engineered by adults. They sometimes involve excruciating contortions to involve all areas of learning and early years practitioners must guard against making topics as incomprehensible to children as subject divisions are.

A particular concern for early childhood educators – particularly teachers – is the expectation that they fit in with the school's cycle of topics. Very often the topic titles are inappropriate for young children and do not meet their current needs and interests. Equally, topics and themes may not last as long for younger children as they do for older pupils and yet early years teachers feel locked into the cycle and compelled to continue with a topic even when it is not bringing about effective learning. Either way, practitioners in the early years should have the flexibility to select topics for the length of time they are relevant and meaningful to the children – or to choose not to use topics at all. Topics should be as expendable and exchangeable as activities and experiences. They are the vehicles for learning, not the purpose of it. If one topic, theme or activity better suits one class or group than another, and either can bring about the intended learning, then any planning system should be sufficiently flexible to accommodate the alternatives.

Short-term planning

It is at this stage that planning moves from concerns with the curriculum and areas of learning or subjects to concerns for the child. It is at this stage that the educator has the opportunity to incorporate the developmental approach to learning, by making first-hand observations of children engaged in active learning and through having conversations with children about what they have experienced and what they are thinking. Through observation of children in action, carrying out open-ended tasks that allow them to explore and investigate, practitioners can gain information about children's knowledge and understanding as well as their skills and strategies. All this information is necessary if practitioners are to plan experiences that have relevance and purpose for each child. Some intentions or objectives may come from the medium-term plans or from more recent analysis of learning needs, but the actual activity or experience will be planned in the light of what the child already knows and can do, and what the practitioner judges he or she needs to know or do next.

Assessment activities

It is at this stage that it would be helpful to look again at the cycle of teaching, assessment and learning that determines the experiences that educators plan for children. As we saw in Chapter 2, assessment activities are often seen as a check against the effectiveness of teaching, a measure of whether children have learnt what it was intended that they should learn. As such, assessment frequently comes at the end of the process and often gets tagged on to the seemingly more important stages of planning and teaching. I would suggest that this model of the cycle is limited and very often ineffectual. If assessment is only ever seen as completing the cycle, then educators lose the powerful and necessary potential of using assessment to inform future planning. It leaves them either predicting or guessing what knowledge or understanding children bring to the introduction of a new concept or the learning of a new skill. Practitioners often make elaborate introductions to new ideas and then use the discussion time following the introduction to elicit a range of understandings from children. However, this knowledge is not always used to inform or to alter planning. If practitioners always begin by teaching, then there is an implicit assumption that what has been planned is appropriate and that, apart from the necessity for differentiated follow-up, the needs of children will be met.

We have seen, however, that children bring with them a whole range of knowledge, understanding and skills that are nothing to do with formal education. Peers, different adults, the television, books, outings and visits all give children a vast array of insights that educators ignore at their peril. It is inappropriate to introduce the concept of magnets to a child whose father is a scientist who has conducted experiments with his young son since age 3 (see Box 3.2). This is a trap that is easy to fall into but can just as easily be avoided.

Box 3.2 Example 4: What William already knew and understood

William, aged 4, stayed at the magnet table for 12 minutes. In that time he did not pick up a single magnet. He became absorbed in the workings of an egg whisk – one of the items that had been left for the investigation. He turned the handle this way and that, watching the blades rotate. He held the whisk upside down and sideways. He tried to engage another child in this investigation, but the boy was too busy discovering for himself that 'you can make it stick through paper ... look!'. William persevered until, having exhausted his investigations, he looked for the teacher and went over to show her what he had discovered. As a result of this she was able to plan for him to use a construction kit that enabled him to make his own 'blades' using cogs and wheels. The child was the son of a scientist. He didn't need to explore the properties of magnets, he knew about them.

By setting up this experience, the teacher not only reminded herself of William's knowledge and understanding in this area – and, to varying levels, that of three other children in the group – but she was able to offer William something to meet his particular and highly specialized needs. The three other children with experience of magnets needed something else, and the remaining children all needed similar experiences because they were new to magnets and their properties and needed time for further investigation and exploration.

Assessment should *begin* the cycle of teaching and learning and plans should remain flexible until precise knowledge of each individual learner is gleaned. There is always a danger that when planning, educators draw on records from previous years or terms and, if an aspect of the curriculum has not been covered, then the assumption is made that an individual child knows nothing about it. All the children then receive the same starting point according to their *presumed* lack of knowledge. As professional educators we must make it our business to find out what individual children already know and can do and ensure that we do not underestimate the skills, knowledge and understandings the children bring to every learning situation. This can be achieved either through the daily observations of children at play or through conversations with them, as an individual or in a group, about what their understandings (and misunderstandings) might be about a new theme or area of learning. What does the child already know, for example, about writing for different purposes; about selecting and using tools; about numerals over 100; about certain living things and how to care for them? Children bring so much knowledge with them from the lives that they lead away from our settings that it is essential that we establish their individual starting points for learning rather than assuming that they all need the same starting points or the same learning experiences.

Differentiation

While long- and medium-term plans are the concern of the staff as a whole and may well be similar in format, short-term planning should be more responsive to the requirements of individual practitioners. Educators need to adopt strategies that allow for these short-term plans to address the issue of *differentiation*. Differentiation is the key to matching experiences to the developmental needs of children.

In the Foundation Stage, differentiation can be addressed in two ways. Firstly, a practitioner can plan to differentiate a learning experience by knowing the stage of development of the children for whom he or she is responsible and then planning an activity or experience that will take that individual or that group to the 'next steps' in their learning. This is called *differentiation by input*. Alongside this more adult-focused learning, early years practitioners also plan activities and provide resources that are very open-ended, and what children learn will be differentiated by the knowledge and understanding that they bring to the experience. *This is called differentiation by outcome.*

The recent emphasis on the value of whole class teaching in schools has challenged this notion of planning to meet individual needs. While both the national literacy and numeracy strategies emphasize the importance of differentiated questioning and some teachers are highly skilled at this, it remains the case that more whole class teaching has resulted in many children receiving the same undifferentiated diet. Whole class teaching is not appropriate for Foundation Stage children. Apart from the joy of a large group singing together, there are few early learning experiences that are not preferential in a smaller group, where individual young voices can be heard. Sitting still and engaging in relatively passive, adult-dominated learning takes a level of physical control and concentration that is simply too much for most 3-, 4- and 5-year-olds to manage. Consultation with children in the Foundation Stage reveals time and again a desire to be active and a dread of being 'on the carpet' for long periods of time (Ofsted 2004; Sanders *et al.* 2005; OCC 2005, 2006). Observation of classroom practice shows all too frequently how often 4- and 5-year-olds sit for registration, followed by assembly, followed by explanations of the day's activities, followed by adult-focused introductory input. Each valid in its own right perhaps but, placed one after another, a numbing experience in more senses than one. While whole class/group experiences can sometimes have a meaningful place in early education, they must not take the place of experiences that specialist educators know would be more effective in smaller, more intimate circumstances.

As differentiation is so critical to children's development and progress, however, it is important that educators clarify what elements of their planning can be matched more closely to children's differing needs. Differentiation may be concerned with:

- the *concepts, skills, knowledge and attitudes* that are the intended outcomes of an activity/experience;
- whether these concepts are to be introduced/developed/consolidated (the *spiral curriculum*);
- the *activity or experience* itself – different activities and experiences can be vehicles for the same outcomes and differ according to the interests of the children;
- the *introduction* of an activity – more or less detailed, verbal or written, etc.;
- the *process* of an activity, determined by the importance of the outcome, not necessarily uniform, but open to the most effective strategy for the child/group;
- the *outcome* of an activity (if indeed there is one at all), determined by the importance of the process; it may be open to interpretation by the child/group;
- the *support* given to an activity by an adult or other children, which may be minimal or substantial;
- the *resources* planned – different levels and different kinds;
- the *evidence* of learning, which varies according to the intended outcomes;
- the *collection* of evidence – which technique, by whom, when;
- the *assessment* of work – by the adult, child or both;
- by whose *criteria* the assessment takes place – adult, child or both;
- follow-up *action* – what, for whom, how, when.

There is no need for every element of this process to be addressed on every occasion, but it is important that all these elements are open to change and adaptation in order to make learning experiences relevant, meaningful and effective for children. A prompt sheet for supporting the planning of differentiated activities is given on pages 58–9. Rather than offering a format for short-term planning, I think a prompt sheet is more helpful so that, irrespective of the format that suits the individual practitioner, plans can be checked against certain indicators of differentiation. Box 3.3 is offered as a starting point. You may find it helpful to formulate your own list with colleagues from your setting.

Box 3.3   Short-term plans

Differentiation by input
- Why are the children doing this activity; why have we set up these resources?
- What do I intend that they should learn?
- What concepts/skills/knowledge/attitudes are to be introduced/developed/consolidated?

Activity/experience
- What activity/experiences will meet the intended learning outcomes?
- Do the children all need the same activity/experiences?
- Do I need to differentiate the introduction/the process/the outcome?
- Who will give the support or will children work independently?
- What grouping is most appropriate?
- What resources are needed? Are they the same for all children?
- Does the activity/experience meet the learning requirements of children with special needs?

Assessment
- What evidence do I need to gather?
- Will this enable me to assess the intended learning outcomes of the activity/experience?
- Will this be done during or after the activity/experience?
- If evidence is to be recorded by an adult, what vocabulary, actions, behaviours are they looking for? How will the adult record this?
- If evidence is to be recorded by children will they be able to select their own method of recording and then explain it to an adult or their peers?
- Should samples of work be saved or photographs or tape recordings taken?
- In what way might children be involved in assessing their own work?
- Were the intended learning outcomes achieved?
- If not, why not? What do I need to change?
- If the learning was not what I expected, what *did* I learn about the children from the outcomes of the activity?

NB be prepared to note unplanned and unexpected assessments too!

Action
- Do I need to change my short-term planning?
- Does a child/group/the class need to revisit a concept or have further practice of a skill?
- Should a child/the children have experience of working with a different child/children?
- Does a child/group need more support at the next stage of development?
- Does the child/group need different resources to support their learning?

Conclusion

This chapter has been concerned with planning a curriculum that acknowledges the developmental needs of children within the constraints of an externally imposed framework. It has been suggested that this is most easily achieved when long- and medium-term planning are seen as meeting the development of the *curriculum* and short-term planning is seen as meeting the development of the *child*. An early years curriculum is concerned with process above product. An appropriate curriculum is one that meets the needs and interests of children and also introduces children to a range of skills and concepts that are deemed, by adults, to be relevant and desirable for their development. The task of the educator is to fuse together these dual interests and to ensure that children's experiences do not lead them to believe that education is something that is imposed by somebody else. Education should be a dynamic and liberating experience. If children are to be lifelong learners, then their independence and motivation to learn must be cultivated at every stage of their educational journey. The next chapter examines how educators achieve a balance in the activities and experiences they provide and explores the role that adults play in supporting the development of competent young learners.

THE ROLE OF THE ADULT

Making the best use of teaching time

Introduction

The role of the adult, as educator, is inextricably bound up with how children are viewed as learners. As has already been shown, once it is acknowledged that children are competent (albeit inexperienced) learners, then this shifts the way in which adults respond to them and their varied and various abilities. Whatever it is intended that children should learn and however it is intended that they should learn it, the most effective learning is rooted in previous experience (Donaldson 1978; Wood 1988; Meadows 1993). Children are active learners, constantly constructing their own internal model of the world (Wells 1986; Wood 1988; Bronson 2000; Kuhn 2000). By acknowledging this, the educator rejects a 'transmission' approach to teaching where the adult is seen as having, or having access to, knowledge and skills that is their responsibility to transmit to the learner. Instead, the adult adopts what Rowland (1984: 4) describes as an 'interpretive' model of teaching, and which involves 'not only the child's attempt to interpret and assimilate the knowledge and skills offered by the teacher, but also the teacher's growing understandings of the world'. This symbiotic relationship (Pascal *et al.* 1997) is identifiable by its reciprocity – with the adult's style of engagement affecting the child's level of involvement and the child's involvement impacting on the adult's style of engagement with them and their learning.

If we ignore what children already know and can do, then their learning will not be embedded in what is already secure and what already makes sense to them. This sends messages to children that their competences and contributions are not valued and this in turn can have a serious impact on their self-esteem.

The educator as observer

We saw in Chapter 2 that in order to incorporate what children already know and can do, educators need to spend a considerable amount of time finding out what that is. Time for observation needs to be found not just at the beginning of the year or term, but throughout the day, so that planning is constantly informed by observations of children in action as learners. The problem for many practitioners is that sitting still, not obviously engaged in interaction with a child or group of children, seems to be almost immoral! Early childhood educators are so used to orchestrating a myriad of different activities and experiences all at the same time and being immersed in the action that sitting back and simply watching children goes against the grain. Time for observation is critical, however. If practitioners do not watch children as they go about the business of learning, then many important moments in their development and understanding may be missed. Of course, practitioners can and do make observations of children when they are playing or working alongside them, but the nature of these observations is different. Children react and respond in different ways when adults are alongside them, and if adults want to see how children approach activities independently or alongside their peers, then they need to remove themselves from the situation and not be distracted by having more than one role at that particular time.

Making time for observation may seem daunting, but without time being set aside for focused observation of children involved in their learning, practitioners will not collect sufficient information about children as learners and planning will not be rooted in strong enough evidence of what children know and can do. Early childhood educators who spend a significant amount of their time observing children say that the knowledge they gain enables them to plan far more appropriately for the individual child, group or class the next day or week. Time is not wasted in planning for a child or group on an activity that is too easy or too difficult and time is not wasted in repeating or revisiting activities unnecessarily. Time is actually *saved*, because practitioners are able to differentiate their planning on the basis of their increased knowledge about the children in their care.

Practitioners need to make time to observe children during the teaching day. As with so many things in the early learning environment, it is a question of prioritizing time, but if time spent on observation saves time in planning and teaching and makes these more effective, then it is time well spent. One successful way that making time for observation can be achieved is by setting time aside at the short-term planning stage when decisions are made about which activities and experiences the adult is going to support most closely – I call these *adult-focused* activities.

Practitioners are all too aware of how short the learning day can seem and the planning of their own time needs to be undertaken carefully. It also needs to be realistic. Planning needs to identify time for observation rather than it being fitted into snatched moments between planned adult tasks. One way of achieving this is to identify on daily plans firstly, what/who is to be *taught* and secondly, what/who is to be *observed*. In this way, the adult can see whether, given the time available, the two sets of adult-focused activities can be realistically achieved. Planning for observation in this deliberate way may mean that time is taken from time that was previously set aside for direct involvement with children. However, observation is part of the role of the early childhood educator and can only be done when children are at work or play and it should regularly be done when children are working independently. In a letter to all reception practitioners, the National Assessment Agency states quite explicitly that:

> When making a judgement for the FSP (the Foundation Stage Profile), practitioners should draw on at least 80 per cent of evidence from knowledge of the child, observations and anecdotal assessments, and no more than 20 per cent of evidence from adult-directed or focused assessments.
>
> (NAA, July 2006)

Having a recorded plan that shows both the teaching and observation tasks for the day can help practitioners raise the status of classroom observation and give it the time it needs.

The balance of classroom experiences

Making good use of time does not, of course, only apply to observation. An early childhood educator has many roles to fulfil. When looking to make the best use of teaching time, it is necessary to be realistic. In pre-schools and nursery settings the problem is less acute. A team of early years educators can work together to identify those who will support the play and learning of the children and those who will observe their activity. But in schools where there is one teacher and possibly 30 children, then the teacher has one of two choices. The easiest option is to teach the class as though it were a single unit, delivering the same curriculum to all children at the same time. This means that the class size is relatively immaterial because the onus is on the children to receive and inwardly digest the curriculum, with the teacher differentiating where possible through questioning during whole class sessions and some differentiated follow-up activities. Any teacher knows, however, that such strategies will not guarantee *learning*. The same diet of experiences can be delivered to a class of children and their digestion of those experiences will be different. Some children will go hungry, some will end up feeling sick, some will turn up their noses because they don't like what's on offer and some will eat the bits they enjoy and leave the rest on the plate. It is the very fact that children cannot be neatly fitted into a curriculum but need a curriculum that fits *them* that makes teaching so challenging.

There are times when effective teaching and learning happens in a large group. The sharing of a big book, planning for a visitor or singing number rhymes can all be effective as a large group/whole class experience. However, whatever the adult:child ratio in a setting, for the majority of their time, young children need to work and play – individually, in pairs or in small groups – on activities that they will carry out independently. This is not only appropriate, in that young children are motivated by being independent and need to discover and experiment alone without adult intervention all the time, but it is also realistic. If there is a class of 30 and one teacher, then for most of the day, 24 or so children will be learning independently. In a reception or Year 1 class, it is essential that this is appreciated. If the teacher is working intensively with a small group of children on an activity differentiated to meet their learning needs, then the rest of the class have got to get on alone. This has many implications, the first of which is how to make the 'rest' of the class (not in the small group with the teacher) independent but not abandoned learners.

The first strategy is to ensure that the majority of the children are not given low-level activities while they 'wait' for the teacher to have finished their adult-focused teaching. This suggests straight away that children cannot learn productively without an adult present and we know this is not the case. Children learn different things when an adult is around. They learn in different ways. They do not draw on their own resources as well, or the support of their peers, when an adult is directing their thought processes and ideas. Learning independently is valuable and necessary and can be achieved by two things. Firstly, the development of a good learning environment. Secondly, the planning of activities that do not need adult support to be effective vehicles for learning.

An effective environment

An effective environment for independent learning must be:

1 *Indoors and out*: there can be few people now who do not realize that an effective early learning environment needs to have an indoors

and an out. Indeed, when there is a choice between the two, I would always choose 'out'. Learning opportunities for children are totally different outdoors and learning out doors is not simply a matter of putting what is indoors out when the weather is fine. Children in every Foundation Stage setting should be entitled to free access to the outdoors throughout the learning day, for without it a child's capacity to learn is inhibited by the constraints of an indoor learning environment that lacks that natural and spontaneous potential of the living, breathing world.

2 *Natural and not fake:* it must be full of natural resources and real-life experiences. It must pose questions that are meaningful and relevant to the children and not manipulated and drawn for someone else's book of ideas. It must draw on what is happening in the children's world – the builders down the street, the fair in town, the violent wind. It must be full of intrigue, surprises and real-life problems to solve.

3 *New and familiar:* children need opportunities and experiences that are familiar. They need to revisit what is known and rehearse and repeat newly acquired skills and understandings. But they also need what is novel and new and intriguing. They need to be surprised and to be amazed. They need to be challenged to think and to try and explain things they haven't met before and do not yet understand. They need to work out how things work and try out and test what is as yet undiscovered.

4 *Flexible and responsive:* space and resources need to be sufficiently flexible to meet the changing needs of large groups of individual children. Space that is cluttered by tables and chairs cannot make way for models that expand across the floor. Rigid demarcated areas can inhibit the child's desire to take resources from one area and use them creatively in role play or model making. Resources should be as adaptable as possible. Boxes, crates and swathes of materials can be used more imaginatively than games and resources that are deigned for only one purpose. Most plastic resources are less responsive and less inspiring than those that are natural.

5 *Positive and respectful:* how the adult responds to children will establish whether this is an environment in which the children's ideas are valued and respected. It will tell the children whether they can explore and experiment in the certain knowledge that their efforts will be respected and appreciated. They can make mistakes and take risks because they have been shown that this can help their learning and is an important part of getting better at things. Treating children as capable of learning independently gives children a sense of self-worth and self-awareness and can only contribute positively to their growing social and emotional development.

The early childhood educator creates all this way before the day begins. It becomes adapted and refined as children live and work and play in the learning spaces. The environment is developed effectively by establishing, firstly, the reciprocal relationships that will underpin successful independent learning. Secondly, by making best use of the available space for active learning. Thirdly, by trying and refining activities, opportunities and experiences that maximize children's capacity to be independent in their learning and the strategies that support their reliance on each other as learning partners.

There are two kinds of experience that can be planned to enhance children's independence as learners. Alongside the adult-focused activities there should be:

- adult-initiated activities;
- child-initiated activities.

Adult-focused activities

It is clearly part of the early childhood educators' repertoire to work directly with children to support their learning and extend their thinking. Once practitioners have carried out observations of children and found out about their interests and preoccupations, then they will want to draw some children together to teach a new skill or introduce a new concept. They may also want to revisit some activity or learning outcome if there have been misunderstandings or if they notice that some children need greater support than others to reach the next stage of learning. They may need to challenge some children whose thinking and understanding is in advance of their peers or work with children who are particularly vulnerable and need to have more adult support than usual. Then, as has been mentioned earlier, practitioners need to plan time for their focused observations and this comes during their adult-focused time. Practitioners are often very skilled at identifying learning intentions, planning an activity for a group of children and supporting them to learn what has been identified for their learning needs. However, as I have said, planning for and ensuring the quality of the activities of the rest of the class is more challenging.

Adult-initiated activities

Adult-initiated activities are one of the three experiences that adults will plan in an effective learning environment. These are activities that are planned by the practitioner but which – once introduced – will be undertaken independently by the children. This has to be the case, of course, as the practitioner has gone to teach the adult-focused activity. The first step towards planning for adult-initiated activities is realizing that the nature of what children do when they are working independently is significantly different from the nature of an activity when children work with the teacher. *Activities that children will be doing independently are not simply the same as adult-focused activities but without the teacher there.* Adult-initiated activities differ from adult-focused activities in various ways.

Adult-initiated activities need to:

- be sufficiently *clear* for children to be able to work without constantly checking that what they are doing is 'right';
- be sufficiently *motivating* that they will sustain the interest and involvement of the children so that they do not interrupt the teacher;
- be sufficiently *open-ended* for children to be able to extend them in ways that interest and engage them until the adult comes alongside again.

These activities are often, though not exclusively, at either end of the learning continuum. They are either repeating or rehearsing what is familiar – giving children the opportunity to try independently that which previously they might have done with support from the adult. Or they are introducing something new – so that children are left to discover the properties of materials or resources, or to test out ideas or solve problems around something that is novel and intriguing.

The key is the open-endedness. The minute that an activity is so tightly prescribed by an adult that there is clearly only one way of doing it – and that's the adult's way – then children will repeatedly come to check that what they are doing is 'right'. If practitioners want uninterrupted teaching time for adult-focused activities, then a great deal of consideration needs to be given to these activities that children are to undertake independently.

This does not mean of course that the *practitioner* will not go to the children working on these adult-initiated activities and have conversations with them about their ideas and solutions and answer their questions, but this will be done *when the practitioner is ready*. The adult should be in control of their own time. This support for the independent activities – 'spinning the plates' as it is sometimes called – will occur after the practitioner has finished one focused activity and before starting the next. There is a world of difference between practitioners being in control of when they move from one role to the next and being at the mercy of the children, doing little more than servicing their needs, because the planned activities all need adult input at much the same level at much the same time.

Most of the children in an early years setting will, most of the time, be working independently, so it is crucial that the activities in which they are engaged are worth while and bring about effective learning. Many children spend far too much of their day on independent activities for these to be mere time-fillers. It is necessary to challenge the notion that the only worthwhile learning occurs when a teacher is there. This implies that any learning that occurs when children are working independently is of little value and this patently is not true, for we have already seen that the learning that children achieve prior to receiving any kind of formal education is very effective and usually self-driven. Children are learning all the time ... and only a small amount of that time is spent anywhere near a 'teacher'!

Child-initiated activity

There is a third kind of activity that is central to high-quality early years settings and that is activity that is initiated by the child. Child-initiated activity is vital to the acknowledgement of children as competent learners. It is through such activity that young children make sense of their world, and learn to explore, experiment and take risks (Moyles 1989). The place of play is fully explored in Chapter 7, but suffice to say in this context that child-initiated activities encourage children to make their own choices and decisions about what they will do, the resources and equipment they will use and the processes and outcomes of the experience. Child-initiated learning is at the cornerstone of good Foundation Stage practice for it allows the child to try new skills, to play alongside other children and develop socially, to use their imagination and creativity and try out things that are fascinating and preoccupying them at the time. Child-initiated activity is not the same as a child being given play resources and then being directed in how to use them by the adult. So, for example, if the adult tells the child to build a castle for Rapunzal from the wooden blocks, or if the adult puts outfits from the Three Bears' story into the home corner and asks a group to act out the story, or when the adult reads *Going On A Bear Hunt* (Rosen 1993) and then tells the children to re-enact the story in the sand-tray – this is not child-initiated learning. The moment that an adult gives a child an outcome to achieve, then the activity ceases to be child-initiated. There are many times when an adult legitimately uses play resources and initiates what children will do with them, but this makes the activity adult-initiated and not child-initiated.

No early learning environment can be effective without high-quality child-initiated learning, but this is the learning that is most often a challenge, particularly for inexperienced practitioners or for those who were not trained to work with young children. Because children can become so easily involved in play, it is often child-initiated learning that is most abandoned. Children are 'occupied' so the adult leaves them to it. Supporting and extending learning through play is a highly skilled business and all early childhood educators need to understand that for play to be of high quality, it needs to be supported in just the same way as adult-initiated learning (see Chapter 7). So, within the learning situation, practitioners must interact with children at play where and when this is appropriate. They must observe the learning that is taking place in play situations and review and revisit this with children at some point in the day that is appropriate. In this way, play is supported and develops and it is given the same status as all the other learning that is taking place. Neither adult-initiated learning nor child-initiated learning will survive or thrive without adult support at key moments in the process. Without adult support and interest, both these activities can rapidly become abandoned learning rather than independent learning.

The balance of classroom activities

In Foundation Stage settings then, there should be a balance between these three types of activity – adult-focused, adult-initiated and child-initiated. I find it helpful to see these three types of activity as the three corners of a triangle (see Fig. 4.1). The differences between the three activities can be summarized as follows:

- *child-initiated:* activity that children control in terms of experience, time and resources;
- *adult-initiated:* activities that arise from adult planning; sufficiently open-ended for children to work on independently until the adult is ready to intervene;
- *adult-focused:* individual, pair or group work, usually differentiated by input; opportunities for observation; the focus of adult time.

How the balance is maintained between these three types of experience will rest with the practitioner and will change from day to day and sometimes session to session. It will certainly change according to the age of the children, because the younger the children the more the emphasis needs to be on child-initiated learning. What is powerful about this triangle model is that it works for whatever kind of learning situation is planned. It makes no difference whether children are engaged in an integrated day – experiencing different areas of learning simultaneously – or in a session where all the children are

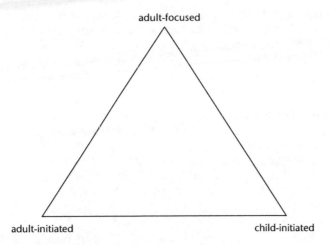

adult-focused

adult-initiated   child-initiated

Figure 4.1 The balance of learning experiences

engaged in mathematical experiences at the same time. The principle of needing a balance of experiences within an early learning environment still applies. When there are a number of adults in the setting – as in a nursery school or day nursery – then this too will change the balance of the experiences. It may be that with two adults constantly available, one engages in adult-focused work while the other undertakes observations. It may be that one leads an adult-focused activity indoors, while another leads one outdoors. The permutations are many and varied. However, for the lone teacher in the school classroom, the movement of the adult between these activities can be summarized as follows:

1 The teacher works with an individual or small group on an adult-focused task.
2 The rest of the children are engaged on either adult-initiated or child-initiated activities.
3 These activities must enable children to be independent of the teacher so that they do not need to interrupt the adult-focused task.
4 The teacher completes the adult-focused task and moves to both the adult-initiated and child-initiated activities in order to support and extend these experiences as appropriate.
5 Independent learning should not be abandoned learning. Adult involvement in all activities is crucial if they are to have status and purpose.
6 Once children working independently have been adequately supported, the teacher returns to the next adult-focused activity.
7 The rest of the children move independently between adult-

initiated and child-initiated activities until/unless the teacher draws them to a adult-focused task. (How children move from one activity to the next is the subject of Chapter 9.)

8 *All* classroom activities are shared at a review time at some point during the day (see Chapter 9).

One interesting feature of the triangle of learning experiences in practice is that different activities sit at different points of the triangle on different occasions. For example, the practitioner may introduce a mathematical game to a group one day as an adult-focused activity and then once children have become familiar with the rules of play, it can become an adult-initiated activity. Equally, the practitioner may lead a discussion with a group of children as an adult-focused session before leaving children to follow up the discussion by designing a layout for the outdoor climbing equipment independently as an adult-initiated task. Sometimes children will have heard a story in an adult-focused session that – several days later – appears in the role-play area as spontaneous play (very different from the adult directing children to play out the story of the Three Bears). Conversely, children may engage in block play or water play that reveals to the adult who is observing them that they would benefit from an adult-focused input around a particular skill or area of knowledge or understanding.

Figure 4.2 summarizes these points and demonstrates the vital interaction between assessment, planning and teaching. Once a practitioner uses the triangle to plan for the balance of learning experiences within the Foundation Stage, then it can be seen that this leads to different learning opportunities. Figure 4.3 shows how:

- *Adult-focused* activities are concerned with **intended learning** – the adult plans an activity and, by and large, that is what the children learn.
- *Adult-initiated* activities are concerned with **potential learning** – the adult has specific learning intentions in mind when he or she selects resources and tasks, but when left to work or play independently, the children may take the learning a different way and end up with different learning outcomes.
- *Child-initiated* activities are concerned with **spontaneous learning** – the adult may have purchased the resources or set up some experiences to begin with, but children approach these in varied and individual ways and follow their own lines of enquiry making their learning spontaneous and unpredictable.

From this explanation it can be seen even more clearly how important it is that the adult observes and evaluates all the learning experiences that are taking place in their setting. If the adult only observes children engaged in adult-focused activity, they are gathering evidence of the

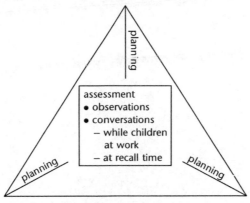

adult-focused: individual, pair or group work, usually differentiated by input; opportunity for observation; the focus of adult time.

Independent, not abandoned learning

adult-initiated: activities that arise from adult planning; sufficiently open-ended for children to work on independently until the adult is ready to intervene.

child-initiated: activities that children control in terms of experience, time and resources.

Figure 4.2 The balance of learning experiences in the Foundation Stage

most predictable kind. While it will be possible to see that some children grasp a new concept or skill more readily than others, the range of what the children are learning is fairly limited to what the adult has introduced. However, when observing adult-initiated activities, the adult can see whether or not the children take the activity or resources where they had intended or change the learning outcomes and become interested in something quite different. This lets the adult know – firstly, whether she picked a good enough challenge for the children to follow independently, or whether the children's minds and imaginations diverted their plans down a more interesting and intriguing (for them) path. Either way, their observations can be used to plan what experiences and opportunities to provide next for that group or individual. Finally, when observing the child-initiated learning, the adult has no idea what they may see children doing or learning. Children at play provide the richest source of observational evidence. Because of the divergent thinking that takes place when children are at play, the adult will find out a whole variety of things about what the children know, are interested in and can do ... and none of it can be predetermined.

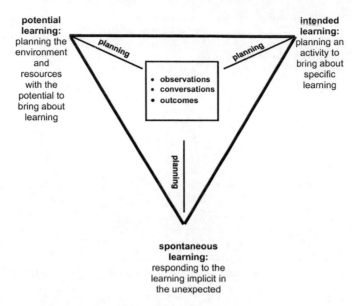

Figure 4.3 The balance of learning opportunities

Adult-initiated learning

There is no doubt that planning effective adult-initiated and child-initiated activities is harder than planning those that are adult-focused. By and large, most practitioners are now skilled at selecting an activity that will bring about intended learning and supporting children to reach that point of learning. It is far more of a challenge to provide for adult-initiated learning and to support and observe child-initiated learning. Chapter 7 looks at the development of play in detail, but here I want to focus some more on adult-initiated activities.

We have seen that effective adult-initiated activities are designed to support children's independence as learners. In the adult's mind is some potential learning that the selection of certain resources might bring about. Adult-initiated activities usually either introduce something very new for children to explore or investigate, or return to something familiar with which children are confident and secure. In either case the activities need to be sufficiently open-ended for the child or children to remain on task until the adult (if they are the only adult in the room) is ready to come and engage with their learning again.

Here are some examples of adult-initiated activities that practitioners have found work well in reception classes with children working near to the Early Learning Goals. Do remember that some of the most effective adult-initiated activities are those that rehearse and repeat what is familiar – a game, the making of a book, the mixing of paints; or what is new – what magnets can do, how to put something, for example, a clock, back together again, what it feels like when you have mixed glue and paint.

Early Learning Goals	Adult-initiated Learning
Personal, social and emotional development	
Be confident to try new activities, initiate ideas and speak in a familiar group	Children devise their own game that they then teach another group later in the day
Have a developing awareness of their own needs, views and feelings and be sensitive to the needs, views and feelings of others	Children plan a picnic meal using magazines from which to cut out pictures. They have to discuss a menu that will include everyone's needs – so being sensitive to allergies, those who do not eat meat and so on
Communication, Language and Literacy	
Use their phonic knowledge to write simple regular words and make phonetically plausible attempts at more complex words	A pretend visitor comes to the classroom during the night – a wolf, an owl … whatever will intrigue your children. The visitor writes to the children and leaves the letters in interesting places – both indoors and outdoors. The children write back independently and leave their messages and letters in a designated place
Attempt writing for different purposes, using features of different forms such as lists, stories and instructions	A group creates a fruit salad. They have a recipe and have to write a shopping list and fetch the ingredients from the school kitchen. The recipe is in pictures and words so that they are all responsible for washing and cutting up the fruit and making the fruit salad for the class to eat later
Problem-solving, Reasoning and Numeracy	
Use everyday words to describe position	Children given card, pens, pencils, etc. Instructions are to plan a route on a map to find some hidden treasure – or the way to the park – or … whatever will interest your children. One child then gives instructions to another child about which directions to take on the map to find … whatever is to be found! They then swap
Use developing mathematical ideas and methods to solve practical problems	Planning a party for the local old folk. How to find out what they want to eat and drink. How many pieces of bread, fillings, strawberries, cups of juice, etc. will be needed. Counting, sorting, estimating, recording

Knowledge and Understanding of the World

Find out about, and identify, some features of living things, objects and events they observe	Give children boxes of the same size with lids. Tell them their task is to go into the outdoor area and find enough XXXX (dependent on season, e.g. leaves, bark, seeds, cones) to fill the box and on return to the classroom identify them and find out some of their key features (from some judiciously selected resource books). Then plan a quiz for their friends about what they found
Find out about their environment, and talk about those features they like and dislike	Go out for a walk in the outdoor area and take photos of their likes and dislikes. Print their most favourite/least favourite and present in a group display for rest of class to discuss

Physical Development

Use a range of large and small equipment	Leave children with a range of small skills equipment, e.g. soft balls, hoops, skittles, etc. Their task is to design, in twos, a circuit of different skills for two other children to complete. The circuit must take at least 3 minutes – and must be timed
Travel around, under, over and through balancing and climbing equipment	Design an assault course. Ensure that there is – 'around', 'under', 'over' and 'through' within in it. Draw cards for each 'station' of the course that explain what is to be done ready for another group to try

Creative Development

Explore shape and form in three dimensions	Give children the challenge of designing and making a chair that will take the weight of a given doll – or toy – or dinosaur – or whatever will interest your children. They have to work in twos and tell them their efforts will be tested at the end of the session
Recognize and explore how sounds can be changed	Leave bottles and water on table. Children to select a simple tune (in pairs) and fill the bottles so that the correct notes are sounded. Rest of class to see if they recognize the tune when everyone together on the carpet

Use of teacher time

Looking at the balance between adult-focused, adult-initiated and child-initiated learning gives each adult action a clear purpose. Each role is planned, it is deliberate and, most of all, for the lone teacher in the Foundation Stage classroom, it acknowledges that the learning that takes place when there is one teacher and 30 children has to be planned for realistically. The aim is to support children's independent learning and to make it of such high quality that the adult is released to focus on their own planned activities and not sidetracked by unnecessary or uncalled for demands. I am not suggesting that, by using this management strategy, children will *never* interrupt! Some children – for justifiable reasons – will occasionally need help or reassurance, but by planning particularly adult-initiated activities with care, the number of interruptions will be minimized. A culture of independence surfaces, where children know that they do not need to rely on the adult at every turn and they come to enjoy their autonomy.

The recorded interactions between a teacher and her reception class (Fisher 1996) provide fascinating data that chronicles the growing independence of children and the changes in their attitudes and behaviour towards their teacher. At the beginning of the school year, in the autumn term, the children related to the teacher in ways that revealed their dependence on them:

Do you want me to do any more?

Can I stop this now please?

As the children became more independent, they seem to revise their concept of what 'being a pupil' meant, started to revel in their new-found independence and ignored the teacher almost completely. During the spring term the teacher was often left alone for 15–25 minutes without interruption, allowing them to get on with their adult-focused activities. Then, towards the end of the spring term, the relationship changed once again and the children began to refer back to the teacher, but the nature of the exchanges had altered. The children were no longer seeking reassurance, but were coming to their teacher simply to share the pleasure of a discovery or an achievement or specifically to request their support:

Child: Do you want to see the model I've made?
Child: I can't do my 'a's.
Teacher: Do you want me to help?
Child: Yes.
Child: Can you help me finish the story I'm writing?

The children's perceptions of the role of the teacher had changed. Because they had independence and a considerable degree of autonomy in the classroom, it seemed as though they came to see the teacher as yet another valuable resource to enable them to complete their tasks in hand.

Worksheets

We cannot leave the subject of independent learning without addressing, head on, the issue of worksheets. Sometimes practitioners feel that they need written evidence that something has been learnt, and I hope that Chapter 2 has dispelled that particular myth. For more than any other reason, worksheets are given to children to keep them occupied while the practitioner does other things. My emphasis on the importance of adult-initiated activities should demonstrate that independent learning must be both dynamic and purposeful. I would suggest that worksheets are neither of these things. When tempted to offer a worksheet to a young child, the following issues should be considered:

1 The difference between many children's literacy skills and their conceptual understanding is great. It is possible for children to have a relatively sophisticated understanding of a concept and yet be unable to record this because the worksheet uses language that they cannot read or don't understand or their own written language is not sufficiently developed.
2 Worksheet answers can be copied or guessed at. Since so many of them require gaps to be filled in, the chances of doing either or both are quite high. All this may give evidence of, is how able another child is on the same table.
3 A worksheet restricts what a young child can tell you about what they know and understand. If children devise their own ways of recording knowledge and understanding, then they will select ways that make sense to them and that give all the information they want to share.
4 Worksheets clone children into producing the same answers to fill in uniform gaps.
5 Children frequently spend more time colouring in worksheets than they do engaging with the concepts behind them. By the time the worksheet is finished, most young children are hard pushed to tell you what it was about.
6 Young children spend far *less* time completing most worksheets than adults spend laboriously drawing – or photocopying – them.

It is unreasonable to criticize things without offering viable alternatives, so:

• if *evidence of learning* is needed, *watch* and *listen* to the child and record what they do and say;
• if *recorded evidence* is needed, let the child devise their own ways of recording;
• if *time-fillers* are needed, think again; address the issue of

independent learning positively and initiate activities that are valuable and valid.

Differentiation

Child-initiated activities will be, by their very nature, differentiated by outcome. Children's own decisions about activities are a reflection of their ability, their knowledge, their understanding and their skill. Observation of these activities will inform the practitioner about these, and about the child's attitudes and motivations. They show the child's confidence and self-esteem, their perseverance and persistence and their willingness to try new things or their need to repeat what is familiar.

Adult-initiated activities are best planned so that differentiation will be by outcome. Sometimes it is appropriate that an activity is planned for a group of children of certain ability and that this activity is targeted exclusively at them. But more often than not, the very nature of an open-ended, problem-solving task is that children will tackle the task at their own level. As long as there is no 'right answer' and children know that their own solution will be valued, then they will differentiate these activities in their own way. Differentiation by outcome places an emphasis on the practitioner learning *about* children through the selected activity, as much as children learning *from* the activity.

Adult-focused activities are most likely to be differentiated by input. In other words, the practitioner has planned to work with a group of children who have reached the same stage at the same time and will benefit from being introduced to, or consolidating, or revisiting an activity, task or experience together. The adult's knowledge of the needs of these children will have come directly from their first-hand observations of them at work or play independently and as they work with adults.

Motivation and perseverance

One of the greatest benefits to early childhood educators of encouraging independent learners is that, by and large, children remain motivated learners. This means that an adult spends less time coercing children to complete a directed task, something that takes up both time and energy. It also means that children usually remain on task for longer and therefore are less likely to make demands on adult time, which is an added bonus. Children, like adults, lack concentration when they are required to do something that they find meaningless and irrelevant. All too often this can happen when the activities that practitioners plan do not take account of children's own experiences and interests. Not that children should only ever engage in activities they *choose* to, but how much easier it is – for both children and adults – when children are motivated to pursue a task rather than having to be coerced to do so. Successful Foundation Stage practitioners 'go with the flow' of children, capturing and using their current interests and absorptions to plan the curriculum. If children's experiences are not embedded in their current needs and interests, then an activity can appear pointless to them and they either rush to finish it or simply do not give it adequate attention. This is when practitioners get interrupted with cries of 'I've finished!' ... and we all know how aggravating that can be.

Status and quality

Some practitioners are concerned that giving children too much independence will result in outcomes of inferior quality, especially if these require recording. There are a number of ways of ensuring that this is not the case and most of these hinge on the adult's own attitudes to the activities that are going on. In order for children to value their own work, whether it is adult-focused, adult-initiated or child-initiated, it has to have status. Status can be conferred by the child and their own involvement and pride in their efforts and ideas. Status is also conferred by the adult, however, who confirms or denies the importance of different activities through a myriad of different messages – given both explicitly and implicitly. All Foundation Stage activities should be worth while. If they are not, then they should not be given houseroom. Adult-focused, adult-initiated and child-initiated activities should all be of value to the adult and to the children, and should all be planned for specific learning purposes. The three kinds of activity will be given equal status if they are:

- *happening at the same time* as each other, not one always preceding the others because it is seen by the practitioner as being more important;
- *observed, monitored and assessed* by the practitioner when children are in action;
- *the subject of conversations* in order to find out what children have done and discovered, and to show interest in their efforts and achievements where observation has not been possible;
- *used to inform future planning*.

In this way, the activities and experiences all have a clear purpose and the use of precious teaching time is maximized.

Conclusion

The role the adult adopts in the Foundation Stage learning environment is the key to the quality of experiences planned for the child. If early childhood practitioners are to emulate the success of children's earliest educators, then their role will be most successful when they facilitate and support children's learning and respond to what children initiate (Sharp 2000). While Foundation Stage practitioners are responsible for transmitting the values of society and introducing children to areas of learning and experience that they might not otherwise discover for themselves, learning is most successful when the strategies that adults use enable children to own the experiences as much as possible and to see the relevance of those experiences to their own lives. Early childhood educators manage a complex orchestration of activities and experiences within the Foundation Stage environment. What is crucial to the success of the enterprise is to remember that when involved in early years education, practitioners will not be directly teaching all of the children all of the time. Indeed, the reality of the situation is that more children will spend more of their day working and playing independently than they will working with an adult. It is vital then for practitioners to focus their attention on those activities that encourage independence and autonomy. They should be demanding and challenging and not planned in order to fill in time until the adult is free. By looking at the balance between adult-focused, adult-initiated and child-initiated activities, early childhood practitioners can make their role both responsive to the children's needs for independence and realistic in terms of their own need to spend targeted time with individuals and groups. The next chapter explores a variety of ways of encouraging children to be independent learners and considers how the learning environment can be organized to facilitate this.

ENCOURAGING INDEPENDENCE

Environments that develop children's learning autonomy

Introduction

Early childhood educators who spend focused time scaffolding the learning of children and making regular observations of children in action have already created a learning environment that encourages independence. But neither of these crucial activities can be achieved satisfactorily if the adult is constantly being interrupted with the well-worn cry 'Please miss ... what do I do next?' In order for children to be independent learners, they need a learning environment that facilitates their independence. As far as possible, children need to manage their own resources, space and time. If children are to work independently, they need to be given systems and strategies that enable them to manage their own learning environment and sustain their own learning.

Children's early experiences

I have already suggested that to adopt effective strategies at school and in other early years settings, we should examine more closely the learning environments in which children have spent time prior to starting their more formal education. In these environments, children have been successful learners because:

- the world around them is an interesting place;
- young children are naturally curious;
- children want to explore, to experiment and to become competent;
- in the home and the community there are countless opportunities to do this as and when children are inspired to do so;

- young children meet new and varied learning experiences in many contexts – the kitchen, the street, on the television, in the park;
- there is almost always an adult on hand to ask questions of and to learn from – responding to the child's queries and questioning.

Children's learning environments, therefore, need to provide the following elements:

- new and interesting experiences;
- activities that encourage children's natural curiosity;
- opportunities to explore, experiment and become competent;
- a timetable that is sufficiently flexible to give the children some control over when and how experiences/activities/tasks are carried out;
- learning that occurs in a range of contexts – the classroom, outside of the classroom, on visits, on trips, in workplaces, in the street;
- access to adults and other expert and experienced people (including other children) who will answer and raise questions and pose challenges to extend learning and understanding.

Creating an environment for independent learners

Learning out of doors

> The best classroom and the richest cupboard are roofed only by the sky
>
> (Margaret McMillan 1919)

The outdoor environment can no longer be thought of as an added extra but should be an entitlement for all children learning in the Early Years Foundation Stage. If we believe that children thrive and learn best in environments that stimulate their curiosity and open up their imagination, then we see this most naturally when children are out of doors. Most children are naturally drawn to the outdoors. There, they find opportunities to explore and to investigate, to observe and to pose questions, to feel free and uninhibited. The outside environment offers a rich world of learning possibilities – usually so much richer than the somewhat fake world of the indoor environment. How much better to use acorns than plastic beads for counting, to hide letter shapes in bushes than write them in 'sounds' books, to investigate a bird or a worm in its natural habitat rather than looking at pictures, to feel the wind in your hair rather than get eye strain from artificial lighting. The EYFS, for example, reminds practitioners to:

> Recognise the mathematical potential of the outdoor environment, for example, for children to discover things about shape, distance,

and measures, through their physical activity (Principles Into Practice card for Problem-solving, Reasoning and Numeracy)

The outdoor learning environment is 'a complete learning environment which can cater for all children's needs – cognitive, emotional, social and physical' (Bilton 2002: ix). Sometimes the outdoor environment mirrors what takes place indoors and sometimes it offers something quite unique. What makes an outdoor area effective, however, is that it is seen as an integral part of the teaching and learning space to be planned for and assessed in exactly the same way as spaces indoors. It should provide for the flow of learning between the two environments. The highly informative ILEA document *A Curriculum for Young Children: Outdoor Play* (1990: 6) identifies three different ways of linking the indoor and outdoor environments:

1 the inside can be *transferred* outside – that is elements from the inside are physically moved outside – like rebuilding the home corner outdoors;
2 the provision is *linked* or *paralleled* – for instance, inside water play using tubes and bottles to move water can be paralleled outside using guttering, drainpipes and buckets;
3 an outside activity can be *contrasted* with an activity indoors – small-scale painting inside can be contrasted with the use of large sheets of paper and decorating brushes outside.

However, there are things that happen outside that simply cannot happen adequately anywhere else. Experiencing weather and the seasons is rich and real outdoors and second-hand if children are inside. The thrill of growing and cultivating living things has so many more possibilities outside than in the indoor environment. The opportunities for being away from adults and finding spaces to be alone and secret are so much greater in a good outdoor area than inside. Most of all, there is a sense of size and scale about being out of doors that cannot be replicated indoors. The chance to run, to leap, to feel free and to use your whole body, so often too cramped and constrained inside, is a compelling reason for most children to be outside for much of the time. And in today's world, of course, there are many reasons why this matters. Too many children as we know are having too little exercise. They are constrained by adult fears for their safety, or by having no garden or green space near their homes to play in, or by having no adult with the time to take them swimming or to play football. Children in our society need outdoor spaces more than ever to offer all the rich and tantalizing possibilities of outdoor learning but within a safe and secure environment. That does not mean, however, an environment without risk. Risk is a valuable part of children's learning experience. It enables children to learn to make judgements about the world and their own capabilities. It gives them opportunities to extend themselves and to try something challenging, exhilarating and satisfying. It is up to staff within a setting to have assessed the environment so that the risks are reasonable and in keeping with the principles of early childhood education that promote challenge, experimentation and error as features of high-quality learning.

The role of the adult

The role of the adult outdoors should mirror precisely the role of the adult indoors. It does not suddenly become supervisory because the space is larger and some of the children are involved in physically challenging activity. The role of the adult remains to work on adult-focused tasks with individuals or groups; to be moving between groups to support and extending children's spontaneous learning as and when required; to observe children at work and play. Managing an outdoor environment in this way is, of course, far harder when there is no second adult. All Foundation Stage settings should have at least two adults, qualified to teach young children and knowledgeable about their learning needs. To expect one adult to manage an indoor and outdoor learning environment is entirely unreasonable and, as has already been said, the UK government should have made a far stronger stand than in the EYFS about ratios in reception classes.

The weather

UK weather is not as bad as we sometimes imagine (just think how relatively few playtimes are lost to bad weather). The provision of a covered veranda should protect the children from both extremes of temperature – the sun in this country is a far greater threat to children's health than rain. The Danish early childhood educators say that there is no such thing as bad weather – only bad clothing. Good-quality provision offers children macs and boots to change into when going outside. Bad weather offers a wealth of learning opportunities that simply cannot be experienced if the weather is always fine. Just think what can be learnt through playing in puddles!

Designing an outdoor area

Clearly, the design of an outdoor learning environment will be dependent on whether or not there is direct access to the outdoors and what opportunities lie outside. Having said that, most classrooms could make better use of the available space – such as it is – than they currently do. It is important to explore the possibilities and to take on board whatever is feasible while lobbying for greater provision.

A high-quality outdoor learning environment should have:

- a landscape with:
  - grassed areas and hard surface areas,
  - tracks using different surfaces (e.g. bricks, cobblestones),
  - shaded areas and sunlit areas,
  - places to run and places to sit,
  - places to hide,
  - areas to cultivate and areas in which to encourage natural habitats,
  - trees, shrubs, bushes, flowers and vegetables,
  - animals and birds to care for,
  - a space for performances;
- areas to encourage the development of gross motor skills:
  - swings and ropes,
  - slides,
  - climbing frames,
  - mats to jump on or over,
  - structures for balancing and jumping between – all sited on appropriate safe surfaces,
  - bicycles and tricycles,
  - wagons and wheelbarrows to push and pull,
  - scooters,
  - bouncing and rocking equipment – and pathways to travel on without interrupting the activities of other children;
- activities that encourage fine motor development:
  - balls and bean bags,
  - hoops,
  - quoits,
  - woodwork table,
  - creative area,
  - small sand and water play area;
- resources that encourage exploration and discovery:
  - construction materials,
  - sand-pit/tray(s),
  - water tray(s),
  - role-play props,
  - roadways and playmats,
  - design and creative materials,
  - unstructured materials,
  - music and rhythm materials; some teachers acquire large carpets that can be put on concrete outside the classroom to enable children to sit and work;

- resources that encourage imagination and expression:
  - drapes for hideaways,
  - a garden shed,
  - boxes and crates,
  - masks, cloaks, hats and shoes,
  - puppets,
  - an old boat,
  - large wheels and long ropes,
  - logs and branches.

Organising the Indoor Learning Environment

Space

When early years practitioners think about what they would like to have in their learning environments to stimulate and extend children's learning, they usually find there simply is not enough space. In discussion with a group of experienced reception and Key Stage 1 teachers about what they would *ideally* like to have, the following list emerged:

The indoor area

- carpeted area(s) for:
  - sharing work,
  - jigsaws,
  - games,
  - construction,
  - grouping together;
- home/imaginative/role-play area;
- sand-tray(s) – wet and dry;
- water tray;
- interest/discovery/exploratory area;
- bed for children to rest;
- quiet area;
- writing/mark-making area;
- reading area;
- listening area;
- music area;
- table tops;
- creative area:
  - gluing,
  - painting,
  - cutting,

- dough,
- clay,
- plasticine,
- modelling;
- computer area.

The outdoor area

- a garden area;
- trees, bushes and seats;
- large apparatus;
- an area for small apparatus (e.g. hoops, bean bags);
- an area for bikes, tricycles and trucks;
- a *large* sand-pit (I now recommend that architects and landscape designers think of golf bunkers!);
- an area for water play;
- an area for construction;
- an area for imaginative play;
- an area, in shade, for mark-making, reading and talking
- an amphitheatre for 'performance'.

It might be useful to draw up your own list about what you believe young children would benefit from in their learning environments. I suspect the lists would be very similar – and equally long. In doing this exercise it is important to concentrate on what children *need* and not, as yet, on the constraints of making this a reality. The chances are that there will not be enough space in many settings for all these areas and experiences. So how should decisions be made about what to leave in and what to take out?

The most important question for early childhood educators to ask is, what do young learners need most? This should provide the foundation for all other decisions that will be made. Sometimes it is all too easy to be distracted by other issues. Our nursery has always been planned like this; the resources and equipment all have to be packed away at the end of our playgroup session; the caretaker hates clearing up sand ... and so on. At the end of the day, however, practitioners are concerned with what is in the best interests of children and should not be swayed from using this as their yardstick. If space is at a premium then, inevitably, some areas will have to be left out ... or at best rotated with other areas. However, those areas that staff have deemed to be invaluable will form the basis of the learning experiences of children and the decisions will have been made using the adults' professional knowledge about the learning needs of young children.

In many early years classrooms, in particular, the majority of space is taken up by tables and chairs. Before decisions are made about prioritizing the use of the rest of the space, it is important to consider whether space given to a table and chair for every child is space well used. Bearing in mind the need for young children to engage in active learning and practical, first-hand experiences, it is worth giving some thought to the following issues:

- tables and chairs take up a great deal of floor space;
- the removal of *one* set of tables and six to eight chairs could create space for:
  - a sand or water tray,
  - a carpet area,
  - an investigation/interactive area,
  - a listening area, etc.;
- any one of these areas might be in use for *most* of the learning day;
- are tables and chairs, for every child at the same time, needed for *most* of the day or only occasionally?
- which use of space is most valuable for the young learner?

Box 5.1 Making decisions about the use of space

- draw up a list of those areas that are valuable for young learners;
- prioritize them in order to make adjustments for the available space;
- eliminate those that are of little value or seldom used;
- plan the remaining areas within the space available;
- be able to justify decisions on sound educational grounds.

Allocating space

Once a list of areas is established, it is helpful to plan these so that the learning environment encourages purposeful, interactive experiences. It is a good idea to experiment with possible design layouts on paper *before* starting to move heavy pieces of furniture around the room. In the outdoors, of course, many decisions will be constrained by the large fixed equipment already in place – such as climbing frames, resilient surfaces or sand-pits.

Once the areas are allocated space, then these can be named and, if appropriate, labelled, so that the children are clear about what areas are appropriate for what activity. The naming and labelling gives a sense of order to what can otherwise be a very confusing environment. It might help to imagine going into an unfamiliar supermarket and looking for washing powders or cereals without signs identifying where these are to be found. Clearly, identified areas for learning make the organization and the management of the learning environment so much more straightforward for both practtioners and children.

Box 5.2 Principles about using space

- some areas will be determined by fixtures such as sinks and floor surfaces (indoors) and resilient surfaces and sand-pits (outdoors) and these need allocating first;
- each area needs sufficient space for children to move around comfortably and safely;
- some learning experiences naturally benefit from being placed alongside others (e.g. the home corner can extend to a café that can benefit from being near the block play area for interrelated play);
- some areas benefit from *not* being near others (e.g. the listening area or book corner will probably be disturbed by the activity in the construction area; bikes and trikes must not be a hazard for other play taking place outside);
- there need to be areas where children can work independently, in small groups and as a large group, both indoors and out.

Resources

Once space has been allocated, then all the resources that will be needed in any one area should be made available. Children who are going to be independent in their learning need to know where to find resources and where to return them once they have been used.

The choice of equipment should once again be determined by the needs of the young learner. If we want children to continue to explore, investigate and discover, then we should select resources and equipment that encourage this to go on. Sometimes the resources that offer some of the greatest learning potential are the most expensive. Wooden blocks, for example, may seem expensive to those operating on a slim budget, but if they provide children with a wealth of experiences in aesthetics, mathematics, the processes of science and problem-solving (Gura 1992), then they offer good value for money. Most times, however, the best and most appealing resources are those that cost nothing at all. The use of natural resources for a whole range of learning is not only aesthetically appealing but means that resources change with the seasons and with children's interests rather than being made of materials that fade, tarnish and deteriorate in quality – but which are not thrown away because their initial cost was so high.

Money can be wasted on resources that might preferably be replaced by natural resources that take time rather than money to collect. A Sunday afternoon walk, a visit to relatives or an outing to certain shops can result in a whole host of wonderful resources for sorting, printing, selling, describing or investigating. A high-quality outdoor learning environment often has these resources in abundance ... and on the 'doorstep'.

The first task in organizing most learning environments is to *gather together* what already exists – and then be quite ruthless with anything that is out of date, inappropriate, chewed or has pieces missing. If space is at a premium, then everything that is in it should be relevant, necessary and in one piece!

It can sometimes be very difficult for early years practitioners to get rid of things, especially if they have been accumulating them 'just in case'. If there is unlimited space and these resources are not making the place look too untidy then, of course, they can be kept. But if keeping some things means there is no space for others, or it is difficult to find or reach others, then the needs of the learners in your classroom should be prioritized. *Throw out* the least useful resources, and those kept 'just in case'. One rule of thumb can be that if something has not been used in the course of a full academic year, it will either be thrown away or given to someone for whom it *is* appropriate and who *will* use it.

Once all unnecessary clutter has been disposed of, it is possible to *identify the gaps* in the available resources and decisions can be made about what needs to be added or ordered. There are many resources that can be found or scrounged rather than bought, but however resources are gathered, there are certain principles to bear in mind (see Box 5.3).

Box 5.3 Principles about gathering resources

- resources should be appropriate for both the girls and the boys in your class;
- resources should encourage girls to play in areas that are traditionally the domain of boys and vice versa (e.g. clothes in the dressing up area that will attract boys to role-play; writing equipment outside);
- resources should reflect a wide range of cultures whether they are represented by the ethnic mix in the class or not; these might include jigsaws, cooking utensils in the home corner or books;
- resources should be appropriate for a range of special needs, interests and circumstances, no child should feel excluded from an activity or experience because the resources available reflect a cultural, gender, social or ability bias.

Having selected and gathered new resources together, these need to be sorted and *allocated* to the areas in the learning environment in which they are most appropriate. It is particularly important that the children see the significance of this sorting process. As with many other stages of this organization of space and resources, the children can be valuably involved in the process and this will be explored later. At this point, it is sufficient to suggest that adults should not make assumptions about what is 'logical' to children. There are a number of resources that can be of use for more than one curriculum area. Therefore, will the allocation be made on the basis of most frequent use or most logical use? Will there be a resource area for each area of learning or is this unrealistic? Is it best to divide curriculum resources between three major areas as suggested by Janet Moyles (1992)?

- *investigation area*: essentially science, maths, technology;
- *language area*: mainly English, history, geography;
- *creative area*: mostly art, design, music.

There are no hard and fast rules about organization. What *is* important is that the decisions that are made make sense to the children who will use them, as well as the adults, and that the organization is consistently applied. In this way, resources are more likely to be found and replaced without confusion.

Once the resources have been allocated to a certain area, they can be *labelled* for further ease of finding and returning. Some adults label both the *resource* and the *location* so that even the youngest children can match the item to its correct home. The labelling can be appropriate to the age and ability of the children using them. The label may be a picture that a child has drawn; it may be a catalogue picture that has been cut out; it may be a word describing the resource; it may be a coloured symbol denoting a certain category of resource. Alternatively, a head-teacher colleague I know and respect feels that it is better that children come to learn where things go *without* such prompts. As with all things, this is a decision for individual practitioners and their children. It is also a decision, along with others to do with the management of the learning environment, that a whole staff might want to discuss. As with most aspects of an effective early years setting, the shared discussion and decision-making within a staffroom can have a very positive impact on children's learning experiences. If children are to be encouraged to be independent, then it is highly beneficial to them – and to their early childhood educators – that there is a consistent approach throughout the setting. Nothing can be more frustrating than being given independence and autonomy in one situation only to have it taken away in the next. So, do raise these issues collaboratively with colleagues. If Foundation Stage children can manage the levels of independence visible in any good-quality early years environment, then just imagine what 7 and 11-year-olds can achieve.

In order to facilitate independence, resources need to be located in *accessible* places. This has implications for the amount of resources in a given space and is the reason for suggesting that cluttered resource areas are not helpful. If resources are cluttered, muddled, piled too high or too deep, then a child or adult may not be able to see a resource, let alone realize that it might be useful. They may know the resource is there somewhere, but be unable to find it and consequently might use something less helpful. Equally, they may not find a space to return it to or may feel that the space is in such a mess that they can put it anywhere ... and the space remains cluttered.

Resources are best placed on uncluttered surfaces that make them easy to be seen and easy to reach. This means that it is better not to have resources in cupboards with doors (except the outdoor storage sheds that will need doors for security purposes). Doors can hide a multitude of clutter and they also take up a lot of space. Cupboard doors have to have space in order to be opened and that space could be so much more effectively used if the doors (indoors) are removed.

Finally, children and adults need to be *trained* to find and replace resources properly. I do not usually use the word 'train' when referring to working with children, but in this context I think it is appropriate. By train I mean, 'reminded repeatedly so that it becomes habit'. It will not happen by chance, neither will it happen instantly! Children need regular reminding about where resources are to be found, how to use them and where to put them back. Such strategies are best made into part of the daily routine, particularly for younger children, so that at some point in each day they watch while someone finds/replaces a certain piece of equipment or resource. This can serve two useful purposes. Firstly, it reinforces the importance of 'a place for everything and everything in its place' and how necessary that is for a space that is being used by a lot of people. Secondly, it is valuable to remind children of what resources *are* available, so that they can include them in their activities as appropriate. Young children need to develop an awareness of their role in the care of the environment, not just within the setting but outside in the community also. They will learn the basic tenets of respect and value for the world around them if there is an expectation that they care for and be responsible for their own learning environment.

Box 5.4 Planning and arranging resources

- *collect* all existing resources together;
- *throw out* all those that are incomplete and/or inappropriate;

- *gather together* new/necessary resources;
- *sort* into categories that fit the arrangement of the learning space;
- *label* by object, catalogue picture, word (possibly label resource *and* location);
- *locate* resources on accessible, open shelving;
- *train* children to locate and return all resources themselves.

Finally, children need to be given *time* at the end of sessions to be responsible for *sorting and tidying* their own areas and activities so that they learn to be responsible for their own learning environment and appreciate the necessity, for everyone's sake, to keep it an organized and efficient working environment. One very helpful strategy is to give children a five-minute warning. If children are told that they have five minutes before they will be asked to stop what they are doing, then it not only gives them the opportunity to start clearing away, but it also gives them time to finish off or to stop an activity at a point that is more appropriate to *them* rather than instantly.

Management

Eliminating the little things

One effective strategy to begin developing children's independence is to keep a log of the interruptions that you get as a practitioner or as a staff team. Interruptions from the children – 'I don't know what to do next'; 'Can I have some more paper'; 'I've spilt some paint'. Interruptions from elsewhere – the school secretary wants dinner numbers; the pre-school supervisor asks to borrow some children for a task; you are asked to show a parent around your setting. All these interruptions take you away from valuable teaching time. Many or most of these interruptions can be eliminated. Children need to be taught the skills of independence. They can be shown how to mix paints, how to find new paper, how to mop up spillages. It may not be perfect at first, but with encouragement and good role modelling children can manage perfectly well and enjoy doing so. As far as the adult interruptions are concerned, very often the adult who has sent the message or the instruction has simply not thought through the ramifications of their request. By raising this at a staff meeting or speaking to the person concerned individually, the level of interruptions can be reduced overnight. The task of early childhood educators is to be educating the children. Now, of course, there are a wealth of social skills to be taught as part of clearing up mess, tidying away resources and so on, but the time for teaching these should not be in the middle of another adult-intensive task when other children will then be waiting for the adult to return to them and the task in hand. Anything that takes you away from that crucial task needs to be questioned and addressed and all those involved in your setting will understand this and should be supportive

If children learn to manage the little things in the learning environment, then it can save them – and staff in the setting – valuable time. But creating time for children to learn these skills can require a change of attitude for some adults. Firstly, it means providing the resources to enable children to manipulate them easily – appropriately sized and shaped pencil sharpeners, for example, or a readily accessible dustpan and brush and mop. It also means allowing children the time and opportunity to find out for themselves that too much water means their pictures look wishy-washy, that using a mop without squeezing out water can make something more slippery not less, that turning the sharpener too often breaks a lead rather than sharpens it. It also means setting time aside when new children arrive to establish this level of independence before focusing on other curriculum areas or focused tasks. To become independent, children need to be taught certain skills and then given time to practise them. It is up to the teacher to set time aside in order to show children how to tie each other's aprons, cut paper or find a new book. Showing children once is, of course, never enough. Experiences like these need repetition, building into the day – perhaps at whole group time – so that children are constantly reminded of the expectations within the learning environment and how to go about looking after themselves. As with many other classroom issues, time invested here will save time later on. In this instance, the time it will save is practitioner time that can then be spent on the valuable business of *teaching* rather than *servicing*. Children feel a great sense of pride and personal achievement when they manage themselves and do not feel that they have to go to an adult. The important thing is that children are taught the skills and strategies for independence and are then given opportunities to practise and use them. It is important too that the children's efforts are seen as valuable parts of the learning process.

Accidents do happen, however. Should the paint go on the floor or the water tray splash over, then valuable adult time can be wasted if it is the classroom expectation that it is an *adult* who clears it up. This, too, is something that – given appropriate training – children are perfectly capable of doing for themselves. The adult simply needs to ensure that children have the wherewithal to clear up. It is helpful if, close to those areas that are prone to getting messy, there is a range of equipment for clearing up. Near the water tray, for example, there should be a mop and bucket and sponges; near the sand tray, a broom and dustpan and brush; near the painting table, more sponges, cloths and a supply of paper towels. It helps enormously if, where appropriate, these are child-sized. It helps the child to manipulate the equipment so much more easily and it gives a clear message that this is the province of the child and not something that an adult automatically manages on their behalf.

Involving children in making decisions

I suggested earlier that it can be beneficial for children to be involved in decisions about space and resources as much as is possible. We all know that, given a sense of ownership and a feeling of responsibility about something, then we are likely to take more interest and effort in maintaining it. There are other important reasons why involving children can be of value to them and their educators. Involving children:

- gives opportunities for real-life problem-solving;
- encourages children to maintain something that they have planned;
- enables children to have an element of control over their own learning environment;
- leads to the development of organization as a life skill;
- gives children a sense of responsibility/self-esteem;
- encourages cooperation and collaboration between children and with adults;
- enables the practitioner to see things from the children's perspectives.

Children can be involved in planning and arranging:

- the use of space;
- the naming of areas within the learning environment;
- the selection of resources;
- the categorizing of resources;
- the sorting of resources;
- the labelling of resources;
- the location of resources.

Reviewing the use of space and resources

The design and management of a learning environment is an ongoing exercise. It requires both children and adults to review their teaching and learning spaces and to be given opportunities for suggesting ways in which improvements can be made. The following are useful questions that practitioners can ask children – and themselves:

Space

- Do children have room to move about the learning environment – both indoors and out – without interfering in other children's activities?
- Is there space for children to engage in active learning, both indoors and out?
- Is there space for a child to sit alone or with a friend as well as in a small group or in a large group, both indoors and out?
- Is there space for a child to be quiet as well as to be interactive, both indoors and out?

Resources

- Can children access resources both indoors and out without interfering with the activities of other children?
- Are resources clearly visible both indoors and out?
- Do resources get put back in the right place both indoors and out?
- Are there enough resources for everyone's needs both indoors and out?

Management

- How often are adults interrupted with queries that are not to do with teaching and learning?
- What is the nature of those interruptions?
- Do children know what to do if paint/paper/glue runs out?
- Do children know how to sharpen pencils?
- Do children know what to do if they need aprons/shoes tied?
- Do children know what to do if things are spilt?
- Do children know what to do with finished work?
- Do children know what to do when they have finished an activity?
- Do children know where to find and return outdoor resources?

Establishing independence

Encouraging children to be independent can take time, but it is time wisely spent. It is very hard to plan a teaching day where adults can spend quality time with individuals or groups of children if the rest of the class is not able to operate independently. It may well be that rather than begin teaching the curriculum from day one, that practitioners spend the early days of a term or year teaching independence. Time can be put aside so that children are taught to find and replace resources, to mix paint, to sharpen pencils, to mop up and tidy away, to move from one activity to the next without recourse to an adult (see Chapter 9 for further details of this). The role of the adult during this time is to watch and support this growing independence. Adults need to have the time to show a child how to do something or to remind them where to find something. This is best achieved if the adult has not planned to spend this time teaching the curriculum. Any attempt to teach individuals or groups while children do not have independence is likely to lead to frustration all round. Children will not know how to manage their time and will become bored or frustrated. Adults will be interrupted from the teaching role by low-level requests for attention. Establishing independence – and seeing this as valuable teaching and learning in its own right – will be of long-term benefit to subsequent teaching and learning of the curriculum and to the focused use of high-quality time.

In order to introduce independent learning and to make it the cornerstone of the balance of learning experiences and opportunities (see Chapter 4), then it is best to start with *child-initiated* activities, then introduce *adult-initiated* activities and then finally introduce *adult-focused* activities. If the practitioner begins with child-initiated activities – that is activities that children can sustain without recourse to an adult – this leaves the adult free to concentrate on supporting independence rather than anything else. Once children are independent, adult-initiated activities can be gradually introduced so that the teacher can see if children can sustain their independence while being required to work at some more prescribed tasks in the course of the day. The adult still needs to leave sufficient breathing space for themselves to remind and support children when they come for help unnecessarily. When independence is established as a part of classroom life, then the adult-intensive activities can be introduced in the knowledge that the rest of the children will be working and playing purposefully without needing adult support for a while. This does not mean that children will never again interrupt an adult, but it does mean that the times when this happens should be dramatically reduced, that children can feel responsible for their own learning and that the adult is able to get on with the business of teaching.

Conclusion

Independent learners are a necessary part of classroom life. Early childhood practitioners are usually responsible for too many children to be able to teach all of them directly, all of the time, and it is inevitable that children spend a large part of their time in a setting working and playing independently. As we shall see in the next chapter, this is not only necessary but also desirable. Children working and playing together, without adult supervision, is an important part of learning and development, for when children are alongside their peers they develop many different skills and understandings. Learning to collaborate and cooperate is a lifelong process and it is crucial that children have the opportunity to rehearse these skills when they are young. Chapter 6 is concerned with the importance of children learning with others; it examines the place of talk in the early years and challenges some established notions about group work.

6

COLLABORATION AND COOPERATION

The importance of talking and learning with others

Introduction

One of the most important elements of an environment appropriate for young learners is the provision of opportunities for children to talk together, and with adults, as they learn. There is now a powerful consensus about the centrality of talk to learning, a consensus brought about by the powerful findings of studies of language in the home and at school (significantly the Bristol study 'Language at home and at school' directed by Gordon Wells (1981, 1986), the research studies of Barbara Tizard and Martin Hughes (1984) and the work of the National Oracy Project). Studies such as these confirm that talking things through is an essential method by which we all make sense of our experience. Vygotsky (1962) saw how young children solve practical tasks with the help of their speech as well as their eyes and hands and use language as a way of sorting out their thoughts. At first, language and action are fused together in this way, and that is why young children are often heard talking to themselves when they are engaged in an activity. Eventually, language and action become separated and the activity can be represented in the medium of words (Bruner 1985).

The realization of the impact of language on thought and learning has had two significant influences on early years practice. The first concerns talk between the children and the adult:

> to be most helpful, the child's experience of conversation should be in a one-to-one situation in which the adult is talking about matters that are of interest and concern to the child ... or about activities in which the child and adult engage together.
>
> (Wells 1985: 44)

The second influence concerns children and their peers and a response to the assertion that:

> collaborative talk not only facilitates the task, it also empowers the learner. Indeed ... it has the potential for promoting learning that exceeds that of almost any other type of talk.
>
> (Chang and Wells 1988: 97)

Communication with adults

In the pre-school years, talking and learning go hand in hand. Children communicate with adults and their siblings and peers about things that are of interest and concern to them. The strategies that children have developed for actively making sense of their experiences have, as we have seen, been highly effective. Yet once children go to school this model of active learning through talk is not always emulated. Instead, children very often meet the vestiges of the learning-by-listening model of teaching with few opportunities to engage in the kinds of dynamic interaction that might bring about the quality of learning described above. Tizard and Hughes (1984: 14) point out that comparisons between conversations at home and in the nursery reveal how differently children can behave in two settings, and that in some cases 'it is hard to believe it is the same child who is talking'. Early childhood educators talk to children in different contexts, as individuals, as members of a small group and as members of a larger group.

Talking to individuals

Conversations with individual children are a critical part of the early childhood educator's repertoire of teaching strategies. It is important that these conversations are not one-sided – that is, on the adult's side. If adults do most of the talking or ask most of the questions, then they leave children few opportunities to express their own ideas or raise their own questions. Louis Malaguzzi (1992), the founder of the pre-schools in Reggio Emilia, Italy, explains that the interactions between adults and children are seen as a reciprocal activity where 'the ball is passed always along. At times the children throw it, at times we do'.

This delightful analogy emphasizes the synergy between the child's contribution and the adult's where both are essential and neither can be effective without the other. The child's energy and ideas, thoughts and feelings are as important as the adult's, and the adult has ideas, thoughts and feelings that can enhance the child's contributions and extend them further.

The studies of conversations in the home environment, cited above, reveal that what is characteristic of them is that they are spontaneous and arise from activities in which one or both of the participants are engaged. The conversations are, therefore, given meaning by the context in which they occur and both adult and child have a vested interest in talking about and putting forward their views about the experience. In early childhood settings it can seem harder to achieve this kind of reciprocity if the adult's agenda predominates. The perception that there is a predetermined list of activities and tasks to cover can sometimes threaten the spontaneity that imbues the experiences within the home, and lead practitioners to follow their own carefully constructed agenda rather than responding to individual interests. But we know that, given a sufficiently stimulating environment, most young children become deeply interested and involved in things of their own choosing and take little notice of adult interventions if they are not on the same wavelength. So, starting from the child, and their interests and concerns, should ensure a higher level of engagement and involvement in learning.

> The strategies that children have developed for actively making sense of their experiences have served them well up to this point; they should now be extended and developed, not suppressed by the imposition of routine learning tasks for which they can see neither a purpose nor a connection with what they already know and can do.
>
> (Wells 1985: 68)

In addition, of course, early childhood educators are recognizing their role in promoting the rights of even very young children to have their interests, their views and their concerns listened to and heeded. In her influential research on *Listening to Children*, Lancaster (2003) reminds us that the quality of our interactions with children are based on a particular view of the child as a learner. Listening to children requires a respectful relationship that stems from a view of the child as powerful and competent. The role of the adult is to promote real opportunities for young children to communicate their experiences, views, concerns and aspirations and then to develop the skills to engage effectively with the children and to take seriously what they have to say (Lancaster 2003: 4).

This notion of 'realness' is central to an effective relationship between adults and children. Carl Rogers (1983), the eminent psychotherapist, identified through his work a number of factors that facilitate learning, the first of which is 'realness' or 'genuineness', that is, when the educator does not present a façade. All too often an adult's response to a child's comment, idea or efforts can be dismissive and patronizing and the child loses the motivation to engage further with their learning and to make any further effort. Some adults can be too busy to stop and really listen to what the child is trying to say, so the child feels belittled and insignificant. Sometimes the adult does not have a very positive view of the child's competence and can brush aside their attempts to explain or describe, leaving the child embarrassed or intimidated. Sometimes the adult falls into the trap of being too positive all the time, leaving the child uncertain about what they have done right or what they could do another time to improve on their efforts. If adults are always saying 'how lovely' to whatever a child attempts to do, then the child will not feel encouraged to try something harder or to attempt something differently. Children need to be motivated by their own inner drive to achieve something, not in order to win the approval of an adult. Young children learn to see through the response that does not truly engage with their efforts of the moment. Rogers says that successful educators understand the learner's reactions 'from the inside' and that their empathy demonstrates that they accept, value and trust the learner, thus bringing out the very best in them.

Talking to individual children gives the practitioner the opportunity to:

- build a closer relationship with the child so that they come to understand them better as a learner;
- know what the child is thinking and feeling about an activity or experience in order to understand what motivates them as a learner
- know what the child understands or can do or will attempt in certain situations;
- extend the child's knowledge and understanding through ideas, explanation, suggestion and questioning.

It is this depth of knowledge about a child that enables the early childhood educator to move that child through Vygotsky's 'zone of proximal development' (see Chapter 1). Unless adults know each child's present levels of understanding, then they cannot know what their potential might be.

In the analysis of *Researching Effective Pedagogy in the Early Years* (REPEY) Project (DfES 2002a) the research team, led by Professor Iram Siraj-Blatchford, highlight that effective learning comes from a process of mutual cognitive co-construction between the adult and the child, 'where each party engages with the understanding of the other ... A necessary condition is that both parties are *involved*' (my italic: p. 10). The project team conclude that effective adult–child interactions stem from what they term 'sustained shared thinking'. This reciprocal learning relationship is what has been variously termed 'joint involvement episodes' by Bruner (1996b); 'a mutual learning encounter' by

SPEEL: *Study of Pedagogical Effectiveness in Early Learning* (DfES 2002b) and 'a passage of intellectual search' by Tizard and Hughes (1984). Whatever term is coined – and the EYFS has gone with 'sustained shared thinking (DfES 2007b: 9), the notion is that skilled adults can intervene in children's learning in ways that are somehow instructive and extend children's understanding. The EYFS (2007b: para 1.28) defines sustained shared thinking in the following way:

- adults are aware of the children's interests and understandings and the adults and children work together to develop an idea or skill;
- in the most effective settings practitioners support and challenge children's thinking by getting involved in the thinking process with them;
- there are positive trusting relationships between adults and children;
- the adults show genuine interest, offer encouragement, clarify ideas and ask open-ended questions that support and extend children's thinking and helps them make connections in learning.

One of the key strategies used by educators to challenge children's thoughts and ideas is questioning. The REPEY project confirms that questioning involves 'an especially important set of strategies for teachers to master'. Traditionally, teachers in school have used questioning as a strategy to discover whether children have either listened to or learnt the information that the teacher has imparted. Many studies of primary classes (e.g., Galton *et al.* 1980; Stodolsky *et al.* 1981; French and Maclure 1983) reveal that during interactions with their teachers, children are required to recall a tremendous number of 'facts'. The teacher asks a question to which they know the answer and to which they want children to give a confirmatory response. Questions are not used to enquire into the wide range of under-standings that children might hold but to elicit the one particular fact that the teacher wants to confirm. In classrooms, the questions raised by teachers overwhelm – and in some cases completely obliterate – the number raised by children. This is because, by and large, the teacher initiates the topic of conversation and is, therefore, in control of the ensuing debate. The conversation follows the agenda of the teacher, it is instigated for the purposes of the teacher and the children learn to adopt the passive role of responder rather than sustain their active role of enquirer (Rowland 1984).

When teachers talk to individual children, it is important to adopt a style of questioning that extends children's understanding and leads them to new ways of thinking for themselves. Questioning that is closed and that requires children to give a correct answer can inhibit the teacher–pupil relationship because children sense that, in a way, the teacher is trying to catch them out. Do they know this, or not? Were they listening, or not? Does this need repeating, or not? Questions that prescribe answers are just as limiting as checklists that prescribe actions. In both cases teachers will only learn what their chosen strategy allows children to reveal. Conversations where the teacher knows the answer and the child does not establish a power base for the teacher that inhibits the kind of collaborative construction of meaning that is mutually relevant. It is this willingness on the part of the teacher to negotiate, says Wells, that gives them the confidence to explore their own understandings. Knowledge has to be 'constructed afresh by each individual knower' and teachers cannot rely on the transmission of their own knowledge as a strategy for successful learning by the child (Wells 1986: 116).

Dillon (1981) claims that excessive questioning makes pupils dependent and passive. In order to make effective use of what is at its best a very valuable teaching strategy, it is as well for teachers to be aware of practices that reduce the effectiveness of questioning as a tool in the repertoire of the effective teacher. In their book *Questioning*, Brown and Wragg suggest that the following are common errors in questioning, and their list is useful in raising teacher awareness of their own questioning strategies:

- asking too many questions at once;
- asking a question and answering it yourself;
- asking questions only of the brightest or most likeable;
- asking a difficult question too early;
- asking irrelevant questions;
- always asking the same type of questions;
- not indicating a change in the type of question;
- not using probing questions;
- not correcting wrong answers;
- ignoring answers;
- failing to see the implications of answers;
- failing to build on answers.

(Brown and Wragg 1993: 18)

Talking to individual children is a skilled activity and one that, if the chosen strategies are appropriate, is vital for the teacher's knowledge and understanding of the child and the child's knowledge and understanding of a whole world of things. Questions such as 'what can you see or hear?'; 'what happens if ...?'; 'how shall we ...?' and 'have you got enough ...?' all elicit thinking skills rather than the mere regurgitation of fact.

Talking to a large group

Of course, early years educators almost always spend some time in the day talking to larger groups of children. These whole group times, or 'carpet' times, can usefully take place at many different points in the day. Whole group times can be valuable, for example:

- introducing a new theme or topic;
- finding out what different children know before beginning a theme or topic;
- sharing rhymes, songs, poems and stories;
- sharing news, events and personal information.

It has to be remembered, however, that young children do not learn effectively in larger groups. Children in the Foundation Stage – and I would suggest into Year 1 and for some children Year 2 – still need to have their voices heard too frequently to be able to wait for an adult's attention when they are managing a large group. Equally, they have not yet learnt to find what others say particularly interesting, and won't learn that easily in a group of 20 or 30. Certainly, to wait while a whole reception class has their say in circle time can be very dull and not in the least edifying when you are just 4 years old. If you want young children to learn rather than to be informed about (the theme) or to share the experience of (the story, the rhymes), then those children need to be in a group small enough for their voices to be heard and their ideas and opinions to be cherished.

One important aspect to think about when planning for whole group sessions is whether they will interrupt some of the more sustained independent learning that is taking place. Whole group times are best planned at the beginning or end of sessions so that the children have as much uninterrupted time as possible to engage in deep-level learning through play and first-hand experience. We know that younger children take longer to come to understand and remember experiences than adults. They are working hard to make connections between their existing knowledge and understanding and what is new, and because they have fewer pieces of their 'cognitive jigsaw' already in place (see Chapter 1), then concentration, time and repetition should be salient characteristics of their learning day. All too often, however, particularly once into school, the time for learning is chopped up into segments that are too short to be helpful to the child's learning journey. Just as they are getting to grips with something they are interrupted to go to the hall for assembly or to the ICT room or to the gym. The most effective early childhood educators try and eliminate as many interruptions to the learning day as they can in order to give children prolonged periods of time to get involved and engaged in their learning. Of course, if children's experiences are not

exciting and intriguing, and learning remains superficial, th
children will readily – and probably happily – break off in order
do something else. But a sign of an outstanding early learnin
environment is where children are reluctant to move away from wha
they are doing and are eager to return to it at the earliest possible
opportunity.

One of the worst uses of whole group times is when the practitioner
uses it to check out what they already know, but what they want to
ensure that the children now know. Research into this kind of dialogue
frequently reveals less of a discussion and more of a diatribe. Most o
the time, Barnes and his colleagues discovered teachers were retainin
the initiative throughout, by a strategy of asking questions a
monopolizing the commentary on the answers that were given (Bar
et al. 1969). My own classroom research with my colleague C
Boulter confirms these findings. The reception teachers we obse
undertaking different whole class sessions showed these teachers
concerned with getting the 'right' answer, given by the 'right' ch
the 'right' way.

The 'right' answer

Our video transcripts revealed that 'discussions' were domi
the teachers' agenda. There was no evidence that they were
find out what the children understood as a starting poi
discussions or for planning the future curriculum. They t
they were concerned with finding out what the children
from the activities they had set up, rather than finding ou
already knew about and would bring to the experience. T
technique of questioning to elicit the 'right' answer,
answers that were in their own heads. They did thi
answers that were not those that were deemed to be 'co
this they sometimes created conceptual confusion in
that they frequently offered no explanation as to wh
accepted or rejected. Therefore, children who had be
answer in the teacher's head' had no idea why they
or right.

The 'right' child

The teachers further controlled the 'discussion
children put their hands up to answer questio
practice, of course, but it does give the t
mechanism. As classroom gender studies show,
ing as a way of including and involving miscrea

back of the class – in an attempt to pre-empt antisocial
ur (e.g. Stanworth 1981; Spender 1982; Clarricoates 1983). The
ild was, therefore, the one named by the teachers, and the
f the child seemed fairly dependent on one of two factors.
were children who were not attending – and, indeed, in
t one, they were boys; or they were children to whom the
d in exasperation or expectation to give them the 'right'
every case this was a girl.

s the right answer, the teachers were not prepared
equently, if children asked questions or made
likely to take them 'off course', they were
re are different examples, particularly in our
ssons, of opportunities to start from the
rests being missed. The 'right' way meant
da, and meeting their intended objectives
e planned curriculum. Such whole class
and exploration not of the children's
vere in marked contrast to the claims
by Alexander *et al.* (1992: para 90)
ted with higher order questioning,
ese in turn correlate with higher

int to remind ourselves that
oom Organisation and Practice
about children and their
en in response to this by
Blatchford (1992) – and
en – comprehensively
and infant children,
ts effectiveness and,
f such whole class
son 1987). None-
for whole group
which is the
ers and with
ing a session
open most
er it, on a
) school
aiding
ed be

counter-productive'. Clearly, if talk between adults and children is such a critical part of the education process, then adults must ensure that the strategies they use extend rather than inhibit children's learning.

Box 6.1 Example 5: Planning for talk

An early years practitioner had identified the following learning outcomes for an activity:

- use language such as 'larger', 'smaller', heavier', 'lighter' to compare quantities;
- use mathematical ideas and methods to solve practical problems.

The activity entailed guessing the contents of several birthday presents that had been wrapped in various colourful pieces of birthday wrapping paper. The five 4-year-old children were sitting on the carpet with the presents in a pile in front of them. The activity had tremendous potential. The children were eager to pick up, feel and shake the presents and a lot of valuable language was already being used as the adult settled down to the activity. Instead of this language being harnessed and extended, the children were told to stop talking. They were then told that they could look but not touch, and the adult proceeded to lift each present in turn and asked for the children's predictions about its contents, which the adult recorded. The children were not asked to justify their responses. Indeed any justification ... 'perhaps you think tha because it's hard ... square ... noisy ...' was given by the adult. the end of the activity (there were seven presents) the children h made their predictions but not had the opportunity to justify th even when they had changed their minds following peer pres The adult had used a great deal of mathematical and sci language, but the children had used virtually none. The aspect for the children was that they were told that they wo find out if they were 'right' until the next day ... when all t children had done the 'guessing' part of the tasks. This se an example of the rich potential for language being so The possibilities for use of language were excellent, t were motivated and the task was highly appropriate. H teaching strategies used made all that potential null a

---

Communicating with other children

Children talking with each other to learn is a relatively new phenomenon – in educational terms. The term 'oracy' was coined in the 1960s by Andrew Wilkinson to stress the importance of the language skills of listening and talking. These separate functions were enshrined in the National Curriculum as 'speaking and listening' and given emphasis in the Area of Learning named 'Communication, Language and Literacy' within the Foundation Stage (QCA/DfEE 2000; DfES, 2007). Recent concern for the level of speech development of children starting in early childhood settings has put the spotlight back on these two crucial skills.

Whatever nomenclature is used, oracy – or speaking and listening – now has a distinctive place in the curriculum not only as a medium of learning in all subjects, but as a 'subject' in its own right – as a critical 'spect of language competence that is taught alongside the tradition-

recognized skills of reading and writing (see DfES 2005). It is of

ular significance for young children for whom 'language plays a

ot only in learning self-control but in the formation of

e' (Pringle 1992: 47). But of course, like most life skills,

eaking and listening develop way before children meet the

urriculum'. Learning to listen and speak emerges out of

munication. This includes body language such as facial

ntact, bending the head to listen, hand gesture and

2007). Babies and young children learn to express

gs in this way and, as they receive responses to

d, so the synergy of interaction begins firstly,

eir significant adult carer, and then between

r family and community.

icate gives children the capacity to

fidence in the social world into which

grow up. In almost all situations in

ople to get on with others in order

their current role or task may be.

er's point of view; to wait and

sider; to negotiate and to be

ion has to be taken; to be

o be tolerant when they

any adults struggle to

they negotiate the

m a very early age

alongside other

y. They need the

ating – very often at

t
by
ad
em,
sure.
entific
worst
uld not
e other
sion was
uandered.
e children
owever, the
d void.

a time when they are still striving to put their
the world. It is an aspect of development
repeated support from adults.

But the importance of speaking and l
children's social development, important
speaking and listening also underpin tl
skills without which children will also
the world. Without rich oral language ᴄ
vocabulary to transfer to the more challenging rᴇᴀ.
word. Through verbal communication children share ᴀ.
feelings and stories that can later be captured on the page. When tʜᴇy
recite rhymes and songs and poetry, they experience the different uses
of language and how words can be manipulated to create different
meanings and emotions. When linking language with physical movement in action songs and rhymes, they not only use language for a
certain purpose but can refine their gross and fine motor skills, so
essential for manipulating the instruments that will help them make
meaningful marks on paper.

It is crucial that we give children time to develop their spontaneous
skills of speaking and listening before we force them towards the less
natural skills of reading and writing. Young children are natural
talkers. In her delightful book *Young Children Talking*, Diane Chilvers
reminds us that children have a 'built-in urge to tell you, in some way,
what they are thinking, feeling, seeing, hearing, smelling, touching.
They are powerful communicators' (2006: 5). This vital and powerful
urge for communication needs only to be compared to the reluctant
struggle many of our children face when being dragged too soon to the
written page. When they experience an overly formal introduction to
phonics, reading and writing before their other skills of speaking,
manipulating a pencil, being able to sit still for an extended period
have developed sufficiently. There are many esteemed educators in this
country who believe that the Early Learning Goals for reading and
writing remain developmentally too high for most children to achieve
naturally.

In other countries in the world there is no expectation on children
to read and write until they are 6 or 7 years of age. This doesn't mean
that children in Denmark or Finland are forbidden from looking at
books or sharing stories! However, they are not introduced to formal
literacy learning because their educators – and parents – know that this
may be beyond their current capabilities and may turn them off the
joys of reading and writing at a very impressionable age. In this
country, by setting achievement goals in linking sounds and letters
and writing at too early an age, many successful young communicators
are finding themselves failures by the yardstick of the Foundation

...le (DfES 2003). These unreasonable and ill-judged expecta-... forcing many educators to teach in ways that they feel are ...opmentally inappropriate for the children in their care. They are ...ing many local authorities to set targets that are at odds with what ...ey would choose to identify as the learning needs of their children. It ...s not that people like me do not want our young children to read and write – nothing could be further from the truth. Indeed, it is because I believe so passionately in the abilities of children and want them to know the lifelong joys of reading and writing that I will continue to challenge the current pressure to introduce these skills too formally too soon. Many early childhood educators believe that higher standards in reading and writing would be achieved, and that children would maintain more positive attitudes to reading and writing into their primary years and beyond, if the current expectations on children at age 5 were pushed forward and applied to children at age 7. If the quality of teaching achieved through the introduction of the literacy strategy was then applied to children at the beginning of Key Stage 2, then we predict that there would be less 'failure' and less need for 'booster' sessions or 'remedial' work. We would be capturing children's developing capacities at a more natural time, and not demanding too much too soon with the resultant strains on children, parents and educators alike.

In the Foundation Stage, talk will arise spontaneously in playful situations. In the role-play area, the home corner, during block play and at the water tray, talk occurs as part of the social and learning process. Children talk to exchange ideas, to ask for help, to commentate on what they are doing and feeling and thinking. Some of these natural and spontaneous opportunities can disappear if children are put into more formal learning situations. However, there are times when children in the final year of the Foundation Stage or in Year 1 and beyond will learn in social situations that the adult manipulates. If the children are to continue to have meaningful conversations with each other, then it is important to monitor that their learning situations continue to facilitate this. Since the early 1970s, primary school classrooms have generally been organized with children sitting around tables in groups of four to seven (Bealing 1972). The Plowden Report (CACE 1967) is usually seen as having legitimized the move towards a more relaxed classroom atmosphere where children no longer sit in rows waiting passively for the teacher to instruct them. A number of major studies, however, have highlighted inconsistencies between the way in which children are seated and the tasks in which they are engaged. The ORACLE Project (Galton *et al.* 1980); the Junior School Project (Mortimore *et al.* 1986); Tizard *et al.*'s (1988) research in infant schools; PRISMS (Curriculum Provision in

Small Primary Schools) (Galton and Patrick 1990) and the Primary Education in Leeds Project (Alexander 1992) all reveal similar findings – that children may sit in groups around tables, but they are usually working on tasks as individuals. I want to look at some of these more contrived learning situations most frequently used once children go to school.

Grouping children

Grouping as an organizational strategy

Managing large classes calls for creative thinking on the part of the teacher. Even at the level of moving children around the classroom and the school, it can be helpful to have children organized in small units. If children are in groups with a collective label such as 'red' group, 'scarf' group or 'leek' group (or any one of the 1001 names that groups are given) some potentially chaotic times such as lining up, getting to the hall and being organized in PE can be managed in a more calm and orderly way.

Grouping as an educational strategy

Many educators feel that children benefit from the sense of belonging to a group, that it gives children security and offers them opportunities to respond collectively and cooperatively. This rationale is essentially social and emotional and does not necessarily fulfil the wider learning needs that a group may have. There is an important difference between children sitting together *in* groups and working together *as* a group. Because research shows that many children sit in groups but work as individuals, it suggests that some teachers may group children for the purposes of their own planning rather than the purposes of children's learning. Rather than plan for the individual needs of a class of 30 or more, the teacher plans work for each of, say, four groups and the children are given tasks that are planned for the whole group to do, but which basically require each child to work as an individual. Some typical examples of such tasks would be completing individual maths workbooks, filling in a worksheet or preparing a design for a model.

To maximize the potential of children being grouped together, and to enhance their skills of speaking and listening with all that this entails, effective tasks require children to collaborate and cooperate. Children who sit together but do not share a common purpose for communication are likely to be distracted by sitting close together (Hastings and Schweiso 1995). This is when talk veers on to topics such as television and pet rabbits. Tasks need to be planned so that children share, discuss, argue, rationalize, find solutions and come to decisions together, just as they did in their earlier years when playing together was a more fluid and spontaneous affair. If children benefit from speaking when formulating concepts, then it is also vital that they talk with peers who will listen and deliberate their ideas. Only if both speaking and listening are a planned part of the curriculum will the social, linguistic and cognitive benefits of group work give an educational rationale for children sitting and working in this context (Box 6.2).

Box 6.2 A rationale for grouping children

Practical (for the teacher)
- time management;
- targeted planning;
- use of scarce resources.

Developmental (for the child)

social

- recognizing strengths and weaknesses in self and others;
- learning to give and take;
- respecting the opinions of others;
- handling conflict;
- developing management/leadership skills.

linguistic

- communicating for a purpose;
- articulating thoughts, ideas and opinions;
- using different kinds of talk for a purpose.

cognitive

- the development of critical attitudes (to evidence, opinion, etc.);
- increase in powers of reasoning;
- opportunities to hypothesize, question and develop ideas collaboratively;
- maximizing thinking power (two heads are better than one);
- the opportunity to go beyond the information given and generate new questions.

The appropriateness of grouping young children

Putting children in groups in order that they should collaborate is certainly not appropriate across the full early years age range or in all early years situations. Younger children will not cooperate simply because it is in the adult's plans. We have seen that young children will cooperate and collaborate with commitment when they see a purpose for doing so. Observations of young children working on construction or in the home corner reveal just how collaborative they can be, if there is a need. It is important that any practitioner working with younger children questions the reasoning behind any grouping that is adult-directed. Is the purpose social, educational or organizational? Will the group aid learning or might it, in fact, hinder it? There is a big difference between being 'put in a group' and working collaboratively alongside other children. We have already seen how crucial it is for children to work alongside and learn from other children. I am challenging the need for young children to be *put* in a group of children *in order to* work collaboratively. To encourage cooperation between young children, early childhood educators throughout the Early Years Foundation Stage should plan activities and experiences that encourage spontaneous interactive learning opportunities in which children see a purpose for talking together, working together and learning together.

Planned grouping

If the educator decides that it is in the interests of the children to be brought together in a specific group in order to experience or to learn something, then the criteria for grouping the children need to reflect the purpose of the task in which the group is to be engaged. There are times when it is beneficial for children with similar interests to work together to inspire and motivate each other. There are times when younger children can beneficially work or play alongside older children who act as models for behaviour and skills. There are times when children of similar ability will benefit from targeted input from an adult at a certain point in their development. If the choice of group is to reflect the nature and purpose of the task then the implication of this is that groupings will *change* in order for that match to be achieved.

Fixed grouping

Because children have different needs at different times, the adult has to plan for those needs to be met, not only through the selection of an activity or experience, but through the social context in which the learning takes place. Grouping that remains fixed and inflexible does not acknowledge the needs of the developing and individual child.

Children develop in highly individualistic ways and although patterns of development can be similar, children make spurts and reach plateaux in ways that are highly idiosyncratic. Their development cannot be catered for by decisions about their ability that remain the same for any period of time, particularly if that decision is held as constant across all subject areas or areas of learning. The needs of any small group of children, however similar their ability at any given time, will not be constant from day to day. Because four children are ready to learn about the concept of 'more than' at the same time, it does not necessarily follow that they will come to understand 'the difference between' at the same time. If different rates of learning mean that children have different learning needs *within* one subject, how much more will those needs vary *across* subjects and areas of learning?

Yet sometimes, particularly in schools, children are grouped with the same children for *all* their learning experiences. Their needs may originally have been assessed in one aspect, such as mathematics, and then presumed to be similar in everything else. How rarely this is the case. Children have such a range of skills and talents and under-standings and to suppose that one child can be 'above average' in all curriculum areas while another is consistently 'below average' is to make inaccurate, not to mention improbable, assessments of children's abilities. Children usually perform according to the expectations of those who influence them. Tell them that they're a 'leek' (one of my bright ones) and they'll perform like a leek. Tell them that they're a 'cabbage' (my slow learners) and they'll perform like a cabbage, even though some children know that given half a chance they could perform like a leek in PE or art or scientific investigation.

Labelling children in fixed *ability* groups can inhibit all manner of opportunities for development. It can restrict the opportunity to shine, gain confidence from and develop in those areas in which the child has strengths. It can also restrict the opportunity to work with a range of peers from whom the child can learn and to whom the child can teach a variety of things. Bringing together children who have the same learning needs at a given time is a constructive use of time. Constraining children to work with the same group of children consistently might, at best, inhibit development and at worst can destroy a child's belief in themselves and their ability in anything.

Flexible grouping

Effective grouping recognizes the ever-changing needs of children and the necessity to be flexible in planning the curriculum and the context in which that curriculum takes place. It means that children are brought together because they have similar needs at that moment in time. Knowledge of those needs comes from observations and conversations that identify every child's stage of development and provides clear evidence on which to base diagnostic assessments and future plans. Early childhood educators need to be flexible in their short-term planning so that whatever they discover about children and their development can be incorporated into weekly and daily reviews of every child's needs.

There are times when children *need to* work alone or want to learn alone, and when it is appropriate that they do so. If, however, one of the purposes of an activity or experience is that children will learn with and from each other, then it is necessary for the practitioner to make a decision. Will children collaborate and cooperate spontaneously because the activity will naturally lead to them doing so? Or is there a need to manipulate the collaborative aspect by bringing certain children together for the purpose of the activity? Children may be set a task to work at as a group, independent of the practitioner, or they may be working with an adult, addressing a specific learning need. The important point is that the activity or experience is relevant at that time to those children who have been grouped together.

The range of learning contexts

Group work is clearly only one context for learning. The early childhood educator has a range of options on which to draw:

- whole class;
- small group plus adult;
- small group minus adult;
- pair with adult;
- pair without adult;
- individual with adult;
- individual alone.

Given the variety of learning situations in any one class and the variety of needs of the children as learners, how does the teacher make decisions about which context is most appropriate? Alexander *et al.* (1992) state that the criteria should be 'fitness for purpose' and this is a helpful starting point. It seems logical that any decision made in a classroom should serve the purpose of the activity for which it is chosen. However, it begs the question – whose purpose? The choice of social context in a classroom situation may be the child's, but may be – and I suggest more often is – the teacher's. Box 6.3 offers a rationale for choosing different social contexts for learning. The suggestions came from a series of in-service sessions with early years teachers.

Box 6.3 Purposes of different learning contexts

Whole class
- introducing a new theme or topic;
- finding out what different children know before beginning a theme or topic;
- enjoying rhymes, songs, poems and stories;
- imparting knowledge;
- enthusing (beginnings);
- sharing (endings).

Small group plus adult (adult-focused activity)
- differentiation – targeting the learning needs of certain children;
- individualized questioning;
- more opportunities to *listen* to individuals;
- opportunities to observe practical activity and social interaction;
- extending knowledge and understanding;
- safety

Small group minus adult (adult-initiated activity)
- revision/rehearsal of the familiar;
- independent discussion;
- collaboration/cooperation (joint outcome);
- motivation of learning independently.

Pair
- mutual support (response partner);
- shared interest;
- motivation (friendships);
- age – older/younger children supporting each other.

Individual
- child's need to focus on individual interests;
- individual progress at own speed;
- maximum concentration.

The child's choice of grouping

What social contexts would the child choose? Unaware of the myriad of learning opportunities presented by their friends, young children tend to play and learn alongside other children for different reasons.

Young children learn best in contexts in which they feel secure. Security comes from being familiar with and trusting those who share the learning space. When given the opportunity to work alongside whomever they choose, children do not always work with a special friend. Often their own interest in an activity will determine where they choose to be. Young children do tend to gravitate towards those with whom they are comfortable and confident, however. Being secure enables children to relax, to experiment, to take risks and to stimulate their own learning. Alongside other children they may ask questions or sound out ideas which, in the company of an adult – however supportive – they may feel inhibited to do. The work of many people who have studied small groups of primary age children's work (Barnes and Todd 1977; Jones 1988; Phillips 1988; Reid *et al.* 1989) shows that children are more likely to generate exploratory questions, hypotheses and explanations on their own than when an adult is present. Working alongside someone with whom you feel secure is a powerful motivating factor. Just think how many adults do not go along to evening classes or join a sports club unless they go with a friend for moral support. Being with someone we like and trust adds to our feelings of enjoyment and security and this affects our application to the task in hand. So, on those occasions when it is possible to enable children to play and learn alongside children of their own choosing, then early childhood educators will find that this is likely to be beneficial both to the children and to the organization and management of the learning environment.

Conclusion

Young children talk to learn and need to have a range of opportunities to talk purposefully to their peers and to adults. Early childhood educators need to ensure that conversations are not one-sided and that children have genuine opportunities to say what they know and what they think and what they feel. When adults group children for educational reasons, these groupings should be flexible and responsive to the changing needs of children. Young children naturally collaborate and cooperate when they see the need to do so, and they do so particularly when they are engaged in self-initiated activities. The following chapter is concerned with child-initiated learning. It explores the place of play in the early years setting and asks why some practitioners can still find it hard to justify time for play at the heart of their learning environments.

7

THE PLACE OF PLAY

The status of child-initiated experiences

Introduction

No book about early childhood education would be complete without a discussion of the place of play. The Early Years Foundation Stage (DfES 2007) says that play 'underpins all development and learning for young children'. While messages such as this are loud and clear in all recent early years documentation (see both *Birth to Three Matters* (DfES 2003a) and *Curriculum Guidance for the Foundation Stage* (DfES 2000), it remains the case that not all play in all settings is of the quality that promotes effective learning, and not all Foundation Stage settings give play the place and status it warrants. This chapter explores why, when so much is said and written about the subject, play across the Early Years Foundation Stage still fails to be the bedrock of high-quality practice in all settings.

Theories surrounding play

Part of the dilemma surrounding play is that when we speak of it we do not always mean the same thing as the next person. There is no single definition of play and, therefore, playful activities in one form or another have been open to interpretation in different ways. There is, however, a plethora of theories as to what play is and what it accomplishes. For a detailed synopsis of the main theories I can do no better than to refer you to Tina Bruce's book *Time to Play in Early Childhood Education* (1991). In addition, the recent PlayEngland/NCB literature review of play entitled 'Free Play in Early Childhood' (Santer *et al.* 2007) offers an excellent summary of different perspectives on play and how play influences children's development and learning.

The classical theories of play explain the *reason* that play exists, and view play as physically very purposeful. For example:

- *Recreation theory*: this theory proposes that play somehow redresses the balance of time spent on work. That play is acknowledged as an appropriate activity for young children but not the same as, and certainly not as important as, work. In this way, play is sometimes used as a reward, as a 'carrot' at the end of a period of work when the child has the opportunity to engage in something of their own choosing once the work for the teacher is finished.
- *Excess energy theory*: here, play is seen as an acceptable way for children to let off steam and this separates 'worktime' from 'playtime'. This theory has given a framework to the infant school day – and indeed to junior and secondary education too – that has changed little over the years. 'Playtime' is given value in that it releases pent-up energies and prepares children to knuckle down to the more static learning experiences to which they will return.
- *Recapitulation theory*: this theory suggests that play reflects the cultural environment in which the child grows up. Play is seen as being deeply embedded in children's personal experiences and a reflection of the influences of children's environments and the significant people within them.
- *Practice or preparation theory*: play helps children to prepare for adult life by letting them practise and explore what they need to be able to do as adults. Young children engage in role play that mimics – often with devastating accuracy – the behaviours of adults who are significant in their lives.

However, there is another school of thought, commonly termed the modern dynamic perspective, which seeks to explain the *content* of play. Here, the theorists often come from a psychodynamic perspective:

- *Play as pleasure theory*: play is seen as a source of pleasure, and in no way dependent on end results or outcomes. This theory emphasizes the importance of play as process, a view strongly held by Bruner (1977: v) who, while not subscribing to the play as pleasure theory, nonetheless asserts that 'Play is an approach to action, not a form of activity'.
- *Play as catharsis theory:* children are believed to communicate and eliminate anxieties and fears by bringing them to a level of consciousness that can then be articulated through play (Santer *et al.* 2007).
- *Affective theories of play:* children are seen to gain control of their lives and to take this competence into adulthood.

Finally, there are theories of play that accentuate children's cognitive development.

- *Piaget (1951):* Piaget saw play as the means by which children unify their experiences, their knowledge and their understanding. His perspective was that children use what is already known (assimilation) and adjust this to take on board what is new (accommodation). Piaget believed that children build up this repertoire of expertise through active engagement with the environment to which they must continuously adapt. He viewed the child's development as leading learning, with play having a strong influence on development.
- *Vygotsky (1966):* Vygotsky, on the other hand, believed that learning led development. His writing emphasized how much children learn in social contexts and how significant language is in children's construction of knowledge and understanding. Because of this he saw adults, and other children, as having a key role in moving children from their current to their potential understandings. Unlike those theorists from the psychodynamic perspective, Vygotsky did not believe that children's play arises from unsatisfied desires, but rather that children create play that has purpose and, which, in turn, determines their affective states.

Different types of play

Now that we have considered some of the theories that have driven the development of play, we need to establish the different types of play in which children engage. Hughes (1996) has identified fifteen types of play in childhood, but I have chosen to focus on just nine as being of most relevance to early childhood educators.

- *Exploratory play:* offers children the opportunity to use their physical skills and their senses to learn more about materials and objects – what they feel like and what they can do.
- *Symbolic play:* children use objects and materials to represent (symbolize) something else, e.g. a piece of wood can symbolize a wand.
- *Dramatic play:* in dramatic play children either take on the actions and activities of others who are often most important to them in their daily lives (e.g. their mum, the shopkeeper, their babysitter or they).
- *Socio-dramatic play:* here children re-enact actual or potential experiences of intense personal meaning to them often becoming another character in order to lay on them the fears or anxieties that these play scenarios express.

- *Pretend play:* children create characters and situations that take them into imaginary and alternative worlds, rich in fantasy and unlikely to happen to the child in real life.
- *Locomotor play:* activities that involve all kinds of physical movement for their own sake and for the sheer physical pleasure of the experience.
- *Rough and tumble play:* playful physical activity that often involves contact, usually between two children, such as touching and tickling and rolling. It is clearly enjoyable and is *not* fighting.
- *Games with rules:* both indoors and out children engage in games with rules that are predetermined by others (usually adults) or rules they determine for themselves. Games with rules can demonstrate great creativity – a bringing together of experiences and ideas from a range of previous experiences and activity. Children have very clear ideas about fairness and police their established rules often with great severity.
- *Freeflow play:* in *Time to Play in Early Childhood Education*, Tina Bruce puts forward a definition of 'freeflow' play as an 'integrating mechanism, which brings together everything we learn, know, feel and understand' (1991: 11) and in which children are 'wallowing in ideas, feelings and relationships'. A key feature of freeflow play is that children use the 'technical prowess, mastery and competence' that they have previously developed and that, in doing so, they are in control of the experience.

Different social contexts for play

Not only are there different types of play but, through observation, we see that children engage in play in different social situations. This does not mean that children's play evolves through simplistic or fixed stages of development. While there is a developmental influence here – with very young children displaying more engagement in play described at the top of the list – children throughout the Foundation Stage choose to be involved in all or any aspects of these social situations according to their mood and the purposes and nature of their play.

- *Solitary play:* children are engaged in their own play, without involvement of or reliance on others;
- *Spectator play:* children are often watching the play of others, onlookers who are absorbing what others are doing;
- *Parallel play:* children playing side by side often with similar resources or in the same space, but with little apparent interaction or engagement one with the other;

- *Co-operative play:* children sharing play space, resources and experiences, talking and playing together with often complementary roles.

Different cultural influences on play

The world in which we live and the culture into which we are born impacts dramatically on our attitudes to all sorts of things, including the role and the status of play. The opportunities for play and the influences upon play come frequently from society's images, ideas and opinions. Some of these are very obvious but others are more insidious, though none-the-less profound for that. Marjatta Kalliala (2006:10) identifies the following list of changes in society currently influencing children's play culture:

- how people earn a living;
- urbanization;
- more middle-aged and elderly people in the population;
- the increasing equality of women;
- the changing work patterns of women outside the home;
- changing class boundaries and social stratification
- changing professions;
- changing sexual behavior;
- changes in the nuclear family and childhood;
- no clear common ideology, religious movements or doctrines to give cohesion and shared understandings;
- changing institutions (e.g. church and state);
- changes in the welfare state and thinking what's best for society.

Changes in society

There are a number of changes in society that have become absorbed in children's play. The increasing number of women out at work and the increasing equality of women in all realms of society; advances in technology and the increasing reliance of all of us on its multiplicity of forms; attitudes to drugs, alcohol and smoking and how these are perceived by children via the media and advertising; the threat of increasing urbanization – pollution, child safety, spaces to play; the loss of influence of the church and the increase in secular behaviour, beliefs and attitudes towards right and wrong, good and evil. In the foundation stage, children are developing their own views about all these things and these are often strongly influenced by the values and beliefs of their family and their community. In their role play, their socio-dramatic play and their pretend play, in particular, children represent their emerging ideas about relationships, about roles, about actions and consequences. They also inhabit roles and create situations that give them fresh powers and possibilities to be someone different or to change the course of events from those in their normal daily lives. These types of play are about alternative worlds. They encourage children to use objects that represent other things and help them separate the difference between make-believe and reality. The key feature of play is that the child remains in control of events. Whether they want to take on a role that is the same as a significant adult in their life, or one that they have seen portrayed on television or on film. Whether they want to imagine another's perspective and try out the powers that this new role might bring. Whether they want to create a character in order to give it feelings of guilt, fear, anxiety or jealousy that they are currently working through. In all these situations, the child has the power to make happen what, in the rest of their lives, they are currently only imagining and feeling and fearing. They have the power to experience the world from another's point of view and to control how much they engage with or discard this alternative persona and its imaginary consequences.

Gender

Attitudes towards gender and what is seen as gender appropriate behaviour are formed in early childhood (Hutt *et al.* 1990; Holland 2003). Children learn most of their ideas from the stereotypes that surround them daily via advertisements, shop displays, television programmes and adult responses. Children begin to label themselves and others as male or female accurately from about age 2 and soon after this they begin to make links between these labels and different activities, toys and behaviours. Many girls will choose to play with dolls when boys will not. Many boys are drawn towards trucks, tractors and trains and girls are not. By age 5 most children have internalized gender-expected roles. Sometimes this is a result of the way in which boys and girls are treated in the family, with adults choosing to dress boys and girls in different colours, for example, and even the way in which adults touch and handle children – bouncing boys vigorously on the knee and cradling girls more gently and rocking them (Livingstone 2005). Vivian Gussin Paley, in her evocative descriptions of play and learning in her classroom, reports that:

Domestic play looks remarkably alike for both sexes at age three ... (but) The four year old boy is far less comfortable in the doll corner than he was the year before; he may occasionally dress up in women's clothes or agree to be Daddy, but the superhero clique has formed and the doll corner is becoming a women's room ... among five and six year olds ... the girls officiate in the doll corner but the presence or absence of boys determines the character of the play ... As the superhero dominates boys' fantasy play the girls turn to dramatic plots that eliminate boys and bring in more sisters and princesses.

(Paley 1984: x–xi)

Paley goes on to pronounce that 'No amount of adult subterfuge or propaganda deflects the five-year-old's passion for segregation by sex' (Paley 1984: ix). Every year, she recounts, 'the girls begin with stories of good little families, while the boys bring us a litany of superheroes and bad guys' (Paley 1984: 3).

Superheroes, war and weapon play:

In the UK, it is the work of Penny Holland (2003) that has most challenged early years practitioners to face their own prejudices and ideologies when encountering superheroes in their settings and classrooms. Her research analysed the experiences of one inner London under-5s centre that decided to relax its 'zero-tolerance' approach to war, weapon and superhero play. In other words, challenging a policy that said 'we don't play with guns here'. Holland explains that, in common with most early years settings she had visited, this was not a policy that was written down. Rather it was a policy adopted consensually by early years staff – predominantly female – who saw their role when confronted with weapons and violent reenactments as peacekeepers, shunning violence or attempting to channel it into something more creative. In seeking to question this policy, Holland firstly established the impact of a policy of zero-tolerance on the children and their play. She found that too many children, particularly boys, were receiving a disproportionate amount of negative attention; that these constantly negative interactions were damaging well-being and self-esteem; that following adult intervention boys were more prone to disruptive behaviour. Finally, for many boys, this was their only outlet for sustained imaginative play and it was being removed. These concerns are echoed by others who write about war and weapon play (Paley 1984; Rich 2003). One key concern is for those children for whom there is a conflict of ideology between the early years setting with a policy of zero-tolerance and the home where such play is tolerated or encouraged or where it is modeled as necessary and appropriate by parents, for example, those serving in the armed forces.

Following the relaxation of the zero-tolerance policy in Holland's own setting, she reports that staff felt that children's self-esteem – especially that of the boys – increased; that children were learning about moral issues such as violence, aggression and justice through their play without this being controlled by adults; that it was giving children conflict resolution strategies in genuine situations and that for boys, in particular, it was 'providing the seeds for rich imaginative play' (Holland 2003).

Media images

It is not only the world of superheroes that impacts on children's play culture. Media coverage of recent violent events has found its way repeatedly into children's homes and into children's play. Adams and Moyles (2005) describe very graphically how, since the events of 9/11, children seem to be struggling to find a response to the different images they have seen portrayed on television in particular, and that many were doing so through their play. Events such as 9/11, the BSE crisis – when many animals were seen being slaughtered – and the Asian Tsunami with its images of panic and destruction, provoke a range of emotions in adults and so we should not underestimate their emotional impact on children. While as adults we may have learnt to manage and control our emotions, this may not be the case for young children and play becomes the only way in which they can act out what may have perturbed, frightened or bewildered them. Adams and Moyles' work sensitively questions practitioners about their responses to children's play, behaviour and language following the viewing of violent events. It challenges all of us to examine our personal prejudices and value systems and asks where we individually draw the line between the tolerable and the unacceptable. Adams and Moyles (2005: 21) suggest 12 underpinning focus points for individuals and staff teams to consider when discussing this delicate subject. They are well worth reproducing here:

1 Violence portrayed in the media is powerful in terms of its visual imagery but can be viewed very impassively (or ignored) by adults. This could lead to adults or children becoming desensitized to violence and then not understanding right or wrong.
2 All children are exposed to violence portrayed through the media in ways that make it extremely pervasive.
3 Violence is promoted through fantasy, (games such as Play Station, and traditional stories and rhymes), as well as news items reporting reality.
4 Practitioners have a responsibility for confronting their own feelings and making informed responses to children's representations of violence.
5 Practitioners are responsible for understanding their local communities and working in the best interest of that community.
6 Practitioners may feel insecure or disturbed by the strongly held

beliefs of others, including children, and need opportunities to talk openly with other professionals.

7 Practitioners should set clear boundaries to protect the rights of all involved in their settings. Conflicts need to be addressed rather than appeased or ignored.

8 Children are more likely to express concerns or fears in an ethos of trust, reassurance and openness. They require time to explore their responses through play and talk.

9 Boys' and girls' experiences affect their attitudes to other people, faiths, cultures and ethnic groups; children's own experiences must be the starting point for discussion.

10 All children should be treated with equal respect and concern, although ways of expressing their feelings may differ. They should be allowed to represent violence through play or other means, in the curriculum.

11 Children are entitled to protected opportunities to express feelings of anger, frustration, fear, sadness or concern.

12 Cultural violence is all pervasive, influencing practitioners' construct of childhood and the role that they have in supporting children's development and learning.

Ethnicity, culture and beliefs

Many of the issues raised in the section above relate to children who are from minority ethnic communities. Much of the confusion of 'right' and 'wrong' in recent media coverage stems from the demonization of certain ethnic groups and the polarization of views as to the outcome of, particularly, terrorist events. Following 9/11, for example, children may have been confused by news that was condemned in America while being sometimes seen to be celebrated in other places. Liz Brooker (2002) reminds us that children can meet conflicting values and expectations between their own culture and that of the school/setting which can lead to confusion in identity and self-esteem. Families and children from minority cultural, religious and ethnic backgrounds may bring very different beliefs and attitudes into the settings they attend and these may not always sit comfortably with those of the practitioners. Furthermore, particularly after 7/7 in London and the increasing hostility to minority ethnic groups generally, children may be made more aware of the way Muslims and others are often portrayed in the media and may be attending settings which such children also attend. Any resulting hostility may be reflected in their play. As Adams and Moyles (2005) argue, we must ensure that as adults working alongside young children, we give children permission to play out their fears and their anxieties, their emotions and their feelings, even when these cut across our own personally held values and beliefs. But racial prejudice and discrimination are not the same as matters of differing (and sometimes conflicting) beliefs and values – they are always unacceptable in any situation. So it is important to distinguish between them. While our concern is for the self-esteem and the well-being of each individual child, it is crucial that practitioners are sufficiently sensitive to intervene when there is evidence of racial prejudice or discrimination from whatever source. Practitioners have to make very informed decisions about when one child's entitlement to express themselves interferes with another child's absolute right not to be oppressed or abused.

Playful environments

What we know about children is that they play naturally and spontaneously. They only need to be observed in parks, in doctor's waiting rooms, in gardens and in shops. Children spontaneously find things to play with and create situations in which to be playful. Whatever is driving this, and the explanations outlined above are only some of many, children find in the most ordinary things, the wherewithal to create alternative, imaginary scenarios that can absorb them for considerable periods of time. So what are the features of an environment that inspires children to be playful?

Time

There is no doubt that high-quality play – using Tina Bruce's definition of freeflow play – needs time to evolve. It can start off as messing about or investigating or what Marjatta Kalliala calls 'dizziness' (2006: 94) but for children to become absorbed, it requires no time constraints and no deadlines. In most of our memories of childhood play there is an ephemeral feeling of timelessness that pervades our images of ourselves in playful situations.

Resources

It takes very little to inspire freeflow play. No toys are necessary. Sticks can be weapons or wands, a bundle of clothes can be a doll or a magic package, a tree can be a hideout, an empty box can be a treasure chest. In fact, the less structured the resources that children use, the more their imaginations can soar and their creativity can flourish. Certain more open-ended resources are often inspirational too – good-quality bricks and blocks, construction equipment, sand and water – but their value as play resources comes from the fact that no adult has determined how they will be used and what their outcome should be.

Outdoors: the outdoor environment is ideal for playfulness. Trees, slopes, grass, logs, streams, sticks and bushes all inspire children to create alternative and fantasy worlds. The greater the expanse the better, the further from adults the better.

Being away from adults

Children do not need adults in order to play. Very often children are at their least inhibited and at their most creative when adults are nowhere in sight. Being alone seems to lead children to be more adventurous, more inventive and to inhabit an imaginary world with less inhibition.

Other children

Other children are not essential to play but, more often than not, children from the age of about 2 years prefer to engage in play when other children are around. Pretend situations are so much easier when there is a friend to be the other witch, to be the baby, to carry your queen's train and to go into battle alongside you. Play that involves construction is easier when there is a friend to lift the other end of the wood, to hold the tower while you try and balance another brick, to dig beside you so that you can get to Australia more quickly. Other children bring out playfulness in their peers. It seems a world that they are instinctively at ease in co-inhabiting and co-constructing. It is a world that they own with confidence and surety.

Boredom

Sometimes children become most creative and playful when they are bored. Many children today are involved in a whole series of adult-constructed play situations – football, karate, dancing, piano lessons and playgrounds. All these are entirely valid but do not give children much opportunity to develop their own creative voice and their own imaginary alternatives. It can be when there are no planned activities, and when there is no television or computer at hand, that children turn to their own resources and develop play situations from the most unlikely beginnings. Very often the cry 'I'm bored' precedes some of the most creative play. It is not that boredom is a prerequisite for play but that being constantly in planned play situations can extinguish children's own imaginative energies.

Creating a playful environment in Foundation Stage settings

The great challenge for Foundation Stage practitioners is, once again, to emulate the most effective features of the best learning environments found in the home and the local community. In working alongside countless practitioners from nursery through to Year 1, I believe that the following are essential points for consideration when planning an effective environment for playful learning:

1 Play has to be the first *consideration in planning the environment*
When play is consigned to the corners of a classroom already set up for more formal learning, it doesn't work. Play needs more space than a squashed-up home corner in the only place not filled with tables. Start by identifying what play spaces children need and make these available. If some of them – for example small world play – need table tops, then that is when to add some tables (see Chapter 5 for more ideas for planning the learning environment in general).

2 Play needs open-ended and adaptable resources
As I have suggested above, play does not rely on resources. Children – especially in the outdoors – will usually find their own. However, the world of the early years setting has, to some extent, to be 'manufactured' for learning and the adults within it must make informed choices about what play resources will stimulate deep-level learning. I believe that any high quality play provision in the Foundation Stage needs the following:

- as large and natural an outdoor space as possible;
- a sand-pit (not just a tray) outside;
- water play and resources such as gutters and pipes and pumps;
- wooden blocks of various sizes;
- a home corner that is lifelike and robust and large enough to accommodate a whole 'family' and their neighbours;
- endless supplies of dressing-up materials.

3 Play needs the opportunity to flow from one place to the next
Like most things in the life of a young child, play is not neat and tidy. One of the reasons that it is inhibited by small spaces is that play often moves about. It goes from the home corner to the 'shop' or 'travel agent' and back again. It goes from the sand-pit into the outdoor house and back again. It goes from the woodwork table to the garden and back again. Play scenarios and play resources get transported from one place to the other and are often discarded en route. Play will flow as it develops, attracting children and losing others, moving from one idea to the next with the purposefulness that is only ever seen in child-initiated activity. Foundation Stage learning environments need to

ensure that play can move about in this way, uninhibited by tables, other resources, adult rules and clutter. 'Only four can play' is a complete anathema to playful behaviour. Rules such as these are an indication of limited space or the adult's desire to control the play situation. If play is dominated by constraints of this nature, then this is what will dominate play and my experience is that children will spend longer talking about 'you can't play' than they will becoming immersed in playful activity.

4 Play must be the bedrock of children's learning experiences
Play will not be effective or of high quality if it is seen as having a different status to work (see Chapters 4 and 9). This means that play is what most children in the Foundation Stage should engage in most of the time. The environment should be set up so that the kind of play resources listed above and the kind of play opportunities listed on page 129 are available every day and so that children learn how to move purposefully and independently from one learning situation to another. Only when the play environment is truly absorbing and engaging for children can the adult then plan more adult-focused interventions. If practitioners attempt to plan this sequence the other way round, that is, if they plan a more structured and adult-dominated environment first and then attempt to offer play opportunities in a limited way – maybe when adult-initiated work is finished or 'just before assembly' – then the play will be as impoverished as the time allowed for it.

5 Play is not 'as well as', 'instead of' or 'what comes after' work
There are some practitioners who say there isn't time for children to play as well as do everything else that the early years curriculum requires. This is to misunderstand entirely the purpose of play in an early years setting. Play is not 'something else'. It is not another Area of Learning but, rather, the *way* in which children will become scientists and designers and writers and mathematicians. It is concerned with the processes of learning and is not some additional subject that has to be covered 'as well as' the rest of the curriculum.

Neither does play take place 'instead of' work. It has different purposes. It has been said that play *is* the child's work (Isaacs 1932), but very often 'work' is seen by children as the activity that adults require them to do, while play is initiated and directed by themselves. We have seen that both adult-initiated and child-initiated experiences are necessary in the effective early years setting. While play is the bedrock of Foundation Stage practice, the 'work' comes when the adult plans activities that focus children's learning on a new skill or the repetition of a developing concept or the rehearsal of newly acquired knowledge.

Finally, play should never 'follow' work. It should not be dangled as the carrot to be won if and when the less appetizing tasks set by the adult are completed. Play will never have the status it needs and deserves if it fits into the spaces left when the work is finished. It needs children to be at their freshest and brightest, not weary from the completion of adult-initiated tasks. Not only do children need play to take place alongside adult-initiated learning, but adults need it too. As we have seen in Chapter 4, if adults plan for only adult-initiated activities to take place all at the same time, they will be torn between which groups and individuals to support. Early years practitioners can give their attention to adult-focused tasks most successfully when the other children are engaged in more independent learning – and the most effective independent learning takes place during high-quality play.

6 Play resources and spaces should not be changed too frequently
One common mistake in the planning of play provision by those who are inexperienced is to change the resources for play too frequently. This is to confuse the fact that the early learning environment needs to be 'stimulating' with the belief that it needs to be ever changing. Stimulation can be maintained for quite some considerable time if the opportunities are the right ones at the right time. A good rule of thumb is that while children are involved or engaged with certain resources or scenarios, then these are providing stimulation and do not need to be interfered with or changed. It is once they lose their cognitive shine that the skilled adult knows that fresh opportunities must be made available or that an existing play situation needs to be refreshed and extended by the addition of new materials or resources.

'Planned' and 'structured' play

One way in which many adults strive to justify play is by prefacing it with the words 'planned' or 'structured'. The two terms are often used interchangeably but, to me, they imply very different things. Firstly, 'planned' play implies that play in an early years setting is not as likely to be as spontaneous or unstructured as it is in home or community environments. By very dint of the fact that all space and resourcing and timetabling are planned by adults, there will always be an element of adult intervention in Foundation Stage play. Nevertheless, adults can facilitate the kind of opportunities described above or constrain and inhibit play opportunities also as described above. Early years educators must make wise choices and have their principles about how young children learn firmly to hand if their planning is to be in the best interests of children's playful experiences.

'Structured' play suggests a very different emphasis. If play is 'structured', then it implies more than adult *intervention* and borders on adult *interference*. If adults structure play – if, for example, they say 'go into the home corner and act out the story of the Three Bears' – then the learning opportunity being provided for the children is not play. The children may be using play resources and they may be in a play space, but the experience they are having is not play. It has become, instead, an adult-initiated activity (see Chapter 4). In other words, the adult has a purpose for the activity; an outcome that they wish the children to achieve and a set of learning intentions that prescribed and constrain what the children will do. Now, once again, there is nothing inherently wrong in an 'act out the Three Bears' activity (although I do sometimes think that certain authors must be grieving for the purposes for which they originally wrote their classic tales), but practitioners must not plan for this kind of 'structure' and then try and pass it off as play.

Why is play challenging to early years practitioners?

One of the most important things to do if early years practitioners want to improve the quality of play in their settings is to confront the fears and anxieties that exist about introducing a more play-based curriculum. Nothing is ever gained by repeatedly extolling the virtues of play, only to leave the planned provision highly structured and controlled by adults rather than children.

Play does not have defined outcomes

Early years practitioners in the UK have identified skills, concepts and knowledge that young children should have acquired by age 5 (see the Early Years Foundation Stage, DfES 2007). Because of this there is a strong concern that if adults do not plan for and cover the curriculum in a structured way, children will not achieve all their Early Learning Goals. There is a belief that when adults direct children's learning, children will learn what the adult has planned that they should learn. Conversely, there is a fear that when children are playing, they will learn something completely unpredictable. That is, of course, the case. By definition, play has no defined outcomes and adults can have no idea what learning will take place when children are engaged in playful experiences. However, the first myth to dispel is that when they are playing, children will not learn anything that relates to the curriculum. The early years curriculum – with the possible exception of the Early Learning Goals related to

Linking Sounds and Letters (DfES 2007a:13) are about key processes and skills and are in evidence whenever children are engaged in high-quality play. Children:

- negotiate when sharing blocks in the block area;
- calculate when constructing models to their own specifications;
- extend their vocabulary when discussing who takes on which roles in the home corner;
- investigate objects and materials when creating a fantasy world in the sand-pit;
- use a range of large and small equipment as they extend their physical skills in the outdoor area;
- express and communicate their ideas, thoughts and feelings as they play alongside each other in fantasy and small world play.

So, when children are playing, they are always learning something that is required by the 'educational programme' of the Early Years Foundation Stage. The task of the adult is to observe what that is and record it appropriately.

Next, however, the notion that adults will know what children will learn if they direct their activity needs to be challenged. As I said in Chapter 4, one adult alone cannot be sure what a whole group of children will learn, even if they are all being 'taught' the same thing at the same time. The larger the group the less likely it is that children will all gain the same from an activity or explanation or discussion, and there are likely to be a number of children who will gain little because the experience is too easy or too demanding. Even when adults direct learning with a small group of children, there is a chance that some children will misunderstand or simply not engage with the adult's agenda. We know that at different points of the day, or week, or their life, children are preoccupied with things that take their concentration away from the focus of the adult's preoccupations and reduce their capacity to learn.

Finally, when learning is directed by adults, then children's experiences are often inhibited by the learning intentions of the activity. In other words, children will learn what the adult has planned, no more and no less. In play, however, the boundaries of what children might learn are limited only by their own creativity and drive. In support of this, Vygotsky asserts that 'a child's greatest achievements are possibly in play' (1966: 92).

Observation and first-hand evidence reveals how, when children are engaged in high-quality play, they will be learning something meaningful and relevant – however unpredictable. So, it may not be that all children will learn what an adult intends all of the time, but at least if some children are engaged in play, then they will be learning something that is meaningful to them at that moment, and are more likely to retain and cherish the skills or knowledge they have learnt because these have meaning and purpose for them.

Play can take a long time

Another grumble about play from those who have yet to observe its potential is that it takes a long time. Give a child a worksheet and they will complete it and then be ready to move on. Give a child an adult-directed task and they will finish as orchestrated by the adult and then move on. It is indeed true that high-quality play takes time to evolve, but early years educators have to ask which is of more value – a large number of 'tasks' that are finished quickly but where learning is relatively superficial and not particularly engaging, or a play scenario that may stretch over days, seemingly concerned with one theme and yet incorporating many if not all of the areas of learning and meeting any number of adult learning objectives (see Box 7.1).

Box 7.1   Example 6 Child-initiated activities involving learning in many curriculum areas

In this Foundation Stage setting, reception children are free to play indoors and out, with about an hour and a half in each session given to uninterrupted child-initiated activity, alongside the other 3 and 4 year-old children. The context for this play, is that building work had been taking place on site, including the building of an extension. The children had been able to watch the whole process through a mesh fence. A few weeks before, a huge cement machine had been used to pour cement into the foundations of the new extension through a large plastic pipe. On one afternoon, a group of reception children had gathered guttering, crates, spades and a wheelbarrow and were transporting sand from the sand pit. They spent an hour patiently bringing sand up to the top of the mound in the school garden which, on the one side, is the back of an 'amphitheatre'. They used the wheelbarrow and poured sand down the guttering angled on the crates with the aid of spades. The steps for the amphitheatre have vertical wooden panels at the front, filled in with 'hogging' – gravelly sand, this had got scattered and had left the panels sticking up and easy to trip over. The children had noticed this and said they were 'making the steps safe'.

In the course of this extended activity, the children were talking to one another, negotiating roles and working as a harmonious team. They were exploring scientific ideas of how to transport and funnel the sand into the right place, and problem-solving the challenge of the hazardous step and how to make it safe. They were drawing on their recent observations of building work and role-playing being builders. They were exploring the physical skills necessary to manoeuvre the wheelbarrow up a steep grassy slope, and how to balance the guttering on the crates. Throughout they were focused, self-motivated, involved and persistent.

Play does not guarantee to 'cover' the curriculum

I hope I have already dispelled this concern. With the exceptions highlighted in the section above, play cannot help but address all aspects of the early years curriculum – especially with the judicious selection of resources and opportunities that early years educators have to make every day in their planning. Play may not 'cover the curriculum' in any prescriptive or predictable manner, but no high quality playful scenario takes place without a wealth of language, social interaction, emotional involvement, mathematical and scientific application, physical manipulation and creative imagination. This does not mean, however, that there is no place for adult intervention! What effective adults do is to observe the emerging patterns or schemas in children's play (Athey 2007; Nutbrown 2006) and use this to plan for extending or supplementing play provision on future occasions. Adults also draw together and emphasize key aspects of learning at appropriate moments. This may be during a review time with an individual child or group of children when play is in flow or when it has drawn to a conclusion. It may be at the end of a session in order to give status to the play experiences children have had as they played independently. It may be that during observation of children's play, the adult observed that a child has struggled with a concept or skill and that this would benefit from direct teaching or explanation. It may become apparent that a number of children have reached a similar point in their conceptual development and would benefit from a more focused activity to reinforce their developing awareness. It may be that the adult wants to introduce their group to some new materials or some different opportunities that are available and can do this best with a group in a more focused way. The skilled early years educator emphasizes, reinforces and rehearses different aspects of the curriculum with children at key moments. But these moments are only identifiable when children's play is observed sufficiently well and understood as the basis for all key learning experiences and opportunities. In this way, adults can ensure that children are introduced to aspects of the curriculum in systematic ways alongside the more spontaneous and unpredictable opportunities offered by play.

Play can be messy

Play has already been identified as 'messy' in the context of planning described above. Play is difficult to manage if you are someone who likes order, control and predictable outcomes. In addition, play can be literally messy. We know that most young children do not place a high priority on tidying up as they go along. Clothes leave a trail from one play space to another. Resources find their way from the inside to the outside, from the sand-pit to the water tray. Resources are used and discarded as other props and materials come to hand. This is part of the creativity of play, this taking up and putting down of tools that serve a purpose and enhance the moment. When play is in full flow, any requests to tidy up can completely cut across children's creative intentions and interfere with their action and activity. There will be time for tidying up at certain points in the day that do not interfere with children's playful preoccupations. Children need to understand that sharing play space means leaving it sufficiently tidy for others to access. However, it is a mistake to expect the tidying up to take place while the play is taking place. Early years practitioners need to be sensitive to the right moment to ask for the communal good to be considered.

There is often an expectation in early years settings for spaces to be tidied at the end of the session or the end of the day. While this can seem necessary or desirable when planning for a different group of children in the afternoon, it can destroy the flow of play for those children who want to pick up where they left off the next day. Where possible, play spaces and play scenarios should be respected and, if the end of the session interrupts a particularly valuable play situation, then adults need to find ways of protecting the space and the resources so that children can start again when they return the next day.

The early years is not the place for adults who are obsessed with tidiness and predictability. It is one of the chief challenges that we face when evaluated or inspected by people who like order and precision and outcomes. The joy of the early years is in its spontaneity. It is what makes working alongside young children such a delight and keeps us so fresh and engaged in our work. Adults should resist the urge to tidy up as they go along or to bring order to the play environment just because it makes *them* feel better or because they think it will persuade a visitor that something more while is going on.

Play can be boisterous

Finally, play can be boisterous. For some early years practitioners this can be as disconcerting as the fact that it can be messy. This has to be confronted. If adults try and stop boisterous play, then they are removing valuable opportunities for children, particularly boys, to let off steam, to use up supplies of testosterone and to develop their physical powers and prowess. Play spaces in the home and the community are under increased threat from urbanization. Traffic, stranger danger and synthetic play areas have reduced play opportunities for children away from adults and out of doors. There is a growing concern among play organisations that the simplistic pursuit of 'safety' across play provision – staffed and unstaffed – has the unintended consequence of making provision so boring that children are denied the opportunity to engage in 'beneficial risk-taking' (e.g. www.playlink.org.uk) in formally provided provision and seek out more dangerous play situations to give themselves the challenge and excitement that play can and should provide. Children need to experience risk and personal challenge in their play and outdoor play can and should provide this. Many early years practitioners who have introduced an open-door policy for using the outside area for learning all session alongside the indoors, report a dramatic improvement in children's behaviour. They describe how children often run around and burn off excess energy to begin with and then settle to something more concentrated and purposeful as the session goes on.

The provision of an outdoor area that is constantly available to children instantly increases the size of the learning environment. If space indoors is cramped, then an outdoor area expands the learning opportunities in a trice. Children become used to moving between the outside and the inside areas and take both resources and experiences from one location to the other. But the outdoor area does not just provide more space, it also provides different opportunities to the inside. Outside there is room for children to experience large-scale movements that are often impractical indoors. They can paint with big brushes, draw and crayon on large rolls of paper, walls or the ground, run and skip and jump and balance, roll down slopes and clamber up ropes. Outdoors children can experience fresh air and vigorous activity. They use more oxygen, strengthen large muscles and increase their blood supply to the brain. At a time when there are such concerns for children's sedentary lives, early years practitioners should be overjoyed that they are being encouraged to provide boisterous play opportunities for children in their settings. However, boisterous play needs to be channelled purposefully and there is no better place to do this than in a good-quality outdoor area for learning. If children are inclined to be boisterous, then the best thing to do is to provide them with the opportunities to be so in the outdoor area and not to suppress this drive as it may only spill out into more aggressive behaviour at another time and in a more negative way.

The role of the adult in supporting children's play

The role of the adult in children's play is difficult to describe. It is as complex and varied as play itself. We have already considered in this chapter how, if adults dominate play or seek to control it, then it becomes another activity altogether. Activities that adults direct are adult-initiated or adult-intensive, they are not play. So how does the adult intervene to improve the quality of play? How does the adult ensure that these interventions do not end up being interference?

Adult as facilitator

The primary role of the adult is in providing an environment conducive to high-quality play. This means facilitating the time, space, resources, experiences and opportunities outlined above. The adult has been responsible for developing the environment – both indoors and out – and selecting the resources, but it is the *environment* that stimulates and entices the child to be playful rather than any adult direction.

Adult as observer

The adult understands that at play, children reveal the true level of their competence and skill. Observation of children in a range of play situations is crucial if the adult is to understand what a child knows, understands and can do. Play also shows the extent of children's social and emotional development. If adults observe children at play, then they will be in the best position to identify what aspects of learning need reinforcement, repetition or extension and these can become the focus of adult-intensive planning at a later date.

Adult as responder

When an adult sits alongside children at play, they can act as a catalyst for questions, conversation and ideas. Sometimes the adult does nothing and the children simply invite the adult into the play through their ideas and suggestions. Sometimes the adult talks aloud as they play, in parallel to begin with, commenting on what they are doing with the blocks, in the water tray and so on. In either case, the adult is alert to the children's ideas, moods and activity and can respond, maybe just by nodding and smiling, but offering reassurance that the play has value.

Adult as protagonist

Following a period of careful observation, the adult may feel that the play has lost its momentum or needs a fresh idea in order to maximize its potential. This can be a very delicate decision. All too often adults can misunderstand the children's purposes or the direction of their play and the adult intervention then destroys the play situation altogether. Sometimes the adult offers an idea or poses a question and children ignore it, preferring to stay with their own focus and their own direction. However, a well-timed comment or question can fan the flames of the play and give it a fresh impetus and new energy.

Adult as co-constructor

Sometimes the adult's parallel play or their close and sensitive attention to children's play results in an invitation to become more closely involved. Children may give the adult a role in pretend play; may invite the adult to join in the construction of a model; and may suggest the adult tries different resources or a new challenge in the water tray. The adult and child together then become playful in their interactions and co-construction of shared playful experiences.

Raising the status of play

In order to raise the status of play, early childhood educators need to have first-hand experience of its value. It is no good reading about play but never seeing it in action; to provide for it in the corners of the environment or the timetable and not observe its potential when resourced and supported in the ways described above. If you have never seen high-quality play, then go and visit a nursery school or a Foundation Stage setting where it is the bedrock of practice. The development of high-quality play needs a commitment to it as being central to the curriculum for young learners. *Box 7.1* suggests a charter for play that may support practitioners in raising the status of play in the Foundation Stage.

Box 7.2 A charter for play

1 *Acknowledge* its unique contribution as a process by which young children learn.
2 *Plan* for it as an integral part of the curriculum and not an 'added extra'.
3 *Facilitate* it with appropriate and high-quality resources.
4 *Act* as a catalyst when intervention is appropriate and a scaffolder when expertise is required.
5 *Observe* it in order to have first-hand evidence of children's learning.
6 *Evaluate* it in order to better understand the needs of the learner.
7 *Value* it through comment and commitment in order for its status to be appreciated.
8 *Fight* for it with rigorous, professional argument in order to bring about deeper understanding and acceptance by colleagues, parents, managers and the community at large.

Conclusion

Play is the natural way in which children go about the business of learning. It enables them to integrate and consolidate a wealth of experiences that enhance their cognitive, physical, social and emotional development. It naturally encourages cooperation and collaboration, requires the use of fine and gross motor skills and demands cognitive application. It is pleasurable, but also helps children face pain and sorrow. It is consuming and challenging and motivating. The relevance of play to early years education is unquestionable and its status in Foundation Stage provision in the classroom should be assured. In Chapter 8 we look at other situations in which children can have power and control in their settings and ask whether children can be motivated by the negotiation of elements of their learning and their learning environment.

THE NEGOTIATED LEARNING ENVIRONMENT

Issues of ownership, power and control

Introduction

The idea of learning being negotiated is a challenge to any curriculum that prescribes the process and content of experiences without taking into account the current needs and interests of children. A developmentally appropriate curriculum, as described in Chapter 3, is built on what individual children know and need to know next. It is a curriculum that starts from the child rather than expecting the child to start from the curriculum. When early years practitioners see the desirability of motivating children in this way, then the learner is placed in a powerful position. Rather than being a passive recipient of someone else's decision-making and control, the learner is an active participant in the formation of their own experiences. When young children exercise control in the learning environment, it determines the relationship between educator and learner. The relationship becomes a partnership in which children can negotiate input and outcomes in ways that increase their autonomy and sense of purpose. This does not diminish the role of the adult but alters it. The idea that learning is controlled by the learner:

> presupposes that knowledge is not transmitted directly from the teacher to the learner. It demands that both teacher and learner recognise that the subject matter of learning resides outside their 'circle of intimacy', rather than exclusively in the teacher.
>
> (Rowland 1984: 149)

Transitions

Transition from home to a new early years setting

When the child moves from the familiar and secure learning environment of the home to a new school or early years setting, they have to make a number of adjustments. The older the child when this transition occurs, then the greater the gap between the informality and spontaneity of the home environment and the more orderly, planned surroundings of the new educational environment. Settings that exclusively care for and educate children below age 5 usually make strenuous efforts to create an environment that mirrors the home and community, with comfy areas for sharing books and talking together, areas for boisterous play, trips out to the shops and all manner of other real-life experiences that offer children rich learning opportunities.

But making the transition from home to a new learning environment is fraught with possible setbacks and needs to be carefully thought through. There are many adjustments that both children and their parents and carers need to make in order to adapt to this new cultural situation. Vygotsky (1978) suggests that the historical, cultural and institutional context shapes children's individual development and their view of the world and yet many practitioners still underestimate the huge cultural shock that children sometimes experience in the transition from home to nursery or early years classroom. Bronfenbrenner (1979) explains that the transition from home to nursery is usually the first and major ecological transition in children's lives. Children are suddenly faced with making new relationships and finding themselves in a new position in the social hierarchy. As home and nursery have different purposes, children may be confronted with a totally different cultural model of expectations from the adults around them.

When thinking about the transition that children make from home to the early years setting or classroom, practitioners might reflect on the following in order to minimize the cultural shock of transition.

- identifying a Key Person (see Elfer *et al.* 2003), who will have a close and loving relationship with the child and their family for the duration of the child's time in the setting;
- undertaking home visits, which will introduce the Key Person to the family at home and enable them to see the child in familiar and secure surroundings so that the Key Person is already a familiar figure;
- having conversations with parents and carers to learn as much about the child as possible before they visit the setting;
- arranging as many visits to the new setting as necessary for the child

and their primary caregiver to be confident and secure before the child begins at the setting;
- offering the opportunity for the parent or caregiver to remain as long as necessary (each day and over days) once the child starts at the new setting until everyone is sure that the transition is secure.

Transition between settings in the foundation stage

Of great concern to many early childhood educators is that, due to a number of social and political pressures, too many children are currently making several transitions during their Foundation Stage career, at a time in their lives when they most need stability and security. It is not just the case that children make a number of significant transitions in a linear way, that is, from a childminder at age 2 to a playgroup at age 3 to a nursery class at age 4 to a primary class at age 5. This would be bad enough with all the social and cultural confusions that this can entail. But our youngest children are also making vertical transitions. In other words, in the course of one day, many of them make the transition from home to a childminder, then to a morning pre-school, then to an afternoon nursery class, then back to the childminder and then home. In her powerful article 'Key Persons in the Early Years Foundation Stage' (2006), Dorothy Selleck describes these transitions as 'serial care', as children are moved from pillar to post very often for the needs of the adults in their lives rather than their own. Selleck challenges these practices by saying that 'I can think of no other adult scenario in which constant transitions would be thought of as desirable, ethical or healthy' (p. 12).

When practitioners realize just how many adjustments and re-adjustments young children are making as they try to settle into their particular setting, then staff need to work hard to reduce the discontinuities children might face. This can only be achieved if practitioners, across all sectors, work more closely together to iron out the discontinuities that are unnecessary and undesirable. The best place to start is from the child's perspective. Many practitioners have revolutionized their practice having once tracked a single child across their Foundation Stage experiences in one day or one week. Only when we see the world through the child's eyes do we truly understand just what is involved in making adjustments from one setting to the next. Early childhood educators who have tackled the issues of transition between settings in the Foundation Stage have found that some of the following prompts have brought about improvements for children's experiences:

Developing a shared understanding of transition

- Transition is the responsibility of all those in the child's foundation stage experience.
- Improving transition means promoting a common language between early years practitioners (e.g. does everyone know what 'child-initiated' learning means?).
- All staff involved in Foundation Stage transition need to respect and know more about each other's work.
- Understanding is enhanced if staff from both settings engage in joint observations of some children to moderate their own judgements about children and their stages of development.

Working with parents

- Parents and carers should be included in all discussions and decisions about the transfer of their children within the Foundation Stage and into Year 1.
- Parents and carers should be involved in developing a policy on transition for the setting their child attends.
- Parents and carers should be consulted about what went well when their child transferred and what could be improved.
- Parents and carers should be asked to talk to their children about their experiences of transition and any concerns – or enjoyable experiences – they might have had.
- So many weeks before the end of the term when transition will take place, parents and carers will be invited to a meeting with staff to hear about transition arrangements and to offer their own ideas about how this can be achieved most successfully.

Visits

- Staff from all settings need to be given time to go and visit and learn about the other Foundation Stage settings in their local area.
- Staff who are 'receiving' children in the Foundation Stage need to visit other settings frequently enough to know what they are building on and what expectations children are used to.
- Before the end of the term when transition will take place, children will have the chance to visit their new foundation stage setting.
- Early in the term following every transition, staff might visit the children they worked with the previous year/term to see how they have settled and progressed.

Observation, assessment and planning

- Staff who share children in the Foundation Stage (across different settings) should agree on consistent ways of observing and recording children's attainment and progress.
- Staff who share children in the Foundation Stage (across different settings) should agree on consistent ways of planning for children's learning experiences (this does not mean that formats have to be identical but that the components should be similar – see Chapter 9).
- Early years teachers in school should ensure that the documentation they use to plan for and record children's progress is relevant and appropriate to the way in which they teach (and not a school format that is inappropriate for a play-based, child-centered curriculum).
- When children make a transition from one Foundation Stage setting to another, the member of staff responsible should send the next early years educator a summary of the child's achievements across the Early Years Foundation Stage Areas of Learning (DfES 2007).

Becoming a 'pupil'

No matter how much work is undertaken to make children's first transitions as smooth as possible, within the first few hours of being in their new early years setting young children pick up messages that life here is going to be different. Most notably, the number of children around is different from home. Also the environment is probably more extensive and there are more adults around. Then there are the expectations of those adults. Not only are these different between home and the early years setting but very frequently they can be different between settings too. One of the hardest points of transfer for children, especially when this is happening in one day, is when expectations of them and their behaviour are different between one set of adults and the other – as confusing as it can be when two parents have different boundaries and sanctions. Where in one setting, for example, children have to ask to go to the toilet and in another, do not. Where in one setting children are expected to find and replace their own resources and in another they are found and replaced by the adults. Where in one setting guns and sword play are permitted and in another they are banned (Fisher 2006). Not only are adult expectations of behaviour frequently a cause of bewilderment, but also young children learn that in their different settings there are expectations to become a different sort of person, to take on new roles. No longer are they culturally secure in their role as daughter, son, granddaughter, nephew, but they become a 'pupil'. While most early years settings outside of the state sector do not use that word, the expectations can be similar. Children find that they have to wait their turn for something rather than receiving it instantly; they have to accommodate the preferences of other children rather than having their own way. They have to wait for certain times to eat or to have a snack. If children make a transition directly into an early years classroom, then the differences can be even more dramatic. This title 'pupil' carries with it attitudes and expectations, now their own, but learnt from the attitudes and expectations of those around them. 'When you're at school you won't be able to do that'; 'at big school they keep you in at dinnertime if you haven't finished your work'; 'now you're at school you'll learn proper things like sums and writing' – a mass of expectations that usually come in the form of well-meaning advice, but can also carry the undertones of threat.

In this way, children arrive at school with a notion, correct to a lesser or greater extent, about what it means to be a pupil. Children believe that they are in school to learn and the teacher to teach. The active role is that of the teacher and the appropriate role for a pupil is to be passive and receive the teaching. In good early years settings children are given as much autonomy as possible, but it is still a very different experience to be one among a large group of other children. This is where the role of the Key Person (Elfer *et al.* 2003) is so essential. If children move from a setting where there is a primary caregiver who has a close and intimate relationship with them to one where they are cared for by everybody rather than somebody, then children can very quickly feel unwanted or lonely. Colwyn Trevarthen says that young children need 'company which is interested and curious and affectionate' (Trevarthen 1998). The Key Person approach intends to give every child and family a loving, secure relationship over the EYFS with a particular practitioner so that each child has the reassurance they need to feel safe and so that parents have regular and consistent opportunities to share and contribute to their child's experiences. The Key Person is different from the Key Worker. The Key Worker is usually the person responsible for the care and education of a group of children, for having them 'at group time' and for keeping records on them. The two roles are not mutually exclusive but the emphasis is quite different. The Key Person makes sure that:

> within the day-to-day demands of the (early years setting) each child feels special and individual, cherished and thought about by someone in particular while they are away from home (Elfer *et al.* 2003: 18)

This role doesn't matter only for babies – although it matters to them most – but is necessary for any young child particularly when making their first transition away from home and home-based care.

Children will find their own ways of managing this new world. We know that they are active in constructing, reconstructing and responding creatively and differently, and will find their own ways of doing this in their new Foundation Stage settings. They may follow, negotiate, transform or reject becoming a 'pupil' but the process of negotiating their position in this new learning environment is a continuous process. Pollard and Filer (1999) point out that adaptation is actively, not passively, fitting in. Therefore, how children cope with and adapt to the new learning environment is crucial to their 'career' as a lifelong learner.

What all early years practitioners can do is to make the learning experiences in the early years setting as similar to those of the home as they can. To make learning lifelike and authentic, and to replicate the positive atmosphere and the genuine responses of parents and carers. All too often children who move directly into school can see few similarities between learning in the home and learning at school. The new learning environment can sometimes be full of second-hand experiences; of interruptions by adults; of writing down rather than acting out; of learning what the adult directs rather than what the children initiate. Good early years practitioners recognize that this is not an effective learning environment for young children. If children are to continue to be 'interested, excited and motivated to learn' (EYFS DfESa: 12), then practitioners must do everything possible to replicate the effective learning environment that has surrounded children since birth. If children are cut off from their previous success and expected to behave in ways that are alien to them, then this can exacerbate the myth that being a *pupil* is different from being a *child*.

Changing a child into a 'pupil'

As we have seen, there are many aspects of a Foundation Stage setting that tell a young child that their role in this place is somehow different from their role at home. Particularly for those practitioners who work in the school sector, it can be illuminating to reflect on how many practices insidiously turn the young enthusiastic spontaneous learner into a more passive and reactive 'pupil'. Some of these changes are necessary if children are to learn the social skills necessary for playing and learning and living alongside others other than their family members. Some, however, are simply designed to maintain the traditional status quo of classrooms, which is that teachers have the power and control, and the role of the child, as pupil, is to learn from the adult's greater skill and knowledge. One of the first rules that children are introduced to – and one of the most entrenched – is that of 'putting your hand up'. Sinclair and Coulthard (1975) call this 'bidding', which is an excellent description. The child is bidding for the adult's time by raising their hand in response to the demand to do so. It is a request to hold the floor and have the adult's attention. Putting up your hand demands an understanding of two basic rules: one, that in order to speak to the adult, this is what you need to do; two, that there are times when you can talk to other children and times when you cannot, and this is one when you cannot unless you are told that you can, in which case you must but only when you're told!

Because the rules and routines are bewildering, many children resort to imitation. Sometimes that imitation is of other children who have been in the setting longer or who have simply cottoned on faster. Children offer responses 'that clearly enough imitate those that have recently been offered and have seemed to please the teacher well enough to get positive feedback' (Willes 1983: 186). Sometimes the imitation is of the adults who, as Mary Willes describes, through their 'intonation, gestures and expression', give out clues that the child is left to guess about and test the meanings.

The rules and routines are frequently non-negotiable. They are the prerogative of the practitioner, and often she does not choose to or think to divulge them. Thus becoming a pupil is seen by Willes as learning these adult initiatives as rapidly as possible:

> The minimal, inescapable requirement that a child must meet if he [*sic*] is to function as a participating pupil is not very extensive. It is necessary to accept adult direction, to know that you say nothing at all unless the teacher indicates that you may, to know that when your turn is indicated you must use whatever clues you can find, and make the best guess you can. There are prerequisites to learning this. It is necessary to want adult attention and approval, and to be able to attend to a person or to a topic for more than a moment or two.
>
> (1983: 83)

This is 'training' in the true sense of the word. It is learning to respond in a given way to a given signal – behaviour with Pavlovian overtones.

Pleasing adults

The notion of pleasing adults is also a very important one in the discussion about power and control in environments for early learning. Holt (1982: 70) suggests that 'it is only when pleasing adults becomes important that the sharp line between success and failure appears'. This implies that children's perceptions of their own success or failure, their own worth and value come from the values and perceptions of the early childhood educators whom they encounter. We know that there is evidence of a self-fulfilling prophecy that operates in any educational environment. Tell a child that they are good, will succeed, are doing well and the child obliges by responding with enthusiasm and proving you right. Tell a child that they are worthless, useless, hopeless or any other damning adjective directed at a certain group of children daily in their educational lives, and lo and behold they prove us right again. Holt suggests that being incompetent has two advantages: firstly, it reduces what others expect of you and secondly, it reduces what you expect or even hope of yourself. When you set out to fail, he says, one thing is certain – you cannot be disappointed.

Chapter 1 showed that, whatever their experiences, most young children arrive at their early childhood class or setting as enthusiastic and energetic learners. Their early experiences in that setting can bring about a transformation in their attitudes and behaviours so that they become a shadow of their former competent selves. Howard Gardner, in his powerful book *The Unschooled Mind*, suggests that somehow

> the natural, universal, or intuitive learning that takes place in one's home or immediate surroundings during the first years of life seems of an entirely different order from the school learning that is now required throughout the literate world.
>
> (1993: 2)

In a similar vein, Janet Meighan (1993: 43) suggests that once children begin school, 'Learning how to learn gives way to learning how to be taught'.

So we return to the main question of this book. Why, when children in their early, formative years have achieved what Gardner calls a 'breathtaking array of competences with little formal tutelage' do some of those same children suddenly become dependent, passive learners, reliant on the adult for success and self-esteem? Gardner (1993: 3) suggests that 'schools were instituted precisely to inculcate those skills and conceptions that, whilst desirable, are not so readily and naturally learned as [their] intuitive capacities'. There is more than an element of truth in this. Schools, and now the whole range of Foundation Stage providers, are devices of society and, therefore, must respond to the requirements of that society and the cultures it serves. Unfortunately, in fulfilling this requirement, these settings can denude children of all their inherent powers as learners and make them feel as though their needs and their interests no longer have a place. For some children, the transition from home to school or setting marks a transition from success as a learner to failure. All too often it is the child who is a truly intuitive learner who is at greatest risk. Early years settings, particularly schools, do not always cater for individuals. Because of their very nature they demand a good deal of conformity, and early childhood settings that are not sufficiently flexible to allow for the idiosyncrasies of learners are likely to alienate some of the most creative and free-thinking children.

Disaffected learners

Feelings of alienation come about when there is a mismatch between the child's expectations of their new early learning setting and the setting's expectations of the child. According to Willes (1983), some children step out of line because they do not know where the line is drawn. Some children, however – those who are already having feelings of alienation because they do not fit with the setting's expectations – know where the lines are drawn, but deliberately cross them. In the introduction to her book on disaffection in the early years, Gill Barrett defines disaffection thus:

> Fundamentally the word implies a negative state of something that was once positive. Thus affection for something has been reversed to become disaffection. Here we are concerned with disaffection in the early years of schooling. Thus, instead of affection for the activities of schooling, disaffection implies a dislike and hence a turning away from the activities and learning expectations of the classroom and school.
>
> (1989: xiv)

If one considers that some children have only just started at school or their new setting, the implication of this definition is that the 'affection' was for learning that happened in contexts prior to and outside the setting. Disaffection, therefore, comes hard on the heels of affection for situations in which the child saw themselves as competent. Running right through this book is the notion of the young child as both a competent and motivated learner, and it is a dreadful indictment of the early childhood setting that can turn that motivation and competence so quickly into disaffection.

So how is this disaffection likely to manifest itself? Young children are unlikely to withdraw themselves from the environment as older children might do, as most young children choose to remain within the security of their early years setting even when feeling very aggrieved. Their most likely response is to reject or withdraw from the activities or tasks that they are being required to perform. If this withdrawal is 'active' the children can throw tantrums, disappear under tables or absent themselves into another room. Barrett (1989: 30) claims that the early years setting or classroom

> with all its new expectations and people, is likely to provoke strong responses such as crying, hitting other children and removing oneself from the source of frustration. If the child knows that these strong responses have always been responded to by an adult in the past, and the cause of frustration removed and dealt with, then it may cause even stronger response behaviour in school when the initial crying or attempted withdrawal fails to remove the expectation.

This is a terrible picture of the distress that some children feel and the anger that they consequently display. If the rebellion is more passive, then children simply stop doing what is asked of them, do it extremely slowly or make sure that they disrupt as many other children as possible in the process.

There can be no doubt that disaffection arises because children are asked to do things that make little sense to them. It is no justification to say that children have to learn to do this in life and, therefore, they should start now. This rationale is used for an astonishing range of experiences, from sitting still for long periods of time to enduring competition in games. Children may have to face a myriad of unpleasant and unhappy experiences before they grow old and die but this is no justification for inflicting such experiences on children just so that they can practise their future unhappiness.

One of the greatest frustrations for young children is that often they cannot articulate their own feelings. They find it hard to explain or describe what they feel and why. Gill Barrett's important study and the more recent work of Penny Lancaster and her team on *Promoting Listening to Children* (2003) shows that if adults are patient enough to ask – and willing to find out the answers – to why children are not responding positively, then they are half-way to resolving the problem for the child and, of course, for themselves and the rest of the children.

A further frustration for young children is the amount of interruption that they get from adults when they are engaged in activities. We have seen that one important principle of early childhood education is that the young learner has time for periods of sustained activity. Whether this is initiated by the child or the teacher, an adherence to the principle is crucial if children's experiences of learning in their early years setting are to emulate their experiences at home and if the practitioner is to give positive messages about the worth of the activity or experience in which the child is engaged. Barrett gives examples of the intense frustration young children feel when their experiences are interrupted:

Daniel and Carl have found a book on New Zealand (Carl's homeland). They start to read when the teacher calls, 'Time to put them away'. Daniel's face and comment show disappointment. 'But I've only just got it.'

There are always too many people in school to take things properly. You have to stop too soon. Someone always spoils it.

(Barrett 1989: 10)

Many early years educators are addressing the issue of interruptions to the learning day. Research by Campbell and Neill (1990) confirmed what all practitioners know that there always seems to be insufficient time in the day for all that has to be done. An audit of how time is spent in school, in particular, can reveal how much learning time is fragmented by the school timetable. Assemblies, playtime, lunches, television and so on, all interrupt the flow of learning for children. Each break requires teachers and children to wind themselves down and then to wind themselves back up again to achieve the momentum that was stopped. This is not an efficient use of time and it is a useful exercise to examine the interruptions in a classroom or within the school, and see if there are ways in which such interruptions can be minimized (see Chapter 5).

The negotiated classroom

The early learning environment, as we have seen, is a place where rules and expectations can be governed exclusively by adults and where children are unable to stake a claim. It is usually adults who create the learning environment for children, who decide what activities and opportunities are available and who decide what should be done where and with whom. But what happens if adults consciously and deliberately give children a stake in the process? What is possible if, in order to maintain and sustain their motivation, application and *rights*, children are taken on as partners in the shared negotiation of practice and behaviour?

The notion of negotiation

Sylvia Warham (1993: 35–6) suggests that in some ways teaching and learning are in themselves a negotiation because 'the process requires the consent of both the teacher and the learner'. The negotiation of the learning context between the early childhood educator and the children is a negotiation of what the children will allow the adult to do and what the adult will allow the children to do. Successful negotiation requires messages to emanate from the adult. When children are listened to and respected (Lancaster, 2003) and their ideas and interests absorbed into the fabric of their learning experiences, then this is a positive starting point for the negotiation of a more reciprocal partnership between educators and learner.

The identity of the adult as educator

There is a whole range of things in the context of the early years setting that can be negotiated with children. The extent to which these are adopted depends very much on the style of the early childhood educator responsible for establishing the learning environment, and her or his personal identity. Warham (1993) identifies educators who have 'dominant identities' and those who have 'less dominant identities'. She suggests that those who have dominant identities 'created inequality. The children found that only one person at a time could be dominant and they had to compete with one another and the teacher if they wanted to take part in the [class] discussion' (Warham 1993: 35–6). On the other hand, the less dominant educators appear to have 'no control over the situation', but in fact use a far greater range of strategies in interaction with children than the dominant educators. By encouraging children to be independent thinkers and learners, the control that less dominant educators exercise is far more subtle, but far more effective. Effective educators, says Warham, adopt both dominant and less dominant strategies in different situations, but she warns that it is important to be conscious of the positive effects of habitually less dominant strategies that she claims:

- foster trust, confidence and security;
- encourage in children a sense of self-worth and respect for others;
- encourage independence and self-reliance;
- encourage children to develop their own initiatives; and foster a sense of equality.

(Warham 1993: 37)

While habitually dominant power strategies may not prevent children from learning, it is possible that they carry with them certain inherent risks. Warham suggests that it is possible they may:

- foster competition to the point of confrontation;
- damage group and individual relationships;
- discourage the children from taking initiatives;
- make the children dependent on their teacher; and risk damaging the child's future attitude towards teachers and education.

(Warham 1993: 37)

The notion of negotiation can only sit comfortably with the less dominant strategies described above. The remainder of this chapter is devoted to looking at ways in which early years practitioners can move towards the kind of learning environments that acknowledge children's competences, respects their rights as individuals and sees education as a collaborative venture between learners.

The negotiated classroom

The possibilities for negotiation within the early learning environment fall into three broad categories:

- *organization*: when and how things are to be learnt;
- *context*: where and with whom they are to be learnt;
- *curriculum*: what is to be learnt.

Organization

The start of the day

At the beginning of the day children are full of energy and, we hope, enthusiasm. If they arrive at their setting and are required to sit down, sit still and – probably – sit quietly, then immediately they are having to adopt behaviours that suit the purposes of the adults rather than themselves. The children's needs are subsumed beneath the needs of the practitioner to sort out the early morning problems, to juggle children and parents, and to be seen as having a calm, controlled group. The beginning of the day does indeed establish the tone for much that will follow. If the day begins in ways that repress children, for whatever purposes, then this sends negative messages to children about those in power and control in the room, and in some children can set up feelings of frustration, alienation and resentment before the day has hardly begun.

In most early learning environments, children on arrival get straight down to activities that they choose themselves. Parents are encouraged to stay for as long as they can or want, and while children are engaged independently or with their parents or carers, the practitioner can get on with her administration or organization in the knowledge that the children are playing purposefully. If a child is new or younger and less settled, then this also gives the practitioner the opportunity to settle and calm them and have conversations on an individual level until the child is reassured and comforted. Some adults are concerned about starting the day in this way because of their responsibilities over completion of the register. However, completion of the register does not rely on children sitting on the carpet and responding to their names. There are a whole range of strategies for recording the arrival of children, from hanging names on a 'tree', to posting names in a letter box, to writing names on a white board. There are a whole variety of strategies that early years practitioners can employ if they feel that a formal registration does not set the tone that they want for the start of the day.

The organization of the learning environment

When I was in my first year of teaching I used to spend days before the beginning of each term organizing my classroom. I drove the caretaker mad by arranging and rearranging my room. I made labels, signs and charts, spent a fortune on card and pens and tacky-backed *everything*. I believed that it was part of my professional responsibility to make the room as 'ready' for the children as I could, so that it would look like a ready and welcoming environment in which we could all get down to work. As I began to give more and more time and thought to the involvement of children in decision-making processes within the classroom, however, I realized just what wonderful learning opportunities I was taking out of the hands of the children. Real-life problem-solving situations frequently stare us in the face in classrooms, and instead of responding to them as heaven-sent opportunities, we subject children to the contortions of 'identifying a need' for a problem for which they will rarely realize a solution and which they would never have identified for themselves.

Early learning environments *need* organizing, however. As Chapter 5 describes, there are decisions about space and resources that are fundamental to the establishment of spaces and areas that are conducive to independent learning. Since these are environments in which children are to learn, then it seems entirely logical that they should be environments that they help to create. Once I realized this I left the furniture where the caretaker had left it – in a heap in the middle of the classroom (yes, that really *was* his practice!). Then when the children arrived, we worked together to decide what learning areas were needed and where resources should go. Then came the business of sorting, locating and labelling resources which, because the children were so involved, gave them a sense of ownership over the classroom that they never had when I made the decisions and took the action, when they were not around.

Discipline: rules and sanctions

One successful way of helping children to respect and adhere to rules and sanctions is not to impose them from on high, but to negotiate them. Children can become involved in establishing rules that they perceive to be necessary in order for their learning environments to run smoothly and for the benefit of all. Children's rules sometimes reveal interesting insights into their perceptions of what is or is not important and what is or is not likely to happen when in their settings. 'The children mustn't spit', said one 4-year-old recently, who had arrived at school – now where did *that* idea come from?

The sanctions that children work out for themselves can be very enlightening. I had endeavoured, as a head teacher, to alter my role within the school in the disciplining of children. Rather than seeing children only when they had been naughty, I asked the staff to send me children with whom I could share something positive and worthwhile. This seemed to be working well, so I was dismayed when the reception class, on negotiating their own sanctions, ended a long list of mounting retribution with 'No. 6: Send them to Miss Fisher for telling off.' Children's perceptions are not altered overnight.

If rules make sense to children and if sanctions seem appropriate, even if not necessarily 'fair' in adult terms, then children are more likely to feel a sense of responsibility in maintaining them. One last word about rules, and that is   it is best to keep them positive. It contributes so much more constructively to the ethos of the classroom if the list talks about what we *will* do and be like rather than what we must *not* do or be like.

Order of experiences

As we have seen, there are many worthwhile reasons for encouraging children to be independent in their movement from one activity or experience to the next. The necessity to do this, of course, will vary according to the age of the children within the Foundation Stage. For the 3- or young 4-year-olds in a pre-school or private nursery or nursery school, children will be encouraged to move from experience to experience, that is either adult or child-initiated, as they choose. If practitioners want to work alongside specific children for an adult-focused activity, then this can be planned for the beginning of sessions so that children's independent learning is not interrupted. For older children in the Foundation Stage, those in their reception year or in Year 1, then there are more constraints over what teachers must teach and these can impinge upon opportunities for children to follow their own interests. Nevertheless, recent research with Year 1 teachers in Oxfordshire shows that those who want to work in more developmentally appropriate ways can still address all the elements of the Year 1 curriculum, including the revised frameworks for Literacy and Numeracy, by extending the amount of time on their timetables for sustained learning (learning not interrupted by playtimes and assemblies, etc.) and by having child-initiated learning taking place alongside adult-initiated learning (just as described in Chapter 4).

Whether or not the learning day incorporates a number of adult-focused or initiated experiences, children should still be given as much autonomy over when they engage in other learning as is possible. If practitioners attempt to organize a 'carousel' of activities so that all children complete the same tasks in a day, then many of children's spontaneous interests and much of their self-initiated learning will fall by the wayside. Not only that, but it sends a message to the children that only adult-directed learning is of value and leads to the kind of alienation and disaffection described earlier in this chapter.

Letting children negotiate the order in which they do things presupposes an element of trust between practitioners and children. If there are some adult-initiated tasks to complete (most likely for older Foundation Stage children), then children have to understand that these have to be fitted into the day. If children know that they are being trusted and are being given the opportunity to make their own choices and decisions, then they also know, because it is a part of the 'negotiation' made explicit by the practitioner, that they have to fulfil their side of the bargain. Negotiation can never be one-sided and a learning environment where children do their own thing, but not the adult's, is not a negotiated environment. Part of the developing relationship between the early years practitioner and the children must include discussions about what choice and decision-making means, and it includes the responsibility to fulfil all sides of the bargain and to complete the tasks that the adult initiates as well as the tasks children want to initiate themselves. On the practitioner's side, the bargain is that they do not set up so many adult-initiated activities that time for child-initiated activity is squeezed out. Planning is critical. If time has been allowed for a balance of activities (see Chapters 4 and 9), then it is perfectly appropriate for an adult to remind a child that there is only x amount of time now in the day/week and there is still y to be done. Most children, given the self-respect that comes from making their own decisions, respect in turn their educators and will complete what is outstanding – even if reluctantly at times. In negotiated early learning environments, where children can choose the order in which they do their various activities, there is a purposeful and dynamic atmosphere. It is rare to see the persuasion and coercion that can go on in classrooms where children are required to complete successive tasks set by the adult with no room for negotiation or using their initiative.

Length of time on different activities

When children can negotiate the order in which they go to different activities and resources, then it is implicit that they will be able to determine how long they will spend there. Time management is something that many adults could usefully learn, but even young children can develop this skill when given experiences that leave decisions in their hands. Most children learn to pace themselves given sufficient experience of having control over time and their own learning activities.

As we have seen earlier in this chapter, children need sustained periods of time in order to produce work or to engage in learning of quality and depth (EYCG 1992). It is up to the early childhood educator to plan for the delicate balance between sufficient time being given to the needs of the child and sufficient time being given to the demands of the external agenda. Some practitioners, particularly working in the reception year, worry about the child who, despite reminders or help with time management, still stays all day on a child-initiated activity. If there are a lot of interesting and absorbing experiences and opportunities both indoors and out, then most children want to experience more than one thing in any one day. However, if a child is genuinely reluctant to move and clearly is gaining something valuable from their self-selected activity then what is this telling us about the child? Children who need to repeat experiences may be in need of reassurance of something familiar. They may be feeling unsettled or unwell and simply find the repetition of something they know offers them the security they temporarily need. If the behaviour is out of character and continues, then this should alert the practitioner to investigate reasons for the child's behaviour. Forcing children simply leads to alienation. It may bring about a temporary result, but will not enhance the children's attitudes or approaches to learning. As Holt says, 'If the situations, the materials, the problems before a child do not interest him [*sic*], his attention will slip off to what does interest him, and no amount of exhortation or threats will bring it back' (1982: 265). Children can be trusted to set their own pace. They will need opportunities from the adult to manage and organize their time, but as with all elements of independent learning, this is time well spent.

Context

Places to learn

Where we choose to engage in activities can have a significant bearing on our application to a task. I am sure I am not alone in feeling that I cannot do my own writing unless I am in the relative tranquillity of my study, and cannot settle to read the Sunday papers unless I have my legs up on the sofa and the cat on my lap. Locations can promote or inhibit learning and, as with everything else, what is desirable for one person can be thoroughly undesirable for someone else. If an early learning environment is designed along the lines of the 'workshop' approach outlined in Chapter 5, then children will already have the freedom to move around the indoor and outdoor space in order to find resources and use equipment. However, this freedom is fettered if children are then required to go back to a predetermined place to complete the task in hand. If a child truly concentrates best sitting alone, lying on the floor, working with a friend, then the environment should be designed so that this can happen. Part of negotiation is being able to justify a decision made (on the part of the adult as well as the child), therefore a child who chooses an unusual location to learn may be required to justify it to their peers and the adult. If the quality of everyone's learning is not compromised, then the decision is justified. If learning is adversely affected, then the practitioner and other children are at liberty to challenge the decision and suggest a different one.

Sometimes, in settings where children are getting used to their independence, there can be children who seem to be 'flitting' – to be going from place to place without settling for long, or who go and watch other children without actually joining in themselves. This situation is another learning opportunity for the practitioner. Children who flit fall generally into two categories. There are those who are unsure of themselves and need to see the range of what is possible but do not yet have the confidence to try something for themselves. In this case flitting is very valuable because it means that the child comes to gain confidence through observations and imitation and almost always joins in once this is achieved. Then there are children who need supporting towards independence. Perhaps they are given little independence at home, are used to having things done for them and need support to make decisions for themselves. In this case the adult needs to make it part of their 'teaching' that the child is helped in small stages to begin to make decisions and to act on their own initiative. One of the most important parts of this is to gain the understanding of parents so that they extend independence to the child's life at home.

With whom to learn

Most of us work, play and learn better when we are alongside people whom we like and trust. You only have to try and separate practitioners who work together at the same setting when they attend in-service training courses to realize just how strong our adult feelings of security in people we know are! If children are not in adult-directed groups for a specific purpose (see Chapter 6), then for most of the day they should be able to learn alongside those with whom they want to learn. If they are working on a task or playing as an individual, then it makes no odds whether they are sitting next to somebody doing something different. However, for most of the time children benefit from playing and learning alongside others. They will collaborate readily when they see the need to do so and will organize themselves very effectively for the purpose. So, being able to be with someone you choose usually gives children an added sense of motivation. Of course there are some exceptions to this. Once again it is part of the negotiation process. If children do not work in cooperative and constructive ways with the person or people whom they have chosen, then the other children and/or the practitioner can suggest alternative ways of learning.

The curriculum

The topic

In Chapter 3, I expressed certain reservations about topic work, in that it can be hijacked by adults and have little relevance to the children. I believe that topics for young children can inhibit and constrain their learning as adults seek to link together areas of the curriculum in ways that become unnatural and illogical. For 3 and young 4-year-olds the cross-curricular nature of their interests can be captured best by short themes that run for a matter of days or for the duration of the children's interests. However, for older children, a topic can usefully emphasize the links between areas of learning and the application of skills and understandings across the curriculum. If the choice of topic is not made too early, then the interests of older Foundation Stage children can and should be incorporated. While planning at the long and medium stage is about addressing the skills, knowledge and understandings that are relevant for certain stages of children's development (see Chapter 3), planning at the short-term stage can address how these are pulled together so that they have meaning and relevance to a particular group of children at a particular time. An individual practitioner can be given the identical set of concepts and skills to address as a colleague in the next room with the same age children but, given their knowledge of their particular needs and interests, may choose to plan for and integrate these elements in quite a different way and through quite a different theme or topic. The topic is a vehicle for learning and should not drive it. Successful negotiation with children encourages adults to consult children as much as possible and to amend their planning to take account of children's opinions, ideas and interests.

The key questions within a topic

One very successful way of involving children in the planning of their topic or theme is to brainstorm with them all the things that they would like to find out about the topic that is being introduced. By raising questions, children come to see that many of the activities, resources and experiences with which they engage are planned for the express purpose of answering these questions. One enterprising setting I know writes their questions on huge pieces of card and suspends them from the ceiling so that everyone is reminded that these are the issues that are to be investigated. This works really well for older Foundation Stage children who love being explorers and investigators on a mission! In this approach, the practitioner is seen as learner alongside the children and the emphasis is on the process of discovery rather than the transmission of facts. When children have ownership of their learning in this way, there are far more opportunities for them to use their initiative both in the setting and at home to come up with answers or pose more questions of their own.

Criteria for success

One of the ways in which early years practitioners display control in their settings is by being in charge of what is deemed to be good, appropriate or sufficient with regard to children's play, work and learning. Children come to rely too much on the adult's judgements for affirmation and approval and do not believe that their own opinion matters. Practitioners sometimes use words like 'good', 'well done', 'brilliant' and so on, and children can be left bemused as to *why* this effort was 'good' and this 'not your best'. Some practitioners draw smiley faces and award stickers, which also send out the message that it is what the adult thinks that matters, judgements about value and worth are by the adult's criteria. When children are reliant on the adult's evaluations in this way they are usually left in no uncertain terms about whether the adult is pleased or not.

In an interesting article called 'In praise of praising less' (1991), the author Mark Tompkins warns against empty praise. The article suggests that practitioners should give their *opinions* rather than their *judgements* and make specific reference to the details of the child's activity or the process the child has used. If children have negotiated the purpose of the work and understand why they are doing what they are doing, then they are far more likely to be able to give a rationale for when something has been undertaken or achieved to their own satisfaction. In some effective settings working with older Foundation Stage children, practitioners negotiate with children the 'success criteria' *before* an adult-focused or adult-initiated activity begins. In other words, they ask 'What do you think will make this an effective chair for the bear to sit on?' 'What do you think will need to happen for you all to collaborate on designing this map?' 'What will make this an interesting story for the readers in Class 4?'

When children select their own 'success criteria' – where this is appropriate to an activity – then it helps give them a clear framework in which to evaluate and review their own efforts. This notion of making explicit what has been achieved and what might be achieved next has, however, been taken to extremes recently in ways that are neither helpful nor beneficial to younger learners. The introduction of the Assessment for Learning initiative (Black *et al.* 2002) and, more recently, target setting with children (DfES 2006), have led to the introduction of practices in Foundation Stage classrooms that were originally designed for older learners and have not always been sensitively or fruitfully adapted for those who are younger. When introduced appropriately, both initiatives encourage children to articulate what they are good at, where they need to improve and what help they need to do so. Such strategies, in the hands of sensitive early years practitioners, can boost children's self-esteem and lead them to new ways of thinking and learning. However, there are real dangers in the use of both initiatives in the hands of those who succumb to practices such as displaying individual targets on the wall of Foundation Stage classrooms, or using a 'traffic light' system that says – I 'must', 'should' or 'could'. Targets (or even 'next steps') for Foundation Stage children should not be displayed, for all the world to see, if they are in any sense pejorative. A public display of what a child cannot do is hardly likely to raise a child's self-esteem. If we want confident and motivated learners, then what goes on the wall should be what that child *can* do and what they *have* achieved. Indeed, the imposition of external criteria for success (for this is what targets are) goes against the grain of promoting intrinsic motivation, which is a fundamental principle of high-quality early education.

Where targets and other external criteria become particularly damaging for children is where they are used to determine the learning for a group of, even worse, a whole class. To begin with it is completely unrealistic to think that a single target can in any way predict the learning trajectory of 30 individual Foundation Stage learners. In addition, these class targets can sometimes be set in order to boost a whole school target that often results in those who have no knowledge of child development, and who do not understand where early learning leads, imposing foundation targets that are not only inappropriate for the learning that they are trying to improve at Key Stage 2 but also which are simply not what a number of children in the Foundation Stage class currently need. In general, target setting in the Foundation Stage should be seen as 'next steps' in children's learning (see Figure 8.1). Observation should support educators in making decisions about what these 'next steps' might be and what provision should be planned to enhance the possibility of these being achieved.

Foundation stage targets come from planning the appropriate 'next steps' for an individual child's development

- Targets for individual children are decided after careful observation of children over a period of time. Observation of child-initiated play and open-ended adult-initiated activities will help to identify children's interests, knowledge, understanding and skills, and ensure that planning for 'target getting' is appropriate.
- Observations will give teachers evidence on which to base the 'next steps' of children's experience and learning. They will be reviewed frequently.
- The targets will be based on the Educational Programme in *the Early Years Foundation Stage* (currently the Stepping stones/ ELGs in the *Curriculum Guidance for the Foundation Stage*). They will be underpinned by an understanding of how children develop and learn.
- The identification of targets may signal a need for additional resources; a need for specific training for staff member/s; a need to structure the timing of the session differently; a need to make time for adults to observe and support child-initiated learning.
- Planning for targets will support children's learning within a broad, rich Foundation Stage curriculum in which all six areas of learning are equally important and interdependent. Activities should be cross-curricular, inside and outside, and meet children's different learning styles.
- Planning for personal, social and emotional development will underpin all other planning.

Figure 8.1 Target setting in the Foundation Stage

What happens to the outcomes of children's efforts?

Sometimes children are pleased with their efforts and want to share what they have done. Sometimes they are dissatisfied and want to start again. Sometimes they are dissatisfied and want to do something else. If children make a decision that their efforts are not acceptable to them, then in almost every case they should be at liberty to dispense with them as they choose. Some children screw up or dismantle what they have been working on because they are so lacking in self-esteem that they cannot believe that they have achieved anything of worth. Whatever the reason for satisfaction or dissatisfaction, choosing what happens to their various efforts should be the child's decision. Yet so often that drawing, or mark-making or number story automatically becomes the property of the adult. 'I just want to borrow it for the colour display'; 'you can take it home at the end of term'; 'mummy will be so pleased to see it on the wall'. The 'I just want to borrow this for the wall/portfolio/ book' puts the adult very firmly back in control of what happens to children and their learning efforts. There are legitimate reasons for adults wanting children's work for display. These should be explained to the children. But if children then decide that they would rather keep their efforts to themselves, or take them home, or throw them away then they should be allowed to do so.

Box 8.1 The negotiated classroom

Long- and medium-term planning
- Long- and medium-term planning identifies the concepts, skills, knowledge and attitudes within each area of learning that the practitioner plans to introduce, revisit and develop over a given period of time.
- The activities, experiences, opportunities and resources identified at this stage should be *possibilities* only.

Short-term planning
- Short-term planning takes account of the needs and interests of a specific group or individual.
- Adult-initiated activities and child-initiated activities should be happening alongside each other.

The adult observes and has conversations
- What can the child tell me about himself/herself as a learner?
- What does each child already know/understand?
- What strategies/skills does each child use?
- How does each child work with others?
- What is the child interested in?

Adult plans	Child plans
• What does the child need to know now? (concepts/skills/knowledge/attitudes)	• What do I want to do today?
• How is this best learnt? (differentiation = activity/process/outcome/ grouping etc.)	• What do I need to do today (what has the adult asked me to do)?
• What support does the child need?	• In what order shall I do this?
• How can I include the spontaneous interests of children? (and who shall give it?)	• Where shall I do it?
• Which activity will be adult-intensive?	• With whom shall I do it?
• Are the other activities/experiences/ resources planned so that the children can be independent learners?	• What resources/equipment do I need?
• What kind of support/intervention do the other activities/experiences need?	• What do I want to do when I have finished?
• Have I planned to revise both adult-initiated and child-initiated activities?	

The adult observes and has conversations

• Have I planned to observe adult-intensive, adult-initiated *and* child-initiated activities?
• Have I planned to involve the child in *self*-assessment?
• What is the focus of my assessment of the adult-intensive task?
• Will I observe or participate?
• Have I identified the evidence on which to base my assessments?
• What strategies have I established for recording unplanned observations/conversations?
• How will I use all the evidence collected to inform future planning?

Conclusion

If children are to emulate their early success as learners once they start in their new early years class or setting, then practitioners need to ensure that there is not a great gulf between being a child and becoming a pupil. Children who are expected to behave in ways that are alien and irrelevant to them may become disaffected as learners and this disaffection frequently occurs when children have no control over their own experiences. When early childhood educators are committed to a learning partnership with their children, then there are many ways in which children can negotiate learning. The power and control this negotiation gives children can be a powerful and motivating force for learning and is likely to lead to positive, lifelong attitudes towards learning and accomplishment (Schweinhart *et al.* 1993). Some practitioners believe that giving children control means that they themselves will lose it. My experience is that this could not be further from the truth. One practitioner in a reception class who evolved a negotiated classroom with her children remarked, 'The more control I give away, the more in control I am'. The next chapter draws together the many practical aspects of previous chapters in suggesting how children can be helped to organize their own learning experiences.

THE ASSESSMENT OF CHILDREN'S LEARNING

What practitioners need to know about their children and their achievements

Introduction

We have already established that assessment should come at the beginning of the cycle of teaching and learning (Chapter 2), as well as at the end of it. It is rather like a sandwich in which observation is the first slice of bread, planning and implementation constitute the filling, and evaluation and assessment are the final slice of bread (Fisher 1998a, 1998b, 1998c). In order to plan effectively, early childhood educators need to know what children already know and can do and this is established through rigorous observation-based assessment of children in action. However, there is also an important place for assessment that comes at the end of the cycle of teaching and learning, when it is used to review what a child has learnt and what progress they have made.

Assessment *for* Learning and Assessment *of* Learning

Recently, the distinction between assessment that takes place *before* learning is planned and implemented and that which takes place afterwards, has been clarified by the use of the terms – Assessment *for* Learning (before) and Assessment *of* Learning (after). These different types of assessment each serve a distinct purpose.

Assessment *for Learning*

As we have already seen in Chapter 2, Assessment *for* Learning (Black *et al.* 2002) happens all the time in early learning environments. It is rooted in the observation of children and the post-its, quick notes, extended observations and ongoing records that practitioners gather as evidence of learning. Importantly, it involves children in their own self-evaluation. Early years practitioners are responsible for ensuring that – in developmentally appropriate ways – children are helped to reflect on what they have done, what skills and materials they used, what they might like to do differently next time and so on. This continuous assessment by both the practitioner and the child ensures that children's development is kept under constant review and the evidence gathered is at hand to inform the ongoing plans that are made for the learning environment and the learning needs of individual children. This ongoing Assessment *for* Learning is often called *'Formative* assessment'.

Assessment *of Learning*

Assessment *of* Learning, on the other hand, is usually carried out once children have been introduced to or experienced something new. It is used to establish what a child *now* knows and can do – after a new topic perhaps, or after the introduction of some adult-focused work on, say, some aspect of calculation. Assessment *of* Learning is also used 'at the end of' a particular phase in children's educational experience, that is, the end of term, the end of a year, when making a transition to a new setting. As such it often means that the practitioner is summing up all the evidence that has been gathered over a period of time in order to make a judgement about where the child is now. Because of this, Assessment *of* Learning is often termed *'Summative* Assessment'.

Different uses of assessment

Early years practitioners then are responsible for using assessments for two key purposes – formative and summative.

1 *Formative Assessment:* used on a daily and weekly basis, by the practitioner, to inform what is planned for the learning environment and for children's individual needs;
2 *Summative Assessment:* used to inform others such as parents, other professionals or the practitioner in the setting to which a child will transfer.

The quality of summative assessment relies on the quality of formative assessment. If a practitioner needs to summarize a child's achievements at a certain point in time, they can do so far more easily if they have good ongoing, formative assessments to refer back to. In addition, the regular and systematic use of observation ensures that practitioners know their children well rather than being uncertain about their skills and knowledge when asked to make a judgement for summative purposes. I want to look at the two purposes of assessment in more detail for, when practitioners are clear about these two types of assessment, then they find it easier to gather appropriate evidence and that evidence is more useful for the purpose to which it is put.

Formative Assessment

Formative records give ongoing information about a child's progress and attainment. Most formative assessments are used *by the practitioner* in everyday practice to 'observe children's learning, strive to understand it, and then put our understanding to good use' (Drummond 1993: 13).

The Early Years Foundation Stage (DfES 2007) says that:

> All effective assessment involves analysing and reviewing what you know about each child's development and learning. You can then make informed decisions about the child's progress and plan next steps to meet their development and learning needs (p. 12, para 2.10).

Formative records are necessary because they give practitioners daily information about what children know and can do and, therefore, provide the necessary information on which to build and adjust short-term plans. As we saw in Chapter 3, short-term plans are concerned with differentiation and in order to plan activities that are appropriate for different children, the adult has to have detailed knowledge of their current learning needs. Ongoing records provide such information and are the foundation of all good planning. By dint of their concern with the detail of children's development, formative records are often quite lengthy, but these records are not for onward transmission to somebody else. The practitioner uses these records either to make plans for the learning environment, or to make decisions about the current learning needs of individual children or to make judgements about children's attainment for summative purposes. The records for formative assessment then can be summarized as follows:

- ongoing, cumulative notes, taken throughout the teaching day;
- narrative records of what children do and what children say;
- including contributions from parents, children and other adults who work with the child;

- providing evidence on which to base future planning;
- incorporating analysis and planned action.

Summative Assessment

By definition, a summative assessment is a summary of achievement. Very often it is required in order to pass on information about a child and, therefore, needs to be brief. In the course of a child's educational life, summative information needs to be passed regularly to a number of different people. Parents have a legal right to receive an annual report on their child's progress including the child's attainment, if appropriate, on the Foundation Stage Profile (DfES 2003). The next Foundation Stage setting or the new school or the next practitioner needs a summary of a child's attainment on transfer in order to help them plan the next stages of the child's education. There are often concerns expressed about how much these transfer records are read. The practitioners who have completed a profile of a child's achievements during their time in the Foundation Stage or during their time in one particular setting often feel that they want to share all their information with the next practitioner. The practitioner who receives the records sometimes feels that they have too much information passed on and cannot possibly absorb all that is being reported. So, there is a necessity for practitioners who are forwarding information to the next setting or practitioner to be sensitive to what is reasonable and practical. The best way to judge this is to have conservations together and decide from one setting to the next, from one practitioner to the next, what is desirable yet manageable.

Even when records are read by the next practitioner, there is another debate about *when* they should be read. Some practitioners say they will not read records before they meet and get to know new children so that they can make up their own minds about the child and form their own relationships. On the other hand, if a practitioner does not know the new children and does not read the information to hand about their abilities on leaving their previous setting, how can they plan appropriately for the first days of the child's new learning environment (these and other issues to do with transition are discussed in Chapter 2). In addition to this, it is important to have a summary of each child's attainment for those times when progress is not smooth and decisions have to be made about appropriate intervention and support. Summative records of progress, written at regular intervals, can give a good indication of strengths and weaknesses, developmental patterns and gaps in knowledge and understanding, all of which provide a foundation for the diagnostic assessment of children's current needs. The records for summative assessment then can be summarized as follows:

- brief statements made to summarize information gained through formative records;
- a summary of the most vital and relevant information about what the child knows, understands and can do;
- often made at a point of transfer (e.g. on entry, change of setting, change of school);
- designed to inform others (e.g. parents, next practitioner/setting, outside agencies).

Recording Formative and Summative Assessments

Formative Assessments

As we have seen, formative assessments are based on the ongoing observations that early years practitioners make of children in action. Recording these is a demanding task, but one that practitioners need to make part of their everyday practice if they are to plan a curriculum that is relevant and appropriate to the children in their class. Many practitioners find it helpful to have a single sheet of paper for each child on which they record:

- date;
- observation;
- analysis of learning;
- action.

The *date* ensures that a child's rate of progress is recorded and that each individual spurt or plateau can be seen as part of the child's overall development. The *observation* captures what the child says and does and sets the action in context. This can be written straight onto the record sheet or it can be written on a post-it, which is then transferred to the record sheet. The *learning analysis* uses the practitioner's professional judgement to identify the skills, concepts, knowledge and attitudes that the observation represents (see below). This analysis will be done at a later stage than the observation and will be used by the practitioner to inform the action column. The *action* column is completed as a result of the analysis by the practitioner, hopefully with other adults who share responsibility for the assessment of the Foundation Stage children, of the learning needs of an individual child. Completion of this column prompts the adult to fine-tune the short-term planning and ensures that assessment influences the curriculum. Sometimes no action is required above and beyond the introduction of the next planned part of the curriculum. At other times, children unexpectedly reveal that they know or do not know something and the practitioner needs to adjust their plans accordingly. When summative records are written they draw on these detailed ongoing notes and this is why the quality of summative records are heavily dependent on the quality of formative assessments.

Summative Assessments

The recording of summative assessments is much more dependent on the purpose of the assessment. It is best if, once a purpose is established; practitioners design a format that will best capture the evidence that is necessary. As electronic data systems come increasingly on line, there is a temptation to try and record children's achievements against prescribed tick boxes, formats and formulae. However appealing these systems may be initially in seeming to save time, they do not work for children in practice. Children are far too individual and idiosyncratic to be summed up by a predetermined list of characteristics, skills and knowledge. If a practitioner was to use such a list, they would soon find that a child had an attribute that was not written down and that there were attributes on the list that did not adequately describe the child. In addition to the failure of pre-designed checklists (electronic or otherwise) to give a full and rounded picture of an individual child's personal achievements, the information gathered is limited in its uses, for it does not offer the richness of ongoing formative assessments that capture all the uniqueness of the individual learner. Without this rounded and individual picture of each child, it is not possible to plan for their individual learning needs. Short cuts rarely deliver qualitative outcomes. Young children deserve better than to be assessed by systems that reduce their various achievements and abilities to a series of ticks in someone else's boxes.

The Foundation Stage Profile

The Foundation Stage Profile (FSP) is the statutory assessment of children completed at the end of their time in the Foundation Stage. It was introduced in 2003 and replaced national baseline assessment on entry to primary school. The Foundation Stage Profile is a combination of both formative and summative assessment. It requires all practitioners working with Foundation Stage children to undertake observations of children in order to record their attainment and progress. It then places a statutory duty on all Foundation Stage providers to make a summative judgement at the end of the Foundation Stage of every child's achievements against 13 assessment scales.

The 13 assessment scales are drawn from the Early Learning Goals

(ELGs) although these may have been split or combined for ease of use. The headings of the assessment scales are as follows:

Personal, Social and Emotional Development
1 Dispositions and attitudes
2 Social development
3 Emotional development

Communication, Language and Literacy
4 Language for communication and thinking
5 Linking sounds and letters
6 Reading
7 Writing

Mathematical Development (soon to be amended to Problem-solving, Reasoning and Numeracy once the EYFS becomes applied)

8 Numbers as labels and for counting
9 Calculating
10 Shape, space and measures
11 Knowledge and understanding of the world
12 Physical development
13 Creative development

Each of the assessment scales has nine points that a child can achieve:

Points 1–3: describe a child who is still working towards the Early Learning Goals and are based currently on the stepping stones in the Foundation Stage curriculum guidance (DfES 2000). Most children are expected to achieve all these three points before they achieve the ELG, but there may be some exceptions to this;

Points 4–8: are drawn from the ELGs. They are presented in approximate order of difficulty; however, they are not viewed as hierarchical as a child may achieve a later point without having achieved some or all of the earlier points;

Point 9: the final scale point describes an exceptional child; one who is working consistently beyond the ELG. It is unlikely that most practitioners will award this scale point.

At the end of the Foundation Stage, practitioners are required to award a numerical score to each child, based on the scoring of that child against the nine points of each assessment scale. This is where the importance of the ongoing, formative assessment becomes apparent. Without a deep knowledge of each individual child, the summative assessment required by the FSP would be very onerous. But for practitioners who use observational assessment as the bedrock of their knowledge of the needs of individual learners, then the task is considerably easier.

The National Assessment Agency (NAA) has given practitioners some valuable guidance when describing the practice best suited to gathering the evidence necessary to complete the FSP.

- The FSP is *not* a test. It is not completed on one day at the same time for all children as, for example, the national tests at the end of Key Stage 2.
- The starting point for assessment is *the child* – not a predetermined list of skills.
- Products such as *test materials* that require Foundation Stage children to respond to a series of pre-set questions using a computer screen or booklet are contradictory to NAA guidance. No supplementary assessments are required in addition to completing the FSP nor is there any expectation that they should take place.
- The FSP is not a *one-off* assessment. It cannot be completed in an instant as it relies on the accumulation of evidence over time. Judgements are made through assessing behaviour that is demonstrated consistently and independently in a range of situations. A judgement will need to demonstrate the child's confidence and ownership of the specific knowledge, skills or concept being assessed. The only part that is completed 'in a moment' is the summative score, which will be completed most easily when the quality of formative assessments is good.
- When *making a judgement* for FSP, practitioners should draw on at least 80 per cent of evidence from knowledge of the child, observations and anecdotal evidence and no more than 20 per cent from adult-directed or focused assessments.
- *Observations and records* show what a child can do – their significant achievements – not what they cannot do.
- Practitioners observe children as part of their *daily routine.*
- *Parents' contributions* to the assessment process are central.
- *Children are involved* and encouraged to express their own views on their achievements.

Moderation

Assessment of children's attainment and progress is a complex and demanding task. While the use of practitioner-based judgements is to be welcomed in the Foundation Stage (rather than the use of more objective tests), there are potential weaknesses in this mode of assessment. The weakness lies in the vast number of practitioners making the judgements, many of whom have different levels of training and expertise in observational assessment of children. While the Foundation Stage Profile documentation has emphasized the great skill involved in this kind of assessment, the Foundation Stage Profile process has highlighted significant variation in the skills demonstrated by the range of practitioners who make the assessments. For this reason, the Foundation Stage Profile process has included the necessity to moderate the assessments made.

Moderation is a way of agreeing the assessment judgements made by different practitioners in order to try and ensure that any practitioner observing the same child engaged in the same learning would make the same judgement. Currently, this is not the case. As schools and settings have started to take moderation more and more seriously, there has been a realization that sometimes *within* the same setting – let alone *between* settings – practitioners are not agreeing about the judgements that they would make. Good moderation comes when practitioners have regular conversations together about children, their learning and the developmental stage that they have reached. It means, in most cases, that practitioners within the same setting need to agree their judgements first. Then, when there is a consensus between practitioners in the same setting, that setting needs to link up with other Foundation Stage providers working in the same community to moderate between settings.

It is important that everyone in the Early Years Foundation Stage becomes confident in the assessments that others are making. Because of the number of transitions that children face during their time in this phase of education (see Chapter 2), practitioners in different settings need to believe that they can rely on the summative assessments passed on to them and to use these with confidence when planning for the child's next learning steps.

One very effective way to strengthen the moderation process is the use of videos. By watching someone else's children at play, it can give practitioners the opportunity to comment on and test out their own theories about what a child knows and can do without this being a judgement about them and their own children. When practitioners in a setting are more confident, then best practice would include videoing themselves and their own children so that the knowledge they bring to the assessments and moderation process are more rounded and extensive. Such confidence takes time, but it is important that all practitioners appreciate that their own judgements can be highly subjective, affected by all manner of prejudices, bias and preference and, therefore, that they need to subject these judgements to scrutiny by others to ensure that their assessments are valid.

Who contributes to observations and assessment?

The guidance from NAA emphasizes that the assessment of children's achievements does not rest with the practitioner alone (see Chapter 2).

All the following people can and should help to build the profile of the individual learner:

The child

Getting the child to evaluate their own learning is an important developmental skill. We know from research (Dweck 1978) that success in learning is based on self-esteem and self-motivation. Those children who believe that they are competent and successful as learners do better than those who are uncertain and rely too much on adults and other children. This is the case even when the more confident child is not necessarily more able. The self-belief overrides the lack of expertise and frequently leads to the child achieving more than the child who is more able but less confident in their own ability. When children believe that intelligence is a malleable quality – something over which they have control – then, says Dweck, they adopt a disposition of 'mastery' over whatever it is that they want to learn. They believe that they can achieve and they do. On the other hand, when children believe that intelligence is a fixed trait, then they often feel 'helpless' in the face of learning that challenges them. They are motivated, not by the drive to succeed that comes from within, but by more external factors, such as the adult's praise or rewards such as stickers or stars. So reliant are they on the adult for a sense of their own worth that 'helpless' children will, in fact, often choose tasks that conceal their ability or protect it from negative evaluation by adults or their peers.

If children are to believe in themselves as learners and if they are to rely on their own judgements about their achievements, then their learning environments need to support their 'mastery' and not create 'helplessness'. Practitioners might consider the following:

- Do I praise children too much? Do I say 'that's lovely' to almost everything in a mistaken attempt to boost children's self-esteem? Will children know *what* I think is good about their work and why?
- Do I rely on external rewards such as stickers or star charts to motivate children? Have children become more anxious to achieve a sticker than they are to achieve something for their own purposes?
- Do I talk to children about what they are trying to achieve, what skills and knowledge they have used that has made them successful and what they might need to know more about?
- Do I support children to reflect on their achievements and activity during a session or a day? Does each child get a regular opportunity to review what they have achieved; where they might want support; what they might want to return to tomorrow; what they felt went really well?

All children need the opportunity to self-assess their own efforts in developmentally appropriate ways. Sitting and listening while a large number of children talk about their own activities is unlikely to lead to greater self-awareness. However, being given the opportunity to talk to an interested adult during or after an activity – with maybe the other children involved at the time – will make a review time far more relevant and meaningful. When adults regularly review children's efforts and achievements with them, then children begin to internalize this for themselves and come to ask the questions internally that adults have asked out loud.

In order to self-assess, children need to be clear about what they were trying to achieve, to have a sense of their own 'success criteria' – what made the activity or experience worth while for them, what they might have learnt from what they have done and how they might like to build on that in the future.

Parents and carers

Both the Early Years Foundation Stage (DfES 2007) and the Foundation Stage Profile documentation (DfES 2003) emphasize the importance of parental contributions to the assessment of their children's learning. The EYFS states that:

> Parents and families are central to the child's wellbeing and practitioners should support this important relationship by sharing information and offering support to learning in the home (DfES 2007a, p. 10, para 1.16).

Later in the same document (para 2.29) it says:

> ... it is expected that ... account will be taken of information provided by parents.

The latter emphasizes that parental contributions to the assessment process do not consist of sitting and listening to a practitioner telling them about their child. The parent or carer has a view of the child that is quite unique. It is usually gained from a lifetime's experience with that child and this knowledge has to be respected and included. Even if the knowledge of the child is gained over a shorter period of time, maybe because the child is adopted or is being looked after by grandparents or a foster family, the knowledge of that child's particular needs will be far greater than any knowledge that can be accumulated by the practitioner alone. It may be that the child has emotional needs that they mask well in the context of the setting and are only known to the parent or carer. It may be that the child responds differently to the learning environment of the home and that this will give insights to the practitioner about how to stimulate and motivate the child in the setting. It may be that the child or the family has cultural expectations of the child that do not match the expectations of the setting. It might be that the child has just experienced something – a trip, a visit, a family occasion – which could provide the stimulus for play or activity in the setting and on which the practitioner might build. There are characteristics and attributes of each child that are only ever seen at home and practitioners must never ignore the parent's perspective even if – and probably especially when – it differs from their own.

It is not unusual to hear a parent say that their view of the child is quite different from the view of the practitioner – and vice versa. Given the different roles that parents and practitioners play and their different intentions for the child, this is not surprising. However, it is all too easy to hide behind a professional smokescreen for fear that parental involvement means parental interference. Sometimes practitioners do not want to know that there is another point of view as it will mean adjusting their own preconceptions, plans and ideas. Early childhood educators must be open to the challenge of parental opinion and be able to value and respect the contribution that they make. In this way, children will come to see that their parents, carers and practitioners all have their interests in common and will be working together to bring about the best educational experiences possible.

Other professionals

Drawing yet again on the EYFS (DfES 2007a, p. 16, para 2.29), the statutory framework says:

> As judgments are based on observational evidence gathered from a wide range of learning and teaching contexts, it is expected that all adults who interact with the child should contribute to the process.

Concern is sometimes expressed by practitioners that assessment should not be in the hands of those who are not adequately trained. However, the EYFS (above) makes the distinction very clearly. It is important to separate out making assessments from making observations. All adults who work alongside a child should be capable of making an observation of what they are doing and saying. The skilled part for the practitioner comes in the analysis of these observations in order to decide what implications there are for future planning of the environment and the curriculum. So, the more views of the child the better as this will only enrich the rounded picture that practitioners are trying to achieve.

Box 9.1   Example 7: Focused teaching and assessment 1

A student had planned that a group of children should bake cakes. Her lesson plan identified the following intended learning outcomes:
1 The children will understand more fully the concept of change.
2 The children will use the scientific skills of observing, hypothesizing, predicting and investigating.
3 The children will record their findings in ways that are relevant to them in order to report back to their peers.

The lesson was well planned and the children became engrossed in their task. The student asked open-ended questions and answered the questions that the children raised. In her profiles, however, the student did not record the achievement of the children in relation to the intended learning outcomes of the lesson. Instead, she recorded the children's success in relation to the quality of the cakes that they had made. While this was important for those tasting the cakes, it was not the purpose of the lesson and the information recorded was of little value when the student came to plan the children's next scientific experience.

Box 9.2   Example 8: Focused teaching and assessment 2

A group of 4-year-olds were to design their own Christmas wrapping paper. The purpose of the activity was for the children to use pattern in their design. The adult had brought into the class a whole range of wrapping paper as a stimulus for the children so that they could see different patterns. Following a look at this wrapping paper, it was put to one side and the child began to print their own paper. From that moment on, the support of the adult lost its focus. Rather than reminding the children about pattern and showing the purchased wrapping paper as a reminder, the adult prompted the children to use more of this colour or that shape, to fill in the spaces and to press harder to get a clearer print. In other words, the adult had become more concerned with artistic rather than mathematical achievements and the potential for reinforcing a key mathematical concept (the purpose of the activity) was lost. When making assessments of that session the adult focused on the quality of the printing rather than the children's understanding and application of pattern.

Box 9.3 Example 9: The cross-curricular nature of learning

When engaged in a cooking activity the children may gain experience of English (when discussing the processes involved or consulting the recipe), maths (when counting out spoonfuls, comparing sizes, weights etc.), science (when observing changes or dissolving substances), design and technology (when observing the effects certain tools such as a whisk have on the ingredients), history (when discussing how cake mixture was beaten before we had whisks), geography (when discussing which part of the world certain recipes come from and finding these on a map), personal and social development (when learning about the hygiene aspects of food preparation, and about which foods are most and least healthy), music (when comparing or imitating vocally sounds made by different utensils), physical education (when learning to control whisks, knives, cutters, etc.) and art (when discussing patterns made by different implements, or decorating cakes or biscuits).

(Hurst and Lally 1992: 55)

Making time for assessment

Chapter 2 explained why observation and conversation are the key strategies on which early years assessments should be based. Both of these require practitioners' close attention and this is not possible in a busy learning environment unless the children are encouraged to be independent learners. Chapter 4 suggested ways in which practitioners can create time for observation by allocating it to the time allocated to 'adult-focused' learning. While some observation clearly takes place when an adult is working alongside a group, this is not sufficient. Some observations require the adult to be independent of children in order to focus on what they know and do independently.

Assessment on entry

On entry to any setting it is important to establish a baseline of what children currently know and can do. Without this, it will not be possible to plan a curriculum to meet the individual child's learning needs nor will it be possible to make judgements later about how much progress they have made while in the setting.

If children are coming from home to a new setting, the gathering of evidence about what they currently know and can do, what they are interested in and what they enjoy is particularly important.

Home visits

Home visits are one key way in which practitioners gather such information for, at this stage, it is the parent or carer who clearly knows the child best and has all the information that the practitioner needs. Home visits should be offered to all parents of children on entry to a new setting in the Foundation Stage, although they should never be mandatory as there are occasionally parents who, for a variety of reasons, choose not to have visitors in their home. However, most parents and most children are more than delighted to welcome a practitioner into their home to find out more about the child, but this visit is a privilege that must not be abused. Such a visit is an occasion for listening to what others have to say and not going in with a predetermined agenda. Practitioners who are sensitive to the invitation into the homes of their new children will learn much if they look and listen to what is being told to them, what they are shown, the toys and books that are around, the way in which children's behaviour is managed, the way in which the family communicates and relates. This rich source of evidence will help a practitioner to understand how much of a transition a child is making from one place to the next – whether expectations of children in the home and the setting are similar or not; whether the language used is similar or not; and whether attitudes towards books and play are similar or not. However, this must not lead to pejorative feelings or comments about the home. It does not make the home 'wrong' and the setting 'right', but it can indicate where the culture of the home and the culture of the school are at variance in which case it may be harder for the child to access the world of the early childhood setting and make progress there without appropriate support.

Home visits give practitioners a privileged insight into the different worlds of family life. They should lead to greater understanding of the adjustments that children sometimes have to make. The child who comes from a minority ethnic group and whose first language is not English, who may be relied upon at a very young age to communicate on behalf of his parents and to translate between the different adults in their life. The only child who isn't played with by the adults in their lives and who may find sharing their possessions with a number of other children a real challenge. The child who doesn't have access to books, doesn't see her parents read and doesn't visit the library and who may find the language of books and stories used in the setting or school difficult to understand and unfamiliar to use. All these insights into children's lives should lead the practitioner to make professional judgements about the needs of the child in the setting rather than prejudicial judgements about the attitudes and approaches and behaviour of the family. If families sense a respect for them, their homes and their communities, then word will soon spread that the home visits help the family as well as the child to feel welcomed and included in the early years setting and will provide a rich reference point for all involved in the child's ongoing learning.

Other strategies on entry

In addition to home visiting, there are a range of other ways to gather evidence about a child on entry to a setting or class. These are just some of the many suggestions that practitioners have made in discussion about this aspect of assessment:

- photographs taken of children before they start at the setting, so that these can be displayed alongside their peg on arrival, or made into a display to greet the new children on arrival;
- visits made to the setting from which the children are transferring (if not the home);
- visits from the child's current practitioner to their new setting (in both these cases practitioners are seeking to ease the discontinuities in some transitions, see Chapter 2);
- observations made of some children in their current setting in order to have some evidence on which to base initial planning;
- joint observations between practitioners from different settings to moderate their judgements of the children that they are 'sharing' in the Foundation Stage;
- records from the previous setting – where the summative information to be passed on has been agreed between practitioners from the two settings as being useful and relevant;
- questionnaires for parents to complete with their child and before the child's arrival at the setting;
- conversations with parents before the child's arrival at the setting;
- information and records from any other professionals who may have already been working with the child (e.g. educational psychologist; pre-school teacher counsellor; social worker; health visitor);
- local cluster meetings between all Foundation Stage providers in an area who 'share' children – to agree (e.g. ways of planning and assessing). Discuss behavioural expectations, routines and procedures.

Planning the use of time for observation

The following is a useful checklist for planning the use of time for Formative Assessment:

- What evidence is required?
- Is the assessment to find out what children *already* know/can do or what they know/can do *after* a period of teaching?
- Is the evidence best gathered during or after the activity?
- Who will gather the evidence?
- What technique best serves the assessment purpose?
- How and by whom will the evidence be recorded?

Gathering evidence of children's learning

What evidence is required?

There is a difference between obtaining *information* about children's learning and gathering *evidence* of their learning. We collect information about children's learning from:

- previous summative records;
- parent consultations;
- conversations with the child.

Previous assessments are important but are not sufficient. Information can be dated or open to misinterpretation. Effective planning is based on current evidence and is gathered in a variety of ways through:

- the collection of tangible end-products;
- photocopying pictures/writing/mark-making etc.;
- taking photographs;
- making audio/video recordings;
- observation of what children do:
  - the process of learning,
  - their learning styles and strategies,
  - their knowledge and understanding,
  - their skills and attitudes;
- through recording what children say:
  - their developing understandings,
  - their misunderstandings,
  - their explanations,
  - their enthusiasms.

Who will gather the evidence, where and when?

- Who? (adults)
  - the practitioner;
  - other adults/practitioners who work with the child;
  - parents/carers;
- With whom? (the children)
  - child alone,
  - children together,
  - children with an adult,
  - children without an adult;
- Where?
  - inside and out,
  - in the hall (if appropriate),
  - in the home (parental and child contributions);
- When?
  - on entry to the setting (establishing a baseline),
  - regularly during the child's time in the setting (tracking progress),
    at the end of the child's time in the setting (judging attainment and progress),
  - before or after teaching (Assessment *for* Learning or Assessment *of* Learning),
  - while working with child/children,
  - while child/children working independently.

What technique best serves the assessment purpose?

There are a variety of assessment techniques that all have their value. The decision that teachers have to make is which technique will give them the evidence that they need. For excellent descriptions of different techniques and their uses, for example, time sampling, frequency sampling, audiotaping and targeted observation, see Drummond *et al.* (1992) Bartholomew and Bruce (1993) and Hutchin (1996, 1999).

Building a profile of the child as a learner

Keeping a record of children's learning throughout their time in the Foundation Stage is more than just completing a series of checklists. As we have seen already in this chapter, the individual child is too rich and complex a learner to be represented by a list of somebody else's predetermined skills.

Certain kinds of evidence 'speaks for itself'. Pieces of writing, photographs, tape recordings and photocopies only need annotation to make them valuable evidence of the stage in a child's development.

The annotation is important, however, for without it the precise context for learning will be forgotten and there will be little evidence of the trajectory of progress made from one piece of evidence to another. A profile should be more than a random selection of paper and photos but show the child's learning journey through words and pictures. Evidence within a child's profile should be annotated with:

- the name of the child;
- the date;
- the learning context;
- child's comments (if any);
- level of support from adult(s)/other children (if any);
- stage of development – using the Early Years Foundation Stage 'Development Matters'.

In different countries, a focus on gathering evidence has resulted in processes that can enrich our understanding and thinking about the assessment process here in England. In particular, the work of Margaret Carr and her colleagues in New Zealand on *Learning Stories* and the work of the educators in Reggio Emilia, Italy on *Documentation*.

Learning Stories

Learning stories are narrative-style observations of children in everyday settings, designed to provide 'a cumulative series of qualitative "snapshots" or written vignettes of individual children' (Carr 2001: 96). As such, they sound similar to the child profiles often created by English early years practitioners. But to complete a Learning Story, the evidence base has to focus on some very particular aspects of learning. Rather than accumulating evidence across all areas of the curriculum, Carr and her colleagues suggest that evidence should concentrate on five particular dispositions that they believe underpin successful learning in all other domains. For the purpose of Learning Stories, these five dispositions are translated into actions:

- taking an interest;
- being involved;
- persisting with difficulty or uncertainty;
- expressing an idea or a feeling;
- taking responsibility or taking another point of view.

Carr proposes that these five dispositions demonstrate to what extent a child is ready (their inclination to learn), willing (their sensitivity to what is around them and what can be investigated) and able (the repertoire of skills that they have) to optimize their learning opportunities. As we have seen earlier in this chapter, it is often those children who are motivated by an inner self-belief who succeed over and above those who are more able but may be inhibited by self-doubt (Dweck 1978).

The completion of Learning Stories lies in the hands of many people:

- the child;
- the practitioners;
- the family.

Each 'story-teller' is seen to have a unique contribution and the emphasis is on participation and a shared enterprise. The Learning Stories provide a discussion point at staff meetings, and at meetings with children and their parents. The purpose of Learning Stories, as with all other formative assessment, is to support practitioners in deciding what to do next in planning for the child's learning.

Learning Stories include photographs, photocopies of mark-making and other recorded work and comments from children and their parents. They also include the context of learning, they highlight the activity or task at hand and they include an interpretation from a 'story-teller' (the person completing that element of the Learning Story), focusing on evidence of new or sustained interest, involvement, challenge, communication and responsibility. Learning Stories, says Carr, need to 'capture the complexity of situated learning strategies plus motivation' (Carr 2001: 95). By doing so, they 'acknowledge the unpredictability of development (thus reflecting) the learning better than performance indicators' (p. 101).

Documentation

This richness of accumulated evidence from a range of significant people is also the characteristic of the Documentation in the pre-schools in Reggio Emilia. The material for the Documentation is gathered during the experience of learning and, as with Learning Stories, read and interpreted at the end of the experience in order to make judgements about children's next steps for learning. Rather than focusing on the developing child as an autonomous learner, the educators in Reggio Emilia see education as a communal activity, a sharing of culture through collaboration among children and also between children and their teachers. Documentation is used for collaborative reflection upon what the evidence might show and enable staff to support the learning process by checking the connections between 'the theories, the hypothesis and their outcomes' (Rinaldi 2001).

> Whenever we can we have these daily reconnaissance meetings while everything is still fresh. In discussing events together our individual interpretations and hypotheses can be compared and consequently take on new substance and meanings (Malaguzzi 1997)

The evidence base is not referred to just once, but brought back for rereading, revisiting and reconstruction of the experience in order to fully understand what the evidence suggests (Rinaldi 2001). The evidence may be in the form of videos, audio recordings, written notes or drawings. There are contributions from staff, parents, children and members of the community. One of the key purposes of Documentation is to support the pre-schools in their search for meaning in addition to supporting the child in their individual and personal search for meaning. The process of Documentation originated through a desire to make visible the way in which the pre-schools approached learning and teaching and, to this end, Documentation is displayed openly on the walls of all the pre-schools and staff, children, parents and the community are encouraged to read about what is taking place and to contribute their thoughts and feelings about it. Though Documentation may have originated as a way to offer children an opportunity to evaluate their own work and to keep parents better informed about pre-school experiences, it was soon discovered to be 'an extraordinary opportunity for teachers to revisit and re-examine their own work with children, offering unquestionable benefits in terms of professional development' (Malaguzzi 1997: 11).

The educators in Reggio believe that Documentation leaves examples of the school's history and gives their institutions a sense of their heritage. But, of course, it is more than simply a record or an archive, for it demonstrates to children the value of their contributions and encourages them to contribute to the process. The evidence that is accumulated evaluates not just what the child knows and can do now, but what they could do 'if ...' As such it builds on the work of Bruner (1986) and Vygotsky (1978), giving the adult a pivotal role in facilitating and scaffolding learning.

The educators in Reggio Emilia stress, as others do (Drummond 1993; Carr 2001), the complexity of assessing young children's learning journeys. They emphasize in particular the difficulty of knowing and understanding what a child is thinking, and are 'suspicious' of the value of Documentation that offers a linear description of a child's development. They admit that what counts in education is often that which escapes being photographed or tape-recorded because it belongs to the world of possible interpretations:

> If we are interested in exploring the genesis and development of means that children construct in their encounters with reality, if we want to know more about the procedures of thought and action used by individual children in their learning processes, then we must document not only that which took place *around* the child, but above all that which we think has taken place *within* the child (Malaguzzi 1997:11)

Using assessment to Inform planning

The whole purpose of observing, assessing and analysing children's learning is in order to plan a learning environment that stimulates children in relevant and appropriate ways, and to plan for the needs of individual children within that learning environment. The paragraphs on Learning Stories and Documentation (above) have emphasized the importance of collaborative reflection on practice. In many early childhood settings there is a team of practitioners who work together to discuss and analyse the impact of their planning on both the learning environment and on individual children.

Planning the learning environment

In weekly staff meetings staff share their views of the learning that has taken place as a result of the planned and the unplanned interactions of children with both the indoor and the outdoor environment. These discussions lead practitioners to extend children's learning through:

- the addition of resources to play that is already in full flow;
- planning new experiences that meet current interests and preoccupations;
- the linking of activities indoors with those outside (or vice versa);
- the removal of some resources in order to give more space and possibilities to others.

Planning for individual children

Planning alone

All early years educators are responsible for planning for a group of children. Sometimes this is a group of 8 or 10 children, sometimes – and often in a reception class – for a whole class of 30 children. Practitioners need to look daily at their notes and 'post-its', gathered during planned and spontaneous observation of children. Planning then needs to be amended if it does not meet the current needs of individual children. Plans are there to be written on. It is not possible to predict with total accuracy what the needs of all children will be even a few days or a week in advance. So practitioners must be sufficiently flexible to change their plans and put something else in their place if this is what is needed.

Planning with the staff team

Many early years educators are fortunate enough to work as part of a team. In this instance, the practitioner responsible for a group of children will not be the only one making observations and gathering evidence. Where there is a Foundation Stage team, then all practitioners in the setting can share their views of individual children whom they may have worked alongside or observed at play. Different staff can bring their 'post-its' and observational notes and support the lead practitioner in planning appropriately for their group or for one individual.

Whatever strategies are used to share information and evidence the single most important thing is that observations and assessments are not wasted. There is no point in gathering information about a child's learning journey if that evidence is not going to be put to good use. The two key processes of assessment and planning should be linked inextricably together for the one cannot be robust without the other.

Conclusion

The assessment of children's learning is a challenging task for early childhood educators. Time must be created to observe each child with care for without time assessments will be superficial and of little value when planning for the next steps in children's learning. But the best early years practitioners not only observe children, but they turn the spotlight on themselves. They reflect on their own practice and the impact it makes to children's learning and children's lives. In the final chapter of this book, we consider what practitioners need to know about themselves and their own practice in order to meet the developmental needs of children and extend their learning.

10

REFLECTION AND EVALUATION

What practitioners need to know about their practice, their provision and themselves

Introduction

Effective early childhood educators are continuously reflecting on their practice. Because the environment of early learning is multi-layered and multifaceted, practitioners need to have a constantly questioning heart and mind in order to evaluate the quality of children's experiences and the quality of their own contribution to children's learning.

Reflective teaching

Some of this reflection takes place in the bath, on the train, walking along the beach or in the middle of a supermarket aisle. The ongoing quest for more appropriate resources, a more interesting way to introduce a mathematical concept, a more challenging way to extent children's physical prowess means that good early childhood educators never miss the opportunity to spot learning potential in the most unlikely places. Sometimes the reflection is about the emotional needs of a child. How can David be encouraged to play less aggressively with other children? How can I support Georgia as she grieves for the loss of her grandma? How can I encourage children to include Sundeep in their play when he doesn't yet communicate in English? All these questions, and thousands more, team through the working mind of the early years practitioner, very often at a subconscious level and most often when we are trying to get to sleep. This constant reflection is necessary because our working environment is neither repetitive nor predictable. We can plan well and with thought and care, but children can hijack that planning and take their learning on a course that we have not anticipated. We can visit other settings – even other countries – to look at different practice, but it is not until those ideas are applied to our children and our learning environments that we can evaluate whether the additions, adjustments and alterations are working. It is one of the main reasons, of course, why working in early childhood education keeps practitioners interested in and stimulated by their jobs. But it means that we will never get it entirely 'right'. There is never a moment when we can say 'I've cracked this now. I can do it like this for ever'. Even if our learning environment is effective and challenging and appropriate this year, it may need complete re-evaluation next year with a different group of children with different needs and expectations.

We saw in Chapter 9 that observation of individual children is central to the planning process in the early years. However, there are times when early childhood educators carry out other observations in their settings that are not specifically to do with the development of individual children. These are concerned with how smoothly the setting runs, how cooperative children are, whether good use is being made of space and resources and whether the environment both indoors and out is contributing to the quality of children's learning.

Observation of resources

This observation provides evidence of different children's responses to a key resource – such as a water tray or the blocks. It shows whether the resource is still used effectively or has become rather 'tired' and the play repetitive:

- How effectively is the resource used by different children?
- Is there any dominant use by, for example, boys as opposed to girls, younger children as opposed to older, children with special needs, children with English as an additional language?
- Is the resource sufficiently challenging for more able children to think creatively, to investigate and to play?
- Are there pieces missing? Do construction toys still fit well together? Are resources a little tatty or bent or 'tired'? Do they need replacing?
- Is the quality of play enhanced by this resource?
- Do resources challenge and stimulate children and do they meet their developmental needs as learners?
- Are resources of a suitable variety and do they encourage choice?
- Are there sufficient resources?

Observation of the environment – indoors and out

This observation is planned to highlight issues of space, resourcing and independence:

- Is there sufficient space in the learning environment – both indoors and out – for children to engage in active learning?
- Is there easy access to an outdoor area for learning and is it constantly in use?
- Is the outdoor area safe and secure?
- Is outdoor equipment suitable for the age of the children?
- Are areas for play indoors constantly available?
- Are tables and heavy furniture (such as cupboards) used, or are some wasting space?
- Are resources – both indoors and out – easily accessible for children?
- Do children find and return resources to their appropriate location?
- Are children able to manage themselves independently?

Observation of children's experiences

This provides evidence of the general quality of planning and provision for children's learning needs:

- Is the planned curriculum based on the Early Years Foundation Stage?
- Is the curriculum planned with full regard to children's gender, race, ability and needs?
- Does planning give children opportunities to work alongside adults who have initiated activities as well as to initiate learning themselves?
- Is the full curriculum represented both indoors and out?
- Do the experiences on offer stimulate, interest, intrigue and engage children?
- Do children have sustained opportunities for learning, without unnecessary interruptions?
- Is there flexibility within the planned curriculum to respond spontaneously to children's interest and preoccupations?
- Is the curriculum inclusive with full regard to the needs of each individual child?
- Do curriculum experiences promote process over product?

Observation of relationships and attitudes to learning

- Do children make constructive relationships with one another and with adults?
- Are children able to concentrate and persevere on both adult-initiated and child-initiated learning?

- Do children show initiative and are they given responsibility?
- Do children have the confidence and motivation to pursue their own play intentions, ideas and interests?
- Does each child feel valued and supported by the care, routines and rhythms of the day?
- Are the rights of children embedded in everyday practice in a way that supports the growth of positive self-esteem, confidence and mutual respect?
- Are children given the freedom to take risks, make mistakes and learn from these?
- Are the diverse needs, abilities, differences and contributions of all children taken into account, valued and respected?

Observation of adult-initiated activity

This observation provides evidence of the responses of different children to an adult-initiated activity (see Chapter 4) where the adult has an intention in mind but the children may take the learning elsewhere:

- How do children's responses to the activity/resource differ?
- Is the activity sufficiently open-ended and does it encourage thought and creativity?
- Is the activity successful in meeting the needs of all the children who engage in it?
- Is the activity capable of being sustained by children until a practitioner is ready to intervene?
- Is the activity posing a problem worth solving?
- Are children learning what was intended?
- If not, does their learning lead the teacher to new understandings about the nature of the activity or the interests of the children?

Observation of the practitioner – by the practitioner!

This is perhaps the most challenging but potentially the most enlightening observation of all. Many early childhood educators are now using video cameras to make a record of their interactions with children in order to evaluate some of the following:

- What do I spend my time doing?
- Do I spend more time talking than the children?
- Do I listen to children as well as initiate conversations?
- Do I respond positively – both in my body language as well as my words?
- Do I ask children questions to which I already know the answers?

- Do I answer children's questions respectfully?
- Do my questions and suggestions challenge and extend children's thinking?
- Am I interrupted unnecessarily by children?
- What strategies am I using to make children more independent?
- Am I having fun? Are the children having fun?

Action research

One way in which some practitioners choose to reflect on their practice in a more systematic way is to engage in some action research in their own classrooms. The work 'research' can sound daunting. But what action research requires of practitioners is very straightforward. In settings and schools, action research gives practitioners a framework to follow a self-reflective cycle (Carr and Kemmis 1986) of:

- planning;
- acting;
- observing;
- reflecting.

In order to undertake action research, the practitioner *plans* what they would like to alter or amend about their current practice or their learning environment. They evaluate what they are doing now and what the children are achieving now, as a baseline against which to judge the impact of any changes.

The practitioner then *acts* to intervene in the current way of working. They may decide to open the doors to the outdoor area for the whole of the teaching time of a session rather than just for an hour in the middle. They may decide to give children greater autonomy in their choices – of where to play or with whom to play. They may decide to ask more open-ended questions and see if this improves children's thinking skills. The subject matter for action research can be whatever a practitioner has identified as being in need of development in their setting.

Next the practitioner *observes* the impact that the intervention has had. It is down to the practitioner to decide how long the intervention needs to last before any change is discernible. But when sufficient time has elapsed, the practitioner observes the child, or the group or the environment and sees how children are behaving now as opposed to at the start of the research.

Finally, the practitioner *reflects* on the changes that have taken place – if any, and asks what impact the evaluation has had. This analysis asks not only whether any changes have occurred but what that might be and whether there have been any surprise outcomes as a result of the intervention. This reflection might lead to another cycle of action research or a period of consolidation while the changes bed down.

In Oxfordshire, some 76 Foundation Stage practitioners took part in a year-long action research project led by Professor Guy Claxton (National Primary Centre 2006). The first term (in the summer) was spent on an initial investigation and this became refined in the autumn and spring terms of the following year. The aim of the project was to increase the 'learning power' of children (Claxton 2002) and enable them to be more resourceful and independent in their learning. We have seen throughout this book that evidence points to young children being naturally both resourceful and independent in their learning. What the project identified is that it is often the practitioners who put barriers in the way of children's competences and the practitioner that has to change the way they plan for and organize learning that permits what Claxton calls 'learnacy' to flourish.

As their contribution to the project, which was called *'Playing for Life'*, each practitioner undertook a piece of action research in their own setting or classroom that they wrote up as a case study. The headings from those case studies reports may prove helpful to others wishing to take a first step into action research:

- Focus of the enquiry: *What is the question you are asking about your practice? What is the planned impact on the development of children as learners?*
- Context of the enquiry: *What kind of setting are you working in? Are there any special circumstances?*
- Initial investigation: *How did you start off? What were you originally interested in? Why was that?*
- Initial findings: *What kind of things did you begin to find out as you studied your children more carefully during the summer term? How did these findings change your question or focus?*
- Main investigation: *What became the final focus for investigation in the autumn and spring terms? What changes in the children as learners did you hope to bring about? What methods did you use? What intervention did you use? How did you evaluate whether there had been any changes?*
- Main findings: *What changes did you actually observe in the children's attitudes to learning? What conclusions can your draw from your study?*
- Implications for our teaching: *How will the outcomes of your study change your teaching in the future?*
- Reflections on our own learning: *What has this project contributed to your own thinking and development?*

The project revealed a great deal about action research. Firstly, that the hardest thing is to decide what you want to research – and sticking to it. The second is – not to make the focus of the enquiry too broad. Time is short and the focus needs to be tight. Thirdly, that good ideas for developing practice often come from others – from the books we read, from the journal articles we see, from the training we attend. No one practitioner can have all the ideas and all the know-how and early childhood educators need to constantly update and refresh their professional knowledge about what research others have written and about what ideas others have tried. We would all be very concerned if a doctor said he didn't know about the latest medical research because he was too busy in his surgery seeing patients! Finally, we learnt that research in the real world is not easy. As Alison Price writes in the project publication (2005: 7), children involved in the project moved out of the class or setting, or out of the area, teachers became pregnant, teaching assistants fell ill. All this meant that practitioners had to revise their plans and adjust their thinking. Any examination of practice in systematic ways can, of course, challenge practitioners' existing theories and beliefs. In action research, say Pollard and Tann (1993), practitioners must be prepared to explore the discrepancies between their current practice and the new insights that might be acquired. Whatever methodology is used, the notion of self-evaluation is every bit as critical for practitioners as it is for children. Reflection should lead to new ways of working (Adelman 1985) and in order for this to happen, early childhood educators need to be explorers and enquirers alongside their children.

Self-evaluation

Another highly effective strategy for reflecting on practice in the early years is to devise a structured programme of self-evaluation. Using a quality assurance scheme or devising a self-evaluation policy for an individual setting can both bring rich rewards in terms of the development of the setting, particularly in relation to staff working together to decide on their judgements about the quality of provision, procedures and practice. Ofsted (the Office for Standards in Education) now requires all settings to complete a self-evaluation of their own practice, which the inspection team will analyse and then seek to scrutinize when the inspection takes place.

Self-evaluation seeks to identify all aspects of the life of the school or setting. The early years practitioner may be responsible for one part of the process or for many aspects, according to the size of the setting and its age range. But the efficacy of the self-evaluation process lies in *analysing the impact* of what is being done in the setting rather than *describing* what is being done. If the analysis is effective, then it gives a clear steer about what steps need to be taken to enable the setting to develop further.

A good self-evaluation or quality assurance programme supports a setting to focus on improvement and to work towards its vision for the future. In Oxfordshire (OCC 2005), the quality assurance programme *'Partners in Quality'* focused on 10 'aspects of quality':

1   interactions and relationships;
2   attitudes and dispositions;
3   opportunities and experiences;
4   support from adults;
5   children's well-being;
6   inclusion;
7   working with parents, carers and the community;
8   the environment;
9   staffing and professional development;
10 leadership and management.

Like the Early Years Foundation Stage, *'Partners in Quality'* built on the National Standards and included the principles from *Birth to Three Matters* (DfES 2003a) and the *Curriculum Guidance for the Foundation Stage* (DfES 2000). It led practitioners through a process of:

- Audit: *Where are we now? What is our evidence?*
- Action: *What do we currently do well? What do we want to develop? Who is going to do this? When do we aim to finish?*
- Evaluation: *What developments did we make? What impact has it made on the quality of our setting? What will we do in the future to further enhance this aspect of our setting?*

Like all good-quality assurance schemes, *'Partners in Quality'* emphasized throughout the importance of staff working together to make their judgements and to gather their evidence. Self-evaluation is not a one-off process but one that continues in a planned cycle so that once one element is evaluated and reflected upon, the next is put under the spotlight. Self-evaluation is a very liberating and empowering process because it gives practitioners the evidence base for making judgements about their own setting and enables staff to challenge any external evaluation that may contradict their own view. It may be that outsiders, such as inspectors and advisers, have a different perspective and arrive at different judgements. But self-evaluation empowers staff to draw on their own findings and their own evidence base and to debate any judgements that they feel are not accurate.

The following prompts offer a framework for discussion between staff about what might constitute 'quality' in their own setting. It is reproduced with grateful thanks to the Oxfordshire County Council Early Learning and Childcare Service:

1 *Interactions and relationships*
- The aims and values of the setting are open and inclusive. All children and adults should be able to participate and contribute to the work of the setting.
- Observations of children and adults are made regularly and are used to improve the quality of social interactions and relationships within the setting, and between home and setting.
- Transitions are handled sensitively.
- Practitioners provide good role models for behaviour and offer support, encouragement and guidance to parents and carers on positive behaviour strategies.
- Practitioners implement a behaviour policy and procedures that are shared with parents.
- Practitioners understand the social and emotional development of children and take into account the age and stage of children in their care.

2 *Attitudes and dispositions*
- Practitioners share observations of the children with each other and use these observations to support children to develop positive attitudes and self-esteem.
- Practitioners ask open-ended questions and encourage children to experiment and ask questions themselves.
- Practitioners provide a secure environment in which children are confident to try new things and learn from their experiences.
- The setting has flexible routine that gives children time to develop their interests.

3 *Opportunities and experiences*
- Practitioners have a good understanding of the developmental needs of the children.
- The environment and activities are planned in response to observations of the children.
- Practitioners respond flexibly to the needs and interests of individual children.
- Children are given time to become involved in their play and learning.
- Opportunities reflect the social and cultural experiences of children and their families.

4 *Support from adults*
- All practitioners are involved in planning broad and balanced activities and experiences and making observations and assessments.

- Practitioners share daily plans and observations with parents and carers and respond to parents' and carers' knowledge of individual children.
- Practitioners plan experiences based on their knowledge of each child.
- Practitioners ensure that all children have access to a carefully planned Early Years Foundation Stage curriculum or planned activities/experiences appropriate to their age and developmental needs.
- Practitioners support and extend children's learning through play.
- Practitioners take part in ongoing professional development.

5 *Children's well-being*
- All practitioners contribute to the writing and implementation of statutory policies and requirements (e.g. child protection policy).
- Provision is made for healthy eating, sleep and exercise.
- Children have daily opportunities for play and learning indoors and out.
- Practitioners are knowledgeable about and respond to children's individual circumstances sensitively.
- Practitioners respond to the physical and comfort needs of children.

6 *Inclusion*
- The Equal Opportunities and Special Educational Needs (SEN) coordinators have discussed their training with the full staff team.
- Practitioners are informed about the cultural, social and personal circumstances of individual families.
- The Inclusion/Equal Opportunities and SEN policies are implemented and evaluated.

7 *Working with parents, carers and the community*
- The setting works in partnership with parents, carers and the local community to identify and respond to the needs of all children.
- Parents and carers are given up-to-date and accessible information about the setting.
- Practitioners are informed about the cultural, social and personal circumstances of individual families.
- All parents and carers feel welcome and are invited to participate in the day to day work of the setting.
- The setting is responsive to the views and concerns of children, parents and carers.

8 *The environment*
- Facilities are provided that support children to develop their exploration, play and learning in all areas indoors and outside and are inclusive for children with special needs.

- Practitioners audit and evaluate the quality, safety and appropriate use of resources in all areas.
- All staff implement health, safety and security procedures.

9 *Staffing and professional development*
- All staff are involved in the self-evaluation process.
- Staff share a common vision and values.
- Staff have a commitment to ongoing training.
- All staff have the opportunity to contribute to panning for children's experiences and to suggest improvements.
- Staff are given support to fulfil their roles and responsibilities.

10 *Leadership and management*
- Procedures for appointing staff, committee members or members of the governing body are in place.
- Policies are regularly reviewed.
- Parents/carers are given information about the setting.
- The quality of education and care is monitored and action plans are created to sustain and improve quality.
- Staff are supported to fulfil their roles and responsibilities.

Every Child Matters

One significant change in the process of self-evaluation – and indeed inspection – is that, in England, any evaluation has to be placed in the context of the Every Child Matters agenda and the five 'outcomes' for children and young people that this policy outlines. The 2003 government Green Paper, called 'Every Child Matters', was published alongside the formal response to the death of Victoria Climbié, the little girl killed in horrific circumstances by her great aunt and the man with whom they lived. The report on Victoria Climbié's death (Laming 2003) made recommendations that would protect other children, particularly those who are vulnerable, from deliberate harm and exploitation. In addition, it recommended dramatic changes in the way in which services for children, young people and families, at national and local level, should be organized. The Green Paper prompted widespread consultation on how to improve these services and in 2004 the government published 'Every Child Matters: the Next Steps' and passed the Children Act 2004 which legislated that every child and young person, whatever their background or circumstances, should have the support they need to:

- be healthy;
- stay safe;
- enjoy and achieve;

- make a positive contribution;
- achieve economic well-being.

These are the 'five outcomes' of the Every Child Matters agenda, and these now permeate all aspects of policy and strategy that touch the lives of children and young people, particularly those from vulnerable families. The vision is to create a joined-up system of health, family support, childcare and education services so that all children get the best start possible in their vital early years. This vision has led to a number of significant government policies and initiatives that are impacting already on early education:

Choice for Parents, the Best Start for Children: a Ten-year Strategy for Childcare (2004)

Set out these key themes:

- *Choice and flexibility*: parents to have greater choice about balancing work and family life;
- *Availability*: for all families with children aged up to 14 who need it, an affordable, flexible, high-quality childcare place that meets their circumstances;
- *Quality*: high-quality provision with a highly skilled childcare and early years workforce, among the best in the world;
- *Affordability*: families to be able to afford flexible, high-quality childcare that is appropriate for their needs.

Childcare Act 2006

The first Act to be exclusively concerned with early education and childcare. The Act takes forward some of the key commitments from the Ten-year Strategy and formalizes the strategic role local authorities play through a set of new duties to:

- improve the five ECM outcomes (see above) for all pre-school children and reduce inequalities in these outcomes;
- secure sufficient childcare for working parents;
- provide a better parental information service.

The Act also reforms and simplifies early years regulation and inspection arrangements, providing for a new integrated education and care quality framework for pre-school children and also for the new Ofsted Childcare Register.

Early support – services for disabled children in the early years

- programme for achieving better coordinated, family-focused services for very young disabled children and their families;
- the role of Early Support is to raise expectations about the way agencies and services work, encourage change, and provide practical tools to support multi-agency service development at local level.

Children's centres

- 'one-stop shops' providing integrated services such as health (antenatal classes); early education (for 3 and 4 year olds); advice (such as Citizen's Advice Bureau outreach) and support for parents and families (e.g. training courses);
- government target to deliver 2,500 children's centres by 2008 and 3,500 children's centres by 2010 ('one in every community');
- many are evolving from existing provision such as local Sure Start programmes, nursery schools and family centres. A few will be new build. Some will be on primary school sites;
- 'full service models' bring together children's services and childcare in the poorest areas, while lighter touch – 'graduated' models will develop in less disadvantaged areas with a focus on information and coordination.

Extended schools

- primary schools will, over time, offer childcare between 8 a.m. and 6 p.m., 48 weeks a year;
- services might include out-of-school hours learning; health and social care; childcare; adult education and family learning, leisure activities and information and communication technology access.

Conclusion

However early childhood educators choose to evaluate their practice, one thing is for certain – it is a process that must never stop. Practitioners who continually question themselves and reflect upon their practice keep children's experiences stimulating, intriguing and absorbing. Throughout this book we have celebrated the competence of young learners. We have considered the central role of the adult in responding to children's learning needs with sensitivity and skill. We have understood that if every child is to be given strong foundations for lifelong learning, then adults must base their planning and their preparation on the daily observation of children. If children's learning experiences are to be relevant and meaningful, then what is taught and learnt in Foundation Stage settings across the country needs to start from the individual learner – it needs to start from the child.

REFERENCES

Abbott, L. and Moylett, H. (1997) *Working with Under-3s: Responding to Children's Needs*. Buckingham: Open University Press.

Adams, S., and Moyles, J. (2005) *Images of Violence*. Lutterworth: Featherstone Education.

Adelman, C. (1985) Action research, in S. Hegarty and P. Evans (eds) *Research Methods in Special Education*. Windsor: NFER.

Adelman, C. (1992) Play as a quest for vocation, *Journal of Curriculum Studies*, 24 (2): 139–51.

Alexander, R. (1992) *Policy and Practice in Primary Education*. London: Routledge.

Alexander, R., Rose, J. and Whitehead, C. (1992) *Classroom Organisation and Classroom Practice in Primary Schools: A Discussion Paper*. London: DES.

Anning, A. (1991) *The First Years at School*. Milton Keynes: Open University Press.

Athey, C. (2007) *Extending Thought in Young Children*, 2nd edn. London: Paul Chapman Publishing.

Aubrey, C. (ed.) (1994) *The Role of Subject Knowledge in the Early Years of Schooling*. Lewes: Falmer Press.

Ball, C. (1994) *Start Right: The Importance of Early Learning*. London: RSA.

Barnes, D., Britton, J. and Rosen, H. (1969) *Language, the Learner and the School*. Harmondsworth: Penguin.

Barnes, D. and Todd, F. (1977) *Communication and Learning in Small Groups*. London: Routledge & Kegan Paul.

Barrett, G. (ed.) (1989) *Disaffection From School? The Early Years*. Lewes: Falmer Press.

Bartholomew, L. and Bruce, T. (1993) *Getting to Know You*. London: Hodder & Stoughton.

Bealing, D. (1972) Organisation of junior school classrooms, *Educational Research*, 14: 231–5.

Belsky, J., Lowe Vandell, D., Burchinal, M., Clarke-Stewart, K.A., McMartney, K. and Tresch Owen M. (2007) Effects of early child care on later development and achievement. *Child Development*, 78 (2): 681–701.

Bennett, N., Desforges, C., Cockburn, A. and Wilkinson, B. (1984) *The Quality of Pupil Learning Experiences*. Hove: Lawrence Erlbaum.

Bennett, N. and Kell, J. (1989) *A Good Start? Four Year Olds in Infant Schools*. Oxford: Basil Blackwell.

Bennett, N., Wood, L. and Rogers, S. (1997) *Teaching Through Play: Teachers' Thinking and Classroom Practice*. Milton Keynes: Open University Press.

Biddulph, S. (2005) *Raising Babies: Should under 3s go to nursery?* London: HarperCollins.

Bilton, H. (1994) Morning and afternoon sessions in the nursery, do they have equal status? With particular reference to story time, *International Journal of Early Years Education*, 2 (2): 54–64.

Bilton, H. (2002) *Outdoor Play in the Early Years*, 2nd edn. London: David Fulton.

Black, P., Harrison, C., Lee, C., Marshall, B. and Wiliam, D. (2002) *Working Inside the Black Box: Assessment for Learning in the Classroom*. London: King's College.

Blenkin, G.M. and Kelly, A.V. (eds) (1987) *Early Childhood Education: A Developmental Curriculum*. London: Paul Chapman.

Blenkin, G.M. and Kelly, A.V. (eds) (1992) *Assessment in Early Childhood Education*. London: Paul Chapman.

Blenkin, G.M. and Kelly, A.V. (eds) (1994) *The National Curriculum and Early Learning*. London: Paul Chapman.

Bowlby, J. (1969) *Attachment*. London: Pelican.

Bowlby, J. (1975) The nature of the child's attachment to the mother, *American Journal of Psychiatry*, 132, 133–7.

Bowly, J. (1981) *Attachment and Loss (vol. 3): Loss, Sadness and Depression*. Harmondsworth: Penguin.

Brierley, J. (1994) *Give Me a Child Until He is Seven*, 2nd edn. Lewes: Falmer Press.

Britton, J. (1970) Speech in the school, *NATE Journal*, Summer: 22–4.

Bronfenbrenner, U. (1979) *The Ecology of Human Development*. Cambridge: Harvard University Press.

Bronson, M.B. (2000) *Self-regulation in Early Childhood*. London: Guilford Press.

Brooker, L. (2002) *Starting School: Young Children Learning Culture*. Milton Keynes: Open University Press.

Brown, D. (1994) Play, the playground and the culture of childhood, in J. Moyles (ed.) *The Excellence of Play*. Milton Keynes: Open University Press.

Brown, S. and Cleave, S. (1990) *Four Year Olds in School: Meeting Their Needs*. Slough: NFER.

Brown, G. and Wragg, E.C. (1993) *Questioning*. London: Routledge.

Bruce, T. (1987) *Early Childhood Education*. Sevenoaks: Hodder & Stoughton.

Bruce, T. (1991) *Time to Play in Early Childhood Education*. Sevenoaks: Hodder & Stoughton.

Bruce, I. (2004) *Developing Learning in Early Childhood* London: Paul Chapman Publishing.

Bruer, J.T. (1999) *The Myth of the First Three Years*. New York: The Free Press.

Bruner, J.S. (1960) *The Process of Education*. Cambridge, MA: Harvard University Press.

Bruner, J.S. (1966a) *Toward a Theory of Instruction*. Cambridge, MA: Harvard University Press.

Bruner, J.S. (1966b) *The Culture of Education*. Cambridge, MA: Harvard University Press.

Bruner, J.S. (1977) Introduction, in B. Tizard and D. Harvey (eds) *The Biology of Play*. London: Spastics International Medical Publications.

Bruner, J.S. (1980) *Under Five in Britain: The Oxford Pre-school Research Project*. Oxford: Grant McIntyre.

Bruner, J.S. (1985) Vygotsky: a historical and conceptual perspective, in J.V. Wertsch (ed.) *Culture, Communication and Cognition: Vygotskian Perspective*. Cambridge: Cambridge University Press.

Bruner, J.S. (1986) *Actual Minds, Possible Worlds*. Cambridge, MA: Harvard University Press.

Bruner. J. (1990) *Acts of Meaning* Cambridge, MA: Harvard University Press.

Bruner, J. and Haste, H. (eds) (1987) *Making Sense: The Child's Construction of the World*. London: Methuen.

Cairns, K. (2002) *Attachment, Resilience and Trauma*. London: BAAF.

Calderhead, J. and Miller, E. (1985) The integration of subject matter knowledge in student teachers' classroom practice. Conference paper, British Educational Research Association, Sheffield.

Calvin, W.H. (1996) *How Brains Think: Evolving Intelligence Then and Now*. London: Weidenfeld & Nicolson.

Campbell, R.J. and Neill, S.R.St.J. (1990) *Thirteen Hundred and Thirty Days: Final Report of a Pilot Study of Teacher Time in Key Stage 1, Commissioned by the Assistant Masters and Mistresses Association*. Warwick: University of Warwick, Department of Education.

Campbell, R.J., Evans, L., Neill, S.R.St.J. and Packwood, A. (1993) *The Use and Management of Infant Teachers' Time: Some Policy Issues*. Stoke-on-Trent: Trentham.

Carnegie Corporation of New York (1994) *Starting Points: Meeting the Needs of our Youngest Children*. New York: Carnegie Corporation.

Carr, M. (2001) *Assessment in Early Childhood Settings*. London: Paul Chapman Publishing.

Carr, W. and Kemmis, S. (1986) *Becoming Critical: Education, Knowledge and Action Research*. Lewes: Falmer Press.

Central Advisory Council for Education (CACE) (1967) *Children and their Primary Schools* (The Plowden Report). London: HMSO.

Chang, G.L. and Wells, G. (1988) The literate potential of collaborative talk, in M. Maclure, T. Phillips and A. Wilkinson (eds) *Oracy Matters*. Milton Keynes: Open University Press.

Chilvers, D. (2006) *Young Children Talking: The Art of Conversation and Why Children Need to Chatter*. London: BAECE.

Clarricoates, K. (1983) Classroom interaction, in J. Whyld (ed.) *Sexism in the Secondary Curriculum*. London: Harper & Row.

Claxton, G. (2002) *Building Learning Power*. Bristol: TLO.

Cohen, D. (1997) *The Secret Language of the Mind*. London: Duncan Baird.

Cousins, J. (1990) Are your little humpty dumpties floating or sinking? *Early Years*, 10 (2): 28–38.

Cousins, J. (1999) *Listening to Four Year Olds*. London: National Early Years Network.

Cox, C.B. and Boyson, R. (eds) (1975) *The Fight for Education: Black Paper 1975*. London: Dent.

Cox, C.B. and Boyson, R. (eds) (1977) *Black Paper 1977*. London: Maurice Temple Smith Ltd.

Cox, C.B. and Dyson, A.E. (eds) (1969a) *Fight for Education: A Black Paper*. London: Critical Quarterly Society.

Cox, C.B. and Dyson, A.E. (eds) (1969b) *Black Paper Two*. London: Critical Quarterly Society.

Cox, C.B. and Dyson, A.E. (eds) (1970) *Black Paper Three: Goodbye Mr Short*. London: Critical Quarterly Society.

Cox, T. and Sanders, S. (1994) *The Impact of the National Curriculum on the Teaching of Five-Year-Olds*. Lewes: Falmer Press.

Curtis, A. (1994) Play in different cultures and different childhoods, in J. Moyles (ed.) *The Excellence of Play*. Milton Keynes: Open University Press.

Darling, J. (1994) *Child-centred Education and its Critics*. London: Paul Chapman.

David, T., Curtis, A. and Siraj-Blatchford, I. (1992) *Effective Teaching in the Early Years: Fostering Children's Learning in Nurseries and in Infant Classes*. OMEP (UK). Stoke-on-Trent: Trentham.

Davies, W.J.K. (1987) *Towards Autonomy in Learning: Process or Product?* London: Council for Educational Technology.

Day, C. (1993) Reflection: a necessary but not sufficient condition for professional development, *British Educational Research Journal*, 19 (1): 83–93.

Department for Education and Employment (DfEE) (1998) *The National Literacy Strategy Framework*. London: DfEE Publications.

Department for Education and Employment (DfEE) (1999) *The National Numeracy Strategy Framework*. London: DfEE Publications.

Department for Education and Employment/Qualifications and Curriculum Authority (DfEE/QCA) (1998) *Desirable Outcomes for Children's Learning on Entering Compulsory Schooling.* London: DfEE Publications.

Department of Education and Science (DES) (1989) *The Education of Children Under Five.* London: HMSO.

Department of Education and Science (DES) (1990) *Starting with Quality* (The Rumbold Report). London: HMSO.

Department for Education and Skills (DfES) (2000) *Curriculum Guidance for the Foundation Stage.* London: DfES Publications.

Department for Education and Skills (DfES) (2002a) *Researching Effective Pedagogy in the Early Years.* London: DfES Publications.

Department for Education and Skills (DfES) (2002b) *Study of Pedagogical Effectiveness in Early Learning.* London: DfES Publications.

Department for Education and Skills (DfES) (2003a) *Birth to Three Matters.* London: DfES Publications.

Department for Education and Skills (DfES) (2003b) *Communicating Matters.* London: DfES Publications.

Department for Education and Skills (DfES) (2004) *Choice for Parents, the Best Start for Children: A Ten Year Strategy for Childcare.* London: DfES Publications.

Department for Education and Skills (DfES) (2005) *Communicating Matters.* London: DfES Publications.

Department for Education and Skills (DfES) (2007) *The Early Years Foundation Stage.* London: DfES Publications.

Department for Education and Skills (DfES) (2007a) *Statutory Framework for the Early Years Foundation Stage*: London: DfES Publications.

Department for Education and Skills (DfES) (2007b) *Practice Guidance for the Early Years Foundation Stage.* London: DfES Publications.

Dewey, J. (1933) *How We Think: A Restatement of the Relation of Reflective Thinking to the Educative Process.* Chicago, IL: Henry Regnery.

Dewey, J. (1938) *Experience and Education.* New York: Macmillan.

Diamond, M. and Hopson, J. (1998) *Magic Trees of the Mind.* New York: Dutton.

Dillon, J.T. (1981) To question or not to question during discussion, *Journal of Teacher Education*, 32 (5): 51–5.

Donaldson, M. (1978) *Children's Minds.* London: Fontana Press.

Donaldson, M. (1992) *Human Minds: An Exploration.* London: Penguin Books.

Dowling, M. (1995) *Starting School at Four: A Joint Endeavour.* London: Paul Chapman.

Dowling, M. (2000) *Young Children's Personal, Social and Emotional Development.* London: Paul Chapman.

Drummond, M.J. (1993) *Assessing Children's Learning*. London: David Fulton.

Drummond, M.J., Rouse, D. and Pugh, G. (1992) *Making Assessment Work*. Nottingham: NES Arnold/National Children's Bureau.

Dunn, J. (1988) *The Beginning of Social Understanding*. Oxford: Blackwell.

Dweck, C. (1978) Children's Interpretation of evaluative feedback: the effect of social cues on learned helplessness *Merrill-Palmer Quarterly*, 22 (2).

Early Years Curriculum Group (EYCG) (1992) *First Things First: Educating Young Children*. Oldham: Madeleine Lindley.

Early Years Curriculum Group (EYCG) (1995) *Four-Year-Olds in School: Myths and Realities*. Oldham: Madeleine Lindley.

Early Years Curriculum Group (EYCG) (1998) *Interpreting the National Curriculum at Key Stage 1: A Developmental Approach*. Milton Keynes: Open University Press.

Edwards, D. and Mercer, N. (1987) *Common Knowledge: The Development of Understanding in the Classroom*. London: Methuen.

Edwards, E. and Knight, P. (1994) *Effective Early Years Education: Teaching Young Children*. Milton Keynes: Open University Press.

Edwards, V. and Redfern, A. (1988) *At Home in School: Parent Participation in Primary Education*. London: Routledge.

Elfer, P. (1996) Building intimacy in relationships with young children in nurseries, *Early Years* 16 (2): 30–4.

Elfer, P., Goldschmied, E. and Selleck, D. (2003) *Key Persons in the Nursery*. London: David Fulton.

Entwhistle, N. (1987) *Understanding Classroom Learning*. Sevenoaks: Hodder and Stoughton.

Fein, G.G. (1981) Pretend play in childhood: an integrative review, *Child Development*, 52 (4): 1095–118.

Fisher, R. (1990) *Teaching Children to Think*. Oxford: Blackwell.

Fisher, J. (1996) Reflecting on the principles of early years practice, *Journal of Teacher Development*, 5 (1): 17–26.

Fisher, J. (1998a) Seen and heard, *Nursery World*, 5 February: 26–7.

Fisher, J. (1998b) All part of the plan, *Nursery World*, 12 February: 12–13.

Fisher, J. (1998c) For good measure, *Nursery World*, 19 February: 14–15.

Fisher, J. (1998d) Fit for the purpose? A critique of the National Framework for Baseline Assessment, *Education 3 to 13*, 26 (3): 9–14.

Fisher, J. (2000) The foundations of learning, *Early Education*, Summer.

Fisher, J. (2002) *The Foundations of Learning*. Milton Keynes: Open University Press.

Fisher, J. (2006) Handle with care! Transitions in the early years, *Early Education*, Autumn.

Fisher, J., Claxton, G. and Price, A. (2005) *Playing for Life*, Birmingham, National Primary Trust.

Forman, E.A. and Cazden, C.B. (1985) Exploring Vygotskian perspectives in education: the cognitive value of peer interaction, in J.V. Wertsch (ed.) *Culture, Communication and Cognition: Vygotskian Perspective*. Cambridge: Cambridge University Press.

French, P. and Maclure, M. (1983) Teacher questions and pupil answers: an investigation of questions and answers in the infant classroom, in M. Stubbs and H. Hillier (eds) *Readings in Language, Schools and Classrooms*, 2nd edn. London: Methuen.

Galton, M. and Patrick, H. (eds) (1990) *Curriculum Provision in Small Primary Schools*. London: Routledge.

Galton, M., Simon, B. and Croll, P. (1980) *Inside the Primary Classroom*. London: Routledge & Kegan Paul.

Galton, M. and Williamson, J. (1992) *Group Work and the Primary Classroom*. London: Routledge.

Gammage, P. (1999) After five, your brain is cooked, *Education Now*, Summer (24).

Gardner, H. (1993) *The Unschooled Mind: How Children Think and How Schools Should Teach*. London: Fontana.

Garvey, C. (1977) *Play*. London: Fontana.

Gerhardt, S. (2004) *Why Love Matters: How Affection Shapes A Baby's Brain*. Hove: Brunner-Routledge.

Gilbert, J.K. and Osborne, R.J. (1982) Studies of pupils' alternative frameworks or misconceptions in science, in W.F. Archenhold *et al.* (eds) *Cognitive Development Research in Science and Mathematics*. Leeds: University of Leeds.

Gipps, C. and Stobart, G. (1993) *Assessment: A Teachers' Guide to Issues*. Sevenoaks: Hodder & Stoughton.

Gipps, C.V. (1994) *Beyond Testing*. Lewes: Falmer Press.

Gopnik, A., Meltzoff, A., and Kuhl, P. (1999) *How Babies Think: The Science of Childhood*. London: Weidenfeld & Nicolson

Greenfield, S. (1997) *The Human Brain: A Guided Tour*. London: Weidenfield & Nicolson.

Gura, P. (ed.) (1992) *Exploring Learning: Young Children and Blockplay*. London: Paul Chapman.

Hall, N. (1987) *The Emergence of Literacy*. Sevenoaks: Hodder & Stoughton.

Harlen, W. (ed.) (1985) *Primary Science ... Taking the Plunge*. Oxford: Heinemann Educational.

Hastings, N. and Schweiso, J. (1995) Tasks and tables: the effects of seating arrangements on task engagement in primary schools, *Educational Research* (NFER), 37 (3): 279–91.

Heath, S.R. (1983) *Ways with Words: Language, Life and Work in Communities and Classrooms.* Cambridge: Cambridge University Press.

Hohmann, M., Banet, B. and Weikart, D.P. (1979) *Young Children in Action.* Ypsilanti, MI: High/Scope Press.

Hohmann, M. and Weikart, D. (1995) *Educating Young Children.* Ypsilanti, MI: High/Scope Press.

Holland, P. (2003) *We Don't Play with Guns Here: War, Weapon and Superhero Play in the Early Years.* Maidenhead: Open University Press.

Holt, J. (1982) *How Children Fail,* 2nd edn. Harmondsworth: Penguin.

Howe, D., Brandon, M., Hings, D. and Schofield, G. (1999) *Attachment Theory, Child Maltreatment and Family Support: A Practice and Assessment Model.* London: Macmillan.

Hughes, B. (1996) *A Playworker's Taxonomy of Play Types.* London: Playlink.

Hughes, M. (1986) *Children and Number.* Oxford: Blackwell.

Hurst, V. (1994) Observing play in early childhood, in J. Moyles (ed.) *The Excellence of Play.* Milton Keynes: Open University Press.

Hurst, V. and Lally, M. (1992) Assessment and the nursery curriculum, in G.M. Blenkin and A.V. Kelly (eds) *Assessment in Early Childhood Education.* London: Paul Chapman.

Huskins, J. (1998) *From Disaffection to Social Inclusion.* Bristol: Jillich.

Hutchin, V. (1996) *Tracking Significant Achievement in the Early Years.* London: Hodder & Stoughton.

Hutchin, V. (1999) *Right from the Start: Effective Planning and Assessment in the Early Years.* London: Hodder & Stoughton.

Hutt, J., Tyler, S., Hutt, C. and Christopherson, H. (1990) *Play, Exploration and Learning: A Natural History of the Pre-school.* London: Routledge.

Inner London Education Authority (ILEA) (1990) *A Curriculum for Young Children: Outdoor Play.* London: Harcourt Brace Jovanovich.

Isaacs, S. (1968) *The Nursery Years.* London: Routledge & Kegan Paul.

Jenson, E. (1998) *Teaching with the Brain in Mind.* Alexandria, VA: ASCD.

Jones, N. (1989) Preface, in G. Barrett (ed.) *Disaffection From School? The Early Years.* Lewes: Falmer Press.

Jones, P. (1988) *Lipservice: The Story of Talk in Schools.* Milton Keynes: Open University Press.

Kagan, S. (1988) *Cooperative Learning: Resources for Teachers.* Riverside, CA: University of California.

Kalliala, M. (2006) *Play Culture in a Changing World.* Maidenhead: Open University Press.

Katz, L. (1998) Enhancing the formative years. Paper presented to the NAEIAC Early Years Conference, Oxford, June.

Kimberley, K. (1990) The third limb: assessment and the national curriculum, *The English Magazine*, 23, Summer: 19–26.

Kuhn, D. (2000) Theory of mind, metacognition, and reasoning: a lifespan perspective, in P. Mitchell and K.J. Riggs (eds) *Children's Reasoning and the Mind*. Hove: Psychology Press.

Laming (2003) *The Victoria Climbié Inquiry*. London: HMSO.

Lancaster, Y. P. (2003) *Promoting Listening to Young Children*. Maidenhead: Open University Press.

Lane, J. (2005a) 'I've just seen a wave as big as our house, Daddy': the importance of providing scope for children to talk about things that worry them, including disasters such as the tsunami. *Early Years Educator*, March.

Lane, J. (2005b) 'Facing terror: terrorist attacks are frightening and can have a big effect on children and adults' *Nursery Education*. November.

Lee, L. (1959) *Cider With Rosie*. London: Hogarth Press.

Lindon, J. (1993) *Child Development from Birth to Eight*. London: National Children's Bureau.

Lindon J. (2000) *Helping Babies and Toddlers Learn: A Guide to Good Practice with Under Threes*. National Early Years Network

Lindon, J, (2001) *Understanding Children's Play*. Cheltenham: Nelson Thornes.

Lindsay, G., Lewis, A. and Phillips, E. (2000) *Evaluation of Accredited Baseline Assessment Schemes 1999–2000*. Warwick: University of Warwick, Psychology and Special Needs Research Unit.

Livingstone T. (2005) *Child of our Time*. London: Bantam Press.

Malaguzzi, L. (1992) *A Message from Loris Malaguzzi*, video transcript , Reggio Emilia: Reggio Children.

Malaguzzi, L. (1993) History, ideas and basic philosophy, in C. Edwards, L. Gandini and G. Foreman (eds) *The Hundred Languages of Children – the Reggio Emilia Approach to Early Childhood Education* Norwood, NJ: Ablex.

Malaguzzi, L. (1997) *Shoe and Meter*. Reggio Emilia: Reggio Children.

Manning, K. and Sharp, A. (1977) *Structuring Play in the Early Years at School*. London: Ward Lock International.

Manning-Morton, J. and Thorp, M. (2001) *Key Times – A Framework for Developing High Quality Provision for Children Under Three Years Old*. Camden Under Threes Development Group and The University of North London.

May, P., Ashford, E. and Bottle, G. (2006) *Sound Beginnings: Learning and Development in the Early Years*. London: David Fulton.

McMillan, M. (1919) *The Nursery School*. London: J.M. Dent & Sons.

Meadows, S. (1993) *The Child As Thinker: The Development and Acquisition of Cognition in Childhood*. London: Routledge.

Meighan, J. (1993) The hijack of young children's learning, in R. Meighan (ed.) *Theory and Practice of Regressive Education*. Nottingham: Educational Heretics Press.

Mortimore, P., Sammons, P., Stoll, L. and Ecob, R. (1986) *The Junior School Project*. London: ILEA.

Moss, P. and Penn, H. (1996) *Transforming Nursery Education*. London: Paul Chapman.

Moyles, J.R. (1989) *Just Playing? The Role and Status of Play in Early Childhood Education*. Milton Keynes: Open University Press.

Moyles, J.R. (1992) *Organising for Learning in the Primary Classroom*. Buckingham: Open University Press.

Moyles, J.R. (ed.) (1994) *The Excellence of Play*. Buckingham: Open University Press.

National Assessment Agency (NAA) (2005) *Continuing the Learning Journey*. London: QCA.

National Commission on Education (1993) *Learning to Succeed*. London: Heinemann.

Nutbrown. C. (2006) *Threads of Thinking,* 3rd edn. London: Sage.

Office for Standards in Education (Ofsted) (1991) *Well Managed Classes in Primary Schools: Case Studies of Six Teachers*. London: DfE.

Office for Standards in Education (Ofsted) (1993a) *Curriculum Organisation and Classroom Practice in Primary Schools: A Follow-up Report*. London: DfE.

Office for Standards in Education (Ofsted) (1993b) *First Class: The Standards and Quality of Education in Reception Classes*. London: HMSO.

Office for Standards in Education (Ofsted) (1994a) *Assessing School Effectiveness*. London: Institute of Education.

Office for Standards in Education (Ofsted) (1994b) *Primary Matters: A Discussion on Teaching and Learning in Primary Schools*. London: HMSO.

Office for Standards in Education (Ofsted) (2000) *Inspecting Subjects 3–11: Guidance for Inspectors and Schools*. London: Ofsted.

Office for Standards in Education (Ofsted) (2004) *Transition from the Reception Year to Year 1: An Evaluation by HMI*. London: Ofsted.

Oxfordshire Early Years Team (1996) *Curriculum Matters 13: Early Years*. Oxford: Oxfordshire Education Department.

Oxfordshire County Council (OCC) (2001) *Early Years Development File*. Oxford: Early Learning and Childcare Service.

Oxfordshire County Council (OCC) (2005) *What We Think about Starting School*. Oxford: Early Learning and Childcare Service.

Oxfordshire County Council (OCC) (2006) *Transition. Foundation Stage to Year 1*. Oxford: Early Learning and Childcare Service.

Paley, V.G. (1984) *Boys and Girls: Superheroes in the Doll Corner*. Chicago: University of Chicago Press.

Pascal, C. (1990) *Under-fives in the Infant Classroom*. Stoke-on-Trent: Trentham.

Pascal, C. and Ghaye, A. (1988) Four year old children in reception classrooms: participant perceptions and practice, *Educational Studies,* 14 (2): 187–208.

Pascal, C., Bertram, A., Ramsden, F. and Saunders, M. (1997) *Evaluating and Improving Quality in Early Childhood Settings (The EEL Programme)*. Worcester: Centre for Research in Early Childhood.

Phillips, T. (1988) On a related matter: why successful small-group talk depends upon not keeping to the point, in M. Maclure, T. Phillips and A. Wilkinson (eds) *Oracy Matters*. Milton Keynes: Open University Press.

Piaget, J. (1929) *The Language and Thought of the Child*. New York: Basic Books.

Piaget, J. and Inhelder, B. (1956) *The Child's Conception of Space*. London: Routledge & Kegan Paul.

Pinker, S. (1997) *How the Mind Works*. London: Allen Lane, The Penguin Press.

Pollard, A. and Tann, S. (1993) *Reflective Teaching in the Primary School,* 2nd edn. London: Cassell.

Pollard, A., Broadfoot, P., Croll, P., Osborn, M. and Abbott, D. (1994) *Changing English Primary Schools? The Impact of the Education Reform Act at Key Stage One*. London: Cassell.

Pollard, A. and Filer, A. (1999) *The Social World of Pupil Career*. London: Cassell.

Postlethwaite, K. (1993) *Differentiated Science Teaching*. Milton Keynes: Open University Press.

Pringle, M.K. (1986) *The Needs of Children*, 3rd edn. London: Routledge.

Pugh, G. (2002) The consequences of inadequate investment in the early years, in J. Fisher (ed) *The Foundations of Learning*. Milton Keynes: Open University Press.

Qualifications and Curriculum Authority (QCA) (1997) *Baseline Assessment Scales*. London: SCAA Publications.

Qualifications and Curriculum Authority (QCA) (2003) *Foundation Stage Profile Handbook*. London: QCA.

Rabain-Jamin, J. (1989) Culture and early social interactions: the example of mother–infant object play in African and native French families, *European Journal of Psychology of Education*, 4 (2): 295–305.

Reggio Emilia Project Zero (2001) *Making Learning Visible: Children as Individual and Group Learners*. Reggio Emilia: Reggio Children.

Reid, J., Forrestal, P. and Cook, J. (1989) *Small Group Learning in the Classroom*. Scarborough, WA: Chalkface Press.

Rich, D. (2003). Bang! Bang! Gun play and why children need it. *Early Education*, Summer.

Richards, M. and Light, P. (1986) *Children of Social Worlds*. Cambridge: Polity Press.

Roberts, R. (1995a) *Self Esteem and Successful Early Learning*. London: Hodder & Stoughton.

Roberts, R. (ed.) (1995b) *A Nursery Education Curriculum for the Early Years*. Oxford: National Primary Centre.

Robinson, M. (2003) *From Birth to One: The Year of Opportunity*. Milton Keynes: Open University Press.

Robinson, E.J. and Beck, S. (2000) What is difficult about counter-factual reasoning?, in P. Mitchell and K.J. Riggs (eds) *Children's Reasoning and the Mind*. Hove: Psychology Press.

Rogoff, B (1997) Cognition as a collaborative process, in L. Duhn and B. Siegler (eds), *Handbook of Child Psychology*. New York: John Wiley & Sons.

Rose, J. (2006) *Independent Review of the Teaching of Early Reading*. London: DfES Publications.

Rose, C. and Nicholl, M.J. (1997) *Accelerated Learning for the 21st Century*. London: Judy Piatkus.

Rosen, M. (1993) *Going On A Bear Hunt*. London. Walker Books.

Rousseau, J.J. ([1762] 1976) *Emile* (translated by Barbara Foxley). London: Dent.

Rowland, S. (1984) *The Enquiring Classroom: An Introduction to Children's Learning*. Lewes: Falmer Press.

Rubin, K., Fein, G. and Vandenberg, B. (1983) Play, in E.M. Hetherington (ed.) *Manual of Child Psychology: Socialization, Personality and Development (Vol. IV)*. New York: Wiley.

Rutter, M. (1995) Clinical implications of attachment concepts, retrospect and prospect, *Journal of Child Psychology and Psychiatry*, 36 (4): 549–71.

Sanders, D., White, W., Burge, B., Sharp, C., Eames, A., McEune, R. and Grayson, H. (2005) *A Study of the Transition from the Foundation Stage to Key Stage 1*. Slough: NFER.

Santer, J., Griffiths, C. and Goodall, D. (2007) *Free Play in Early Childhood*. London: Play England/NCB.

School Curriculum and Assessment Authority (SCAA) (1995) *Planning the Curriculum at Key Stages 1 and 2*. London: SCAA.

School Curriculum and Assessment Authority (SCAA) (1997) *The National Framework for Baseline Assessment: Criteria and Procedures for the Accreditation of Baseline Assessment Schemes*. London: SCAA.

Schön, D.A. (1987) *Educating the Reflective Practitioner*. San Francisco, CA: Josey-Bass.

Schweinhart, L.J., Barnes, H. and Weikart, D.P. (1993) *Significant Benefits: The High/Scope Perry Preschool Study Through Age 27.* Ypsilanti, MI: High/Scope Press.

Selleck, D. (2006) Key Persons in the Early Years Foundation Stage, in *Early Education*, Autumn.

Sestini, E. (1987) The quality of the learning experiences of four year olds in nursery and infant classes, in NFER/SCDC (eds) *Four Year Olds in School.* Slough: NFER.

Shaffer, D.R. (1993) *Developmental Psychology: Childhood and Adolescence*, 3rd edn. Pacific Grove, CA: Brooks/Cole Publishing.

Sharp, C. (2000) When should children start school and what should we teach them?, *Topic*, 23, Spring.

Sinclair, J.McH. and Coulthard, R.M. (1975) *Towards an Analysis of Discourse: The English Used by Teachers and Pupils.* London: Oxford University Press.

Siraj-Blatchford, I. (1994) *The Early Years: Laying the Foundations for Racial Equality.* Stoke-on-Trent: Trentham Books.

Smith, A.B. (1993) Early childhood educare: seeking a theoretical framework in Vygotsky's work, *International Journal of Early Years Education*, 1 (1): 47–61.

Smith, H. (1995) *Unhappy Children.* London: Free Association Books.

Smith, P.K. and Cowie, H. (1991) *Understanding Children's Development*, 2nd edn. Oxford: Basil Blackwell.

Spaggiari, S. (1997) The invisibility of the essential, in Reggio Children *Shoe and Meter: First Approaches to the Discovery, Function and Use of Measurement*, Reggio Emilia: Reggio Children.

Spender, D. (1982) *Invisible Women: The Schooling Scandal.* London: Writers and Readers.

Stanworth, M. (1981) *Gender and Schooling: A Study of Gender Divisions in the Classroom.* London: Women's Research and Resources Centre.

Stern, D. (1985) *The Interpersonal World of the Infant: A View from Psychoanalysis and Developmental Psychology.* New York: Basic Books.

Stevenson, C. (1987) The young four-year-old in nursery and infant classes: challenges and constraints, in NFER/SCDC (eds) *Four Year Olds in School.* London: NFER/SCDC.

Stodolsky, S.S., Ferguson, T.L. and Wimpelberg, K. (1981) The recitation persists; but what does it look like? *Journal of Curriculum Studies*, 13: 121–30.

Sutton-Smith, B. and Kelly-Byrne, D. (1984) The idealization of play, in P.K. Smith (ed.) *Play in Animals and Humans.* Oxford: Basil Blackwell.

Sylva, K. (1994) The impact of early learning on children's later development, Appendix C, in C. Ball (ed.) *Start Right: The Importance of Early Learning.* London: RSA.

Sylva, K. and Lunt, I. (1982) *Child Development: A First Course*. Oxford: Basil Blackwell.

Sylwester, R. (1995) *A Celebration of Neurons: An Educator's Guide to the Brain*. Alexandria, VA: ASCD.

Thomas, I. (1987) The Bedfordshire 4+ pilot scheme: some issues and implications, in NFER/SCDC (eds) *Four Year Olds in School*. Slough: NFER.

Tizard, B., Blatchford, D., Burke, J., Farquar, C. and Plewis, I. (1988) *Young Children at School in the Inner City*. Hove: Lawrence Erlbaum.

Tizard, B. and Hughes, M. (1984) *Young Children Learning: Talking and Thinking at Home and At School*. London: Fontana.

Tompkins, M. (1991) In praise of praising less, *Extensions* (newsletter of the High/Scope Curriculum), 6 (1): 1–3.

Torgerson, C., Brooks, G. and Hall, J. (2006) A systematic review of the research literature on the use of phonics in the teaching of reading and spelling. *Research Report 711*. London: Department for Education and Skills.

Trevarthean, C. (1977) Descriptive analyses of infant communicative behaviour, in H.R. Schaffer (ed.) *Studies in Mother–Infant Interaction*. London: Academic Press.

Trevarthen, C. (1980) The foundations of intersubjectivity: development of interpersonal and cooperative understanding in infants, in D. Olsen (ed.) *The Social Foundations of Language and Thought*. New York: W.W. Norton.

Trevarthen, C. (1992) An infant's motives for speaking and thinking in the culture, in A.H.Wold (ed.) *The Dialogical Alternative*. Oslo/Oxford: Scandinavian University Press/Oxford University Press.

Trevarthen, C. (1998) Excerpt from an interview recorded for BBC Radio 4 , in L. Puriv and D. Selleck (1999) *Tuning in to Children: Understanding a Child's Development from Birth to Five Years*. London: BBC Education, 62.

United Nations Convention on the Rights of the Child (1989) Geneva: Office of the High Commissioner for Human Rights.

Vygotsky, L.S. (1962) *Thought and Language*. Cambridge, MA: MIT Press.

Vygotsky, L.S. (1966) Play and its role in the mental development of the child (translated by Catherine Mulholland), *Voprosy psikhologi*, 12 (6): 62–76.

Vygotsky, L.S. (1978) *Mind in Society: The Development of Higher Psychological Processes*. Cambridge, MA: Harvard University Press.

Warham, S.M. (1993) *Primary Teaching and the Negotiation of Power*. London: Paul Chapman.

Watson, R. (1998) Rethinking readiness for learning, in D. Olson and N. Torrance (eds) *Handbook of Education and Human Development: New Models of Learning, Teaching and Schooling*. London: Blackwell.

Wells, G. (ed.) (1981) *Learning Through Interaction*. Cambridge: Cambridge University Press.

Wells, G. (1985) *Language, Learning and Education*. Windsor: NFER/ Nelson.

Wells, G. (1986) *The Meaning Makers: Children Learning Language and Using Language to Learn*. Sevenoaks: Hodder & Stoughton.

Whitehead, M. (1992) Assessment at Key Stage 1: core subjects and the developmental curriculum, in G.M. Blenkin and A.V. Kelly (eds) *Assessment in Early Childhood Education*. London: Paul Chapman.

Whitehead, M. (1993) Why not happiness? Reflections on change and conflict in early childhood education, in P. Gammage and J. Meighan (eds.) *Early Childhood Education: Taking Stock*. Ticknall: Education Now Publishing.

Willes, M.J. (1983) *Children Into Pupils: A Study of Language in Early Schooling*. London: Routledge & Kegan Paul.

Wolfe, P. and Brandt, R. (1998) What do we know from brain research? *Educational Leadership*. November: 8–13.

Wolfendale, S. (1993) *Baseline Assessment: A Review of Current Practice, Issues and Strategies for Effective Implementation*. OMEP (UK). Stoke-on-Trent: Trentham.

Wood, D. (1988) *How Children Think and Learn*. Oxford: Blackwell

Wood, D., Bruner, J.S. and Ross, G. (1976) The role of tutoring in problem solving, *Journal of Child Psychology and Psychiatry*, 17 (2): 89–100.

Woods, P. (1990) *Teacher Skills and Strategies*. Basingstoke: Falmer Press.

Wyse, D., and Styles, M. (in press) Synthetic phonics and the teaching of reading: the debate surrounding England's 'Rose Report', *Literacy*, 47 (1).

INDEX

Locators shown in *italics* refer to case studies.